# The Sackett Novels
## of
## Louis L'Amour

# THE SACKETT NOVELS
## OF
# LOUIS L'AMOUR

## Volume II

**The Daybreakers
Sackett
Lando
Mojave Crossing**

NELSON DOUBLEDAY, INC.
Garden City, New York

THE SACKETT NOVELS OF LOUIS L'AMOUR, VOLUME II

Originally published as four separate works
THE DAYBREAKERS
Copyright © 1960 by Bantam Books, Inc.
SACKETT
Copyright © 1961 by Bantam Books, Inc.
LANDO
Copyright © 1962 by Bantam Books, Inc.
MOJAVE CROSSING
Copyright © 1964 by Bantam Books, Inc.

Published by arrangement with Bantam Books

PRINTED IN THE UNITED STATES OF AMERICA

# Contents

# Foreword

Following the Civil War many of the more adventurous young men, veterans from both the Union and the Confederacy, moved westward. Pioneer movement was strong in all parts of the country but from the South there was the added incentive of a shattered economy. The West offered fresh opportunity, land for the taking, and a chance for individual growth.

Above all, with the war over, the country was permeated with restlessness, an urge to get on with it. The war had held up the growth of the country but now destiny awaited.

The restlessness was evident in more ways than just the desire for land, for cattle, for gold. Men were no longer content to be what they had been. During the war they had often fought beside men who were better educated, men of wider experience, and men who talked of lands that mountain and city boys had never even heard of. As their horizons broadened many were becoming irritated with what they had been.

Moving west, they left behind the narrow streets, the clearings in the forest, or the small farms where they had grown up. Suddenly they were moving out into a vast land, out upon prairies that seemed to roll away forever, and they were appalled. Some wished to turn back. They hunched their shoulders and kept their eyes on the ground.

Others began to take bigger steps on the land. They dragged their heavy wagons up long and muddy slopes, they swam rivers in flood, and where they had to they made rafts. They hunted buffalo or antelope on the open plains, and occasionally in one of the river bottoms, they killed a bear. They no longer feared the land nor were they awed by the distances or the vastness of the sky. They knew they had come home, that this land was theirs.

These are stories of what was happening to thousands who came west. Tyrel and Orrin Sackett were not heroes, nor did they think of themselves as such. They were young men trying to make a living and to find a place for themselves in a changing world, and theirs were the problems of young men the world over, in all times.

The Sacketts came from mountains where they had to hunt for the meat they ate. Their wounds and illnesses were treated with the remedies or herbs traditional in their lands or learned from Indians. All their lessons were learned the hard way. They were good shots because they did not have powder and lead to throw away. From childhood they learned to make every shot count. Men of their kind were often poor but they had lost neither pride nor dignity. They wanted nothing they did not earn, and would be beholden to no man.

Nothing in these stories is "made-up" or invented. The threads of these lives are woven into an existing tapestry of plains, cattle, people, and the westward movement.

The Sacketts' first job was with a cattle drive to Kansas. It could scarcely have been otherwise. Further west they became involved in a land-grant fight in New Mexico, and such fights are history.

Tell Sackett found gold in Colorado and it is still found there. If you wish to see where he found it you have three choices: walk in with a back-pack, ride in by a round-about trail, or fly in with a helicopter. There was no easy way in then and there is none now.

All gold mining is based on great expectation. During my own gold mining days I was constantly meeting someone who had "a million dollars, just under the ground, just waiting to be taken out." I remember none of them that ever yielded so much as a good living. Many a man has been killed over a hole in the ground that produced nothing but dreams.

Yet fantastic discoveries were made in the old West, and nothing seemed impossible. A doctor, travelling through Arizona in the very early days, was told by a Mexican mule-driver whom he befriended that there was gold atop a nearby hill. In his diary the doctor comments, "So I walked up the hill and picked up six thousand dollars worth of nuggets before breakfast."

Of course, then as now, there were those who wanted the gold but not to dig for it. They preferred to let somebody else sweat and strain, then to steal the gold. As western men were long on tolerance but short on patience, it isn't to be expected that the thieves would long enjoy good health.

Each period of history has different standards by which to judge morality, and we in these later years must not presume to look back upon another time with too critical an eye. This is especially true as the man of the early West could point to our own time as a less than honest, less than moral age.

The settling of disputes with weapons did not originate in the American West but existed from the beginning of time. Moreover, it is doubtful that any western gunfighter even approached the record for killings of the famous swordsman, the Chevalier d'Andrieux who killed at least seventy-seven men in duels.

Most duels were fought over trivial things, and the only major difference in the West was that they lacked the precise formality of those on the eastern seaboard or in Europe. In the West such things were settled at once, on the spot, wherever the antagonists happened to be.

Men who moved westward were ambitious or they would not have started west in the first place. The wiser ones began to see that more was needed than luck, or courage, or sheer physical endurance.

The Sacketts in my stories came west from the Tennessee mountains where English, Scotch and Irish traditions remained strong. They had come to the mountains bringing their songs, their folklore, their religion and their pride. When they moved westward they carried all this with them.

Being observant and perceptive individuals they soon understood the need for learning. They wanted it and they sought it, and along the trail they learned how to read and write, and began to understand some of the larger aspects of the world into which they were growing.

They understood, so very well, that it is not enough to be just a man. In our kind of world one must also be a citizen.

# THE DAYBREAKERS

# Chapter 1

My brother, Orrin Sackett, was big enough to fight bears with a switch. Me, I was the skinny one, tall as Orrin, but no meat to my bones except around the shoulders and arms. Orrin could sing like an angel, or like a true Welshman which was better than any angel. Far away back and on three sides of the family, we were Welsh. Orrin was a strapping big man, but for such a big man he was surprising quick.

Folks said I was the quiet one, and in the high-up hills where we grew up as boys, folks fought shy of me come fighting time. Orrin was bigger than me, fit to wrassle a bull, but he lacked a streak of something I had.

Maybe you recall the Sackett-Higgins feud? Time I tell about, we Sacketts were just fresh out of Higginses.

Long Higgins, the mean one, was also the last one. He came hunting Sackett hide with an old squirrel rifle. It was Orrin he was hunting, being mighty brave because he knew Orrin wouldn't be packing anything in the way of sidearms at a wedding.

Orrin was doing no thinking about Higginses this day with Mary Tripp there to greet him and his mind set on marrying, so I figured it was my place to meet Long Higgins down there in the road. Just as I was fixing to call him to a stand, Preacher Myrick drove his rig between us, and by the time I got around it Long Higgins was standing spraddlelegged in the road with a bead on Orrin.

Folks started to scream and Long Higgins shot and Mary who saw him first pushed Orrin to save him. Only she fell off balance and fell right into the bullet intended for Orrin.

*"Long!"*

He turned sharp around, knowing my voice, and he had that rifle waist high and aimed for me, his lips drawed down hard.

Long Higgins was a good hip shot with a rifle and he shot quick . . . maybe too quick.

That old hog-leg of mine went back into the holster and Long Higgins lay there in the dust and when I turned around, that walk up into the trees was the longest I ever did take except one I took a long time later.

Ollie Shaddock might have been down there and I knew if Ollie called I'd have to turn around, for Ollie was the Law in those mountains and away back somewheres we were kin.

When Ma saw me cutting up through the woods she knew something was cross-ways. Took me only a minute to tell her. She sat in that old rocker and looked me right in the eye while I told it. "Tye," she was almighty stern, "was Long Higgins looking at you when you fetched him?"

"Right in the eye."

"Take the dapple," Ma said, "he's the runningest horse on the mountain. You go west, and when you find a place with deep, rich soil and a mite of game in the hills, you get somebody to write a letter and we'll come down there, the boys an' me."

She looked around at the place, which was mighty rundown. Work as we would, and us Sacketts were workers, we still hadn't anything extra, and scarcely a poor living, so Ma had been talking up the west ever since Pa died.

Most of it she got from Pa, for he was a wandering and a knowing man, never to home long, but Ma loved him for all of that, and so did we young-uns. He had a Welshman's tongue, Pa did, a tongue that could twist a fine sound from a word and he could bring a singing to your blood so you could just see that far land yonder, waiting for folks to come and crop it.

Those old blue eyes of Ma's were harder to face than was Long Higgins, and him with a gun to hand. "Tye, do you reckon you could kill Ollie?"

To nobody else would I have said it, but to Ma I told the truth. "I'd never want to, Ma, because we're kin but I could fetch him. I think maybe I can draw a gun faster and shoot straighter than anybody, anywhere."

She took the pipe from her lips. "Eighteen years now I've seen you growing up, Tyrel Sackett, and for twelve of them you've been drawing and shooting. Pa told me when you was fifteen that he'd never seen the like. Ride with the law, Tye, never against it." She drew the shawl tighter about her knees. "If the Lord wills we will meet again in the western lands."

The way I took led across the state line and south, then west. Ollie Shaddock would not follow beyond the line of the state, so I put Tennessee behind me before the hills had a shadow.

It was wild land through which the trail led, west out of Tennessee, into Arkansas, the Ozarks, and by lonely trails into Kansas. When I rode at last into the street at Baxter Springs folks figured me for one more mountain renegade coming to help keep tick-infected Texas cattle out of the country, but I was of no such mind.

It was eight miles to where the Texas men held their cattle, so there I rode, expecting no warm welcome for a stranger. Riding clear of the circling riders I rode up to the fire, the smell of grub turning my insides over. Two days I'd been without eating, with no money left, and too proud to ask for that for which I could not pay.

A short, square man with a square face and a mustache called out to me. "You there! On the gray! What do you want?"

"A job if one's to be had, and a meal if you've grub to spare. My name is Tyrel Sackett and I'm bound westward from Tennessee toward the Rockies, but if there's a job I'll ride straight up to it."

He looked me over, mighty sharp, and then he said, "Get down, man, and come to the fire. No man was ever turned from my fire without a meal inside him. I'm Belden."

When I'd tied Dapple I walked up to the fire, and there was a big, handsome man lying on the ground by the fire, a man with a golden beard like one of those Vikings Pa used to tell of. "Hell," he said agreeably, "it's a farmer!"

"What's wrong with farming?" I asked him. "You wouldn't have your belly full of beans right now if they'd not been farmed by somebody."

"We've had our troubles with farmers, Mr. Sackett," Belden said, "there's been shooting, the farmers killed a man for me."

"So," said a voice alongside, "so maybe we should kill a farmer."

He had an itch for trouble and his kind I'd met before. He was a medium-tall man with a low hanging shoulder on his gun side. His black brows met over his nose and his face was thin and narrow. If it was trouble he was hunting he was following the right trail to get it.

"Mister," I told him, "any time you think you can kill this farmer, you just have at it."

He looked across the fire at me, surprised I think, because he had expected fear. My clothes showed I was from the hills, a patched, old homespun shirt, jeans stuffed into clumsy boots. It was sure that I looked like nothing at all, only if a man looked at the pistol I wore he could see there'd been a sight of lead shot out of that barrel.

"That's enough, Carney!" Mr. Belden said sharply. "This man is a guest at our fire!"

The cook brought me a plate of grub and it smelled so good I didn't even look up until I'd emptied that plate and another, and swallowed three cups of hot black coffee. Up in the hills we like our coffee strong but this here would make bobwire grow on a man's chest in the place of hair.

The man with the golden beard watched me and he said to Mr. Belden,

"Boss, you better hire this man. If he can work like he can eat, you've got yourself a hand."

"Question is," Carney broke in, "can he fight?"

It was mighty quiet around that fire when I put my plate aside and got up. "Mister, I didn't kill you before because when I left home I promised Ma I'd go careful with a gun, but you're a mighty tryin' man."

Carney had the itch, all right, and as he looked across the fire at me I knew that sooner or later I was going to have to kill this man.

"You promised Ma, did you?" he scoffed. "We'll see about that!" He brought his right foot forward about an inch and I durned near laughed at him, but then from behind me came a warm, rich voice and it spoke clear and plain. "Mister, you just back up an' set down. I ain't aimin' to let Tyrel hang up your hide right now, so you just set down an' cool off."

It was Orrin, and knowing Orrin I knew his rifle covered Carney.

"Thanks, Orrin. Ma made me promise to go careful."

"She told me . . . an' lucky for this gent."

He stepped down from the saddle, a fine, big, handsome man with shoulders wide enough for two strong men. He wore a belt gun, too, and I knew he could use it.

"Are you two brothers?" Belden asked.

"Brothers from the hills," Orrin said, "bound west for the new lands."

"You're hired," Mr. Belden said, "I like men who work together."

So that was how it began, but more had begun that day than any of us could guess, least of all the fine-looking man with the beard who was Tom Sunday, our foreman on the drive. From the moment he had spoken up all our lives were pointed down a trail together, but no man could read the sign.

From the first Orrin was a well-loved man. With that big, easy way of his, a wide smile, as well as courage and humor enough for three men, he was a man to ride the trail with. He did his share of the work and more, and at night around the fire he would sing or tell yarns. When he sang to the cows in that fine Welsh baritone of his, everybody listened.

Nobody paid me much mind. Right off they saw I could do my work and they let me do it. When Orrin told them I was the tough one of the two they just laughed. Only there was one or two of them who didn't laugh and of these one was Tom Sunday, the other Cap Rountree, a thin, wiry old man with a walrus mustache who looked to have ridden a lot of trails.

The third day out, Tom Sunday fetched up alongside me and asked, "Tye, what would you have done if Reed Carney had grabbed his gun?"

"Why, Mr. Sunday," I said, "I'd have killed him."

He glanced at me. "Yes, I expect you would have."

He swung off then, only turned in his saddle. "Call me Tom. I'm not much on long-handled names."

Have you seen those Kansas plains? Have you seen the grass stretch away from you to the horizon? Grass and nothing but grass except for flowers here and there and maybe the white of buffalo bones, but grass moving gentle under the long wind, moving like a restless sea with the hand of God upon it.

On the fifth day when I was riding point by myself, and well out from the herd a dozen men came riding out of a ravine, all bunched up. Right off I had a smell of trouble, so instead of waiting for them to come up, I rode right to meet them.

It was a mighty pleasant day and the air was balmy with summer. Overhead the sky was blue and only a mite of cloud drifting like a lost white buffalo over the plain of the sky.

When they were close I drew up and waited, my Spencer .56 cradled on my saddle, my right hand over the trigger guard.

They drew up, a dirty, rough-looking bunch—their leader mean enough to sour cream.

"We're cuttin' your herd," he was a mighty abrupt man, "we're cuttin' it now. You come through the settlements an' swept up a lot of our cattle, an' they've et our grass."

Well, I looked at him and I said, "I reckon not."

Sort of aimlesslike I'd switched that Spencer to cover his belt buckle, my right finger on the trigger.

"Look here, boy," he started in to bluster.

"Mister," I said, "this here Spencer ain't no boy, an' I'm just after makin' a bet with a fellow. He says one of those big belt buckles like you got would stop a bullet. Me, I figure a chunk of lead, .56 caliber, would drive that buckle right back into your belly. Mister, if you want to be a sport we can settle that bet."

He was white around the eyes, and if one of the others made a wrong move I was going to drop the bull of the herd and as many others as time would allow.

"Back," it was one of the men behind the leader, "I know this boy. This here is one of them Sacketts I been tellin' you about."

It was one of those no-account Aikens from Turkey Flat, who'd been run out of the mountains for hog stealing.

"Oh?" Back smiled, kind of sickly. "Had no idea you was friends. Boy," he said, "you folks just ride on through."

"Thanks. That there's just what we figured to do."

They turned tail around and rode off and a couple of minutes later hoofs drummed on the sod and here came Mr. Belden, Tom Sunday, Cap

Rountree, and Reed Carney, all a-sweat an' expecting trouble. When they saw those herd cutters ride off they were mighty surprised.

"Tye," Mr. Belden asked, "what did those men want?"

"They figured to cut your herd."

"What happened?"

"They decided not to."

He looked at me, mighty sharp. Kneeing Dapple around I started back to the herd.

"Now what do you make of that?" I could hear Belden saying. "I'd have sworn that was Back Rand."

"It was," Rountree commented dryly, "but that there's quite a boy."

When Orrin asked me about it at the fire that night, I just said, "Aiken was there. From Turkey Flat."

Carney was listening. "Aiken who? Who's Aiken?"

"He's from the mountains," Orrin said, "he knows the kid."

Reed Carney said nothing more but a couple of times I noticed him sizing me up like he hadn't seen me before.

There would be trouble enough, but man is born to trouble, and it is best to meet it when it comes and not lose sleep until it does. Only there was more than trouble, for beyond the long grass plains were the mountains, the high and lonely mountains where someday I would ride, and where someday, the Good Lord willing, I would find a home.

How many trails? How much dust and loneliness? How long a time until then?

# Chapter 2

There was nothing but prairie and sky, the sun by day and the stars by night, and the cattle moving westward. If I live to be a thousand years old I shall not forget the wonder and the beauty of those big longhorns, the sun glinting on their horns; most of them six or seven feet from tip to tip. Some there were like old brindle, our lead steer, whose horns measured a fair nine feet from point to point, and who stood near to seventeen hands high.

It was a sea of horns above the red, brown, brindle, and white-splashed backs of the steers. They were big, wild, and fierce, ready to fight anything that walked the earth, and we who rode their flanks or the drag, we loved them and we hated them, we cussed and reviled them, but we moved them westward toward what destination we knew not.

Sometimes at night when my horse walked a slow circle around the bedded herd, I'd look at the stars and think of Ma and wonder how things were at home. And sometimes I'd dream great dreams of a girl I'd know someday.

Suddenly something had happened to me, and it happened to Orrin too. The world had burst wide open, and where our narrow valleys had been, our hog-backed ridges, our huddled towns and villages, there was now a world without end or limit. Where our world had been one of a few mountain valleys, it was now as wide as the earth itself, and wider, for where the land ended there was sky, and no end at all to that.

We saw no one. The Plains were empty. No cattle had been before us, only the buffalo and war parties of Indians crossing. No trees, only the far and endless grass, always whispering its own soft stories. Here ran the antelope, and by night the coyotes called their plaintive songs to the silent stars.

Mostly a man rode by himself, but sometimes I'd ride along with Tom Sunday or Cap Rountree, and I learned about cattle from them. Sunday knew cows, all right, but he was a sight better educated then the rest of us, although not one for showing it.

Sometimes when we rode along he would recite poetry or tell me stories

from the history of ancient times, and it was mighty rich stuff. Those old
Greeks he was always talking about, they reminded me of mountain folk
I'd known, and it fair made me ache to know how to read myself.

Rountree talked mighty little, but whatever he said made a sight of
sense. He knew buffalo . . . although there was always something to learn
about them. He was a mighty hard old man, rode as many hours as any of
us, although he was a mighty lot older. I never did know how old he was,
but those hard old gray eyes of his had looked on a sight of strange things.

"Man could make some money," Rountree said one day, "over in the
breaks of western Kansas and Colorado. Lots of cows over there, belongin'
to nobody, stuff drifted up from the Spanish settlements to the south."

When Rountree spoke up it was because there was an idea behind it.
Right then I figured something was stirring in that coot's skull, but nothing more was said at the time.

Orrin and me, we talked it over. Each of us wanted a place of our own,
and we wanted a place for Ma and the boys. A lot of cattle belonging to
no man . . . it sounded good to us.

"It would take an outfit," Orrin said.

Tom Sunday, I was sure, would be for it. From things he'd said on
night herd I knew he was an ambitious man, and he had plans for himself
out west. Educated the way he was, there was no telling how far he would
go. Time to time he talked a good deal about politics . . . out west a man
could be whatever he was man enough to be, and Tom Sunday was smart.

"Orrin and me," I said to Rountree, "we've been talking about what
you said. About those wild cows. We discussed the three of us and maybe
Tom Sunday, if you're willing and he wants to come in."

"Why, now. That there's about what I had in mind. Fact is, I talked to
Tom. He likes it."

Mr. Belden drove his herd away from the Kansas-Missouri border, right
out into the grassy plains, he figured he'd let his cows graze until they were
good and fat, then sell them in Abilene; there were cattle buyers buying
and shipping cattle from there because of the railroad.

Anybody expecting Abilene to be a metropolis would have been some
put out, but to Orrin and me, who had never seen anything bigger than
Baxter Springs, it looked right smart of a town. Why, Abilene was quite a
place, even if you did have to look mighty fast to see what there was of it.

Main thing was that railroad. I'd heard tell of railroads before, but had
never come right up to one. Wasn't much to see: just two rails of steel
running off into the distance, bedded down on crossties of hewn logs.
There were some stock pens built there and about a dozen log houses.
There was a saloon in a log house, and across the tracks there was a spank-

ing-new hotel three stories high and a porch along the side fronting the rails. Folks had told me there were buildings that tall, but I never figured to see one.

There was another hotel, too. Place called Bratton's, with six rooms to let. East of the hotel there was a saloon run by a fat man called Jones. There was a stage station . . . that was two stories . . . a blacksmith shop and the Frontier Store.

At the Drovers' Cottage there was a woman cooking there and some rooms were let, and there were three, four cattle buyers loafing around.

We bunched our cows on the grass outside of town and Mr. Belden rode in to see if he could make a deal, although he didn't much like the look of things. Abilene was too new, it looked like a put-up job and Kansas hadn't shown us no welcome signs up to now.

Then Mr. Belden came back and durned if he hadn't hired several men to guard the herd so's we could have a night in town . . . not that she was much of a place, like I said. But we went in.

Orrin and me rode down alongside the track, and Orrin was singing in that big, fine-sounding voice of his, and when we came abreast of the Drovers' Cottage there was a girl a-setting on the porch.

She had a kind of pale blond hair and skin like it never saw daylight, and blue eyes that made a man think she was the prettiest thing he ever did see. Only second glance she reminded me somehow of a hammer-headed roan we used to have, the one with the one blue eye . . . a mighty ornery horse, too narrow between the ears and eyes. On that second glance I figured that blonde had more than a passing likeness to that bronc.

But when she looked at Orrin I knew we were in for trouble, for if ever I saw a man-catching look in a woman's eyes it was in hers, then.

"Orrin," I said, "if you want to run maverick a few more years, if you want to find that western land, then you stay off that porch."

"Boy," he put a big hand on my shoulder, "look at that yaller hair!"

"Reminds me of that hammer-headed, no-account roan we used to have. Pa he used to say, 'size up a woman the way you would a horse if you were in a horse trade'; and Orrin, you better remember that."

Orrin laughed. "Stand aside, youngster," he tells me, "and watch how it's done."

With that Orrin rides right up to the porch and standing up in his stirrups he said, "Howdy, ma'am! A mighty fine evening! Might I come up an' set with you a spell?"

Mayhap he needed a shave and a bath like we all did, but there was something in him that always made a woman stop and look twice.

Before she could answer a tall man stepped out. "Young man," he spoke mighty sharp, "I will thank you not to annoy my daughter. She does not consort with hired hands."

Orrin smiled that big, wide smile of his. "Sorry, sir, I did not mean to offend. I was riding by, and such beauty, sir, such beauty deserves its tribute, sir."

Then he flashed that girl a smile, then reined his horse around and we rode on to the saloon.

The saloon wasn't much, but it took little to please us. There was about ten feet of bar, sawdust on the floor, and not more than a half-dozen bottles behind the bar. There was a barrel of mighty poor whiskey. Any farmer back in our country could make better whiskey out of branch water and corn, but we had our drinks and then Orrin and me hunted the barrels out back.

Those days, in a lot of places a man might get to, barrels were the only place a man could bathe. You stripped off and you got into a barrel and somebody poured water over you, then after soaping down and washing as best you could you'd have more water to rinse off the soap, and you'd had yourself a bath.

"You watch yo'se'f," the saloon keeper warned, "feller out there yestiddy shot himself a rattler whilst he was in the barrel."

Orrin bathed in one barrel, Tom Sunday in another, while I shaved in a piece of broken mirror tacked to the back wall of the saloon. When they finished bathing I stripped off and got into the barrel and Orrin and Tom, they took off. Just when I was wet all over, Reed Carney came out of the saloon.

My gun was close by but my shirt had fallen over it and there was no chance to get a hand on it in a hurry.

So there I was, naked as a jaybird, standing in a barrel two-thirds full of water, and there was that trouble-hunting Reed Carney with two or three drinks under his belt and a grudge under his hat.

It was my move, but it had to be the right move at the right time, and to reach for that gun would be the wrong thing to do. Somehow I had to get out of that tub and there I was with soap all over me, in my hair and on my face and dribbling toward my eyes.

The rinse water was in a bucket close to the barrel so acting mighty unconcerned I reached down, picked it up, sloshing it over me to wash off that soap.

"Orrin," Carney said, grinning at me, "went to the *ho*-tel and it don't seem hardly right, you in trouble and him not here to stand in front of you."

"Orrin handles his business. I handle mine."

He walked up to within three or four feet of the barrel and there was something in his eyes I'd not seen before. I knew then he meant to kill me.

"I've been wonderin' about that. I'm curious to see if you can handle your own affairs without that big brother standing by to pull you out."

The bucket was still about a third full of water and I lifted it to slosh it over me.

There was a kind of nasty, wet look to his eyes and he took a step nearer. "I don't like you," he said, "and I—" His hand dropped to his gun and I let him have the rest of that water in the face.

He jumped back and I half-jumped, half-fell out of the barrel just as he blinked the water away and grabbed iron. His gun was coming up when the bucket's edge caught him alongside the skull and I felt the *whiff* of that bullet past my ear. But that bucket was oak and it was heavy and it laid him out cold.

Inside the saloon there was a scramble of boots, and picking up the flour-sack towel I began drying off, but I was standing right beside my gun and I had the shirt pulled away from it and easy to my hand it was. If any friends of Carney's wanted to call the tune I was ready for the dance.

The first man out was a tall, blond man with a narrow, tough face and a twisted look to his mouth caused by an old scar. He wore his gun tied to his leg and low down the way some of these fancy gunmen wear them. Cap Rountree was only a step behind and right off he pulled over to one side and hung a hand near his gun butt. Tom Sunday fanned out on the other side. Two others ranged up along the man with the scarred lip.

"What happened?"

"Carney here," I said, "bought himself more than he could pay for."

That blond puncher had been ready to buy himself a piece of any fight there was left and he was just squaring away when Cap Rountree put in his two-bit's worth. "We figured you might be troubled, Tye," Cap said in that dry, hard old voice, "so Tom an' me, we came out to see the sides were even up."

You could feel the change in the air. That blond with the scarred lip—later I found out his name was Fetterson—he didn't like the situation even a little. Here I was dead center in front of him, but he and his two partners, they were framed by Tom Sunday and Cap Rountree.

Fetterson glanced one way and then the other and you could just see his horns pull in. He'd come through that door sure enough on the prod an' pawin' dust, but suddenly he was so peaceful it worried me.

"You better hunt yourself a hole before he comes out of it," Fetterson said. "He'll stretch your hide."

By that time I had my pants on and was stamping into my boots. Believe me, I sure hate to face up to trouble with no pants on, and no boots.

So I slung my gun belt and settled my holster into place. "You tell him to draw his pay and rattle his hocks out of here. I ain't hunting trouble, but he's pushing, mighty pushing."

The three of us walked across to the Drovers' Cottage for a meal, and the first thing we saw was Orrin setting down close to that blond girl and she was looking at him like he was money from home. But that was the least of it. Her father was setting there listening himself . . . leave it to Orrin and that Welsh-talking tongue of his. He could talk a squirrel right out of a walnut tree . . . I never saw the like.

The three of us sat down to a good meal and we talked up a storm about that country to the west, and the wild cattle, and how much a man could make if he could keep Comanches, Kiowas, or Utes from lifting his hair.

Seemed strange to be sitting at a table. We were all so used to setting on the ground that we felt awkward with a white cloth and all. Out on the range a man ate with his hunting knife and what he could swab up with a chunk of bread.

That night Mr. Belden paid us off in the hotel office, and one by one we stepped up for our money. You've got to remember that neither Orrin or me had ever had twenty-five dollars of cash money in our lives before. In the mountains a man mostly swapped for what he needed, and clothes were homespun.

Our wages were twenty-five dollars a month and Orrin and me had two months and part of a third coming.

Only when he came to me, Mr. Belden put down his pen and sat back in his chair.

"Tye," he said, "there's a prisoner here who is being held for the United States Marshal. Brought in this morning. His name is Aiken, and he was riding with Back Rand the day you met them out on the prairie."

"Yes, sir."

"I had a talk with Aiken, and he told me that if it hadn't been for you Back Rand would have taken my herd . . . or tried to. It seems, from what he said, that you saved my herd or saved us a nasty fight and a stampede where I was sure to lose cattle. It seems this Aiken knew all about you Sacketts and he told Rand enough so that Rand didn't want to call your bluff. I'm not an ungrateful man, Tye, so I'm adding two hundred dollars to your wages."

Two hundred dollars was a sight of money, those days, cash money being a shy thing.

When we walked out on the porch of the Drovers' Cottage, there were three wagons coming up the trail, and three more behind them. The first three were army ambulances surrounded by a dozen Mexicans in fringed buckskin suits and wide Mexican sombreros. There were another dozen riding around the three freight wagons following, and we'd never seen the like.

Their jackets were short, only to the waist, and their pants flared out at the bottom and fitted like a glove along the thighs. Their spurs had rowels like mill wheels on them, and they all had spanking-new rifles and pistols. They wore colored silk sashes like some of those Texas cowhands wore, and they were all slicked out like some kind of a show.

Horses? Mister, you should see such horses! Every one clean-limbed and quick, and every one showing he'd been curried and fussed over. Every man Jack of that crowd was well set-up, and if ever I saw a fighting crowd, it was this lot.

The first carriage drew up before the Drovers' Cottage and a tall, fine-looking old man with pure white hair and white mustaches got down from the wagon, then helped a girl down. Now I couldn't rightly say how old she was, not being any judge of years on a woman, but I'd guess she was fifteen or sixteen, and the prettiest thing I ever put an eye to.

Pa had told us a time or two about those Spanish *dons* and the *señoritas* who lived around Santa Fe, and these folks must be heading that direction.

Right then I had me an idea. In Indian country the more rifles the better, and this here outfit must muster forty rifles if there was one, and no Indian was going to tackle that bunch for the small amount of loot those wagons promised. The four of us would make their party that much stronger, and would put us right in the country we were headed for.

Saying nothing to Sunday or Rountree, I went into the dining room. The grub there was passing fine. Situated on the rails they could get about what they wanted and the Drovers' Cottage was all set up to cater to cattlemen and cattle buyers with money to spend. Later on folks from back east told me some of the finest meals they ever set down to were in some of those western hotels . . . and some of the worst, too.

The don was sitting at the table with that pretty girl, but right away I could see this was no setup to buck if a man was hunting trouble. There were buckskin-clad riders setting at tables around them and when I approached the don, four of them came out of their chairs like they had springs in their pants, and they stood as if awaiting a signal.

"Sir," I said, "from the look of your outfit you'll be headed for Santa Fe. My partners and me . . . there are four of us . . . we're headed west. If we could ride along with your party we'd add four rifles to your strength and it would be safer for us."

He looked at me out of cold eyes from a still face. His mustache was beautifully white, his skin a pale tan, his eyes brown and steady. He started to speak, but the girl interrupted and seemed to be explaining something to him, but there was no doubt about his answer.

She looked up at me. "I am sorry, sir, but my grandfather says it will be impossible."

"I'm sorry, too," I said, "but if he would like to check up on our character he could ask Mr. Belden over there."

She explained, and the old man glanced at Mr. Belden across the room. There was a moment when I thought he might change his mind, but he shook his head.

"I am sorry." She looked like she really was sorry. "My grandfather is a very positive man." She hesitated and then she said, "We have been warned that we may be attacked by some of your people."

I bowed . . . more than likely it was mighty awkward, it was the first time I ever bowed to anybody, but it seemed the thing to do.

"My name is Tyrel Sackett, and if ever we can be of help, my friends and I are at your service." I meant it, too, although that speech was right out of a book I'd heard read one time, and it made quite an impression on me. "I mean, I'll sure come a-foggin' it if you're in trouble."

She smiled at me, mighty pretty, and I turned away from that table with my head whirling like somebody had hit me with a whiffletree.

Orrin had come in, and he was setting up to a table with that blond girl and her father, but the way those two glared at me you'd have sworn I'd robbed a hen roost.

Coming down off the steps I got a glimpse into that wagon the girl had been riding in. You never seen the like. It was all plush and pretty, fixed up like nothing you ever saw, a regular little room for her. The second wagon was the old man's, and later I learned that the third carted supplies for them, fine food and such, with extra rifles, ammunition, and clothing. The three freight wagons were heavy-loaded for their rancho in New Mexico.

Orrin followed me outside. "How'd you get to know Don Luis?"

"That his name? I just up an' talked to him."

"Pritts tells me he's not well thought of by his neighbors." Orrin lowered his voice. "Fact is, Tyrel, they're getting an outfit together to drive him out."

"Is that Pritts? That feller you've been talking to?"

"Jonathan Pritts and his daughter Laura. Mighty fine New England people. He's a town-site developer. She wasn't pleased to come west and leave their fine home behind and all their fine friends, but her Pa felt it his duty to come west and open up the country for the right people."

Now something about that didn't sound right to me, nor did it sound like Orrin. Remembering how my own skull was buzzing over that

Spanish girl I figured he must have it the same way over that narrow-be-tween-the-eyes blond girl.

"Seems to me, Orrin, that most folks don't leave home unless they figure to gain by it. We are going west because we can't make a living out of no sidehill farm. I reckon you'll find Jonathan Pritts ain't much different."

Orrin was shocked. "Oh, no. Nothing like that. He was a big man where he came from. If he had stayed there he would be running for the Senate right now."

"Seems to me," I said, "that somebody has told you a mighty lot about her fine friends and her fine home. If he does any developin' it won't be from goodness of his heart but because there's money to be had."

"You don't understand, Tyrel. These are fine people. You should get acquainted."

"We'll have little time for people out west rounding up cows."

Orrin looked mighty uncomfortable. "Mr. Pritts has offered me a job, running his outfit. Plans to develop town sites and the like; there's a lot of old Spanish grants that will be opened to settlement."

"He's got some men?"

"A dozen now, more later. I met one of them, Fetterson."

"With a scarred lip?"

"Why, sure!" Orrin looked at me mighty curious. "Do you know him?"

For the first time then I told Orrin about the shindig back of the saloon when I belted Reed Carney with the bucket.

"Why, then," Orrin said quietly, "I won't take the job. I'll tell Mr. Pritts about Fetterson, too." He paused. "Although I'd like to keep track of Laura."

"Since when have you started chasing girls? Seems to me they always chased after you."

"Laura's different . . . I never knew a city girl before, and she's mighty fine. Manners and all." Right then it seemed to me that if he never saw them again it would be too soon . . . all those fancy city manners and city fixings had turned Orrin's head.

Another thing. Jonathan Pritts was talking about those Spanish land grants that would be opened to settlement. It set me to wondering just what would happen to those Spanish folks who owned the grants?

Sizing up those riders of the don's I figured no rawhide outfit made up of the likes of Fetterson would have much chance shaking the dons loose from their land. But that was no business of ours. Starting tomorrow we were wild-cow hunters.

Anyway, Orrin was six years older than me and he had always had luck with girls and no girl ever paid me much mind, so I was sure in no position to tell him.

This Laura Pritts was a pretty thing . . . no taking that away from her. Nonetheless I couldn't get that contrary hammerheaded roan out of mind. They surely did favor.

Orrin had gone back into the cottage and I walked to the edge of the street. Several of the don's riders were loafing near their wagons and it was mighty quiet.

Rountree spoke from the street. "Watch yourself, Tye."

Turning, I looked around.

Reed Carney was coming up the street.

# Chapter 3

Back in the hills Orrin was the well-liked brother, nor did I ever begrudge him that. Not that folks disliked me or that I ever went around being mean, but folks never did get close to me and it was most likely my fault. There was always something standoffish about me. I liked folks, but I liked the wild animals, the lonely trails, and the mountains better.

Pa told me once, "Tyrel, you're different. Don't you ever regret it. Folks won't cotton to you much, but the friends you will make will be good friends and they'll stand by you."

Those days I thought he was wrong. I never felt any different than anybody else, far as I could see, only now when I saw Reed Carney coming up the street, and knowing it was me he was coming to kill, something came up in me that I'd never felt before, not even when Long Higgins started for Orrin.

It was something fierce and terrible that came up and liked to choke me, and then it was gone and I was very quiet inside. The moments seemed to plod, every detail stood out in sharp focus, clear and strong. Every sense, every emotion was caught and held, concentrated on that man coming up the street.

He was not alone.

Fetterson was with him, and the two who had come from the saloon when I laid Carney low with the bucket. They were a little behind him and spread out.

Orrin was inside somewhere and only that dry, harsh old man with his wolf eyes was there. He would know what was to be done, for nobody needed to tell him how to play his cards in a situation like this . . . and no one needed to tell me. Suddenly, with a queer wave of sadness and fatality, I realized that it was for moments such as this that I had been born.

Some men are gifted to paint, some to write, and some to lead men. For me it was always to be this, not to kill men, although in the years to come I was to kill more than I liked, but to command such situations as this.

Reed was coming up the street and he was thinking what folks would say when they told the story in the cow camps and around the chuck wagons. He was thinking of how they would tell of him walking up the street to kill Tyrel Sackett.

Me, I wasn't thinking. I was just standing there. I was just me, and I knew some things were inevitable.

On my right a door closed and I knew Don Luis had come out on the porch. I even heard, it was that still, the scratch of the match when he lit his cigar.

When Reed started at me he was more than a hundred yards off, but when he had covered half the distance, I started to meet him.

He stopped.

Seems like he didn't expect me to come hunting it. Seems like he figured he was the hunter and that I would try to avoid a shoot out. Seems like something had happened to him in that fifty yards, for fifty yards can be a lifetime.

Suddenly, I knew I didn't have to kill him. Mayhap that was the moment when I changed from a boy into a man. Somewhere I'd begun to learn things about myself and about gunfights and gunfighters. Reading men is the biggest part; drawing fast, even shooting straight, they came later. And some of the fastest drawing men with guns were among the first to die. That fast draw didn't mean a thing . . . not a thing.

The first thing I was learning was there are times when a man had to kill and times when he had no need to.

Reed Carney wanted a shoot out and he wanted to win, but me, I'm more than average contrary.

Watching Reed come up the street, I knew I didn't need a gun for him; suddenly it came over me that Reed Carney was nothing but a tinhorn. He fancied himself as a tough man and a gunfighter, but he didn't really want anybody shooting at him. The trouble with having a reputation as a tough man is that the time always comes when you have to be a tough man. It's a whole lot different.

Nothing exciting or thrilling about a gunfight. She's a mighty cold proposition for both parties. One or t'other is to be killed or hurt bad, maybe both.

Some folks take chances because they've got it in their minds they're somebody special, that something will protect them. It is always, they figure, somebody else who dies.

Only it ain't thataway. *You* can die. You can be snuffed out like you never existed at all and a few minutes after you're buried nobody will care except maybe your wife or your mother. You stick your finger in the water and you pull it out, and that's how much of a hole you leave when you're gone.

Reed Carney had been thinking of himself as a mighty dangerous man and he had talked himself into a shoot out.

Maybe it was something in his walk or the way he looked or in the fact that he stopped when I started toward him. Mayhap it was something sensed rather than seen, that something within me that made me different than other men. Only suddenly I knew that by the time he had taken ten steps toward me the time had begun to peter out of him, that for the first time he was realizing that I was going to be shooting at him to kill.

Panic can hit a man. You never really know. You can have a man bluffed and then something wild hits him and you're in a real honest-to-warchief shooting.

Those others were going to wait for Reed, but I'd leave them to Cap. Reed was my problem and I knew he wanted to kill me. Or rather, he wanted it known around that he'd killed me.

As I walked toward him I knew Reed knew he should draw, and he felt sure he was going to draw, but he just stood there. Then he knew that if he didn't draw it would be too late.

The sweat was streaming down his cheeks although it wasn't a hot evening. Only I just kept walking up on him, closing in. He took a step back and his lips parted like he was having trouble breathing, and he knew that if he didn't draw on me then he would never be the same man again as long as he lived.

When I stopped I was within arm's length of him and he was breathing like he'd run a long way uphill.

"I'd kill you, Reed."

It was the first time I'd ever called him by his first name and his eyes looked right into mine, startled, like a youngster's.

"You want to be a big man, Reed, but you'll never make it with a gun. You just ain't trimmed right for it. If you'd moved for that gun you'd be dead now . . . cold and dead in the dust down there with only the memory of a gnawing rat of pain in your belly.

"Now you reach down mighty careful, Reed, and you unbuckle your belt and let it fall. Then you turn around and walk away."

It was still. A tiny puff of wind stirred dust, then died out. Somewhere on the porch of the Drovers' Cottage a board creaked as somebody shifted weight. Out on the prairie a meadow lark sang.

"Unbuckle the belt!"

His eyes were fastened on mine, large and open. Sweat trickled down his cheeks in rivulets. His tongue fumbled at his lips and then his fingers reached for his belt buckle. As he let the belt fall there was a gasp from somewhere, and for a split second everything hung by a hair. There was a moment then when he might have grabbed for a gun but my eyes had him and he let the belt go.

"Was I you I'd straddle my bronc and light a shuck out of here. You got lots of country to choose from."

He backed off, then turned and started to walk away, and then as he realized what he'd done he walked faster and faster. He stumbled once, caught himself, and kept going.

After a moment I scooped up the gun belt with my left hand and turned back toward the Drovers' Cottage.

They were all on the porch. Orrin, Laura Pritts and her Pa, and Don Luis . . . even his granddaughter.

Fetterson stood there, mad clear through. He had come itching for trouble and he was stopped cold. He had no mind to tackle Cap Rountree for fun . . . nobody wanted any part of that old wolf. But he had a look in those gun-metal eyes of his that would frighten a body.

"I'll buy the drinks," I said.

"Just coffee for me," Cap replied.

My eyes were on Fetterson. "That includes you," I said.

He started to say something mean, and then he said, "Be damned if I won't. That took guts, mister."

Don Luis took the cigar from his lips and brushed away the long ash that had collected there during the moments just past. He looked at me and spoke in Spanish.

"He says we can travel west with him if we like," Cap translated, "he says you are a brave man . . . and what is more important, a wise one."

"*Gracias*," I said, and it was about the only Spanish word I knew.

In 1867, the Santa Fe Trail was an old trail, cut deep with the ruts of the heavy wagons carrying freight over the trail from Independence, Missouri. It was no road, only a wide area whose many ruts showed the way the wagons had gone through the fifty-odd years the trail had been used. Cap Rountree had come over it first in 1836, he said.

Orrin and me, we had an ache inside us for new country, and a longing to see the mountains show up on the horizon.

We had to find a place for Ma, and if we had luck out west, then we could start looking for a place.

Back home we had two younger brothers and one older, but it had been a long time since we'd seen Tell, the oldest of our brothers who was still alive and should be coming home from the wars soon. When the War between the States started he joined up and then stayed on to fight the Sioux in the Dakotas.

We rode west. Of a night we camped together and it sure was fine to

set around the fire and listen to those Spanish men sing, and they did a lot
of it, one time or another.

Meantime I was listening to Rountree. That old man had learned a lot
in his lifetime, living with the Sioux like he did, and with the Nez Perce.
First off he taught me to say that name right, and he said it *Nay-Persay.*
He taught me a lot about their customs, how they lived, and told me all
about those fine horses they raised, the Appaloosas.

My clothes had give out so I bought me an outfit from one of the
Spanish men, so I was all fixed out like they were, in a buckskin suit with
fringe and all. In the three months since I'd left home I'd put on nearly
fifteen pounds and all of it muscle. I sure wished Ma could see me. Only
thing that was the same was my gun.

The first few days out I'd seen nothing of the don or his granddaughter,
except once when I dropped an antelope with a running shot at three
hundred yards. The don happened to see that and spoke of it . . .

Sometimes his granddaughter would mount her horse and ride alongside the wagons, and one day when we'd been out for about a week, she
cantered up on a ridge where I was looking over the country ahead of us.

A man couldn't take anything for safe in this country. From the top of a
low hill that country was open grass as far as you could see. There might
be a half-dozen shallow valleys out there or ditches, there might be a canyon or a hollow, and any one of them might be chock full of Indians.

This time that Spanish girl joined me on the ridge, I was sizing up the
country. She had beautiful big dark eyes and long lashes and she was
about the prettiest thing I ever did see.

"Do you mind if I ride with you, Mr. Sackett?"

"I sure don't mind, but what about Don Luis? I don't expect he'd like
his granddaughter riding with a Tennessee drifter."

"He said I could come, but that I must ask your permission. He said
you would not let me ride with you if it was not safe."

On the hill where we sat the wind was cool and there was no dust. The
train of wagons and pack horses was a half mile away to the southeast.
The first Spanish I learned I started learning that day from her.

"Are you going to Santa Fe?"

"No, ma'am, we're going wild-cow hunting along the Purgatoire."

Her name it turned out was Drusilla, and her grandmother had been
Irish. The *vaqueros* were not Mexicans but Basques, and like I'd figured,
they were picked fighting men. There was always a *vaquero* close by as we
rode in case of trouble.

After that first time Drusilla often rode with me, and I noticed the
*vaqueros* were watching their back trail as carefully as they watched out

for Indians, and sometimes five or six of them would take off and ride back along the way we had come.

"Grandfather thinks we may be followed and attacked. He has been warned."

That made me think of what Jonathan Pritts had told Orrin, and not knowing if it mattered or not, I told her to tell the don. It seemed to me that land that had been granted a family long ago belonged to that family, and no latecomer like Pritts had a right to move in and drive them off.

The next day she thanked me for her grandfather. Jonathan Pritts had been to Santa Fe before this, and he was working through political means to get their grant revoked so the land could be thrown open to settlement.

Rountree was restless. "By this time we should have met up with Injuns. Keep those rides closer in, Tye, d'you hear?"

He rode in silence for a few minutes, then he said, "Folks back east do a sight of talkin' about the noble red man. Well, he's a mighty fine fighter, I give him that, but ain't no Injun, unless a Nez Perce, who wouldn't ride a couple hundred miles for a fight. Folks talk about takin' land from the Injuns. No Injun ever *owned* land, no way. He hunted over the country and he was always fightin' other Injuns just for the right to hunt there.

"I fought Injuns and I lived with Injuns. If you walked into an Injun village of your own will they'd feed you an' let you be as long as you stayed . . . that was their way, but the same Injun in whose tipi you slept might follow you when you left an' murder you.

"They hadn't the same upbringin' a white man has. There was none of this talk of mercy, kindness and suchlike which we get from the time we're youngsters. We get it even though most folks don't foller the teachin'. An Injun is loyal to nobody but his own tribe . . . an' any stranger is apt to be an enemy.

"You fight an Injun an' whup him, after that maybe you can trade with him. He'll deal with a fightin' man, but a man who can't protect hisself, well, most Injuns have no respect for him, so they just kill him an' forget him."

Around the fires at night there was talk and laughter. Orrin sang his old Welsh and Irish ballads for them. From Pa he'd picked up some Spanish songs, and when he sang them you should have heard them Spanish men yell! And from the far hills the coyotes answered.

Old Rountree would find a spot well back from the flames and set there watching the outer darkness and listening. A man who stares into flames is blind when he looks into outer darkness, and he won't shoot straight . . . Pa had taught us that, back in Tennessee.

This was Indian country and you have to figure, understanding Indians, that his whole standing in his tribe comes from how many coups he's counted, which means to strike an enemy, a living enemy, or to be the first one to strike a man who has fallen . . . they figure that mighty daring because the fallen man may be playing possum.

An Indian who was a good horse thief, he could have the pick of the girls in the tribe. Mostly because marriage was on the barter system, and an Indian could have all the wives he could afford to buy . . . usually that wasn't more than two or three, and mostly one.

Orrin hadn't forgotten that Laura girl. He was upset with me, too, for leading him off again when he was half a mind to tie up with Pritts.

"He's paying top wages," Orrin said, one night.

"Fighting wages," I said.

"Could be, Tyrel," Orrin said, and no friendly sound to his voice, "that you're holding something against Mr. Pritts. And against Laura, too."

Go easy, boy, I told myself, this is dangerous ground. "I don't know them. Only from what you've said he's planning to horn in on land that doesn't belong to him."

Orrin started to speak but Tom Sunday got up. "Time to turn in," he spoke abruptly, "gettin'-up time comes early."

We turned in, both of us with words we were itching to say that were better unsaid.

It rankled, however. There was truth about me having a holding against Pritts and his daughter. That I had . . . she didn't look right to me, and I've always been suspicious of those too-sanctimonious men like Jonathan Pritts.

The way he looked down that thin New England nose of his didn't promise any good for those who didn't agree with him. And what I said to Orrin that time, I'd believed. If Pritts had been so much back home, what was he doing out here?

We filled our canteens at daybreak with no certain water ahead of us. A hot wind searched the grass. At Mud Creek there was enough water in the creek bottom for the horses, but when we left it it was bone dry. It was seven miles to the Water Holes, and if there was no water there it was a dry day's travel to the Little Arkansas.

The sun was hot. Dust lifted from the feet of the horses and mules, and we left a trail of dust in the air. If any Indians were around, they'd not miss us.

"A man would have to prime himself to spit in country like this," Tom Sunday remarked. "How about the country we're heading toward, Cap?"

"Worse . . . unless a man knows the land. Only saving thing, there's no travel up thataway except for Comanches. What water there is we'll likely have to ourselves."

Every day then, Drusilla was riding with me. And every day I felt myself looking for her sooner than before. Sometimes we were only out for a half hour, at most an hour, but I got so I welcomed her coming and dreaded her going.

Back in the mountains I'd known few girls. Mostly I fought shy of them, not figuring to put my neck in any loops I couldn't pull out of . . . only I had a feeling I was getting bogged down with Drusilla.

She was shy of sixteen, but Spanish girls marry that young and younger, and in the mountains they did also. Me, I had nothing but a dapple horse, a partnership in some mules, and my old Spencer and a Colt pistol. It didn't count up to much.

Meanwhile, I'd been getting to know the *vaqueros*. I'd never known anybody before who wasn't straightout American, and back in the hills we held ourselves suspicious of such folk. Riding with them, I was finding they were good, solid men.

Miguel was a slim, wiry man who was the finest rider I ever knew, and maybe a couple of years older than me. He was a handsome man with a quick laugh, and like me he was always ready to ride far afield.

Juan Torres was the boss of the lot, a compact man of forty-three or four, who rarely smiled but was always friendly. Maybe he was the finest rifle shot I ever saw . . . he had worked for Don Luis Alvarado since he, Torres, was a boy, and thought of him like he was a god.

There was Pete Romero, and a slim, tough young devil called Antonio Baca . . . the only one who didn't have the Basque blood. It seemed to me he thought he was a better man than Torres, and there was something else I figured was just my thinking until Cap mentioned it.

"Did you ever notice how young Baca looks at you when you ride with the *señorita?*"

"He doesn't seem to like it. I noticed that."

"You watch yourself. That boy's got a streak of meanness."

That was all Cap said, but I took it to mind. Stories I'd heard made out these Spanish men to be mighty jealous, although no girl was going to look serious at me when there were men around like Orrin and Tom Sunday.

There's no accounting for the notions men get, and it seems to me the most serious trouble between men comes not so much from money, horses, or women, but from notions. A man takes a dislike to another man for no reason at all but they rub each other wrong, and then something, a horse or a woman or a drink sets it off and they go to shooting or cutting or walloping with sticks.

Like Reed Carney. Only a notion. And it could have got him killed.

At the Little Arkansas we camped where a little branch flowed from a spring in the bluff and ran down to the river. It was good water, maybe a mite brackish.

After night guard was set I slipped out of camp with a rifle and canteen and went down to the Little Arkansas. Dark was coming on but a man could see. Moving down to the river's edge . . . there was more sand than water . . . I stood listening.

A man should trust his senses and they'll grow sharper from use. I never took it for granted that the country was safe. Not only listening and watching as I moved, but testing the air for smells. Out on the prairie where the air is fresh a man can smell more than around people, and after awhile he learns to smell an Indian, a white man, a horse, or even a bear.

Off in the distance there was heat lightning, and a far-off rumble of thunder.

Waiting in the silence after the thunder a stone rattled across the river and a column of riders emerged from the brush and rode down into the river bed.

There might have been a dozen, or even twenty, and although I could not make them out I could see white streaks on their faces that meant they were painted for war.

Crossing the stream sixty, seventy yards below me they rode out across the prairie. They would not be moving this late unless there was a camp not far off, and that meant more Indians and a possible source of trouble.

When they had gone I went back to camp and got Cap Rountree. Together, we talked to Torres and made what plans we could.

Daylight came, and on the advice of Torres, Drusilla remained with the wagons. We moved slowly, trying to keep our dust down.

It was dry . . . the grass was brown, parched and sun-hot when we fetched up to Owl Creek and found it bone-dry. Little and Big Cow Creeks, also dry.

This last was twenty miles from our last night's camp and no sign of water, with another twenty to go before we reached the Bend of the Arkansas.

"There'll be water," Rountree said in his rasping voice, "there's always water in the Arkansas."

By that time I wasn't sure if there was any water left in Kansas. We took a breather at Big Cow Creek and I rinsed out Dapple's mouth with my handkerchief a couple of times. My lips were cracked and even Dapple seemed to have lost his bounce. That heat and the dry air, with no water, it was enough to take the spry out of a camel.

Dust lifted from the brown grass . . . white buffalo bones bleached in the sun. We passed the wrecks of some burned-out wagons and the skull of a horse. In the distance clouds piled up enormous towers and battlements, building dream castles in the sky. Along the prairie, heat waves danced and rippled in the sun, and far off a mirage lake showed the blue of its dream water to taunt our eyes.

From the top of a low hill I looked around at miles of brown emptiness with a vast sweep of sky overhead where the sun seemed to have grown enormously until it swept the sky. From my canteen I soaked my handkerchief and sponged out the Dapple's mouth, again. It was so dry I couldn't spit.

Far below the wagons made a thin trail . . . the hill on which I sat was low, but there was a four-mile-long slope leading gradually up to it.

The horizon was nowhere, for there was only a haze of heat around us, our horses slogging onward without hope, going because their riders knew no better.

The sky was empty, the land was still . . . the dust hung in the empty air. It was very hot.

# Chapter 4

Rountree humped his old shoulders under his thin shirt and looked ready to fall any minute but the chances were he would outlast us all. There was iron and rawhide in that old man.

Glancing back I saw a distant plume of dust, and pointed it out to Orrin who gave an arm signal to Torres. We got down from our horses, Orrin and I, and walked along to spell our mounts.

"We got to get that place for Ma," I said to Orrin, "she ain't got many years. Be nice if she could live them in comfort, in her own home, with her own fixin's."

"We'll find it."

Dust puffed from each step. Pausing to look back, he squinted his eyes against the glare and the sting of sweat. "We got to learn something, Tye," he said suddenly, "we're both ignorant, and it ain't a way to be. Listening to Tom makes a man think. If a body had an education like that, no telling how far he'd go."

"Tom's got the right idea. In this western land a man could make something of himself."

"The country makes a man think of it. It's a big country with lots of room to spread out . . . it gives a man big ideas."

When we got back into the saddle the leather was so hot on my bottom I durned near yelled when I settled down into my seat.

After awhile, country like that, you just keep moving, putting one foot ahead of the other like a man in a trance. It was dark with the stars out when we smelled green trees, grass, and the cool sweetness of water running. We came up to the Arkansas by starlight and I'd still a cup of brackish water in my canteen. Right away, never knowing what will happen, I dumped it out, rinsed the canteen and filled it up again.

Taking that canteen to Drusilla's wagon I noticed Baca watching me with a hard look in his eyes. She was too good for either of us.

The four of us built our own fire away from the others because we had business to talk.

"The don has quite a place, Torres tells me. Big grant of land. Mountains, meadows, forest . . . and lots of cattle." Cap had been talking to Torres for some time. "Runs sheep, too. And a couple of mines, a sawmill."

"I hear he's a land hog," Orrin commented. "Lots of folks would like to build homes there, if he'd let 'em."

"Would you, Orrin, if you owned the land?" Tom asked mildly.

"Nobody has a right to all that. Anyway, he ain't an American," Orrin insisted.

Rountree was no hand to argue but he was a just old man. "He's owned that land forty years, and he got it from his father who moved into that country back in 1794. Seems they should have an idea of who it belongs to."

"Maybe I was mistaken," Orrin replied. "That was what I'd heard."

"Don Luis is no pilgrim," Rountree told us, "I heard about him when I first come west. He and his pappy, they fought Utes, Navajo, and Comanches. They worked that land, brought sheep and cattle clear from Mexico, and they opened the mines, built the sawmill. I reckon anybody wants to take their land is goin' to have to dig in an' scratch."

"It doesn't seem to me that Jonathan Pritts would do anything that isn't right," Orrin argued. "Not if he knows the facts."

Pawnee Rock was next . . . Torres came over to our fire to tell us Don Luis had decided to fight shy of it.

Orrin wanted to see it and so did I, so the four of us decided to ride that way while the wagons cut wide around it.

Forty or fifty men were camped near the Rock, a tough, noisy, drunken crowd, well supplied with whiskey.

"Looks like a war party," Rountree commented.

Suddenly I had a bad feeling that this was the Pritts crowd, for I could think of no reason why a bunch of that size should be camping here without wagons or women. And I saw one of them who had been with the Back Rand crowd the other side of Abilene.

When they saw us riding up, several got up from where they'd been loafing. "Howdy! Where you from?"

"Passing through." Tom Sunday glanced past the few men who had come to greet us at their camp, which was no decent camp, but dirty, untidy and casual. "We're headed for the upper Cimarron," he added.

"Why don't you step down? We got a proposition for you."

"We're behind time," Orrin told him, and he was looking at their faces as if he wanted to remember them.

Several others had strolled toward us, sort of circling casually around as if they wanted to get behind us, so I let the dapple turn to face them.

They didn't take to that, not a little bit, and one redhead among them took it up. "What's the matter? You afraid of something?"

When a man faces up to trouble with an outfit like that you get nowhere either talking or running, so I started the dapple toward him, not saying a word, but walking the horse right at him. My right hand was on my thigh within inches of my six-shooter, and it sized up to me like they figured to see what would happen if Red crowded me.

Red started to side-step but the dapple was a cutting horse Pa had used working stock, and once you pointed that horse at anything, man or animal, he knew what his job was.

Red backed off, and long ago I'd learned that when you get a man to backing up it's hard for him to stop and start coming at you. Every move he made the dapple shifted and went for him, and all of a sudden Red got desperate and grabbed for his gun and just as he grabbed I spurred the dapple into him. The dapple hit him with a shoulder and Red went down hard. He lost grip on the pistol which fell several feet away.

Red lay on the ground on his back with the dapple right over him, and I hadn't said a word.

While everybody was watching the show Red and the dapple were putting on, Orrin had his pistol lying there in his lap. Both Tom Sunday and Cap Rountree had their rifles ready and Cap spoke up. "Like I said, we're just passing through."

Red started to get up and the dapple shifted his weight and Red relaxed. "You get up when we're gone, Red. You're in too much of a sweat to get killed."

Several of the others had seen what was going on and started toward us. "All right, Tye?" Orrin asked.

"Let's go," I said, and we dusted out of there.

One thing Cap had in mind and I knew it was what he was thinking. If they were watching us they wouldn't have noticed the passing of the wagons, and they didn't. We watered at Coon Creek and headed for Fort Dodge.

The Barlow, Sanderson Company stage came in while we were in Fort Dodge. Seems a mighty fine way to travel, sitting back against the cushions with nice folks around you.

We were standing there watching when we heard the stage driver talking to a sergeant. "Looks like a fight shaping up over squatters trying to move in on the Spanish grants," he said.

Orrin turned away. "Good thing we're straying shut of that fight," he said. "We'll be better off hunting cows."

When we rode back to camp everything was a-bustle with packing and loading up.

Torres came to us. "We go, *señores*. There is word of trouble from home. We take the dry route south from here. You will not come with us?"

"We're going to the Purgatoire."

"Then it will be *adios*." Torres glanced at me. "I know that Don Luis will wish to say good-by to you, *señor*."

At the wagons Don Luis was nowhere in sight, but Drusilla was. When she saw me she came quickly forward. "Oh, Tye! We're going! Will I ever see you again?"

"I'll be coming to Santa Fe. Shall I call on you then?"

"Please do."

We stood together in the darkness with all the hurry around us of people packing and getting ready to move, the jingle of trace chains, the movement and the shouts.

Only I felt like something was going right out from my insides, and I'd never felt this way before. Right then I didn't want to hunt wild cows. I wanted to go to Santa Fe. Was this the way Orrin felt about Laura Pritts?

But how could I feel any way at all about her? I was a mountain boy who could scarcely read printing and who could not write more than his name.

"Will you write to me, Tyrel?"

How could I tell her I didn't know how? "I'll write," I said, and swore to myself that I'd learn. I'd get Tom to teach me.

Orrin was right. We would have to get an education, some way, somehow.

"I'll miss you."

Me, like a damned fool I stood there twisting my hat. If I'd only had some of Orrin's easy talk! But I'd never talked much to any girl or even womenfolks, and I'd no idea what a man said to them.

"It was mighty fine," I told her, "riding out on the plains with you."

She moved closer to me and I wanted to kiss her the worst way, but what right had a Tennessee boy to kiss the daughter of a Spanish don?

"I'll miss the riding," I said, grasping at something to say. "I'll sure miss it."

She stood on her tiptoes suddenly and kissed me, and then she ran. I turned right around and walked right into a tree. I backed off and started again and just then Antonio Baca came out of the darkness and he had a knife held low down in his hand. He didn't say anything, just lunged at me.

Talking to girls was one thing, cutting scrapes was something else. Pa had brought me up right one way, at least. It was without thinking, what I did. My left palm slapped his knife wrist over to my right to get the blade out of line with my body, and my right hand dropped on his wrist as my left leg came across in front of him, and then I just spilled him over my leg and threw him hard against a tree trunk.

He was in the air when he hit it, and the knife fell free. Scooping it up, I just walked on and never even looked back. One time there, I figured I heard him groan, but I was sure he was alive all right. Just shook up.

Tom Sunday was in the saddle with my dapple beside him. "Orrin and Cap went on. They'll meet us at the Fort."

"All right," I said.

"I figured you'd want to say good-by. Mighty hard to leave a girl as pretty as that."

I looked at him. "First girl ever paid me any mind," I said. "Girls don't cotton to me much."

"As long as girls like that one like you, you've nothing to worry about," he said quietly. "She's a real lady. You've a right to be proud."

Then he saw the knife in my hand. Everybody knew that knife who had been with the wagons. Baca was always flashing it around.

"Collecting souvenirs?" Tom asked dryly.

"Wasn't planning on it." I shoved the knife down in my belt. "Sort of fell into it."

We rode on a few steps and he said, "Did you kill him?"

"No."

"You should have," he said, "because you'll have it to do."

Seems I never had a difficulty with a man that made so little impression. All I could think of was Drusilla Alvarado, and the fact that we were riding away from her. All the time I kept telling myself I was a fool, that she was not for me. But it didn't make a mite of difference, and from that day on I understood Orrin a lot better and felt sorry for him.

Nothing changed my mind about that narrow-between-the-ears blonde, though. That roan horse never had been any account, and miserable, contrary and ornery it was, too.

We could see the lights of the Fort up ahead and behind me the rumble of those wagon wheels as the train moved out, the rattle of trace chains, and the Mexicans calling to each other.

"Tom," I said, "I got to learn to write. I really got to learn."

"You should learn," he told me seriously, "I'll be glad to teach you."

"And to read writing?"

"All right."

We rode in silence for a little while and then Tom Sunday said, "Tye, this is a big country out here and it takes big men to live in it, but it gives every man an equal opportunity. You're just as big or small as your vision is, and if you've a mind to work and make something of yourself, you can do it."

He was telling me that I could be important enough for even a don's daughter, I knew that. He was telling me that and suddenly I did not need to be told. He was right, of course, and all the time I'd known it. This was a country to grow up in, a land where a man had a chance.

The stars were bright. The camp lay far behind. Somebody in the settlement ahead laughed and somebody else dropped a bucket and it rolled down some steps.

A faint breeze stirred, cool and pleasant. We were making the first step. We were going after wild cows.

We were bound for the Purgatoire.

# Chapter 5

Cap Rountree had trapped beaver all over the country we were riding toward. He had been there with Kit Carson, Uncle Dick Wootton, Jim Bridger, and the Bents. He knew the country like an Indian would know it.

Tom Sunday . . . I often wondered about Tom. He was a Texan, he said, and that was good enough. He knew more about cattle than any of us.

Orrin and me, well, most of what we'd had all our lives came from our own planting or hunting, and we grew up with a knowledge of the herbs a man can eat and how to get along in the forest.

The country we were riding toward was Indian country. It was a place where the Comanches, Utes, Arapahos, and Kiowas raided and fought, and there were Cheyennes about, too. And sometimes the Apaches raiding north. In this country the price for a few lazy minutes might be the death of every man in the party. It was no place for a loafer or one lacking responsibility.

Always and forever we were conscious of the sky. City folks almost never look at the sky or the stars but with us there was no choice. They were always with us.

Tom Sunday was a man who knew a sight of poetry, and riding across the country thataway, he'd recite it for us. It was a lonely life, you know, and I expect what Sunday missed most was the reading. Books were rare and treasured things, hard to come by and often fought over. Newspapers the same.

A man couldn't walk down to the corner and buy a paper. Nor did he have a postman to deliver it to him. I've known cowhands to memorize the labels off canned fruit and vegetables for lack of reading.

Cap knew that country, knew every creek and every fork. There were no maps except what a man had in his skull, and nobody of whom to ask directions, so a body remembered what he saw. Cap knew a thousand miles of country like a man might know his kitchen, to home.

These mornings the air was fresher. There was a faint chill in the air, a sign we were getting higher. We were riding along in the early hours when we saw the wagons.

Seven wagons, burned and charred. We moved in carefully, rifles up and ready; edged over to them, holding to a shallow dip in the prairie until we were close up.

Folks back east have a sight to say about the poor Indian but they never fought him. He was a fighter by trade, and because he naturally loved it, mercy never entered his head.

Mercy is a taught thing. Nobody comes by it natural. Indians grew up thinking the tribe was all there was and anybody else was an enemy.

It wasn't a fault, simply that nobody had ever suggested such a thing to him. An enemy was to be killed, and then cut up so if you met him in the afterlife he wouldn't have the use of his limbs to attack you again. Some Indians believed a mutilated man would never get into the hereafter.

Two of the men in this outfit had been spreadeagled on wagon wheels, shot full of arrows, and scalped. The women lay scattered about, their clothing ripped off, blood all over. One man had got into a buffalo wallow with his woman and had made a stand there.

"No marks on them," I said, "they must have died after the Indians left."

"No," Cap indicated the tracks of moccasins near the bodies. "They killed themselves when their ammunition gave out." He showed us powder burns on the woman's dress and the man's temple. "Killed her and then himself."

The man who made the stand there in the wallow had accounted for some Indians. We found spots of blood on the grass that gave reason to believe he'd killed four or five, but Indians always carry their dead away.

"They aren't mutilated because the man fought well. Indians respect a fighter and they respect almost nobody else. But sometimes they cut them up, too."

We buried the two where they lay in the wallow, and the others we buried in a common grave nearby, using a shovel found near one of the wagons.

Cap found several letters that hadn't burned and put them in his pocket. "Least we can do," he said, "the folks back home will want to know."

Sunday was standing off sizing up those wagons and looking puzzled. "Cap," he said, "come over here a minute."

The wagons had been set afire but some had burned hardly at all before the fire went out. They were charred all over, and the canvas tops were burned, of course.

"See what you mean," Orrin said, "seems to be a mighty thick bottom on that wagon."

"Too thick," Sunday said, "I think there's a false bottom."

Using the shovel he pried a board until we could get enough grip to pull it loose. There was a compartment there, and in it a flat iron box, which we broke into.

Inside were several sacks of gold money and a little silver, coming to more than a thousand dollars. There were also a few letters in that box.

"This is better than hunting cows," Sunday said. "We've got us a nice piece of money here."

"Maybe somebody needs that money," Orrin suggested. "We'd better read those letters and see if we can find the owner."

Tom Sunday looked at him, smiling, but something in his smile made a body think he didn't feel like smiling. "You aren't serious? The owner's dead."

"Ma would need that money mighty bad if it had been sent to her by Tyrel and me," Orrin said, "and it could be somebody needs this money right bad."

First off, I'd thought he was joking, but he was dead serious, and the way he looked at it made me back up and take another look myself. The thing to do was to find who the money rightfully belonged to and send it to them . . . if we found nobody then it would be all right to keep it.

Cap Rountree just stood there stoking that old pipe and studying Orrin with care, like he seen something mighty interesting.

There wasn't five dollars amongst us now. We'd had to buy pack animals and our outfit, and we had broke ourselves, what with Orrin and me sending a little money to Ma from Abilene. Now we were about to start four or five months of hard work, and risk our hair into the bargain, for no more than this.

"These people are dead, Orrin," Tom Sunday said irritably, "and if we hadn't found it years might pass before anybody else did, and by that time any letter would have fallen to pieces."

Standing there watching the two of them I'd no idea what was happening to us, and that the feelings from that dispute would affect all our lives, and for many years. At the time it seemed such a little thing.

"Not in this life will any of us ever find a thousand dollars in gold. Not again. And you suggest we try to find the owner."

"Whatever we do we'd better decide somewheres else," I commented. "There might be Indians around."

Come dusk we camped in some trees near the Arkansas, bringing all the stock in close and watering them well. Nobody did any talking. This was

no place to have trouble but when it came to that, Orrin was my brother
. . . and he was in the right.

Now personally, I'm not sure I'd have thought of it. Mayhap I wouldn't
have mentioned it if I did think of it . . . a man never knows about
things like that. Rountree hadn't done anything but listen and smoke that
old pipe of his.

It was when we were sitting over coffee that Tom brought it up again.
"We'd be fools not to keep that money, Orrin. How do we know who
we'd be sending it to? Maybe some relative who hated him. Certainly,
nobody needs it more than we do."

Orrin, he just sat there studying those letters. "Those folks had a
daughter back home," Orrin said, finally, "an' she's barely sixteen. She's
living with friends until they send for her, and when those friends find
out she isn't going to be sent for, and they can expect no more money,
then what happens to that girl?"

The question bothered Tom, and it made him mad. His face got red
and set in stubborn lines, and he said, "You send your share. I'll take a
quarter of it . . . right now. If I hadn't noticed that wagon the money
would never have been found."

"You're right about that, Tom," Orrin said reasonably, "but that money
just ain't ours."

Slowly, Tom Sunday got to his feet. He was mad clear through and
pushing for a fight. So I got up, too.

"Kid," he said angrily, "you stay out of this. This is between Orrin and
me."

"We're all in this together, Cap an' me as much as Orrin and you. We
started out to round up wild cattle, and if we start it with trouble there's
no way we can win."

Orrin said, "Now if that money belonged to a man, maybe I'd never
have thought of returning it, but with a girl as young as that, no telling
what she'll come to, turned loose on the world at that age. This money
could make a lot if difference."

Tom was a prideful and stubborn man, ready to take on the two of us.
Then Rountree settled matters.

"Tom," he said mildly, "you're wrong, an' what's more, you know it.
This here outfit is four-sided and I vote with the Sackett boys. You ain't
agin democracy, are you, Tom?"

"You know darned well I'm not, and as long as you put it that way, I'll
sit down. Only I think we're damned fools."

"Tom, you're probably right, but that's the kind of a damned fool I
am," said Orrin. "When the cows are rounded up if you don't feel
different about it you can have my share of the cows."

THE DAYBREAKERS

Tom Sunday just looked at Orrin. "You damned fool. Next thing we know you'll be singing hymns in a church."

"I know a couple," Orrin said. "You all set down and while Tyrel gets supper, I'll sing you a couple."

And that was the end of it . . . or we thought it was. Sometimes I wonder if anything is ever ended. The words a man speaks today live on in his thoughts or the memories of others, and the shot fired, the blow struck, the thing done today is like a stone tossed into a pool and the ripples keep widening out until they touch lives far from ours.

So Orrin sang his hymns, and followed them with *Black, Black, Black, Lord Randall, Barbara Allan* and *Sweet Betsy*. When Orrin finished the last one Tom reached over and held out his hand and Orrin grinned at him and shook it.

No more was said about the gold money and it was put away in the bottom of a pack and to all intents it was forgotten. If that amount of gold is ever forgotten.

We were getting into the country of the wild cattle now. Cap Rountree as well as others had noticed these wild cattle, some of them escaped from Spanish settlements to the south, and some escaped or stampeded by Indians from wagon trains bound for California.

No doubt Indians had killed a few, but Indians preferred buffalo, and many of these cattle had come south with buffalo herds. There was no shortage of buffalo in 1867, and the Indians only killed the wild cattle when there was nothing else.

The country we were going to work lay south of the Mountain Branch of the Santa Fe Trail, between the Purgatoire and Two Buttes Creek, and south to the Mal Pais. It was big country and it was rough country. We rode south through sage plains with some mesquite, with juniper and piñon on the hills.

Cap had in his mind a hidden place, a canyon near the base of a mountain where a cold spring of sweet water came out of the rocks. There was maybe two hundred acres of good grass in the bottom, grass belly-high to a horse, and from the look of it nobody had seen it since Cap Rountree stumbled on it twenty years back.

First off, we forted up. Behind us the cliffs lifted sheer with an overhang that provided shelter from above. Right out in front there was four or five acres of meadow with good grass, edged on the far side by trees and rocks. Beyond that was the bowl with the big pasture as we called it, and in an adjoining canyon was a still larger area where we figured to trap the wild cattle and hold them.

We spent that first day gathering fuel, adding a few rocks to our fort, and generally scouting the country close around our hide-out. Also, I killed a deer and Cap got a buffalo. We brought the meat into camp and started jerking it.

Next morning at daybreak we started out to scout the country. Within an hour's riding we'd seen sixty or seventy head. A man never saw such cattle. There was a longhorn bull in that crowd that must have stood seven feet and would have weighed sixteen hundred pounds. And horns? Needle sharp.

By nightfall we had a good bunch of cattle in the bowl or drifted toward it. By the third day we had more than a hundred head in that bowl and we were beginning to count our money.

It was slow, patient work. Push them too fast and they would stampede clear out of the country, so we tried to move them without them guessing what we planned.

We had two things to accomplish: to catch ourselves some wild cattle and to stay alive while doing it. And it wasn't only Indians we had to think about, but the cattle themselves, for some of those tough old bulls showed fight, and the cows could be just as mean if they caught a man afoot. Of a night we yarned around the fire or belly-ached about somebody's cooking. We took turn about on that job.

We kept our fires small, used the driest wood, and we moved around only when we had to. We daren't set any patterns of work so's Indians could lay for us. We never took the same trail back that we used on the way out, and we kept our eyes open all the time.

We gathered cattle. We sweated, we swore, and we ate dust, but we gathered them up, six one day, twelve another, nineteen, then only three. There was no telling how it would be. We got them into the bowl where there was grass and plenty of water and we watched them get fat. Also, it gave them time to settle down.

Then trouble hit us. Orrin was riding a sorrel we had picked up in Dodge. He was off by himself and he started down a steep hillside and the sorrel fell. That little sorrel got up fast with Orrin's foot caught in the stirrup and he buckled down to run. There was only one way Orrin could keep from being dragged to death, and that was one reason cowhands always carried pistols. He shot the sorrel.

Come nightfall there was no sign of Orrin. We had taken to coming in early so if anything went wrong with any of us there would be time to do something before night.

We set out to look. Tom went south, swinging back toward the east, Cap went west, and I followed up a canyon to the north before topping out on the rim. It was me found him, walking along, packing his saddle and his Winchester.

When he put down the saddle on seeing me, I rode up to him. "You took long enough," he grumbled, but there was no grumble in his eyes, "I was fixing to cache my saddle."

"You could have fired a shot."

"There were Indians closer than you," he said.

Orrin told us about it around the fire. He had shucked his saddle off the dead sorrel and started for camp, but being a sly one, he was not about to leave a direct trail to our hide-out, so he went downhill first and stumbled on a rocky ledge which he followed sixty or seventy yards.

There had been nine or ten Indians in the party and he saw them before they saw him, so he just laid right down where he was and let them pass by. They were all warriors, and the way they were riding they might miss his dead horse.

"They'll find it," Cap told us, "it's nigh to dark now, so they won't get far tonight. Likely they'll camp somewhere down the creek. At daybreak they'll see the buzzards."

"So?"

"That's a shod horse. It isn't likely they'd pass up a chance to get one man afoot and alone."

Any other time we could have high-tailed it out of the country and left them nothing but tracks, but now we were men of property and property ties a man down.

"Think they'll find us?"

"Likely," Cap said. "Reckon we better hold to camp a day or two. Horses need the rest, anyway."

We all sat there feeling mighty glum, knowing the chances were that if the Indians didn't find us they would stay around the country, looking for us. That meant that our chance of rounding up more cattle was coming down to nothing.

"You know what I think?" They waited for me to speak up. "I think we should cash in our chips. I think we should take what we've got and hit the trail for Santa Fe, sell what we've got and get us a proper outfit. We need three or four horses per man for this kind of work."

Tom Sunday flipped his bowie knife into the sand, retrieved it and studied the light on the blade while he gave it thought. "Not a bad idea," he said.

"Cap?"

"If Orrin's willin'." Cap hesitated. "I figure we should dust out of here, come daybreak."

"Wasn't what I had in mind," I said, "I meant to leave right now . . . before those Indians find that sorrel."

The reason I hadn't waited for Orrin to speak was because I knew he

was pining to see that yellow-haired girl and I had some visiting in mind
my own self.

Only it wasn't that . . . it was the plain, common-sense notion that
once those Indians knew we were here, starting a herd might be tough to
do. It might take them a day or two to work out our trail. Chances were
by the time they found we were gone we'd be miles down the trail.

So I just picked up my saddle and headed for my horse. There is a time
that calls for action and when debate makes no sense. Starting a herd in
the middle of the night isn't the best thing to do, but handling cattle we'd
be scattered out and easy picking for Indians, and I wanted to get started.

We just packed up and lit out. Those cattle were heavy with water and
grass and not in the mood for travel but we started them anyhow. We put
the north star at our backs and started for Santa Fe.

When the first sun broke the gray sky we had six miles behind us.

# Chapter 6

We had our troubles. When that bunch began to realize what was happening they didn't like it. We wore our horses to a frazzle but we kept that herd on the trail right up to dusk to tire them out as much as to get distance behind us. We kept a sharp lookout, but we saw no Indians.

Santa Fe was a smaller town than we expected, and it sure didn't shape up to more than a huddle of adobe houses built around a sunbaked plaza, but it was the most town I'd ever seen, or Orrin.

Folks stood in the doorways and shaded their eyes at us as we bunched our cows, and then three riders, Spanish men, started up the trail toward us. They were cantering their horses and staring at us, then they broke into a gallop and came charging up with shrill yells that almost started our herd again. It was Miguel, Pete Romero, and a rider named Abreu.

"Ho!" Miguel was smiling. "It is good to see you, *amigo*. We have been watching for you. Don Luis has asked that you be his guests for dinner."

"Does he know we're here?" Orrin was surprised.

Miguel glanced at him. "Don Luis knows most things, *señor*. A rider brought news from the Vegas."

They remained with the herd while we rode into town.

We walked over to the La Fonda and left our horses in the shade. It was cool inside, and quiet. It was shadowed there like a cathedral, only this here was no cathedral. It was a drinking place, and a hotel, too, I guess.

Mostly they were Spanish men sitting around, talking it soft in that soft-sounding tongue of theirs, and it gave me a wonderful feeling of being a travelled man, of being in foreign parts. A couple of them spoke to us, most polite.

We sat down and dug deep for the little we had. Wasn't much, but enough for a few glasses of wine and mayhap something to eat. I liked hearing the soft murmur of voices, the clink of glasses, and the click of heels on the floor. Somewhere out back a woman laughed, and it was a mighty fine sound.

While we sat there an Army officer came in. Tall man, thirtyish with a

clean uniform and a stiff way of walking like those Army men have. He
had mighty fancy mustaches.

"Are you the men who own those cattle on the edge of town?"

"Are you in the market?" Orrin said.

"That depends on the price."

He sat down with us and ordered a glass of wine.

"I will be frank, gentlemen, there has been a drought here and a lot of
cattle have been lost. Most of the stock is very thin. Yours is the first fat
beef we've seen."

Tom Sunday glanced up and smiled. "We will want twenty-five dollars
per head."

The captain merely glanced at him. "Of course not," he said, then he
smiled at us and lifted his glass. "Your health—"

"What about Don Luis Alvarado?" Orrin asked suddenly.

The captain's expression stiffened a little and he asked, "Are you one of
the Pritts crowd?"

"No," Tom Sunday said, "we met the don out on the Plains. Came
west from Abilene with him, as a matter of fact."

"He's one of those who welcomed us in New Mexico. Before we took
over the Territory the Mexican government was in no position to send
troops to protect these colonies from the Indians. Also, most of the trade
was between Santa Fe and the States, rather than between Santa Fe and
Mexico. The don appreciated this, and most of the people here welcomed
us."

"Jonathan Pritts is bringing in settlers," Orrin said.

"Mr. Pritts is a forceful and energetic man," the captain said, "but he is
under the false impression that because New Mexico has become a possession of the United States . . . I should say, a part of the United States
. . . that the property rights of all Spanish-speaking people will be tossed
out the window."

There was a pause. "The settlers—if one wishes to call them that—that
Jonathan Pritts is bringing in are all men who bring their guns instead of
families."

I had me another glass of wine and sat back and listened to the captain
talking with Tom Sunday. Seems the captain was out of that Army
school, West Point, but he was a man who had read a sight of books. A
man never realizes how little he knows until he listens to folks like that
talk. Up where I was born we had the Bible, and once in awhile somebody would bring a newspaper but it was a rare thing when we saw any
other kind of reading.

Politics was a high card up in the hills. A political speech would bring
out the whole country. Folks would pack their picnic lunches and you'd

see people at a speech you'd never see elsewhere. Back in those days most every boy grew up knowing as much about local politics as about coon dogs, which was about equal as to interest.

Orrin and me, we just set and listened. A man can learn a lot if he listens, and if I didn't learn anything else I was learning how much I didn't know. It made me hungry to know it all, and mad because I was getting so late a start.

We'd picked up a few more head of cattle coming south and the way it was going to figure out, each of us would have more than a thousand dollars of his own when we'd settled up. Next day Orrin and Cap went to the stage office and arranged to ship east the gold we'd found in the wagon.

The itch to see the town got the best of me so I walked outside. Those black-eyed *señoritas* was enough to turn a man's good sense. If Orrin would look at some of these girls he'd forget all about Laura. It was no wonder he fell for her. After a man has been surrounded for months by a lot of hard-handed, hairy-chested men even the doggiest kind of female looks mighty good.

Most of all right now I wanted a bath and a shave. Cap, he followed me.

"Seems to me there's things around town need seeing to," I suggested.

"You look here, Tyrel, if you're thinkin' of what I think you're thinkin' you'd better scout the country and study the sign before you make your move. If you figure to court a Spanish gal you'd also better figure to fight her man."

"Seems like it might be worth it."

This was siesta time. A dog opened one eye and wagged a tail to show that if I didn't bother him he'd be pleased. Me, I wasn't of a mind to bother anybody.

Taking it slow, I walked down the dusty street. The town was quiet. A wide door opened into a long, barnlike building with a lot of tubs and water running through in a ditch. There was homemade soap there and nobody around. There was a pump there, too. It was the first time I ever saw a pump inside a house. Folks are sure getting lazy . . . won't even go outside the house to pump.

This here must be a public bathhouse, but there was nobody around to take my money. I filled a tub with water, stripped off and got in and when I'd covered with soap, head to foot, three women came in with bundles of clothes on their heads.

First off I stared and they stared and then I yelled. All of a sudden I realized this here was no bathhouse but a place to wash clothes.

Those Spanish girls had taken one look and then they began to shriek, and first off I figured they were scared, but they weren't running, they were just standing there laughing at me.

*Laughing!*

Grabbing a bucket of water I doused myself with it and grabbed up a towel. Then they ran outside and I could hear screams and I never crawled into my clothes so fast in all my born days. Slinging gun belt around me at a dead run I beat it for my horse.

It must have been a sight, me all soapy in that tub. Red around the gills. I started Dapple out of town on a run and the last thing I could hear was laughter. Women sure do beat all.

Anyway, I'd had a bath.

Morning was bright and beautiful like nine mornings out of ten in the high desert country. We met the captain and turned the cattle over to him. We'd finally settled on twenty dollars a head, which was a very good price at the time and place.

First off, as we rode into town, a girl spotted me. She pointed her finger at me, gasped, and spoke excitedly to the girl with her, and then they both began to look at me and laugh.

Orrin was puzzled because the girls always noticed him first and paid me no mind. "Do you know those girls?"

"Me? I never saw them before in my life." But it gave me a tipoff as to what it was going to be like. That story must be all over Santa Fe by now.

Before we reached the La Fonda we'd passed a dozen girls and they all laughed or smiled at me. Tom Sunday and Orrin, they hadn't an idea of what was going on.

The La Fonda was cool and pleasant again, so we ordered wine and a meal. The girl who took our order realized all of a sudden who I was and she began to giggle. When she went out with our order, two or three girls came from the kitchen to look at me.

Picking up a glass of wine, I tried to appear worldly and mighty smug about it all. Fact was, I felt pretty foolish.

Orrin was getting sore. He couldn't understand this sudden interest the girls were taking in me. He was curious, interested and kind of jealous all to once. Only thing I could do was stand my ground and wear it out or high-tail it for the brush.

Santa Fe was a small town, but it was a friendly town. Folks here all wanted the good time that strangers brought. Those years, it was a town at the end of things, although it was old enough to have been a center of everything. And the girls loved a fandango and enjoyed the presence of the Americans.

There was a cute little button of a Mexican girl and every time I'd see her she'd give me a flashing glance out of those big dark eyes, and believe me, I'd get flustered.

This one had a shape to take a man's eye. Every time she'd pass me on the streets she'd give a little more swish to her skirts and I figured we could get acquainted if I just knew how to go about it. Her name was Tina Fernandez.

Night of the second day, there was a knock at the door and when I opened it Fetterson was standing there.

"Mr. Pritts wants to see you, all of you. He wants to talk business."

We looked at each other, then Orrin got up to go. The rest of us followed him and a Mexican standing at the bar turned his back on us. Anybody who was friendly to Jonathan Pritts would find few friends in Santa Fe.

It wasn't just that which worried me. It was Orrin.

Jonathan Pritts had four men outside the adobe where he lived and a few others loafing near the corral. Through the bunkhouse door I could see several men, all armed.

One thing you've got to watch, Tyrel, I told myself, is a man with so many fighters around. He wouldn't have all those men unless he figured he'd need them.

Rountree glanced at me. He was badger tough and coon smart. Sunday paused on the porch and took out a cigar; when he reached back and struck the match on his pants three chairs creaked as men put their hands to their guns. Tom didn't let on he noticed but there was a sly smile around his mouth.

Laura came to meet us in a blue dress that brought out the blue in her eyes, so she looked like an angel. The way she offered both hands to Orrin and the way she looked at him . . . it was enough to make a man gag. Only Orrin wasn't gagging. He was looking like somebody had hit him with a fence post.

Cap was uncommon sour but Sunday—always a hand with the ladies—gave her a wide smile. Sometimes I thought it irritated him that Laura had chosen to fall for Orrin and not him.

Her eyes looked past Orrin at me and our minds were hitched to the same idea. We simply did not like each other.

Jonathan Pritts entered wearing a preacher's coat and a collar that made you wonder whether he was going to offer prayer or sell you a gold brick.

He passed around a box of cigars and I was glad I didn't smoke. Orrin accepted a cigar, and after the slightest hesitation, Tom did too.

"I don't smoke," I said.

"Will you have a drink?"

"I don't drink," I said.

Orrin looked at me, because while I don't care for the stuff I sometimes drink with friends.

"You boys have done well with your cattle," Pritts said, "and I like men with business minds. However, I am wondering what you plan to do with the proceeds of your success. I can use men who want to invest business brains and capital, men who can start something and carry it through."

Nobody said anything and he brushed the ash from his cigar and studied the glowing end for a minute.

"There may be a little trouble at first. The people on the land are not Americans and may resent our moving in."

Orrin spoke slowly. "Tyrel and me came west hunting land. We're looking for a home."

"Good! New Mexico is now a part of the United States, and it's time that we American citizens had the benefits."

He drew deep on his cigar. "The first comers will be first served."

"The way it sounds," I said, "you plan to shove out the first comers and move in yourself."

Pritts was mad. He was not accustomed to straight talk—least of all from men like us. He said nothing for a moment and Laura sat down near Orrin and I got a whiff of her perfume.

"The Mexicans have no rights," Pritts replied. "The land belongs to us freeborn Americans, and if you come in with us now you will have shares in the company we are forming."

"We need a home for Ma," Orrin said, "we do need land."

"If we get it this way, there'll be blood on it," I said, "but first we should get Mr. Pritts' proposition in writing, just what he has in mind, and how he aims to settle up." That was Pa talking. As Pa always said, "Get it in writing, boy."

"A gentleman's word," Pritts replied stiffly, "should be enough."

I got up. I'd no idea what the others figured to do and didn't much care. This sanctimonious old goat was figuring to steal land from folks who'd lived on it for years.

"A man who is talking on stealing land with guns," I said, "is in no position to talk about himself as being a gentleman. Those people are American citizens now as much as you or me."

Turning around, I started for the door, and Cap Rountree was only a step behind me. Tom Sunday hesitated, being a polite man, but the four of us were four who worked and travelled together, so he followed us. Orrin lagged a little, but he came.

Pritts yelled after us, his voice trembling he was so mad. "Remember this! Those who aren't with me are against me! Ride out of town and don't come back!"

None of us were greenhorns and we knew those men on the porch weren't knitting so when we stopped, the four of us faced out in four directions. "Mr. Pritts," I said, "you've got mighty big ideas for such a small head. Don't you make trouble for us or we'll run you back to the country they run you out of."

He was coming after us and he stopped in midstride, stopped as though I'd hit him with my fist. Right then I knew what I'd said was true . . . somebody had run him out of somewhere.

He was an arrogant man who fancied himself important, and mostly he carried it off, but now he was mad. "We'll see about that!" he shouted. "Wilson, *take them!*"

Rountree was facing the first man who started to get out of a chair, which was Wilson, and there was no mercy in old Cap. He just laid a gun barrel alongside of Wilson's head and Wilson folded right back into his chair.

The man facing Orrin had a six-shooter in his stomach and I was looking across a gun barrel at Pritts himself.

"Mr. Pritts," I said, "you're a man who wants to move in on folks with guns. Now you just tell them to go ahead with what they've started and you'll be dead on the floor by the time you've said it."

Laura stared at me with such hatred as I've ever seen on a woman's face. There was a girl with a mighty big picture of her pa and anybody who didn't see her pa the way she did couldn't be anything but evil. And whoever she married was always going to play second fiddle to Jonathan Pritts.

Pritts looked like he'd swallowed something that wasn't good for him. He looked at that Navy Colt and he knew I was not fooling. And so did I.

"All right." He almost choked on it. "You can go."

We walked to our horses with nobody talking and when we were in our saddles Orrin turned on me. "Damn you, Tye, you played hell. You the same as called him a thief."

"That land belongs to Alvarado. We killed a lot of Higginses for less."

That night I slept mighty little, trying to figure out if I'd done right. Anyway I looked at it, I thought I'd done the right thing, and I didn't believe my liking for Drusilla had a thing to do with it. And believe me, I thought about that.

Next morning I saw Fetterson riding out of town with a pack of about forty men, and Wilson was with him. Only Wilson's hat wasn't setting right because of the lump on his skull. They rode out of town, headed northeast.

About the time they cleared the last house a Mexican boy mounted on a speedy looking sorrel took off for the hills, riding like the devil was on his tail.

Looked to me like Don Luis had his own warning system and would be ready for Fetterson before he got there. Riding that fast he wouldn't be riding far, so chances were a relay of horses was waiting to carry the word. Don Luis had a lot of men, lots of horses, and a good many friends.

Orrin came out, stuffing his shirt into his pants. He looked mean as a bear with a sore tooth. "You had no call to jump Mr. Pritts like that."

"If he was an honest man, I'd have nothing to say."

Orrin sat down. One thing a body could say for Orrin, he was a fair man. "Tyrel," he said at last, "you ought to think before you talk. I like that girl."

Well . . . I felt mighty mean and low down. I set store by Orrin. Most ways he was smarter than me, but about this Pritts affair, I figured he was wrong.

"Orrin, I'm sorry. We never had much, you and me. But what we had, we had honest. We want a home for Ma. But it wouldn't be the home she wants if it was bought with blood."

"Well . . . damn it, Tyrel, you're right, of course. I just wish you hadn't been so rough on Mr. Pritts."

"I'm sorry. It was me, not you. You ain't accountable for the brother you've got."

"Tyrel, don't you talk thataway. Without you that day back home in Tennessee I'd be buried and nobody knows it better than me."

# Chapter 7

This was raw, open country, rugged country, and it bred a different kind of man. The cattle that went wild in Texas became the longhorn, and ran mostly to horns and legs because the country needed a big animal that could fight and one who could walk three days to get water. Just so it bred the kind of man with guts and toughness no eastern man could use.

Most men never discover what they've got inside. A man has to face up to trouble before he knows. The kind of conniving a man could get away with back east wouldn't go out here. Not in those early years. You can hide that sort of behavior in a crowd, but not in a country where there's so few people. Not that we didn't have our own kinds of trickery and cheating.

Jonathan Pritts was one of those who mistook liberty for license and he figured he could get away with anything. Worst of all, he had an exaggerated idea of how big a man he was . . . trouble was, he wasn't a big man, just a mean one.

We banked our money with the Express Company in Santa Fe, and then we saddled up and started back to Purgatoire after more cattle. We had us an outfit this time. Dapple was still my horse, and a better no man was likely to have, but each of us now had four extra mounts and I'd felt I'd done myself proud.

The first was a *grulla*, a mouse-colored mustang who, judging by disposition, was sired out of a Missouri mule by a mountain lion with a sore tooth. That *grulla* was the most irritating, cantankerous bit of horseflesh I ever saw, and he could buck like a sidewinder on a red-ant hill. On the other hand he could go all day and night over any kind of country on less grass and water than one of Beale's camels. My name for him was Sate, short for Satan.

There was a buckskin, a desert horse used to rough going, but steady. In many ways the most reliable horse I had. His name was Buck, like you might expect.

Kelly was a big red horse with lots of bottom. Each horse I paid for out of my own money, although Sate they almost gave me, glad to be rid of him, I expect.

First time I straddled Sate we had us a mite of a go-around. When I came off him I was shook up inside and had a nosebleed, but I got off when I was good and ready and from that time on Sate knew who was wearing the pants.

My fourth horse I bought from an Indian.

We'd spent most of the day dickering with Spanish men, and this Indian sat off to one side, watching. He was a big-framed Nez Perce from up Idaho, Montana way.

He was at the corral at sunup and by noontime I'd not seen him have a bite to eat.

"You're a long way from home," I said, slicing off a chunk of beef I'd had fixed for a lunch and handed it to him.

He looked at me, a long, careful look, then he accepted it. He ate slow like a starving man who can't eat a lot at first because his stomach shrinks up.

"You speak English?"

"I speak."

Splitting my grub down the middle, I gave him half, and we ate together. When we'd finished he got up. "Come—you see horse."

The horse was a handsome animal, a roan with a splash of white with red spots on the white, the kind of horse they call an Appaloosa. Gaunt as his owner he stood a good sixteen hands. Looked like this Indian had come a long way on short rations.

So I swapped him my old rifle (I'd bought a .44 Henry the day before) and some grub. I threw in my old blanket.

We were a week out of Santa Fe when we found a spot in the bend of a creek among some rocks. When we'd forted up they left it to me to scare up some fresh meat as we planned to live off the country and stretch our store-bought rations.

That Montana horse could move. He could get out and go, lickety-brindle, and he was smart. We passed up antelope because no matter what folks tell you it's the worst kind of Rocky Mountain meat. Old-timers will tell you that cougar meat is best. Lewis and Clark said that, and Jim Bridger, Kit Carson, Uncle Dick Wootton, Jim Baker . . . they all agreed.

Morning, with a bright sun over far hills, shadows lying in the folds and creases of the country, sunlight on cottonwood leaves and sparkling on the river water . . . a meadow lark calling. Montana horse and me, we sure loved it. We took off along an old deer trail. This was higher country than before, the plateaus giving way to long ridges crested with pines and slopes dotted with juniper or piñon.

Suddenlike, I saw a deer . . . and then another. Tethering Montana horse I moved up with my rifle.

Feeding deer are easy to stalk if a man is careful on his feet and doesn't let them get wind of him. When deer put their heads down to graze, you can move up on them, and you can keep moving, very quiet. When their tails start to switch they're going to look up, so you freeze in position. He may be looking right at you when he looks up, and he might look a long time, but if you stand right still, after awhile he will decide you're a harmless tree or stump and go back to feeding.

I worked my way up to within fifty yards of a good big buck and then I lifted my rifle and put a bullet behind the left foreleg. There was another deer no further off and on my left, and as I fired at the first one I swung the rifle just as he was taking his first jump and my bullet broke his neck as he hit ground.

Working fast, I butchered those deer, loaded the choice cuts into their hides and mounted Montana horse. When I came out of the trees a couple of miles further on a half-dozen buffalo were running across the wind. Now no buffalo runs without reason.

Pulling up on the edge of the trees I knew we'd be hard to see, for that roan and me with my buckskin outfit fitted into the country like part of it. No man in this country ever skylines himself if he can help it.

Sometimes the first man to move is the first to die, so I waited. The sun was bright on the hillside. My horse stamped a foot and switched his tail. A bee hummed around some leaves on a bush nearby.

They came in a single file, nine of them in a row. Utes, from the description I'd heard from Cap. They came out of the trees and angled along the slope in front of me.

Now most times I prefer to stand my ground and fight it out, for running can make your back a broad target, but there are times to fight and times to run and the wise man is one who can choose the right time for each.

First off, I sat still, but they were riding closer and closer to me, and if they didn't see me their horses would. If I tried to go back into the trees they'd hear me.

Sliding my rifle across my saddle I said a prayer to the guardian angel of fools and covered maybe thirty yards before they saw me. One of them must have spoken because they all looked.

Indians can make mistakes like anybody. If they had all turned and come at me I'd have had to break for the brush and I'd have been fairly caught. But one Indian got too anxious and threw up his rifle and fired.

Seeing that rifle come up, I hit the spurs to Montana horse and went away from there, but in the split seconds before I hit him with the spurs, I fired. As I'd been timing my horse's steps I'd shot at the right time and I didn't miss.

My shot took out, not the Indian shooting at me but the one who seemed to be riding the best horse. My shot was a hair ahead of his and he missed when Montana horse jumped.

We took out . . . and I mean we really lit a shuck. There was nothing around there I wanted and what I wanted most was distance from where I was.

With that first Indian down I'd cut my sign right across their trail and now they wanted me mighty bad, but that horse didn't like Utes any better than I did. He put his ears back and stretched out his tail and left there like a scared rabbit.

My next shot was a miss. With Montana horse travelling like he'd forgot something in Santa Fe, there wasn't much chance of a hit. They had all come right at me with the shooting and I saw unless I did something drastic they had me so I swung and charged right at the nearest Indian. He was fifty yards ahead of the nearest Ute and which shot got his horse I don't know, but I fired three or four shots at him.

Dust jumped from the horse's side and the horse went down throwing his rider over his head into the grass, and when I went by at a dead run I shot into that Indian as I rode.

They were all messed up for a minute or two, switching directions and running into each other, but meanwhile I rode through a small creek and was out on the open prairie beyond.

We were eight to ten miles from camp and I wasn't about to lead these Utes full tilt into my friends. And then I saw a buffalo wallow.

Slowing Montana horse we slid into that wallow and I hit ground and threw my shoulder into the horse and grabbed his off foreleg, hoping to throw him, but Montana horse seemed to know just what I wanted and he went down and rolled on his side like he had been trained for it . . . which he probably had, the Nez Perce using Appaloosas for war horses.

Dropping to one knee, the other leg stretched out ahead of me, I drew a careful bead on the chest of the nearest Ute and squeezed off my shot.

There was a minute when I believed I'd missed, and him coming right into my sights, then his horse swung wide and dumped a dead Ute into the grass. There was a bright stain of blood on the horse's side as he swung away.

It was warm and still. Patting Montana horse I told him, "You rest yourself, boy, we'll make out."

He rolled his eyes at me like he understood every word.

You would never have believed that a moment ago there was shooting and killing going on, because suddenly everything was still. The hillside was empty, those Indians had gone into the ground faster than you would believe. Lying there, knowing any moment might be my last, I liked the feel of the warm sun on my back, the smell of parched brown grass and of dust.

Three of the Utes were down in the grass and there were six left. Six to one might seem long odds but if a man has nerve enough and if he thinks in terms of combat, the advantage is often against sheer numbers. Sheer numbers rob a man of something and he begins to depend . . . and in a fighting matter no man should depend. He should do what has to be done himself.

My canteen was full and I'd some jerked meat in my saddlebag, lots of fresh meat, and plenty of ammunition.

They would try to come over the rise behind me. That crest, only a couple of feet away, masked my view of the far slope. So I had out my bowie knife and began cutting a trench. That was a nine-inch blade, sharp enough to shave with, and I worked faster than ever in my born days.

It took me only minutes to have a trench that gave me a view of the back slope, and I looked around just in time. Four of them were coming up the slope toward me on foot and running bent over. My shot was a miss . . . too quick. But they hit dirt. Where there had been running Indians there was only grass stirring in the wind.

They would be creeping on their bellies now, getting closer. Taking a chance, I leaped up. Instantly, I spotted a crawling Indian and fired, then dropped into my hole with bullets spearing the air where I'd been. That was something I couldn't try again, for now they'd be expecting.

Overhead there were high streamers of white clouds. Turning around I crawled into my trench, and just in time. An Indian was coming up that back slope, bent over and coming fast and I let him come. It was high time I shortened the odds against me, so I put my rifle in position, reached down to ease my Colt for fast work in case the others closed in at the same time. That Ute was going to reach me with his next rush.

Some were down, but I doubted if more than one was actually dead. I wasn't counting any scalps until I had them.

Minutes loitered. Sweat trickled down my cheeks and my neck. I could smell the sweat of my own body and the hot dust. Somewhere an eagle cried. Sweat and dust made my skin itch, and when a big horsefly lit on Montana, my slap sounded loud in the hot stillness.

Eastern folks might call this adventure, but it is one thing to read of adventure sitting in an easy chair with a cool drink at hand, and quite another thing to be belly down in the hot dust with four, five Indians coming up the slope at you with killing on their minds.

A grasshopper flew into the grass maybe fifteen yards down slope, then took off at once, quick and sharp. That was warning enough. Lifting the rifle I steadied it on that spot for a quick shot, then chanced a glance over my shoulder. Just as I looked back that Ute charged out of the grass like he was bee-stung.

My guess had been right, and he came up where that grasshopper had lit. My sights were on the middle of his chest when I squeezed off my shot and he fell in plain sight.

Behind me their feet made a whisper in the dry grass and rolling over I palmed my Colt and had two shots off before I felt the slam of the bullet. The Utes vanished and then I was alone but for a creeping numbness in my left shoulder and the slow welling of blood.

Sliding back from the trench I felt sickish faint and plugged the hole with a handkerchief. The bullet had gone through and I was already soaked with blood on my left side. With bits of handkerchief I plugged the bullet hole on both sides and knew I was in real trouble.

Blinking against the heat and sudden dizziness I fed shells into my guns. Then I took the plug from my canteen and rinsed my mouth. It was luke-warm and brackish.

My head started to throb heavily and it was an effort to move my eye-brows. The smell of sweat and dried grass grew stronger and overhead the sky was yellow and hot as brass. From out of an immeasurable distance a buzzard came.

Suddenly I hated the smells, hated the heat, hated the buzzard circling and patient—as it could be patient—knowing that most things die.

Crawling to the rim of the buffalo wallow my eyes searched the terrain before me, dancing with heat waves. I tried to swallow and could not, and Tennessee and its cool hills seemed very far away.

Through something like delirium I saw my mother rocking in her old chair, and Orrin coming up from the spring with a wooden bucket full of the coldest water a man could find.

Lying in a dusty hole on a hot Colorado hillside with a bullet hole in me and Utes waiting to finish the job, I suddenly remembered what day it was.

It had been an hour . . . or had it been more? It had been at least an hour since the last attack. Like the buzzards, all those Utes needed was time, and what is time to an Indian?

Today was my birthday . . . today I was nineteen years old.

# Chapter 8

Long fingers of shadow reached out from the sentinel pines before I took my next swallow of water. Twice I'd sponged out the mouth of that Montana horse, who was growing restless and harder to keep down.

No chance to take a cat nap, or even take my eyes off the country for more than a minute because I knew they were still out there and they probably knew I was hurt. My shoulder was giving me billy-hell. Even if I'd had a chance to run for it Montana horse would be stiff from lying so long.

About that time I saw the outfit coming up the slope. They rode right up to that buffalo wallow bold as brass and sat their horses grinning at me, and I was never so glad to see anybody.

"You're just in time for tea," I said, "you all just pull up your chairs. I've got the water on and she'll be ready any minute."

"He's delirious," Tom Sunday grinned like a big ape. "He's gone off his rocker."

"It's the heat," Orrin agreed. "The way he's dug in you'd think he'd been fighting Indians."

"Hallucinations," Rountree added, "a plain case of prairie sickness."

"If one of you will get off his horse," I suggested, "I'll plain whip him till his hair falls out, one-handed at that. Where've you been? Yarning it in the shade?"

"He asks us where we've been?" Sunday exclaimed. "And him sitting in a nice cool hole in the ground while we work our fool heads off."

Rountree, he cut out and scouted around, and when he rode back he said, "Looks like you had yourself a party. By the blood on the grass you got two, anyway."

"You should backtrack me." I was feeling ornery as a stepped-on baby. "If I didn't score on five out of nine Utes, I'll put up money for the drinks."

"Only three took off when we showed up," Sunday agreed.

Grabbing my saddle horn I pulled myself into the leather; for the first time since I'd sighted those Utes I could count on another day of living.

For the next three days I was cook which comes of having a bum wing on a cow outfit. Cap was a fair hand at patching up wounds and he made a poultice of herbs of some kind which he packed on my shoulder. He cleaned the wound by running an arrow shaft through with a cloth soaked in whiskey, and if you think that's entertainment, you just try it on for size.

On the fifth day I was back in the saddle but I fought shy of Sate, reckoning he'd be too much for me, feeling like I was. So I worked Dapple and Buck to a frazzle, and ended up riding Montana horse who was turning into a real cow horse.

This was rougher country than before. We combed the breaks and drifted the cattle into a rough corral. It was hot, rough, cussing work, believe you me. Here and there we found some branded stock, stuff that had stampeded from trail herds further east, or been driven off by Indians.

"Maybe we should try Abilene this time," I suggested to the others. "The price would be better. We just happened to be lucky in Santa Fe."

Seven hundred head of cattle was what we started out with, and seven hundred head can be handled by four men if they work like dogs and are passing lucky.

As before, we let them graze as they moved. What we wanted was fat cattle at selling time. In that box canyon they had steadied down a good bit with plenty of water and grass and nothing much to do but eat and lie around.

First night out from the Purgatoire we bedded down after a long drive with the cattle mighty tired. After awhile Orrin stopped near me.

"Tyrel, I sure wish you and Laura cottoned to each other more'n you do."

"If you like her, Orrin, that's what matters. I can't be no different than I am, and something about her doesn't ring true. Orrin, the way I see it, you'd always play second fiddle to her old man."

"That's not true," he said, but there wasn't much force in it.

After awhile we met again and stopped together. "Ma's not getting younger," he said, "and we've been gone a year."

A coyote made talk to the stars, but nothing else seemed to be stirring.

"If we sell this herd we'll have more money than any Sackett ever heard of, and I figure we should buy ourselves an outfit and start ranching. Then we ought to get some book learning. Especially you, Orrin. You could make a name for yourself."

Orrin's thoughts were afar off for a minute or two, gathering dreams somewhere along tomorrow's road.

"I've had it in mind," he said finally.

"You've a talking way with you, Orrin. You could be governor."

"I haven't the book learning."

"Davy Crockett went to Congress. Andrew Johnson was taught to read and write by his wife. I figure we can get the book learning. Hell, man, if youngsters can learn we should be able to throw it and hog-tie it. I figure you should study law. You've got a winning way with that Welsh tongue of yours."

We drove through Dodge on to Abilene, and that town had spread itself all over the prairie, with saloons side by each, all of them going twenty-four hours to the day, and packed most of the time.

Everywhere a man looked around the town there were herds of Texas cattle. "We came to the wrong market," Cap said dourly, "we should have sold out in Dodge."

We swung the herd into a tight circle and saw several riders coming toward us. Two of them looked like buyers and the other two looked like trouble. Orrin did his talking to the first two, Charlie English and Rosie Rosenbaum. Rosenbaum was a stocky man with mild blue eyes, and I could tell by the way he was sizing up our cattle that he knew beef.

"How many head have you got?" he asked Orrin.

"Seven hundred and forty, as of last night," Orrin said, "and we want a fast deal."

The other two had been studying our herd and sizing us up.

"I should think you would," one of them said, "those are stolen cattle."

Orrin just looked at him. "My name is Orrin Sackett, and I never stole anything in my life." He paused. "And I never had anything stolen from me, either."

The man's face shadowed. "You've got Two-Bar cattle in that herd," he said, "and I'm Ernie Webb, foreman of the Two-Bar."

"There are Two-Bar cows in that herd, and we rounded them up in the Colorado country along with a lot of wild cattle. If you want to claim them get your boss and we'll talk a deal, but he'll pay for the rounding up and driving."

"I don't need the boss," Webb replied, "I handle my own trouble."

"Now see here," Rosenbaum interfered quietly. "There's no need for this. Sackett is reasonable enough. Get your boss and when the matter is settled, I'll buy."

"You stay out of this." Webb was staring at Orrin, a trouble-hunting look on his face. "This is a rustled herd and we're taking it over."

Several rough-looking riders had been drifting closer, very casually. I knew a box play when I saw one.

Where I was sitting Webb and his partner couldn't see me because Sunday was between us. They'd never seen Orrin before but they'd both seen me that day on the plains of east Kansas.

"Cap," I said, "if they want it, let's let them have it."

"Tom," I wheeled my horse around Sunday which allowed me to flank Webb and his partner, "this man may have been foreman for Two-Bar once, but he also rode with Back Rand."

Cap had stepped down from his saddle and had his horse between himself and the oncoming riders, his rifle across his saddle. "You boys can buy the herd," Cap said, "but you'll buy it the hard way."

The riders drew up.

Rosenbaum was waiting right in the middle of where a lot of lead could be flying but there wasn't a quiver in him. For a man with no stake in the deal, he had nerve.

Webb had turned to look at me, and Orrin went on like he hadn't been interrupted. "Mr. Rosenbaum, you buy these cattle and keep track of any odd brands you find. I think they'll check with those in our tally books, and we'll post bond for their value and settle with any legitimate claimant but nobody is taking any cattle from us."

Ernie Webb had it all laid out for him nice and pretty, and it was his turn to call the tune. If he wanted to sashay around a bit he had picked himself four men who could step to the music.

"It's that loudmouth kid," Webb said, "somebody will beat it out of him someday, and then rub his nose in it."

"You try," Orrin invited. "You can have any one of us, but that kid will blow you loose from your saddle."

We sold out for thirty-two dollars a head, and Rosenbaum admitted it was some of the fattest stock brought into Abilene that year. Our herd had grazed over country no other herds travelled and with plenty of water. We'd made our second lucky drive and each of us had a notion we'd played out our luck.

When we got our cash we slicked out in black broadcloth suits, white shirts, and new hats. We were more than satisfied and didn't figure to do any better than what we had.

Big John Ryan showed up to talk cattle. "This the Sackett outfit?"

"We're it."

"Hear you had Tumblin' R stock in your herd?"

"Yes, sir. Sit down, will you?" Orrin told him about it. "Seven head, including a brindle steer with a busted horn."

"That old devil still alive? Nigh cost me the herd a few times and if I'd caught him I'd have shot him. Stampede at the drop of a hat and take a herd with him."

"You've got money coming, Mr. Ryan. At thirty-two dollars a head we figure—"

"Forget it. Hell . . . anybody with gumption enough to round up those cows and drive them over here from Colorado is entitled to them. Besides, I just sold two herds of nearly six thousand head . . . seven head aren't going to break me."

He ordered a drink. "Fact is, I'd like to talk to you boys about handling my herd across the Bozeman Trail."

Orrin looked at me. "Tom Sunday is the best cattleman among us. Orrin and me, we want to find a place of our own."

"I can't argue with that. My drive will start on the Neuces and drive to the Musselshell in Montana. How about it, Sunday?"

"I think not. I'll trail along with the boys."

There I sat with almost six thousand dollars belonging to me and about a thousand more back in Santa Fe, and I was scared. It was the first time in my life I'd ever had anything to lose.

The way I saw it unless a man knows where he's going he isn't going anywhere at all. We wanted a home for Ma, and a ranch, and we also wanted enough education to face the changing times. It was time to do some serious thinking.

A voice interrupted. "Aren't you Tyrel Sackett?"

It was the manager of the Drovers' Cottage. "There's a letter for you."

"A letter?" I looked at him stupidly. Nobody had ever written me a letter.

Maybe Ma . . . I was scared. Who would write to me?

It looked like a woman's handwriting. I carefully unfolded the letter. It scared me all hollow.

Worst of it was, the words were handwritten and the letters were all which-way and I had a time making them out. But I wet my lips, dug in my heels, and went to work—figuring a man who could drive cattle could read a letter if he put his mind to it.

First off there was the town: Santa Fe. And the date. It was written only a week or so after we left Santa Fe.

*Dear Mr. Sackett:*

Well, now! Who was calling me mister? Mostly they called me Tyrel, or Tye, or Sackett.

The letter was signed *Drusilla.*

Right about then I started to get hot around the neck and ears, and took a quick look to see if anybody noticed. You never saw so many people paying less attention to anybody.

They heard I was in Santa Fe and wondered why I did not visit them. There had been trouble when some men had tried to take part of the ranch but the men had gone away. All but four, which they buried. And then her grandfather had gone to town to see Jonathan Pritts. In my mind's eyes I could see those two old men facing each other, and it must have been something to see, but my money was on the don. She ended with an invitation to visit them when I was next in Santa Fe.

Time has a way of running out from under a man. Looked like a man would never amount to much without book learning and every day folks were talking of what they read, of what was happening, but none of it made sense to me who had to learn by listening. When a man learns by listening he is never sure whether he is getting the straight of things or not.

There was a newspaper that belonged to nobody and I took that; it took me three days to work my way through its four pages.

There was a man in town with gear to sell, and figuring on buying an extra pistol, I went to see him. The gun I bought, and some boxes of shells, but when I saw some books in his wagon I bought them without looking.

"You don't want to know what they are?"

"Mister, I don't see that's your business, but the fact is, I wouldn't know one from the other. I figured if I studied out those books I'd learn. I'd work it out."

He had the look of a man who knew about writing and printing. "These aren't the books I'd recommend for a beginner, but you may get something out of them."

He sold me six books and I took them away.

Night after night I sat by the campfire plugging away at those books, and Tom Sunday sure helped a lot in telling me what words were about. First off, I got a surprise by learning that a man could learn something about his own way of living from a book. This book by an Army man, Captain Randolph Marcy, was written for a guide to parties traveling west by wagon. He told a lot of things I knew, and a good many I didn't.

Cap Rountree made out like he was sour about the books. "Need an extry pack horse for all that printed truck. First time I ever heard of a man packin' books on the trail."

# Chapter 9

Santa Fe lay lazy in the sun when we rode into town. Nothing seemed to have changed, yet there was a feeling of change in me. And Drusilla was here, and this time I would call at her home. I'd never called on a girl before.

My letter from Drusilla was my own secret and I had no idea of telling anyone about it. Not even Orrin.

When Drusilla wrote I didn't answer because I couldn't write and if I'd traced the letters out—well, it didn't seem right that a man should be writing like a child.

First off when we got to Santa Fe I wanted to see Drusilla, so I went about getting my broadcloth suit brushed and pressed out. It was late afternoon when I rode to the ranch. Miguel was loafing at the gate with a rifle across his knees.

"*Señor!* It is good to see you! Every day the *señorita* has asked me if I have seen you!"

"Is she in?"

"*Señor*, it is good that you are back. Good for them, and good for us too." He indicated the door.

The house surrounded a patio, and stood itself within an adobe wall fifteen feet high. There was a walk ran around the inside near the top of the wall, and there were firing positions for at least thirty men on that wall.

Don Luis sat working at a desk. He arose. "Good afternoon, *señor*. It is good to see you. Was your venture a success?"

So I sat down and told him of our trip. A few of the cattle had carried his brand and we had kept the money for him and this I now paid.

"There is much trouble here," Don Luis said. "I fear it is only the beginning."

It seemed to me he had aged a lot in the short time since I'd last seen him. Suddenly, I realized how much I liked that stern, stiff old man with his white mustache.

Sitting back in his chair, he told me how Pritts' men made their first move. Forty in the group had moved on some flat land well within the Grant and had staked claims there, then they had dug in for a fight. Knowing the manner of the men he faced, Don Luis held back his *vaqueros*.

"There are, *señor*, many ways to victory, and not all of them through violence. And if there was a pitched battle, some of my men would be hurt. This I wished to avoid."

The invaders were watched, and it was noted when Pritts and Fetterson returned to Santa Fe on business that several bottles appeared and by midnight half the camp was drunk. Don Luis was close by, but he held back his *vaqueros* who were eager for a fight.

By three in the morning when all were in a drunken sleep, Don Luis' *vaqueros* moved in swiftly.

The invaders were tied to their horses and started back down the road toward Santa Fe. Their tents and equipment were burned or confiscated, their weapons unloaded and returned to them. They were well down the trail when several riders returning from Mora engaged in a running gun battle with the *vaqueros*. Four of the invaders were killed, several wounded. Don Luis had two men wounded, none seriously.

"The advantage was ours," Don Luis explained, "but Jonathan Pritts is a very shrewd man and he is making friends, nor is he a man to suffer defeat without retaliation. It is difficult," he added, "to carry out a project with the sort of men he uses. They are toughs and evil men."

"Don Luis," I said, "have I your permission to see Miss Drusilla?"

He arose. "Of course, *señor*. I fear if the privilege were denied that I should have another war, and one which I am much less suited to handle.

"We in New Mexico," he added, "have been closer to your people than our own. It is far to Mexico City, so our trade has been with you, our customs affected by yours. My family would disapprove of our ways, but on the frontier there is small time for formality."

Standing in the living room of the lovely old Spanish home, I felt stiff in my new clothes. Abilene had given me time to get used to them, but the awkwardness returned now that I was to see Drusilla again.

I could hear the click of her heels on the stone flags, and turned to face the door, my heart pounding, my mouth suddenly so dry I could scarcely swallow.

She paused in the doorway, looking at me. She was taller than I had remembered, and her eyes were larger. She was beautiful, too beautiful for a man like me.

"I thought you had forgotten us," she said, "you didn't answer my letter."

I shifted my hat in my hands. "It looked like I'd get here as fast as the letter, and I'm not much hand at writing."

An Indian woman came in with some coffee and some little cakes and we both sat down. Drusilla sat very erect in her chair, her hands in her lap, and I decided she was almost as embarrassed as I was.

"Ma'am, I never called on a girl before. I guess I'm almighty awkward."

Suddenly, she giggled. "And I never received a young man before," she said.

After that we didn't have much trouble. We both relaxed and I told her about our trip, about rounding up wild cattle and my fight with the Indians.

"You must be very brave."

Well, now. I liked her thinking that about me but fact is, I hadn't thought of much out there but keeping my head and tail down so's not to get shot, and I recalled being in something of a sweat to get out of there.

I've nothing against a man being scared as long as he does what has to be done . . . being scared can keep a man from getting killed and often makes a better fighter of him.

We sat there in that cool, spacious room with its dark, massive furniture and tiled floors and I can tell you it was a wonderful friendly feeling. I'd never known a house like that before, and it seemed very grand and very rich.

Dru was worried about her grandfather. "He's getting old, Tyrel, and I'm afraid for him. He doesn't sleep well, and sometimes he paces the floor all night long."

Torres was waiting for me when I went to get my horse almost an hour later. "Señor," he said carefully, "Don Luis likes you and so does the señorita. Our people, they like you too."

He studied me searchingly. "Señor Pritts hates us, and he is winning friends among your people. He spends much money. I believe he would take everything from us."

"Not while I'm alive."

"We need a sheriff in this country, a man who will see justice done." He looked at me. "We ask only for justice."

"What you say is true. We do need a sheriff."

"The don grows old, and he does not know what to do, but all my life I have been with him, señor, and I do not think that to fight is enough. We must do something else, as your people would. There are, señor, still more Mexicans than Anglos. Perhaps if there was an election. . . ."

"A Mexican sheriff would not be good, Juan. The Americans would not be willing to recognize him. Not those who follow Pritts."

"This I know, señor. We will talk of this again."

\* \* \*

When I walked into the La Fonda that night Ollie Shaddock was standing at the bar having a drink. He was a broad man with a shock of blond hair and a broad, cheerful face.

"Have a drink," he said, "I resigned my sheriffing job to bring your Ma and the boys west."

"You brought Ma?"

"Sure enough. Orrin's with her now."

He filled my glass from the bottle. "Don't you be thinkin' of me as sheriff. You done right in killin' Long. I'd have had to arrest you but the law would have freed you. He had a gun pointed when you killed him."

We didn't say anything more about it. It was good to have Ollie Shaddock out here, and I owed him a debt for bringing Ma. I wanted to see her the worst way but Ollie had something on his mind.

"Folks talk you up pretty high," he said.

"It's Orrin they like."

"You know something, Tyrel? I've been giving some thought to Orrin since I got here. He's a man should run for office."

It seemed a lot of folks had running for office on their minds, but this was a new country and in need of law. "He's got it in mind," I said.

"I've been in politics all my years. I was a deputy sheriff at seventeen, sheriff at nineteen, justice of the peace at twenty-four and served a term in the state legislature before I was thirty. Then I was sheriff again."

"I know it."

"Orrin looks to me like a man who could get out the vote. Folks take to him. He talks well, and with a mite more reading he could make something of himself, if we managed it right."

"We?"

"Politics ain't much different, Tyrel, than one of these icebergs you hear tell of. Most of what goes on is beneath the surface. It doesn't make any difference how good a man is, or how good his ideas are, or even how honest he is unless he can put across a program, and that's politics.

"Statesmanship is about ten percent good ideas and motives and ninety percent getting backing for your program. Now I figure I know how to get a man elected, and Orrin's our man. Also, you can be a big advantage to him."

"Folks don't take to me."

"Now that's as may be. I find most of the Mexicans like you. They all know you and Orrin turned Pritts down when he invited you to join him, and the *vaqueros* from the Alvarado ranch have been talking real friendly about you."

He chuckled. "Seems the women like you too. They tell me you provided more entertainment in one afternoon than they had in years."

"Now, look—!" I could feel myself getting red around the ears.

"Don't let it bother you. Folks enjoyed it, and they like you. Don't ask me why."

"You seem to have learned a lot since you've been here."

"Every man to his job, mine's politics. First thing is to listen. Learn the issues, the personalities, where the votes are, where the hard feelings are."

Ollie Shaddock tasted his whiskey and put the glass back on the bar. "Tyrel, there's trouble brewing and it will come from that Pritts outfit. That's a rough bunch of boys and they'll get to drinking and there'll be a killing. Chances are, it will be a riot or something like that."

"So?"

"So we got to go up there. You and me and Orrin. When that trouble comes Orrin has to handle it."

"He's no officer."

"Leave that to me. When it happens, folks will want somebody to take over the responsibility. So Orrin steps in."

He tossed off his whiskey. "Look . . . Pritts wants Torres killed, some of the other key men. When the shooting starts some of those fur thieves and rustlers he's got will go too far.

"Orrin steps in. He's Anglo, so all the better Americans will be for him. You convince the Mexicans Orrin is their man. Then we get Orrin appointed marshal, run him for sheriff, start planning for the legislature."

Ollie made a lot of sense, and it beat all how quickly he had got hold of the situation, and him here only a few weeks. Orrin was the man for it all right. Or Tom Sunday.

"What about Tom Sunday?"

"He figures he's the man for the job. But Tom Sunday can't talk to folks like Orrin can. He can't get down and be friends with everybody the way Orrin can. Orrin just plain likes people and they feel it . . . like you like Mexicans and they know it. Anyway," he added, "Orrin is one of ours and one thing about Orrin. We don't have to lie."

"Would you lie?"

Ollie was embarrassed. "Tyrel, politics is politics, and in politics a man wants to win. So he hedges a little."

"Whatever we do has to be honest," I said. "Look, I'm no pilgrim. But there's nothing in this world I can't get without lying or cheating. Ma raised us boys that way, and I'm glad of it."

"All right, honesty is a good policy and if a man's honest it gets around. What do you think about Orrin?"

"I think he's the right man."

Only as I left there and started to see Ma, I was thinking about Tom Sunday. Tom was our friend, and Tom wasn't going to like this. He was a mite jealous of Orrin. Tom had the best education but folks just paid more mind to Orrin.

Ma had aged . . . she was setting in her old rocker which Ollie had brought west in his wagon, and she had that old shawl over her knees. When I walked in she was puffing on that old pipe and she looked me up and down mighty sharp.

"You've filled out. Your Pa would be proud of you."

So we sat there and talked about the mountains back home and of folks we knew and I told her some of our plans. Thinking how hard her years had been, I wanted to do something for her and the boys. Bob was seventeen, Joe fifteen.

Ma wasn't used to much, but she liked flowers around her and trees. She liked meadow grass blowing in the wind and the soft fall of rain on her own roof. A good fire, her rocker, a home of her own, and her boys not too far away.

Ollie Shaddock wasted no time but rode off toward Mora. He was planning on buying a place, a saloon, or some such place where folks could get together. In those days a saloon was a meeting place, and usually the only one.

Of the books I'd bought I'd read Marcy's guide books first, and then that story, *The Deerslayer*. That was a sure enough good story too. Then I read Washington Irving's book about traveling on the prairies, and now was reading Gregg on *Commerce of the Prairies*.

Reading those books was making me talk better and look around more and see what Irving had seen, or Gregg. It was mighty interesting.

Orrin and me headed for the hills to scout a place for a home. Sate was feeling his oats and gave me a lively go-around but I figured the trip would take some of the salt out of him. That Satan horse really did like to hump his back and duck his head between his legs.

We rode along, talking land, cattle, and politics, and enjoying the day. This was a far cry from those blue-green Tennessee mountains, but the air was so clear you could hardly believe it, and I'd never seen a more beautiful land. The mountains were close above us, sharp and clear against the sky, and mostly covered with pines.

Sate wasn't cutting up any more. He was stepping right out like he wanted to go somewhere, but pretty soon I began to get a feeling I didn't like very much.

Sometimes a man's senses will pick up sounds or glimpses not strong enough to make an impression on him but they affect his thinking anyway. Maybe that's all there is to instinct or the awareness a man develops when he's in dangerous country. One thing I do know, his senses become tuned to sounds above and below the usual ranges of hearing.

We caught, of a sudden, a faint smell of dust on the air. There was no wind, but there was dust.

We walked our horses forward and I watched Sate's ears. Those ears picked up, like the mustang he was, and I knew he was aware of something himself.

My eyes caught an impression and I walked my horse over for a look where part of the bark was peeled back from a branch. There were horses' tracks on the ground around the bush.

"Three or four, wouldn't you say, Tyrel?"

"Five. This one is different. The horses must have stood here around two hours, and then the fifth one came up but he didn't stop or get down."

Several cigarette butts were under a tree near where the horses had been tethered, and the stub of a black cigar.

We were already further north than we had planned to go and suddenly it came to me. "Orrin, we're on the Alvarado grant."

He looked around, studied our back trail and said, "I think it's Torres. Somebody is laying for him."

He walked his horse along, studying tracks. One of the horses had small feet, a light, almost prancing step. We both knew that track. A man who can read sign can read a track the way a banker would a signature. That small hoof and light step, and that sidling way of moving was Reed Carney's show horse.

Whoever the others had been, and the chances were Reed Carney had joined up with Fetterson and Pritts, they had waited there until the fifth man came along to get them. And that meant he could have been a lookout, watching for the man they were to kill.

Now we were assuming a good deal. Maybe. But there was just nothing to bring a party up here . . . not in those days.

Orrin shucked his Winchester.

It was pine timber now and the trail angled up the slope through the trees. When we stopped again we were high up and the air was so clear you could see for miles. The rim was not far ahead.

We saw them.

Four riders, and below on the slope a fifth one, scouting. And off across the valley floor, a plume of dust that looked like it must be the one who was to be the target.

The men were below us, taking up position to cover a place not sixty yards from their rifles. They were a hundred feet or so higher than the rider, and he would be in the open.

Orrin and me left our horses in the trees. We stood on the edge of the mesa with a straight drop of about seventy feet right ahead of us, then the talus sloped away steeply to where the five men had gathered after leaving their horses tied to the brush a good hundred yards off.

They were well concealed from below. There was no escape for them, however, except to right or left. They could not come up the hill, and they could not go over the rim.

Orrin found himself a nice spot behind a wedged-up slab of rock. Me, I was sizing up a big boulder and getting an idea. That boulder sat right on the edge of the mesa, in fact it was a part of the edge that was ready to fall . . . with a little help.

Now I like to roll rocks. Sure, it's crazy, but I like to see them roll and bounce and take a lot of debris with them. So I walked to the rim, braced myself against the trunk of a gnarled old cedar and put my feet against the edge of that rock.

The rider they were waiting for was almost in sight. When I put my boots against that rock my knees had to be doubled up, so I began to push. I began to straighten them out. The rock crunched heavily, teetered slightly, and then with a slow, majestic movement it turned over and fell.

The huge boulder hit with a heavy thud and turned over, gained speed, and rolled down the hill. The riders glanced around and seemed unable to move, and then as that boulder turned over and started to fall, they scattered like sheep.

At the same instant, Orrin lifted his rifle and put a bullet into the brush ahead of their horses. One of the broncs reared up and as Orrin fired again, he jerked his head and ripped off a branch of the brush, broke free and started to run, holding his head to one side to keep from tripping on the branch.

The lone horseman had come into sight, and when he stared up the mountain, I lifted my hat and waved, knowing from his fawn-colored sombrero that it was Torres. Doubtfully, he lifted a hand, unable to make us out at that distance.

One of the men started for their horses and Orrin put a bullet into the ground ahead of him and the man dove for shelter. Orrin levered another shot into the rocks where he disappeared then sat back and lighted up one of those Spanish cigars.

It was downright hot. Settling in behind some rocks I took a pull at my canteen and figured down where they were it had to be hotter than up here where we had some shade.

"I figure if those men have to walk home," Orrin said, "it might cool their tempers some."

A slow half hour passed before one of the men down below got ambitious. My rifle put a bullet so close it must have singed his whiskers and he hunkered down in the rocks. Funny part of it was, we could see them plain as day. Had we wanted to kill them we could have. And then we heard a horse coming through the trees and I walked back to meet Torres.

"What happens, *señor?*" He looked sharply from Orrin to me.

"Looks like you were expected. Orrin and me were hunting a place for ourselves and we found some tracks, and when we followed them up there were five men down there." I showed him where. Then I explained our idea about the horses and he agreed.

"It will be for me to do, *señor.*"

He went off down the slope and after awhile I saw him come out of the trees, untie the horses and run them off.

When Torres rode back Orrin came up to join us. "It is much you have done for me," Torres said. "I shall not forget."

"It is nothing," I said, "one of them is Reed Carney."

"*Gracias, Señor* Sackett," Torres said. "I believed I was safe so far from the hacienda, but a man is safe nowhere."

Riding back toward Mora I kept still and let Orrin and Torres get acquainted. Torres was a solid man and I knew Orrin would like him, and Torres liked people, so the contrary was true.

Torres turned off toward the ranch and we rode on into Mora. We got down in front of the saloon and strolled inside. It took one glance to see we weren't among friends. For one thing there wasn't a Mex in the place and this was mostly a Mexican town, and there were faces I remembered from Pawnee Rock. We found a place at the bar and ordered drinks.

There must have been forty men in that saloon, a dusty, dirty lot, most of them with uncut hair over their collars, and loaded down with six-shooters and bowie knives. Fetterson was at the other end of the bar but hadn't seen us.

We finished our drinks and edged toward the door and then we came face to face with Red . . . the one my horse had knocked down at Pawnee Rock.

He started to open his mouth, but before he could say a word, Orrin clapped him on the shoulder. "Red! You old sidewinder! Come on outside and let's talk!"

Now Red was a slow-thinking man and he blinked a couple of times, trying to decide what Orrin was talking about, and we had him outside before he could yell. He started to yell but Orrin whooped with laughter and slapped Red on the back so hard it knocked all the breath out of him.

Outside the door I put my knife against his ribs and he lost all impulse to yell. I mean he steadied down some.

"Now wait a minute," he protested, "I never done you boys any harm. I was just—"

"You just walk steady," I told him, "I'm not in the mood for trouble myself. I got a backache and I don't feel up to a shooting, so don't push me."

"Who's pushing?"

"Red," Orrin said seriously, "you're the kind of a man we like to see. Handsome, upstanding . . . and alive."

"Alive!" I added, "but you'd make a handsome corpse, Red."

By now we had him out in the dark and away from his friends, and he was scared, his eyes big as pesos. He looked like a treed coon in the lanternlight.

"What you goin' to do to me?" he protested. "Look, I—"

"Red," Orrin said, "there's a fair land up north, a wide and beautiful land. It's a land with running water, clear streams, and grass hip-high to a tall elk. I tell you Red, that's a country."

"And you know something, Red?" I put in my two-bits' worth. "We think you should see it."

"We surely do." Orrin was dead serious. "We're going to miss you if you go, Red. But Red, you stay and we won't miss you."

"You got a horse, Red?"

"Yeah, sure." He was looking from one to the other of us. "Sure, I got a horse."

"You'll like that country up north. Now it can get too hot here for a man, Red, and the atmosphere is heavy . . . there's lead in it, you know, or liable to be. We think you should get a-straddle of that cayuse of yours, Red, and keep riding until you get to Pike's Peak, or maybe Montana."

"To—tonight?" he protested.

"Of course. All your life you've wanted to see that country up north, Red, and you just can't wait."

"I—I got to get my outfit. I—"

"Don't do it, Red." Orrin shook his head, big-eyed. "Don't you do it." He leaned closer. "Vigilantes, Red. Vigilantes."

Red jerked under my hand, and he wet his lips with his tongue. "Now, look here!" he protested.

"The climate's bad here, Red. A man's been known to die from it. Why, I know men that'd bet you wouldn't live to see daybreak."

We came to a nice little gray. "This your horse?"

He nodded.

"You get right up into the saddle, Red. No—keep your gun. If somebody should decide to shoot you, they'd want you to have your gun on to make it look right. Looks bad to shoot an unarmed man. Now don't you feel like traveling, Red?"

By this time Red may have been figuring things out, or maybe he never even got started. Anyway, he turned his horse into the street and went out of town at a fast canter.

Orrin looked at me and grinned. "Now there's a traveling man!" He looked more serious. "I never thought we'd get out of there without a shooting. That bunch was drinking and they would have loved to lynch a couple of us, or shoot us."

We rode back to join Cap and Tom Sunday. "About time. Tom has been afraid he'd have to go down and pull you out from under some Settlement man," Cap said.

"What do you mean . . . Settlement man?"

"Jonathan Pritts has organized a company which he calls the Settlement Company. You can buy shares. If you don't have money you can buy them with your gun."

Orrin had nothing to say, he never did when Pritts' name was mentioned. He just sat down on his bed and pulled off a boot.

"You know," he said reflectively, "all that talk about the country up north convinced me. I think we should all go."

# Chapter 10

Mora lay quiet in the warm sun, and along the single street, nothing stirred. From the porch of the empty house in which we had been camping, I looked up the street, feeling the tautness that lay beneath the calm.

Orrin was asleep inside the house, and I was cleaning my .44 Henry. There was trouble building and we all knew it.

Fifty or sixty of the Settlement crowd were in town, and they were getting restless for something to do, but I had my own plans and didn't intend they should be ruined by a bunch of imported trouble makers.

Tom Sunday came out on the porch and stopped under the overhang where I was working on my rifle. He took out one of those thin black cigars and lighted up.

"Are you riding out today?"

"Out to the place," I said, "we've found us a place about eight or nine miles from here."

He paused and took the cigar from his mouth. "I want a place too, but first I want to see what happens here. A man with an education could get into politics and do all right out here." He walked on down the street.

Tom was no fool; he knew there was going to be a demand for some law in Mora, and he intended to be it. I knew he wouldn't take a back seat because of Orrin.

It worried me to think of what would happen when Orrin and Tom found out each wanted the same office, although I doubted if Orrin would mind too much.

When I finished cleaning my rifle I saddled up, put my blanket roll behind the saddle and got ready to ride out. Orrin crawled out of bed and came to the door.

"I'll be out later, or Cap will," he said. "I want to keep an eye on things here." He walked to the horse with me. "Tom say anything?"

"He wants to be marshal."

Orrin scowled. "Damn it, Tyrel, I was afraid of that. He'd probably make a better marshal than me."

"There's no telling about that, but I'd say it was a tossup, Orrin, but you can win in the election. I just hate to see you two set off against each other. Tom's a good man."

Neither one of us said anything for a while, standing there in the sun, thinking about it. It was a mighty fine morning and hard to believe so much trouble was building around us.

"I've got to talk to him," Orrin said at last, "this ain't right. We've got to level with him."

All I could think of was the fact that the four of us had been together two years now, and it had been a good period for all of us. I wanted nothing to happen to that. Friendships are not so many in this life, and we had put rough country behind us and kicked up some dust in our passing, and we had smelled a little powder smoke together and there's nothing binds men together like sweat and gunsmoke.

"You go ahead, Orrin. We'll talk to Tom tomorrow."

I wanted to be there when it was talked out, because Tom liked me and he trusted me. He and Orrin were too near alike in some ways, and too different in others. There was room enough for both of them, but I was quite sure that Tom would want to go first.

It took me a shade more than an hour to ride down to where we figured to start ranching. There were trees along the river there, and some good grass, and I bedded down at the mouth of the gap, in a corner among the rocks. Picketing Montana horse, I switched from boots to moccasins and scouted around, choosing the site for the house and the corrals.

The bench where the house was to be was only twenty feet above the river, but above the highest watermark. The cliff raised up behind the bench, and the location was a good one.

Peeling off my shirt, I worked through the afternoon clearing rocks and brush off the building site and pacing it off. Then I cut poles and began building a corral for our horses, for we would need that first of all.

Later, when dark began to come, I bathed in the creek and putting on my clothes, built a small fire and made coffee and chewed on some jerked beef.

After I'd eaten I dug into my saddlebags for a book and settled down to read. Time to time I'd get up and look around, or stand for a spell in the darkness away from the fire, just listening. By the time the fire was burning down I moved back from the fire and unrolled my bed. A bit of wind was blowing up and a few clouds had drifted over the stars.

Taking my rifle I went out to check on Montana horse who was close by. I shifted his picket pin a little closer and on fresh grass. There was a feel to the night that I didn't like, and I found myself wishing the boys would show up.

When I heard a sound it was faint, but Montana horse got it, too. His head came up and his ears pricked and his nostrils reached out for the smell of things. Putting a hand on his shoulder, I said, "All right, boy. You just take it easy."

Somebody was out there in the night, calling to me.

Now a man who goes rushing out into the night will sooner or later wind up with a bullet in his belly. Me, I circled around, scouting, and moving mighty easy. I had a sight more enemies in this country than friends.

It wasn't any time at all until I saw a standing horse, heard a low moan, and then I moved in. It was a man on the ground, and he was bad hurt.

"*Señor!*" the voice was faint. "Please . . . it is Miguel. I come to you . . . I bring you troubles."

So I scooped him off the ground and put him on his horse. "You hang on," I said. "Only a few yards."

"Men come to kill me, *señor*. It will be trouble for you."

"I'll talk to them," I said, "I'll read 'em from the Scriptures."

He passed out, but I got him to camp and unloaded him. He was shot all right. He'd had the hell shot out of him. There was a bullet hole in his thigh and there was another high in his right chest that had gone clean through. His clothes were soaked with blood and he was all in.

There was water by the fire so I peeled back his clothes and went to work. First off, I bathed away the blood and plugged the holes to stop the bleeding. Come daylight, if he made it, I was going to have to do more.

With the tip of my bowie I slit the hide and eased a bullet out from under the skin of his back, then bathed the wound and fixed it up as best I could. I could hear riders working their way down the country, a-hunting him. Sooner or later they'd see the reflection of my fire and then I'd have to take care of that.

Moving Miguel back out of the firelight, I got him stashed away when I heard them coming, and they came with a rush.

"Hello, the fire!"

"You're talking. Speak your piece."

"We're hunting a wounded greaser. You seen him?"

"I've seen him and he's here, but you can't have him."

They rode up to the fire then and I stepped up to the edge of the light. Trouble was, one of those riders had a rifle and it was on me, and the range wasn't fifteen feet.

That rifle worried me. They had me sweating. A fast man on the draw can beat a man who has to think before he can fire, but that first shot better be good.

"It's Sackett. The kid they say is a gunfighter."

"So it's Sackett." It was a sandy-haired man with two tied-down guns like one of these here show-off gunmen. "I ain't seen none of his grave-yards."

"You just ride on," I said, "Miguel is here. He stays here."

"Talking mighty big, ain't you?" That man was Charley Smith, a big man, bearded and tough, hard to handle in a difficulty it was said. The one with the rifle was thin, angular, with a bobbing Adam's apple and a shooting look to him.

"He's wounded," I said, "I'll take care of him."

"We don't want him alive," Smith said. "We want him dead. You give him to us and you're out of it."

"Sorry."

"That's all right," Sandy said, "I like it this way. I prefer it this way."

That Sandy didn't worry me as much as the man with the rifle. Although the chances were that Sandy had practiced some with those guns. Even a show-off may be pretty fast, and I had that to think about.

Of one thing I was sure. There was no talking my way out of this. I could stand by and see them kill Miguel or I could fight them.

Now I'm not a smoking man myself, but Miguel's makings had fallen from his pocket and I'd picked them up, so I got them out and started to roll a smoke and while I talked I went right on building that smoke.

What I needed was an edge, and I needed it bad. There was the man with the rifle and Charley Smith and there was this Sandy lad who fancied himself with six-shooters. There might be more back in the dark but those three I had to think about.

"Miguel," I said, and I was talking for time, "is a good man. I like him. I wouldn't interfere in any fight of his, but on the other hand, I don't like to see a wounded man shot without a chance, either."

Smith was the cagey one. He was looking around. I guessed Smith was worried about Orrin. He knew we were a team, and he knew there was four of us, and there might be, just might be, somebody out there in the dark.

Now I was doing some serious thinking. A man who holds a gun on somebody is all keyed up and ready to shoot when he first gets the drop on you, but after awhile his muscles get a little heavy, and his reactions will be a little slower. Moreover, these fellows outnumbered me three to one. They had the advantage, so they just didn't think anybody would be fool enough to tackle them. That there was against them too. It sort of made them relax mentally, if you get what I mean.

Only any move I made must be timed just right and I had to slicker them into thinking of something else.

If they killed Miguel when he was wounded in my camp, I'd never feel right again . . . even if I lived.

"Miguel," Smith said, "is one of Alvarado's men. We're running them out."

"Where's your brother?" The man with the rifle was asking. He'd had some of his attention on the shadows out there. In his place I'd have been giving them plenty of thought.

"He's around. Those boys are never far off."

"Only one bed." That was Sandy shooting off his fat mouth. "I can see it." That was the man with the two big pistols who wanted to kill me. He could make it sound mighty big, later.

Charley Smith was going to kill me because he didn't want anybody around taking a shot at him later.

Putting that cigarette between my lips I stooped down and picked up a burning twig to light it. I lifted it to my cigarette, holding it in my fingers while I had my say.

"The four of us," I said, "never spread out very far. We work together, we fight together, and we can win together."

"They ain't around," Sandy-boy said, "only one bed, only his horse and the greaser's."

Up on the hills there was a stirring in the pines and because I'd been hearing it all evening I knew it was a wind along the ridge, but they stopped talking to listen.

"I'm a Sackett," I said conversationally, "out of Tennessee. We finished a feud a couple of years ago . . . somebody from the other outfit shot a Sackett and we killed nineteen Higginses in the next sixteen years. Never stop huntin'. I got a brother named Tell Sackett . . . best gunshot ever lived."

I was just talking, and the twig was burning. Charley Smith saw it. "Hey!" he said. "You'll burn—!"

The fire touched my fingers and I yelped with pain and dropped the twig and with the same continuing movement I drew my gun and shot that rifleman out of the saddle.

Sandy was grabbing iron when I swung my gun on him and thumbed my hammer twice so it sounded like one shot and he went backwards off his horse like he'd been hit with an axe.

Swinging my gun on Smith I saw him on the ground holding his belly and Tom Sunday came riding up with a Henry rifle.

"Smartest play I ever saw," he said, watching Smith on the ground. "When I saw you lighting up I knew there had to be something . . . knowing you didn't smoke."

"Thanks, you sure picked a good time to ride up."

Sunday got down and walked over to the man who'd held the rifle. He was dead with a shot through the heart and Sandy had taken two bullets through the heart also. Sunday glanced at me. "I saw it but I still don't believe it."

Thumbing shells into my gun I walked over to Miguel. He was up on one elbow, his face whiter than I'd have believed and his eyes bigger. "*Gracias, amigos,*" he whispered.

"Orrin told me you'd come out here and I was restless so I figured I'd ride out and camp with you. When I saw you in the middle of them I was trying to figure out what to do that wouldn't start them shooting at you. Then you did it."

"They'd have killed us."

"Pritts will take your helping Miguel as a declaration of war."

There was more sound out in the darkness and we pulled back out of the light of the fire. It was Cap Rountree and two of Alvarado's hands. One of them was Pete Romero, but the other was a man I didn't know.

He was a slim, knifelike man in a braided leather jacket, the most duded-up man I ever saw, but his pearl-handled six-shooter was hung for business and he had a look in his eyes that I didn't like.

His name was Chico Cruz.

Cruz walked over to the bodies and looked at them. He took out a silver dollar and placed it over the two bullet holes in Sandy's chest. He pocketed the dollar and looked at us.

"Who?"

Sunday jerked his head to indicate me. "His . . . and that one too." He indicated the man with the rifle. Then he explained what had happened, not mentioning the burning twig, but the fact that I'd been covered by the rifle.

Cruz looked at me carefully and I had a feeling this was a man who enjoyed killing and who was proud of his ability with a gun. He squatted by the fire and poured a cup of coffee. It was old coffee, black and strong. Cruz seemed to like it.

Out in the darkness, helping Romero get Miguel into the saddle, I asked, "Who's he?"

"From Mexico. Torres sent for heem. He is a bad man. He has kill many times."

Cruz looked to me like one of those sleek prairie rattlers who move like lightning and kill just as easily, and there was nothing about him that I liked. Yet I could understand the don sending for him. The don was up against a fight for everything he had. It worried him, and he knew he was getting old, and he was no longer sure that he could win.

When I came back to the fire, Chico Cruz looked up at me. "It was good shooting," he said, "but I can shoot better."

Now I'm not a man to brag, but how much better can you get?

"Maybe," I said.

"Someday we might shoot together," he said, looking at me through the smoke of his cigarette.

"Someday," I said quietly, "we might."

"I shall look forward to it, *señor*."

"And I," I smiled at him, "I shall look back upon it."

# Chapter 11

We expected trouble from Pritts but it failed to show up. Orrin came out to the place and with a couple of men Don Luis loaned us and help from Cap and Tom we put a house together. It was the second day, just after work finished when we were setting around the fire that Orrin told Tom Sunday he was going after the marshal's job.

Sunday filled his cup with coffee. His mouth stiffened up a little, but he laughed. "Well, why not? You'd make a good marshal, Orrin . . . if you get the job."

"I figured you wanted it . . ." Orrin started to say, then his words trailed off as Tom Sunday waved a hand.

"Forget it. The town needs somebody and whoever gets it will do a job. If I don't get it and you do, I'll lend a hand . . . I promise that. And if I get it, you can help me."

Orrin looked relieved, and I knew he was, because he had been worried about it. Only Cap looked over his coffee cup at Tom and made no comment, and Cap was a knowing man.

Nobody needed to be a fortuneteller to see what was happening around town. Every night there were drunken brawls in the street, and a man had been murdered near Elizabethtown, and there had been robberies near Cimarron. It was just a question of how long folks would put up with it.

Meanwhile we went on working on the house, got two rooms of it up and Orrin and me set to making furniture for them. We finished the third room on the house and then Orrin and me rode with Cap over to the Grant where we bought fifty head of young stuff and drove it back and through the gap where we branded the cattle and turned them loose.

Working hard like we had, I'd not seen much of Drusilla, so I decided to ride over. When I came up Antonio Baca and Chico Cruz were standing at the gate, and I could see that Baca was on duty there. It was the first time I'd seen him since the night he tried to knife me on the trail.

When I started to ride through the gate, he stopped me. "What is it you want?"

"To see Don Luis," I replied.

"He is not here."

"To see the *señorita*, then."

"She does not wish to see you."

Suddenly I was mad. Yet I knew he would like nothing better than to kill me. Also, I detected something in his manner . . . he was insolent. He was sure of himself.

Was it because of Chico Cruz? Or could it be that the don was growing old and Torres could not be everywhere?

"Tell the *señorita*," I said, "that I am here. She will see me."

"It is not necessary." His eyes taunted me. "The *señorita* is not interested in such as you."

Chico Cruz moved his shoulders from the wall and walked slowly over. "I think," he said, "you had better do like he say."

There was no burned-match trick to work on them, and anyway, I wasn't looking for a fight with any of Don Luis' people. The don had troubles of his own without me adding to them. So I was about to ride off when I heard her voice.

"Tye!" She sounded so glad I felt a funny little jump inside me. "Tye, why are you waiting out there? Come in!"

Only I didn't come in, I just sat my horse and said, "*Señorita*, is it all right if I call here? At any time?"

"But of course, Tye!" She came to the gate and saw Baca standing there with his rifle. Her eyes flashed. "Antonio! Put that rifle down! *Señor* Sackett is our friend! He is to come and go as he wishes, do you understand?"

He turned slowly, insolently away. "*Si*," he said, "I understand."

But when he looked at me his eyes were filled with hatred and I glanced at Cruz, who lifted a hand in a careless gesture.

When we were inside, she turned on me. "Tye, why have you stayed away? Why haven't you been to see us? Grandfather misses you. And he wanted to thank you for what you did for Juan Torres, and for Miguel."

"They were my friends."

"And you are our friend."

She looked up at me, then took my hand and led me into another room and rang a little bell.

She had grown older, it seemed, in the short time since I had last seen her. She looked taller, more composed, yet she was worried too, I could see that.

"How is Don Luis?"

"Not well, Tye. My grandfather grows old. He is more than seventy, you know. I do not even know how old, but surely more than that, and he finds it difficult to ride now.

"He fears trouble with your people. He has many friends among them, but most of them resent the size of the ranch. He wants only to keep it intact for me."

"It is yours."

"Do you remember Abreu?"

"Of course."

"He is dead. Pete Romero found him dead last week, ten miles from here. He had been shot in the back by someone with a Sharps buffalo gun."

"That's too bad. He was a good man."

We drank tea together, and she told me all that had been happening. Some days now it was difficult for the don to get out of bed, and Juan Torres was often off across the ranch. Some of the men had become hard to handle and lazy. Apparently, what had happened today was not the only such thing.

Don Luis was losing his grip when he needed desperately to be strong, and his son, Drusilla's father, had long been dead.

"If there is any way that I can help, you just call on me."

She looked down at her hands and said nothing at all, and I sort of felt guilty, although there was no reason why. There was nobody I loved so much as Drusilla, but I'd never talked of love to anybody, and didn't know how to go about it.

"There's going to be trouble at Mora," I said, "it would be well to keep your men away from there."

"I know." She paused. "Does your brother see *Señorita* Pritts?"

"Not lately." I paused, uncertain of what to say. She seemed older.

So I told her about the place we had found, and thanked her for the help of the men the don had sent to help us with the adobe bricks. Then I told her about Tom Sunday and Orrin, and she listened thoughtfully. All the Mexicans were interested in the selection of the marshal, for it was of great importance to them. His authority would be local, but there was a chance he could move into the sheriff's job and in any case, the selection of a man would mean a lot to the Mexicans who traded in Mora and who lived there, as many did.

What I was saying wasn't at all what I wanted to say, and I searched for the words I wanted and they would not come. "Dru," I said suddenly, "I wish—"

She waited but all I could do was get red in the face and look at my hands. Finally, I got up, angry with myself. "I've got to be going," I said, "only—"

"Yes?"

"Can I come back? I mean, can I come to see you often?"

She looked straight into my eyes. "Yes, you can, Tye. I wish you would."

When I rode away I was mad with myself for saying nothing more. This was the girl I wanted. I was no hand with women but most likely Drusilla considered me a man who knew a lot about women, and figured if I had anything to say, that I'd say it.

She had a right to think that, for a man who won't speak his mind at a time like that is no man at all. More than likely she would think I just didn't want to say anything. If she thought of me that way at all.

That was a gloomy ride home, and had anybody been laying for me that night I'd have been shot dead I was that preoccupied. When I rode up to the house I saw Ollie's horse tied outside.

Ollie was there, along with a man who operated a supply store in Mora. His name was Wilson. "The time is now, Orrin. You've got to come in and stay in town a few days. Charley Smith and that sandy-haired man who was with him have done a lot to rile folks around town, and they were mighty impressed the way Tyrel handled them."

"That was Tyrel, not me."

"They know that, but they say you're two of a kind. Only," . . . Ollie looked apologetically at me, "they don't figure you're as mean as your brother. I mean they like what happened out here, only they don't hold with killing."

Orrin glanced at him. "There wasn't another thing Tyrel could have done, and mighty few who could have done what he did."

"I know that, and you know it. The fact remains that these folks want law enforced against killers but without killing. The Mexicans . . . they understand the situation better than the Americans. They know that when a man takes a weapon in hand he isn't going to put it down if you hand him a bunch of roses. Men of violence only understand violence, most times."

Orrin rode into town and for two days I stayed by the place, working around. I cleared rocks using a couple of mules and a stone boat. I dragged the rocks off and piled them where they could be used later in building a stable.

Next day I rode into town, and it looked like I'd timed things dead right. There was quite a bunch gathered outside the store Ollie was running and Ollie was on the porch, and for the first time since he came out here he had a gun where you could see it.

"It's getting so a decent person can't live in this country," he was saying. "What we need is a town marshal that will send these folks packing. Somebody we can trust to do the right thing."

He paused, and there were murmurs of agreement. "Seems to me this could be a fine, decent place to live. Most of the riffraff that cause the trouble came from Las Vegas."

Across the way on the benches I could see some of the Settlement crowd loafing and watching. They weren't worried none, it seemed like it was a laughing matter with them for they'd played top dog so long, here and elsewhere.

I went on into the saloon, and Tom Sunday was there. He glanced at me, looking sour.

"I'll buy a drink," I suggested.

"And I'll take it."

He downed the one he had and the bartender filled our glasses for us.

"You Sacketts gang up on a man," Tom declared. "Orrin's got half the town working for him. Take that Ollie Shaddock. I thought he was a friend of mine."

"He is, Tom. He likes you. Only Ollie's sort of a cousin of ours and came from the same country back in the mountains. Ollie's been in politics all his life, Tom, and he's been wanting Orrin to have a try at it."

Tom said nothing for a little while, and then he said, "If a man is going to get any place in politics he has to have education. This won't help Orrin a bit."

"He's been studying, Tom."

"Like that fool Pritts girl. All she could see was Orrin. She never even looked at you or me."

"Womenfolks pay me no mind, Tom."

"They sure gave you all their attention in Santa Fe."

"That was different." He needed cheering up, so for the first time I told him—or anybody—of what happened that day. He grinned in spite of himself.

"No wonder. Why, that story would have been all over town within an hour." He chuckled. "Orrin was quite put out."

He tossed off his drink. "Well, if he can make it, more power to him."

"No matter what, Tom," I said, "the four of us should stick together."

He shot me a hard glance and said, "I always liked you, Tye, from the first day you rode up to the outfit. And from that day I knew you were poison mean in a difficulty."

He filled his glass. I wanted to tell him to quit but he was not a man to take advice and particularly from a younger man.

"Why don't you ride back with me?" I suggested. "Cap should be out there, and we could talk it up a little."

"What are you trying to do? Get me out of town so Orrin will have a clear field?"

Maybe I got a little red around the ears. I hadn't thought anything of the kind. "Tom, you know better than that. Only if you want that job, you'd better lay off the whiskey."

"When I want your advice," he said coolly, "I'll ask for it."

"If you feel like it," I said, "ride out. I'm taking Ma out today."

He glanced at me and then he said, "Give her my best regards, Tye. Tell her I hope she will be happy there." And he meant it, too.

Tom was a proud man, but a gentleman, and a hard one to figure. I watched him standing there by the bar and remembered the nights around the campfire when he used to recite poetry and tell us stories from the works of Homer. It gave me a lost and lonely feeling to see trouble building between us, but pride and whiskey are a bad combination, and I figured it was the realization that he might not get the marshal's job that was bothering him.

"Come out, Tom, Ma will want to see you. We've talked of you so much."

He turned abruptly and walked out the door, leaving me standing there. On the porch he paused.

Some of the Settlement gang were gathered around, maybe six or eight of them, the Durango Kid and Billy Mullin right out in front. And the Durango Kid sort of figured himself as a gunman.

More than anything I wanted Tom Sunday to go home and sleep it off or to ride out to our place. I knew he was on edge, in a surly mood, and Tom could be hard to get along with.

Funny thing. Ollie had worked hard to prepare the ground work all right, and Orrin had a taking way with people, and the gift of blarney if a man ever had it.

It was a funny thing that with all of that, it was Tom Sunday who elected Orrin to the marshal's job.

He did it that day there in the street. He did it right then, walking out of that door onto the porch. He was a proud and angry man, and he had a few drinks under him, and he walked right out of the door and faced the Durango Kid.

It might have been anybody. Most folks would have avoided him when he was like that, but the Kid was hunting notches for his gun. He was a lean, narrow-shouldered man of twenty-one who had a reputation for having killed three or four men up Colorado way. It was talked around that he had rustled some cows and stolen a few horses and in the Settlement outfit he was second only to Fetterson.

Anything might have happened and Tom Sunday might have gone by, but the Durango Kid saw he had been drinking and figured he had an edge. He didn't know Tom Sunday like I did.

"He wants to be marshal, Billy," the Durango Kid said it just loud enough, "I'd like to see that."

Tom Sunday faced him. Like I said, Tom was tall, and he was a handsome man, and drinking or not, he walked straight and stood straight. Tom had been an officer in the Army at one time, and that was how he looked now.

"If I become marshal," he spoke coolly, distinctly, "I shall begin by arresting you. I know you are a thief and a murderer. I shall arrest you for the murder of Martin Abreu."

How Tom knew that, I don't know, but a man needed no more than to look at the Kid's face to know Tom had called it right.

"You're a liar!" the Kid yelled. He grabbed for his gun.

It cleared leather, but the Durango Kid was dead when it cleared. The range was not over a dozen feet and Tom Sunday—I'd never really seen him draw before—had three bullets into the Kid with one rolling sound.

The Kid was smashed back. He staggered against the water trough and fell, hitting the edge and falling into the street.

Billy Mullin turned sharply. He didn't reach for a gun, but Tom Sunday was a deadly man when drinking. That sharp movement of Billy's cost him, because Tom saw it out of the tail of his eye and he turned and shot Billy in the belly.

I'm not saying I mightn't have done the same. I don't think I would have, but a move like that at a time like that from a man known to be an enemy of Tom's and a friend to the Kid . . . well, Tom shot him.

That crowd across the street saw it. Ollie saw it. Tom Sunday killed the Durango Kid, and Billy Mullin was in bed for a couple of months and was never the same man again after that gunshot . . . but Tom Sunday shot himself right out of consideration as a possible marshal.

The killing of the Kid . . . well, they all knew the Kid had it coming, but the shooting of Billy Mullin, thief and everything else that he was, was so offhand that it turned even Tom's friends against him.

It shouldn't have. There probably wasn't a man across the street who mightn't have done the same thing.

It was a friend of Tom's who turned his back on him that day and said, "Let's talk to Orrin Sackett about that job."

Tom Sunday heard it, and he thumbed shells into his gun and walked down the middle of the street toward the house where he'd been sharing with Orrin, Cap, and me when we were in Mora.

And that night, Tom Sunday rode away.

# Chapter 12

Come Sunday we drove around to the house where Ma was living with the two boys and we helped her out to the buckboard. Ma was all slicked out in her Sunday-go-to-meeting clothes—which meant she was dressed in black—and all set to see her new home for the first time.

Orrin, he sat in the seat alongside her to drive, and Bob and Joe, both mounted up on Indian ponies, they brought up the rear. Cap and me, we led off.

Cap didn't say much, but I think he had a deep feeling about what we were doing. He knew how much Orrin and me had planned for this day, and how hard we had worked. Behind that rasping voice and cold way of his I think there was a lot of sentiment in Cap, although a body would never know it.

It was a mighty exciting thing at that, and we were glad the time of year was right, for the trees were green, and the meadows green, and the cattle feeding there . . . well, it looked mighty fine. And it was a good deal better house than Ma had ever lived in before.

We started down the valley, and we were all dressed for the occasion, each of us in black broadcloth, even Cap. Ollie was going to be there, and a couple of other friends, for we'd sort of figured to make it a house-warming.

The only shadow on the day was the fact that Tom Sunday wasn't there, and we wished he was . . . all of us wished it.

Tom had been one of us so long, and if Orrin and me were going to amount to something, part of the credit had to be Tom's, because he took time to teach us things, and especially me.

When we drove up through the trees, after dipping through the river, we came into our own yard and right away we saw there were folks all around, there must have been fifty people.

The first person I saw was Don Luis, and beside him, Drusilla, looking more Irish today, than Spanish. My eyes met hers across the heads of the crowd and for an instant there we were together like we had never been, and I longed to ride to her and claim her for my own.

Juan Torres was there, and Pete Romero, and Miguel. Miguel was looking a little pale around the gills yet, but he was on his own feet and looked great.

There was a meal all spread out, and music started up, and folks started dancing a fandango or whatever they call it, and Ma just sat there and cried. Orrin, he put his arm around her and we drove all the rest of the way into the yard that way, and Don Luis stepped up and offered Ma his hand, and mister, it did us proud to see her take his hand and step down, and you'd have thought she was the grandest lady ever, and not just a mountain woman from the hills back of nowhere.

Don Luis escorted her to a chair like she was a queen, and the chair was her own old rocker, and then Don Luis spread a serape across her knees, and Ma was home.

It was quite a shindig. There was a grand meal, with a whole steer barbecued, and three or four *javelinas*, plenty of roasting ears, and all a man could want. There was a little wine but no drinking liquor. That was because of Ma, and because we wanted it to be nice for her.

Vicente Romero himself, he was there, and a couple of times I saw Chico Cruz in the crowd.

Everybody was having themselves a time when a horse splashed through the creek and Tom Sunday rode into the yard. He sat his horse looking around, and then Orrin saw him and Orrin walked over.

"Glad you could make it, Tom. It wouldn't have been right without you. Get down and step up to the table, but first come and speak to Ma. She's been asking for you."

That was all. No words, no explanations. Orrin was that way, though. He was a big man in more ways than one, and he liked Tom, and had wanted him there.

We had a fiddle going for the dancing, and Orrin took his old geetar and sang up some songs, and Juan Torres sang, and we had us a time. And I danced with Dru.

When I went up to her and asked her to dance, she looked right into my eyes and accepted, and then for a minute or two we danced together and we didn't say much until pausing for a bit when I looked at her and said, "I could dance like this forever . . . with you."

She looked at me and said, her eyes sparkling a little, "I think you'd get very hungry!"

Ollie was there and he talked to Don Luis, and he talked to Torres, and he got Torres and Jim Carpenter together, and got them both with Al Brooks. They talked it over, and Torres said the Mexicans would support Orrin, and right then and there, Orrin got the appointment.

Orrin, he walked over to me and we shook hands. "We did it, Tyrel," Orrin said, "we did it. Ma's got herself a home and the boys will have a better chance out here."

"Without guns, I hope."

Orrin looked at me. "I hope so, too. Times are changing, Tyrel."

The evening passed and folks packed into their rigs or got back into the saddle and everybody went home, and Ma went inside and saw her house.

We'd bought things, the sort of things Ma would like, and some we'd heard her speak of. An old grandfather's clock, a real dresser, some fine tables and chairs, and a big old four-poster bed. The house only had three rooms, but there would be more—and we boys had slept out so much we weren't fit for a house, anyway.

I walked with Dru to her carriage, and we stood there by the wheel. "I've been happy today," I told her.

"You have brought your mother home," she said. "It is a good thing. My grandfather admires you very much, Tye. He says you are a thoughtful son and a good man."

Watching Dru drive away in that carriage it made me think of money again. It's a high card in a man's hand when he goes courting if he has money, and I had none of that. True, the place we had belonged to Orrin and me but there was more to it than that. Land wasn't of much value those days nor even cattle. And cash money was almighty scarce.

Orrin was going to be busy, so the money question was my chore.

Orrin, he worked hard studying Blackstone. From somewhere he got a book by Montaigne and he read Plutarch's *Lives*, and subscribed to a couple of eastern papers, and he read all the political news he could find, and he rode around and talked to folks or listened to them tell about their troubles. Orrin was a good listener who was always ready to give a man a hand at whatever he was doing.

That was after. That was after the first big night when Orrin showed folks who was marshal of Mora. That was the night he took over, the night he laid down the law. And believe you me, when Orrin takes a-hold, he takes a-hold.

At sundown, Orrin came up the street wearing the badge, and the Settlement men were around, taking their time to look him over. Having a marshal was a new thing in town and to the Settlement outfit it was a good joke. They just wanted to see him move around so they could decide where to lay hold of him.

The first thing Orrin done was walk through the saloon to the back door and on the inside of the back door he tacked up a notice. Now that notice was in plain sight and what was printed there was in both Spanish and English.

*No gun shall be drawn or fired within the town limits.*
*No brawling, fighting or boisterous conduct will be tolerated.*
*Drunks will be thrown in jail.*
*Repeat offenders will be asked to leave town.*
*No citizen will be molested in any way.*
*Racing horses or riding steers in the street is prohibited.*
*Every resident or visitor will be expected to show visible means of sup-*
*port on demand.*

That last rule was pointed right at the riffraff which hung around the streets, molesting citizens, picking fights, and making a nuisance of themselves. They were a bad lot.

Bully Ben Baker had been a keel-boat man on the Missouri and the Platte and was a noted brawler. He was several inches taller than Orrin, weighed two hundred and forty pounds, and Bully Ben decided to find what the new marshal was made of.

Bully Ben wasted no time. He walked over to the notice, read it aloud, then ripped it from the door.

Orrin got to his feet.

Ben reached around, grinning cheerfully, and took a bottle from the bar, gripping it by the neck.

Orrin ignored him, picked up the notice and replaced it on the door, and then he turned around and hit Ben Baker in the belly.

When Orrin had gone by him and replaced the notice, Bully Ben had waited to see what would happen. He had lowered his bottle, for he was a man accustomed to lots of rough talk before fighting, and Orrin's punch caught him off guard right in the pit of the stomach and he gasped for breath, his knees buckling.

Coolly, Orrin hit him a chopping blow to the chin that dropped Ben to his knees. The unexpected attack was the sort of thing Ben himself had often done but he was not expecting it from Orrin.

Ben came up with a lunge, swinging his bottle and I could have told him he was a fool. Blocking the descending blow with his left forearm, Orrin chopped that right fist down to Ben's jaw. Deliberately then, he grabbed the bigger man and threw him with a rolling hip-lock. Ben landed heavily and Orrin stood back waiting for him to get up.

All this time Orrin had acted mighty casual, like he wasn't much interested. He was just giving Bully Ben a whipping without half trying.

Ben was mighty shook up and he was astonished too. The blood was dripping from a cut on his jawbone and he was stunned, but he started to get up.

Orrin let him get up and when Ben threw a punch, Orrin grabbed his wrist and threw him over his shoulder with a flying mare. This time Baker got up more slowly, for he was a heavy man and he had hit hard. Orrin waited until he was halfway to his feet and promptly knocked him down.

Ben sat on the floor staring up at Orrin. "You're a fighter," he said, "you pack a wallop in those fists."

The average man in those years knew little of fist-fighting. Men in those days, except such types as Bully Ben, never thought of fighting with anything other than a gun. Ben had won his fights because he was a big man, powerful, and had acquired a rough skill on the river boats.

Pa had taught us and taught us well. He was skilled at Cornish-style wrestling and he'd learned fist-fighting from a bare-knuckle boxer he'd met in his travels.

Ben was a mighty confused man. His strength was turned against him, and everything he did, Orrin had an answer for. On a cooler night Orrin would never have worked up a sweat.

"You had enough?" Orrin asked.

"Not yet," Ben said, and got up.

Now that was a mighty foolish thing, a sadly foolish thing, because until now, Orrin had been teaching him. Now Orrin quit fooling. As Ben Baker straightened up, Orrin hit him in the face with both fists before Ben could get set. Baker made an effort to rush and holding him with his left, Orrin smashed three wicked blows to his belly, then pushed Ben off and broke his nose with an overhand right. Ben backed up and sat down and Orrin grabbed him by the hair and picking him off the floor proceeded to smash three or four blows into his face, then Orrin picked Ben up, shoved him against the bar and said, "Give him a drink." He tossed a coin on the bar and walked out.

Looked to me like Orrin was in charge.

After that there was less trouble than a man would expect. Drunks Orrin threw in jail and in the morning he turned them out.

Orrin was quick, quiet, and he wasted no time talking. By the end of the week he had jailed two men for firing guns in the town limits and each had been fined twenty-five dollars and costs. Both had been among the crowd at Pawnee Rock and Orrin told them to get out of town or go to work.

Bob and me rode down to Ruidoso with Cap Rountree and picked up a herd of cattle I'd bought for the ranch, nigh onto a hundred head.

Ollie Shaddock hired a girl to work in his store and he devoted much of his time to talking about Orrin. He went down to Santa Fe, over to Cimarron and Elizabethtown, always on business, but each time he managed to say a few words here and there about Orrin, each time mentioning him for the legislature.

After a month of being marshal in Mora there had been no killings, only one knifing, and the Settlement crowd had mostly moved over to Elizabethtown or to Las Vegas. Folks were talking about Orrin all the way down to Socorro and Silver City.

On the Grant there had been another killing. A cousin of Abreu's had been shot . . . from the back. Two of the Mexican hands had quit to go back to Mexico.

Chico Cruz had killed a man in Las Vegas. One of the Settlement crowd.

Jonathan Pritts came up to Mora with his daughter and he bought a house there.

It was two weeks after our housewarming before I got a chance to go see Dru. She was at the door to meet me and took me in to see her grandfather. He looked mighty frail, lying there in bed.

"It is good to see you, *señor*," he said, almost whispering. "How is your ranch?"

He listened while I told him about it and nodded his head thoughtfully. We had three thousand acres of graze, and it was well-watered. A small ranch by most accounts.

"It is not enough," he said, at last, "to own property in these days. One must be strong enough to keep it. If one is not strong, then there is no hope."

"You'll be on your feet again in no time," I said.

He smiled at me, and from the way he smiled, he knew I was trying to make him feel good. Fact was, right at that time I wouldn't have bet that he'd live out the month.

Jonathan Pritts, he told me, was demanding a new survey of the Grant, claiming that the boundaries of the Grant were much smaller than the land the don claimed. It was a new way of getting at him and a troublesome one, for those old Grants were bounded by this peak or that ridge or some other peak, and the way they were written up a man could just about pick his own ridges and his own peak. If Pritts could get his own surveyor appointed they would survey Don Luis right out of his ranch, his home, and everything.

"There is going to be serious trouble," he said at last. "I shall send Drusilla to Mexico to visit until it is over."

Something seemed to go out of me right then. If she went to Mexico she would never come back because the don was not going to win his fight. Jonathan Pritts had no qualms, and would stop at nothing.

I sat there with my hat in my hand wishing I could say something, but what did I have to offer a girl like Drusilla? I was nigh to broke. Right then I was wondering what we could do for operating expenses, and it was no time to talk marriage to a girl, even if she would listen to me, when that girl was used to more than I could ever give her.

At last the don reached for my hand, but his grip was feeble. "*Señor,* you are like a son to me. We have seen too little of you, Drusilla and I, but I have found much in you to respect, and to love. I am afraid, *señor,* that I have not long, and I am the last of my family. Only Drusilla is left. If there is anything you can do, *señor,* to help her . . . take care of her, *señor.*"

"Don Luis, I'd like . . . I mean . . . I don't have any money, Don Luis. Right now I'm broke. I must get money to keep my ranch working."

"There are other things, my son. You have strength, and you have youth, and those are needed now. If I had the strength. . . ."

Drusilla and I sat at the table together in the large room, and the Indian woman served us. Looking down the table at her my heart went out to her, I wanted her so. Yet what could I do? Always there was something that stood between us.

"Don Luis tells me you are going to Mexico?"

"He wishes it. There is trouble here, Tye."

"What about Juan Torres?"

"He is not the same . . . something has happened to him, and I believe he is afraid now."

*Chico Cruz . . .*

"I will miss you."

"I do not want to go, but what my grandfather tells me to do, I must do. I am worried for him, but if I go perhaps he will do what must be done."

"Any way I can help?"

"No!" She said it so quickly and sharply that I knew what she meant. What had to be done we both knew: Chico Cruz must be discharged, fired, sent away. But Dru was not thinking of the necessity, she was thinking of me, and she was afraid for me.

*Chico Cruz . . .*

We knew each other, that one and I, and we each had a feeling about the other.

If this had to be done, then I would do it myself. There was no hope that the don would recover in time, for we both knew that when we parted tonight we might not meet again. Don Luis did not have the strength, and his recovery would take weeks, or even months.

What was happening here I understood. Torres was afraid of Cruz and the others knew it, so their obedience was half-hearted. There was no leader here, and it was nothing Cruz had done or needed to do. I doubted if he had thought of it . . . it was simply the evil in him and his willingness to kill.

Whatever was to be done must be done now, at once, so as we ate and talked I was thinking it out. This was nothing for Orrin, Cap, or anyone but me, and I must do it tonight. I must do it before this went any further.

Perhaps then she would stay, for I knew that if she ever left I would never see her again.

At the door I took her hand . . . it was the first time I had found courage to do it. "Dru . . . do not worry. I will come to see you again." Suddenly, I said what I had been thinking. "Dru . . . I love you."

And then I walked swiftly away, my heels clicking on the pavement as I crossed the court. But I did not go to my horse, but to the room of Juan Torres.

It seemed strange that a man could change so in three years since we had met. Three years? He had changed in months. And I knew that Cruz had done this, not by threats, not by warnings, just by the constant pressure of his being here.

"Juan . . . ?"

"Señor?"

"Come with me. We are going to fire Chico Cruz."

He sat very still behind the table and looked at me, and then he got up slowly.

"You think he will go?"

He looked at me, his eyes searching mine. And I told him what I felt. "I do not care whether he goes or stays."

We walked together to the room of Antonio Baca. He was playing cards with Pete Romero and some others.

We paused outside and I said, "We will start here. You tell him."

Juan hesitated only a minute, and then he stepped into the room and I followed. "Baca, you will saddle your horse and you will leave . . . do not come back."

Baca looked at him, and then he looked at me, and I said, "You heard what Torres said. You tried it once in the dark when my back was turned. If you try it now you will not be so lucky."

He put his cards into a neat, compact pile, and for the first time he seemed at a loss. Then he said, "I will talk to Chico."

"We will talk to Chico. You will go." Taking out my watch, I said, "Torres has told you. You have five minutes."

We turned and went down the row of rooms and stopped before one that was in the dark. Torres struck a light and lit a lantern. He held the light up to the window and I stepped into the door.

Chico Cruz had been sitting there in the darkness. Torres said, "We don't need you any longer, Chico, you can go . . . now."

He looked at Torres from his dark, steady eyes and then at me.

"There is trouble here," I said, "and you do not make it easier."

"You are to make me go?" His eyes studied me carefully.

"It will not be necessary. You will go."

His left hand and arm were on the table, toying with a .44 cartridge. His right hand was in his lap.

"I said one day that we would meet."

"That's fool talk. Juan has said you are through. There is no job for you here, and the quarters are needed."

"I like it here."

"You will like it elsewhere." Torres spoke sharply. His courage was returning. "You will go now . . . tonight."

Cruz ignored him. His dark, steady eyes were on me. "I think I shall kill you, *señor*."

"That's fool talk," I said casually and swung my boot up in a swift, hard kick at the near edge of the table. It flipped up and he sprang back to avoid it and tripped, falling back to the floor. Before he could grasp a gun I kicked his hand away, then grabbed him quickly by the shirt and jerked him up from the floor, taking his gun and dropping him in one swift movement.

He knew I was a man who used a gun and he expected that, but I did not want to shoot him. He clung to his wrist and stared at me, his eyes unblinking like those of a rattler.

"I told you, Cruz."

Torres walked to the bunk and began stuffing Chico's clothes into his saddlebags, and rolling his bedroll. Chico still clung to his wrist.

"If I go they will attack the hacienda," Cruz said, "is that what you want?"

"It is not. But we will risk it. We cannot risk you being here, Chico. There is an evil that comes with you."

"And not with you?" He stared at me.

"Perhaps . . . anyway, I shall not be here."

We heard the sound of a horse outside, and glanced out to see Pete Romero leading Chico's horse.

Chico walked to the door and he looked at me. "What of my gun?" he said, and swung into the saddle.

"You may need it," I said, "and I would not want you without it."

So I handed him the gun, nor did I take the shells from it. He opened the loading gate and flipped the cylinder curiously, and then he looked at me and held the gun in his palm, his face expressionless.

For several seconds we remained like that, and I don't know what he was thinking. He had reason to hate me, reason to kill me, but he held the gun in his hand and looked down at me, and my own gun remained in its holster.

He turned his horse. "I think we will never meet," he said, "I like you, señor."

Juan Torres and I stood there until we could hear the gallop of his horse no longer.

# Chapter 13

Jonathan Pritts had brought with him an instrument more dangerous than any gun. He brought a printing press.

In a country hungry for news and with a scarcity of reading material, the newspaper was going to be read, and people believe whatever they read must be true—or it would not be in print.

Most folks don't stop to think that the writer of a book or the publisher of a newspaper may have his own axe to grind, or he may be influenced by others, or may not be in possession of all the information on the subject of which he writes.

Don Luis had known about Pritts' printing press before anybody else, and that was one reason he wanted his granddaughter out of the country, for a paper can be used to stir people up. And things were not like they had been.

Don Luis sent for me again, and made a deal to sell me four thousand acres of his range that joined to mine. The idea was his, and he sold it to me on my note.

"It is enough, *señor*. You are a man of your word, and you can use the range." He was sitting up that day. He smiled at me. "Moreover, *señor*, it will be a piece of land they cannot take from me, and they will not try to take it from you."

At the same time, I bought, also on my note, three hundred head of young stuff. In both cases the notes were made payable to Drusilla.

The don was worried, and he was also smart. It was plain that he could expect nothing but trouble. Defeat had angered Jonathan Pritts, and he would never quit until he had destroyed the don or been destroyed himself.

His Settlement crowd had shifted their base to Las Vegas although some of them were around Elizabethtown and Cimarron, and causing trouble in both places. But the don was playing it smart . . . land and cattle sold to me they would not try to take, and he felt sure I'd make good, and so Drusilla would have that much at least coming to her.

These days I saw mighty little of Orrin. Altogether we had a thousand or so head on the place now, mostly young stuff that would grow into money. The way I figured, I wasn't going to sell anything for another three years, and by that time I would be in a position to make some money.

Orrin, the boys, and me, we talked it over. We had no idea of running the big herds some men were handling, or trying to hold big pieces of land. All the land I used I wanted title to, and I figured it would be best to run only a few cattle, keep from overgrazing the grass, and sell fat cattle. We had already found out we could get premium prices for cattle that were in good shape.

Drusilla was gone.

The don was a little better, but there was more trouble. Squatters had moved into a valley on the east side of his property and there was trouble. Pritts jumped in with his newspaper and made a lot more of the trouble than there had been.

Then Orrin was made sheriff of the county, and he asked Tom to become a deputy.

Now we had a going ranch and everything was in hand. We needed money, and if I ever expected to make anything of myself it was time I had at it. There was nothing to do about the ranch that the boys could not do, but I had notes to Don Luis to pay and it was time I started raising some money.

Cap Rountree rode out to the ranch. He got down from his horse and sat down on the step beside me.

"Cap," I said, "you ever been to Montana?"

"Uh-huh. Good country, lots of grass, lots of mountains, lots of Indians, mighty few folks. Except around Virginia City. They've got a gold strike up there."

"That happened some years back."

"Still working." He gave me a shrewd look out of those old eyes. "You gettin' the itch, too?"

"Need money. We're in debt, Cap, and I never liked being beholden to anybody. Seems to me we might strike out north and see what we can find. You want to come along?"

"Might's well. I'm gettin' the fidgets here."

So we rode over to see Tom Sunday. Tom was drinking more than a man should. He had bought a ranch for himself about ten miles from us. He had him some good grass, a fair house, but it was a rawhide outfit, generally speaking, and not at all like Tom who was a first-rate cattleman.

"I'll stay here," he told me finally. "Orrin offered me a job as deputy sheriff, but I'm not taking it. I think I'll run for sheriff myself, next election."

"Orrin would like to have you," I said. "It's hard to get good men."

"Hell," Tom said harshly, "he should be working for me. By rights that should be my job."

"Maybe. You had a chance at it."

He sat down at the table and stared moodily out the window.

Cap got to his feet. "Might's well come along," he said, "if you don't find any gold you'll still see some fine country."

"Thanks," he said, "I'll stay here."

We mounted up and Tom put a hand on my saddle. "Tye," he said, "I've got nothing against you. You're a good man."

"So's Orrin, Tom, and he likes you."

He ignored it. "Have a good time. If you get in trouble, write me and I'll come up and pull you out of it."

"Thanks. And if you get in trouble, you send for us."

He was still standing there on the steps when we rode away, and I looked back when I could barely make him out, but he was still standing there.

"Long as I've known him, Cap," I said, "that was the first time I ever saw Tom Sunday without a shave."

Cap glanced at me out of those cold, still eyes. "He'd cleaned his gun," he said. "He didn't forget that."

The aspen were like clusters of golden candles on the green hills, and we rode north into a changing world. "Within two weeks we'll be freezin' our ears off," Cap commented.

Nonetheless, his eyes were keen and sharp and Cap sniffed the breeze each morning like a buffalo-hunting wolf. He was a new man, and so was I. Maybe this was what I was bred for, roaming the wild country, living off it, and moving on.

In Durango we hired out and worked two weeks on a roundup crew, gathering cattle, roping and branding calves. Then we drifted west into the Abajo Mountains, sometimes called the Blues. It was a mighty big country, two-thirds of it standing on edge, seemed like. We rode through country that looked like hell with the fires out, and we camped at night among the cool pines.

Our tiny fire was the only light in a vast world of darkness, for any way we looked there was nothing but night and the stars. The smell of coffee was good, and the smell of fresh wood burning. We hadn't seen a rider for three days when we camped among the pines up there in the Blues, and we hadn't seen a track in almost as long. Excepting deer tracks, cat or bear tracks.

Out of Pioche I got a job riding shotgun for a stage line with Cap Rountree handling the ribbons. We stayed with it two months.

Only one holdup was attempted while I rode shotgun because it seemed I was a talked-about man. That one holdup didn't pan out for them because I dropped off the stage and shot the gun out of one of the outlaw's hands—it was an accident, as my foot slipped on a rock and spoiled my aim—and put two holes in the other one.

We took them back into town, and the shot one lived. He lived but he didn't learn . . . six months later they caught him stealing a horse and hung him to the frame over the nearest ranch gate.

At South Pass City we holed up to wait out a storm and I read in a newspaper how Orrin was running for the state legislature, and well spoken of. Orrin was young but it was a time for young men, and he was as old as Alexander Hamilton in 1776, and older than William Pitt when he was chancellor in England. As old as Napoleon when he completed his Italian campaign.

I'd come across a book by Jomini on Napoleon, and another by Vegetius on the tactics of the Roman legions. Most of the time I read penny dreadfuls as they were all a body could find, except once in a while those paperbound classics given away by the Bull Durham company for coupons they enclosed. A man could find those all over the west, and many a cowhand had read all three hundred and sixty of them.

We camped along the mountain streams, we fished, we hunted, we survived. Here and yonder we had a brush with Indians. One time we outran a bunch of Blackfeet, another time had a set-to with some Sioux. I got a nicked ear out of that one and Cap lost a horse, so we came into Laramie astride Montana horse, the both of us riding him.

Spring was coming and we rode north with the changing weather and staked a claim on a creek in Idaho, but nothing contented me any more. We had made our living, but little more than that. We'd taken a bunch of furs and sold out well, and I'd made a payment to Don Luis and sent some money home.

There was a two-by-four town near where we staked our claim. I mean, there was no town but a cluster of shacks and a saloon called the Rose-Marie. A big man with a square red face, sandy-red hair and small blue eyes ran the place. He laid his thick hands on the bar and you saw the scars of old fist fights there, and those little eyes studied you cruel . . . like he was figuring how much you'd be worth to him.

"What'll you have, gents? Something to cut the dust?"

"Out of that bottle in the cabinet," I said, as I'd seen him take a drink out of it himself. "We'll have a shot of that bourbon."

"I can recommend the barrel whiskey."

"I bet you can. Give it to us from the bottle."

"My own whiskey. I don't usually sell it."

There were two men sitting at a back table and they were sizing us up. One thing I'd noticed about those men. They got their service without paying. I had a hunch they worked for the firm, and if they did, what did they do?

"My name is Brady," the red-haired man said, "Martin Brady."

"Good," I said, "a man should have a name." We put our money on the bar and turned to go. "You keep that bottle handy. We tried that river whiskey before."

After three days we had only a spot or two of color. Straightening up from my pick I said, "Cap, the way I hear it we should have a burro, and when the burro strays, we follow him, and when we find that burro he's pawing pay dirt right out of the ground, or you pick up a chunk to chuck at the burro and it turns out to be pure-dee gold."

"Don't you believe all you hear." He pushed his hat back. "I been lookin' the ground over. Over there," he indicated what looked like an old stream bed, "that crick flowed for centuries. If there's gold in the crick there's more of it under that bench there."

Up on the bench we cut timber and built a flume to carry water and a sluice box. Placer mining isn't just a matter of scooping up sand and washing it out in a pan. The amount of gold a man can get that way is mighty little, and most places he can do as well punching cows or riding shotgun on a stage.

The thing to do is locate some color and then choose a likely spot like this bench and sink a shaft down to bedrock, panning out that gravel that comes off the bedrock, working down to get all the cracks and to peel off any loose slabs and work the gravel gathered beneath them. Gold is heavy, and over the years it works deeper and deeper through loose earth or gravel until it reaches bedrock and can go no further.

When we started to get down beyond six feet we commenced getting some good color, and we worked all the ground we removed from there on down. Of a night I'd often sit up late reading whatever came to hand, and gradually I was learning a good bit about a lot of things.

On the next claim there was a man named Clark who loaned me several books. Most of the reading a man could get was pretty good stuff . . . nobody wanted to carry anything else that far.

Clark came to our fire one night. "Cap, you make the best sour-dough bread I ever ate. I'm going to miss it."

"You taking out?"

"She's deep enough, Cap, I'm leaving tomorrow. I'm going back to the States, to my wife and family. I worked in a store for six, seven years and always wanted one of my own."

"You be careful," Cap said.

Clark glanced around, then lowered his voice. "Have you heard those yarns, too? About the killings?"

"They found Wilton's body last week," I said, "he'd been buried in a shallow grave but the coyotes dug him out."

"I knew him." Clark accepted another plate of beans and beef and then he said, "I believe those stories. Wilton was carrying a heavy poke, and he wasn't a man to talk it around."

He forked up some more beans, then paused. "Sackett, you've been talked up as a man who's good with a gun."

"It's exaggerated."

"If you'll ride with me I'll pay you a hundred dollars each."

"That's good money, but what about our claim?"

"This means everything to me, boys. I talked to Dickey and Wells, and they're reliable men who will watch your claim."

Cap lit up his pipe and I poured coffee for all of us. Clark just wasn't a-woofin'. Most of the miners who gambled their money away at the Rose-Marie in town had no trouble leaving. It was only those who tried to leave with their money. At least three were sitting a-top some fat pokes of gold wondering how to get out alive and still keep what they'd worked for.

"Clark," I said, "Cap and me, we need the money. We'd help even if you couldn't afford to pay."

"Believe me, it's worth it."

So I got up off the ground. "Cap, I'll just go in and have a little talk with Martin Brady."

Clark got up. "You're crazy!"

"Why, I wouldn't want him to think us deceitful, Clark, so I'll just go tell him we're riding out tomorrow. I'll also tell him what will happen if anybody bothers us."

There were thirty or forty men in the Rose-Marie when I came in. Brady came to me, drying his big hands on his apron. "We're fresh out of bourbon," he said, "you'll have to take bar whiskey."

"I just came to tell you Jim Clark is riding out of the country tomorrow and he's taking all that gold he didn't spend in here."

You could have heard a pin drop. When I spoke those words I said them out loud so everybody could hear. Brady's cigar rolled between his teeth and he got white around the eyes, but I had an eye on the two loafers at the end of the bar.

"Why tell me?" He didn't know what was coming but he knew he wouldn't like it.

"Somebody might think Clark was going alone," I said, "and they might try to kill him the way Wilton and Jacks and Thompson were killed, but I figured it would be deceitful of me to ride along with Clark and let somebody get killed trying to get his gold. You see, Clark is going to make it."

"I hope he does," Brady rolled that cigar again, those cold little eyes telling me they hated me. "He's a good man."

He started to walk away but I wasn't through with him.

"Brady?"

He turned slowly.

"Clark is going through because I'm going to see that he gets through, and when he's gone, I'm coming back."

"So?" He put his big hands on the edge of the bar. "What does that mean?"

"It means that if we have any trouble at all, I'm going to come back here and either run you out of town or bury you."

Somebody gasped and Martin Brady's face turned a kind of sick white, he was that mad.

"It sounds like you're calling me a thief." He kept both hands in plain sight. "You'd have to prove that."

"Prove it? Who to? Everybody knows what killing and robbery there has been was engineered by you. There's no court here but a six-shooter court and I'm presiding."

So nothing happened. It was like I figured and it was out in the open now, and Martin Brady had to have me killed, but he didn't dare do it right then. We put Clark on the stage and started back to our own claims.

We were almost to bedrock now and we wanted to clean up and get out. We were getting the itch to go back to Santa Fe and back to Mora. Besides, I kept thinking of Drusilla.

Bob Wells was sitting on our claim with a rifle across his knees when we came in. "I was gettin' spooked," he said, "it don't seem like Brady to take this layin' down."

Dickey came over from his claim and several others, two of whom I remembered from the Rose-Marie Saloon the night I told off Martin Brady.

"We been talking it around," Dickey said, "and we figure you should be marshal."

"No."

"Can you name anybody else?" Wells asked reasonably. "This gold strike is going to play out, but a few of the mines will continue to work, and I plan to stay on here. I want to open a business, and I want this to be a clean town."

The others all pitched in, and finally Dickey said, "Sackett, with all respect, I believe it's your public duty."

Now I was beginning to see where reading can make a man trouble. Reading Locke, Hume, Jefferson, and Madison, had made me begin to think mighty high of a man's public duty.

Violence is an evil thing, but when the guns are all in the hands of the men without respect for human rights, then men are really in trouble.

It was all right for folks back east to give reasons why trouble should be handled without violence. Folks who talk about no violence are always the ones who are first to call a policeman, and usually they are sure there's one handy.

"All right," I said, "on two conditions: first, that somebody else takes over when the town is cleaned up. Second, that you raise money enough to buy out Martin Brady."

"*Buy* him out? I say, run him out!"

Who it was yelled, I don't know, but I spoke right up in meeting. "All right, whoever you are. You run him out."

There was a silence then, and when they had gathered the fact that the speaker wasn't going to offer I said, "We run him out and we're no better than he is."

"All right," Wells agreed, "buy him out."

"Well, now," I said, "we can be too hasty. I didn't say we should buy him out, what I say is we should *offer*. We make him a cash offer and whatever he does then is up to him."

Next day in town I got down from my horse in front of the store. Wind blew dust along the street and skittered dry leaves along the boardwalk. It gave me a lonesome feeling. Looking down the street I had a feeling the town would die.

No matter what happened here, what I was going to do was important. Maybe not for this town, but for men everywhere, for there must be right. Strength never made right, and it is an indecency when it is allowed to breed corruption. The west was changing. One time they would have organized vigilantes and had some necktie parties, but now they were hiring a marshal, and the next step would be a town meeting and a judge or a mayor.

Martin Brady saw me come in. His two men standing at the bar saw me too, and one of them moved a mite so his gun could be right under his hand and not under the edge of the bar.

There was nothing jumpy inside me, just a slow, measured, waiting feeling.

Around me everything seemed clearer, sharper in detail, the shadows and lights, the grain of wood on the bar, the stains left by the glasses, a slight tic on the cheek of one of Brady's men, and he was forty feet away.

"Brady, this country is growing up. Folks are moving in and they want schools, churches, and quiet towns where they can walk in the streets of an evening."

He never took his eyes from me, and I had a feeling he knew what was coming. Right then I felt sorry for Martin Brady, although his kind would outlast my kind because people have a greater tolerance for evil than for violence. If crooked gambling, thieving, and robbing are covered over, folks will tolerate it longer than outright violence, even when the violence may be cleansing.

Folks had much to say about the evil of those years, yet it took hard men to live the life, and their pleasures were apt to be rough and violent. They came from the world around, the younger sons of fine families, the ne'er-do-wells, the soldiers of fortune, the drifters, the always-broke, the promoters, the con men, the thieves. The frontier asked no questions and gave its rewards to the strong.

Maybe it needed men like Martin Brady, even the kind who lived on murder and robbery, to plant a town here at such a jumping-off place to nowhere. An odd thought occurred to me. Why had he called the saloon and the town Rose-Marie?

"Like I said, the country is growing up, Martin. You've been selling people rot-gut liquor, you've been cheating them out of hide an' hair, you've been robbing and murdering them. Murdering them was going too far, Martin, because when you start killing men, they fight back."

"What are you gettin' at, Sackett?"

"They elected me marshal."

"So?"

"You sell out, Martin Brady, they'll pay you a fair price. You sell out, and you get out."

He took the cigar from his teeth with his left hand and rested that hand on the bar. "And if I don't want to sell?"

"You have no choice."

He smiled and leaned toward me as if to say something in a low tone and when he did he touched that burning cigar to my hand.

My hand jerked and I realized the trick too late and those gunmen down the bar, who had evidently seen it done before, shot me full of holes.

My hand jerked and then guns were hammering. A slug hit me and turned me away from the bar, and two more bullets grooved the edge of the bar where I'd been standing.

Another slug hit me and I started to fall but my gun was out and I rolled over on the floor with bullets kicking splinters at my eyes and shot the big one with the dark eyes.

He was coming up to me for a finishing shot, and I put a bullet into his brisket and saw him stop dead still, turn half around and fall.

Then I was rolling over and on my feet and out of the corner of my eye I saw Martin Brady standing with both hands on the bar and his cigar in his teeth, watching me. My shirt was smoldering where it had caught fire from that black powder, but I shot the other man, taking my time, and my second bullet drove teeth back into his mouth and I saw the blood dribble from the corner of his mouth.

They were both down and they weren't getting up and I looked at Martin Brady and I said, "You haven't a choice, Martin."

His face turned strange and shapeless and I felt myself falling and remembered Ma asking me about Long Higgins.

There were cracks in the ceiling. It seemed I lay there staring at them for a dozen years, and remembered that it had been a long time since I'd been in a house and wondered if I was delirious.

Cap Rountree came into the room and I turned my head and looked at him. "If this here is hell, they sure picked the right people for it."

"Never knew a man to find so many excuses to get out of his work," Cap grumbled. "How much longer do I do the work in this shebang?"

"You're an old pirate," I said, "who never did an honest day's work in his life."

Cap came back in with a bowl of soup which he started spooning into me. "Last time I recollect they were shooting holes in me. Did you plug them up?"

"You'll hold soup. Only maybe all your sand run out."

On my hand I could see the scar of that cigar burn, almost healed now. That was one time I was sure enough outsmarted. It was one trick Pa never told me about, and I'd had to learn it the hard way.

"You took four bullets," Cap said, "an' lost a sight more blood than a man can afford."

"What about Brady?"

"He lit a shuck whilst they were huntin' a rope to hang him." Cap sat down. "Funny thing. He showed up here the next night."

"*Here?*"

"Stopped by to see how you was. Said you were too good a man to die like that—both of you were damned fools but a man got into a way of livin' and there was no way but to go on."

"The others?"

"Those boys of his were shot to doll rags."

Outside the door I could see the sunshine on the creek and I could hear the water chuckling over the rocks, and I got to thinking of Ma and Drusilla, and one day when I could sit up I looked over at Cap.

"Anything left out there?"

"Ain't been a day's wages in weeks. If you figure to do any more minin' you better find yourself another crick."

"We'll go home. Come morning you saddle up."

He looked at me skeptically. "Can you set a saddle?"

"If I'm going home. I can sit a saddle if I'm headed for Santa Fe."

Next morning, Cap and me headed as due south as the country would allow, but it is a long way in the saddle from Idaho to New Mexico.

From time to time we heard news about Sacketts. Men on the trail carried news along with them and everybody was on the prod to know all that was going on. The Sackett news was all Orrin . . . it would take awhile for the story of what happened at Rose-Marie to get around and I'd as soon it never did. But Orrin was making a name for himself. Only there was a rumor that he was to be married.

Cap told me that because he heard it before I did and neither of us made comments. Cap felt as I did about Laura Pritts and we were afraid it was her.

We rode right to the ranch.

Bob came out to meet us, and Joe was right behind him. Ma had seen us coming up the road.

She came to the steps to meet me. Ma was better than she had been in years, a credit to few worries and a better climate, I suppose. There was a Navajo woman helping with the housework now, and for the first time Ma had it easier.

There were bookshelves in the parlor and both the boys had taken to reading.

There was other news. Don Luis was dead . . . had been buried only two days ago, but already the Settlement crowd had moved in. Torres was in bad shape . . . he had been ambushed months ago and from what I was told there was small chance he'd be himself again.

Drusilla was in town.

And Orrin was married to Laura Pritts.

# Chapter 14

Orrin came out to the ranch in the morning, driving a buckboard. He got down and came to me with his hand out, a handsome man by any standards, wearing black broadcloth now like he was born to it.

He was older, more sure of himself, and there was a tone of authority in his voice. Orrin had done all right, no doubt of that, and beneath it all he was the same man he had always been, only a better man because of the education he had given himself and the experience behind him.

"It's good to see you, boy." He was sizing me up as he talked, and I had to grin, for I knew his way.

"You've had trouble," he said suddenly, "you've been hurt."

So I told him about Martin Brady and the Rose-Marie, my brief term as marshal, and the showdown.

When he realized how close I'd come to cashing in my chips he grew a little pale. "Tyrel," he said slowly, "I know what you've been through, but they need a man right here. They need a deputy sheriff who is honest and I sure know you'd never draw on anybody without cause."

"Has somebody been saying the contrary?" I asked him quietly.

"No . . . no, of course not." He spoke hastily, and I knew he didn't want to say who, which was all the answer I needed. "Of course, there's always talk about a man who has to use a gun. Folks don't understand."

He paused. "I suppose you know I'm married?"

"Heard about it. Has Laura been out to see Ma?"

Orrin flushed. "Laura doesn't take to Ma. Says a woman smoking is indecent, and smoking a pipe is worse."

"That may be true," I replied carefully. "Out here you don't see it much, but that's Ma."

He kicked at the earth, his face gloomy. "You may think I did wrong, Tyrel, but I love that girl. She's . . . she's different, Tyrel, she's so pretty, so delicate, so refined and everything. A man in politics, he needs a wife like that. And whatever else you can say about Jonathan, he's done everything he could to help me."

I'll bet, I said to myself. I'll just bet he has. And he'll want a return on it too. So far I hadn't noticed Jonathan Pritts being freehanded with anything but other folks' land.

"Orrin, if Laura suits you, and if she makes you happy, then it doesn't matter who likes her. A man has to live his own life."

Orrin walked out of the corral with me and leaned on the rail and we stood there and talked the sun out of the sky and the first stars up before we went in to dinner. He had learned a lot, and he had been elected to the legislature, and a good part of it had been the Mexican vote, but at the last minute the Pritts crowd had gotten behind him, too. He had won by a big majority and in politics a man who can command votes can be mighty important.

Already they were talking about Orrin for the United States Senate, or even for governor. Looking at him across the table as he talked to Ma and the boys, I could see him as a senator . . . and he'd make a good one.

Orrin was a smart man who had grown smarter. He had no illusions about how a man got office or kept it, yet he was an honest man, seeking nothing for himself beyond what he could make in the natural way of things.

"I wanted Tom Sunday for the deputy job," Orrin said, "he turned it down, saying he didn't need any handouts." Orrin looked at me. "Tye, I didn't mean it that way. I liked Tom, and I needed a strong man here."

"Tom could have handled it," Cap said. "That's bad, Tom feelin' that-away."

Orrin nodded. "It doesn't seem right without Tom. He's changed, Cap. He drinks too much, but that's only part of it. He's like an old bear with a sore tooth, and I'm afraid there'll be a killing if it keeps up."

Orrin looked at me. "Tom always liked you. If there is anybody can keep him in line it will be you. If anybody else even tried, and that includes me, he would go for his gun."

"All right."

Miguel rode over on the second day and we talked. Drusilla did not want to see me—he'd been sent to tell me that.

"Why, Miguel?"

"Because of the woman your brother has married. The *señorita* believes the hatred of Jonathan Pritts killed her grandfather."

"I am not my brother's keeper," I replied slowly, "nor did I choose his wife." I looked up at him. "Miguel, I love the *señorita*."

"I know, *señor*. I know."

The ranch was moving nicely. The stock we had bought had fattened out nicely, and some had been sold that year.

Bill Sexton was sheriff, and I took to him right off, but I could also see that he was an office man, built for a swivel chair and a roll-top desk.

Around Mora I was a known man, and there was mighty little trouble. Once I had to run down a couple of horse thieves, but I brought them in, without shooting, after trailing them to where they had holed up, then—after they'd turned in—I Injuned down there and got their guns before I woke them up.

Only once did I see Tom Sunday. He came into town, unshaven and looking mighty unpleasant, but when he saw me he grinned and held out his hand. We talked a few minutes and had coffee together, and it seemed like old times.

"One thing," he said, "you don't have to worry about. Reed Carney is dead."

"What happened?"

"Chico Cruz killed him over to Socorro."

It gave me a cold feeling, all of a sudden, knowing that gun-slinging Mexican was still around, and I found myself hoping that he did not come up this way.

When I'd been on the job about a week I was out to the ranch one day when I saw that shining black buckboard coming, only it wasn't Orrin driving. It was Laura.

I walked down from the steps to meet her. "How are you, Laura? It's good to see you."

"It isn't good to see you." She spoke sharply, and her lips thinned down. Right at that moment she was a downright ugly woman. "If you have any feeling for your brother, you will leave here and never come back!"

"This is my home."

"You'd better leave," she insisted, "everybody knows you're a vicious killer, and now you've wheedled the deputy's job out of Sexton, and you'll stay around here until you've ruined Orrin and me and everybody."

She made me mad so I said, "What's the difference between being a killer and hiring your killing done."

She struck at me, but I just stepped back and she almost fell out of the buckboard. Catching her arm, I steadied her, and she jerked away from me. "If you don't leave, I'll find a way to make you. You hate me and my father and if it hadn't been for you there wouldn't have been any of this trouble."

"I'm sorry. I'm staying."

She turned so sharply that she almost upset the buggy and drove away, and I couldn't help wondering if Orrin had ever seen her look like that. She wasn't like that hammer-headed roan I'd said she was like. That roan was a whole damned sight better.

Ma said nothing to me but I could see that she missed Orrin's visits, which became fewer and fewer. Laura usually contrived to have something important to do or somewhere important for him to be whenever he thought about coming out.

There was talk of rustling by Ed Fry who ranched near Tom's place, and we had several complaints about Tom Sunday. Whatever else Tom might be, he was an honest man. I got up on Kelly and rode the big red horse out to Sunday's place.

It was a rawhide outfit. I mean it the western way where a term like that is used to mean an outfit that's held together with rawhide, otherwise it would fall apart.

Tom Sunday came to the door when I rode up and he stood leaning against the doorjamb watching me tie my horse.

"That's a good horse, Tye," he said. "You always had a feeling for a good horse."

He squatted on his heels and began to build a smoke. Hunkering down beside him I made talk about the range and finally asked him about his trouble with Fry.

He stared at me from hard eyes. "Look, Tye, that's my business. You leave it alone."

"I'm the law, Tom," I said mildly. "I want to keep the peace if I can do it."

"I don't need any help and I don't want any interference."

"Look, Tom, look at it this way. I like this job. The boys do all there is to do on the ranch, so I took this job. If you make trouble for me, I may lose out."

His eyes glinted a little with sardonic humor. "Don't try to get around me, Tye. You came down here because you've been hearing stories about me and you're worried. Well, the stories are a damned lie and you know it."

"I do know it, Tom, but there's others."

"The hell with them."

"That may be all right for you, but it isn't for me. One reason I came down was to check on what's been happening, another was to see you. We four were mighty close for a long time, Tom, and we should stay that way."

He stared out gloomily. "I never did get along with that high-and-mighty brother of yours, Tye. He always thought he was better than anybody else."

"You forget, Tom. You helped him along. You helped him with his reading, almost as much as you did me. If he is getting somewhere it is partly because of you."

I figured that would please him but it didn't seem to reach him at all.

He threw his cigarette down. "I got some coffee," he said, and straightening up he went inside.

We didn't talk much over coffee, but just sat there together, and I think we both enjoyed it. Often on the drives we would ride for miles like that, never saying a word, but with a kind of companionship better than any words.

There was a book lying on the table called *Bleak House* by Charles Dickens. I'd read parts of some of Dickens' books that were run as serials in papers. "How is it?" I asked.

"Good . . . damned good."

He sat down opposite me and tasted the coffee. "Seems a long time ago," he said gloomily, "when you rode up to our camp outside of Baxter Springs."

"Five years," I agreed. "We've been friends a long time, Tom. We missed you, Cap and me, on this last trip."

"Cap and you are all right. It's that brother of yours I don't like. But he'll make it all right," he added grudgingly, "he'll get ahead and make the rest of us look like bums."

"He offered you a job. That was the deal: if you won you were to give him a job, if he won he would give you a job."

Tom turned sharply around. "I don't need his damned job! Hell, if it hadn't been for me he'd never have had the idea of running for office!"

Now that wasn't true but I didn't want to argue, so after awhile I got up and rinsed out my cup. "I'll be riding. Come out to the house and see us, Tom. Cap would like to see you and so would Ma." Then I added, "Orrin isn't there very much."

Tom's eyes glinted. "That wife of his. You sure had her figured right. Why, if I ever saw a double-crossing no-account female, she's the one. And her old man . . . I hate his guts."

When I stepped into the saddle I turned for one last word. "Tom, stay clear of Ed Fry, will you? I don't want trouble."

"You're one to talk." He grinned at me. "All right, I'll lay off, but he sticks in my craw."

Then as I rode away, he said, "My respects to your mother, Tye."

Riding away I felt mighty miserable, like I'd lost something good out of my life. Tom Sunday's eyes had been bloodshot, he was unshaven and he was careless about everything but his range. Riding over it, I could see that whatever else Tom might be, he was still a first-rate cattleman. Ed Fry and some of the others had talked of Tom's herds increasing, but by the look of things it was no wonder, for there was good grass, and he was keeping it from overgrazing, which Fry nor the others gave no thought to

. . . and his water holes were cleaned out, and at one place he'd built a dam in the river to stop the water so there would be plenty to last.

There was no rain. As the months went by, the rains held off, and the ranchers were worried, yet Tom Sunday's stock, in the few times I rode that way, always looked good. He had done a lot of work for a man whose home place was in such rawhide shape, and there was a good bit of water dammed up in several washes, and spreader dams he had put in had used the water he had gotten to better effect, so he had better grass than almost anybody around.

Ed Fry was a sorehead. A dozen times I'd met such men, the kind who get something in their craw and can't let it alone. Fry was an ex-soldier who had never seen combat, and was a man with little fighting experience anywhere else, and in this country, a man who wasn't prepared to back his mouth with action was better off if he kept still. But Ed Fry was a big man who talked big, and was too egotistical to believe anything could happen to him.

One morning when I came into the office I sat down and said, "Bill, you could do us both a favor if you'd have a talk with Ed Fry."

Sexton put down some papers and rolled his cigar in his jaws. "Has he been shooting off his mouth again?"

"He sure has. It came to me secondhand, but he called Tom Sunday a thief last night. If Tom hears about that we'll have a shooting. In fact, if Cap Rountree heard it there would be a shooting."

Sexton glanced at me. "And I wouldn't want you to hear it," he said bluntly, "or Orrin, either."

"If I figured to do anything about it, I'd take off this badge. There's no place in this office for personal feelings."

Sexton studied the matter. "I'll talk to Ed. Although I don't believe he'll listen. He only gets more bullheaded. He said the investigation you made was a cover-up for Sunday, and both you and Orrin are protecting him."

"He's a liar and nobody knows it better than you, Bill. When he wants to bear down, Tom Sunday is the best cattleman around. Drunk or sober he's a better cattleman than Ed Fry will ever be."

Sexton ran his fingers through his hair. "Tye, let's make Ed put up or shut up. Let's demand to know what cattle he thinks he has missing, and what, exactly, makes him suspect Sunday. Let's make him put his cards on the table."

"You do it," I said, "he would be apt to say the wrong thing to me. The man's a fool, talking around the way he is."

Since taking over my job as deputy sheriff and holding down that of town marshal as well, I'd not had to use my gun nor had there been a shooting in town in that time. I wanted that record to stand, but what concerned me most was keeping Tom Sunday out of trouble.

Only sometimes there isn't anything a man can do, and Ed Fry was a man bound and determined to have his say. When he said it once too often it was in the St. James Hotel up at Cimarron, and there was quite a crowd in the saloon.

Clay Allison was there, having a drink with a man from whom he was buying a team of mules. That man was Tom Sunday.

Cap was there, and Cap saw it all. Cap Rountree had a suspicion that trouble was heading for Sunday when he found out that Fry was going to Cimarron. Cap already knew that Sunday had gone there, so he took off himself, and he swapped horses a couple of times but didn't beat Fry to town.

Ed Fry was talking when Cap Rountree came into the St. James. "He's nothing but a damned cow thief!" Fry said loudly. "That Tom Sunday is a thief and those Sacketts protect him."

Tom Sunday had a couple of drinks under his belt and he turned slowly and looked at Ed Fry.

Probably Fry hadn't known until then that Sunday was in the saloon, because according to the way Cap told it, Fry went kind of gray in the face and Cap said you could see the sweat break out on his face. Folks had warned him what loose talk would do, but now he was face to face with it.

Tom was very quiet. When he spoke you could hear him in every corner of the room, it was that still.

"Mr. Fry, it comes to my attention that you have on repeated occasions stated that I was a cow thief. You have done this on the wildest supposition and without one particle of evidence. You have done it partly because you are yourself a poor cowman as well as a very inept and stupid man."

When Tom was drinking he was apt to fall into a very precise way of speaking as well as using all that highfalutin language he knew so well.

"You can't talk to me like—"

"You have said I was a cow thief, and you have said the Sacketts protect me. I have never been a cow thief, Mr. Fry, and I have never stolen anything in my life, nor do I need protection from the Sacketts or anyone else. Anyone that says I have stolen cattle or that I have been protected is a liar, Mr. Fry, a very fatheaded and stupid liar."

He had not raised his voice but there was something in his tone that lashed a man like a whip and in even the simplest words, the way Tom said them, there was an insult.

Ed Fry lunged to his feet and Tom merely watched him. "By the Lord—"

Ed Fry grabbed for his gun. He was a big man but a clumsy one, and when he got the gun out he almost dropped it. Sunday did not make a move until Fry recovered his grip on the gun and started to bring it level, and then Tom palmed his gun and shot him dead.

Cap Rountree told Bill Sexton, Orrin, and me about it in the sheriff's office two days later. "No man ever had a better chance," Cap said, "Tom, he just stood there and I figured for a minute he was going to let Fry kill him. Tom's fast, Tye, he's real fast."

And the way he looked at me when he said it was a thing I'll never forget.

# Chapter 15

It was only a few days later that I rode over to see Drusilla.

Not that I hadn't wanted to see her before, but there had been no chance. This time there was nobody to turn me away and I stopped before an open doorway.

She was standing there, tall and quiet, and at the moment I appeared in the door she turned her head and saw me.

"Dru," I said, "I love you."

She caught her breath sharply and started to turn away. "Please," she said, "go away. You mustn't say that."

When I came on into the room she turned to face me. "Tye, you shouldn't have come here, and you shouldn't say that to me."

"You know that I mean it?"

She nodded. "Yes . . . I know. But you love your brother, and his wife's family hate me, and I . . . I hate them too."

"If you hate them, you're going about it as if you tried to please them. They think they've beaten your grandfather and beaten you because you live like a hermit. What you should do is come out, let people see you, go to places."

"You may be right."

"Dru, what's happening to you? What are you going to do with yourself? I came here today to pay you money, but I'm glad I came and for another reason.

"Don Luis is gone, and he was a good man, but he would want you to be happy. You are a beautiful girl, Dru, and you have friends. Your very presence around Santa Fe would worry Laura and Jonathan Pritts more than anything we could think of. Besides, I want to take you dancing. I want to marry you, Dru."

Her eyes were soft. "Tye, I've always wanted to marry you. A long time ago I would have done it if you had asked me, that first time you visited us in Santa Fe. . . ."

"I didn't have anything. I was nobody. Just another drifter with a horse and a gun."

"You were you, Tye."

"Sometimes there were things I wanted to say so bad I'd almost choke. Only I never could find the words."

So we sat down and we had coffee again like we used to and I told her about Laura and Ma, which made Dru angry.

"There's trouble shaping, Dru. I can't read the sign clear enough to say where it will happen, but Pritts is getting ready for a showdown.

"There's a lot could happen, but when it happens, I want you with me."

We talked the sun down, and it wasn't until I got up to go that I remembered the money.

She pushed it away. "No, Tyrel, you keep it for me. Invest it for me if you want to. Grandfather left me quite a bit, and I don't know what to do with it now."

That made sense, and I didn't argue with her. Then she told me something that should have tipped me off as to what was coming.

"I have an uncle, Tye, and he is an attorney. He is going to bring an action to clear the titles to all the land in our Grant. When they are clear," she added, "I am going to see the United States Marshal moves any squatters off the land."

Well . . . what could I say? Certainly it was what needed to be done and what had to be done sooner or later, but there was nothing I could think of that was apt to start more trouble than that.

Jonathan Pritts had settled a lot of his crowd on land belonging to the Alvarado Grant. Then he had bought their claims from them, and he was now laying claim to more than a hundred thousand acres. Probably Pritts figured when the don died that he had no more worries . . . anyway, he was in it up to his ears and if the title of the Alvarado Grant proved itself, he had no more claim than nothing. I mean, he was broke.

Not that I felt sorry for him. He hadn't worried about what happened to the don or his granddaughter, all he thought of was what he wanted. Only if there was anything that was figured to blow the lid off this country it was such a suit.

"If I were you," I advised her, "I'd go to Mexico and I'd stay there until this is settled."

"This is my home," Dru said quietly.

"Dru, you don't seem to realize. This is a shooting matter. They'll kill you . . . or they'll try."

"They may try," she said quietly. "I shall not leave."

When I left the house I was worried about Dru. If I had not been so concerned with her situation I might have given some thought to myself.

They would think I had put her up to it.

From the day that action was announced I would be the Number-One target in the shooting gallery.

When I was expecting everything to happen, nothing happened. There were a few scattered killings further north. One was a Settlement man who had broken with Jonathan Pritts and the Settlement Company . . . it was out of my bailiwick and the killing went unsolved, but it had an ugly look to it.

Jonathan Pritts remained in Santa Fe, Laura was receiving important guests at her parties and fandangos most every night. Pritts was generally agreed to have a good deal of political power. Me, I was a skeptic . . . because folks associate in a social way doesn't mean they are political friends, and most everybody likes a get-together.

One Saturday afternoon Orrin pulled up alongside me in a buckboard. He looked up at me and grinned as I sat Sate's saddle.

"Looks to me like you'd sell that horse, Tyrel," he said. "He was always a mean one."

"I like him," I said. "He's contrary as all get-out, and he's got a streak of meanness in him, but I like him."

"How's Ma?"

"She's doing fine." It was a hot day and the sweat trickled down my face. The long street was busy. Fetterson was down there with the one they called Paisano, because he gave a man a feeling that he was some kin to a chaparral cock or road runner. Folks down Mexico way called them *paisanos*.

Only I had a feeling about Paisano. I didn't care for him much.

"Ma misses you, Orrin. You should drive out to see her."

"I know . . . I know. Damn it, Tyrel, why can't womenfolks get along?"

"Ma hasn't had any trouble with anybody. She's all right, Orrin, the same as always. Only she still smokes a pipe."

He mopped his face, looking mighty harried and miserable. "Laura's not used to that." He scowled. "She raises hell every time I go out to the place."

"Womenfolks," I said, "sometimes need some handling. You let them keep the bit in their teeth and they'll make you miserable and themselves too. You pet 'em a little and keep a firm hand on the bridle and you'll have no trouble."

He stared down the sun-bright street, squinting his eyes a little. "It sounds very easy, Tyrel. Only there's so many things tied in with it. When we become a state I want to run for the Senate, and it may be only a few years now."

"How do you and Pritts get along?"

Orrin gathered the reins. He didn't need to tell me. Orrin was an easygoing man, but he wasn't a man you could push around or take advantage of. Except maybe by that woman.

"We don't." He looked up at me. "That's between us, Tyrel. I wouldn't even tell Ma. Jonathan and I don't get along, and Laura . . . well, she can be difficult."

"You were quite a bronc rider, Orrin."

"What's that mean?"

"Why," I pushed my hat back on my head, "I'd say it meant your feet aren't tied to the stirrups, Orrin. I'd say there isn't a thing to keep you in the saddle but your mind to stay there, and nobody's going to give you a medal for staying in the saddle when you can't make a decent ride of it.

"Take Sate here," I rubbed Sate's neck and that bronc laid back his ears, "you take Sate. He's a mean horse. He's tough and he's game and he'll go until the sun comes up, but Orrin, if I could only have one horse, I'd never have this one. I'd have Dapple or that Montana horse.

"It's fun to ride a mean one when you don't have to do it every day, but if I stay with Sate long enough he'll turn on me. And there's some women like that."

Orrin gathered the reins. "Too hot . . . I'll see you later, Tyrel."

He drove off and I watched him go. He was a fine, upstanding man but when he married that Laura girl he bought himself a packet of grief.

Glancing down the street I saw Fetterson hand something to Paisano. It caught the sunlight an instant, then disappeared in Paisano's pocket. But the glimpse was enough. Paisano had gotten himself a fistful of gold coins from Fetterson, which was an interesting thought.

Sometimes a man knows something is about to happen. He can't put a finger on a reason, but he gets an itch inside him, and I had it now.

Something was building up. I could smell trouble in the making, and oddly enough it might have been avoided by a casual comment. The trouble was that I did not know that Torres was coming up from Socorro, and that he was returning to work for Dru.

Had I known that, I would have known what Jonathan Pritts' reaction was to be.

If Dru had happened to mention the fact that Torres was finally well and able to be around and was coming back, I would have gone down to meet him and come back with him.

Juan Torres was riding with two other Mexicans, men he had recruited in Socorro to work for Dru, and they were riding together. They had just ridden through the gap about four miles from Mora when they were shot to doll rags.

Mountain air is clear, and sound carries, particularly when it has the hills behind it. The valley was narrow all the way to town, and it was early morning with no other sound to interfere.

Orrin had come up from Santa Fe by stage to Las Vegas and had driven up to town from there. We had walked out on the street together for I'd spent the night in the back room at the sheriff's office.

We all heard the shots, there was a broken volley that sounded like four or five guns at least, and then, almost a full half minute later, a single, final shot.

Now nobody shoots like that if they are hunting game. For that much shooting it has to be a battle, and I headed for Orrin's buckboard on the run with him right behind me. His Winchester was there and each of us wore a belt gun.

Dust lingered in the air at the gap, only a faint suggestion of it. The killers were gone and nobody was going to catch up with them right away, especially in a buckboard, so I wasted no time thinking about that.

Juan Torres lay on his back with three bullet holes in his chest and a fourth between his eyes, and there was a nasty powder burn around that.

"You know what that means?" I asked Orrin.

"Somebody wanted him dead. Remember that final shot?"

There was a rattle of hoofs on the road and I looked around to see my brother Joe and Cap Rountree riding bareback. The ranch was closer than the town and they must have come as fast as they could get to their horses.

They knew better than to mess things up.

Juan Torres had been dead when that final shot was fired, I figured, because at least two of the bullets in the chest would have killed him. The two others were also dead.

I began casting for sign. Not thirty feet off the trail I found where several men had waited for quite some time. There were cigarette stubs there and the grass was matted down.

Orrin had taken one look at the bodies and had walked back to the buckboard and he stood there, saying no word to anybody, just staring first at the ground and then at his hands, looking like he'd never seen them before.

A Mexican I knew had come down the road from town, and he was sitting there on his horse looking at those bodies.

"*Bandidos?*" he looked at me with eyes that held no question.

"No," I said, "assassins."

He nodded his head slowly. "There will be much trouble," he said, "this one," he indicated Torres, "was a good man."

"He was my friend."

"Sí."

Leaving the Mexican to guard the road approaching the spot—just beyond the gap—I put Joe between the spot and the town. Only I did this after we loaded the bodies in the buckboard. Then I sent Orrin and Cap off to town with the bodies.

Joe looked at me, his eyes large. "Keep anybody from messing up the road," I said, "until I've looked it over."

First I went back to the spot in the grass where the drygulchers had waited. I took time to look all around very carefully before approaching the spot itself.

Yet even as I looked, a part of my mind was thinking this would mean the lid was going to blow off. Juan Torres had been a popular man and he had been killed, the others, God rest their souls, were incidental. But it was not that alone, it was what was going to happen to my own family, and what Orrin already knew. Only one man had real reason to want Juan Torres dead. . . .

One of the men had smoked his cigarettes right down to the nub. There was a place where he had knelt to take aim, the spot where his knee had been and where his boot toe dug in was mighty close. He was a man, I calculated, not over five feet-four or -five. A short man who smoked his cigarettes to the nub wasn't much to go on, but it was a beginning.

One thing I knew. This had been a cold-blooded murder of men who had had no chance to defend themselves, and it had happened in my bailiwick and I did not plan to rest until I had every man who took part in it . . . no matter where the trail led.

It was a crime on my threshold, and it was a friend of mine who had been killed. And once before Orrin and I had prevented his murder . . . and another time Torres had been shot up and left for dead.

I was going to get every man Jack of them.

There had been five of them here and they had gathered up all the shells before leaving . . . or had they?

Working through the tall grass that had been crushed down by them, I found a shell and I struck gold. It was a .44 shell and it was brand, spanking new. I put that shell in my pocket with a mental note to give some time to it later.

Five men . . . and Torres himself had been hit by four bullets. Even allowing that some of them might have gotten off more than one shot, judging by the bodies there had been at least nine shots fired before that final shot.

Now some men can lever and fire a rifle mighty fast, but it was unlikely you'd find more than one man, at most two, who could work a lever and aim a shot as fast as those bullets had been, in one group of five men.

Torres must have been moving, maybe falling after that first volley, yet somebody had gotten more bullets into him. The answer to that one was simple. There were more than five.

Thoughtfully, I looked up at the hill crested with cedar which arose behind the place where they'd been waiting. They would have had a lookout up there, someone to tell them when Torres was coming.

For a couple of hours I scouted around. I found where they had their horses and they had seven of them, and atop the ridge I found where two men had waited, smoking. One of them had slid right down to the horses, and a man could see where he had dug his heels into the bank to keep from sliding too fast.

Cap came and lent me a hand and after a bit, Orrin came out and joined us.

One more thing I knew by that time. The man who had walked up to Torres's body and fired that last shot into his head had been a tall man with fairly new boots and he had stepped in the blood.

Although Orrin held off and let me do it—knowing too many feet would tramp everything up—he saw enough to know here was a plain, outright murder, and a carefully planned murder at that.

First off, I had to decide whether they expected to be chased or not and about how far they would run. How well did they know the country? Were they likely to go to some ranch owned by friends, or hide out in the hills?

Cap had brought back Kelly all saddled and ready, so when I'd seen about all I could see there, I got into the saddle and sent Joe back to our ranch. He was mighty upset, wanting to go along with a posse, but if it was possible I wanted to keep Joe and Bob out of any shooting and away from the trouble.

"What do you think, Tyrel?" Orrin watched me carefully as he spoke.

"It was out-and-out-murder," I said, "by seven men who knew Torres would be coming to Mora. It was planned murder, with the men getting there six to seven hours beforehand. Two of them came along later and I'd guess they watched Torres from the hills to make sure he didn't turn off or stop."

Orrin stared at the backs of his hands and I didn't say anything about what I suspected nor did Cap.

"All right," Orrin said. "You go after them and bring them in, no matter how long it takes or what money you need."

I hesitated. Only Cap, Orrin, and me were there together. "Orrin," I said, "you had me hired, and you can fire me. You can leave it to Bill Sexton or you can put in someone else."

Orrin seldom got mad but he was angry when he stared back at me. "Tyrel, that's damn-fool talk. You do what you were hired to do."

Not one of the three of us could have doubted where that trail would lead, but maybe even then Orrin figured it would lead to Fetterson, maybe, but not Pritts.

Bill Sexton came up just then. "You'll be wanting a posse," he said, "I can get a few good men."

"No posse . . . I want Cap, that's all."

"Are you crazy? There's seven of them . . . at least."

"Look, if I take a posse there's apt to be one in the crowd who's trigger happy. If I can avoid it I don't want any shooting. If I can take these men alive, I'm going to do it."

"You're looking to lose your scalp," Sexton said doubtfully, "but it's your hair. You do what you've a mind to."

"Want me to come along?" Orrin asked.

"No." I wanted him the worst way but the less involved he was, the better. "Cap will do."

The way I looked at it, the chances were almighty slim that the seven would stay together very long. Some of them would split off and that would shorten the odds.

The Alvarado Ranch lay quiet under low gray clouds when Cap and I rode up to the door. Briefly, I told Miguel about Torres. "I will come with you," he said instantly.

"You stay here." I gave it to him straight. "They thought by killing Torres they would ruin any chance the *señorita* would have. Torres is killed but you are not. You're going to take his place, Miguel. You are going to be foreman."

He was startled. "But I—"

"You will have to protect the *señorita*," I said, "and you will have to hire at least a dozen good men. You'll have to bunch what cattle she has left and guard them. It looks to me like the killing of Juan Torres was the beginning of an attempt to put her out of business."

I went on inside, walking fast, and Dru was there to meet me. Quietly as possible, I told her about Juan Torres' death and what I had told Miguel.

"He's a good man," I said, "a better man than he knows, and this will prove it to him and to you. Give him authority and give him responsibility. You can trust him to use good judgment."

"What are you going to do?"

"Why, what a deputy sheriff has to do. I am going to run down the killers."

"And what does your brother say?"

"He says to find them, no matter what, no matter how long, and no matter who."

"Tyrel—be careful!"

That made me grin. "Why, ma'am," I said, grinning at her, "I'm the most careful man you know. Getting myself killed is the last idea in my mind . . . I want to come back to you."

She just looked at me. "You know, Dru, we've waited long enough. When I've caught these men I am going to resign and we are going to be married . . . and I'm not taking no for an answer."

Her eyes laughed at me. "Who said no?"

At the gap Cap and I picked up the trail and for several miles it gave us no trouble at all. Along here they had been riding fast, trying to put distance between themselves and pursuit.

It was a green, lovely country, with mountain meadows, the ridges crested with cedar that gave way to pine as we climbed into the foothills. We camped that night by a little stream where we could have a fire without giving our presence away.

Chances were they would be expecting a large party and if they saw us, would not recognize us. That was one reason I was riding Kelly. Usually I was up on Dapple or Montana horse, and Kelly was not likely to be known.

Cap made the coffee and sat back into the shadows. He poked sticks into the fire for a few minutes the way he did when he was getting ready to talk.

"Figured you'd want to know. Pritts has been down to see Tom Sunday."

I burned my mouth on a spoonful of stew and when I swallowed it I looked at him and said, "Pritts to see Tom?"

"Uh-huh. Dropped by sort of casual-like, but stayed some time."

"Tom tell you that?"

"No . . . I've got a friend down thataway."

"What happened?"

"Well, seems they talked quite some time and when Pritts left, Tom came out to the horse with him and they parted friendly."

Jonathan Pritts and Tom . . . it made no kind of sense. Or did it?

The more thought I gave to it the more worried I became, for Tom Sunday was a mighty changeable man, and drinking as he was, with his temper, anything might happen.

Orrin had had trouble with Pritts—of this I was certain sure—and Pritts had made a friendly visit to Tom Sunday. I didn't like the feel of it. I didn't like it at all.

# Chapter 16

There was a pale lemon glow over the eastern mountains when we killed the last coals of our fire and saddled up. Kelly was feeling sharp and twisty, for Kelly was a trail-loving horse who could look over big country longer than any horse I ever knew, except maybe Montana horse.

Inside me there was a patience growing and I knew I was going to need it. We were riding a trail that could only bring us to trouble because the men we were seeking had friends who would not take lightly to our taking them. But the job was ours to do and those times a man didn't think too much of consequences but crossed each bridge as he came to it.

It was utterly still. In this, the last hour before dawn, all was quiet. Even with my coat on, the sharp chill struck through and I shivered. There was a bad taste in my mouth and I hated the stubble on my jaws . . . I'd gotten used to shaving living in town and being an officer. It spoiled a man.

Even in the vague light we could see the lighter trail of pushed-down grass where the riders had ridden ahead of us. Suddenly, the trail dipped into a hollow in the trees and we found their camp of the night before.

They were confident, we could see that, for they had taken only the usual, normal precaution in hiding their camp, and they hadn't made any effort to conceal that they'd been there.

We took our time there for much can be learned of men at such a time, and to seek out a trail it is well to know the manner of men you seek after. If Cap Rountree and me were to fetch these men we would have to follow them a far piece.

They ate well. They had brought grub with them and there was plenty of it. At least a couple of them were drinking, for we found a bottle near the edge of camp . . . it looked like whoever was drinking didn't want the others to know, for the bottle had been covered over with leaves.

"Fresh bottle," I said to Cap and handed it to him. He sniffed it thoughtfully. "Smells like good whiskey, not none of this here Indian whiskey."

"They don't want for anything. This outfit ıs traveling mighty plush."

Cap studied me carefully. "You ain't in no hurry."

"They finished their job, they'll want their pay. I want the man who pays them."

"You figured out who it'll be?"

"No . . . all I want is for these men to take me there. Twice before they tried to kill Juan and now they got him. I'm thinking they won't stop there and the only way to stop it is to get the man who pays out the money."

As I was talking a picture suddenly came to mind. It was Fetterson passing out gold to that renegade Paisano. It was a thing to be remembered.

"Bearing west," Cap said suddenly, "I think they've taken a notion."

"Tres Ritos?"

"My guess." Cap considered it. "That drinkin' man now. Supposin' he's run out of whiskey? The way I figure, he's a man who likes his bottle and whoever is bossin' the bunch has kept him off it as much as possible.

"Drinkin' man now, he gets mighty canny about hidin' his stuff. He figures he got folks fooled . . . trouble is, it becomes mighty obvious to everybody but the one drinkin'. They may believe that because the job's finished they can have a drink, and Tres Ritos is the closest place."

"I'd guess it's about an easy two-hour ride from here," I looked ahead, searching out the way the riders had gone. "They've taken themselves a notion, all right. Tres Ritos, it is."

Nevertheless, we kept a close watch on the trail. Neither of us had a good feeling about it. A man living in wild country develops a sense of the rightness of things . . . and he becomes like an animal in sensing when all is not well.

So far it had been easy, but I was riding rifle in hand now and ready for trouble. Believe me, I wanted that Henry where I could use it. We had seven tough men ahead of us, men who had killed and who did not wish to be caught. I believe we had them fooled, for they would expect to be followed by a posse, but only a fool depends on a feeling like that.

Against such men you never ride easy in the saddle, you make your plans, you figure things out, and then you are careful. I never knew a really brave man yet who was reckless, nor did I ever know a red fighting man who was reckless . . . maybe because the reckless ones were all dead.

Cap drew up. "I think I'll have a smoke," he said. Cap got down from his saddle, keeping his rifle in his hand.

He drew his horse back under the trees out of sight and I did likewise. Only one fault with Kelly. That big red horse stood out like a forest fire in this green country.

We sat there studying the country around but doing no talking until

Cap smoked his pipe out. Meanwhile both of us had seen a long bench far above the trail that led in the direction of Tres Ritos.

"We might ride along there," I suggested, "I'm spooky about that trail ahead."

"If they turn off we'll lose 'em."

"We can come back and pick up the trail."

We started off at an easy lope, going up through the trees, cutting back around some rocks. We'd gone about a mile when Cap pointed with his rifle.

Down the hill, not far off the trail, we could see some horses tied in the trees. One of them was a dark roan that had a familiar look. Reminded me of a horse I'd seen Paisano riding. And Paisano had taken money from Fetterson. This trail might take us somewhere at that.

We dusted the trail into Tres Ritos shy of sundown. We had taken our own time scouting around and getting the country in our minds.

We headed for the livery stable. The sleepy hostler was sitting on the ground with his back to the wall. He had a red headband and looked like a Navajo. He took our horses and we watched him stall them and put corn in the box. Cap walked down between the rows of stalls and said, "Nobody . . . we beat 'em to town."

The barkeep in the saloon was an unwashed halfbreed with a scar over his left eye like somebody had clouted him with an axe.

We asked for coffee and he turned and yelled something at a back door. The girl his yell brought out was Tina Fernandez. She knew me all right. All those Santa Fe women knew me.

Only she didn't make out like she knew me. She was neat as a new pin, and she brought a pot of coffee and two cups and she poured the coffee and whispered something that sounded like *cuidado*—a word meaning we should be careful.

We drank our coffee and ate some chili and beans with tortillas and I watched the kitchen door and Cap watched the street.

The grub was good, the coffee better, so we had another cup. "Behind the corral," she whispered, "after dark."

Cap chewed his gray mustache and looked at me out of those old, wise-hard eyes. "You mixin' pleasure with business?"

"This is business."

We finished our coffee and we got up and I paid the bartender while Cap studied the street outside. The bartender looked at my face very carefully and then he said, "Do I know you?"

"If you do," I said, "you're going to develop a mighty bad memory."

The street was empty. Not even a stray dog appeared. Had we guessed wrong? Had they gone around Tres Ritos? Or were they here now, waiting for us?

Standing there in the quiet of early evening I had a dry mouth and could feel my heart beating big inside of me. Time to time I'd seen a few men shot and had no idea to go out that way if I could avoid it.

We heard them come into town about an hour later. Chances are they grew tired of waiting for us, if that was what they had been doing. They came down the street strung out like Indians on the trail, and from where we lay in the loft over the livery stable we could not see them but we could hear their horses.

They rode directly to the saloon and got down there, talking very little. As we had ridden into Tres Ritos by a back trail they would have seen no tracks, so unless they were told by the bartender they were not likely to realize we were around.

Lying there on the hay, listening out of the back of my mind for any noise that would warn us they were coming our way, I was not thinking of them, but of Orrin, Laura, Tom Sunday, Dru, and myself. And there was a lot to think about.

Jonathan Pritts would not be talking to Tom Sunday unless there was a shady side to his talk, for Jonathan was a man who did nothing by accident. I knew Tom had no use for the man, but as far back as the night Jonathan had sent for us in Santa Fe there had been a streak of compromise in Tom. He had hesitated that night, recognizing, I think, that Jonathan was a man who was going to be a power.

What was Jonathan Pritts up to? The thought stayed with me and I worried it like a dog at a bone, trying to figure it out. Of one thing I was sure: it promised no good for us.

Cap sat up finally and took out his pipe. "You're restless, boy."

"I don't like this."

"You got it to do. A man wants peace in a country he has to go straight to the heart of things." He smoked in silence for a few minutes. "Time to time I've come across a few men like Pritts . . . once set on a trail they can't see anything but that and the more they're balked the stiffer they get." He paused a moment. "As he gets older he gets meaner . . . he wants what he's after and he knows time is short."

The loft smelled of the fresh hay and of the horses below in their stalls. The sound of their eating was a comfortable sound, a good sleeping sound, but I could not sleep, tired as I was.

If I was to do anything with my life it had to be now and when this trail had been followed to the end I was going to quit my job, marry Dru, and settle down to build something.

We'd never rightly had a real home and for my youngsters I wanted one. I wanted a place they could grow up with, where they could put down roots. I wanted a place they'd be proud to come back to and which they could always call home . . . no matter how far they went or what happened.

Getting up I brushed off the hay, hitched my gun belt into position, and started for the ladder.

"You be careful."

"I'm a careful man by nature."

At the back of the corral I squatted on my heels against a corral post and waited.

Time dragged and then I heard a soft rustle of feet in the grass and saw a shadow near me and smelled a faint touch of woman-smell.

"You all right?"

It was scarcely a whisper but she came to me and I stood up keeping myself in line with that corral post at the corner.

"They are gone," Tina said.

"*What?*"

"They are gone," she repeated. "I was 'fraid for you."

She explained there had been horses for them hidden in the woods back of the saloon, and while they were inside drinking, their saddles had been switched and they had come out one by one and gone off into the woods.

"Fooled us . . . hornswoggled us."

"The other one is there. He is upstairs but I think he will go in the morning."

"Who?"

"The man who gave them money. The blond man."

Fetterson? It could be.

"You saw the money paid?"

"Yes, *señor*. With my two eyes I saw it. They were paid much in gold . . . the balance, he said."

"Tina, they killed Juan Torres . . . did you know him?"

"*Si* . . . he was a good man."

"In court, Tina. Would you testify against them? Would you tell you saw money paid? It would be dangerous for you."

"I will testify. I am not afraid." She stood very still in the darkness. "I know, *señor*, you are in love with the *Señorita* Alvarado, but could you help me, *señor*? Could you help me to go away from here? This man, the one you talked to, he is my . . . how do you call it? He married my mother."

"Stepfather."

"*Si* . . . and my mother is dead and he keeps me here and I work, *señor*.

Some day I will be old. I wish now to go to Santa Fe again but he will not let me."

"You shall go. I promise it."

The men had gone and we had not seen them but she told me one had been Paisano. Only one other she knew. A stocky, very tough man named Jim Dwyer . . . he had been among those at Pawnee Rock. But Fetterson was here and he was the one I wanted most.

We slept a little, and shy of daybreak we rolled out and brushed off the hay. I felt sticky and dirty and wanted a bath and a shave the worst way but I checked my gun and we walked down to the hotel. There was a light in the kitchen and we shoved open the back door.

The bartender was there in his undershirt and pants and sock feet. There was the tumbled, dirty bedding where he had slept, some scattered boots, dirty socks, and some coats hung on the wall, on one nail a gun belt hung. I turned the cylinder and shucked out the shells while the bartender watched grimly.

"What's all this about?"

Turning him around we walked through the dark hall with a lantern in Cap's hand to throw a vague light ahead.

"Which room is he in?"

The bartender just looked at me, and Cap, winking at me, said, "Shall I do it here? Or should we take him out back where they won't find the body so soon?"

The bartender's feet shifted. "No, look!" he protested. "I ain't done nothing."

"He'd be in the way," I said thoughtfully, "and he's no account to us. We might as well take him out back."

Cap looked mean enough to do it, and folks always figured after a look at me that killing would be easier for me than smiling.

"Wait a minute . . . he ain't nothin' to me. He's in Room Six, up the stairs."

Looking at him, I said, "Cap, you keep him here." And then looking at the bartender I said, "You know something? That had better be the right room."

Up the stairs I went, tiptoeing each step and at the top, shielding the lantern with my coat, I walked down the hall and opened the door to Room Six.

His eyes opened when I came through the door but the light was in his eyes when I suddenly unveiled the lantern and his gun was on the table alongside the bed. He started to reach for it and I said, "Go ahead, Fetterson, you pick it up and I can kill you."

His hand hung suspended above the gun and slowly he withdrew it.

He sat up in bed then, a big, rawboned man with a shock of rumpled blond hair and his hard-boned, wedgelike face. There was nothing soft about his eyes.

"Sackett? I might have expected it would be you." Careful to make no mistakes he reached for the makings and began to build a smoke. "What do you want?"

"It's a murder charge, Fett. If you have a good lawyer you might beat it, but you make a wrong move and nothing will beat what I give you."

He struck a match and lit up. "All right . . . I'm no Reed Carney and if I had a chance I'd try shooting it out, but if that gun stuck in the holster I'd be a dead man."

"You'd never get a hand on it, Fett."

"You takin' me in?"

"Uh-huh. Get into your clothes."

He took his time dressing and I didn't hurry him. I figured if I gave him time he would decide it was best to ride along and go to jail, for with Pritts to back him there was small chance he would ever come to trial. My case was mighty light on evidence, largely on what Tina could tell us and what I had seen myself, which was little enough.

When he was dressed he walked ahead of me down the hall to where Cap was waiting with a gun on the bartender. We gathered up Fetterson's horse and started back to town. I wasn't through with that crowd I'd trailed, but they would have to wait.

Our return trip took us mighty little time because I was edgy about being on the trail, knowing that the bartender might get word to Fetterson's crowd. By noon the next day we had him behind bars in Mora and the town was boiling.

Fetterson stood with his hands on the bars. "I won't be here long," he said, "I'd nothing to do with this."

"You paid them off. You paid Paisano an advance earlier."

There was a tic in his eyelid, that little jump of the lid that I'd noticed long ago in Abilene when he had realized they were boxed and could do nothing without being killed.

"You take it easy," I said, "because by the time this case comes to court I'll have enough to hang you."

He laughed, and it was a hard, contemptuous laugh, too. "You'll never see the day!" he said. "This is a put-up job."

When I walked outside in the sunlight, Jonathan Pritts was getting down from his buckboard.

One thing I could say for Jonathan . . . he moved fast.

# Chapter 17

It had been a long time since I'd stood face to face with Jonathan Pritts. He walked through the open door and confronted me in the small office, his pale blue eyes hard with anger. "You have Mr. Fetterson in prison. I want him released."

"Sorry."

"On what charge are you holding him?"

"He is involved in the murder of Juan Torres."

He glared at me. "You have arrested this man because of your hatred for me. He is completely innocent and you can have no evidence to warrant holding him. If you do not release him I will have you removed from office."

He had no idea how empty that threat was. He was a man who liked power and could not have understood how little I wanted the job I had, or how eager I was to be rid of it.

"He will be held for trial."

Jonathan Pritts measured me carefully. "I see you are not disposed to be reasonable." His tone was quieter.

"There has been a crime committed, Mr. Pritts. You cannot expect me to release a prisoner because the first citizen who walks into my office asks me to. The time has come to end crimes of violence, and especially," I added this carefully, "murder that has been paid for."

This would hit him where he lived, I thought, and maybe it did, only there was no trace of feeling on his face. "Now what do you mean by that?"

"We have evidence that Fetterson paid money to the murderers of Juan Torres."

Sure, I was bluffing. We had nothing that would stand up in court, not much, actually, on which to hold him. Only that I had seen him paying money to Paisano, and he had been at Tres Ritos when the killers arrived, and that Tina would testify to the fact that he had paid money there.

"That is impossible."

Picking up a sheaf of papers, I began sorting them. He was a man who demanded attention and my action made him furious.

"Mr. Pritts," I said, "I believe you are involved in this crime. If the evidence will substantiate my belief you will hang also, right along with Fetterson and the others."

Why, he fooled me. I expected him to burst out with some kind of attack on me, but he did nothing of the kind.

"Have you talked to your brother about this?"

"He knows I have my duty to do, and he would not interfere. Nor would I interfere in his business."

"How much is the bail for Mr. Fetterson?"

"You know I couldn't make any ruling. The judge does that. But there's no bail for murder."

He did not threaten me or make any reply at all, he just turned and went outside. If he had guessed how little I had in the way of evidence he would have just sat still and waited. But I have a feeling about this sort of thing . . . if you push such men they are apt to move too fast, move without planning, and so they'll make mistakes.

Bill Sexton came in, and Ollie was with him. They looked worried.

"How much of a case have you got against Fetterson?" Sexton asked me.

"Time comes, I'll have a case."

Sexton rubbed his jaw and then took out a cigar. He studied it while I watched him, knowing what was coming and amused by all the preliminaries, but kind of irritated by them, too.

"This Fetterson," Sexton said, "is mighty close to Jonathan Pritts. It would be a bad idea to try to stick him with these killings. He's got proof he wasn't anywhere around when they took place."

"There's something to that, Tye," Ollie said. "It was Jonathan who helped put Orrin in office."

"You know something?" I had my feet on the desk and I took them down and sat up in that swivel chair. "He did nothing of the kind. He jumped on the band wagon when he saw Orrin was a cinch to win. Fetterson stays in jail or I resign."

"That's final?" Ollie asked.

"You know it is."

He looked relieved, I thought. Ollie Shaddock was a good man, mostly, and once an issue was faced he would stand pat and I was doing what we both believed to be right.

"All right," Sexton said, "if you think you've got a case, we'll go along."

It was nigh to dark when Cap came back to the office. There was no light in the office and sitting back in my chair I'd been doing some thinking.

Cap squatted against the wall and lit his pipe. "There's a man in town," he said, "name of Wilson. He's a man who likes his bottle. He's showing quite a bit of money, and a few days ago he was broke."

"Pretty sky," I said, "the man who named the Sangre de Cristos must have seen them like this. That red in the sky and on the peaks . . . it looks like blood."

"He's getting drunk," Cap said.

Letting my chair down to an even keel I got up and opened the door that shut off the cells from the office. Walking over to the bars and stopping there, I watched Fetterson lying on his cot. I could not see his face, only the dark bulk of him and his boots. Yes, and the glow of his cigarette.

"When do you want to eat?"

He swung his boots to the floor. "Any time. Suit yourself."

"All right." I turned to go and then let him have it easy. "You know a man named Wilson?"

He took the cigarette from his mouth. "Can't place him. Should I?"

"You should . . . he drinks too much. Really likes that bottle. Some folks should never be trusted with money."

When I'd closed the door behind me Cap lit the lamp. "A man who's got something to hide," Cap said, "has something to worry about."

Fetterson would not, could not know what Wilson might say, and a man's imagination can work overtime. What was it the Good Book said? "The guilty flee when no man pursueth."

The hardest thing was to wait. In that cell Fetterson was thinking things over and he was going to get mighty restless. And Jonathan Pritts had made no request to see him. Was Jonathan shaping up to cut the strings on Fetterson and leave him to shift for himself? If I could think of that, it was likely Fetterson could too.

Cap stayed at the jail and I walked down to the eating house for a meal. Tom Sunday came in. He was a big man and he filled the door with his shoulders and height. He was unshaved and he looked like he'd been on the bottle. Once inside he blinked at the brightness of the room a moment or two before he saw me and then he crossed to my table. Maybe he weaved a mite in walking . . . I wouldn't have sworn to it.

"So you got Fetterson?" He grinned at me, his eyes faintly taunting. "Now that you've got him, what will you do with him?"

"Convict him of complicity," I replied. "We know he paid the money."

"That's hitting close to home," Sunday's voice held a suggestion of a sneer. "What'll your brother say to that?"

"It doesn't matter what he says," I told him, "but it happens it has been said. I cut wood and let the chips fall where they may."

"That would be like him," he said, "the sanctimonious son-of-a-bitch."

"Tom," I said quietly, "that term could apply to both of us. We're brothers, you know."

He looked at me, and for a moment there I thought he was going to let it stand, and inside me I was praying he would not. I wanted no fight with Tom Sunday.

"Sorry," he said, "I forgot myself. Hell," he said then, "we don't want trouble. We've been through too much together."

"That's the way I feel," I said, "and Tom, you can take my say-so or not, but Orrin likes you, too."

"Likes me?" he sneered openly now. "He likes me, all right, likes me out of the way. Why, when I met him he could scarcely read or write . . . I taught him. He knew I figured to run for office and he moved right in ahead of me, and you helping him."

"There was room for both of you. There still is."

"The hell there is. Anything I tried to do he would block me. Next time he runs for office he won't have the backing of Jonathan Pritts. I can tell you that."

"It doesn't really matter."

Tom laughed sardonically. "Look, kid, I'll tip you to something right now. Without Pritts backing him Orrin wouldn't have been elected . . . and Pritts is fed up."

"You seem to know a lot about Pritts' plans."

He chuckled. "I know he's fed up, and so is Laura. They're both through with Orrin, you wait and see."

"Tom, the four of us were mighty close back there awhile. Take it from me, Tom, Orrin has never disliked you. Sure, the two of you wanted some of the same things but he would have helped you as you did him."

He ate in silence for a moment or two, and then he said, "I have nothing against you, Tye, nothing at all."

After that we didn't say anything for a while. I think both of us were sort of reaching out to the other, for there had been much between us, we had shared violence and struggle and it is a deep tie. Yet when he got up to leave I think we both felt a sadness, for there was something missing.

He went outside and stood in the street a minute and I felt mighty bad. He was a good man, but nobody can buck liquor and a grudge and hope to come out of it all right. And Jonathan Pritts was talking to him.

I arrested Wilson that night. I didn't take him to jail where Fetterson could talk to him. I took him to that house at the edge of town where Cap, Orrin, and me had camped when we first came up to Mora.

I stashed him there with Cap to mount guard and keep the bottle away. Joe came in to guard Fetterson and I mounted up and took to the woods, and I wasn't riding on any wild-goose chase . . . Miguel had told me that a couple of men were camped on the edge of town, and one of them was Paisano.

From the ridge back of their camp I studied the layout through a field glass. It was a mighty cozy little place among boulders and pines that a man might have passed by fifty times without seeing it had it not been for Miguel being told of it by one of the Mexicans.

The other man must be Jim Dwyer—a short, thickset man who squatted on his heels most of the time and never was without his rifle.

There was no hurry. There was an idea in my skull to the effect these men were camping here for the purpose of breaking Fetterson out of jail. I wanted those men the worst way but I wanted them alive, and that would be hard to handle as both men were tough, game men who wouldn't back up from a shooting fight.

There was a spring about fifty yards away, out of sight of the camp. From the layout I'd an idea this place had been used by them before. There was a crude brush shelter built to use a couple of big boulders that formed its walls. All the rest of the day I lay there watching them. From time to time one of them would get up and stroll out to the thin trail that led down toward Mora.

They had plenty of grub and a couple of bottles but neither of them did much drinking.

By the time dark settled down I knew every rock, every tree, and every bit of cover in that area. Also I had spotted the easiest places to move quietly in the dark, studying the ground for sticks, finding openings in the brush.

Those men down there were mighty touchy folks with whom a man only made one mistake.

Come nightfall I moved my horse to fresh grass after watering him at the creek. Then I took a mite of grub and a canteen and worked my way down to within about a hundred feet of their camp.

They had a small fire going, and coffee on. They were broiling some beef, too, and it smelled almighty good. There I was, lying on my belly smelling that good grub and chewing on a dry sandwich that had been packed early in the day. From where I lay I could hear them but couldn't make out the words.

My idea was that with Fetterson in jail it was just a chance Jonathan Pritts might come out himself.

He was a cagey man and smart enough to keep at least one man between himself and any gun trouble. But Pritts wanted Fetterson out of jail.

It seemed to me that in the time I'd known Jonathan Pritts he had put faith in nobody. Such a man was unlikely to have confidence in Fetterson's willingness to remain silent when by talking he might save his own skin. Right now I thought Pritts would be a worried man, and with reason enough.

Fetterson had plenty to think about too. He knew that we had Wilson, and Wilson was a drinker who would do almost anything for his bottle. If Wilson talked, Fetterson was in trouble. His one chance to get out of it easier was to talk himself. Personally, I did not believe Fetterson would talk—there was a loyalty in the man, and a kind of iron in him, that would not allow him to break or be broken.

I was counting on the fact that Pritts believed in nobody, was eternally suspicious and would expect betrayal.

What I did not expect was the alternative on which Jonathan Pritts had decided. I should have guessed, but did not. Jonathan was a hard man, a cold man, a resolute man.

Now it can be mighty miserable lying up in the brush, never really sleeping, and keeping an eye on a camp like that. Down there, they'd sleep awhile and then rouse up and throw some sticks on the fire, and go back to sleep again. And that's how the night run away.

It got to be the hour of dawn with the sun some time away but crimson streaking the sky, and those New Mexico sunrises . . . well, there's nothing like the way they build a glory in the sky.

Paisano stood up suddenly. He was listening. He was lower in the canyon and might hear more than I.

Would it be Jonathan Pritts himself? If it was, I would move in, taking the three of them in a bundle. Now that might offer a man a problem, and I wanted them all alive, which would not be a simple thing. Yet I had it to do.

What made me turn my head, I don't know.

There was a man standing in the brush about fifty feet away, standing death-still, his outline vague in the shadowy brush. How long that man had been there I had no idea, but there he was, standing silent and watching.

It gave me a spooky feeling to realize that man had been so close all the while and I'd known nothing about it. Not one time in a thousand could that happen to me. Trouble was, I'd had my eyes on that camp, waiting, watching to miss nothing.

Suddenly, that dark figure in the brush moved ever so slightly, edging forward. He was higher than I, and could see down the canyon, although he was not concealed nearly so well as I was. My rifle was ready, but what I wanted was the bunch of them, and all alive so they could testify. And I'd had my fill of killing and had never wished to use my gun against anyone.

It was growing lighter, and the man in the brush was out further in the open, looking down as if about to move down there into the camp. And then he turned his head and some of the light fell across his face and I saw who it was.

It was Orrin.

# Chapter 18

Orrin. . . .

It was so unexpected that I just lay there staring and then I began to bring my thoughts together and when I considered it I couldn't believe it. Sure, Orrin was married to Pritts' daughter, but Orrin had always seemed the sort of man who couldn't be influenced against his principles. We'd been closer even than most brothers.

So where did that leave me? Our lives had been built tightly around our blood ties for Lord knows how many years. Only I knew that even if it was Orrin, I was going to arrest him. Brother or not, blood tie or not, it was my job and I would do it.

And then I had another thought. Sure, I could see then I was a fool. There had to be another reason. My faith in Orrin went far beyond any suspicion his presence here seemed to mean.

So I got up.

His attention was on that camp as mine had been, and I had taken three steps before he saw me.

He turned his head and we looked into each other's eyes, and then I walked on toward him.

Before I could speak he lifted a hand. "Wait!" he whispered, and in the stillness that followed I heard what those men down below must have heard some time before . . . the sound of a buckboard coming.

We stood there with the sky blushing rose and red and the gold cresting the far-off ridges and the shadows still lying black in the hollows.

We stood together there, as we had stood together before, against the Higginses, against the dark demons of drought and stones that plagued our hillside farm in Tennessee, against the Utes, and against Reed Carney. We stood together, and in that moment I suddenly knew why he was here, and knew before the buckboard came into sight just who I would see.

The buckboard came into the trail below and drew up. And the driver was Laura.

Paisano and Dwyer went out to meet her and we watched money pass between them and watched them unload supplies from the back of the buckboard.

Somehow I'd never figured on a woman, least of all, Laura. In the west in those years we respected our women, and it was not in me to arrest one although I surely had no doubts that a woman could be mighty evil and wrong.

Least of all could I arrest Laura. It was a duty I had, but it was her father I wanted and the truth was plain to see. A man who would send his daughter on such a job . . . he was lower than I figured.

Of course, there were mighty few would believe it or even suspect such a frail, blond, and ladylike girl of meeting and delivering money to murderers.

Orrin shifted his feet slightly and sighed. I never saw him look the way he did, his face looking sick and empty like somebody had hit him in the midsection with a stiff punch.

"I had to see it," he said to me, "I had to see it myself to believe it. Last night I suspected something like this, but I had to be here to see."

"You knew where the camp was?"

"Jonathan gave her most careful directions last night."

"I should arrest her," I said.

"As you think best."

"It isn't her I want," I said, "and she would be no good to me. She'd never talk."

Orrin was quiet and then he said, "I think I'll move out to the ranch, Tyrel. I'll move out today."

"Ma will like that. She's getting feeble, Orrin."

We went back into the brush a mite and Orrin rolled a smoke and lit up. "Tyrel," he said after a minute, "what's he paying them for? Was it for Torres?"

"Not for Torres," I said, "Fetterson already paid them."

"For you?"

"Maybe . . . I doubt it."

Suddenly I wanted to get away from there. Those two I could find them when I wanted them for they were known men, and the man I had wanted had been cagey enough not to appear.

"Orrin," I said, "I've got to head Laura off. I'm not going to arrest her, I just want her to know she has been seen and I know what's going on. I want them to know and to worry about it."

"Is that why you're holding Wilson apart?"

"Yes."

We went back to our horses and then we cut along the hill through the bright beauty of the morning to join the trail a mile or so beyond where Laura would be.

When she came up, for a minute I thought she would try to drive right over us, but she drew up.

She was pale, but the planes of her face had drawn down in hard lines and I never saw such hatred in a woman's eyes.

"Now you're spying on me!" There was nothing soft and delicate about her voice then, it was strident, angry.

"Not on you," I said, "on Paisano and Dwyer."

She flinched as if I'd struck her, started to speak, then pressed her lips together.

"They were in the group that killed Juan Torres," I said, "along with Wilson."

"If you believe that, why don't you arrest them? Are you afraid?"

"Just waiting . . . sometimes if a man lets a small fish be his bait he can catch a bigger fish. Like you, bringing supplies and money to them. That makes you an accessory. You can be tried for aiding and abetting."

For the first time she was really scared. She was a girl who made much of position, a mighty snooty sort, if you ask me, and being arrested would just about kill her.

"You wouldn't dare!"

She said it, but she didn't believe it. She believed I would, and it scared the devil out of her.

"Your father has been buying murder too long, and there is no place for such men. Now you know."

Her face was pinched and white and there was nothing pretty about her then. "Let me pass!" she demanded bitterly.

We drew aside, and she looked at Orrin. "You were nothing when we met, and you'll be nothing again."

Orrin removed his hat. "Under the circumstances," he said gently, "you will pardon me if I remove my belongings?"

She slashed the horses with the whip and went off. Orrin's face was white as we cut over across the hills. "I'd like to be out of the house," he said, "before she gets back."

The town was quiet when I rode in. Fetterson came to the bars of his cell and stared at me when I entered. He knew I'd been away and it worried him he didn't know what I was doing.

"Paisano and Dwyer are just outside the town," I said, "and no two men are going to manage a jail delivery, but Pritts was paying them . . . what for?"

His eyes searched my face and suddenly he turned and looked at the barred window. Beyond the window, three hundred yards away, was the wooded hillside . . . and to the right, not over sixty yards off, the roof of the store.

He turned back swiftly. "Tye," he said, "you've got to get me out of here."

Fetterson was no fool and he knew that there was no trust in Jonathan Pritts. Fetterson would die before he would talk, but Pritts did not for a minute believe that. Consequently he intended that Fetterson should die before he could talk.

"Fett," I said, "it's up to you not to get in front of that window. Or," I paused and let the word hang for a minute, "you can talk and tell me the whole story."

He turned sharply away and walked back to his cot and lay down. I knew that window would worry him, Wilson would worry him, and he would worry about how much I knew.

"You might as well tell me and save your bacon," I said, "Wilson hasn't had a drink in three days and he'll tell all he knows any day now. After that we won't care about you."

Right then I went to Ceran St. Vrain. He was the most influential man in Mora, and I had Vicente Romero come in, and we had a talk. Ollie Shaddock was there, Bill Sexton, and Orrin.

"I want ten deputies," I said, "I want Ceran to pick five of them and Romero to pick the other five. I want solid, reliable men. I don't care whether they are good men with guns or not, I want substantial citizens."

They picked them and we talked the whole thing over. I laid all my cards on the table. Told them just what the situation was and I didn't beat around the bush.

Wilson was talking, all right. He had a hand in the killing of Torres and the others and he named the other men involved, and I told them that Paisano and Dwyer were out in the hills and that I was going after them myself. I made good on my word to Tina Fernandez and got a promise from Ceran himself to go after her with a couple of his riders to back him up. He was a man respected and liked and feared.

On Jonathan Pritts I didn't pull my punches. Telling them of our meeting with him in Abilene, of our talk with him in Santa Fe, of the men waiting at Pawnee Rock, and of what he had done since. St. Vrain was an old friend to the Alvarado family . . . he knew much of what I said.

"What is it, señor? What do you wish to do?"

"I believe Fetterson is ready to talk," I said. "We will have Wilson, we will have Tina, and Cap's evidence as well as my own, for we trailed the killers to Tres Ritos."

"What about Mrs. Sackett?" St. Vrain asked.

Right there I hesitated. "She's a woman and I'd like to keep her out of it."

They all agreed to this and when the meeting broke up, I was to have a final talk with Fetterson.

So this was to be an end to it. There was no anger in me any more. Juan Torres was gone and another death could not bring him back. Jonathan Pritts would suffer enough to see all his schemes come to nothing, and they would, now. I knew that Vicente Romero was the most respected man in the Spanish-speaking group, and St. Vrain among the Anglos. Once they had said what they had to say, Jonathan Pritts would no longer have influence locally nor in Santa Fe.

Orrin and me, we walked back to the jail together and it was good to walk beside him, brothers in feeling as well as in blood.

"It's tough," I said to him, "I knew how you felt about Laura, but Orrin, you were in love with what you thought she was. A man often creates an image of a girl in his mind but when it comes right down to it that's the only place the girl exists."

"Maybe," Orrin was gloomy, "I was never meant to be married."

We stopped in front of the sheriff's office and Cap came out to join us.

"Tom's in town," he said, "and he's drunk and spoilin' for a fight."

"We'll go talk to him," Orrin said.

Cap caught Orrin's arm. "Not you, Orrin. You'd set him off. If you see him now there'll be a shootin' sure."

"A shooting?" Orrin smiled disbelievingly. "Cap, you're clean off the trail. Why, Tom's one of my best friends!"

"Look," Cap replied shortly, "you're no tenderfoot. How much common sense or reason is there behind two-thirds of the killings out here? You bump into a man and spill his drink, you say the wrong thing . . . it doesn't have to make sense."

"There's no danger from Tom," Orrin insisted quietly. "I'd stake my life on it."

"That's just what you're doing," Cap replied. "The man's not the Tom Sunday that drove cows with us. He's turned into a mighty mean man, and he's riding herd on a grudge against you. He's been living alone down there and he's been hitting the bottle."

"Cap's right," I told him. "Tom's carrying a chip on his shoulder."

"All right. I want no trouble with him or anyone."

"You got an election comin' up," Cap added. "You get in a gun battle an' a lot of folks will turn their backs on you."

Reluctantly, Orrin mounted up and rode out to the ranch, and for the first time in my life, I was glad to see him go. Things had been building toward trouble for months now, and Tom Sunday was only one small part of it, but the last thing I wanted was a gun battle between Tom and Orrin.

At all costs that fight must be prevented both for their sakes and for Orrin's future.

Ollie came by the office after Orrin had left. "Pritts is down to Santa Fe," he said, "and he's getting himself nowhere. Vicente Romero has been down there, and so has St. Vrain and it looks like they put the kibosh on him."

Tina was in town and staying with Dru and we had our deposition from Wilson. I expect he was ready to get shut of the whole shebang, for at heart Wilson was not a bad man, only he was where bad company and bad liquor had taken him.

He talked about things clear back to Pawnee Rock, and we took that deposition in front of seven witnesses, three of them Mexican, and four Anglos. When the trial came up I didn't want it said that we'd beaten it out of him, but once he started talking he left nothing untold.

On Wednesday night I went to see Fetterson for I'd been staying away and giving him time to think. He looked gaunt and scared. He was a man with plenty of sand but nobody likes to be set up as Number-One target in a shooting gallery.

"Fett," I said, "I can't promise you anything but a chance in court, but the more you cooperate the better. If you want out of this cell you'd better talk."

"You're a hard man, Tyrel," he said gloomily. "You stay with a thing."

"Fett," I said, "men like you and me have had our day. Folks want to settle affairs in court now, and not with guns. Women and children coming west want to walk a street without stray bullets flying around. A man has to make peace with the times."

"If I talk I'll hang myself."

"Maybe not . . . folks are more anxious to have an end to all this trouble than to punish anybody."

He still hesitated so I left him there and went out into the cool night. Orrin was out at the ranch and better off there, and Cap Rountree was some place up the street.

Bill Shea came out of the jail house. "Take a walk if you're of a mind to, Tyrel," he suggested, "there's three of us here."

Saddling the Montana horse I rode over to see Dru. It was a desert mountain night with the sky so clear and the stars so close it looked like you could knock them down with a stick. Dru had sold the big house that lay closer to Santa Fe, and was spending most of her time in this smaller but comfortable house near Mora.

She came to the door to meet me and we walked back inside and I told her about the meeting with Romero and St. Vrain, and the situation with Fetterson.

"Move him, Tye, you must move him out of there before he is killed. It is not right to keep him there."

"I want him to talk."

"Move him," Dru insisted, "you must. Think of how you would feel if he was killed."

She was right, of course, and I'd been thinking of it. "All right," I said, "first thing in the morning."

Sometimes the most important things in a man's life are the ones he talks about least. It was that way with Dru and me. No day passed that I did not think of her much of the time, she was always with me, and even when we were together we didn't talk a lot because so much of the time there was no need for words, it was something that existed between us that we both understood.

The happiest hours of my life were those when I was riding with Dru or sitting across a table from her. And I'll always remember her face by candlelight . . . it seemed I was always seeing it that way, and soft sounds of the rustle of gowns, the tinkle of silver and glass, and Dru's voice, never raised and always exciting.

Within the thick adobe walls of the old Spanish house there was quiet, a shadowed peace that I have associated with such houses all my years. One stepped through the door into another world, and left outside the trouble, confusion, and storm of the day.

"When this is over, Dru," I said, "we'll wait no longer. And it will soon be over."

"We do not need to wait." She turned from the window where we stood and looked up at me. "I am ready now."

"This must be over first, Dru. It is a thing I have to do and when it is finished I shall take off my badge and leave the public offices to Orrin."

Suddenly there was an uneasiness upon me and I said to her, "I must go."

She walked to the door with me. *"Vaya con Dios,"* she said, and she waited there until I was gone.

And that night there was trouble in town but it was not the trouble I expected.

# Chapter 19

It happened as I left my horse in front of the saloon and stepped in for a last look around. It was after ten o'clock and getting late for the town of Mora, and I went into the saloon and stepped into trouble.

Two men faced each other across the room and the rest were flattened against the walls.

Chico Cruz, deadly as a sidewinder, stood poised and negligent, a slight smile on his lips, his black eyes flat and without expression.

And facing him was Tom Sunday.

Big, blond, and powerful, unshaven as always these days, heavier than he used to be, but looking as solid and formidable as a blockhouse.

Neither of them saw me. Their attention was concentrated on each other and death hung in the air like the smell of lightning on a rocky hillside. As I stepped in, they drew.

With my own eyes I saw it. Saw Chico's hand flash. I had never believed a man could draw so fast, his gun came up and then he jerked queerly and his body snapped sidewise and his gun went off into the floor and Tom Sunday was walking.

Tom Sunday was walking in, gun poised. Chico was trying to get his gun up and Tom stopped and spread his legs and grimly, brutally, he fired a shot into Chico's body, and then coolly, another shot.

Chico's gun dropped, hit the floor with a thud. Chico turned and in turning his eyes met mine across the room, and he said very distinctly into the silence that followed the thundering of the guns, "It was not you."

He fell, then, fell all in a piece and his hat rolled free and he lay on the floor and he was dead.

Tom Sunday turned and stared at me and his eyes were blazing with a hot, hard flame. "You want me?" he said, and the words were almost a challenge.

"It was a fair shooting, Tom," I said quietly. "I do not want you."

He pushed by me and went out of the door, and the room broke into wild talk. "Never would have believed it. . . . Fastest thing I ever saw. . . . But *Chico!*" The voice was filled with astonishment. "He killed *Chico Cruz!*"

Until that moment I had always believed that if it came to a difficulty that Orrin could take care of Tom Sunday, but I no longer believed it.

More than any of them I knew the stuff of which Orrin was made. He had a kind of nerve rarely seen, but he was no match for Tom when it came to speed. And there was a fatal weakness against him, for Orrin truly liked Tom Sunday.

And Tom?

Somehow I didn't think there was any feeling left in Tom, not for anyone, unless it was me.

The easy comradeship was gone. Tom was ingrown, bitter, hard as nails.

When Chico's body was moved out I tried to find out what started the trouble, but it was like so many bar-room fights, just sort of happened. Two tough, edgy men and neither about to take any pushing around. Maybe it was a word, maybe a spilled drink, a push, or a brush against each other, and then guns were out and they were shooting.

Tom had ridden out of town.

Cap was sitting in the jail house with Babcock and Shea when I walked in. I could see Fetterson through the open door, so walked back to the cells.

"That's right? What they're saying?"

"Tom Sunday killed Chico Cruz . . . beat him to the draw."

Fetterson shook his head unbelievingly. "I never would have believed it. I thought Chico was the fastest thing around . . . unless it was you."

Fetterson grinned suddenly. "How about you and Tom? You two still friends?"

It made me mad and I turned sharply around and he stepped back from the bars, but he was grinning when he moved back. "Well, I just asked," he said, "some folks never bought that story about you backin' Cruz down."

"Tom is my friend," I told him, "we'll always be friends."

"Maybe," he said, "maybe." He walked back to the bars. "Looks like I ain't the only one has troubles."

Outside in the dark I told Cap about it, every detail. He listened, nodding thoughtfully.

"Tyrel," Cap said, "we've been friends, and trail dust is thicker'n blood, but you watch Tom Sunday. You watch him. That man's gone loco like an old buffalo bull who's left the herd."

Cap took his pipe out of his mouth and knocked out the ashes against the awning post. "Tyrel, mark my words! He's started now an' nuthin's goin' to stop him. Orrin will be next an' then you."

That night I got into the saddle and rode all the way out to the ranch to sleep, pausing only a moment at the gap where the river flowed through, remembering Juan Torres who died there. It was bloody country and time it was quieted down. Inside me I didn't want to admit that Cap was right, but I was afraid, I was very much afraid.

As if the shooting, which had nothing to do with Pritts, Alvarado, or myself, had triggered the whole situation from Santa Fe to Cimarron, the lid suddenly blew off. Maybe it was that Pritts was shrewd enough to see his own position weakening and if anything was to be done it had to be done now.

Jonathan and Laura, they moved back up to Mora and it looked like they had come to stay.

Things were shaping up for a trial of Wilson and Fetterson for the murder of Juan Torres.

We moved Fetterson to a room in an old adobe up the street that had been built for a fort. We moved him by night and the next morning we stuck a dummy up in the window of the jail. We put that dummy up just before daylight and then Cap, Orrin, and me, we took to the hills right where we knew we ought to be.

We heard the shots down the slope from us and we went down riding fast. They were wearing Sharps buffalo guns. They both fired and when we heard those two rifles talk we came down out of the higher trees and had them boxed. The Sharps buffalo was a good rifle, but it was a single shot, and we had both those men covered with Winchesters before they could get to their horses or had time to load.

Paisano and Dwyer. Caught flat-footed and redhanded, and nothing to show for it but a couple of bullets through a dummy.

That was what broke Jonathan Pritts' back. We had four of the seven men now and within a matter of hours after, we tied up two more. That seventh man wasn't going to cause anybody any harm. Seems he got drunk one night and on the way home something scared his horse and he got bucked off and with a foot caught in the stirrup there wasn't much he could do. Somewhere along the line he'd lost his pistol and couldn't kill the horse. He was found tangled in some brush, his foot still in the stirrup, and the only way they knew him was by his boots, which were new, and his saddle and horse. A man dragged like that is no pretty sight, and he had been dead for ten to twelve hours.

Ollie came down to the sheriff's office with Bill Sexton and Vicente Romero. They were getting up a political rally and Orrin was going to speak. Several of the high mucky-mucks from Santa Fe were coming up, but this was to be Orrin's big day.

It was a good time for him to put himself forward and the stage was being set for it. There was to be a real ol' time fandango with the folks coming in from back at the forks of the creeks. Everybody was to be there and all dressed in their Sunday-go-to-meeting clothes.

In preparation for it I made the rounds and gave several of the trouble makers their walking papers. What I mean is, I told them they would enjoy Las Vegas or Socorro or Cimarron a whole sight better and why didn't they start now.

They started.

"Have you heard the talk that's going around?" Shea asked me.

"What talk?"

"It's being said that Tom Sunday is coming into town after Orrin."

"Tom Sunday and Orrin are friends," I said, "I know Tom's changed, but I don't believe he'll go that far."

"Put no faith in that line of thought, Tyrel. Believe me, the man hasn't a friend left. He's surly as a grizzly with a sore tooth, and nobody goes near him any more. The man's changed, and he works with a gun nearly every day. Folks coming by there say they can hear it almost any hour."

"Tom never thought much of Orrin as a fighter. Tom never knew him like I have."

"That isn't all." Shea put his cigar down on the edge of the desk. "There's talk about what would happen if you and Tom should meet."

Well, I was mad. I got up and walked across the office and swore. Yes, and I wasn't a swearing man.

Oddly enough, thinking back, I can't remember many gunfighters who were. Most of them I knew were sparing in the use of words as well as whiskey.

But one thing I knew: Orrin must not meet Tom Sunday. Even if Orrin beat him, Orrin would lose. A few years ago it would not have mattered that he had been in a gun battle, now it could wreck his career.

If Orrin would get out of town . . . but he couldn't. He had been selected as the speaker for the big political rally and that would be just the time when Tom Sunday would be in town.

"Thanks," I said to Shea, "thanks for telling me."

Leaving Cap in charge of the office I mounted up and rode out to the ranch. Orrin was there, and we sat down and had dinner with Ma. It was good to have our feet under the same table again, and Ma brightened up and talked like her old self.

Next day was Sunday and Orrin and me decided to take Ma to church.

It was a lazy morning with bright sunshine and Orrin took Ma in the buckboard and we boys rode along behind.

We wore our broadcloth suits and the four of us dressed in black made a sight walking around Ma, who was a mighty little woman among her four tall sons, and Dru was with us, standing there beside Ma and me, and I was a proud man.

It was a meeting I'll not soon forget, that one was, because when Ollie heard the family was going, he came along and stood with us at the hymn singing and the preaching.

Whether or not Orrin had heard any of the stories going round about Tom I felt it necessary to warn him. If I expected him to brush it off, I was wrong. He was dead serious about it when I explained. "But I can't leave," he added, "everybody would know why I went and if they thought I was afraid, I'd lose as many votes as if I actually fought him."

He was right, of course, so we prepared for the meeting with no happy anticipation of it, although this was to be Orrin's big day, and his biggest speech, and the one that would have him fairly launched in politics. Men were coming up from Santa Fe to hear him, all the crowd around the capital who pulled the political strings.

Everybody knew Orrin was to speak and everybody knew Tom would be there. And nothing any of us could do but wait.

Jonathan Pritts knew he had been left out and he knew it was no accident. He also knew that it was to be Orrin's big day and that Laura's cutting loose had not hurt him one bit.

Also Jonathan knew the trial was due to come off soon, and before the attorney got through cross-examining Wilson and some of the others the whole story of his move into the Territory would be revealed. There was small chance it could be stopped, but if something were to happen to Orrin and me, if there was to be a jail delivery. . . .

He wouldn't dare.

Or would he?

# Chapter 20

The sun was warm in the street that morning, warm even at the early hour when I rode in from the ranch. The town lay quiet and a lazy dog sprawled in the dust opened one eye and flapped his tail in a I-won't-bother-you-if-you-don't-bother-me sort of way, as I approached.

Cap Rountree looked me over carefully from those shrewd old eyes as I rode up. "You wearing war paint, boy? If you ain't, you better. I got a bad feeling about today."

Getting down from the saddle I stood beside him and watched the hills against the skyline. People were getting up all over town now, or lying there awake and thinking about the events of the day. There was to be the speaking, a band concert, and most folks would bring picnic lunches.

"I hope he stays away."

Cap stuffed his pipe with tobacco. "He'll be here."

"What happened, Cap? Where did it start?"

He leaned a thin shoulder against the awning post. "You could say it was at the burned wagons when Orrin and him had words about that money. No man likes to be put in the wrong.

"Or you could say it was back there at the camp near Baxter Springs, or maybe it was the day they were born. Sometimes men are born who just can't abide one another from the time they meet . . . don't make no rhyme nor reason, but it's so."

"They are proud men."

"Tom's gone killer, Tyrel, don't you ever forget that. It infects some men like rabies, and they keep on killing until somebody kills them."

We stood there, not talking for awhile, each of us busy with his own thoughts. What would Dru be doing about now? Rising at home, and planning her day, bathing, combing her long dark hair, having breakfast.

Turning away I went inside and started looking over the day's roundup of mail. This morning there was a letter from Tell, my oldest brother. Tell was in Virginia City, Montana, and was planning to come down and see us. Ma would be pleased, mighty pleased. It had been a sorry time since we had seen Tell.

There was a letter from that girl, too. The one we had sent the money we found in that burned wagon . . . she was coming west and wanted to meet us. The letter had been forwarded from Santa Fe where it had been for weeks . . . by this time she must be out here, or almost here.

It gave me an odd feeling to get that letter on this morning, thinking back to the trouble it had caused.

Cap came in from outside and I said, "I'm going to have coffee with Dru. You hold the fort, will you?"

"You do that, boy. You just do that."

Folks were beginning to crowd the streets now, and some were hanging out bunting and flags. Here and there a few rigs stood along the street, all with picnic baskets in the back. There were big, rawboned men in their Sunday-go-to-meeting clothes and women in fresh-washed ginghams and sunbonnets. Little boys ran and played in the streets, and their mothers scolded and called after them while little girls, starched and ribboned, looked on enviously and disdainfully.

It was good to be alive. Everything seemed to move slow today, everything seemed to take its time . . . was this the way a man felt on his last day? Was it to be my last day?

When I knocked on the door Dru answered it herself. Beyond the welcome I could see the worry.

"How's about a poor drifter begging a cup of coffee, ma'am? I was just passin' through and the place had a kindly look."

"Come in, Tye. You don't have to knock."

"Big day in town. Biggest crowd I ever saw. Why, I've seen folks from Santa Fe . . . as far as Raton or Durango."

The maid brought in the coffee and we sat at the breakfast table looking out the low-silled window over the town and the hillside and we sat talking for awhile and at last I got up and she came with me to the door. She put her hand on my sleeve. "Stay here, Tye . . . don't go."

"Got to . . . busy day today."

Folks were crowded along the street and there were wagons drawn up where the speaking was to be—with many people taking their places early so they could be close enough to hear. When I got down to the office Orrin was there in his black frock coat and string tie. He grinned at me, but beyond the grin his eyes were serious. "You get up there and talk," I said, "you're the speaker of this family."

Me, I stayed at the office. Cap was out and around, nosing after news like a smart old coon dog looking up trails in the dust or the berry patches.

There was no sign of Tom Sunday, and around the jail everything was quiet. Nor was Jonathan Pritts anywhere in sight. My guards were rest-

less, most of them men with families who wanted to be with them on a
big day like this.

Ma and the boys came in about noon, Ma riding in the buckboard with
Joe driving. Ollie had held a place for them where Ma could hear the
speaking, and it would be the first time she had ever heard Orrin make a
speech. Folks were mighty impressed with speech-making those days, and
a man who could talk right up and make his words sound like something,
well, he rated mighty high up there. He was a big man.

That day I was wearing black broadcloth pants down over my boots, a
style just then coming in, and I had on a gray shirt with a black string tie
and a black, braided Spanish-style jacket and a black hat. My gun was on,
and I was carrying a spare tucked into my waistband out of sight under
my jacket.

About noon Caribou Brown rode into town with Doubleout Sam. Shea
saw them ride in and reported to me at once and I went down to the saloon where they had bellied up to the bar.

"All right, boys. Finish your drink and ride out."

They turned around on me, the both of them, but they knew me pretty
well by then. "You're a hard man," Brown said. "Can't a man stay around
for the fun?"

"Sorry."

They had their drinks but they didn't like it and when they finished
them I was standing right there. "If you boys start right now you can
make Vegas," I told them. "You'll have trouble if you think you can stay.
I'll throw you both in jail and you'll be there next month at this time."

"On what charge?" Sam didn't like it.

"Loitering, obstructing justice, interfering with an officer, peddling
without a license . . . I'll think of something."

"Oh, damn you!" Brown said. "Come on, Sam . . . let's ride."

They started for the door.

"Boys?"

They turned. "Don't circle around. I've got some deputies who are
mighty concerned about the town today. You're known men and if you
come back they'll be shooting on sight."

They rode out of town and I was glad to see them go. Both were known
trouble makers of the old Settlement crowd and they had been in several
shootings.

The streets began to grow empty as folks drifted toward the speech-making and the band concert, which was going full blast. Going slow along
the walks the streets were so empty the sound of my heels was loud.
When I reached the adobe where Fetterson was held, I stopped by. Shea
was on guard there.

"Hello, Fett," I said.

He got up and came to the bars. "That right? That they shot into my cell? Into a dummy?"

"What did you expect? You can hang him, Fetterson, and he knows that. He's got to do something . . . or run!"

Fetterson rubbed his jaw. The man looked worried. "How does a man get into these things?" he asked suddenly. "Damn it, I played square with him."

"He's wrong, Fett. He cares nothing for you except in so far as you are useful and when your usefulness is ended, so's his interest. You're too good a man to be wasted, Fett . . . you're loyal to a man who does not understand loyalty."

"Maybe . . . maybe."

He listened to the band, which was playing *My Darling Nelly Gray*. "Sounds like a good time," he said wistfully.

"I've got to go," I said, "the speaking starts in a few minutes."

He was still standing by the bars when I went out. Shea got up and walked outside with me. "Are you expecting trouble?"

"At any minute."

"All right," he cradled the shotgun in his arms, "I just don't want to miss all the fun."

From the gathering place beyond the buildings I could hear Ollie introducing somebody. Pausing, I listened. It was the speaker from Santa Fe—the one who preceded Orrin—and I could hear his rolling tones, although he was too far away to distinguish more than a word or two, and when it happened, it happened so suddenly that I was taken by surprise.

They came into the street below the jail and they came suddenly and they were on foot. Obviously they had been hidden during the night in the houses of some of the citizens, and there were eight of them and they had rifles. Every one of them was a familiar face, all were from the old Settlement crowd, and they had me dead to rights.

They were near the jail and there was a man inside. There were probably two men inside. Up the street behind me Shea could do little unless I gave him room, but I had to be where I could do the most damage.

Turning at right angles I walked into the middle of the street and then I faced them. Sixty yards separated us. Looking at those rifles and shotguns I knew I was in trouble and plenty of it, but I knew this was what I had been waiting for.

There were eight of them and they would be confident, but they would also be aware that I was going to get off at least one shot and probably one man would be killed . . . nobody would want to be that man.

"What are you boys getting out of this?" I asked them coolly. "Fifty

dollars apiece? It's a cinch Jonathan isn't going to pay more than that . . .
hope you collected in advance."

"We want the keys!" The man talking was named Stott. "Toss them
over here!"

"You're talking, Stott . . . but are you watching? You boys are going to
get it from the jail."

"The keys!"

Stott I was going to kill. He was the leader. I was going to get him and
as many more as possible.

There was a rustle of movement down the street behind them. There
was movement down there but I didn't dare take my eyes off them. So I
started to walk. I started right down the street toward them, hoping to get
so close they would endanger each other if they started shooting. Beyond
them I could see movement and when I realized who it was I was so startled they might have killed me.

It was Dru.

She wasn't alone. She had six buckskin-clad riders with her and they all
had Winchesters and they looked like they wanted to start shooting.

"All right," I said, "the fun's over. Drop your gun belts."

Stott was angry. "What are you trying—" Behind him seven Winchesters were cocked on signal, and he looked sharply around. And after
that it was settled . . . they were not nearly so anxious for trouble and
when they were disarmed, they were jailed along with the others.

Dru walked her horse up to the front of the jail. "Miguel saw them
coming," she said, "so we rode down to help."

"Help? You did it all."

We talked there in the street and then I walked beside her horse over to
the speaking. When this was over I was going to go after Jonathan Pritts.
I was going to arrest him but oddly enough, I did not want him jailed. He
was an old man, and defeat now would ruin him enough and he was
whipped. When this was over he would be arrested, but if St. Vrain,
Romero, and the others agreed, I'd just send him out of town with his
daughter and a buckboard . . . they deserved each other.

Orrin was introduced. He got up and walked to the front of the plat-
form and he started to speak in that fine Welsh voice of his. He spoke
quietly, with none of that oratory they had been hearing. He just talked to
them as he would to friends in his own home, yet as he continued his
voice grew in power and conviction, and he was speaking as I had never
heard him speak.

Standing there in the shade of a building I listened and was proud.
This was my brother up there . . . this was Orrin. This was the boy I'd

grown up with, left the mountains with, herded cattle, and fought Indians beside.

There was a strange power in him now that was born of thought and dream and that fine Welsh magic in his voice and mind. He was talking to them of what the country needed, of what had to be done, but he was using their own language, the language of the mountains, the desert, the cattle drives. And I was proud of him.

Turning away from the crowd, I walked slowly back to the street and between the buildings and when I emerged on the sunlit street, Tom Sunday was standing there.

I stopped where I stood and could not see his eyes but as flecks of light from the shadow beneath his hat brim.

He was big, broad, and powerful. He was unshaved and dirty, but never in my life had I seen such a figure of raw, physical power in one man.

"Hello, Tom."

"I've come for him, Tyrel. Stay out of the way."

"He's building his future," I said, "you helped him start it, Tom. He's going to be a big man and you helped him."

Maybe he didn't even hear me. He just looked at me straight on like a man staring down a narrow hallway.

"I'm going to kill him," he said, "I should have done it years ago."

We were talking now, like in a conversation, yet something warned me to be careful. What had Cap said? He was a killer and he would go on killing until something or somebody stopped him.

This was the man who had killed the Durango Kid, who had killed Ed Fry and Chico Cruz . . . Chico never even got off a shot.

"Get out of the way, Tye," he said, "I've nothing against you, I—"

He was going to kill me.

I was going to die . . . I was sure of it.

Only he must not come out of it alive. Orrin must have his future. Anyway, I was the mean one . . . I always had been.

Once before I had stepped in to help Orrin and I would now.

There was nobody there on the street but the two of us, just Tom Sunday, the man who had been my best friend, and me. He had stood up for me before this and we had drunk from the same rivers, fought Indians together. . . .

"Tom," I said, "remember that dusty afternoon on that hillside up there on the Purgatoire when we. . . ."

Sweat trickled down my spine and tasted salt on my lips. His shirt was open to his belt and I could see the hair on his big chest and the wide buckle of his belt. His hat was pulled low but there was no expression on his face.

This was Tom Sunday, my friend . . . only now he was a stranger.

"You can get out of the way, Tye," he said, "I'm going to kill him."

He spoke easily, quietly. I knew I had it to do, but this man had helped teach me to read, he had loaned me books, he had ridden the plains with me.

"You can't do it," I said. Right then, he went for his gun.

There was an instant before he drew when I knew he was going to draw. It was an instant only, a flickering instant that triggered my mind.

My hand dropped and I palmed my gun, but his came up and he was looking across it, his eyes like white fire, and I saw the gun blossom with a rose of flame and felt my own gun buck in my hand, and then I stepped forward and left—one quick step—and fired again.

He stood there looking across his gun at me and then he fired, but his bullet made a clean miss. Thumbing back the hammer I said, "Damn it, Tom . . ." and I shot him in the chest.

He still stood there but his gun muzzle was lowering and he was still looking at me.

A strange, puzzled expression came into his eyes and he stepped toward me, dropping his gun. "Tyrel . . . Tye, what . . ." He reached out a hand toward me, but when I stepped quickly to take it, he fell.

He went full face to the dust, falling hard, and when he hit the ground he groaned, then he half-turned and dropping to my knees I grabbed his hand and gripped it hard.

"Tye . . . Tye, damn it, I . . ." He breathed hoarsely, and the front of his shirt was red with blood.

"The books," he whispered, "take the . . . books."

He died like that, gripping my hand, and when I looked up the street was full of people, and Orrin was there, and Dru.

And over the heads of some of the nearest, Jonathan Pritts.

Pushing through the crowd I stopped, facing Jonathan. "You get out of town," I told him, "you get out of the state. If you aren't out of town within the hour, or if you ever come back, for any reason at all, I'll kill you."

He just turned and walked away, his back stiff as a ramrod . . . but it wasn't even thirty minutes until he and Laura drove from town in a buckboard.

"That was my fight, Tye," Orrin said quietly, "it was my fight."

"No, it was mine. From the beginning it was mine. He knew it would be, I think. Maybe we both knew it . . . and Cap. I think Cap Rountree knew it first of all."

*       *       *

We live on the hill back of Mora, and sometimes in Santa Fe, Dru and me . . . we've sixty thousand acres of land in two states and a lot of cattle. Orrin, he's a state senator now, and pointing for greater things.

Sometimes of an evening I think of that, think when the shadows grow long of two boys who rode out of the high hill country of Tennessee to make a home in the western lands.

We found our home, and we graze and work our acres, and since that day in the street of Mora when I killed Tom Sunday I have never drawn a gun on any man.

Nor will I. . . .

# SACKETT

*To Mamu*

# Chapter 1

It wasn't as if he hadn't been warned. He got it straight, with no beating around the mesquite.

"Mister," I said, "if you ain't any slicker with that pistol than you were with that bottom deal, you'd better not have at it."

Trouble was, he wouldn't be content with one mistake, he had to make two; so he had at it, and they buried him out west of town where men were buried who die by the gun.

And me, William Tell Sackett, who came to Uvalde a stranger and alone, I found myself a talked-about man.

We Sacketts had begun carrying rifles as soon as we stood tall enough to keep both ends off the ground. When I was shy of nine I fetched my first cougar . . . caught him getting at our pigs. At thirteen I nicked the scalp of a Higgins who was drawing a bead on Pa . . . we had us a fighting feud going with the Higginses.

Pa used to say a gun was a responsibility, not a toy, and if he ever caught any of us playing fancy with a gun he'd have our hide off with a bullwhip. None of us ever lost any hide.

A gun was to be used for hunting, or when a man had a difficulty, but only a tenderfoot fired a gun unless there was need. At hunting time Pa doled out the ca'tridges and of an evening he would check our game, and for every ca'tridge he'd given us we had to show game or a mighty good reason for missing. Pa wasn't one to waste a bullet. He had trapped the western lands with Kit Carson and Old Bill Williams, and knew the value of ammunition.

General Grant never counted ca'tridges on me, but he was a man who noticed. One time he stopped close by when I was keeping three Rebel guns out of action, picking off gunners like a 'possum picking hazelnuts, and he stood by, a-watching.

"Sackett," he said finally, "how does it happen that a boy from Tennessee is fighting for the Union?"

"Well, sir," I said, "my country is a thing to love, and I set store by being an American. My greatgrandpa was one of Dearborn's riflemen at the second battle of Saratoga, and Grandpa sailed the seas with Decatur and Bainbridge.

"Grandpa was one of the boatmen who went in under the guns of the Barbary pirates to burn the *Philadelphia*. My folks built blood into the foundations of this country and I don't aim to see them torn down for no reason whatsoever."

Another Rebel was fixing to load that cannon, so I drew a bead on him, and the man who followed him in the chow line could move up one place.

"Come fighting time, General," I said, "there'll always be a Sackett ready to bear arms for his country, although we are peaceful folks, unless riled."

And that was still true, but when they buried that gambling man out west of Uvalde it marked me as a bad man.

In those days what they called a "bad man" was one who was a bad man to have trouble with, and a lot of mighty good men were known as bad men. The name was one I hadn't hankered for, but Wes Bigelow left me no choice.

Fact of the matter was, if it hadn't been me it would have been somebody else, because Bigelow's bottom deal was nothing like so good as I'd seen on the river-boats.

Nevertheless, I had got a reputation in Uvalde, and this seemed a good time to become a wandering man. Only I was fed up with drifting ever since the war, and wanted a place to light.

Outside of town I fell in with a cow outfit. North from Texas we rode, driving a herd to Montana grass, with never a thought of anything but grief while riding the Bozeman Trail.

North of the Crazy Woman three men rode into camp hunting beef to buy. The boss was not selling but they stayed on, and when my name was mentioned one of them looked at me.

"Are you the Sackett who killed Bigelow?"

"He wasn't much good with a bottom deal."

"Nor with a gun, I guess."

"He was advised."

"Unless you're fit to handle his two brothers, you'd best not ride into Montana. They come up by steamboat and they're waiting for you."

"I wasn't planning on staying around," I said, "but if they find me before I leave, they're welcome."

"Somebody was wondering if you were kin to Tyrel Sackett, the Mora gunfighter."

"Tyrel Sackett is my brother, but this is the first I've heard of him gunfighting. Only, if he was put to it, he could."

"He cleaned up Mora. He's talked about in the same breath with Hickok and Hardin."

"He's a hand with any kind of shooting iron. Back to home he used to outshoot me sometimes."

"Sometimes?"

"Sometimes I outshot Tyrel . . . but I was older than him, and had done more shooting."

We drove our cattle to Gallatin Valley and scattered them on Montana grass, and Nelson Story, whose cattle they were, rode out to camp with the mail. There was a letter for me, the first one I ever got.

All through wartime I watched folks getting letters and writing them, and it was a hard thing, a-yearning to have mail and receiving none. Got so when mail call came around that I used to walk away and talk with the cook. He had lost his family to a war party of Kiowas, out Texas way.

This letter that Story brought me from town looked mighty fine, and I turned it in my hands several times, sizing it up and wishing it could speak out. Printing I could read, but writing was all which-ways and I could make nothing of it.

Mr. Story, he stopped by, and noticed. "Maybe I can help you," he suggested.

Shame was upon me. Here I was a grown man and couldn't read enough to get the sense out of a letter. My eyes could make sense of a Cheyenne or Comanche war trail, but reading was something I couldn't handle.

Mr. Story, he read that letter to me. Orrin and Tyrel each had them a ranch, and Ma was living at Mora in New Mexico. Tyrel was married to the daughter of a Don, one of those rich Spanish men, and Orrin was in politics and walking a wide path.

All I had was a wore-out saddle, four pistols, a Winchester carbine, and the clothes I stood up in. Yes, and I had me a knife, an Arkansas toothpick, good for hand-fighting or butchering meat.

"Your brothers seem to have done well," Mr. Story said. "I would learn to read, if I were you, Tell. You're a good man, and you could go far."

So I went horse-hunting and wound up making a dicker with an Indian. He had two appaloosa horses and he dearly wanted a .36-calibre pistol I had, so we settled down to outwait each other. Every boy in Tennessee grows up horse-trading or watching horse trades, and no Red Indian was going to outswap me.

He was a long, tall Indian with a long, sad face and he had eyes like an old wore-out houn' dog, and I could only talk swap with him when I didn't look him in the eye. Something about that Indian made me want to give him everything I had. However, he had a thirst on and I had me a jug of fighting whiskey.

So I stalled and fixed grub and talked horse and talked hunting and avoided the subject. Upshot of it was, I swapped the .36 pistol, twenty ca'tridges, an old blanket, and that jug of whiskey for those two horses.

Only when I took another look at the pack horse I wasn't sure who had the better of the swap.

That letter from home stirred me to moving that way. There's folks who don't hold with women-folks smoking, but I was honing to see Ma, to smell her old pipe a-going, and to hear the creak of that old rocker that always spelled home to me. When we boys were growing up that creak was the sound of comfort to us. It meant home, and it meant Ma, and it meant understanding . . . and time to time it meant a belt with a strap.

Somehow, Ma always contrived to put a bait of grub on the table, despite drouth that often lay upon the hills, or the poor soil of our side-hill farm. And if we came home bear-scratched or with a bullet under our skins, it was Ma who touched up the scratches or probed for the bullet.

So I lit a shuck for New Mexico, and the folks.

That's an expression common down Texas way, for when a man left his camp to walk to a neighbor's, he would dip a corn shuck into the flames to light his path, and he would do the same when he started back. Folks came to speak of anybody who was leaving for somewhere as "lighting a shuck."

Well, most of my life I'd been lighting a shuck. First, it was hungering for strange country, so I took off down the Natchez Trace for New Orleans. Another time I rode a flatboat down river to the same place.

Had me a time aboard those flatboats. Flatboat men had the name of being tough to handle. Lean and gangling like I was, they taken me for a greener, but away back of yonder in the hills boys take to fighting the way they take to coon dogs or making 'shine, so I clobbered them good.

I'm named for William Tell, whom Pa held in admiration for his arrow-shooting and his standing on principle. Speaking of standing, I stand six feet and three inches in my sock feet, when I have socks, and weigh one hundred and eighty pounds, most of it crowded into chest and shoulders, muscled arms, and big hands. Back to home I stood butt of all the funning because of my big hands and feet.

No Sackett was ever much on the brag. We want folks to leave us alone and we leave them alone, but when fighting time comes, we stand ready.

Back in the mountains, and in the army, too, I threw every man I tackled at wrestling. Pa raised us on Cornish-style wrestling and a good bit of fist work he'd learned from an Englishman prizefighter.

"Boys," Pa used to say, "avoid conflict and trouble, for enough of it fetches to a man without his asking, but if you are attacked, smite them hip and thigh."

Pa was a great man for Bible speaking, but I never could see a mite of sense in striking them hip and thigh. When I had to smite them I did it on the chin or in the belly.

It is a far piece from Montana to New Mexico astride of a horse, but I put together a skimpy outfit and headed west for Virginia City and Alder Gulch. A day or two I worked there, and then pulled out for Jackson's Hole and the Teton Mountains.

It came over me I wanted to hear Orrin singing the old songs, the songs our people brought from Wales, or the songs we had from others like us traveling from Ireland, Scotland and England. Many happy thoughts of my boyhood time were memories of singing around the fire at home. Orrin was always the leader in that, a handsome, singing man, the best liked of us all. We held no envy, being proud to call him brother.

When I started for New Mexico the last thing I was hunting was gold or trouble, and usually they come as a pair. Gold is a hard-found thing, and when a man finds it he's bound to fetch trouble a-keeping it.

Seems like a man finds gold only when he ain't hunting it. He picks up a rock to throw at something and that rock turns out to be mostly gold, or he trips over a ledge and finds himself sitting astride the Mother Lode.

This whole shooting match of a thing started because I was a curious man. There I was, dusting my tail down a south-going trail with no troubles. A time or two I cut Indian sign, but I fought shy of them.

Back in my army days I heard folks tell of what a bad time the Indians were getting, and some of them, like the Cherokee, who settled down to farming and business, did get a raw deal; but most Indians would ride a hundred miles any time to find a good fight, or a chance to steal horses or take a scalp.

When the war ended I joined up to fight the Sioux and Cheyenne in Dakota after the Little Crow massacre in Minnesota. The Sioux had moved off to the west so we chased them, and a couple of times we caught them . . . or they caught us. Down Texas way I'd had trouble with the Kiowa, Comanche, Arapahoe, and even the Apache, so I had respect for Indians.

It was a slow-riding time. Of a morning the air was brisk and chill with a hint of frost in the higher altitudes, but the days were warm and lazy, and by night the stars were brighter than a body would believe.

There's no grander thing than to ride wild country with time on your hands, so I walked my horses down the backbone of the Rockies, through the Tetons and south to South Pass and on to Brown's Hole. Following long grass slopes among the aspen groves, camping in flowered meadows beside chuckling streams, killing only when I needed grub, and listening then to the long echo of my rifle shot—believe me, I was having me a time.

Nothing warned me of trouble to come.

Thinking of Orrin's mellow Welsh voice a-singing, I came fresh to hear my own voice, so I took a swallow from my canteen and tipping my head back, I gave out with song.

It was "Brennan on the Moor," about an Irish highwayman, a song I dearly loved to hear Orrin sing.

I didn't get far. A man who plans to sing while he's riding had better reach an understanding with his horse. He should have him a good voice, or a horse with no ear for music.

When my voice lifted in song I felt that cayuse bunch his muscles, so I broke off short.

That appaloosa and me had investigated the capabilities of each other the first couple of times I got up in the saddle, and I proved to him that I could ride. That horse knew a thing or two about bucking and pitching, and I had no notion of proving myself again on a rocky mountainside.

And then we came upon the ghost of a trail.

# Chapter 2

It was a sliver of white quartz thrust into a crack in a wall of red sandstone.

Riding wild country, a man who wants to keep his hair will be wary for anything out of the ordinary. He learns to notice the bent-down grass, the broken twig, the muddied water of a stream.

Nature has a way that is simple, direct, and familiar. Animals accept nature pretty much as they find it. Although they build lairs and nests for themselves they disturb their surroundings mighty little. Only the beaver, who wants to make his home in water, and so builds his dams, will try to alter nature. If anything is disturbed the chances are a man did it.

This was lonesome country, and that quartz had not come there by accident. It had to be put there by hand.

The last settlement I'd seen was South Pass City, far away to the north, and the last human had been a greasy trapper who was mostly hair and wore-out buckskins. He and his pack asses went by me like a pay wagon passing a tramp. They simply paid me no mind.

That was two weeks ago. Since then I'd seen neither men nor the tracks of men, although I'd passed up lots of game, including one old silver-tip grizzly that was scooping honey out of a hollow tree.

That bear was minding his business so I minded mine. We Sackett boys never killed anything we didn't need to eat unless it was coming at us. A mountain man tries to live with the country instead of against it.

However, this quartz, being where it was, struck me as an interesting thing. If it was to mark a trail of some kind there was no indication of that trail on the ground, and some kinds of soil will hold trail marks for years.

Prying that sliver of quartz from its crack, I gave it study. It seemed to have been there for years and years.

I put it back where I'd found it and unlimbered my field glasses. These were war booty, taken from the body of a Rebel colonel down near Vicksburg, he being in no shape to object. Sure enough, some distance off I saw another gleam of white in the face of a rock.

Homesickness had started me south, but it was plain old-fashioned curiosity that led me to follow that white-quartz trail.

No doubt about it, I'd stumbled upon a trail the like of which I'd never seen before, and whoever conceived the idea must have been mighty knowing, for it was unlikely to be noticed. Yet it could easily be followed for, even in the almost dark, those white fragments would catch the light.

For more than an hour I followed the strange trail up the mountainside, through the trees. The pines thinned out and I rode around groves of aspen, and soon I was close to timberline in the wildest, loneliest country a man was likely to see.

Above me were gray granite shoulders of bare rock, streaked with occasional snow. There were stunted trees, more often than not lightning-blasted and dead, and many fallen ones. The air was so fresh it was like drinking cold water to breathe it, and there was a touch of chill. It was very clear, and a body could see for miles.

Nowhere did I see a track, nor horse-droppings, nor any sign of an old campfire or of wood cutting. From time to time, where there was no place to put the quartz, a cairn of stones had been set up.

It began to look as if I'd stumbled on an old, an awfully old trail, older than any I had followed or even heard tell of.

Pa had wintered south of here on the Dolores River, one time, with a party of trappers. Many a time he had told us boys about that, and over a campfire in Texas I'd been told of Father Escalante's trip through this region, hunting a trail to the California missions from Santa Fe. But he never would have come as high as this.

Only riches of some kind would have brought men this far into the back country, unless they were hiding. Nobody needed to tell me that the trail I had taken might lead to blood and death, for when gold comes into a man's thinking, common sense goes out.

It was getting close to sundown when I fetched through a keyhole pass into a high mountain valley without growth of any kind. Bleak and lonely under the sky, it was like a granite dish, streaked here and there with snow or ice that lay in the cracks.

Timberline was a thousand feet below me, and I was close under the night-coming sky, with a shivering wind, scarcely more than a breath for strength, blowing along the valley. All I could hear was the sound of my horses' hoofs and the creak of my saddle. There was a spooky feeling to the air, and my horse walked with ears pricked to the stillness.

Off to the left lay a sheet of ghost water, a high cold lake fed by melting snow, scarcely stirred by that breath of wind. It lay flat and still, and that lake worried me, for I had heard stories of ghost water lakes in the high-up mountains.

Then there came a sound, and my horses heard it first. Riding lonesome country a man does well to give heed to his horses, for they will often see or hear things a man will miss, and these appaloosas were mountain-born and -bred, captured wild and still wild at heart, and, like me, they had a love for the lost, the wild, and the lonely.

It was a far-off sound, like rushing wind in a great forest, or like the distant sound of steam cars running on rails. It grew as we moved nearer, and I knew it for the sound of falling water.

I came to another keyhole pass, even narrower than the first, and the trail led into it. Alongside the narrow trail rushed the outflow of that ghost lake, spilling down the chute in a tumble of white water.

I could see it falling away in a series of falls, steep slides, and rapids. The pass was no more than a crack, not a canyon or ravine, just a gash in the face of the mountain wall, a gloomy place, shadowed and spattered by spray. A thread of trail skirted the rushing stream, a trail that must, much of the time, be under water.

Believe me, I took a good long look down that dark, narrow crack, filled with the roar of the water. Yet on the wall, in a place dug out for the purpose, was a sliver of quartz, and now I had come too far to turn back.

My horses shied from that opening, liking it not at all, but I was less smart than my horses, and urged them on, starting gingerly down the slide.

That trail was narrow . . . it was almighty narrow. If it played out there would be no way of turning back. No mustang was ever taught to back up, and I'd no way of controlling the pack horse, anyway.

Once I got him started, that appaloosa was as big a fool as I was. Ears pricked, he started down, sliding on his rump in spots, it was that steep. A body couldn't hear a thing beyond the roar of the water.

Rock walls towered hundreds of feet overhead, closing in places until there was scarcely a crack above us, and it was like riding through a cave. Ferns overhung the water in places, and there was more than thirty yards in one place and twice as far in another where a thin sheet of water actually ran over the trail.

In other places, where the stream fell away into a deep chasm beside the trail, I lost all sight of the water, and could only hear it. In two or three spots, near waterfalls, the mist and spray was thick enough to soak a man and blot out everything. It was a death trap, all right, and I felt it. A man who says he has never been scared is either lying or else he's never been anyplace or done anything.

For about three miles I followed that trail. I went down it more than a thousand feet, judging by the vegetation in the valley that I found. It opened on my right, narrow at first, and then widening. The creek tumbled off and disappeared into a narrow, deep canyon shrouded by ferns and trees growing from the rock walls. But the trail turned into the valley.

At that point the valley was no more than twenty yards wide, with steep walls rising on either side. A man on foot might have climbed them; a horse couldn't have gone six feet. The last of the sunlight was tinting the canyon wall on the east, but for maybe a hundred and fifty yards I rode in deep shadows.

Then the valley broadened. It looked to be a couple of miles long, and from a quarter- to a half-mile wide. A stream ran along the bottom and emptied into that run-off stream beside which I had been riding.

The bottom was as pretty a high mountain meadow as a body would care to see, and along the stream there were clumps of aspen, some dwarf willows, and other trees whose names I couldn't call to mind. A few elk were feeding not far off and they looked up at me. It was likely there was another way into the valley, but a body wouldn't know it from their actions. When I rode nearer they moved off, but seemed in no way frightened.

The pack horse was pulling back on the lead rope, not at all sure he wanted to go into that valley. My mount was going, all right, but he hadn't decided whether he liked it or not. Me, I was feeling spooky as an eight-year-old at a graveyard picnic in the evening.

So I shucked my Winchester, expecting I've no idea what.

We walked it slow. Horse, he was stepping high, ears up and spooky as all get out, but you never saw a prettier little valley than this one, caught as now with the late shadows on it, and a shading of pink and rose along that rocky rim, high above us.

And then I saw the cave.

Actually, it was only a place hollowed out by wind and water from the face of the cliff, but it cut back maybe eight or ten feet at its deepest, and there were some trees, mostly aspen, growing in front, masking the entrance.

Getting down, I tied my horses to a tree, not risking them taking off and leaving me afoot.

No tracks . . . nobody had been around here for a long time.

Part of the opening had been walled up with stone the way cliff dwellers sometimes do, and the inside was all black with the smoke of forgotten fires. There was nothing much there but broken stone where part of the wall had fallen, and in back, at the deepest part, a polished log that had been cut off at both ends with an axe.

That big old log was polished smooth from folks a-setting on it, but at one end there were several rows of small notches. Counting them, they added up to groups of thirty and thirty-one and, figuring each notch as a day, they came out to about five months. In a place like this, that's a long time.

Sand had blown into the cave, and my toe stubbed against something on the floor at the back. Digging around it with my hand, I pulled out one of those old breastplates like the Spanish men wore. It was rusted, but it had been made of good steel, tempered to take the force of a blow.

All I knew about the Spanish men I'd heard from Pa when he used to yarn with us about his old days as a mountain man. He told us much of Santa Fe, where he had lived for a spell, and I knew that Santa Fe was ten, eleven years old before the Pilgrims landed at Plymouth Rock.

Those Spanish men had done a sight of exploring, and much of it was only a matter of record away over in Spain. How many expeditions had gone exploring, nobody rightly knew, and this might have been the tag end of one of them.

The trail I'd been hunting as I rode south was one Pa had told me about, and of which I heard more from miners in Montana. Spanish men had used that trail for trading expeditions to the Ute country. Traders had traveled that route to the north before Father Escalante, even before Captain John Smith sighted the Virginia shore, but they left little record. Rivera had scouted through here in 1765, but he was a late-comer.

Studying around in the little time I had before it got dark, I figured that no more than three or four men had reached this valley, and two of them had never left it, because I found their graves. One of them had a stone marker, and the date of death was 1544.

Maybe I was the first to see that grave in three hundred years.

That shelter might have slept four in a pinch, certainly no more. Yet at least one man had to get out of here to leave the trail I'd found, and I had a hunch it was two men. The only puzzle was how they had come upon this valley in the first place.

On the wall, half concealed by aspen leaves, was carved a Spanish word: *Oro*. Beside it an arrow pointed up the valley.

*Oro* is a word that most men recognize, even those who know no other Spanish. Serving in the army with a couple of men who spoke the Spanish tongue, I'd learned a bit of the language, and much more while in Texas.

The shadows were long now, but there was still light, and I had that word to lead me on. Stepping into the saddle, I walked my horses up the valley. Sure enough, a half-mile up I found a tunnel dug into the side of the hill, and broken rock around it.

Picking up a chunk from a pile stacked against the wall of the tunnel, I found it heavy—heavy with gold. It was real gen-u-ine high-grade, the kind a body hears tell of, but rarely sees.

Those Spanish men had found gold all right. No matter how they came to be here, they had found it, and now it was mine.

All I had to do was get it out.

# Chapter 3

So there I was, up to my ears in a strange country, with gold on my hands.

We Sacketts never had much. Mostly we wanted land that we could crop and graze, land where we could rear a family. We set store by kinfolk, and when trouble showed we usually stood against it as a family.

The Higgins feud, which had cost our family lives, had ended while I was away. Tyrel ended that feud on the day when Orrin was facing up to marriage. Long Higgins had come laying for Orrin, figuring Orrin's mind would be all upset with marrying. Long Higgins missed Orrin when his bride pushed Orrin out of the way, but she took the lead meant for a Sackett.

Trouble was, Long never figured on Tyrel, and you always had to figure on Tyrel.

He was a man who could look right along the barrel of your gun at you just like you'd look across a plate of supper. He would look right down your gun barrel and shoot you dead. Only Tyrel never hunted trouble.

We were nip and tuck with a pistol. Maybe I was a shade better with a rifle, but it was always a question.

Right now the question was one of gold. Pa, he always advised us boys to take time to contemplate. I taken it now.

First off, I had to figure what to do. The gold was here, but it had to be kept secret until I could get it laid claim to officially, and get it out.

Gold is never a simple thing. Many a man has wished he had gold, but once he has it he finds trouble. Gold causes folks to lose their right thinking and their common sense. It had been lied for and killed for, and I was in a lawless land.

Gold has weight, and when a body carries it, it is hard to hide. Gold seems almost to have an odor. Folks can smell it out even faster than gossip.

Finding the gold had been one thing, but getting it out was another. I'd no tools, and nothing in which to carry it but my saddlebags. Nearly all my money had gone to buy grub and gear for this trip south. I wanted to take enough gold out now to buy a mining outfit.

Seemed to be a sight of gold here, near as I could judge, as much as a body could want, but mostly I wanted enough for cattle and a place of my own, and enough to buy time for a little book learning.

It ain't right for a man to be ignorant, but in the hills we had school only one year out of three, and the time might not last over two, three months. When I got all squared away with a pencil I could write my name . . . Pa and Tyrel could read it, too. Only one of my officers in the army could read it, but he told me not to worry. "A man who can shoot like you can," he said, "isn't likely to have anybody question the way he signs his name."

But even if a man pays no mind to himself, he has to think of his youngsters, when and if. We Sacketts were healthy breeders, running long on tall boys. Counting ourselves, we had forty-nine brothers and cousins. Pa had two sisters and five brothers living. Starting a feud with us didn't make any kind of sense. If we couldn't outshoot them we could outbreed them.

A man who expects to sire children doesn't want to appear the fool in front of them. We Sacketts believed young folks should respect their elders, but their elders had to deserve respect. Finding the gold could mean all the difference to me.

While I was contemplating, I was unsaddling my horses and settling down for the night. The season was well into spring and fetching up to summer. The snow was almost off the mountains although in this kind of country it never seemed to leave entirely, and there was no telling when it might snow again.

If I went out, got an outfit and came back, it would be a close thing to get out some gold and leave before snow fell. High up as I was, snow could be expected nine months out of the year. And when snow fell, that valley up above would fill up and the stream would freeze over. Anybody caught in this valley would be stuck for the winter.

Yet a heavy rain could make that narrow chute impassable for days. Allowing for rain spells and snow, there were probably not over fifty or sixty days a year when a man could get in or out of the valley. . . . Unless there was another way in.

It left me with a worried, uneasy feeling to think I was in a jug that might be stoppered at any time.

Making coffee over my fire, I studied about my situation. Those Bigelows now, the brothers of the man I'd had to shoot . . . they might think I had run from them, and they might try to follow me.

During that ride south I'd taken no more than usual precautions with my trail, and it fretted me to think that they might follow me south, and bother Orrin and Tyrel. Our family had had enough of feuding, and I'd no right to bring trouble to their door.

That the Bigelows would follow me to this place I did not expect. From my first discovery of the strange trail, I had taken care to cover my tracks and leave nothing for anybody to find.

A wind scurried my fire, just a mite of wind, and my eyes strayed to that old breastplate against the wall. Did the ghosts of men really prowl in the night? Never a man to believe in ha'nts, I was willing to believe that if a place was to be ha'nted, this was a likely one.

Empty as this valley seemed, I had the feeling of somebody looking over my shoulder, and the horses were restless too. Come sleeping time, I brought them in off the grass where they had been picketed and kept them closer to the fire. A horse makes the best sentinel in many cases, and I had no other. However, I was a light sleeper.

At daylight I shagged it down to the stream and baited a hook for trout. They snagged onto my hook and put up a fight like they were sired by bulldogs, but I hauled them in, fried them out, and made a tasty breakfast.

Making a handle out of a stick I split the end and wedged in a rounded stone, then lashed it in place. Using that and a few blades of stone, I started to work on that ore in the end of the tunnel. By sundown I had broken my axe handle twice at the hammer end, but had knocked off about three hundredweight of ore.

Long after nightfall I sat beside my fire and broke up that quartz. It was rotten quartz, some of which I could almost pull apart with my fingers, but I hammered it down and got some of the gold out. It was free gold, regular jewelry store stuff, and I worked until after midnight.

The crackling of my fire in the pine-scented night was a thing to pleasure me, but I walked down to the bank of the stream in the darkness and bathed in the cold water of the creek. Then I went back to the cave where I was camped and went to work on a bow.

Growing up with Cherokees like we did, all of us boys hunted with bows and arrows, even more than with guns. Ammunition was hard to come by when Pa was off in the western lands, and sometimes the only meat we had was what we killed with a bow and arrow.

My fire was burning wood that held the gathered perfume of years, and it smelled right good, and time to time the flames would strike some pitch and flare up, changing color, pretty as all get-out. Suddenly the heads of my horses came up and I was over in the deep shadows with my Winchester cocked.

Times like that a man raised to wild country doesn't think. He acts without thinking . . . or he may never get a chance to think again.

For a long time I waited, not moving a muscle, listening into the night. Firelight reflected from the flanks of my horses. It could be a bear or a lion, but from the way the horses acted I did not think so.

After a while the horses went back to eating, so I took a stick and snaked the coffeepot to me and had some coffee and chewed some jerked beef.

Awakening in the gray morning light, I heard a patter of rain on the aspen leaves, and felt a chill of fear . . . if it started to rain and that chute filled up with run-off water it might be days before I could get out.

So I sacked up my gold. The horses seemed happy to have me moving around. There was about three pounds of gold, enough and over for the outfit I'd need.

When I went outside I saw that the trout I'd cleaned and hung in a tree against breakfast were gone. The string with which I'd suspended the meat had been sawed through by a dull blade . . . or gnawed by teeth.

I stood looking at the ground. Under the tree there were several tracks. They were not cat tracks, they were the tracks of little human feet. They were the tracks of a child or a small woman.

My skin crawled . . . nothing human could be in a place like this; yet come to think of it, I couldn't recall ever hearing of a ha'nt with a taste for trout.

We Welsh, like the Irish and the Bretons, have our stories of the Little People, all of which we love to yarn about, but we do not really believe in such things. But in America a man heard other tales. Not often, for Indians did not like to talk of them, and never spoke of them except among themselves. But I'd talked to white men who took squaws to wife, and they lived among Indians, and heard the tales.

Up in Wyoming I rode by to look at the Medicine Wheel, a great wheel of stone with twenty-odd spokes, well over a hundred feet across. The Shoshones copied their medicine lodge from that wheel, but all they can say about who built the wheel is that it was done by "the people who had no iron."

A hundred miles away to the southwest there was a stone arrow pointing toward the wheel. It pointed a direction for someone—but who?

My gold was sacked to go, but I needed meat, and disliked to fire a gun in that valley. So I stalked a young buck and killed him with an arrow, butchered him, and carried the meat back to the cave, where I cut a fair lot of it into strips and hung them on a pole over a fire to smoke.

Then I broiled a steak of venison and ate it, decided that wasn't enough for a man my size, and broiled another.

Hours later the wind awakened me. The fire was down to red coals and I was squirming around to settle down for sleep again when my mustang blew.

Me, I came out of those blankets like an eel out of greased fingers, and was back in the shadows again with my rifle hammer eared back before you could say scat.

"All right, boy." The horses would know I was awake and they were not alone. At first there was no sound but the wind, then after a bit a stirring made by no bear or deer in the world.

My bronc snorted and my pack horse blew. I could see their legs in the faint glow of the coals, and nothing moved near them . . . but something was out there in the night.

A long slow time dragged by and the coals glowed a duller red. Leaning back against the wall, I dozed a little, but alert for trouble if need be.

There was no other sound.

Morning was painting a sunrise on a storm-gored ridge beyond the dark sentinel pines when I got up, stretched my stiff muscles. Studying the trees across the valley and the slope above them, I failed at first to notice what was closest to home. The rest of that meat had been pulled from the tree and a good-sized hunk had been cut off.

Whoever had cut it off had made work of it with a dull blade, and to take the risk of approaching a man's camp whoever it was must have been hungry.

Hanging the meat up again, I went out and killed and dressed another buck. I hung it in a tree also, and rode away. I wanted nobody going hungry where I could lend a hand. Whoever or whatever it was would have meat as long as that buck lasted.

The trail going out was worse than coming in, but with some scrambling and slipping we reached the high basin. We rode past that lake of ghost water and headed for the lowlands once more. But once through the keyhole pass I did not follow the same trail, taking a rough, unlikely way that nobody was apt to find, unless maybe a mountain goat.

Turning in my saddle, I looked back in the peaks. "Whoever you are," I said aloud, "expect me back, for I'll be riding the high trails again, a-hunting for gold."

# Chapter 4

When I sighted the ranch, I drew up on the trail and looked across the bottom. There was a rocky ridge where the Mora River cut through, and the ranch was there beside it. That light over there was home, for home is where the heart is, and my heart was wherever Ma was, and the boys.

Walking the appaloosa down the trail, I could smell the coolness rising from the willows along the Mora, and the hayfields over in the big valley called La Cueva.

A horse whinnied, and a dog started to bark, and then another dog. Yet no door opened and the light continued to burn. Chuckling, I walked my horse along and kept my eyes open. Unless I was mistaken, one of the boys or somebody would be out in the dark watching me come up, maybe keeping me covered from the darkness until my intentions were clear.

Getting down from the saddle, I walked up the steps to the porch. I didn't knock, I just opened the door and stepped in.

Tyrel was sitting at a table with an oil lamp on it, and Ma was there, and a girl who had to be Tyrel's wife.

The table was set for four, and I stood there, long and tall in the door, feeling my heart inside me so big I felt choked and awkward. My clothes were stiff and I knew I was trail-dusty and mighty mean-looking.

"Howdy, Ma. Tyrel, if you'll tell that man behind me to take his gun off my back, I'll come in and set."

Tyrel got up. "Tell . . . I'll be damned."

"Likely," I said, "but don't blame it on me. When I rode off to the wars I left you in good hands."

Turning toward Tyrel's wife, a lovely, dark-eyed, dark-haired girl who looked like a princess out of a book, I said, "Ma'am, I'm William Tell Sackett, and you'll be Drusilla, my brother's wife."

She put her hands on mine and stood on tiptoe and kissed me, and my face colored up and I went hot clean to my boots. Tyrel laughed, and then he looked past me into the darkness and said, "It's all right, Cap. This is my brother Tell."

He came in out of the darkness then, a thin old man with cold gray eyes and a gray mustache above a hard mouth. There was no give to this man, I figured. Had I been a wrong one I would have been killed.

We shook hands and neither of us said anything. Cap was not a talkative man, and I am only at times.

Ma turned her head. "Juana, come get my son his supper."

I couldn't believe it—Ma with household help. Long as I could recall, nobody had done for us boys but Ma herself, working early and late and never complaining.

Juana was a Mexican-Indian girl and she brought the food in fancy plates. I looked at it and commenced to feel mighty uncomfortable. I'd not eaten a meal in the presence of a woman for a long time, and was embarrassed and worried. I'd no idea how to eat proper. In a trail camp a body eats because he's hungry and doesn't think much of the way he does it.

"If it's all the same to you," I said, "I'll go outside. Under a roof like this I'm mighty skittish."

Drusilla took my sleeve and led me to the chair. "You sit down, Tell. And don't you worry. We want you to eat with us and we want you to tell us what you've been doing."

First I thought of that gold.

I went out and fetched it. Putting my saddlebags down on the table, I took out a chunk of the gold, still grainy with quartz fragments, but gold.

It shook them. Nothing, I'd figured, would ever shake Tyrel, but this did.

While they looked at the gold I went to the kitchen and washed my hands in a big basin and dried them on a white towel.

Everything was spotless and clean. The floor was like the deck of a steamboat I traveled on one time on the Mississippi. It was the kind of living I'd always wanted for Ma, but I'd had no hand in this. Orrin and Tyrel had done it.

While I ate, I told them about the gold. I'd taken a big slab of bread and buttered it liberal, and I ate it in two bites, while talking and drinking coffee. First real butter I'd tasted in more than a year, and the first real coffee in longer than that.

Through the open door into the parlor I could see furniture made of some dark wood, and shelves with books. While they talked, I got up and went in there, taking the lamp along. I squatted on my heels to look at the books, fair hungering for them. I taken one down and turned the leaves real slow, careful not to dirty them, and tested the weight of the book in my hand. A book as heavy as one of these, I figured, must make a lot of sense.

I rested a finger on a line of print and tried to get the way of it, but there were words I'd never seen before. Back to home we'd had no books but an almanac and the Bible.

There was a book there by a man named Blackstone, seemed to be about the law, and several others. I felt a longing in me to read them all, to know them, to have them always at my hand. I looked through book after book, and sometimes I would find a word I could recognize, or even a sentence I could make out.

Such words would catch my eye like a deer taking off into the woods or the sudden lift of a gun barrel in the sun. One place I found something I puzzled out, and I do not know why it was this I chose. It was from Blackstone.

> ". . . that the whole should protect all its parts, and that every part should pay obedience to the will of the whole; or, in other words, that the community should guard the rights of each individual member, and that (in return for this protection) each individual should submit to the laws of the community; without which submission of all it was impossible that protection could be extended to any."

It took me a spell, working that out in my mind, to get the sense of it. Yet somehow it stayed with me, and in the days to come I thought it over a good bit.

Returning the books to their places, I stood up, and I looked around very carefully. This was Ma's home, and it was Tyrel's and Orrin's. It was not mine. They had earned it with their hands and with their knowing ways, and they had given this place to Ma.

Tyrel was no longer the lean, hungry mountain boy. He stood tall now, and carried himself very straight and with a kind of style. He wore a black broadcloth coat and a white shirt like a man born to them and, come to think of it, he was even better-looking than Orrin.

I stared at myself in the mirror. No getting around it, I was a homely man. Over-tall and mighty little meat, with a big-boned face like a wedge. There was an old scar on my cheekbone from a cutting scrape in New Orleans. My shoulders were heavy with muscle, but a mite stooped. In my wore-out army shirt and cow-country jeans I didn't come to much.

My brothers were younger than me, and probably brighter. Hands and a strong back were all I had. I could move almost anything I put a hand to, and I could ride and rope, but what was that?

My mind turned back to that passage in the book. There was the kind of rule for men to live by. I'd no idea such things were written down in books.

Orrin had come while I was inside, and he'd taken his gee-tar and was singing. He sang "Black, Black, Black," "Barb'ry Allen," and "The Golden Vanity."

It was like old times . . . only it wasn't old times and the boys had left me far, far behind. Twenty-eight years old in a few days—with years of brute hard living behind me—but if Orrin and Tyrel could do it, I was going to try.

Come daylight, I was going to shape my way for the mountains, for the high far valley, and the stream. First I must sell my gold and buy an outfit. Then I would light out. And it was best I go soon, for the Bigelows might come hunting me. Turned out less simple than that.

Las Vegas was the nearest place I could get the kind of outfit I wanted. We hitched up, Tyrel and me, and we drove down to Las Vegas with Cap riding horseback along with us. That old coot was a man to ride the river with, believe me.

"Wherever you go," Cap told me, "if you show that gold you'll empty the town. They'll foller you . . . they'll track you down, and if they get a chance, they'll kill you. That's the strike of a lifetime."

Riding to Las Vegas I got an idea. Somewhere on that stream that ran down from the mountains I would stake a claim, and folks would think the gold came from *that* claim and never look for the other.

"You do that," Cap's old eyes twinkled a mite, "and I'll give you a name for it. You can call it the Red Herring."

When I showed my gold in the bank at Las Vegas the man behind the wicket turned a little pale around the eyes, and I knew what Cap Rountree had said was truth. If ever there was greed in a man's eyes, it was in his. "Where did you get this gold?" he demanded.

"Mister," I said, "if you want to buy it, quote me a price. Otherwise I'll go elsewhere."

He was a tall, thin man with sharp gray eyes that seemed to have only a black speck for a pupil. He had a thin face and a carefully trimmed mustache.

He touched his tongue to his lips and lifted those eyes to me. "It might be st——"

When he saw the look in my eyes he stopped, and just at that moment, Tyrel and Orrin came in. Orrin had come down earlier than we had for some business. They walked over.

"Is anything wrong, Tell?"

"Not yet," I said.

"Oh, Orrin. " The banker's eyes flickered to Tyrel and back to me. The family resemblance was strong.

"I was about to buy some gold. A brother of yours?"

"Tell, this is John Tuthill."

"It is always a pleasure to meet one of the Sackett family," Tuthill said, but when our eyes met we both knew it was no pleasure at all. For either of us.

"My brother has just come down from Montana," Orrin said smoothly. "He's been mining up there."

"He looks like a cattleman."

"I have been, and will be again."

After that we shopped around, buying me an outfit. There was no gainsaying the fact that I'd need a pick and a shovel, a single-jack, and some drills. That is mining equipment in any man's figuring, and there was no way of sidestepping it. I'm not overly suspicious, but no man ever lost his hair by being careful, and I kept an eye on my back trail as we roamed about town.

After a while Tyrel and Orrin went about their business, and I finished getting my outfit together. Cap was nowhere to be seen, but he needed no keeper. Cap had been up the creek and over the mountain in his time. Anybody who latched onto that old man latched onto trouble.

Dark came on. I left my gear at the livery stable and started up the street. I paused to look over toward the mountains and I got a look behind me. Sure enough, I'd picked up an Indian.

Only he was no Indian, he was a slick-looking party who seemed to have nothing to do but keep an eye on me. Right away it came to mind that he might be a Bigelow, so I just turned down an alley and walked slow.

He must have been afraid I would get away from him, for he came running, and I did a boxer's sidestep into the shadows. My sudden disappearance must have surprised him. He skidded to a stop, and when he stopped I hit him.

My fists are big, and my hands are work-hardened. When I connected with his jaw it sounded like the butt end of an axe hitting a log.

Anybody who figures to climb my frame is somebody I wish to know better, so I took him by the shirt front with my left hand and dragged him into the saloon where I was to meet the boys.

Folks looked up, always interested in something coming off, so I taken a better grip and one-handed him to a seat on the bar.

"I hadn't baited no hook, but this gent's been bobbin' my cork," I said. "Any of you know him? He just tried to jump me in the alley."

"That's Will Boyd. He's a gambler."

"He put his money on the wrong card," I said. "I don't like being followed down alleys."

Boyd was coming out of it, and when he realized where he was he started to slide down off the bar, only I held him fast. From my belt scabbard I took that Arkansas toothpick of mine, which I use for any manner of things.

"You have been led upon evil ways," I explained, "and the way of the transgressor is hard. Seems to me the thing led you down the wrong road is that mustache."

He was looking at me with no favor, and I knew he was one man would try to kill me first chance he had. He was a man with a lot to learn, and he wouldn't learn it any younger.

Balancing that razor-sharp knife in my hand I said, "You take this knife, and you shave off that mustache."

He didn't believe me. You could see he just couldn't believe this could be happening to him. He didn't even want to believe it, so I explained.

"You come hunting me," I said, "and I'm a mild man who likes to be left alone. You need something to remind you of the error of your ways."

So I held out the knife to him, haft first, and I could see him wondering if he dared try to run it into me. "Mister, don't make me lose my patience. If I do I'll whup you."

He took the knife, carefully, because he didn't feel lucky, and he started on that mustache. It was a stiff mustache and he had no water and no soap and, mister, it hurt.

"Next time you start down an alley after a man, you stop and think about it."

I heard the saloon door close. Boyd's eyes flickered. He started to speak, then shut up. The man was John Tuthill.

"Here!" His voice had authority. "What's going on?"

"Man shaving a mustache," I said. "He decided he'd rather shave it than otherwise." Turning my eyes momentarily, I said, "How about you? You want to shave, Mr. Tuthill?"

His face turned pink as a baby's, then he said, "If that man did something unlawful, have him arrested."

"You'd send a man to *prison?*" Seemed like I was mighty upset. "That's awful! You'd imprison a fellowman?"

Nobody around seemed likely to side him and he shut up, but he didn't like it. Seemed likely he was the man who set Boyd to following me, but I had no proof.

Boyd was making rough work of the shaving, hacking away at it, and in places his lip was raw. "When he gets through," I said, "he's leaving town. If he ever finds himself in another town where I am, he'll ride out of that one too."

By sun-up the story was all over town, or so I heard—I wasn't there. I was on my way back to Mora, riding with Tyrel and Cap.

Orrin followed us by several hours, and when he came into the yard in the buckboard Cap was watching me arrange my gear in bundles.

"If you're a man who likes company," Cap said, "I'm a man to ride the hills. I'm getting cabin fever."

"Pleased," I said. "Pleased to have you."

Orrin got down from the buckboard and walked over. "By the way, Tell. There was a man in Las Vegas inquiring for you. Said his name was Bigelow."

# Chapter 5

We started up Coyote Creek in the late hours of night, with the stars hanging their bright lanterns over the mountains. Cap was riding point, our six pack horses trailing him, and me riding drag. A chill wind came down off the Sangre de Cristos, and somewhere out over the bottom a quail was calling.

Cap had a sour, dry-mouthed look to him. He was the kind if you got in trouble you didn't look to see if he was still with you—you knew damned well he was.

Not wishing to be seen leaving, we avoided Mora, and unless somebody was lying atop that rocky ridge near the ranch it was unlikely that we were seen.

The Mora River flowed through a narrow gap at the ranch and out into the flatlands beyond, and we had only to follow the Mora until it was joined by Coyote Creek, then turned up Coyote and across the wide valley of La Cueva.

We circled around the sleeping village of Golondrinos, and pointed north, shivering in the morning cold. The sky was stark and clear, the ridges sharply cut against the faintly lightening sky. Grass swished about our horses' hoofs, our saddles creaked, and over at Golondrinos a dog barked inquiringly into the morning.

Cap Rountree hunched his shoulders in his wore-out homespun coat and never once looked back to see if we were coming along. He did his part and expected others to do theirs.

I had a lot to think about, and there's no better time for thinking than a day in the saddle. There'd been many changes in life for Orrin and Tyrel and Ma, and my mind was full of them.

I had rolled out of my soogan at three o'clock that morning. It was cold, believe me. Any time you think summer is an always warm time, you try a high country in the Southwest with mountains close by.

After rolling my bed for travel, I went down to the corral, shook out a loop, and caught up the horses. They were frosty and wild-eyed and suspected my notions, liking their corral.

Before there was a light in the house I had those horses out and tied to the corral with their pack saddles on them. Then I stepped into the leather on my appaloosa to top him off and get the kinks out of him. By the time I had him stopped pitching and bucking, Cap was around.

The door opened, throwing a rectangle of light into the yard. It was Drusilla, Tyrel's wife. "Come and get it," she said, and I never heard a prettier sound.

Cap and me, we came in out of the dark, our guns belted on, and wearing jackets. We hung our hats on pegs and rinsed our hands off in the wash basin. Cap had a face on that would sour milk.

Tyrel was at table, fresh-shaved and looking fit as a man could. How he found the time, I didn't know, but sizing him up, I decided it was mighty becoming in a man to be fresh-shaved at breakfast. Seemed like if I was going to fit myself for living with a woman I'd have to tone up my manners.

Women-folks were something I'd seen little of, and having them around was unsettling, sort of. But I could see the advantages. It's a comforting thing to hear a woman about tinkling dishes, and stepping light, and looking pretty.

Ma was up, too. She was no youngster any more, and some crippled by rheumatism, but Ma would never be abed when one of us boys was taking off. The room was warm from the fire and there was a fine smell of bacon frying and coffee steaming. Drusilla had been raised right. She had a mug of steaming coffee before Cap and me as soon as we set down to table.

Drusilla looked slim and pretty as a three-month-old fawn, her eyes big and dark and warm. That Tyrel was a lucky man.

Cap was a good eater and he leaned into his food. I ate seven eggs, nine strips of bacon and six hot-cakes, and drank five cups of coffee. Tyrel watched me, no smile on his face. Then he looked over at Dru. "I'd sooner buy his clothes than feed him," he said.

Finally I got up and took up my Winchester. At the door I stopped and looked at Ma, then around the room. It was warm, comfortable, friendly. It was home. Ma'd never had much until now, and what she had now wasn't riches, but it was better than ever before, and she was happy. The boys had done well by her, and well by themselves.

Me? The least I could do was try to make something of myself. The eldest-born, the last to amount to anything, if ever.

Tyrel came outside when I stepped into the saddle and handed me up that copy of Blackstone he'd seen me looking at. "Give it study, Tell," he said. "It's the law we live by, and a lot of men did a lot of thinking for a lot of years to make it so."

I'd never owned a book before, or had the loan of one, but it was a friendly feeling, knowing it was there in my saddlebag, waiting to give me its message over a lot of campfires to come.

The proper route to the country where we were headed was up the old Spanish Trail, but Cap suggested we head north for San Luis and old Fort Massachusetts, to avoid anybody who might be laying for us. We made camp that night in the pines a half-mile back from Black Lake.

Earlier, we had ridden through the village of Guadalupita without stopping. In a country where folks are few they make up for it with curiosity. News is a scarce thing in the far hills. Two men riding north with six pack horses were bound to cause comment.

It was a quiet night, and we weren't to see too many of that kind for a long, long time.

Coyotes talked inquiringly to the moon and cocked their ears for the echo of their own voices. Somewhere up the slope an old grizzly poked around in the brush, but he paid us no mind, muttering to himself like a grouchy old man.

About the time coffee water was on, Cap opened up and started to talk. He had his pipe going and I had some steaks broiling.

"Coolest man I ever saw in a difficulty is your brother Tyrel. Only time he had me worried was when he faced up to Tom Sunday.

"You've heard tell of Sunday? He was our friend. As good a man as ever stretched a buffalo hide, but when Orrin commenced getting the things Tom Sunday figured should come to him, trouble showed its hand.

"Sunday was a big, handsome, laughing man, a man of education and background, but hell on wheels in any kind of a fight. Only when Orrin edged him out on things, though Orrin wanted to share everything, or even step aside for him, Tom turned mean and Tye had to get tough with him."

"Tye's a good man with a gun."

"Shooting's the least of it," Cap said irritably. "Any man can shoot a gun, and with practice he can draw fast and shoot accurately, but that makes no difference. What counts is how you stand up when somebody is shooting back at you."

I hadn't heard Cap talk much before but Tyrel was one of his few enthusiasms, and I could see why.

Gold is a hard-kept secret.

The good, the bad, the strong, and the weak all flock to the kind of warmth that gold gives off.

Come daylight we moved out, and soon we had Angel Fire Mountain abreast of us, with Old Taos Pass cutting into the hills ahead and on our left. Cap was troubled in his mind about our back trail, and he was giving it attention.

Wind was talking in the pines along the long slopes when we rode into the high valley called Eagle Nest. The trail to Cimarron cut off into the mountains east of us, so I broke away from the pack train and scouted the ground where the trail came out into the valley. Several lone riders and at least one party had headed north toward Elizabethtown.

We hauled rein and contemplated. We could follow Moreno Creek right into town, or we could cut around a mountain by following Comanche Creek, but it would be better to seem unconcerned and to ride right on into town and stop for a meal, giving out that we were bound up the trail for Idaho where I had a claim.

Elizabethtown was still a supply point for a few prospectors working the hills, and a rough crowd, left over from the Land Grant fighting, hung out there. We turned our stock into an abandoned corral and paid a Mexican to look after them and our outfits.

As we walked toward the nearest bar Cap told me that eight or ten men had been killed in there, and I could see why. There was twenty feet of bar in forty feet of room. The range was so short that a man could scarcely miss.

"The grub's good," Cap said. "They've got a cook who used to be chef in a big hotel back east—until he killed a man and had to light out."

The men at the bar were a rugged lot, which meant nothing, for good men can look as rough as bad men, and often do.

"The one with the General Grant beard," Cap commented, "that's Ben Hobes . . . he's on the wanted list in Texas."

The bartender came over. "What's it for you?" He glanced at Cap Rountree. "Ain't seen you in a while."

"And you won't," Cap said, "not unless you come to Idaho. We got us a claim. . . . Who's that white-headed kid at the bar with Ben?"

The bartender shrugged. "Drifter . . . figures he should be considered a bad man. I ain't seen any graveyards yet."

"You got some of those oysters? Fix me up a stew."

"Same for me," I said, "only twice as much, and a chunk of beef, if you've got it."

"Cookie's got a roast on—best you ever ate."

The bartender walked away, and Cap said, "Sam's all right. He's neutral, the way he should be. Wants no trouble."

The white-headed kid that Cap had asked about leaned his elbows on the bar, hooking a heel over the brass rail. He was wearing two guns, tied down. He had a long, thin face, his eyes were close-set, and there was a twist to his mouth.

He said something to Ben Hobes, and the older man said, "Forget it."
Cap looked at me, his eyes grim.

After a few minutes the bartender came in with the grub and we
started to eat. Cap was right. This man could sure put the groceries together.

"He can cook, all right," I said to Cap. "How'd he kill that man?"

"Poisoned him," Cap said, and grinned at me.

# Chapter 6

We were hungry. Nobody savors his own cooking too much, and in the months to come we figured to have too much of ours, so we enjoyed that meal. Whatever else the cook was, he understood food.

All the time there was talk at the bar. Folks who live quiet in well-ordered communities probably never face up to such a situation. It was a time of free-moving, independent men, each jealous of his own pride, and touchy on points that everybody is touchy about.

And there are always those who want to be thought big men, who want to walk with great strides across the world, be pointed out, and looked up to. Trouble is, they all don't have what it takes to be like that.

Up there at the bar was this white-headed youngster they were calling Kid Newton, feeling his oats and wanting to stack up against somebody. Cap could see it just as I could; and Ben Hobes, who stood up there beside him, was made nervous by it.

Ben Hobes was a hard man. Nobody needed to point that out, but a man should be wary of the company he keeps, because a trouble-hunter can get you into a bind you'd never get into by yourself. And that Kid Newton was hunting a handle for trouble. He wanted it, and wanted it bad, feeling if he could kill somebody folks would look up to him. And we were strangers.

The thing wrong with strangers, you never know who they are. Cap now, he was a thin old man, and to Newton he might look like somebody to ride over, instead of an old buffalo hunter and Indian fighter who'd seen a hundred youngsters like Kid Newton get taken down.

Me, I'm so tall and thin for my height (Ma says I should put on thirty pounds) that he might figure me as nothing to worry about.

Trouble was the last thing I wanted. Back in Uvalde I'd killed Bigelow in a showdown I couldn't get out of any other way—unless I wanted to die. That was likely to give me all the difficulty I'd want.

Newton was looking at Cap. He grinned, and I heard Hobes say again, "Forget it."

"Aw, what's the matter?" I heard the Kid say, "I'm just gonna have some fun." Ben whispered to him, but the Kid paid him no mind.

"Hey, old man! Ain't you kind of old to be traipsin' over the country?"

Cap didn't even look up, although the lines in his face deepened a little. I reached down real slow and taken my pistol out and laid it on the table. I mean I taken one pistol out. I was wearing another in my waistband.

When I put that pistol on the table beside my plate, the Kid looked over at me, and so did Ben Hobes. He threw me a sharp look, and kind of half squared around toward us. Me, I didn't say anything or look around. I just kept eating.

The Kid looked at the gun and he looked at me. "What's that for?"

Surprised-like, I looked up. "What's what for?"

"The gun."

"Oh? *That?* That's for killing varmints, snakes, coyotes, and such-like. Sometimes frogs."

"You aimin' that at me?" He was really asking for it.

"Why, now. Why would I do a thing like that? A nice boy like you." He was young enough to get mad at being called a boy, but he couldn't make up his mind whether I was makin' fun, or what.

"I'll bet you got a home somewheres, and a mother." I looked at him thoughtfully. "Why, sure! I see no reason . . . *exactly*, why you shouldn't have a mother like anybody else."

Taking a big bite of bread, I chewed it for a minute while he was thinking of something to say. I waited until he was ready to say it and then said, "You had your supper, son? Why don't you set down here with us and have a bite? And when you go out of a night you should bundle up more. A body could catch his death of cold."

He was mad now, but ashamed, too. Everybody was starting to smile a little. He dearly wanted a fight, but it's pretty hard to draw a gun on a man who's worried about your welfare.

"Here . . ." I pushed back a chair. "Come and set down. No doubt you've been long from home, and your mama is worried about you. Maybe you feel troubled in your mind, so you just set up and tell us about it. After you've had something to eat, you'll feel better."

Whatever he had fixed to say didn't fit any more, and he groped for words and finally said, "I'm not hungry."

"Don't be bashful, son. We've got a-plenty. Cap here . . . he has youngsters like you . . . he must have, he's been gallopin' around over the country so much. He must have left some like you somewhere."

Somebody laughed out loud, and the Kid stiffened up. "What do you mean by that?" His voice shrilled a little, and that made him still madder. "Damn you—"

"Bartender," I said, "why don't you fix this boy a little warm broth? Something that will rest easy on his stomach?"

Pushing back my chair, I got up and holstered my gun. Cap got up, too, and I handed the bartender the money, then added an extra quarter. "This is for the broth. Make it hot, now."

Turning around, I looked at the Kid mildly and held out my hand. "Good-bye, son. Walk in the ways of righteousness, and don't forget your mother's teaching."

Almost automatically he took my hand, then jerked his back like it was bee-stung.

Cap had started toward the door, and I followed him. At the door I turned and looked back at the Kid again. I've got big eyes and they are serious most times. This time I tried to make them especially serious. "But really, son, you should bundle up more."

Then I stepped outside and we walked back to our outfit. I said to Cap, "You tired?"

"No," he said, "and a few miles will do us no harm."

We rode out. Couple of times I caught Cap sizing me up, like, but he said nothing at all. Not for several miles, anyway, then he asked, "You realize you called that boy a bastard?"

"Well, now. That's strong language, Cap, and I never use strong language."

"You talked him out of it. You made him look the fool."

"A soft answer turneth away wrath," I said. "Or that's what the Good Book says."

We rode on for a couple of long hours and then camped in the woods on Comanche Creek, bedding down for a good rest.

We slept past daylight and took our time when we did get up, so we could watch our trail and see if anybody was behind us.

About an hour past daylight we saw a half-dozen riders going north. If they were following us, they did not see our tracks. We had made our turn in the creek bottom, and by this time any tracks left there had washed away.

It was on to midday before we started out, and we held close to the east side of the valley where we could lose our shape against the background of trees, rocks, and brush. We were over nine thousand feet up, and here the air was cool by day and right cold by night.

We cut across the sign of those riders and took the trail along Costilla Creek, and up through the canyon. At Costilla Creek the riders had turned right on the most obvious trail, but Cap said there was an old Indian trail up Costilla, and we took it.

We rode into San Luis late in the afternoon. It was a pleasant little town where the folks were all of Spanish descent. We corralled our stock, hiring a man to watch over our gear again. Then we walked over to Salazar's store. Folks all over this part of the country came there for supplies and news. A family named Gallegos had founded that store many years back, and later this Salazar took it over.

These were friendly, peaceful folks. They had settled in here years before, and were making a good thing of it. We were buying a few things when all of a sudden a woman's voice said, "Señor?"

We turned around; she was speaking to Cap. Soon as he saw her, he said, "Buenos dias, Tina. It has been a long time."

He turned to me. "Tina, this is Tell Sackett, Tyrel's brother."

She was a pretty little woman with great big eyes. "How do you do, Señor? I owe your brother much thanks. He helped me when I had need."

"He's a good man."

"Si . . . he is."

We talked a mite, and then a slender whip of a Mexican with high cheek bones and very black eyes came in. He was not tall, and he wouldn't have weighed any more than Cap, but it took only a glance to see he was mucho hombre.

"It is my hoosband, Esteban Mendoza." She spoke quickly to him in Spanish, explaining who we were. His eyes warmed and he held out his hand.

We had dinner that night with Tina and Esteban, a quiet dinner, in a little adobe house with a string of red peppers hanging on the porch. Inside there was a black-eyed baby with round cheeks and a quick smile.

Esteban was a *vaquero,* or had been. He had also driven a freight team over the road to Del Norte.

"Be careful," he warned. "There is much trouble in the San Juans and Uncomphagre. Clint Stockton is there, with his outlaws."

"Any drifters riding through?" Cap asked.

Esteban glanced at him shrewdly. "Si. Six men were here last night. One was a square man with a beard. Another"—Esteban permitted himself a slight smile, revealing beautiful teeth and a sly amusement—"another had two pistols."

"Six, you said?"

"There were six. Two of them were larger than you, Señor Tell, very broad, powerful. Big blond men with small eyes and big jaws. One of them, I think, was the leader."

"Know them?" Cap asked me.

"No, Cap, I don't." Yet even as I said it, I began to wonder. What did the Bigelows look like?

I asked Esteban, "Did you hear any names?"

"No, Señor. They talked very little. Only to ask about travelers."

They must know that either we were behind them, or had taken another trail. Why were they following us, if they were?

The way west after leaving Del Norte lay through the mountains, over Wolf Creek Pass. This was a high, narrow, twisting pass that was most difficult to travel, a very bad place to run into trouble.

It was a pleasant evening, and it did me good to see the nice home the Mendozas had here, the baby, and their pleasure in being together. But the thought of those six men and why they were riding after us worried me, and I could see Cap had it in mind.

We saddled up and got moving. During the ride west Cap Rountree, who had lived among Indians for years, told me more about them than I'd ever expected to know. This was Ute country, though the Comanches had intruded into some of it. A warlike tribe, they had been pushed out of the Black Hills by the Sioux and had come south, tying up with the still more warlike and bloody Kiowa. Cap said that the Kiowa had killed more whites than any other tribe.

At first the Utes and the Comanches, both of Shoshone ancestry, had got along all right. Later they split and were often at war. Before the white man came the Indians were continually at war with one another, except for the Iroquois in the East, who conquered an area bigger than the Roman empire and then made a peace that lasted more than a hundred years.

Cap and I rode through some of the wildest and most beautiful country under the sun, following the Rio Grande up higher and still higher into the mountains. It was hard to believe this was the same river along which I'd fought Comanches and outlaws in Texas—that we camped of a night beside water that would run into the Gulf one day.

Night after night our smoke lifted to the stars from country where we found no tracks. Still, cold, and aloof, the snow-capped peaks lifted above us. Cap, he was a changed man, gentler, somehow, and of a night he talked like he'd never done down below. And sometimes I opened up my Blackstone and read, smelling the smoke of aspen and cedar, smelling the pines, feeling the cold wind off the high snow.

It was like that until we came down Bear Creek into the canyon of the Vallecitos.

West of us rose up the high peaks of the Grenadier and Needle Mountains of the San Juan range. We pulled up by a stream that ran cold and swift from the mountains. Looking up at the peaks I wondered again: what was it up there that got the meat I left handing in that tree?

Cap, he taken a pan and went down to the creek. In the late evening he washed it out and came back to the fire.

There were flecks of gold in the pan . . . we'd found color. Here we would stake our claim.

# Chapter 7

We forted up for trouble.

Men most likely had been following us. Sooner or later they would find us, and we could not be sure of their intentions. Moreover, the temper of the Utes was never too certain a thing.

Riding up there, I'd had time for thinking. Where gold was found, men would come.

There would be trouble—we expected that—but there would be business too. The more I thought, the more it seemed to me that the man who had something to sell would be better off than a man who searched for gold.

We had made camp alongside a spring not far from the plunging stream that came down the mountainside and emptied into the Vallecitos. I was sure this was the stream I had followed into the high valley where my gold was. Our camp was on a long bench above the Vallecitos, with the mountainside rising steeply behind it and to the east. We were in a clump of scattered ponderosa pine and Douglas fir.

First, we shook out our loops and snaked some deadfall logs into spaces between the trees. Next we made a corral by cutting some lodgepole pine —the lodgepole pine grew mostly, it seemed, in areas that had been burned over—and laying the ends of the poles in tree forks or lashing them to trees with rawhide. It was hard work, but we both knew what needed to be done and there was little talk and no waste effort.

Short of sundown I walked out of the trees and along the bench. Looking north, we faced the widest spot we had so far seen in the canyon of the Vallecitos. It was a good mile north of our camp.

"That's where we'll build the town," I told Cap.

He took his pipe out of his mouth. "Town?"

"Where there's gold, there'll be folks. Where folks are, there's wanting. I figure we can set up store and supply those wants. Whether they find gold or not, they will be eating and needing tools, powder, blankets—all that sort of thing. It seems to be the surest way, Cap, if a man wants to make him a living. Gold is found and is mined, but the miners eat."

"You won't find me tending store," Cap said.

"Me, neither. But we'll lay out the town site, you and me. We'll stake the lots, and we'll watch for a good man. Believe me, he'll come along. Then we'll set him up in business."

"You Sacketts," Cap said, "sure play hell once you get out of the mountains. Only thing puzzles me is, what kept you there so long?"

The next few days we worked sunrise to sundown. We paced off a street maybe four hundred yards long, we laid out lots, and planned the town. We figured on a general store, a livery stable, a hotel and boarding house, and two saloons. We spotted a place for a blacksmith shop, and for an assayer.

We cut logs and dragged some of them down to the site for the store, and we put up signs indicating that any folks who came along were to see us about the lots.

Meantime, we worked a little on the claim—rarely more than a pan or two a day because we had much else to do. But we found color—not a lot, but some.

We also improved our fort. Not that it looked much like one, and we didn't want it to, but we were set up to fight off an attack if it came.

Neither one of us had much trust in the peaceful qualities of our fellowmen. Seems to me most of the folks doing all the talk about peace and giving the other fellow the benefit of the doubt were folks setting back to home in cushy chairs with plenty of grub around and the police nearby to protect them. Back there, men would set down safe of an evening and write about how cruel the poor Indian was being treated out west. They never come upon the body of a friend who had been staked out on an ant hill or had a fire built on his stomach, nor had they stood off a charge of Indians.

Personally, I found Indians people to respect. Their ways weren't our ways, and a lot of virtues they were given credit for by white men were only ideas in a white man's head, and no Indian would have considered them virtues. Mercy rarely had any part in the make-up of an Indian.

Folks talk about human nature, but what they mean is not human nature, but the way they are brought up. It seems to me that folks who are brought up to Christian ways of thought don't believe in the taking of life, but the Indian had no such conception. If you were a stranger you were an enemy. If you gave him gifts it was usually because you were afraid of him . . . or that's how he thought.

Indians were fighting men. Fighting was their greatest sport and occupation. Our people look up to athletes of one kind or another, but the Indian saved all his respect for fighting men. And an Indian would count the scalp of a woman or a child as well as a man's.

This was wrong to our way of thinking, but his thinking was altogether different.

The Indian, before the white man took up the West, was physically cleaner than the white man. He bathed often, and it wasn't until white man's liquor and poverty caught up with him that he lost the old ways. But the Indian warrior would have been ashamed of all the milk-sop talk about the poor Indian. He was strong, he was proud, and he was able to handle his own problems.

It was Sunday before trouble showed. Sunday was a quiet time for us. Cap was busy scraping and tanning some elk and deer hides, and after cleaning my weapons and catching a bait of trout, I settled down to study Blackstone.

It was a warm, lazy day, with sunlight sparkling on the creek waters, and scarce a breeze stirring the pines overhead. Time to time my thoughts would drift from my study to that high valley. If I wanted to go up and get some of that gold I would have to find another way into that valley before snow fell and closed it off.

"Tell . . ."

Cap spoke softly, and I got up and walked over to him. He was looking off through the trees, and we could see four riders over by the town site. They turned toward us, and I got out my field glasses. There was nothing familiar about any of them. While I watched they started in our direction, and the last man in line checked his pistol.

Down the bench, maybe fifty yards or so, they slowed to a stop, seeing the corral with the horses in it, and the smoke from our fire. Then they came on up.

Me, I was wearing an old U.S. Army hat, a wore-out blue army shirt and jeans, and I had me a belt gun on. When I sighted them coming I taken up my Winchester, and Cap and me stood out to greet them.

"'Light," I said. "Ain't often we have visitors."

"Looks of that town site, you must be expectin' plenty," one of them said. "What would a man want with a town here?"

"Well, sir," I said, "we took a notion. Cap Rountree an' me, we like to go to town of an evening when the chores are done. There ain't no town close up, so we decided to build our own. We laid her out and started cuttin' timber. Then we held an election."

"An *election?*"

"Town ought to have a mayor. We elected Cap by acclamation. Cap never has been a mayor before, and the town never had one. We figured they could start off together."

While I was talking, I was looking them over. One was riding a horse branded with a pitchfork over a bar. The owner used to call it the Pitch-fork Bar, but folks who knew the ways of the outfit called it the Fork Over, because that was what you had to do if you crossed their range. The man on this horse was a big man with a wide face and thick, blond hair. He kept staring at me, and at what remained of my uniform.

There was a stoop-shouldered man with narrow black eyes, and a square-set one with an open, friendly face, and a fat man with a round face—round and mighty hard.

"You must be proud of that uniform," the big one said. "The war's been over a long time."

"Ain't had money enough to shed it," I said.

The fat man walked his horse toward the creek, then called back, "Kitch, lookit here!"

They all rode over, and Cap and me followed.

Kitch looked over our shaft, which was only down a few feet. "Gold?" He was amazed. "This here's silver country."

"Spot of color," I said. "Nothing much yet, but we've got hopes."

The fat man paid us no mind. "Kitch," he said, "they've got a good thing here. That's why they've laid out the town. Once folks hear of a strike, they'll come running, and that town will be a gold mine itself."

"Only there hasn't been any strike," Cap said. "We're scarcely making wages."

He turned and walked off, saying, "I'll put some coffee on, Tell."

At the name, Kitch turned sharply around and looked at me. "Tell? Are you Tell Sackett?"

"Uh-huh."

He chuckled. "Mister, you're going to have company. Seen a couple of men in Silverton who were hunting you."

"I'll be here."

"They tell me you can sure run." Kitch had a mean look to his eyes. "I seen many a-running with that uniform on."

"All the way to Lee's surrender," I said. "We stopped running then."

He started to say something and his face hardened up and he commenced getting red around the gills.

"The Bigelows say every time you get stopped somewhere they come along and you take out like a scared rabbit. "

*Tell Sackett,* I told myself, *this man aims to get you into a fight. Have no part of it.* "Any man who wants to kill me," I said, "can do it on his own time. I got too many things to do to waste time."

Cap was back behind the logs near the fire, and I knew what he would be doing back there.

"Now I tell you what you do," I said. "You go back to Silverton and you tell the Bigelow boys I'm here. You tell them their brother tried dealing off the bottom with the wrong man, and if they're of a mind to, they can find me here. This is as far as I'm going."

I added, more quietly, "And, Kitch, you said something about running. You come back with them. I'll be right here."

Kitch was startled, then angry. But the fat man spoke up. "Let's get out of here."

They started off. Only the square-built man lingered. "Mr. Sackett, I'd like to come back and talk to you, if I may."

"Any time," I said, and he rode off.

We worked our claim, got out some gold, and built a rocker. Meanwhile I cut a hidden trail up the steep mountainside behind our camp. About two hundred feet above, covering the bench, I built a rifle-pit, of brush, dead-falls, and rocks—a shelter where two or three men could cover all approaches to our camp.

The following day, switching back and forth to make it an easier climb, I opened a way further up the ridge.

"What's the idea?" Cap asked me, come nightfall.

"If I have to start running," I said, "I don't want anything in the way. I've got big feet."

Over the fire that night, Cap looked at me.

"When you going back up on that mountain?"

"And leave you with trouble shaping up?"

"Forget it. Trouble is no stranger to me. You go ahead, only don't be gone too long."

I told him I didn't know exactly how to get up there from where we were. We were close, that much I knew.

Cap said the way I came before, judging from my description, had brought me over Columbine Pass and up to the Vallecitos along Johnson Creek. That was south of us, so if I rode south I might recognize something or come on one of the markers.

The idea of leaving Cap alone worried me. Sure, he was an old wolf, but I had many enemies around, what with the Bigelows, Ben Hobes, and that white-haired kid with the two guns. To say nothing of Tuthill, back in Las Vegas, and his gambler friend. Trouble just naturally seemed to latch onto me and hang on with all its teeth.

On the other hand, Cap had plenty of ca'tridges, he had meat, and there was a spring. Unless they caught him away from camp he could stand off a good-sized force, and we were not expecting anything of the kind.

From worrying about Cap, I turned to thinking back to home, and

Tyrel and Dru. It was a fine thing for a man to have a woman love him like that, a fine thing. But who would I ever find? It was complete and total unlikely that any female woman in her right mind would fall into love with the likes of me. It was likely all I'd ever have would be a horse and maybe a dog.

Lying there, I could smell the smoke of the dying fire, see the stars through the tops of the pines, and hear the wind along the ranges. The moon came up and, off to the west, I could see the towering, snow-capped peaks of the Needle Mountains.

Suddenly I sat up. "Cap!" I whispered. "You hear that?"

"I hear it."

"Sounds like somebody crying." I got up and pulled on my boots. The sound had died away, but it seemed to have come from somewhere upwind of us.

We walked to the edge of the trees and listened, but we heard it no more. Putting my hands to my mouth, I called, not too loud. "Come on into camp! No use to be out there alone!"

"How do you know it's alone?" Cap asked mildly. "Come on back to sleep. You believe in ha'nts? A trick of the wind, that's all."

I heard no further sound, so I followed Cap and turned in. And, although I lay awake for what seemed like long hours, I heard nothing more.

Maybe it was, like Cap suggested, a trick of the wind. But I didn't believe it.

# Chapter 8

Nor was it a trick of the wind. Somewhere in those mountains I knew there was something . . . or somebody. . . .

When daylight came I was high in the hills. There was no trail where I rode. To the south there was, but I had switched off. I rode up into the trees, then got down from my horse and switched to moccasins. I went back over my tracks and smoothed them out. Then I mounted up again and headed higher.

Pines grew thick, giving way to spruce. Sometimes I was weaving among trees so close there was scarce room to pass, and half the time I was bent down low to get under branches, or was walking on the soft pine needles and leading that appaloosa.

It was in my mind that I would come out on the ridge not far from that first keyhole pass, and it worked out that way. I found myself on a crest where I could see far and away in all directions.

To the north a huge peak called Storm King shouldered against the bright sky, with sunlight on the snow. The canyon of the Vallecitos, through which I'd climbed, fell away steeply below me, and on my right I could look for miles over some of the most rugged country I ever saw.

I rode into the high valley where that ghost lake was. It looked unchanged until I got near it. My old trail was partly covered over by water. There had been rains since my last trip, and the lake was acres larger despite the run-off.

The trail down the chute was about the same. Maybe there was a mite more water over the trail, but not enough to interfere. Riding into my lonely valley, I felt like I was coming home.

First off, I checked the tree where I had left the meat hanging. The meat was gone, but there were no bones about, as there would have been if a wild animal had pulled it down. If there had been any tracks the rain had beat them out.

Next I went on to the mine, and scouted around. I left everything as it was, only I staked a claim, marking down its limits on a piece of tanned hide so's I'd have a map if it came to trouble.

Then I set out to scout that valley, for it was in my mind that there must be an easier way out. And I discovered that the stream flowing down the chute actually flowed *north*. Then it took a sharp bend to the west and flowed down from the mountain to join the Vallecitos. For the first time I realized that the stream beside which Cap and I had camped was not the one that fell down the chute.

A dim trail, maybe left by ancient Indians, headed off to the east, and far off I could see several other high lakes. And, riding up through the trees to the ridge top, where I could look the country over, I found that across the valley and beyond a ridge was still another long, high valley. Through it a stream flowed almost due north.

Among the trees that lined the ridges which bordered these valleys there was some grass, but in the valley bottoms there were meadows, rich and green. Remembering the short-grass range country of Texas and the high plains, I thought what magnificent summer range these high valleys would make.

But my concern now was to find a new trail down to the Vallecitos and, if possible, to learn who lived up here and had taken my meat.

Riding north, I looked along the ridge toward the end. The valley seemed to be completely enclosed but, farther on, I discovered that it took a sharp turn, narrowed, and came to an end in a wall of forest.

It was there, under the trees, that I found a fresh footprint.

Dismounting, I followed the faint tracks. Here and there grass was still pressed down, so the trail must have been made while the dew was on it, early that very morning. Suddenly I found a snare. Here there were several footprints, but no blood and no hair, so evidently the snare had caught nothing. Squatting on my heels, I studied it. Cunningly done, it resembled no Indian snare I had seen.

I walked my horse across the high meadow that lay beyond the curtain of trees. The ground was nigh covered by alpine gold-flower, bright yellow, and almighty pretty to look at. And along some of the trickles running down from the melting snow a kind of primrose was growing.

The trees were mostly blue spruce, shading off into aspen and, on the high ridges above timberline, there were a few squat bristle-cone pines, gnarled from their endless war with the wind.

A couple of times I found where whoever it was I was trailing had stopped to pick some kind of herb out of the grass, or to drink at a stream.

All of a sudden I came to a place where the tracks stopped. Here the person had climbed a big rock, and grass stains had rubbed off the moccasins onto the rock. The meaning was plain enough. He, she, it, or whatever, had caught sight of me trailing it.

From atop the boulder I sighted back down the way I had come and, sure enough, my back trail could be seen at a dozen points in the last few miles.

So I sat down on the rock and took time to study the country. Unless I was mistaken, that party was somewhere not too far off, a-looking me over. What I wished was for them to see I meant no harm.

After a while, I went back to my horse, which had been feeding on the good meadow grass. I rode across a trickle of water and up a long gouge in the mountainside until I topped out where there was nothing but a few bristle-cone pines, a kind of gray gravel, and some scattered, lightning-struck trees.

Off to my right, and some distance ahead, I could see a stream running down the mountain to the northeast. It looked like here was another way out of this jumble of ridges and mountain meadows.

Starting the appaloosa ahead, I saw his ears come up. Following his look, I saw a movement, far off, at the edge of a clump of aspen on a slope. But before I could get out my glasses, whatever it was had gone.

Riding on, I came to a place where somebody had been kneeling beside a snow-stream, evidently for a drink. If my guessing was right that was the third drink in the last couple of hours. Possibly it was less time than that . . . and in this high country, with moisture in the air, it seemed too much drinking. Nor was the weather that warm.

Puzzled, I started on again. All of a sudden the tracks weren't hard to follow. Whoever it was had headed straight for some place, and was too busy getting there to think of covering trail . . . or else I was believed to be lost down below somewhere.

A moment later I saw where the person I followed had fallen down, then got up, and gone on.

Sick . . . that drinking could mean fever.

Sick and, unless I missed my guess, all alone.

The tracks disappeared. It took me several minutes of circling and scouting to find the likely spot. From here on it was judgment more than tracks, for the person had taken to rock, and there was a-plenty of it.

The appaloosa made work of scrambling over that rock, so I got down and walked.

It was coming up to night, and there was no way I knew of to get down off the mountain at night.

Time to time I stopped, trying the air for smoke or sound, but there was none.

Whatever I was hunting had taken off in a wild area of boulders and lightning-struck trees, where the gray ridges had been lashed and whipped by storm.

Off on the horizon I could see great black thunderheads piling up, and

I knew this place would be hell during an electrical storm. Somehow I had to get down from there, and fast. Time or two before, I'd been caught in high peaks by a storm, although never so high as this. I'd seen lightning leaping from peak to peak, and sometimes in sheets of blue flame.

The boulders were a maze. Great slabs of rock stood on knife edges, looking like rows of broken molars, split and rotten. Without warning, a canyon dropped away in front of me for maybe five hundred feet of almost sheer fall. Off to the left I could see an eyebrow of trail.

Anywhere off that bald granite ridge would look like heaven to me, and I hurried to the trail. Once I heard rocks fall behind my horse, but we kept going down, with me walking and leading.

When I reached the meadow at the foot of the trail, I looked up. It was like standing on the bottom of a narrow trough with only the dark sky above me.

The trail led out of the meadow, and on it were those same tracks. Hurried by the storm, I followed them.

Thunder rumbled like great bowling balls in an empty hall of rock. Suddenly, an opening appeared in the wall ahead of me and I drew up, calling out.

There was no answer.

Leaving the appaloosa, I shucked my gun. In front of the opening there was a ledge, maybe thirty yards along the face of the cliff, and a dozen yards deep. A body could see folks had lived and worked there for some time. I called out again, and my voice echoed down the canyon.

There was only the fading echo, only the silence, and emptiness. A few large drops of rain fell. I went slowly across to the mouth of the cave.

A sort of wall had been fixed up, closing off part of the opening. It was made of rocks, fitted together without mortar. Stepping around it, I looked inside.

On the wall hung an old bridle. In a corner was a dried-up saddle and a rifle. Dead coals were in a fireplace that had seen much use. Over against the wall was a pallet, and on the pallet a girl was lying.

I struck a match, and got the shock of my life. She was a young girl, a little thing, and she was mighty pretty. A great mass of red-gold hair spilled over the worn blankets and bearskins on which she was lying. She wore a patched-up dress, and moccasins. Her cheeks were flushed red.

I spoke to her, but she made no sound. Bending over, I touched her brow. She was burning up with fever.

And then the storm broke.

It took me only a couple of minutes to rush outside and get my horse. There was an adjoining cave—actually part of the one the girl was in—that had a crude manger. At one time a horse or mule had been kept there.

When I had tied my horse I went back and, taking wood from a stack by the entrance, I kindled a fire and put some water on to heat.

With a fire going I could see better, and I found another blanket to cover her over with. It was plain enough that two folks had been living here, though there was only one now. Likely there had been only one for quite a stretch.

The rifle had been cleaned, but the chamber was empty and there was no ammunition anywhere I looked. There was a flint knife with quite an edge to it—probably the knife used to cut my meat that first time.

Looked to me this girl had been living here quite some time, and by the look of her, not living too well. She was mighty slight, almighty slight.

When that water was boiling I fixed some coffee and, with my own jerked beef, made some broth.

Outside the thunder was rolling something awful and there were lightning flashes almost two or three a minute, seemed like, lighting up that gorge where the cave was. Rain was falling in great sheets, and when the lightning flashed I could see the rocks glistening with it.

Cap was down at our camp by himself, and the country would be filling up with mighty unpleasant folks. I was realizing that after a rain like this nobody could get back up that chute, and unless there was another way out, I was stuck. And me with a sick girl on my hands.

When I had that broth hot, I held the girl in my arms and fed her some of it. She was out of her head, delirious-like. It seemed to me she had got back to the cave with her last strength, but she tasted that broth and liked it.

After a while she went back to sleep.

Back home on the Cumberland we did for ourselves when it came to trouble and sickness, but in a storm like this there was no chance to go out and get any herbs or suchlike. All I could do was keep her from getting chilled and build up her strength with broth.

Might be she only had a cold, and I was praying it wasn't pneumonia or anything like that. She was run down some, and probably hadn't been eating right. What she could get from her snares wouldn't amount to much, and she had no weapons to kill anything larger. What bothered me was how she got into this wild country in the first place.

While she slept I hunted around the cave and found a man's wore-out boots, and a coat hanging on the wall. I taken that down and used it for more cover over her.

Hours later, while the storm was still blowing and lightning jumped peak to peak, crashing like all get-out, she awakened and looked around, and called to somebody whose name I couldn't make out. All I could do was feed her some more of that broth, but she took to it like a baby to mother's milk.

All night long I sat by that fire, keeping it bright in case she awakened and was scared. Toward daylight the storm played itself out and went rumbling away far off down the mountains.

I rigged a line and went down to the creek. The chances of getting fish after the storm didn't look too good, with the water all riled. Nonetheless, I threw out a hook. After a while I hooked a trout and, about a half-hour later, another one.

Up at the cave the red-haired girl was sleeping quietly, so I went to work and cleaned those trout and fried them up. I started some coffee and then went outside.

Wandering around, I came on a grave. Actually, I could see it wasn't a dug grave, but a wide crack in the rock. Rocks had been rolled in at each end and the cracks tamped in with some kind of clay which had settled hard. Over the grave was scratched a name and a date.

### JUAN MORALES
#### 1790–1874

He had died last year, then.

And that meant this girl had been here in this canyon all alone for almost a year. No wonder she was run down.

Juan Morales had been eighty-four years old when he died. Too old a man to be traipsing around the mountains with a young girl. From his name he had been a Spanish man, but she did not look like any Spanish girl I'd ever seen. Yet I'd heard it said that some of them were blonde, so maybe they were red-headed, too.

I went back to the cave and looked at my patient. She was lying there looking at me, and the first thing she said was, "Thank you for the venison."

She had the bluest eyes.

"Ma'am," I said, "I'm William Tell Sackett, Tell for short, and leaving the meat was little enough to do."

"I'm Ange Kerry," she said, "and I'm most glad you found me."

Only thing I couldn't figure out was how a girl that pretty ever got lost.

# Chapter 9

Ange had gone to sleep again so, after adding sticks to the fire, I went out and sat down in the mouth of the cave. It was the first good chance I'd had to look around me.

The valley where I found the gold was lonely but peaceful . . . this was wild. Sheer black cliffs surrounded it on nearly all sides, broken here and there as though cracked by some thunderous upheaval of the mountain. The foot of each crack ended in a slope of talus, with broken, barkless tree trunks, their branches thrown wide and white against the rock like skeleton arms.

The stream descended through the valley in a series of ripples and miniature cascades, gathering here and there in a pool, only to go tumbling off down into the wild gorge that seemed to end in space.

The trees that rimmed the canyon were dwarfed and twisted, leaning away from prevailing winds, trees that the years gave no stature, only girth and a more tenacious grip on the rock from which they grew.

Landslides had carried away stands of aspen and dumped them among the tumbled boulders along the bottom. Slabs and crags of rock had broken off from the cliff faces and lay cracked and riven upon the canyon floor. There was scarcely a stretch of level land anywhere, only here and there an arctic meadow or stretch of tundra. The rocks were colored with lichen—green, orange, reddish, black, or gray—crusting the rocks, forever working at them to create from their granite flanks the soil that would build other growth.

The matlike jungles of arctic willow hedged the stream in places, and streaks of snow and ice lay along cracks where the sun could not reach.

About an hour short of noon the sun came over the mountain and warmed the cave mouth. New streams melted from the snow banks, and I watched several mountain sheep go down a narrow thread of trail. A big old black bear showed on the mountain opposite. Had I shot him it would have taken me all day to get where he was. Anyway, he wasn't bothering me.

Despite the quiet of the place, there was something wild and terrible about it that wouldn't let me settle down. Besides that, I couldn't keep from worrying about Cap.

It was midafternoon when Ange Kerry woke up again, and I went back in and fixed her a cup of coffee.

She looked up at me. "You've no idea how good that tastes. I've had no coffee for a year."

"Thing puzzles me," I said, "is why you came up here in the first place. You came with that Juan Morales?"

"He was my grandfather. He and my grandmother raised me, and when she died he began to worry about dying and leaving me with nothing. Grandfather had an old map that had been in our family for years, telling of gold in the San Juans, so he decided to find it for me. I insisted on coming with him.

"He was very strong, Tell. It seemed nothing was too much for him. But we couldn't follow the map, and we got lost in the mountains. We were short of ammunition. Some of it we lost in a rock slide that injured his shoulder.

"We found this place, and he was sure it was close by—the gold, I mean. He never told me why he believed it, but there was some position in relation to two mountain peaks. One was slightly west of north, the other due west.

"Grandfather must have been hurt worse in the slide than he let me know. He never got better. One of his shoulders was very bad, and he limped after that, and worried about me. He said we must forget the gold and get out as best we could.

"Then he became ill . . . that was when you came into the valley, and when I took some venison from you at night."

"You should have awakened me."

"I—I was afraid."

"Then when you came back and found the venison I left for you . . . you knew I was all right then?"

"I thought—oh, I don't know what I thought! When I came back here after getting that first piece of meat, that was when grandfather died. I told him about you."

"He died then?"

"He told me to go to you, that you would take me out of here, and that most men were good to women."

"When I saw the grave I thought he'd been dead longer than that."

"I wasn't sure of the date. We lost track of time, up here."

She must have had a rough time of it. I thought of that while I went to work and made some more broth, only this time with chunks of meat in it.

"How did you get into this place?"

"We came up a trail from the north—an ancient trail, very steep, or perhaps it was a game trail."

From the north, again. What I wanted was a way down on the west. The way I figured, we couldn't be much more than a mile from Cap right now, but the trouble was that mile was almost straight down.

Ange Kerry was in no shape to leave, and with all the men hunting me that had a figuring to fill me full up with lead, I wasn't planning to go down until I could take Ange along. Suppose I was killed before anybody knew where she was?

Just in case, I told her how things were. "We got us a camp, Cap Rountree and me, down on the Vallecitos, west of here. If something happens to me, you get to him. He'll take you to my folks down to Mora."

Seemed likely that with another few days of rest she might be ready to try coming down off that mountain. Mostly she was starved from eating poorly.

I went out and went across the canyon. There I looked back, taking time to study that cliff. A man might climb that slope of talus and work his way to the top of the cliff through the crack that lay behind it. A man on foot might.

Chances were that right down the other side was camp. Studying it out, I decided to have a try at it. Down by the stream I had seen an outcropping of talc, so I broke off a piece and scratched out *Back Soon* on a slab of rock.

Taking my rifle, I rigged myself a sling from a rawhide strip, and headed for that slope. Climbing the steep talus slope was work, believe me. That rock slid under my feet and every time I took three steps I lost one, but soon I got up to that crack.

Standing there looking up, I was of a mind to quit, though quitting comes hard to me. That crack was like a three-sided chimney, narrow at the bottom, widening toward the top. The slope above the chimney looked like it was just hanging there waiting for a good reason to fall. Yet by holding to the right side a man might make it.

I hung my rifle over my back to have my hands free, and started up that chimney and made it out on the slope. Holding on to catch my breath, I looked down into the canyon.

It made a man catch his breath. I swear, I had no idea I'd climbed so high up. The creek was a thread, the cave mouth looked no bigger than the end of a fingernail, and I was a good two thousand feet above the floor of the valley. My horse, feeding in the meadow where I'd left him on a picket-rope, looked like an ant.

Clinging to the reasonably solid rock along the side of the rock slide, I worked my way to the top, and was wringing wet by the time I got there.

Nothing but sky and cloud above me, and around me bare, smooth granite, with a hollow where there was snow, but nowhere any trees or vegetation. I walked across the top of that ridge, scoured by wind and storm . . . the air was fresher than a body could believe, and a light wind was blowing.

In a few minutes I was looking down into the valley of the Vallecitos. A little way down the forest began, first scattered, stunted trees, then thick stands of timber. Our camp—I could see a thin trail of smoke rising— was down there among them.

From where I stood to the point where camp was, I figured it to be a half-mile, if it was level ground. But the mountain itself was over a mile high, which made the actual distance much greater. Here and there were sheer drops. And there would be no going straight down. One cliff I could see would take a man almost a mile north before he could find a place to get down.

Off where Cap and me had laid out the town site there was a stir of activity. There were several columns of smoke, and it looked like some building going on, but it was too far to make out, even in that clear air.

It was sundown when I got back to the cave, and Ange broke into a smile when I showed up.

"Worried?"

She smiled at me. "No . . . you said you'd come back."

She was looking better already. There was color in her cheeks and she had started to make coffee. Coming back I had killed a big-horn sheep, and we roasted it over the fire, and had us a grand feast. That night we sat talking until the moon came up.

After she went to sleep I sat in the door of the cave and watched the moon chin itself on the mountains, and slowly slide out of sight behind a dark fringe of trees.

At dawn, five days later, we pulled out.

We crossed toward that stream that ran down to the north or northeast and followed the old game trail Ange had mentioned. She showed me where they had lost their pack mule with some of their grub, and then she told me that there was a way which would lead down to our camp, a deer and sheep trail off to the south of the canyon.

With Ange riding and me leading the appaloosa among those rocks and thick forests, it was slow going and it took a long time to get to the bottom. I led the horse on through the trees until I reached a point maybe a half-mile from the town site.

There must have been forty men working around over there, with buildings going up, but I could see no sign of Cap. Somehow the setup didn't look right to me.

I helped Ange down from the horse. "We'll rest," I said. "Come dark, we'll go to our camp. That bunch over there look like trouble." I'd no idea of facing up to a difficulty with a sick girl on my hands.

Dark came on slowly. Finally, thinking of Cap, it wasn't in me to wait longer. I helped Ange back into the saddle, and took my Winchester from the scabbard.

It was a short walk across a meadow and into the willows. Nothing stirred except the nighthawks which dipped and swung in the air above us. Somewhere a wolf howled. The sun was down, but it was not yet dark.

We turned south. Wearing my moccasins, I made little sound in the grass, and the appaloosa not much more. There was a smell of smoke in the air, and a gentle drift of wind off the high peaks.

All I could think of was Cap Rountree. If that crowd at the town site were the wrong bunch—and I had a feeling they were—then Cap was bad hurt or killed. And if he was killed I was going up to that town and read them from the Book. I was going to give that bunch gospel.

The first of the three men who came out of the brush ahead of me was Kitch.

"We been waiting for you, Sackett," he said, and he lifted his gun. He thought sure enough he had me.

Trouble was, he hadn't seen that Winchester alongside my leg. I just tilted it with my right hand, grabbed the barrel with my left, and shot from the hip. While he was swinging that gun up, nonchalant and easy, I shot him through the belly. Without moving from my tracks I fired at the second man, and saw him go spinning.

The third one stood there, white-faced and big-eyed, and I told him, "Mister, you unloose that gun belt. If you want to, you just grab that pistol . . . I'm hoping you do."

He dropped his gun belt and backed off a step.

"Now we're going to talk," I said. "What's your name?"

"Ab Warren . . . I didn't mean no harm." He hesitated. "Mister, Kitch ain't dead . . . can I do for him?"

"He'll get another bullet 'less he lies still," I replied. "You want to help him, you talk. Where's my partner?"

The man shifted his feet. "You better high-tail it. The others'll be down here to see."

"Let 'em come. You going to talk?"

"No, I ain't. By—"

By that time I'd moved in close and I backhanded him across the mouth. It was a fairly careless blow but, like I said, my hands are big and I've worked hard all my life.

He went down, and I reached over and took him by the front of his shirt and lifted him upright.

"You talk or I'll take you apart. I'll jump down your throat and jollop your guts out."

"They ambushed him, but he ain't dead. That ol' coon Injuned away in the brush and downed two before they pulled off. He's back at your camp, but I don't think he's doing so good."

"Is he alone?"

"No . . . Joe Rugger's there with him." Warren paused. "Rugger took up for him."

Kitch was moaning. I walked over to him. "I didn't run, did I, Kitch?" I turned on Warren. "If he lives, and I ever see him carrying a gun, here, in Texas or Nebraska, I'm going to kill him on sight. That goes for you, too. If you want to stay around, stay. But if you wear a gun, I'll kill you."

Taking up the bridle, I added, "You go back up there and tell that outfit that all those who didn't make a deal with Cap for their lots can move, or be moved by me. We staked and claimed that town site and we cut timber for the buildings."

"There's forty men up there!" Warren said.

"And there's one of me. But you tell them. I hope they are gone before I have to come read them from the Book."

Scooping up his guns and the others, I started off.

It was full dark by the time we got to the camp, and I heard a challenge. The voice sounded familiar, but it wasn't Cap.

"Sackett here," I said, "and I got a lady for company. I'm coming in."

Falling back beside her, I said, "Ma'am, I'm sure sorry about back yonder. Folks never reckoned me a quarrelsome man, but I'd trouble with these men before."

She did not reply and suddenly scared, I said, "Look—you ain't hurt, are you?"

"No . . . I'm not hurt."

Her voice sounded different, somehow, but I didn't think much of it until I reached up and helped her down. She felt stiff in my hands, and she wouldn't look at me.

A man stepped up beside us. "Sackett? I'm Joe Rugger. Remember? I spoke of coming back to see you. I've been trying to keep them off Cap."

Rugger was the square-set man who had ridden with Kitch. Brushing past him, I went to the lean-to. Cap was lying there on his blankets, and he was so pale it scared me.

"Most times we haven't dared have a light," Rugger said. "They've been pot-shooting around here at night."

"Put the light out."

For a few minutes I sat there, scared to death. That old man looked bad off, mighty bad off. We hadn't been together long, but I'd come to be fond of him. He was a solid, true-blue old man.

"They ambushed him . . . four, five of them. They shot him out of his saddle and then went hunting him like an animal. Only Cap was clear conscious and he let them come in close where he couldn't miss. He killed two and the rest took off like scared pole-cats."

"Where's he hit?"

"Missed the lung, I think. Took him high, but he lost a lot of blood before he got here. I didn't know of it until the next morning. Then I came right up.

"When they came to finish him off, I stopped them before they could get to the trees. Cap, he came out of it and managed to get off a shot . . . they think he's in better shape than he is."

I walked outside and stood under the trees. If that old man died I'd hunt every man-jack of them down and gut-shoot them.

By now they had seen Kitch and they knew I was back. If I knew that crowd over there, tonight they would argue, they would threaten, and they would make wartalk, but unless I was completely wrong, they wouldn't come down here in the dark. Not after what happened to Kitch. Tomorrow I could expect trouble.

However I would be ready, and if they wanted it tonight instead of tomorrow, they could have it.

Last thing I'd wanted was trouble, but they'd called the turn, and now they would get a bellyful of it. If they wanted to start the town with a line of graves in boot hill, it would be that way.

Joe Rugger came up behind me. "You want I should ride south for Orrin and Tyrel?"

"No, sir. No, I don't. This here is myself, and I don't think there's going to be enough of it to go around."

They could have forty-eight hours. Then I was riding down.

# Chapter 10

Morning broke with an overcast sky and a hint of rain, and rain worried me because down here rain could mean snow in the mountains where the gold was.

First off, I walked out to the edge of the timber that surrounded our camp and looked toward the town site. There were several tents, one building already up, and a couple more on the way.

Nobody seemed to be pulling out.

Joe Rugger was squatting over the fire with a long fork, working on some venison steaks. Ange was helping him, but when she looked at me her eyes were bleak and frightened.

Not that I could blame her. It must have come as a shock to come out of the peace of those hills and run into a gunfight . . . and my way of doing things must have been a shock. Folks who live sheltered or quiet lives, away from violent men, have no idea how they have to be dealt with. And I never was one to stand around and talk mean . . . if there's fighting to be done the best thing is have at it and get it over with.

Those men at the town site had had their warning, and I gave them time to think about it. In any such number of men a few of them with nerve will stand up to trouble; they will be tough, resolute men. A few will be talkers willing to ride along with the crowd; a few will be camp-followers ready to pick up the leavings of stronger men. And of course, there is always the kind who is himself a tough man, if given leadership.

Such a warning as I had given was apt to thin their ranks somewhat. A few of the camp-followers would shy from trouble, and some of the talkers would make an excuse and ride out.

Cap was in bad shape. He had lost a lot of blood, like Rugger said, and he was a thin, tough old man without too much blood in him. He ran mostly to bone and sinew.

It scared me when I looked at him. His cheeks were sunken in and his eyes were hollow. He looked a sight.

"Ange," I said, "will you see what you can do for him?"

"Yes."

"Ange, I'm sorry about last night."

"You didn't have to shoot those men. That was wicked! It was an awful thing!"

"They were mighty bad men. They came out there to kill me, Ange."

"I don't believe it. They were just talking."

"Ange, when men carry guns they don't just talk about killing. When a man mentions killing, and has in his hands or on his person the means to kill, then you have a right to believe he means to do what he says. I've helped bury a few men who tried to argue at times like that."

Ange wasn't doing any trading on that kind of talk. She walked away from me and left me standing, and all that sort of nice feeling between us was gone.

Only girl I ever felt likely to care for, and she would have none of me.

And after I did what I would have to do, she was going to like me even less. But the fact of the matter is, no man can shape his life according to woman's thinking. Nor should any woman try to influence a man toward her way. There must be give and take between them, but when a man faces a man's problems he has to face them a man's way.

We had come up here asking trouble of no one. We had staked a claim, measured out a town site, and staked out building sites. We had cut timber and prepared to build; and then strangers came in, jumped our town site, and tried to jump our claim. They had shot Cap, and they had tried to kill me.

Nobody talked much over breakfast. After breakfast I taken Blackstone and sat down under a tree where I could watch that town site, and I read. Reading was not easy for me, but I hooked both spurs in the girth and settled down for a long ride, determined not to let it throw me. When words showed up that wore an unfamiliar brand, I passed them by and went on, but usually they made sense to me after some study.

After an hour I toted my book back to camp and, rounding up a pick and shovel, headed for the creek.

Cap had sunk a shaft to bedrock and started a cleanup. Going down into the shaft I widened it out a mite and got out some gravel. At the edge of the stream I went to work with the pan, filling it with gravel, dipping it into the water, and starting the water swirling to wash the sand over the edge. I found color, but not much.

Several times I walked to the edge of the woods. Noon came and I could see no sign of work around the town, so evidently they were drinking and talking. Cap was breathing easier, and Ange was feeding him when I came into camp, but she paid me no mind and I sat down to eat what there was.

If they made an all-out attack on us, we might be able to hold them off, but if we had to get out of there our only chance was up the mountain, and with a sick man on our hands we weren't likely to get far.

Taking an axe, I went out to check our defenses. I added a few logs, and rooted out some brush here and there to give us a better field of fire.

Joe Rugger was worried, I could see that, but there was no rabbit in him. He had come in with us and he planned to stick.

"What led you to throw in with us, Joe?" I asked him.

"Drifted in here with the wrong crowd before I measured them for calibre. Seemed to me you and Rountree were more my type. Fact was, I figured to try leasing that store from you. Back in Ohio I operated a small store for another man, but it seemed to me I'd get nowhere working for the other fellow, so I quit. I've done some mining, but a store is what I always wanted."

"Joe, you've just bought yourself a lease. Cap and me, we want to build a town that shapes up to something, and we would be proud to lease that store to you."

"Thanks, Tell."

It made a body restless, wondering what they were cooking up down there in town. Same time, I never was one to keep a serious view of things. Time to time folks get the idea I'm slighting my problems because ofttimes they strike me as funny. Now I kept thinking of all those men down there, arguing and drinking and drinking and arguing, and working up a nerve to come after us. It struck me, a man might sort of wander down there of a nighttime and have himself some fun.

Rousting around in our gear I found about a hundred feet of rope Cap had packed along, on account of rope is always handy. Joe had some more, and I knotted the two together and went inside and got my field glasses and studied that town.

There were four tents—one large, like the saloon tents at the end of the tracks in railroad towns, and the others small. A couple of horses were saddled, with packs behind the saddles . . . some men were in the street.

Something about it bothered me. If there actually were forty men around the town, where were they?

I took my Winchester and scouted around the edge of the trees, studying the bench, searching every possible approach. It scarcely seemed likely that they would try another attack with me here, when Cap and Joe had driven them off alone. But they might.

Thinking of it worried me, with Ange Kerry at the camp, and Cap Rountree a sick man. Looked to me like I was going to have to go after them, after all.

Come evening time, Joe Rugger came out to stand watch, and I went into camp for grub. Cap was conscious and he looked up at me. "You've got it all on your hands, Tell. I'll be no help to you."

"You've been a help." I squatted on my heels beside his pallet, nursing a cup of coffee in my hands. "Cap, I'm going to take it to them tonight."

"You be careful."

"Else they'll come a-hunting. We can't have them shooting around with Ange here, and you laid up."

"That's a fine girl."

"You should see that country up yonder. Blessed if I can see how she made it . . . months up there, all alone."

I could see Cap was done up. He would need time and plenty of good food to get his strength back . . . it was lucky Ange was there.

She came in, bringing a cup of soup for Cap, but she kept her eyes away from me. What did she expect me to do? Stand still and get shot? Sure, I got the jump, but Kitch had warning. And when he came out of the trees like that he wasn't looking to play patty-cake.

She was mighty pretty. A little thing, slim and lovely. Though the only clothes she had were wore-out things, and she was not likely to have better until one of us could cut loose for Silverton or Del Norte.

Her face had taken on some color, and she had combed out that hair of hers and done it up like some of those fancy pictures I'd seen in *Godey's Lady's Book*. I declare, she was pretty!

"See you," I said, and stood up. "You take care."

There was a moment there I thought of talking with her, but what could I say? Seemed to me she didn't want any words from me, and I went away feeling mighty miserable inside. Walking out to the edge of the trees, I stood looking toward the two or three lights and thinking what a fool a man could be.

What was she, after all? Just a slim girl with a lot of red-gold hair . . . nothing to get upset about.

The humor of what I'd been thinking of doing there in town went out of me. I looked at that town and felt like walking over there and shooting it out.

Only there was no sure way I could win if I did that, and I had to win. Joe was a solid man, but he was no gunfighter. First time in my life I wished I could look up and see Tyrel coming down the pike.

Only Tyrel was miles away and days away, and whatever happened now was up to me. Anyway, it never does a man much good to be thinking of what he could do if he had help . . . better spend his time figuring a way of doing it himself.

Gathering up that rope, I taken it to my horse and saddled up.

"Joe," I said, "you be careful. They may come a-winging it over this way. If they do, and if I'm able, I'll come a-smoking, but you stand 'em off until I get here."

Ange was standing with the fire behind her and I couldn't see her face. Only when I rode out, I lifted a hand. "See you," I said, and let the palouse soft-foot it off the bench and into the stream bed.

It was cool, with no wind. The clouds were low, making it especial dark. There was a smell of pine woods in the air, and a smell of wood smoke and of cooking, too.

Nigh the town site I drew up and got down, tying the appaloosa to some willows in the stream bed. I put my hand on his shoulder. "Now you stand steady, boy. I won't be gone long."

But I wondered if that was truth or not.

Maybe it would be just as well if I was to get the worst of them. That Ange, now—she had no use for me, and sure as shooting I was getting a case on her.

Not that it was likely she could ever see me. Girl that pretty had her choice of men. Nobody ever said much about me being good-looking—except Ma—and even Ma, with the best intentions in the world, looked kind of doubtful when she said it.

I didn't shape up to much except for size. Only thing I could do better than anybody else I knew was read sign . . . and maybe shoot as good as most. Otherwise, all I had was a strong back.

That Blackstone, now. I'd been worrying that book like a dog worries a bone, trying to get at the marrow of it, but it was a thing took time. Days now I'd been at it, off and on, and everything took a sight of thinking out.

He said a lot of things that made a man study, although at the wind-up they made a lot of sense. If I could learn to read . . . I would never get to be a lawyer like Orrin there, but . . .

This was no time for dreaming. Pa, he always advised taking time for contemplating, but this was the wrong time.

Taking that rope and my Winchester, I edged in close. Working soft on moccasin feet, I ran my rope through the guy ropes of that big tent, up behind about four guy ropes, and then a loop clean around one of the smaller tents and around the guy ropes of another. Then I walked back to my horse and loosed him, mounting up and taking a dally around the pommel with the loose end.

Everything at the town seemed mighty peaceful. Inside I could hear folks a-cutting up some touches, the clatter of glasses and poker chips. Seemed almost a shame to worry them.

Walking my horse alongside the building, I stood up on the saddle and pulled myself to the roof. I slid out of my shirt, and shoved it into the chimney. Then I stepped back to the eaves and, about time I touched saddle, all hell broke loose inside. The room had started to fill up with wood smoke and I heard folks a-swearing something awful and coughing.

Turning my horse, I taken a good hold on that rope, let out a wild Comanche yell, and slapped spurs to that palouse.

Those spurs surprised him. He taken out like a scared rabbit. Ripping down those guy ropes and collapsing the other tents, I lit out. When I'd done what I could that way, I rode back through between the tents at a dead run. As I came through, a gang of men rushed up and caught themselves in a loop of rope.

It tumbled the lot of them, and dragged some. I let go the rope and, leaning from the saddle, I wrenched loose a length of tent stake. I rode up on that bunch and rapped a skull here and there.

A man on the stoop of the store building grabbed his pistol. I tossed that stake at his face and said, "Catch!"

He jumped back, fell over the last step and half inside the door.

Riding by, I drew up in the shadow. I'd sure enough played hob. Two small tents had collapsed and folks were struggling under them. The big tent was leaning away over. There was a lot of shouting, and somebody yelled, "No, you don't! Drop that money!" A shot was fired.

I remembered Pa's advice then, and taken time to contemplate. Setting my horse there in the shadows, I watched that mess-up and enjoyed it.

There was swelling under those tents, everybody arguing and swearing. Nobody was making any kind of sense.

One tent flattened down as the men struggled from under it. I decided they needed light, so I taken a flaming stick from the outside fire and tossed it at that flattened-out tent.

Somebody saw me and yelled. I turned sharp and trotted my horse away just as he let go with a shotgun. Then that tent burst into flame and I had to move back further.

They wanted to settle on my town site without paying, did they? They wanted to shoot up my camp?

I happened to notice their corral on the edge of the wash. A couple of saddles, a rope . . . Shaking out a loop, I caught a corner post of the corral with my rope and rode off, pulling it down. Horses streamed by me.

Surely does beat all what a man can do when he sets his mind to being destructive.

One leg hooked around my saddlehorn, I spoke gentle to my horse to warn him of trouble to come, and then I turned my head to the sky.

"*When I walked out on the streets of Laredo, when I—*"

A bullet cut wind near me, and I taken off. Seemed like nobody liked my singing.

# Chapter 11

There was a faint lemon color edging the gray of the clouds when I rolled out of my blankets. Joe Rugger had teased the fire into flame and put water on for coffee. Sticking my feet into my boots, I stomped them into place and slung my gun belt around my hips. Expecting trouble, that was all I had taken off, except for my vest.

I put on my vest and tucked another gun behind my belt and then walked out to the edge of the woods. Oh, sure, I had my hat on—first thing a cowboy does when he crawls out of bed in the morning is to put his hat on.

Looked to me like somebody was leaving over yonder.

Ange was up, her hair combed as pretty as might be, and sunlight catching the gold of it through a rift in the clouds. She brought me a cup of coffee.

"I suppose you're satisfied with what you've done," she said.

"Thank you, ma'am. . . . Satisfied? Well, now. Takes a lot to satisfy a man, takes a lot to please him if he's any account. But what I did, I did well . . . yes, ma'am, I'm pleased."

"I thought you were a good man."

"Glad to hear you say so. It's an appearance I favor. Not that I've ever been sure what it was made a good man. Mostly I'd say a good man is one you can rely on, one who does his job and stands by what he believes."

"Do you believe in killing people?"

"No, ma'am, not as a practice. Trouble is, if a body gets trouble out here he can't call the sheriff . . . there isn't any sheriff. He can't have his case judged by the law, because there aren't any judges. He can't appeal to anybody or anything except his own sense of what's just and right.

"There's folks around believe they can do anything they're big enough to do, no matter how it tromples on other folks' rights. That I don't favor.

"Some people you can arbitrate with . . . you can reason a thing out and settle it fair and square. There's others will understand nothing but force.

"Joe Rugger now, there's a good man. Cap Rountree is another. They are trying to build something. Those others, they figure to profit by what other people do, and I don't aim to stand by in silence."

"You have no authority for such actions."

"Yes, ma'am, I do. The ideas I have are principles that men have had for many a year. I've been reading about that. When a man enters into society—that's living with other folks—he agrees to abide by the rules of that society, and when he crosses those rules he becomes liable to judgment, and if he continues to cross them, then he becomes an outlaw.

"In wild country like this a man has no appeal but to that consideration, and when he fights against force and brutality, he must use the weapons he has.

"Take Joe Rugger now. He rode in here with a lot of mighty mean, shiftless folks. He broke with them and came over to us when we were shorthanded. He knew when he made that choice that it might be the death of him.

"Ma'am, I'm not an educated man, but I'm trying to make up for it. Thing is, when folks started to live together, a long time ago, they worked out certain laws, like respecting the rights of others, giving folks the benefit of the doubt, sharing the work of the community . . . that sort of thing.

"Cap and me figured to start a town, and we wanted it to be a good town where there would someday be women-folks walking the streets to stores and where youngsters could play. And you know something? We've got our first citizen. We've got Joe Rugger."

"I never thought of it that way." She said it grudgingly, and she riled me.

"No, ma'am, folks don't," I said with considerable heat. "People who live in comfortable, settled towns with law-abiding citizens and a government to protect them, they never think of the men who came first, the ones who went through hell to build something.

"I tell you, ma'am, when my time comes to ride out, I want to see a school over there with a bell in the tower, and a church, and I want to see families dressed up of a Sunday, and a flag flying over there. And if I have to do it with a pistol, I'll do it!"

This time I riled her. She walked away stiff-like, and I could see that I'd said the wrong thing.

When I finished my coffee Joe came out to stand guard, and I went back and ate some venison and some sour-dough bread dipped in sorghum molasses.

Cap looked a sight better. His eyes were brighter, and there was color in his faded cheeks.

"Well, Cap," I said, "I never had any doubt. You're too mean and

onery to die like this. Way I figure, you'll die in a corner just snapping
and grabbing and cutting around you. You'll die with your teeth in somebody if I know you right.

"Now you hurry up and get out of there. Joe and me are getting almighty tired of you laying up while we do all the work."

"How're things?"

"Sober. Looks to me like those folks have started to settle down to
think things out. Time I went over and had a talk with them. Time to
make a little medicine."

"You be careful."

"I'm a careful man. Time comes to run, I ain't afraid to run. When I
ride down there this morning, I'm going for a showdown."

"Wish I could go along."

"You set tight . . . I think they'll stand for reasoning now. I plan to get
them to sit down and contemplate. And if they can't cut the mustard that
way, they'll get their walking papers."

"All of them?"

"Shucks, there ain't no more than forty."

With my Winchester across my saddle, I rode down. They saw me coming, but I was walking my horse in plain sight and they waited for me.
With the exception of that fat man who had come with Kitch to our
camp, I saw nobody I knew until Ab Warren came outside. He was not
wearing a gun.

"You men have moved into a town site staked and claimed by Cap
Rountree and myself. You took it on yourselves to occupy building sites
we had laid out. You taken our timber. Last night you found out a little of
what trouble can be. Now I've come down here to arbitrate this matter,
and I'm going to do it right here in my saddle.

"When Cap and me moved in here, we had an election. He became
mayor and I became town marshal by popular acclamation. It was popular
with both of us.

"As Cap is laid up, I'm acting mayor as well as marshal. I am also the
town council and the vigilante committee, and any time during these pro-
ceedings that anybody wants to challenge my authority, he can have at it.

"We're going to have a town here. I think it's going to be a rich town;
but rich or poor, it's going to be law-abiding. Any who aren't ready to
stand for that had better saddle up, because until we get some constituted
authority (I wasn't real sure what "constituted" meant but it sounded
mighty good) I am going to run it with a six-shooter.

"Whoever has occupied that building will move out, starting now. That
is to be the general store, and Joe Rugger has a lease on it."

The fat man spoke up. "I'm in that building, and I had it built."

"Who paid for the lumber?"

He hesitated, then blustered. "That's no matter. We found it here and we—"

"It belongs to Cap and me. We valued it at one thousand dollars. Pay for it here and now, or get out of the building. As for the work involved, you can charge that up to poor judgment on your part, and know better next time."

"You can't get away with that!"

"You've got ten minutes to start moving. After that I throw things out—you included."

Ignoring him, I looked the others over. They were a bunch of toughs for the most part, although here and there were some men that looked likely.

"We're going to need a saloon—a straight one. And we're going to need a hotel and an eating house. If any of you want to have a try at it, you'll get cooperation from us."

The fat man was the leader, I could see that, but he was red-faced and mad, not sure of how much backing he would get. Several had pulled out already. Kitch and his partner were dead. Ab Warren was here to tell them how that happened.

Suddenly a burly, unshaved man stepped out of the crowd. "I cooked for a railroad construction crew one time. I'd like to handle that eating house."

"All right, you trim that beard and wash your shirt, and you've got thirty days to prove you can cook grub fit to eat. If you can't, you get somebody who can."

A slim young fellow who looked pale around the gills, like he hadn't been west long, spoke up. "I'm a hotel man, and I can also run a saloon. I can run it honest."

"All right." With my left hand I took a paper from my shirt front. "Here's the plan Cap and me laid out. You two study that and choose your sites. When you get your plans made, you draw straws to see who builds first; the other helps, and turn about."

It was time to settle things with that fat man. Somebody was speaking low to him and I heard the fat man called Murchison.

"Murchison," I said, "you have about three minutes to get started. And this time I don't mean cleaning out that building. I mean down the road."

"Now, look here—"

My horse walked right up to him. "You came in here to ride roughshod over what you thought was a helpless old man. You showed no respect for the rights of others or the rights of property. You'd be no help to a town. Get on your horse and start traveling."

Pushing my horse forward another step, I backed Murchison up. The appaloosa stepped right up on the stoop after him.

"I'll be back," Murchison said angrily. "The Bigelows are in Silverton."

"We'll hold a place for you," I said, "right alongside of Kitch."

Ab Warren stayed.

Murchison rode from town that morning and about fifteen men rode with him.

There was a Texas Ranger one time who said that there's no stopping a man who knows he's in the right and keeps a-coming. Well, I've often been wrong, but this time I was right and they had to pay mind to me or bury me, and mine is a breed that dies hard.

In the days that followed, other folks began to drift in. The second week a rider came, and then two wagons. Claims were taken up along the creek and one man drove in about thirty head of sheep which he started feeding along the mountainside. Joe Rugger got his store going, Allison his hotel, which he started in the big gambling tent that had been abandoned. Briggs ran a good eating house. Nothing fancy, but simple food, mighty well-cooked. Aside from beef and beans, he served up bear meat, venison, and elk.

We saw nothing of the Bigelows, but we heard aplenty. Tom and Ira were the two we heard most about. They were suspected of holding up a stage near Silverton. Tom had killed a man in Denver City, and had been in a shooting in Leadville. Ira was a gambler, dividing his time between Silverton and some other boom camps.

They had made their brags about me. They would take care of me when they found time. I'd as soon they never found it.

Twice I made trips into the mountains and came back down with gold . . . two muleloads the last time.

Esteban Mendoza and Tina came over and built a cabin in town, near the foot of the mountain, and Esteban had two freight wagons working along the Silverton road.

Ange Kerry moved away from our camp and got a little place in town where she lived, and she worked with Joe Rugger in the store, which combined with the post office and Wells Fargo express. She had never been the same toward me since I killed Kitch and his partner.

She was prettier than ever, and mighty popular around town. Nearly everybody sort of protected her. Joe Rugger brought his wife out and they built a home on the back end of the store.

Cap took a long time mending, and he hadn't much energy when he was able to walk, so it was up to me to do what was done.

Of an evening I read what newspapers I could find, and kept hammering away at Blackstone. Time to time somebody would drift into camp, stay a while, and drift out again, leaving books behind. I read whatever there was. But mostly I worked.

I built us a three-room log house high on the bench, with my old trail up the mountain right behind it, and the spring close by. I built a strong stable and corral against the coming winter, and I cut a few tons of hay in the meadow.

There was snow on some of the peaks now where I hadn't seen it before. A time or two, early in the morning, there was frost in the bottom, and once ice slicked over a bucket of left-out water.

The old barricades I let lie, and I kept the brush trimmed off the mesa. Grass was growing high out there, and there was good grazing for our stock.

When I went to town now there were few whom I knew. Joe Rugger was acting mayor, Allison and Briggs were loyal men. Murchison had come back and started a small gambling house. There were at least two hundred people in town, and she was running like a top.

The aspen began to turn yellow . . . seemed like I'd been here years, though it was only a few months.

There was little trouble. Two men killed each other over a poker game in Murchison's joint, and there was a cutting down on the creek, some private affair over a woman.

One night Cap came in and sat down. "You stay at the books," he said, "and you'll ruin your eyes."

"I've got to learn, Cap."

"You take after those brothers of yours. As soon as they learned to read there was no holding them."

"They've done well."

"Yes, they have. Married, too."

I didn't answer right away, but finally I said, "Well, it takes two."

"You seen Ange lately?"

"You know I haven't."

"That's a mighty fine girl. She won't be around always. I hear that Ira Bigelow is paying her mind."

"Bigelow? Is he in town?"

"Rode in a few days ago while you were in the mountains. Only stayed a few hours, but he managed to meet Ange, and he talked it up to her. He's a handsome man."

Didn't cut much ice, reading about ethics and all. Inside, I could feel myself getting mean. The thought of any of those Bigelows around Ange . . . well, sir, a thing like that could make me mean as an old bear.

Of an evening I would walk outside and look toward the town lights, but I didn't often go down to the street. And it was time for me to make my last trip of the season into the high peaks. I wanted one more load out of there before snow fell. Not that there hadn't been snow up that high, but I had a hunch there was time for one trip. With the new route in, and no need to go by way of the chute, I might make it in and back.

"Going up the mine tomorrow," I told Cap. I stood there a moment. "You know, Ange should come in for a share of that. Her grandpa was hunting it when he died up there . . . he had him a map, and one of those dead Spanish men must have been a relative of his . . . or one of the live ones."

"I was thinking that. Wondered if you'd get around to it."

Picking up my hat, I said, "I think I'll go talk to her."

"You do that," Cap said. "You surely do it."

Anyway, it was time I bought me an outfit—new clothes, and the like. I had money now.

Turning to leave, I stopped. Esteban Mendoza was in the doorway. "Señor Tell? I must speak with you."

He came on into the room. "I was working at my freight wagons fixing some harness, and it became very dark while I sat there, and when I am through I put out the lantern and then sit for a while, enjoying the coolness.

"Beyond the wagon are several men, and they are talking. They do not know I am there, and so I keep very still, for one of them speaks of you. He says you have gold that is not placer gold, but from quartz, from a lode. They believe the mine is in the mountains."

"Who were the men?"

"One is named Tuthill . . . they call him Meester. Another is called Boyd."

Cap looked over at me. "The banker and that gambler from Las Vegas."

"How about the others?"

He shrugged. "I do not know. But I think they plan to follow you into the mountains if you go again."

"Thanks, 'Steban. Thanks very much."

After he left I gave it some thought. It was important to make one more trip up there. I not only wanted to get enough gold to start buying my ranch, but I wanted to cover up the work I'd done at the mine in case somebody found the way up to the valley. The trip was a risk I would have to take.

Cap was getting around pretty good now, better than before, and Esteban would look in on him from time to time. He was well enough to care for himself, and he had friends in the town.

"You going down to see Ange?" Cap asked suddenly. "It's getting late."

I got into my saddle and started for town. The lights seemed brighter than before, and there was excitement in me.

Ange. . . .

A shadow stirred in the brush and I waited a moment before riding on. It was a man all right, and he was watching our camp.

Esteban had been right.

# Chapter 12

Late as it was, the store was crowded. Joe waved a hand to me from where he stood waiting on a customer, and I glanced toward the other counter where Ange was. If she had noticed me, she gave no sign of it.

Most of the people in the store seemed like newcomers, although there were a couple of familiar faces.

"Mr. Sackett, I believe?"

Turning around, I faced Tuthill. He was a handsome man, no question of it, tall and well-dressed in storebought clothes.

"How are you?" I asked. "I wasn't expecting to see you this far from home. What happened to the bank?"

"I left it in good hands."

Glancing toward Ange, I saw she was no longer busy, so I excused myself and walked over to her. "Ange," I said, "I want to buy some clothes."

Her eyes met mine for the merest instant. "All right."

So I gave her my order, aware that Tuthill was watching from a short distance away. She brought me some shirts, jeans, socks, and a sheepskin coat.

". . . And two boxes of .44s," I said.

Her eyes lifted to mine and her face stiffened. Abruptly, she turned and walked to the ammunition shelf and took down two boxes and came back, placing them on the counter before me.

"Ange," I said, "I've got to talk to you."

"You brought me out of the mountains and I'm very grateful," she said, "but I don't think—"

"Ange, part of that gold belongs to you. Your grandpa was hunting it, and it was probably some ancestor of his who found it first. So you should have a share."

"Whatever you think is right. There's no need for talk."

She turned away from me with my money and made change.

"Ange," I said, "I had to shoot those men."

"Did you? It was the most brutal, the most callous thing I ever saw! And I thought you were so gentle, so nice—"

She broke off and walked away from me. A moment I stood there. When I turned around, Tuthill was beside me. "I didn't know you knew Ange Kerry," he said.

"You make a habit of listening in when folks are talking?" I was mad. "Look, Tuthill, I think you're no gentleman. I also think you're a thief, and that you travel with thieves. You keep that Boyd out of my sight—do you hear? If I see him, I'll come looking for you both."

Brushing past him, I started for the door. Rugger was there. "Something wrong, Tell?"

Ange was looking at me with something mighty close to horror in her eyes. She could not know about Will Boyd following me down that street in Las Vegas, or about his connection with Tuthill, or what Esteban had overheard. All she knew was what she heard now—that I had made what looked like an unprovoked attack on an innocent and respectable man.

"Nothing, Joe." My voice lowered. "Only Tuthill's curious about me and that claim of mine. So are the people with him. He followed me here from Las Vegas."

Riding back to the claim, I made up my mind. I would head for the high hills now, before daybreak, get a lead on anybody who might try to follow me, and keep it. Once I came down with the gold, I would head south to Mora or somewhere and buy myself a ranch. Ange could do what she had a mind to.

Every time I came to be near her something happened to make me look worse than I had before. She probably had never seen anyone killed before that night I shot Kitch.

Back at camp, Cap could see I was mad, and he made no comment when I threw a pack together and brought out pack saddles. I was taking two pack horses, and the appaloosa. There was no need to take much gear . . . I would be gone only two or three days.

Yet, just on chance, I took enough food for a week, and four boxes of .44s, aside from what was in my belt. It was an hour short of day when I mounted up to ride out.

"You be careful," Cap warned.

"I saw Tuthill," I told him. "He smells gold. Through some bank, or Wells Fargo, or something, he's had a smell of that gold . . . and he knows it isn't placer gold."

Holding close against the wall of the mountain, I rode north, weaving among the scattered trees on the bench. It was still overcast and there was a smell of dampness in the air.

Where Rock Creek entered the Vallecitos I turned southeast, riding in the creek bed. By daylight that water would have washed away what tracks I made.

The sun was painting the sky with a lavish brush when I topped out on a rise in the trees and looked back. Far below, several miles back, I saw movement. Sun gleamed for an instant on a rifle barrel.

No use taking a chance on leading them to the mine. So, turning off to my left I went up a rocky ridge, using several switchbacks, and rode over the saddle to the east. About a half-mile off I saw a lake, larger than the one in the high valley. Riding swiftly in that direction, I held to a good pace.

Near the shore of that lake I bedded down for the night, and made camp without a fire.

Awakening to a patter of rain on the leaves overhead, I crawled out on the ground, put on my hat and boots, slung on my gun belt and then rolled my bed.

Without even waiting for coffee, I saddled up and left the woods at a fast trot. Working my way around a dozen small lakes and ponds, I topped out on a ridge overlooking miles upon miles of the most magnificent country under heaven.

Nothing moved through the gray veil of the rain. I rode down into my valley. The mine was as I left it. But the trail along the chute was two feet deep in water, and the rain would soon make it impassable. The other route would have to be my way out.

Picketing my horses, I went into the mine and went to work with my pick. The gold was richer than ever, and the quartz so rotten that it crumbled under my boots.

The rain continued . . . a steady, persistent downfall that could easily turn to snow.

No time to think of Ange . . . nor of Cap, or anything but getting the gold out and down the mountains.

When next I came out the rain had ceased, but there was an odd lightness to the air that left me uneasy, and it bothered the horses also.

Several deer and an elk were feeding in the meadows across the valley, and that might mean a storm was coming. They usually came out about sundown. The valley was quiet, the clouds pressing low down over the peaks. The rain started again, scarcely more than a mist.

Returning to the mine, I worked hard for another hour, and then built a fire and made coffee. My head ached a little from not eating, and it was hard to settle down, with that feeling in the air.

But part of my uneasiness was the fear of being trapped.

Beside my fire I worked long into the night, pounding up the quartz. Maybe the gold I'd come upon was only a pocket. Maybe the quartz would be harder farther on into the rock, or the gold might change its character and require milling to get it out. Of such things I knew next to nothing.

When night came I brought the horses in close to the cave, built a fire deeper inside, and mixed a batch of sourdough bread. I made a good meal before I turned in.

Middle of the night I woke up.

It was cold. I mean, it was really cold. It was colder than I'd ever believed it could be. The horses were crowded together, heads down. I stepped out of the cave into a strange, weird world of ice.

Ice . . . crystal ice in the moonlight that fell through torn clouds. Ice on the trees, ice on the rocks, gleaming ice on the meadow grass. Ice on the willows, making them like a forest of slim glass sticks.

It was strange, and it was beautiful, and it had the shine of death.

Nobody would be traveling any trail in the mountains until that ice was gone. Those eyebrow trails . . . those brink-of-the-precipice trails, those rocky crossings, those sheets of rock—all would be sheets of ice now, where no horse could maintain its footing, where even a man in moccasins would scarcely dare to move.

The thought of the trail into the valley where Ange had been made my hair stand on end.

If the sun came out it would melt fast enough. But it was late in the season . . . suppose it snowed first? Any step might start an avalanche.

Going back inside I built my fire bigger, and than I came out with a piece of sacking and commenced to clean off the horses. Ice was on their winter coats, and it crackled when I broke it free. They knew I was trying to help them and they stood very still, their eyes helpless and frightened.

It was the worst sleet storm I'd ever seen, worse even than the *pogonips* in Nevada. A lot of tree branches had broken under the weight of the ice. It was a white, crystalline world . . . like glass, everywhere.

Food . . . I would need food the worst way. With the intense cold I would need more than usual to keep warm, and there was no telling how long I'd be stuck here. Maybe all winter.

There was no sense wasting time. Every step, even on the flat, would be taken at the risk of a broken leg. The trails were out of the question now, the gold itself was unimportant. From now on, it would be a fight to survive.

It was still a couple of hours until daylight, but I got my axe, went outside, and cut a couple of good chunks from a log that I'd dragged up, and built a fire that would last.

The horses stood stiff-legged, afraid to move on the slick ground, so with a shovel I went around and broke up the ice and shoveled some of the waste rock from my mine over the ice.

Then I went to the woods, knocked the ice loose from a tree trunk, cut off the heavier limbs, and packed them back to the cave. The moonlight was gone. I added fuel to my fire, put on the coffeepot, and commenced to study out the situation. There might be some way of getting out that I'd overlooked.

With daylight, the first thing would be to find and kill a deer or two. As long as the cold held I'd not have to worry about the meat spoiling.

Dawn came under a sky of cold gray clouds. I went out and started to hunt for a deer. The appaloosa moved to the edge of the ice that sparkled on the grass and began to paw at it to get at the grass. He was a Montana horse and used to such things.

Shortly before noon I found a buck.

By nightfall it was colder, if anything. I'd butchered my deer and hung the meat up. I'd skinned him properly and saved the hide. If I was here for the winter I was going to need as many such hides as I could get. And all the game I would have a chance at was right there in the valley now.

Huddled in my blankets, I sat over the fire all night long. I was going to have to wall up the mouth of that cave. The wind crept in there, fluttered my fire, and brought the cold with it. The morning broke with the flat gray clouds still shielding the sun, the wind knife-edged and raw, the glassy branches shaking slightly, clashing one against the other like skeleton arms.

The horses tugged woefully at the frozen grass, and the ice cut their lips until they came to me, whimpering. Down by the stream where the grass grew taller, I shattered the ice and cut the grass to take back to them.

This could not go on. Somehow I was going to have to get down the mountain. I wanted to take the horses with me if it could be done. Yet I knew it could not. . . . And without me in this high valley they would die.

That night I broiled a venison steak, and ate it, hunched over the fire, cutting it in strips to handle it better.

Snow fell that night, and when day came one of my pack horses was down with a broken leg. The shot that killed him echoed down the ice-choked valley.

Through lightly falling snow, I went down the valley to the chute. The stream was frozen over, and the chute was a solid mass of ice. The water had risen still more, and the ledge down which the trail wound was now under several feet of water. To get out by that route was out of the question.

Ange had lasted out a winter up here with her grandfather. How had they done it?

Their cave was bigger and better sheltered, and there was a lifetime of firewood in the huge old logs that lay among the boulders . . . but could I get down the trail to the bottom?

Could I even get *to* the canyon? Up where the bristle-cone pines grew the wind had a full sweep, and it would be even colder than here. The trail, if I could reach it, was five hundred feet down a sheer face that was probably sheeted in ice.

That would be a last resort. For the time being I would remain where I was and try to last out the storm.

Taking the shovel, I went out and knocked more ice from the grass to give the horses a fighting chance. They knew how to get at it themselves, but the ice roughed up their lips and bloodied their hocks.

The snow kept falling, covering the ice with a thin mantle, making the ice all the more dangerous.

Suddenly the appaloosa's head came up sharply and his ears pricked.

I got out my Winchester. Nothing moved within the limited area I could see through the drifting snow. Listening, I could hear nothing.

Walking with extreme care, I went to the willows at the edge of the creek and cut several long slender lengths which I carried back to the cave and placed on the floor not too close to the fire.

Always, on the range, I carried with me a bundle of rawhide strips, most of them "piggin strings" for tying the legs of cattle when branding. Every cowhand carried some for emergencies on the range. And I was going to have a use for them now.

The horses showed no tendency to wander, but remained close to the cave. All through the morning and into the afternoon I kept busy reducing the rest of the quartz to gold I could pack out.

When the willow strips were pliable again, I took each of them and bent them into an oval and tied them, selecting the two best ovals to keep. Then with the rawhide strips tied across them, I made rough snowshoes.

Before nightfall I took the rifle, strapped on the snowshoes, and went out to give them a test run. They were not the first pair I had made, and they worked well. Trailing down the valley toward the chute, I saw it was rapidly choking with snow over the ice. Escape by that route was completely out of the question.

I circled around, and ventured toward the valley of Ange's cave. When almost to the bare shoulder where the bristle-cone pines grew, I turned back to reach my cave before dark. It was at that moment that I heard the shot.

Stunned with the shock, I stood stock-still listening to the echo of it racketing against the solemn hills.

The echo lost itself against the snow-clad hillsides and I remained still, shivering a little in the cold, alone in a vast world of sky and snow, scarcely willing to accept what my ears had heard.

A shot . . . here!

It had come from the canyon below. Someone was down there! Someone was at or near Ange's cave.

*Here? In this place?*

# Chapter 13

The sudden crack of ice . . . the breaking of a tree branch laden with snow? . . . No. This had been a shot, clear, sharp, unmistakable.

*Tell,* I said, *you ain't . . . aren't . . . alone.*

Who knew of the cave below? Or of the valley? Only Ange, so far as I knew. Cap knew what I'd told him, but Cap couldn't have made it up there even if I'd given exact directions, which I hadn't. He was still too weak.

Ange . . . ? That was mighty foolish to consider. She had no reason for coming up.

Whoever had been following me down below? Could they have found some way into that valley? That seemed the most likely.

If I started for the canyon now it would be full dark before I got there, and I'd see nothing anyway. The thing to do would be to go back to the mine and hole up there until daybreak.

One thing was a copper-riveted cinch. If those men were in the canyon they were snowed in like I was, and, unless I was much mistaken, they were a lot less able to cope with it.

We Sacketts had never had much to do with, and back in the mountains we learned to make out on mighty little, but we learned how to rustle. There wasn't one of us boys who hadn't traveled miles by himself and lived off the country before he was sixteen.

Since then I'd had very little but rough time, what with soldiering and all. A Montana-from-Texas cattle drive is not exactly a place for softening up, and it seemed like I'd spent half my life getting along on less than nothing.

Hardship was a way of life to me, and there were few times when I wasn't hungry, cold, or fighting rough country for a living. Being snowed in up here in these mountains wasn't a pleasant thing, but somehow I'd survive. But those others now . . . ?

When I got back to camp the horses were close around the cave. I brought them inside and wiped them off. Mostly I fussed over them to keep their spirits up. They were smart enough to know we were in trouble, but being cared for made them confident that all was well.

I wished I could be so sure myself.

When I had my fire going I took off my sheepskin coat and shed my vest before putting the coat back on. I always try to have a little something extra to put on when out in cold weather. Main thing a man has to avoid is sweating. When he stops moving that sweat can freeze into an icy sheet inside the clothes.

I fixed myself some grub, and sat by the fire with Blackstone open. Time to time, I'd squint in the firelight to make something out.

These last few months, after I went to bed, sometimes I'd lie awake into the night, a-contemplating things I'd read, or trying to say things, using the words taken from that book. By the time spring came I had hoped my talking would be better.

And, time to time, I had thought of Ange. . . . About the time I was doing for her and she was half-dead from starvation and exhaustion, when I thought maybe this was my woman. I spent a sight of time daydreaming around, just contemplating her, and all about her.

But there wasn't much left to think about. She'd made that plain the other night in the store. Might have been better to let Kitch shoot me. Only I didn't believe that. I've heard of men killing themselves over a woman—most fool thing I ever heard tell of.

Women are practical. They get right down to bedrock about things, and no woman is going to waste much time remembering a man who was fool enough to kill himself. Thing to do is live for love, not die for it.

Though most women-folks would a sight rather see a man dead than with another woman.

Only that evening alone, with the fire bright in the cave, I got something all bunched up in my throat, just a-wishing and a-dreaming over Ange and that red-gold hair.

After I'd eaten, I packed a bait of grub for morning, fixed over my snowshoes a mite, and settled down for the night, stowing the book away in my saddlebag.

A good hour before suntime I rolled out of my soogan and stowed it away. I fixed myself some breakfast and went down to the creek with the horses. Breaking a hole with my axe, I watered them there. I knocked some grass free of snow and ice, but it wasn't enough . . . the day wasn't long enough to get enough.

Strapping on the snowshoes and slinging a pack, I took a length of rope and my Winchester and started out. It was shy of daybreak when I reached the trail into the canyon.

The first thing I saw was a smear on the snow of the trail, almost half-way down. Something had fallen on the trail.

Carefully, using hand-holds on the rock wall where I could find them, I started down the trail, and when I got to the smear I could see a little snow had already blown over it. So it must have happened during the night. And whatever it was had fallen over the edge.

I edged close to the rim. Here and there the wind had piled the snow until it had built up a cornice. If a man should rest his weight on it, down he would go. Leaning over, I looked down.

It was Ange.

She was lying on a ledge maybe twenty feet down. Snow had blown over her. That red-gold hair lay like a flame on the snow, caught in the first light that filtered through the dawn clouds.

Putting my rifle down, I hunted around, till I found a mess of bristle-cone roots exposed by a slide. I knotted my rope to them and went over the side, landing beside her in a shower of snow. The ledge on which she lay was deep in snow and not over six or seven feet across, and maybe three times that long.

She was not dead.

I picked her up in my arms and held her close, trying to get her warm, and whispered all sorts of nonsense to her.

I tied a bowline around her body under her arms, snug enough so she couldn't slip through. Then, hand over hand, clambering for footholds in the rock, I pulled myself back up to the trail. When I had caught my breath, I hoisted her up.

By the time I had her on the trail it was day and there was plenty of light. Unknotting the bowline, I coiled my rope, strapped on my snow-shoes, and picked her up. She had a bad knot on her head, but the thickness of her hair and the snow had probably cushioned the blow, so I doubted if she was hurt much.

I hadn't taken two steps before I heard a shout, far below, and a rifle shot that must have been very low, because it came nowhere near me. I turned, and saw several black figures against the snow of the canyon, far below.

Ange stirred, and opened her eyes. Quickly, pulling back as far as I could against the cliff wall, I put her down on her feet.

"Tell? Tell, is it really you? I thought—"

"You all right?"

"I fell . . . I thought I fell over the edge."

"You did." Rifle in one hand, and her hand in the other, I eased along the trail, hugging the rocks. Another shot put a bullet close to me, and I could see men running for the trail's end. One of them fell, but the others did not stop.

"Who is it down there?"

"It's Mr. Tuthill and those others. Ira Bigelow and Tom. That man named Boyd and two others I don't know. One of them they call Ben."

*Ben Hobes?*

"They made me bring them, Tell. They threatened me. Besides . . . you hadn't come back and I was afraid."

It was growing colder. The clouds were breaking and the wind was mounting. It was slow going because of the ice beneath the snow. At the top of the trail, I got out of the snowshoes and tied them on Ange.

I thought back to the men who by now were making their way up the trail. There were six men down there, and they wanted the gold; but most of all, they wanted to kill me. Under the circumstances, they must kill Ange, too.

"Who knows you came with them?"

"Nobody does. Mr. Tuthill heard us talking, and he must have known about the gold already. But from what I said to you, he could tell that I knew about it too. He came to my cabin and offered to become my partner and get all the gold for us. I refused.

"He went away, and then when it was dark he came back with those other men. He told me to get dressed, and to dress warmly. He said he would kill me if I didn't . . . and he meant it.

"I had no idea what he intended to do until we were outside. And then I found out what had happened. They tried to follow you, and you got away from them, so they came back after me.

"The only way I knew was back the way we came out, and I was not very sure of that. When we got in the mountains it was turning colder and the rain was falling. We got to the cave, and by that time, they were half-frozen and arguing among themselves.

"Boyd stayed on watch, but he fell asleep and I slipped out. I knew you were up here somewhere."

We struggled through the snow, with her talking fast, nervous and scared. "Tell, they mean to kill you. I was wrong. Tell! I didn't understand what kind of men they were!"

The fire was down to the merest coals when we got to the cave. From my stacked fuel I built up the fire to warm the place, and put some snow on to melt for coffee water.

When I looked up from the fire, Ange was standing there looking at me. "Tell, I'm sorry. I didn't understand."

"What could you think? I just up and shot those men. Of course, they were hunting it. They figured to kill me. I'm sorry you had to see it."

I walked to the opening and looked out. The sky was bright, the air was sharp with cold, but there was no sign of Tuthill and the others.

"Back east," I said, "folks still have duels now and again, only they arrange them . . . everything all laid out pretty and conducted like a ceremony. Only difference is that out here we don't bother with fixing it up proper. Back where most every man is known, it's different. Out here most of us are strangers and nobody knows if the man he has a difficulty with is a gentleman, or not. So he just ups and shoots."

"That's what Joe told me. I . . . I wouldn't listen at first. It seemed so . . . so brutal."

"Yes, ma'am. It is brutal. Only I never could see the sense in having folks look at your tombstone and say, 'He was a man who didn't believe in violence. He's a good man . . . and dead.'"

I paused, peering at the trees opposite. "No, Ange, if the folks who believe in law, justice, and a decent life for folks are to be shot down by those who believe in violence, nothing makes much sense. I believe in justice, I believe in being tolerating of other folks, but I pack a big pistol, ma'am, and will use it when needed."

There was no sign of those men yet. Either they were having trouble on the trail, or they were Injuning up on me and would settle down to shooting most any time. The snow and ice had covered the piles of waste rock thrown out of the tunnel so it wasn't likely they would guess first off that this was where the mine was.

Ange saw my Blackstone and picked it up. "Are you studying this?" She looked up me curiously.

"Yes, ma'am. It's books like that which make a man proud of being a man."

"Are you going to be a lawyer?"

"No . . . my brother Orrin made himself into one, but Orrin always was a talker. He had the gift, the Welsh tongue. I don't have any gift, ma'am, I'm just a man tries to do the right thing as well as he knows. Only, the way I figure, no man has the right to be ignorant. In a country like this, ignorance is a crime. If a man is going to vote, if he's going to take part in his country and its government, then it's up to him to understand.

"I had no schooling, ma'am, so I'm making out with this book and a few others. Some day"—I felt myself getting red around the gills—"I hope to have children and they'll have schooling, and I don't aim they should be ashamed of their Pa."

"How could they be?" Ange demanded. "You're good, you're brave, and—"

"Here they come," I said, and settled down behind the woodpile.

We could hear their boots crunching through the snow. There were five of them. Tuthill I recognized at once, and the two men beside him were probably the Bigelows. Will Boyd looked done up from the climbing and the cold. Behind him was Ben Hobes. The only one missing was that white-haired youngster with the guns.

I watched them come, chewing on a bit of stick, my Winchester in my hands. They were playing the fool, for at that distance . . .

"Come on out, Sackett! We want to talk."

"I can hear you."

"Come on out here."

"And leave this warm fire? I'm comfortable."

They started arguing among themselves. Then Tuthill started toward the cave, so I put a bullet into the snow at his feet and he stopped so quick he almost fell.

"You boys have got bigger problems than me," I commented, conversationally. "A sight of snow fell since you came into the mountains. How do you plan to get out?"

"Look here, Sackett," Tuthill said, "we know you're sitting on a rich claim. Well, all we want is a piece of it. Why be foolish? There's enough for us all."

"Why share it? I've got it, and all you boys have got is a chance to die in the snow."

I eased my position a little. "Tuthill, you don't seem to understand. When you came in here you came into a trap. The passes are closed, and we're all going to spend the winter. I hope you brought grub for five or six months."

"If you don't come out, Sackett," Tuthill threatened, "we're coming in."

"If I shoot again, Tuthill, I'll shoot to kill."

It was cold. Knowing this kind of country as I did, I knew what we could expect. It had cleared off. It was cold now—at least ten below. In a few hours it might drop to fifty below.

"Ben," I called, "you're no pilgrim. Tell them how cold it can get at ten or eleven thousand feet on a still night. We are all stuck for the winter, and you might as well get used to the idea.

"You're going to need shelter, fuel, and food. The game won't stay this high, it will all head for lower ground. If you make a run for it, you might still get out."

The pile of firewood covered half the tunnel mouth to a height of more than four feet, and made a crude windbreak and shelter from gunfire. The tunnel, in following the vein, had taken a slight bend—enough to shelter one person—and I whispered to Ange to get back behind it.

While partly open, the walls of rock acted as reflectors and threw heat back upon us. Moreover, in our struggle to live, I would have three price-less assets not available to them—the pick, shovel, and axe.

They had come to take a mine away from me. I had come to work the mine.

I knew there were at least two things they could do that would be terri-bly dangerous to us. They could direct a heavy fire at the walls and roof of the tunnel, causing the bullets to ricochet within the small space. Such bullets tear like the jagged pieces of hot metal they are.

And they could kill the horses.

Killing them in the tunnel mouth could obscure our vision, and might even block escape. It might be they were doomed to die anyway, but I was going to get them out if I could.

Somewhere up on the slope a tree branch cracked in the cold. It was very still . . . an icy stillness.

Boyd stamped his feet and complained. Boyd would be the first to go. He simply hadn't the guts for the long pull. Of them all, Ben Hobes was the one to last.

Suddenly, they turned around and started for the trees. *I should nail one of them*, I thought. Then it was too late, and they were under three large trees and behind some brush where I could hear branches breaking as they built a fire. They would need more than a fire.

Where was the kid?

There had been six . . . one had tripped and fallen down below. That whole lower canyon was a vast snare of boulders and logs, covered now with snow.

The bullet hit the butt end of a cut log just an instant before the report racketed against the hills. I reached over for the coffeepot and filled my cup. Nursing it in my hands to keep my fingers warm, I sat tight. A volley of shots came next, and one of them struck above the entrance, showering the woodpile with chipped rock.

"Stay back there, Ange. Don't move unless you have to."

"Tell? Are we going to get out of this?"

"Ange, I could lie to you, but I don't know. If any of us get out, we'll be lucky."

For several minutes they kept up a hammering fire and I let them shoot, holding my cup in my hands and waiting. Finally, they stopped, and we could hear them arguing.

Would they believe us dead? That was what I hoped.

Tuthill called out, but I made no sound. A couple of searching shots came then, one striking the rock above the opening again, the other hit-ting just inside.

Again Tuthill yelled, and I finished my coffee, peering through openings in the woodpile.

Another shot. This one struck deep into the cave with an angry smack.

There was more arguing. The voices could be heard, but not the words. Then the bushes parted and Tom Bigelow was coming toward the cave, a pistol in his hand.

He slowed as he came nearer, worried by what he was doing. He paused, threw up his pistol, and fired. It was a quick, testing shot, and it struck the rock at the side of the opening.

Bigelow hesitated, then came on, walking fast. He was within a dozen steps when I spoke out. "All right, Bigelow. Drop that gun!"

He pulled up sharp, starting to tilt the gun.

*"Drop it!"*

He could see the rifle muzzle now. At that distance even a child couldn't miss with a Winchester. He dropped the gun.

"Your brother was killed because he tried to bottom deal on me, and I told him he'd better not grab iron. He tried it. I didn't want to kill him."

Tom Bigelow said nothing.

"Unloose your gun belt," I said.

He unfastened the belt and let it fall.

"All right, I'm letting you go back. But before you go, you might tell me what you boys are going to do for something to eat. Your passes are closed. You can't take our grub, and if you could, there isn't enough to last out a week."

"We can get back."

"Ask Ben Hobes. Ask him about Al Packer."

"Who's he?"

"He started across the mountains in the winter with a party. They ran out of grub. He ate all five of the others. These same mountains. Are you ready for that, Bigelow?"

"You're lyin'!"

"All right, go on back."

One less gun they had, and maybe eighteen to twenty less ca'tridges. Come night time they would try and close in on me. Of course, on the white snow . . .

"Did they bring any pack horses?" I asked Ange.

"No," she said, "they planned to go right back."

They would be short of grub then. Whatever they did, they must do at once.

Suddenly, as Bigelow disappeared into the trees, I levered three fast, searching shots over there, waited an instant, then fired again, holding the rifle a little lower.

Shivering, I added fuel to the fire. The hungry flames crept slowly along the branches, then finding a piece of pitch pine, blazed up. A shot struck the roof, ricocheted down, and scattered fire. I brushed the sparks from my clothing and the bed, and felt a sharp tug at my sleeve as a second bullet came, striking just beyond the fire.

Through the trees I could see their fire. Lying prone on the cold floor, and taking my time, I drew a careful bead on a dark spot at the edge. It might be a log or a stump. It might also be a man.

For a moment I relaxed. Then, taking a long breath, I gathered trigger-slack, let the breath out slowly, and squeezed off the shot.

The cry was hoarse, choking . . . followed by a horrible retching sound such as I had never heard from anything, animal or human.

There was a volley in reply. I fired four more shots that covered an area about four feet back from the fire, and then a final shot across the fire itself.

"Ange," I said, "you'll find some cold flour in my pack. Take it and some of that meat and cook them up together. When it gets dark, we're going to get out."

"Can we?"

"We can try."

Worried as I was about what Tuthill and the rest of them might do, I was more worried about the cold.

Somehow we had to escape. We had to try. We had to try while we had our strength.

Ange was in no condition to attempt a winter in the mountains. We lacked the food for it, lacked the proper clothing and equipment. Yet bad off as we were, those others must be suffering more by now. For his own sake, I hoped the man I shot was dead.

Frightened by the firing, the horses had drawn away from the cave mouth. Now they started back, but before they could reach us, two quick shots put them down. The pack horse first, then the appaloosa.

For the first time in months I swore. Pa was never strong on cussing, and Ma was dead set against it, so we boys kind of grew up without doing much of that, but I said some words this time. They were good horses, and they had done no harm to anyone. But I knew why they were killed. Those men over there, they were realizing how much they needed grub . . . and horse meat was still meat, and not bad eating at that.

Night came. Stars appeared, wind came flowing like icy water over the rim of the mountain. The moon was not visible to us yet, but shone white upon the mountain tops. Twice I dusted the woods with gunfire; and then Ange and me, we ate what we could. What was left of the jerked meat I stowed away in a pack, and made another pack of our blankets and the ammunition.

With a long pole I'd used a couple of times for fishing, I reached out and snagged Tom Bigelow's gun belt, then the pistol. I shucked the shells from the gun belt, and used them to fill empty loops in my own belt. Emptying the shells into my hand from the cylinder, I took my axe and smashed the firing pin.

Then I made a loop on my pack from which to hang the axe, and covered over the shovel and pick with rock waste from the floor of the tunnel. They would probably find them, but I had no intention of making anything easy.

Occasionally a shot hit the back wall or struck into the woodpile. Only at long intervals I returned their fire . . . I wanted them to become accustomed to long waiting.

There was every chance they would try an attack under cover of darkness, although their dark figures would be visible on the snow for a time. However if they managed to cross far down the valley and worked toward us along the wall . . .

"Be ready to move," I whispered to Ange. "I think they will try something now, and after that we're pulling out."

Getting up from behind the stacked wood, I moved outside and eased along the rock wall until I could look both ways. Nothing at first . . . then a faint whisper of coarse cloth brushing on branches. Waiting until I detected a movement, I lifted the rifle, located the movement again, and fired.

There was a grunt, a heavy fall, and a bullet struck rock near my face. I ducked and half fell back into the tunnel. Outside there was cursing, and several shots. Catching up the packs, I slung one on my back. Ange already had the small one. An instant we paused. I levered a shot at a stab of flame from the trees, and then we slipped out.

The area around the tunnel lay in heavy darkness. We went swiftly along the wall and, when well away from the tunnel, turned up through the trees.

We had to go down the trail up which they had come, and go down it in darkness. Then we had to go up the opposite side, climb that steep talus slope to the bare, icy ridge that overlooked the Vallecitos. Whether Ange could make this, I did not know.

Once into the trees and moving, working away from the valley of the mine, we slowed down, holding to a steady pace. The snow had frozen, and we moved now across a good surface where there was no need for snowshoes.

The crude pair had been abandoned, as they were in bad shape anyway after the rough usage they had. As long as the cold held the snow would remain solid, but when it began to get warmer the ice beneath the snow, left from the sleet storm, would melt. Once that happened, travel would become impossible. At the lightest step, snow might slide, bringing down all the snow upon an entire mountainside in one gigantic avalanche. The cold was a blessing, severe as it was.

We traveled steadily. Nobody would be too anxious to investigate the mine, even when they began to believe we had escaped. And when they did investigate, they would start at once to seek for gold. Most of that in sight had been taken by me, and they were going to have to do some digging to get at the rest.

And before long they would have other things on their minds.

Time to time I stopped to give Ange a chance to catch her breath and ease her muscles. She didn't complain, and seemed to be holding up.

The moon was bright on the canyon wall when we came to the path down. Ange caught my sleeve. "Tell? Do we have to?"

"We have to."

I tried a foot on the trail. The frozen snow might make it a lot easier going down than loose snow over that sleet. Moving carefully, like a man walking on eggs, I started down.

Wind bit at exposed flesh, stiffening our muscles. The canyon below was a great open mouth of darkness. Above us the ridges and peaks towered pure, white, and glittering with wild beauty in the moonlight. It's rare in a man's life to see such a sight, and I stopped for a minute, just taking it in. Ange was standing close behind, her hands on my back.

"I wish Ma would see that," I said. "She favors lovely things."

The wind gnawed at our faces with icy teeth, as we moved along. Snow crunched as we put our feet down, each step a lifetime of risk and doubt.

The path was scarce three feet wide, widening to four at the most but looking broader in spots because of the cornices of snow that hung over the lip. It was a steep path where every step had to be separate, the foot put carefully down, the weight rested gradually, and then the other foot lifted.

The sky above was amazingly bright; the moon made the hills and peaks like day. High above, on a frosty ridge where I hoped to be by daylight, the snow blew, throwing a brief veil across the sky. The snow hanging on the slopes above the trail made me mighty uneasy. Snow like that can start to slide on the slightest provocation, and with daylight it would become worse.

When we were halfway down, we stopped again, and Ange came up beside me. "You ready for it?" I asked her. "They'll be coming soon, Ange."

"How long has it been?"

"Couple of hours . . ."

We hit bottom with our knees shaking, and headed for the cave. By daylight they would realize we were gone. With the fire out, they would soon guess that we'd lit a shuck, and they would come a-helling after us.

We were almost to the cave before we smelled smoke. Catching a whiff of it, I pulled up short. Somebody was in the cave.

Stepping into the opening, gun up and ready, I found myself looking into the muzzle of a .44 gun. That gun muzzle looked as great as the cave mouth, as black as death itself.

"Mister," I said, "you put down that .44 gun. If you don't, I'm sure going to kill you."

And all the while he had the drop on me.

# Chapter 14

Kid Newton was holding that pistol—that white-headed kid I'd talked out of trouble back down the line.

He was lying on his back, looking sick, and the gun in his hand was shaky. A blanket was pulled over him, and I could see from the fire that he had been feeding sticks into it without getting up.

"What's the matter, Kid? You in trouble?"

He kept the gun on me. Could I swing that Winchester up in time to nail him? I was hoping I wouldn't have to try.

"Busted my leg."

"And they left you? That ain't hardly decent, Kid." Using up all the nerve I had in store, I put my rifle down. "Kid, put that gun away and let me look at your leg."

"You got no cause to help me," he said, but I could see he wanted help more than anybody I'd ever seen.

"You're hurt, that's cause enough. Maybe when you get well I'll have cause to shoot you, but right now I wouldn't leave no man in your kind of trouble."

I said to Ange, "You stay in the opening and keep a lookout. We may have to shoot our way out of here yet."

Taking the pistol from his hand, I pulled back the blanket. He had made a try at splinting his leg, but the splints had come loose. The leg was swollen and looked a fright.

I cut a split in his pants leg, and cut his boot to get it off. No cowhand likes to have a good pair of boots ruined, but there was no other way about it. Looked like a clean break a few inches below the knee, but those splints had been a lousy job. I cut some fresh ones, then I made a try at doing something to ease him.

I heated some water, and put hot cloths on that leg. To tell the truth, I wasn't sure how much good they'd do, but they would make him think he was being helped, a comfort to a man that's been lying alone, half-froze to death in a lonely cave.

"You drag yourself here?"

"They left me."

"That's a rawhide outfit, Kid. They aren't worth shootin'. You ought to cut loose from them and line up with a real bunch."

Breaking some sticks, I built up the fire, and all the time I was thinking what a pickle we were in. We had it bad enough, Ange and me, trying to take out over that ridge. And as if we weren't in trouble enough, we were now saddled with a man with a broke . . . broken leg.

Folks might say it was none of my business, that my first duty was to get Ange out of here, and myself. It was nip and tuck whether we would make it or not—I'd say we were on the short end of the odds. The Kid had come with men who intended to rob me, probably murder me. And before that he had tried to pick a fight with me. Someday, somebody was going to have to shoot him, more than likely.

But left here, he would freeze to death before he could starve. There was no two ways about that. And none of that gold-hungry crowd would lift a hand to help.

Taking the axe, I walked down to the trees. The moon was gone now, but day was not too far off. Searching through a bunch of second-growth timber, stuff that had grown up after a slide had ripped it down, I found in a thick cluster of aspen just what I wanted, and cut two slim poles about eight feet long.

I carried them back to the cave, after trimming the branches off, and then took the axe and smoothed off one side. My axe was sharp and I'd split enough rails for fences back in Tennessee to know how to trim up a young tree. On the bottom end I made a bevel, curving the end upward a mite.

Going to the woodpile, I cut some crosspieces, notched the poles to take four of them, and then fitted them into the notches.

"What you fixin'?"

"You set quiet. Can't pack you out of here on my back, so I'm fixing a toboggan . . . such as it is."

"You'd take me out of here?" The Kid was not expecting any favors, seemed like.

"Can't let you lie here and freeze," I told him irritably. "Best thing you can do is stay quiet. If we get out at all, you'll be with us, but don't get your hopes up. Our chances are mighty poor."

For several minutes, while I wove some rawhide around the crosspieces, Kid Newton had nothing to say. Finally, he eased his leg a mite. "Sackett, you and that girl better take out. I mean, I'm no account. Why, I was fixin' to kill you back along the trail."

"Kid, you'd never have cleared leather. I wasn't hunting trouble, but I cut my teeth on a six-shooter."

"You can make it, you two. You're never going to get me over any trail on that sled."

"We aren't going by trail." I sat back on my heels. "Kid, if you get out of this alive you can sure tell folks you've been up the creek and over the mountain, because that's where we're going."

He didn't get it. And reason enough he couldn't. No man in his right mind would try what I figured to do.

Some of the trails by which we had come into the mountains would by now be a dozen feet under the snow. What I figured to do was go over the ridge . . . to go right down the steep side of the mountain into camp.

Crazy? Sure . . . but the chute was choked with snow and ice, the upper valley was full by now, and the other trails, the one by which Ange came in . . . the passes would be choked with snow there.

We had all come in on horseback, but no horse could get out. In places the snow might carry the weight of a man alone, but never the weight of men and horses. We might make it out, but it was a risk scarcely worth thinking about.

It is one thing to ride a horse through unknown country; it is another to go back afoot. It would take twice, maybe three times as long. The gang up there had figured to come in and go right out. . . .

"What do you mean?" The Kid was looking at me now like he was afraid he did know.

Pausing in my work, I gestured at the mountain opposite. "The one above us is higher, and we're going over it."

He knew I was crazy now. One lone man taking a girl and a wounded man over that mountain!

The sky was gray overhead when we started out of there, me towing that crude toboggan behind me. The slope of talus was steep, but easier going with the snow on it, for the rock did not slide under me. Still, it was a struggle to get up to the foot of that chimney.

Ange looked up at it, and her eyes were mighty big when she turned back to me. "Tell," she whispered, "you can't do it. It's impossible."

To tell the truth, I didn't feel very good about it myself. That was a high mountain, and that climb was going to be something. Slinging my rifle around my shoulders and hanging a coil of rope to my belt, I told Ange to come on.

The Kid, he was tied onto the sled, and he laid there looking at me. "You going to leave me, Sackett? I don't blame you. Unless you can fly, you ain't going up there."

I made one end of the rope fast to the head of the toboggan, and got ready to climb. The rope was made fast by taking a round turn on each runner, then tying the end of the rope to the standing part, so the sled would hang straight when I started to pull it.

Going up ahead, I cut a few toe-holds in the ice, and found a couple I'd used before where no ice had collected. When at last I climbed the chimney, I guided Ange.

She was little, but mighty lithe and strong when it came right down to it, and she made easier work of that climb up the chimney than I had.

The old, gnarled bristle-cone was standing there where I'd remembered it, atop that chimney and rooted deep in the rock. Taking a turn around that old tree, I dug my heels in and started to hand over hand that rope. Like I said, I'm a big man with a lot of beef in my shoulders and arms, but when I took the strain of that full weight, I surely knew I was in trouble.

Getting him clear of the ground was only part of it. He had to fend himself off the rocky face with his hands. A time or two, I could feel him helping me where he could get a hand-hold.

Ange stood behind me and cleared the rope around the trunk of the pine so we could hold what we had got. My hands were stiff, and I didn't think I'd ever get my fingers unwound from about that rope. But I hauled away.

Stopping to rest myself, with the Kid hanging there like a papoose slung on a pack board, I looked off across the valley.

Somebody was coming down the trail. How far? Maybe a quarter of a mile, a bit more or less. There were only four of them, the man behind was making a slow thing of it.

One of them jerked up his rifle and we heard the sound of a shot. What happened to that bullet I never could say, but it came nowhere near us. Judging distance across a canyon like that, when the target is higher than you—that's quite a stunt. Why, I've missed a few shots like that my own self.

Digging in my heels, I took hold of that rope. My arms ached and I was fighting for breath. Those high-up ridges surely took a man's wind. But I got him up a couple of feet farther, beat my hands to warm them, and started at it again.

There was no time to look across the canyon. There was only time to haul away. Heave, and heave again . . . catch a breath, and heave again.

Then the toboggan brought up against something and stuck.

"Ange," I said, straightening up, "I'm going down. When I clear the sled, you get as much rope around that pine as can be."

"Tell?"

Turning around, I looked at her. She was looking right at me. "Why are you doing this? Is it because of the way I acted?"

Well, I declare! I hadn't thought of that. "No, Ange, I never gave thought to that. No man can abide much by what a woman thinks, at times like this. He does what it's his nature to do. That man down there . . . we had words one time. He was figuring to shoot me, and I was planning to beat him to it.

"That there's one thing, this here's another. That's a helpless man, and when I get him up here and get him safe, then maybe he'll come a-gunning for me. So I'll have to shoot him."

I started down the slope, then stopped and looked back. "Seems a lot of trouble to go to, doesn't it?"

Well, I cleared him, and we hoisted him out on top of the ridge, using the same route I'd found on that day when I left Ange in the cave.

Down below was Cap, our log house, and our claim—down there in those trees. And up here the wind was blowing a gale, and a man could scarcely stand erect. One thing I knew: we had to get off that mountain, and fast.

It was clouding up again—great banks of gray, solid cloud. That could mean more snow. That canyon could be twenty feet deep in snow before the week was out.

Camp was a half-mile as the crow flies, but a good five thousand feet down. Looking north to where I'd spotted what looked like a way down, I could still see it, despite the snow. Once into the trees, we could make it all right, although it would be work.

This ridge was about thirteen thousand feet up, and the wind was roaring along it. All the gray granite was swept clean, although there were flurries of snow in the air from time to time. Leaning into the wind, we started on, towing the sled. Finally we got down over the edge of the ridge. Right away, the wind seemed to let up.

My face was raw from the wind, my hands were numb. My fingers in their gloves felt stiff, and I was afraid that the Kid, held immovable the way he was, would freeze to death.

Lowering the sled away ahead of us, we made it down. One time the wind came around a shoulder of the mountain and lifted the sled, man and all, like it was a leaf, but set it down again before the rope tore from my hands. We both heard the Kid scream when the drop jolted his broken leg.

Bracing myself on great shattered rocks, I lowered him. Climbing after, lowering Ange, I lost all sense of time, and could not remember when it ever had been warm.

Below us was a huge old tree, ripped from the rock by its roots. It sprawled like a great spider, petrified in the moment of death, legs writhing. A little below it were some wind-tortured trees, and then the forest.

We could see the tops of the trees and, far off below, a white, white world of snow, with here and there a faint feather of smoke rising from some house.

Hugging that wind-torn mountainside, and looking down into those treetops, I could hardly believe there was a house with a fire burning in it, or Ma a-rocking in her old rocker, or Orrin a-singing. It was a world far away from the wind, the cold, and snow that drove at your face like sand.

But, easing the sled down a little farther, we got into the trees. From there to the bottom it was mostly a matter of guiding the sled, belaying the rope around a tree here and there to ease it, and working our way through. One time Ange almost dropped, and my own knees were buckling most of the way.

By the time we reached the path I'd cut to build a little fort above the camp, I had fallen down a couple of times, and I was so numb with cold and so exhausted I could scarce think. The draw rope over my shoulder, and one arm around Ange, I started through the tall pines toward the house.

The snow was deep under the trees, but there was a slow lift of smoke from the chimney, and a light in the window. Seemed like only a short time ago it was coming daylight, and now it was nighttime again.

Then I fell, face down in the snow. Seemed to me I tried to get up . . . seemed to get my hands under me and push. I could see that light in the window and I could hear myself talking. I hauled away and got to the door, where I couldn't make my fingers work the latch.

The door opened of a sudden and Cap was standing there with a six-gun in his hand, looking like he was the old Cap and ready to start shooting.

"It ain't worth the trouble, Cap. I think I'm dead already."

Joe Rugger was there, and between them they got Kid Newton off the sled and into the house. Ange, she just sat down and started to cry, and I knelt on the floor and put my arm around her and kept telling her everything was all right.

Kid Newton caught my sleeve. "By God," he said, "today I seen a man! I thought—"

"Get some sleep," I said. "Joe's going for the doctor."

"I seen a man," the Kid repeated. "Why, when I hung those guns on me I thought I was something, I thought—"

"Shut up," I said. And I reached my hands toward the fire a distance off. I could feel the million tiny needles starting to dance in my fingers as the cold began to leave them.

"Speaking of men"—I looked over at Newton—"if you ever get down to

Mora, I've got two brothers down there, Tyrel and Orrin. Now there's a couple of men!

"Always figured to make something of myself," I said, "but I guess I just ain't got it in me."

Sitting on the edge of the bed, I just let the heat soak into me, every muscle feeling stretched out and useless. Ange had quit her crying and dropped off to sleep there beside me, her face drawn, dark hollows under her eyes.

"You been through it," Cap said. He looked at Newton. "What did you bring him back for?"

"I got no better sense, Cap. I brought him down off that mountain because there was nobody else to do it."

"But he wanted to kill you!"

"Sure . . . he had him a notion, that was all. I reckon since then he's had time to contemplate."

Cap Rountree took his pipe out of his teeth and dumped coffee in the pot.

"Then you take time to contemplate about this," he said. "There's another Bigelow down in town. He's asking for you."

# Chapter 15

It wasn't in me to lie abed. Come daylight, I was on my feet, but I wasn't up to much. What I really got up for was vittles. Seemed like I hadn't been so hungry in years.

Ange was still sleeping in the other room, and Joe Rugger and his wife, just out from Ohio, had come out to the place.

"That Bigelow worries me," Rugger said. "He's a man hunting trouble like you never saw."

"Those Bigelows," I said, "they remind me of those little animals a Swede told me about one time. Called them lemmings or something like that. Seems as if all of a sudden they take out for the ocean . . . millions of them, and they run right into the ocean and drown. Those Bigelows seem bound and determined to get themselves killed just as fast as they can manage."

"Don't take him lightly, Tell," Rugger warned me. "He killed a man in Denver City, and another in Tascosa. Benson Bigelow, he's the oldest, biggst, and toughest of all of them."

"Heard of him," Cap said. "I didn't know he was kin."

"He's been asking questions about his brothers. They haven't come back out of the mountains, and he says you murdered them."

"Them and three more? That's quite a lot to take on. Believe me, they haven't come out of the mountains, and it will surprise me if they ever do."

The warmth of the room felt good and after a while I stretched out and slept some more.

When I opened my eyes Ange was fixing something at the stove. I got up and pulled on my boots. I spilled some water in the basin and washed my face and hands. The water felt good on my face, and I decided I needed a shave.

Cap was off somewhere, and just the two of us were there. The doctor had taken the Kid away. It was nice, shaving, with Ange fussing over something at the fire. Finally she called me to dinner and I was ready. Cap came in, stomping the snow from his boots on the stoop.

"Snowing," he said. "You were lucky. A few hours more, and you might never have made it."

Ange brought me a cup of coffee and I held it in my hands, thinking about those men up there. They brought it on themselves, and despite their ill feeling for me, I was wishing they would make it.

They never did.

Cap accepted coffee too, and he looked over at me. "That Benson Bigelow is telling it around that you're yellow, afraid to meet him."

Some folks are bound and determined to make fools of themselves.

All I wanted was a ranch of my own, some cattle, and a little land I could crop. Only when I looked up there at Ange I knew that wasn't all I wanted.

I had no idea how to put it, and hated to risk it, knowing how little I had to offer. Here I was a grown man, just learning to read proper, and although I'd found some gold there was no telling how deep that vein would run. In fact, it acted to me like a pocket. That was why as soon as spring came I was going to light out for Mora to see the boys.

I said as much to Cap.

"You needn't worry," he said. "Tyrel and Orrin, they're riding up here. Them and Ollie Shaddock."

Ollie was from the Cumberland too. Sheriff back there one time, and some kin of ours. He was the one who got Orrin into politics, although Tennessee boys take to politics like they do to coon hunting.

"When do you expect them?"

"Tonight or tomorrow, if all goes well. They heard you were fetching trouble and they sent word they were coming up."

They would ride into town and, unknown to them, that Bigelow would be there, and he might hear one of them called Sackett and just open up and start shooting.

If he faced them, I wasn't worried. Tyrel now, Tyrel was hell on wheels with a pistol.

I finished my coffee and got up. Then I took down my gun belt and slung it around my hips and took down my coat and hat. "Riding up to town," I said. "A little fresh air."

"Kind of stuffy in here," Cap Rountree said. "Mind if I ride along?"

Ange had turned from the fire with a big spoon in her hand.

"What about supper? After I've gone to all this trouble?"

"We'll be back," I said. "You keep it warm, Ange."

I shrugged into my coat and put on my hat. I was going to have to get me a coonskin for this weather. "Anyway," I said, "the way I figure, I shouldn't get used to your cooking, nohow. A man can form a habit."

She was looking me right in the eye, her face flushed a mite from the fire, looking pretty as all get-out.

"Trouble is, no woman in her right mind would marry a fool, and I'm certainly one."

"A lot you know about women!" she scoffed. "Did you ever see a fool who didn't have a wife?"

Come to that, I hadn't.

"Keep it warm," I said.

She didn't say a word about shooting or Benson Bigelow. She just said, "You come back, Tell Sackett, I won't have my supper wasted. Not after all this trouble."

It was cool in the outside air, and Cap led the horses out. He had them saddled. "Figured you wouldn't want the boys to come up against it, unexpected," he said.

The saloon was hot and crowded, and up at the bar a big man was standing. He had a broad, hard-boned face and it took only one look to see this was no ordinary Bigelow, this was the Old Man of the Woods, right from Bitter Creek, tough and mean and not all talk.

He turned around and looked at me and I walked over and leaned on the bar alongside him.

You never saw a saloon lose customers so fast. Must have been fifty, sixty men in there when I leaned on that bar, and a half-minute later there weren't but five or six, the kind who just have to stay and see what happens, men determined to be innocent bystanders.

This Bigelow sized me up and I looked back at him kind of mild and round-eyed, and I said, "Nice mustache you have there, Mr. Bigelow."

"What's wrong with my mustache?"

"Why, nothing . . . exactly."

"What's that mean?"

"Buy you a drink?"

"What's wrong with my mustache? No, I'll buy my own drinks!"

For the first time he realized the crowd was gone. The skin under his eyes seemed to tighten.

Outside I thought I could hear horses coming. It was late for travel in this weather, which made me wonder if it wasn't Tyrel and Orrin.

Those brothers of mine . . . ride hundreds of miles—well, maybe a couple hundred—through rough country because they figured I was standing alone against trouble.

"Are you Tell Sackett?"

"That brother of yours, Wes, he never was no hand with cards. Nor a pistol, either."

"What happened to Tom and Ira?"

"You look long enough, you'll find them in the spring," I told him. "They had no more sense than to come chasing me back into the hills, with winter coming on and snow in the air."

"Did you see them?"

"They tried to kill me a couple of times. They weren't any better shots than Wes. Tom, he lost his gun up there."

Bigelow was quiet, and I could see him studying things out in his mind.

"Hear you came up here hunting me," I said mildly. "It's a long ride for the trouble."

He couldn't quite make me out. Nothing I had said showed I was troubled about anything, just talking like to any passer-by.

"You know something, Bigelow? You better just straddle your horse and ride out of here. What happened to your brothers was brought on them by their own actions."

"Maybe you're right," he said. "I'll buy the drink."

So we had a drink together, and then I ordered one. When I got rid of that I drew back. "Well, I've got a good supper waiting for me. See you around, Bigelow."

Turning, I started for the door and then he said, "Sackett?"

His gun cocked when it cleared leather and a sound like that is plain to hear in an empty room. I drew as I turned and his first bullet whiffed by my ear. Steadying down, I shot him through the belly, and it slammed him against the bar. But he caught the edge with his left hand and pulled himself around. I did not hear the report, but I felt the slug take me low and hard. I braced myself and shot him again.

He did not go down . . . . .44 or not, you have to hit a man right through the heart, through the head, or on a big bone to stop him if he's mad, and Bigelow was killing mad. He was a big bear of a man and he looked tough as a winter on the cap-rock of west Texas.

For what seemed like minutes he stood there, and I could see the blood soaking his shirt front and pants, and then great red drops of it began to hit the floor between his feet.

He lifted his gun, taking his time, his left hand still clinging to the bar, and he took dead aim at me. He started to cock the gun, and I shot him again. He jolted the bar when he slammed against it. A bottle tipped over and rolled down the bar, spilling whiskey. He reached over and took up the bottle and drank out of it, holding it in his left hand, never taking his eyes off me.

He put the bottle down, and I said, "That drink was on me."

"I made a mistake," he said. "I guess you shot them honest."

"Only Wes . . . the cold got the others."

"All right," he said, and turned his back on me. I could hear running outside.

For a long minute I stood there with my gun in my hand looking at his back, and then his knees began to sag and he fell slowly, his fingers clinging as long as they could to the bar. Then he let go and rolled over on the floor and he was dead.

He lay there face up in the sawdust, his eyes open to the lights, and there was sawdust in his beard.

There was a wet feeling inside my pants where the blood was running down. I thumbed shells into my gun, holstered it, and Cap came up to me.

"You're hit," he said.

"Seems like," I said, and caught hold of the wall.

The door opened and Tyrel came in, with Orrin right behind him, both of them ready for trouble.

"We'd better get back to the place," I said. "Supper will get cold."

They looked past me at Bigelow.

"Any more of them?" Tyrel asked.

"If there are, they won't have to shoot me. I'll shoot myself."

Cap pulled my shirt open and they could see the blood oozing from a hole in the flesh over my hip. The bullet had cut itself a place without hitting a bone or doing much harm. Tyrel took out a silk handkerchief and plugged it up, and we went outside.

"The doctor's here," Cap protested. "You'd better see him."

"Bring him along. There's a lady waiting dinner."

When I came in the door of the cabin, Ange stood with her back to it. I could see her shoulders hunch a mite as if she expected to be hit, and I said, "This fool ain't married."

She turned around and looked at me. "He will be," she said, and dropped her spoon on the floor and came across the room and right into my arms.

So I taken her in my arms and for the first time in my life I had something that was really mine.

Seems like even a long, tall man who ain't much for looks can find him a woman, too.

# LANDO

# Chapter 1

We Sacketts were a mountain folk who ran long on boy children and gun-shooting, but not many of us were traveled men. And that was why I envied the Tinker.

When first I caught sight of him he was so far off I couldn't make him out, so I taken my rifle and hunkered down behind the woodpile, all set to get in the first shot if it proved to be a Higgins.

Soon as I realized who it was, I turned again to tightening my mill, for I was fresh out of meal and feeling hunger.

Everybody in the mountains knew the Tinker. He was a wandering man who tinkered with everything that needed fixing. He could repair a clock, sharpen a saw, make a wagon wheel, or shoe a horse.

Fact was, he could do almost anything a body could think of that needed doing, and he wandered up and down the mountains from Virginia to Georgia just a-fixing and a-doing. Along with it, he was a pack peddler.

He carried a pack would have put a crick in a squaw's back, and when he fetched up to my cabin he slung it down and squatted on his heels beside it.

"If you reckoned I was a Higgins," he said, "you can put it out of mind. Your Cousin Tyrel cut his notch for the last Higgins months ago. You Sacketts done cleaned them out."

"Not this Sackett. I never shot 'ary a Higgins, although that's not to say I wouldn't had they come at me."

"Tyrel, him an' Orrin, they taken out for the western lands. Looks to me like you're to be the last of the Sacketts of Tennessee."

"Maybe I will and maybe I won't," said I, a-working at my mill. "I've given thought to the western lands myself, for a man might work his life away in these mountains, and nothing to show for it in the end."

The Tinker, he just sat there, not saying aye, yes, or no, but I could see he had something on his mind, and given time would have his say.

"You're the one has the good life," I said. "Always a-coming and a-going along the mountains and down to the Settlements."

There was a yearning in me to be off the mountain, for I'd lived too long in the high-up hills, knowing every twisty creek to its farthest reaches, and every lightning-struck tree for miles.

Other than my cabin, the only places I knew were the meetinghouse down to the Crossing where folks went of a Sunday, and the schoolhouse at Clinch's Creek where we went of a Saturday for the dancing and the fighting.

"Tinker," I said, "I've been biding my time until you came along, for come sunup it is in my mind to walk away from the mountains to the western lands."

Filling the mill's hopper, I gave the handles a testing turn, then added, "If you've a mind to, I'd like you to come with me."

Now, the Tinker was a solitary man. A long-jawed man, dark as any Indian, but of a different cast, somehow, and he'd an odd look to his yellow eyes. Some said he hailed from foreign lands, but I knew nothing of that, nor ought of the ways of foreign folk, but the Tinker knew things a body could scarcely ken, and held a canny knowledge of uncanny things.

Beside a fire of an evening his fingers worked a magic with rope or yarn, charming queer, decorative things that women took fancy to, but the likes of which none of us had ever seen.

"I have given it thought, 'Lando," he answered me, "but I am a lone man with no liking for company."

"So it is with me. But now it is in my mind to go to the western lands and there become rich with the things of this earth. You have the knack for the doing of things, and I have a knack for trade, and together we might do much that neither could do alone."

"Aye . . . you have a knack for trade, all right. A time or two you even had the better of me."

A time or two he said? *Every* time. And well he knew it, too, but it was not in me to bring that up.

"Except for one thing," I said. "You never would trade me a Tinker's knife."

He took out his pipe and settled to smoke, and I knew it was coming, this thing he had on his mind. "You have enemies. Is that why you have chosen to leave at this time?"

It ired me that he should think so, but I held my peace, and when I spoke at last, my voice was mild.

"Will Caffrey and his son? They have reason to fear me, and not I to fear them. It was my father's mistake to leave me with Will Caffrey to be reared by him, but pa was not himself from the grief that was on him, and in no condition for straight thinking."

"Caffrey had a good name then," the Tinker said, "although a hard-fisted man and close with money. Only since he became a rich man has he become overbearing."

"And it was the gold I claimed from him at Meeting that made him rich, and none of his earning. He had it from my father to pay for my keep and education."

"You put your mark upon his son."

"He asked it of me. He came at me, a-swinging of his fists."

When I had emptied the meal from the hopper, I tightened the mill and filled the hopper again, for such a mill as that of mine could grind only to a certain coarseness on the first grinding, and then the mill must be tightened and the meal reground before it was fit for the baking or for gruel.

"They are saying how you faced Will Caffrey at Meeting, and him a deacon of the church and all, and demanded he return the money your father left with him, and all the interest he had from its use.

"They tell how he flustered and would give you the lie, but all knew how five years ago you ran from his farm and have lived alone in this cabin since, and how, suddenly, after your father left Will Caffrey had money with which to buy farms and cattle.

"You'll not be forgiven this side of the grave, not by Will Caffrey. He is a proud man and you have shamed him at Meeting."

"The money is rightfully mine, Tinker. When he decided my father would not return, he took me from school and put me to work in the fields, and sent his son to school in my place."

The mill was ready, and again I ground my meal, the noise allowing for no talk, but when I'd emptied the hopper I said, "If it is enemies I have, it is the Caffreys. I know of no others."

He shot me a curious glance, which puzzled me with its content. "Not three tall, mustached men with dark hair and long faces? Three tall men as alike as peas in a pod . . . named Kurbishaw?"

"It was my mother's name."

"They are riding to kill you."

"You saw them where?"

"In the Cherokee towns. They asked questions there."

"The Indians are my friends. They will tell them nothing."

"When last I saw them they had old Midah Wolf and were buying him drink."

Midah was an old man with a love for the bottle and a memory of youth that only drink could bring back. When drunk, he was enemy to no man and would surely talk. He would be sorry after, but that would be of no help.

"The Kurbishaws are my mother's folk. They will surely be coming for other reasons."

"I have heard them say, 'We have killed the wolf, now we shall kill the whelp.'"

They had killed the wolf? If by that they meant my father, I did not believe them. My father might have many faults, but lack of shrewdness was not one of them. As I grew older I had remembered his actions around our mountain cabin, and now I knew that he had been aware of danger, that he had lived no moment without that awareness.

Yet he had not returned . . . had they killed him, indeed?

"I have only my father's worn-out rifle," I said, "and a dislike for shooting men I do not know, nor have I any appetite for violence."

The Tinker glanced at me shrewdly, and I wondered what went on behind those yellow eyes. Was he my friend, in truth? Had I learned this doubt of people? Was it acquired by brief but hard experience?

"If they find their way to the Crossing, Caffrey will be quick to tell them where you are." The Tinker turned his yellow eyes straight at me. "Did you never wonder why your pa came to this lonely place with his bride? There's a story told in the lowland towns."

"There was trouble when he married ma. Her family objected to him."

"Objected is a mild word. They objected so much they hired a man to kill him when his brothers-in-law decided against trying it. Your pa killed the man and then lit out for the hills so he would not have to kill her brothers and have their blood between them.

"Or so the story is told. Yet there is a whisper of something else, of something beyond pride of family. There is a tale that they hated your father for a reason before he even met your mother."

We Sacketts had come early to the mountains. Welsh folk we were, Welsh and Irish, and my family had come to America one hundred and fifty years before the Colonies fought for their independence. A relative of mine had been killed in the fierce fighting in North Carolina in the revolt that failed.

We settled on the frontier, as it then was, along the flanks of the Blue Ridge and Smoky mountains, and there we made ourselves part of the rocky hills and the forests. Pa was the first of our family to run off to the lowlands and return with a bride.

The Kurbishaws made much of themselves and cut a wide swath among the lowland folk, looking down their long noses at us who lived in the hills.

We Sacketts set store by kinfolk, but we never held up our family with pride. A mill grinds no corn with water that is past. Come trouble, we

Sacketts stand shoulder to shoulder as long as need be, but we made no talk of ancestors, nor how high they stood in the community.

Yet it was no wonder that pa took the eye of the lowland girls, for he was a fine, upstanding man with a colorful way about him, and he cut quite a dash in the lowland towns.

He rode a fine black gelding, his pockets filled with gold washed from a creek the Cherokees showed him, and he dressed with an elegance and a taste for fine tailoring. There was gold from another source, too, and as a child I saw those hoarded coins a time or two.

My father showed me one of them and I loved the dull reflection of the nighttime firelight upon it. "There is more where that came from, laddie, more indeed. One day we shall gather it, you and I."

"Let it lie," ma said. "The earth is a fit place for it."

Such times pa would flash her that bright, quick smile of his and show her that hard light in his black eyes. "I might have told them where it was, had they acted differently about us," he would say; "but if they have it now it shall cost them blood."

How long since I had thought of that story? How long since I had even seen that gold until pa brought it out to turn over to Caffrey for my education and keep?

Her brothers had planned for ma to marry wealth and power, and when she ran off with pa they were furious, and challenged him. He refused them, and as he refused them he held two finely wrought pistols in his hands.

"You do not wish to fight me," he said, and tossed a bottle into the air. With one pistol he smashed the bottle, and with the second he hit a falling fragment. It was after that they hired a man to kill him.

Pa and ma would have lived their lives among the lowland folk had the Kurbishaws let them be, but they used their wealth and power to hound them out of Virginia and the Carolinas, until finally they took refuge in the mountain cabin among the peaks, which pa built with his own hands.

The cabin was a fair, kind place among the rocks and trees, with a cold spring at the back and a good fishing stream not a hundred yards off. And happily they lived there until ma died.

"If you stay here," the Tinker went on, "they will kill you. You have but the one barrel of your old rifle and they are three armed men, and skilled at killing."

"They are my uncles, after all."

"They are your enemies, and you are not your father. These men are fighters, and you are not."

My head came up angrily, for he spoke against my pride. "I can fight!"

Impatience was in his voice and attitude when he answered. "You have fought against boys or clumsy men. That is not fighting. Fighting is a skill to be learned. I saw you whip the three Lindsay boys, but any man with skill could have whipped you easily."

"There were three of them."

The Tinker knocked the ash from his pipe. "'Lando, you are strong, one of the strongest men I know, and surprising quick, but neither of these things makes you a fighter. Fighting is a craft, and it must be learned and practiced. Until you know how to fight with your head as well as with heart and muscle, you are no fighting man."

"And I suppose you know this craft?"

I spoke contemptuously, for the idea of the Tinker as a fighting man seemed to me laughable. He was long and thin, with nothing much to him.

"I know a dozen kinds. How to fight with the fists, the open hand, and Japanese- as well as Cornish-style wrestling. If we travel together, I will teach you."

Teach *me*? I bit my tongue on angry words, for my pride was sore hurt that he took me so lightly. Had I not, when only a boy, whipped Duncan Caffrey, and him two years older and twenty pounds heavier? And since then I'd whipped eight or nine more, men and boys; and at Clinch's Creek was I not cock of the walk? And he spoke of teaching *me!*

Opening his pack, the Tinker brought out a packet of coffee, for he carried real coffee and not the dried beans and chickory we mountain folk used. Without moving from where he was, he reached out and brought together chips, bark, and bits of twigs left from my woodcutting and of them he made a fire.

He was a man who disliked the inside of places, craving the freeness of the open air about him. Some said it was because he must have been locked up once upon a time, but I paid no mind to gossip.

While he started the fire and put water on to boil, I went to a haunch of venison hanging in the shed and cut a healthy bait of it into thick slices for roasting at the fire. Then I returned to grind more meal.

Such mills as mine were scarce, and the corn I ground would be the last, for I planned to trade the mill for whatever it would bring as I passed out of the country.

If it was true the Kurbishaws sought to kill me they could find me here, for mountains are never so big that a man is not known.

But the thought of leaving this place brought a twinge of regret, for all the memories of ma and pa concerned this place. Yonder was the first tree I'd climbed, and how high the lowest branch had seemed then! And nearby was the spring from which I proudly carried the first bucket of water I could hold clear of the ground.

No man cuts himself free of old ties without regret; even scenes of hardship and sadness possess the warmth of familiarity, and within each of us there is a love for the known. How many times at planting had my shovel turned this dark earth! How many times had I leaned against that tree, or marveled at the cunning with which pa had fitted the logs of our house, or put all the cabinets together with wooden pins!

The Tinker filled my plate and cup. "We shall talk of fighting another time."

Suddenly my quieter mood was gone and irritation came flooding back. No man wishes to be lightly taken, and I was young and strong, and filled with the pride of victories won.

"Talk of it now," I said belligerently, "and if you want to try me on, you've no cause to wait."

"You talk the fool!" he said impatiently. "I am your friend, and I doubt if you have another. Wait, and when you have taken your whipping, come to me and I will show you how it should be done."

Putting down the coffee cup, I got to my feet. "Show me," I said, "if you think you can."

With a pained expression on his lean, dark face he got slowly to his feet. "This may save you a beating, or I'd have no part of it. So come at me if you will."

He stood with his arms dangling, and suddenly I thought what a fool I was to force such a fight on a friend; but then my pride took command and my fingers clenched into a fist and I swung at him.

End it with a blow, I thought, and save him a bad beating. That was in my mind when I swung. Suddenly long fingers caught my wrist with a strength I'd never have believed, and the next thing I knew I was flying through the air, to land with a thump on the hard ground. It fairly knocked the wind from me, and the nonsense from my brain as well; but then I saw him standing a few feet away, regarding me coolly.

Anger surged through me and I lunged up from the ground, prepared for that throw he had used upon me. This time I struck the ground even harder—he had thrown me in another way, and so suddenly and violently that I had no idea how it was done.

There was some sense in me after all, for I looked up at him and grinned. "At least you know a few tricks. Are these what you would show me?"

"These, and more," he said. "Now drink your coffee. It grows cold."

My anger was gone, and my good sense warned me that had he been my enemy I should now have been crippled or dead. For once down, he could put the boots to me and kick in my ribs, crush my chest or crush my skull. In such fighting there is no sportsmanship, for it is no game but is in deadly earnest, and men fight to win.

"Have you heard of Jem Mace?" he asked me.

"No."

"He was the world champion prize fighter, an Englishman and a gypsy. He whipped the best of them, and he was not a large man, but he was among the first to apply science to the art of fist fighting. He taught me boxing and I have sparred with him many times.

"Footwork is not mere dancing about. By footwork you can shift a man out of position to strike you effectively, and still leave yourself in position to strike him. By learning to duck and slip punches, you can work close to a man and still keep your hands free for punching. Certain blows automatically create openings for the blows to follow."

He refilled his cup. "A man who travels alone must look out for himself."

"You have your knives."

"Aye, but a hand properly used can be as dangerous as a knife." He was silent for a moment, and then added, "And a man is not lynched for what he does with his hands."

We both were still, letting the campfire warm our memories. What memories the Tinker had, what strange thoughts might come into his head, and of what strange things he had seen, I knew nothing, but my own memories went back to the day pa left me with Will Caffrey.

Three heavy sacks of gold he passed over to Caffrey that day, and then he said, "This is my son, of whom I have spoken. Care for him well, and every third coin is your own."

"You'll be leaving now?"

"Yes . . . to wander is a means to forgetting, and we were very close, my wife and I." He put his hand on my shoulder. "I'll come back, son. Do you be a good boy now."

Pa advised Caffrey to send me to the best schools and treat me well, and in due time he would return.

For the first year I was treated well enough, yet long before the change came I had seen shadows of it. Often at night I would hear Mrs. Caffrey complaining of the extra burden I was, and how much the money would mean to them if they had not to think of me. And Caffrey would speculate aloud on how much interest the money would bring, and what could be bought of lands and cattle with such an amount of gold.

Her words bothered me more than his, for I sensed an evil in her that was not in him. He was a greedy, selfish man, close with money and hard-fisted as well as self-righteous; but as for her—I think she would have murdered me. Indeed, I think it was in her mind to do so.

Caffrey had a reputation for honesty, but many a man with such a reputation simply has not been found out or tested, and for Will Caffrey the test of those bags of gold was too much for his principles to bear. The year after pa had gone they took me from school—their own son continued—and they put me to work with the field hands. Eleven years old I was then, and no place to go, nor anyone to turn to.

The day came when Duncan struck me.

Contemptuous of me he was, taking that from his parents' treatment of me, and he often sneered or cursed at me, but when he struck me we had at it, knuckle and skull.

It was even-up fighting until I realized all his blows were struck at my face, so I scrooched down as he rushed at me and struck him a mighty blow in the belly.

It taken his wind. He let go a grunt and his mouth dropped open, so I spread wide my legs and let go at his chin.

With his mouth open and jaw slack, a girl might have broken his jaw, and I did, for I was a naturally strong boy who had worked hard and done much running and climbing in the forest.

He fell back against the woodpile where I had been working, his face all white and strange-looking, but my blood was up and I swung a final fist against his nose, which broke, streaming blood over his lips and chin.

The door slammed and his ma and pa were coming at me, Will Caffrey with his cane lifted, and her with her fingers spread like claws.

I taken out.

So far as I could see, nothing was keeping me, and by the time I stopped running I was far off in the piney woods and nighttime a-coming on.

By that time I was twelve years old and knew only the mountains. The towns I feared, so it never occurred to me to leave all I had known behind.

The one place I knew was the cabin, and there I had known happiness, so I turned up through the woods, hunting the way.

It was thirty-odd miles of rough mountain and forest, and I slept three nights before I got there, the first nights I ever spent in the forest alone.

When at last I came to the cabin I was a tuckered-out boy.

If they ever came seeking me, I never knew. They might have come before I got back, or after, when I was off a-hunting. More than likely they were pleased to be free of me, for now they had the gold.

Five years I lived there alone.

That isn't to say I didn't see anybody in all that time. Long before ma died I used to go hunting with the Cherokee boys, and I could use a bow and arrow or set a snare as good as the best of them. These were wild

Cherokees who took to the mountains when the government moved the Indians west.

Pa had been friendly with them, and they liked me. Whenever I was over that way I was sure of a meal, and many a time during that first year I made it a point.

Whilst working with Caffrey I had done most of the kitchen-garden planting, and there was seed at the house. The Cherokees were planting Indians, so I got more seed from them, and I spaded up garden space and planted melons, corns, potatoes, and suchlike. For the rest, I hunted the woods for game, berries, nuts, and roots.

It would be a lie to say I was brave, for of a night I was a scared boy, and more than once I cried myself to sleep, remembering ma and wishing pa would come home.

Those first years it was only the thought of pa coming back that kept me going. Caffrey had been sure pa was dead and had never left off telling me so, although why he should be so sure I never knew. It wasn't until I was past fifteen that I really gave up hope. In my thinking mind I was sure after that that he would not come back, but my ears pricked every time I heard a horse on the trail.

Travel was no kind thing those days, what with killers along the Natchez Trace and the Wilderness Road, Bald Knobbers, and varmints generally. Many a man who set out from home never got back, and who was to say what became of him?

First off, I swapped some dress goods ma had in her trunk for a buckskin hunting shirt and leggings; and after I had trapped, I traded my muskrat and red-fox skins with the Cherokees for things I needed. The cornmill was there, and after my first harvest I always had corn.

My fourteenth birthday came along and ma wasn't there to bake me a cake like she'd done, so I fried myself up a batch of turkey eggs. And that was a big day, because just shy of noon when I was fixing to set up to table, the Tinker came along the trail.

It was the first time I'd seen him, although I'd heard tell of him. He sat up to table with me and told me the news of the Settlements. After that he always stopped by.

The Tinker hadn't very much to say that first time, but he did a sight of looking and seeing. So I showed him around, proud of the cabin pa had built and the way he'd used water from the creek to irrigate the fields when they needed water—although rain usually took care of that.

The Tinker noticed everything, but it wasn't until a long time after, that some of his questions started coming back to mind to puzzle me. Especially, about the gold.

Once he asked me if I had any gold money . . . said he could get a lot for gold.

So I told him about all our gold going to Will Caffrey, and he got me to draw him a picture of what those gold pieces looked like.

"Your pa," he said, "must have been a traveled man."

"Sacketts haven't taken much to travel," I said, "although we hear tell that a long time ago, before they came over to the Colonies, some of them were sailors."

"Like your pa," he said.

"Pa? If he was a sailor he never said anything about it to me. Nor did ma ever speak of it."

He looked at a knot I had made in a piece of rope. "Good tight knot. Your pa teach you that?"

"Sure—that's a bowline. He taught me to tie knots before he taught me letters. Two half-hitches, bowline, bowline-on-a-bight, sheep's bend—all manner of knots."

"Sailor knots," the Tinker said.

"I wouldn't know. I expect a good knot is useful to a lot of folks beside sailors."

Aside from the cornmill and ma's trunk filled with fixings, there wasn't much left at the cabin beside pa's worn-out Ballard rifle and the garden tools. In the trunk was ma's keepsake box. It was four inches deep, four inches wide and eight inches long, and was made of teakwood. Inside she kept family papers and a few odds and ends of value to her.

The Ballard was old, and no gun to be taking to the western lands, so I figured to swap it off when I did the mill, or at the first good chance. If I˙ was going to meet up with Bald Knobbers or wild Indians I would need a new, reliable gun.

Now the Tinker, he sat there smoking, and finally as the fire died down he said, "Daylight be all right for you?"

It was all right, so come daylight we taken off down the mountain for the last time.

One time, there on the trail, I stopped and looked back. There was a mist around the peaks, and the one that marked the cabin was hidden. The cabin was up there in those trees. I reckoned never to see it again, or ma's grave, out where pa dug it under the big pine.

A lot of me was staying behind, but I guess pa left a lot up there, too.

And then we rounded the last bend in the trail and my mountain was hidden from sight. Before us lay the Crossing, and I had seen the last of the place where I was born.

# Chapter 2

We fetched up to the Crossing in a light spatter of rain, and I made a dicker with the storekeeper, swapping my cornmill for a one-eyed, spavined mare.

It was in my mind to become rich in the western lands, but a body does not become rich tomorrow without starting today, so I taken my mare to a meadow and staked her out on good grass. A man who wants to become rich had better start thinking of increase, and that mare could have a colt.

The Tinker was disgusted with me. "You bragged you'd a mind for swapping, but what can a man do with a one-eyed, spavined mare?"

Me, I just grinned at him. Two years now I'd had it in my mind to own that little mare. "Did you ever hear of the Highland Bay?"

"She was the talk of the mountains before she broke a leg and they had to shoot her."

"Seven or eight years ago the Highland Bay ran the legs off everything in these parts, and won many a race in the lowlands, too."

"I recall."

"Well, when I was working in the fields for Caffrey, the Highland Bay was running loose in the next pasture. A little scrub stallion tore down the fence and got to her."

"And you think this no-'count little mare is their get?"

"I know it. Fact is, I lent a hand at her birthing. Old Heywood, he who owned the Highland Bay, he was so mad he gave the colt to a field hand."

There was a thoughtful look in the Tinker's eyes. "So you have a one-eyed, spavined mare out of the Highland Bay by a scrub stallion. Now where are you?"

"I hear tell those Mexicans and Indians out west hold strong to racing. I figure to get me a mule that will outrun any horse they've got."

"Out of that mare?" he scoffed.

"Her get," I said. "She can have a colt, and sired by the right jack stud I reckon to turn up a fast mule."

We sat there on the bank watching that little mare feed on green meadow grass, and after a bit, I said to the Tinker, "When a man owes me, one way or another I figure to collect. Do you know where Caffrey keeps his prize jack?"

He didn't answer, but after a bit he said, "Nobody ever races a mule."

"Tinker, where there's something will run, there's somebody will bet on it. Why, right in these mountains you could get a bet on a fast cow, and many a mule is faster than a horse, although mighty few people believe it. The way I see it, the fewer folk who believe a mule can run, the better."

Caffrey's jackass could kill a man or a stallion, and had sired some of the best mules ever set foot. Before dark we were hidden in a clump of dogwood and willow right up against the Caffrey pasture fence.

The wind was across the pasture and from time to time the jack could catch scent of my mare, and while he couldn't quite locate her, he was stomping around in there, tossing his head and looking.

"Two things," I said, "had to work right for me to leave this here country—the timing had to be right: You had to come up the trail, and that mare of mine had to be ready. And this here jack will work the charm."

"You're smarter than I thought," he said, and then we sat quiet, slapping mosquitoes and waiting until it was full dark. Crickets sang in the brush, and there was a pleasant smell of fresh-mown hay.

Watching the lights of that big white house Caffrey had built just two years ago, I got to thinking how elegant it must be behind those curtains. Would I ever live in a house like that? And have folks about who loved me? Or would I always be a-setting out in the dark, looking on?

Caffrey had done well with pa's money. He had it at a time when gold had great value, and he'd bought with a shrewd eye there at the war's last years. He was one of the richest men around.

When I called on him at Meeting to return the money I had no hope I would get it, but I wanted to put it square before the community that he had wrongfully used money with which he had been trusted. I'd no money nor witnesses to open an action for recovery . . . but almost everybody around had wondered where he got that gold money.

He had talked large of running for office, but I felt a man who would be dishonest with a boy was no man to trust with government. It always seemed to me that a man who would betray the trust of his fellow citizens is the lowest of all, and I wanted no such man as Will Caffrey to have that chance. When I called upon him at Meeting I had my plans made to leave the mountains, for now he would not rest until he had me jailed or done away with.

Right now I was risking everything, for if I was caught I would be in real trouble.

Slapping at a mosquito, I swore softly and the Tinker commented, "It's the salt. They like the salt in your blood. On jungle rivers mosquitoes will swarm around a white man before going near a native, because a white man uses more salt."

"You've been to the jungle?"

"I've heard tell," he said.

That was the Tinker's way. He would not speak of himself. Right then he was probably smiling at me in the dark, but all I could see was the glint of those gold earrings. Only man I ever did see who wore earrings.

His being there worried me some. He was an outlander, and Tinker or not, mountain folks are suspicious of outlanders. The Tinker was a needful man in the mountains, but folks had never rightly accepted him . . . so why had he come away with me?

When the barnyard noises ceased—the sounds of milking and doors slamming—we went up to the white rails of that fence and I taken a pickhead from my gear and pried loose that rail. That one, and the next.

The mare went into that pasture like she knew what she was there for, and against the sky we saw the jack's head come up and we heard him blow. Then we heard the preen and prance of his hoofs as he came toward the mare.

We waited under the dogwood, neither of us of a mind to get shot in another man's pasture. We were half dozing and a couple of hours had gone by. Even the mosquitoes were tiring.

Of a sudden the Tinker put a hand to my arm. "Somebody coming," he said, and I caught the flicker of the shine on a blade in his hand.

We listened . . . horses coming. Two, maybe three. The first voice we heard was Duncan Caffrey's.

"We've got to have a good horse or two in those races out west," he was saying. "The Bishop wouldn't like it if he lost money. The Bishop is touchy about money."

They had drawn up right beside the grove where we were hidden.

The older man spoke. "Now tell me about that gold. You say your pa had it from a man named Sackett? Where's that man now?"

"He left out of here. Pa thinks he's dead."

The Tinker cupped his hands to my ear. "Let's get out of this."

The trouble was that my mare was out in that pasture and I didn't want to leave her. No more did I want to leave off listening to that talk.

"You go ahead," I whispered. "I'll catch up or meet you at the crossing of the Tombigbee."

He hoisted his pack, then took up mine. How he disappeared so quick with those packs, I'll never guess. And at the time I thought nothing of his taking up my pack, for I'd have trouble getting it and the mare both out of there.

"What difference does it make?" Dun Caffrey sounded impatient. "He's nobody."

"You got it to learn," the other man said irritably. "You're a damn' fool, Dun. Falcon Sackett is one of the most dangerous men on earth, and to hear the Bishop talk about it, he's almighty important. So much so the Bishop has spent years hunting down every piece of that Spanish gold to find him."

"But he's dead!"

"You see the body? Nothing else would convince the Bishop. I ain't so sure he'd even believe it then."

"Are you goin' to talk all night about a dead man? Let's go get the horses," and they moved on.

It was no use waiting any longer. If I was going to get away from here it had to be now. Stepping through the opening, I started out into that pasture after my mare and not feeling any too good about it, either. Jacks are a mean lot. If I was caught in the middle of this pasture by either the stud or the owner I might be lucky to get out alive.

It was almighty dark, and every step or two I'd hold up to listen. Once I thought I heard hoof-beats off to my left; but listening, I heard nothing more. Back behind me I heard rustling in the brush.

Suddenly, something nudged my elbow and there was my mare. All day I'd been feeding her bits of a carrot or some turnips, so she found me her ownself. More than likely it was the first time anybody'd ever fussed over her.

Hoisting myself to her back, I turned her toward that opening in the fence.

The Bishop had been mentioned, and he was a known man. Riverboat gambler, river pirate, and bad actor generally, he was one of the top men at Natchez-under-the-Hill, and one of the most feared men along the river.

"Whoever went in there," somebody said, "is still there."

A light glowed close to the ground as he spoke, then vanished.

Didn't seem no call to be wasting around, so I booted the mare in the ribs and she jumped like a deer and hit the ground running—and brother, she had plenty of scat.

She went through that fence opening and when a man reared up almost in front of her she hit him with her shoulder, knocking him rump over teakettle into the brush. The other man jumped to grab me and I stiff-legged him in the belly and heard the *ooof* as his breath left him. He went back and down out of sight, and the mare and me, we dusted around that clump of brush and off down the pike.

There was no need to meet the Tinker at the crossing of the Tombigbee, for I came up to him just as false dawn was spreading a lemon-yellow across the gray sky. He had stopped alongside the road and put both packs down. It looked to me like he was about to open mine when I came up to him.

"You got the wrong pack there," I said.

He turned sharp around, braced for trouble. He'd been so busy he'd not heard the mare coming in that soft dust. When he saw it was me he eased up and let go his hold on my pack.

"I was looking for the coffee," he said. "I thought you put it in your pack last night."

I didn't believe he thought anything of the kind, but I was not going to argue with him. Only it started me thinking and trying to add together two and two, which is not always as easy as it seems.

"Take it from me," I advised, "and let's get back off the trail before we coffee-up. We may be sought after."

He pointed ahead. "There's an old trace runs up over the hills yonder. I was only down this way once, but I traveled it for a day or so."

Two days later I swapped my old Ballard for a two-wheeled cart. The Ballard wasn't much of a gun but I knew it so well I could make it shoot, and I let a farmer see me bark a squirrel with it. Now barking a squirrel is a neat trick, but most mountain boys could do it. A squirrel has little meat, and so's not to spoil any of it you don't shoot the squirrel, you shoot the branch he's setting on or one close by. It knocks him out of the tree, stuns him, and sometimes kills him with flying chips.

"You've a straight-shootin' gun," this farmer said to me. "Would you be of a mind to swap?"

We settled down to dicker. He was a whittler and a spitter, but I was natural-born to patience, so I waited him out. He was bound and determined to make a trade, and few folks came that way. That beat-up old cart hadn't been used in years, but the Tinker and me, we could fix it up. From now on we'd be in the flat-lands where it would be handy.

Between story-telling and talk of the Settlements, we dickered. We dickered again over hominy grits and sidemeat for supper, and we dickered at breakfast, but about that time I got awful busy making up my pack, talking to the Tinker and the like, and he began to think he'd lost me.

Upshot of it was, I let him have that Ballard and I taken the cart, three bushels of mighty fine apples, a worn-out scythe, and a couple of freshly tanned hides. The Tinker and me turned to and tightened the iron rims and the spokes, and loaded our gear.

It took two weeks of walking to reach the river, but by that time we had done a sight of swapping.

The little mare was looking good. Our daily marches were not long and the load she carried most of the way was light. We babied her along on carrots, turnips, slices of watermelon, and greens from along the road, and she fattened up on it.

We saw no sign of the three Kurbishaws, but they were never out of mind.

All the time I kept trying to dicker the Tinker out of one of his knives. He carried a dozen in his pack, and two belted at his waist. A third was slung down the back of his neck under his collar. They were perfectly balanced and the steel tempered to a hardness you wouldn't believe. We both shaved with them, they were that good. In the mountains a man would trade most anything for a Tinker-made knife.

Walking along like that, neither of us much to talk, I had time to think, and I remembered back to the Tinker asking about that gold. A man has a right to be interested in gold, but why that gold in particular? And Spanish gold, they said.

Why was the Tinker starting to open my pack? If he had found what he wanted, would he have made sure I didn't come up to him at the Tombigbee or anywhere?

Was it something about that gold that started the Kurbishaws after me?

I had no gold, and never had had any. So what did I have that they might want?

Nothing.

Nothing, unless maybe there was something in ma's keepsake box. The first time I was alone I'd go through that stuff of ma's again. I never had really looked at it—mostly, I kept it because it was all I had of hers.

All I had else was some worn-out clothes, some Indian blankets, and a couple of extra shirts.

Like I've said, walking gives a man time to think, and a couple of things began to fit. Pa had never spent any of that gold that I could recall, but after Caffrey got it, some was spent. Not much right at first—he was afraid of pa coming back. And it was not long after Caffrey started to spend it that the Tinker showed up.

Not right away . . . it must have taken him some time to find out where that gold came from.

The Tinker was not a sociable man, but he had made a point of being my friend. He had spent time with me, and I believed he was really my friend, but I now believed he had some other interest in that gold.

That night we reached the Mississippi and the ferry. We were avoiding main-traveled roads, and the ferry we came up to was operated by a sour, evil-smelling old man who peered suspiciously at us. We dickered with him until he agreed to take us across for a bushel of apples.

He stared at our packs as if he was trying to see right through them, but mostly he looked at Tinker's knives. Neither of us had any other kind of a weapon, except that I carried a long stick to chase off mean dogs, of which we'd met a-plenty.

"Country's full of movers," the ferryman said. "Where mought you folks be goin'?"

"Where folks don't ask questions," I told him.

He threw me a mean look. "Doubtless you've reason," he said. "We git lots of 'em don't want questions asked."

"Tinker, did you ever operate a ferry?"

"Not that I recall."

"I've got a feeling there's going to be a job open around here—unless somebody can swim with a knot on his head."

The ferryman shut up, but when we made shore near a cluster of miserable-looking shacks I thought I saw him make a signal to some rough-looking men loitering on the bank.

"Trouble," I said, low-voiced, to the Tinker.

A bearded man with a bottle in his hand, his pants held up by a piece of rope, started toward us. Several others followed.

The bearded man was big, and he was wearing a pistol, as were some of the others.

My walking staff was a handy weapon, if need be. A Welshman in the mountains had taught me the art of stick fighting, and I was ready.

The bearded man stopped in our path as we drove off the ferry. He glanced from the Tinker to me, and it was obvious that neither of us had a gun.

Four men behind him . . . a dirty, boozing lot, but armed and confident. My mouth was dry and my belly felt empty.

"Stoppin' around?"

"Passin' through," I said.

One end of my stick rested on my boot toe, ready to flip and thrust. A stick fighter never swings a wide blow—he thrusts or strikes with the end, and for the belly, the throat, or the eyes.

"Have a drink!" The big man thrust the bottle at the Tinker.

"Never touch it," the Tinker replied.

Two of the other men were closing in on me, about as close as I could afford for them to get.

"You'll drink and like it!" The big man suddenly swung with the bottle, but he was too slow. The Tinker's hand shot out, flicking this way and that as though brushing the big man with his fingers' ends, but the big man screamed and staggered back, his face streaming blood.

Even as he lifted the bottle, the two men nearest me jumped to get close. My stick barely had room, but the end caught the nearest man in the throat and he fell back gasping horribly. As he did so, without withdrawing the stick I struck sidewise with it, not a hard blow, but the other man threw up an arm to block it and staggered. Instantly I jerked back the stick, which was all of five feet long and broom-handle size, and grasping it with both hands, struck him in the face with the end of it.

The fight was over. The Tinker glanced at the other two men, who were withdrawing. Then he coolly leaned over and thrust the blade into the turf near the road to cleanse it of blood.

Three men were down and the fight gone out of the others, and it hadn't been twenty seconds since they stopped us. No doubt they'd robbed many a traveler at this point and believed us easily handled.

We paid them no more mind, starting off up the rise toward the high ground back of the river. And that big man was dead. From time to time I'd seen fighting done, but not a man killed before, and it seemed there ought to be more to it. One moment he was coming at us blustering and confident, and the next he was dying in the trail mud.

We did not stop that night, but went on, wanting distance between us and trouble. West and south we kept on going, through sunlight and rain, the Tinker plying his trade, and me swapping here and there.

The mare was filling out, carrying her colt, and I was in fine shape.

Down at Jefferson in Texas, we laid in supplies. We walked out of town before we made camp, and we were just setting up to eat when we heard horses soft-footing it along the trail.

Turning to warn the Tinker, I saw him standing outside the firelight, a blade in his hand.

Me, I held to my place at the fire, letting them think me alone.

The riders stopped out beyond the firelight and a voice called out, not loud, "Hello, the fire! Can we come in?"

"If you're friendly, you're welcome. Coffee's on."

Those days nobody rode right up to a fire or a house. It was customary to stop off a bit and call in—it was also a whole lot safer.

There were three of them, one about my own age, the other two a mite older. They were roughly dressed, like men who were living out in the brush, and they were heavily armed. These men, by the look of them, were on the dodge.

"'Light and set. We're peaceful folk."

They sat their horses, their eyes missing nothing, noting the Tinker there, knife in hand.

"You with the knife." The speaker was a handsome big man with a shock of dark, untrimmed hair. "You wishin' trouble?"

"Fixed for it. Not hunting it."

The big man swung down, keeping his horse between himself and the fire. "You look like movers," he said pleasantly. "I was a mover one time . . . moved to Texas from Tennessee." He gestured to the others. "These here are gen-u-ine Texans."

He hunkered down beside the fire as the others dismounted, and I passed him the coffee pot. He was wearing more pistols than I ever did see, most men being content with one. He had two belted on in holsters and a third shoved down in his waistband. Unless I was mistaken, he had another, smaller one in his coat pocket.

Loading a cap-and-ball pistol took time, so a man apt to need a lot of shooting often took to packing more than one gun. There was an outlaw up Missouri way who sometimes carried as many as six when on a raid. Others carried interchangeable cylinders so they could flip out an empty and replace it with a loaded one.

When the Tinker walked up to the fire they saw the other knives.

"You don't carry a pistol?"

"I can use these faster than any man can use a gun."

The youngest of them laughed. "You're saying that to the wrong man. Cullen here, he's learned to draw and fire in the same instant."

The Tinker glanced at the big man. "Are you Cullen Baker?"*

"That I am." He indicated the quiet-seeming man beside him. "This here's Bob Lee, and that's Bill Longley."

"I'm the Tinker, and this here is Orlando Sackett."

"You're dark enough for an Indian," Cullen Baker said to the Tinker, "but you don't shape up to be one."

"I am a gypsy," Tinker said, and I looked around, surprised. I'd heard tell of gypsies, but never figured to know one. They were said to be a canny folk, wanderers and tinkerers, and he was all of that.

Cullen Baker and his friends were hungry, but they were also tired, and nigh to falling asleep while they ate.

"If you boys want to sleep," I said, "you just have at it. The Tinker and me will stand watch."

"You're borrowing trouble just to feed us," Bob Lee said. "We've stood out against the Carpetbag law, so Governor Davis' police are out after us."

"We're outcasts," Baker said.

* *The First Fast Draw,* Bantam Books, 1959.

"My people have been outcasts as long as the memory of man," the Tinker said.

"No Sackett," I said, "so far as I know, was ever an outlaw or an outcast. On the other hand, no Sackett ever turned a man from his fire. You're welcome to stop with us."

When they had stripped the gear from their horses the other two went back into the brush to sleep, avoiding the fire; but Cullen Baker lingered, drinking coffee.

"What started you west?" he asked.

"Why," I told him, "it was one of those old-timey gospel-shouters set me to considering it. He preached lively against sin. He was a stomper and a shouter, but a breast-beater and a whisperer, too.

"When he got right down to calling them to the Lord, he whispered and he pleaded, and right there he lost me. Seems if the Lord really wants a man it doesn't need all that fuss to get him worked up to it. If a man isn't ready for the Lord, then the Lord isn't ready for him, and it's a straight-forward proposition between man and God without any wringing of the hands or hell-fire shouting.

"When that preacher started his Bible-shouting and talking large about the sins of Sodom and Gomorrah, I was mighty taken with him. He seemed more familiar with the sins of those foreign places than he did with those of Richmond or Atlanta, but mostly he was set against movers.

"Sinful folk, he said, and the Lord intended folks to stay to home, till the earth, and come to church of a Sunday. By moving, they set their feet on unrighteous paths.

"Fact was, he talked so much about sin that I got right interested, and figured to look into it. A man ought to know enough to make a choice; and pa, he always advised me to look to both sides of a proposition.

"Back in the hills mighty few folks ever got right down to bedrock sinning. Here and there a body drank too much 'shine and took to fighting, but rarely did he covet his neighbor's wife up to doing anything about it, because his neighbor had a squirrel rifle.

"That parson ranted and raved about painted women, but when I looked around at Meeting it seemed to me a touch of paint here and there might brighten things up. He talked about the silks and satins of sin until he had me fairly a-sweating to see some of that there. Silks and satins can be almighty exciting to a man accustomed to homespun and calico. So it came on me to travel."

Baker cupped his hands around the bottom of his coffee cup, and taken his time with that coffee. So I asked him about that fast draw I'd heard them speak about.

"Studied it out by my ownself," he said. "Trouble is apt to come on a man sudden-like, and he needs a weapon quick to his hand. When Mr. Sam Colt invented his revolving pistol he done us all a favor.

"Best way is just to draw and fire. Don't aim . . . point your gun like you'd point your finger. You need practice to be good, and I worked on it eight or nine months before I had to use it. The less shooting you've done before, the better. Then you have to break the habit of aiming.

"It stands to reason. Just like you point your finger. How many times have you heard about some female woman grabbing up a pistol—something she maybe never had in her hands before—and plumb mad, she starts shooting and blasts some man into doll rags. Nobody ever taught her to shoot—she just pointed at what she was mad at and started blazing away."

He reached inside his shirt and fetched out a gun. "This I taken from a man who was troubling me—and you'll need a gun in the western lands, so take it along. This here is a Walch Navy, .36 caliber, and she fires twelve shots."

"*Twelve?* It looks like a six-shooter."

"Weighs about the same. See? Two triggers, two hammers. She's a good pistol, but too complicated for me. Take it along."

She was a mite over twelve inches long and weighed just over two pounds, had checkered walnut grips, and was a beautiful weapon. Stamped 1859, it looked to be in mint condition.

"Thanks. I've been needing a weapon."

"Practice . . . practice drawing and pointing a long time before you try firing. Don't try to aim. Just draw and point."

He put down his cup and got to his feet. "And one thing more." He looked at me out of those hard green eyes. "You wear one of those and you'll be expected to use it. When a man starts packing a gun nobody figures he wears it just for show."

Come daybreak, they saddled and rode away, and the Tinker and me went west afoot. And as we walked, I tried my hand with that gun. I practiced and practiced. A body never knew when it would come in handy.

Somewhere behind me three Kurbishaws were riding to kill me.

# Chapter 3

We were six months out of the piney woods of Tennessee when we walked into San Augustine, Texas. It was an old, old town.

Seemed like we'd never left home, for there were pines growing over the red clay hills, and everywhere we looked there were Cherokee roses.

We camped among the trees on the outskirts, and the Tinker set to work repairing a broken pistol I had taken in trade. An old man stopped by to watch. "Shy of gunsmiths hereabouts," he said. "A man could make a living."

"The Tinker can fix anything. Even clocks and suchlike."

"Old clock up at the Blount House—a fine piece. Ain't worked in some time."

The Tinker filled a cup and passed it across the fire to him, and the old man hunkered down to talk. "Town settled by Spanish men back around 1717. Built themselves a mission, they did, and then fifty, sixty years later when it seemed the Frenchies were going to move in, they built a fort.

"Been a likely place ever since. The Blount and Cartwright homes are every bit of thirty year old, and up until the War between the States broke out we had us a going university right here in town."

He was sizing us up, making up his mind about us, and after a while he said, "If I was you boys I'd keep myself a fancy lookout. You're being sought after."

"Three tall men who look alike?"

"Uh-huh. Rode through town yestiddy. Right handy men, I'd say, come a difficulty."

"They're his uncles," the Tinker explained, "and they're all laid out to kill him."

"No worse fights than kinfolk's." The old man finished his coffee and stood up. "Notional man, m'self. Take to folks or I don't. You boys take care of yourselves."

The Tinker glanced over at me. "You wearing that gun?"

Pulling my coat back, I showed it to him, shoved down inside my pants behind my belt. "I ain't much on the shoot," I said, "but come trouble I'll have at it."

San Augustine was further south in Texas than I'd any notion of coming, but the Tinker insisted on it. "The biggest cow ranches are south," he said, "down along the Gulf coast, and some of them are fixing to trail cattle west to fresh grass, or north to the Kansas towns."

Now we'd come south and here the Kurbishaws were, almost as if they'd known where we were coming.

"No use asking for it," I said, "we'd better dust off down the pike."

"Didn't figure you would run from trouble," the old man said. "Best way is to hunt it down and have it out."

"They're still my uncles, and I never set eye on them. If they're fixing for trouble they'll have to bring it on themselves."

The old man bit off a chew of tobacco, regarded the plug from which he had bitten, and said, "You ain't goin' to dodge it. Those fellers want you bad. They offered a hundred dollars cash money for you. And they want you *dead.*"

That was more actual money than a man might see in a year's time, and enough to set half the no-goods in Texas on my trail. Those Kurbishaws were sure lacking in family feeling. Well, if they wanted me they'd have to burn the stump and sift the ashes before they found me.

San Augustine was a pleasant place, but I wasn't about to get rich there. The mare was far along, but it would be a few weeks before she dropped her colt.

The Tinker started putting that pistol together and I went to rolling up my bed, such as it was. The Tinker said to the old man, "Isn't far to the Gulf, is it?"

"South, down the river."

The Tinker put the pistol away and started putting gear in the cart while I went for the mare. It was just as I was starting back that I heard him say, "This is the sort of place a man could retire . . . say a seafaring man."

The old man spat, squinting his eyes at the Tinker. "You thinkin' or askin'?"

"Why"—the Tinker smiled at him—"when it comes to that, I'm asking."

The old man indicated a road with a gesture of his head. "That road . . . maybe thirteen, fourteen mile. The Deckrow place."

We taken out with our fat little mare, and the cart painted with signs to advise that we sharpened knives, saws, and whatever.

We walked alongside, the Tinker with his gold earrings, black hat, and black homespun clothes, and me with a black hat, red shirt, buckskin coat, and black pants tucked into boots. Him with his knives and me with my pistol. We made us a sight to see.

Ten miles lay behind us when we came up to this girl on horseback, or rather, she came up to us. She was fourteen, I'd say, and pert. Her auburn hair hung around her shoulders and she had freckles scattered over her nose and cheekbones. She was a pretty youngster, but like I say, pert.

She looked at the Tinker and then at the sign on the wagon, and last she looked to me, her eyes taking their time with me and seeming to find nothing of much account.

"We have a clock that needs fixing," she said. "I am Marsha Deckrow."

The way she said it, you expected no less than a flourish of trumpets or a roll of drums, but until the old man mentioned them that morning I'd never heard tell of any Deckrows and wouldn't have paid it much mind if I had. But when we came to the house I figured that if means gave importance to a man, this one must cut some figure.

That was the biggest house I ever did see, setting back from the road with great old oaks and elms all about, and a plot of grass out front that must have been five or six acres. There was a winding drive up to the door, and there were orchards and fields, and stock grazing. The coach-house was twice the size of the schoolhouse back at Clinch's.

"Are you a tinker?" she asked me.

"No, ma'am. I am Orlando Sackett, bound for the western lands."

"Oh?" Her nose tilted. "You're a *mover!*"

"Yes, ma'am," I said. "Most folks move at one time or another."

"A rolling stone gathers no moss," she said, nose in the air.

"Moss grows thickest on dead wood," I said, "and if you're repeating the thoughts of others, you might remember that 'a wandering bee gets the honey.'"

"*Movers!*" she sniffed.

"Looks like an old house," I said. "Must be the finest around here."

"It is," she said proudly. "It is the oldest place anywhere around. The Deckrows," she added, "came from *Virginia!*"

"Movers?" I asked.

She flashed an angry look at me and then paid me no mind. "The servants' entrance," she said to the Tinker, "is around to the side."

"You're talking to the wrong folks," I said, speaking before the Tinker could. "We aren't servants, and we don't figure to go in by the side door. We go in by the front door, or your clock won't be fixed."

The Tinker gave me an odd look, but he made no objection to my speaking up thataway. He said nothing at all, just waiting.

"I was addressing the Tinker," she replied coolly. "Just what is it that you do? Or do you do anything at all?"

One of the servants had come up to hold her stirrup and she got down from the saddle. "Mr. Tinker," she said sweetly, "will you come with me?" Then, without so much as glancing my way, she said, "You can wait . . . if you like."

When I looked up at that house I sobered down some. Here I was in a worn-out buckskin coat and homespun, dusty from too many roads, and my boots down at heel. I'd no business even talking to such a girl.

So I sat down on a rock beside the gravel drive and looked at my mare. "You hurry up," I said, "and have that colt. We'll show them."

Hearing footsteps on the gravel, I looked up to see a tall man coming toward me. His hair and mustaches were white, his skin dark as that of a Spanish man, his eyes the blackest I'd ever seen.

He was thin, but he looked wiry and strong, and whatever his age might be it hadn't reached to his eyes . . . or his mind.

He paused when he saw me, frowning a little as if something about me disturbed him. "Are you waiting for someone?" His voice had a ring to it, a sound like I'd heard in the voices of army officers.

"I travel with the Tinker," I said, "who's come to fix a clock, and that Miss Deckrow who lives here, she wanted me to come in by the servants' entrance, I'll be damned if I will."

There was a shadow of a smile around his lips, though he had a hard mouth. He taken out a long black cigar and clipped the end, then he put it between his teeth. "I am Jonas Locklear, and Marsha's uncle. I can understand your feelings."

So I told him my name, and then for no reason I could think of, I told him about the mare and the colt she would have and some of my plans.

"Orlando Sackett . . . the name has a familiar sound." He looked at me thoughtfully. "There was a Sackett who married a Kurbishaw girl from Carolina."

"My father," I said.

"Oh? And where is he now?"

So I told him how ma died and pa taken off, leaving me with the Caffreys, and how I hadn't heard from pa since.

"I don't believe he's dead," I explained, "nor that those Kurbishaws killed him. He seemed to me a hard man to kill."

Jonas Locklear's mouth showed a wry smile. "I would say you judge well," he said. "Falcon Sackett was indeed a hard man to kill."

"You knew him?" I was surprised—and then right away I was no longer surprised. This was the Deckrow plantation, the place the Tinker had inquired about. At least, he had inquired about a seafaring man.

"I knew him well." He took the cigar from his mouth. "We were associated once, in a manner of speaking." He turned toward the door. "Come in, Mr. Sackett. Please come in."

"I am not welcome here," I said stiffly.

The way his face tightened showed him a man of quick temper. "You are *my* guest," he replied sharply. "And I say you are welcome. Come in, please."

Almost the first person I laid eyes on when we stepped through the door was Marsha Deckrow.

"Uncle Jonas," she said quickly, "that boy is with the Tinker."

"Marsha, Mr. Sackett is my guest. Will you please tell Peter that he will be staying for dinner? And the Tinker also."

She started to say something, but whatever it was, Jonas Locklear gave her no time. "Peter must know at once, Marsha."

Nobody who ever heard that voice would doubt that it was accustomed to command—and to be obeyed.

"Yes, uncle."

Her backbone was ramrod stiff when she walked away, anger showing in every line of her slim figure. I wanted to smile, but I didn't. I kept my face straight.

Locklear beckoned me to follow and led the way into a wing of the house. The moment we passed through the tall doors I knew I had entered the rooms of a man of a very different kind from any I had known.

We went into a small hallway where, just inside the door, there hung on the wall a strange shield made of some kind of thick hide, and behind it two crossed spears. "Zula—from South Africa," he said.

The large square, high-ceilinged room beyond was lined with books. On a table was a stone head, beautifully carved and polished. He noticed my attention and said, "It is very ancient—from Libya. Beautiful, is it not?"

"It is. I wish the Tinker could see it."

"He is a lover of beautiful things?"

"I was thinking more of the craft that went into it. The Tinker can do anything with his hands, and you should see his knives. We—we both shave with them."

"Fine steel." He rubbed out his cigar on a stone of the fireplace. "This tinker of yours—where is he from?"

"We came together from the mountains. He was a tinker and a pack peddler there."

When I had washed up in the bathroom I borrowed a whisk broom to brush some of the dust from my clothing, and when I got back to the library he was sitting there with a chart in his hands. When he put it down it rolled up so that I had no more chance to look at it.

He crossed to a sideboard and filled two wine glasses from a bottle. One of them he handed to me. "Madeira," he said, "the wine upon which this country was built. Washington drank it, so did Jefferson. Every slave ship from Africa brought casks of it ordered by the planters."

When we were seated and had tasted our wine, he said, "What are your plans, Mr. Sackett? You are going west, you said?"

"California, or somewhere west."

"It is a lovely land, this California. Once I thought to spend my days there, but strange things happen to a man, Mr. Sackett, strange things, indeed."

He looked at me sharply. "So you are the son of Falcon Sackett. You're not so tall as he was, but you have the shoulders." He tasted his wine again. "Did he ever speak to you of me?"

"No, sir. My father rarely talked of himself or his doings. Not even to my mother, I think."

"A wise man . . . a very wise man. Those who have not lived such a life could not be expected to understand it. He was not a tame man, your father. He was no sit-by-the-fire man, no molly-coddle. His name was Falcon, and he was well named."

He lighted another cigar. "He never talked to you of the Mexican War, then? Or of the man he helped to bury in the dunes of Padre Island?"

"No."

"And when he went away . . . did he leave anything with you? I mean, with you personally?"

"Nothing. A grip on the shoulder and some advice. I am afraid the grip lasted longer than the advice."

Locklear smiled, and then from somewhere in the house a bell sounded faintly. "Come, we will go in to dinner now, Mr. Sackett." He got to his feet. "I am afraid I must ask you to ignore any fancied slights—or intentional ones, Mr. Sackett.

"You see"—he paused—"this is my house. This is my plantation. Everything here is mine, but I was long away and when I returned my health was bad. My brother-in-law, Franklyn Deckrow, seems to have made an attempt to take command during my absence. He is not altogether pleased that I have returned."

He finished his wine and put down his glass. "Mr. Sackett, face a man with a gun or a sword, but beware of bookkeepers. They will destroy you, Sackett. They will destroy you."

At the door of the dining room we paused, and there for a minute I was ready to high-tail it out of there, for I'd eaten in no such room before. True, I'd heard ma speak of them, but I'd never imagined such a fine long table or such silver or glassware. Right then I blessed ma for teaching me to eat properly.

"Will the Tinker be here, sir?"

"It has been arranged."

Marsha swept into the library in a white gown, looking like a young princess. Her hair was all combed out and had a ribbon in it, and I declare, I never saw anything so pretty, or so mean.

She turned sharply away from me, her chin up, but that was nothing to the expression of distaste on her father's face when he looked up and down my shabby, trail-worn clothes.

He was short of medium height, with square shoulders and a thin nose. No man I had seen dressed more carefully than he, but there were lines of temper around his eyes and mouth, and a hollow look to his temples that I had learned to distrust.

"Really, Jonas," he said, "we are familiar with your habits and ways of life, but I scarcely think you should bring them here, in your own home, with your sisters and my niece present."

Jonas ignored him, just turning slightly to say, "Orlando Sackett, my brother-in-law, Franklyn Deckrow. When he would destroy a man he does it with red ink, not red blood, with a bookkeeper's pen, not a sword."

Before Deckrow could reply, two women came into the room. They were beautifully gowned, and lovely. "Mr. Sackett, my sister . . . Lily Anne Deckrow."

"My pleasure," I said, bowing a little.

She looked her surprise, but offered her hand. She was a slender, graceful young woman of not more than thirty, with a pleasant but rather drawn face.

"And my other sister . . . Virginia Locklear."

She was dark, and a beauty. She might have been twenty-four, and had the kind of a figure that no dress can conceal, and well she knew it.

Her lips were full, but not too full. Her eyes were dark and warm; there was some of the tempered steel in her that I had recognized in Jonas.

"Mr. Sackett," she asked, "would you take me in to dinner?"

Gin Locklear—for that was how she was known—had a gift for making a man feel important. Whether it was an art she had acquired, or something natural to her, I did not know, nor did it matter. She rested her hand upon my arm and no king could have felt better.

Then a Negro servant stepped to the door. "Mr. Cosmo Lengro!" he said, and I'll be damned if it wasn't the Tinker.

It was he, but a far different Tinker than any I had seen before this, for he wore a black tailored suit that was neatly pressed (he'd bribed a servant to attend to that for him) and a white ruffled shirt with a black string tie. His hair was combed carefully, his mustache trimmed. All in all, he was a dashing and romantic-looking man.

Jonas Locklear was within my range of vision when he turned and saw the Tinker. I swear he looked as if he'd been pin-stuck. He stiffened and his lips went tight, and for a moment I thought he was about to swear. And the Tinker wasn't looking at anybody but Jonas Locklear. I knew that stance . . . in an instant he could pick a steel blade to kill whatever stood before him.

The Tinker bowed from the hips. "After all these years, Captain!"

Virginia Locklear threw a quick, startled look at her brother, and Franklyn Deckrow's expression was tight, expectant. They were surprised, but no more than I was.

It was the first time I'd heard the Tinker's name, if that was indeed it, nor had I any idea he had that black suit in his pack, or that he could get himself up like that.

Jonas spoke to me without turning his head. "Were you a party to this? Did you know he knew me?" His tone was unfriendly, to say the least.

"I never even heard his right name before, nor have I known of anybody who knew him outside the mountains."

Not until we were seated did I again become conscious of my appearance. This table was no place for a buckskin hunting shirt, and Deckrow was probably right. I vowed then that this should not happen to me again.

That snip of a Marsha did not so much as glance my way, but Virginia Locklear made up for it. "Virginia does not suit me," she said, in reply to a question about her name. "Call me Gin. Jonas calls me that, and I prefer it."

The talk about the table was of things of which I knew nothing, and those who spoke might well have talked a foreign tongue for all the good it did me. Fortunately, I had never been one to speak much in company, for I'd seen all too little of it. I'd no need to be loose-tongued, so I held my silence and listened.

But Gin Locklear would not have it so. She turned to me and began asking me of my father, and then of the cabin where I had lived so long alone. So I told her of the forest and the game I had trapped, and how the Indians built their snares.

"Tell me about your father," she said finally. "I mean . . . *really* tell me about him."

It shamed me that I could say so little. I told her that he was a tall man, four inches taller than my five-ten, and powerful, thirty pounds heavier than my one hundred and eighty.

She looked at me thoughtfully. "I would not have believed you so tall."

"I am wide in the shoulders," I said. "My arms are not long, yet I can reach seventy-six inches—the extra breadth is in my shoulders. I am usually guessed to be shorter than I am.

"Pa," I went on, "was skillful with all sorts of weapons, with horses, too."

"He would be a man to know," she said thoughtfully. "I think I'd like to know him."

It was not in me to be jealous. She was older than me, and a beautiful woman as well, and I did not fancy myself as a man in whom beautiful women would be interested. I knew none of the things about which they seemed to interest themselves.

Yet, even while talking to Gin, I sensed the strange undercurrent of feeling at the table. At first I believed it was between Jonas and the Tinker, and there was something there, to be sure; but it was Franklyn Deckrow of whom I should have been thinking.

After dinner, we three—Locklear, the Tinker, and I—stood together in Locklear's quarters. Deckrow had disappeared somewhere, and the three of us faced each other. Suddenly all the guards were down.

"All right, Lengro," Locklear said sharply, "you have come here, and not by accident. . . . Why?"

"Gold," the Tinker said simply. "It is a matter of gold, and we have waited too long."

"We?"

"In the old days we were not friends," the Tinker said quietly, "but all that is past. The gold is there, and we know it is there. I say we should drop old hatreds and join forces."

Jonas indicated me. "How much does he know?"

"Very little, I think, but his father knew everything. His father is the one man alive who knew where it was."

"And is he alive?"

"You," the Tinker said carefully, "might be able to answer that question. Is he alive?"

"If you suggest that I may have killed him, I can answer that. I did not. In fact, he is the one man I have known about whom I have had doubts—I might not be able to kill him."

"I don't know what you're talking about," I said, "but I am sure my father is alive—somewhere."

"You told me he planned to come back," the Tinker said. "Do you think he would purposely have stayed away?"

For a moment I considered that in the light of all I knew of him. A hard, dangerous man by all accounts, yet a loving and attentive father and husband. At home I had never heard his voice lifted in anger, had never seen a suggestion of violence from him.

"If he could come," I said, "he would come."

"Then he must be dead," the Tinker said reluctantly.

"Or prevented from returning," Jonas interposed dryly, "as I was for four years."

Far into the night we talked, and much became plain which I had not understood until then—why the Tinker had come to the mountains, and where he had come from; and why, when we reached Jefferson, he had insisted upon turning south instead of continuing on to the west.

I knew now that he had never intended going further west than Texas, and that he had thought of little else for nearly twenty years.

This was 1868 and the War with Mexico lay twenty years behind, but it was during that war that it all began.

Captain Jonas Locklear had sailed from New York bound for the Rio Grande, with supplies and ammunition for the army of General Zachary Taylor. There the cargo would be transshipped to a river steamer and taken upstream nearly two hundred miles to Camargo. The Tinker had been bosun on the ship.

Captain Jonas had run a taut ship, respected but not liked by his crew—and that included the Tinker.

They had dropped the hook first off *El Paso de los Brazos de Santiago,* the Pass of the Arms of St. James. From there orders took them south a few miles to *Boca del Rio,* the Mouth of the River—the Rio Grande.

It was there, on their first night at anchor, when all the crew were below asleep except the Captain and the Tinker, that Falcon Sackett emerged from the sea.

The Tinker was making a final check to be sure all gear was in place. The sea was calm, the sky clear. There was no sound anywhere except, occasionally, some sound of music from the cluster of miserable shacks and hovels that was the smugglers' town of Bagdad, on the Mexican side of the river.

Captain Jonas Locklear was wakeful, and he strolled slowly about the deck, enjoying the pleasant night air after the heat of the day.

Both of them heard the shots.

The first shot brought them up sharp, staring shoreward. They could see nothing but the low, dark line. More shots followed—the flash of one of them clearly visible, a good half-mile away.

Then there were shouts, arguments. These were dying down when they heard the sound of oars in oarlocks, and a boat pulled alongside.

There was a brief discussion in Spanish, the Tinker doing the talking. At that time Jonas knew very little Spanish, although later he learned a good deal. There was plenty of time to learn . . . in prison.

There were soldiers in the boat. They were looking for an escaped criminal, a renegade. As the boat started to pull away they backed on their oars and the officer in command called back. "There will be a reward . . . five hundred pesos . . . *alive!*"

"Whoever he is," the Tinker had said, "they want him badly, to pay that much. And they want him alive. He knows something, Captain."

"That he does," said a voice, speaking from the sea. And then an arm reached up, caught the chains, and pulled its owner from the dark water. He crouched there in the chains for a moment to catch his breath, then reached up and pulled himself to the top of the bowsprit, and came down to the deck. He was a big man, splendidly built, and naked to the waist as well as bare-footed.

"That I do, gentlemen," he had said quietly. "I know enough to make us all rich."

He was talking for his life, or at least for his freedom, and he knew he must catch their attention at once. There on the deck, the water dripping from him, he told them enough to convince them. And to his arguments he added one even more convincing—a Spanish gold piece, freshly minted.

By that time they were in the Captain's own cabin, a pot of coffee before them. The stranger dropped the gold coin on the table, then pushed it toward them with his forefinger. "Look at it," he said. "It's a pretty thing—and where that comes from, there's a million of them."

Not a million dollars—a million of such coins, each of them worth many dollars.

There in the cabin of the brig, the three men sat about the Captain's table—Jonas Locklear, the Tinker, and the man who was to become my father, Falcon Sackett. Jonas was the only one who was past twenty-five, but the story they heard that night was to effect a change in all their lives.

Thirty-odd years before, Jean LaFitte, pirate and slave trader, was beating north along the Gulf coast with two heavily laden treasure ships. During a gale one of these ships was driven ashore, its exact position unknown. LaFitte believed, or professed to believe, that the vessel had gone ashore on Padre Island, that very long, narrow island that parallels many miles of the Gulf coast of Texas. As a matter of fact, the ship had gone ashore some sixty miles south of Padre.

Six men, and six only, made it to shore. Of these, one died within a matter of hours of injuries sustained during the wreck, and a second was slain by roving Karankawa Indians while struggling through the brush just back from the shore.

The four who reached a settlement were more thirsty than wise. Staggering exhausted into the tiny village, rain-soaked and bedraggled, coming from out of nowhere, they hurried to the *cantina*, where they proceeded to get roaring drunk on the gold they carried in their pockets.

They woke up in prison.

The commandant at the village was both a greedy and a cruel man, and the four drunken sailors carried in their pockets more than three hundred dollars . . . a veritable fortune at that place and time.

Upon a coast where tales of buried treasure and lost galleons are absorbed with the milk of the mother, this gold could mean but one thing: the four sailors had stumbled upon such a treasure and could be, by one means or another, persuaded to tell its location.

The commandant had no idea with what kind of men he dealt, for the four were pirates and tough men, accustomed to hardship, pain, and cruelty. They were also realistic. They knew that as soon as the commandant knew what they knew, he would no longer have any need for them. They wanted the gold, and they wanted to live, and both these things were at stake. So they kept their secret well. They denied knowing anything of pirate treasure . . . they had won the money playing cards in Callao, in Peru.

Much of what they were asked could be denied with all honesty, for the commandant was positive they had stumbled upon gold long buried, and never suspected that they themselves might have brought the gold to the shores of Mexico.

Under the torture one man died, and the commandant grew frightened. If the others died, he might never learn their secret. Torture, then, was not the answer.

He would get them drunk. Under the influence, they would talk.

The trouble was, he underestimated their capacity, and overestimated that of himself and his guards. He judged their capacity by the effect of the first drinks, not realizing they had been taken on stomachs three days empty of food.

The result was that he got drunk, his guards got drunk, and the prisoners escaped. And before they escaped they cleaned out the pockets of the commandant and his guards, as well as the office strongbox (their own gold had been hidden elsewhere), and then they fled Mexico.

The border was close and they nearly killed their horses reaching it. Splashing across the Rio Grande, alternately wading or swimming, they arrived in Texas.

The year was 1816.

Texas was still Mexico, so they stole horses and headed northeast for Louisiana. En route one of the three men was killed by Indians, and now only two remained who knew exactly where the gold lay, and each was suspicious of the other.

Knowing where a treasure is, is one thing; going there to get it, quite another. Financing such a wildcat venture is always a problem; moreover, a "cover" is needed in the event the authorities ask what you are doing there. And there is always the question: who can be trusted?

Both men intended to go back at once, either together or each by himself, but neither could manage it. Both were out of funds, which meant work, and their work was on the sea. So they went to sea, on separate ships, and neither ever saw the other again. Each knew where there was a vast treasure in gold, but it lay upon a lonely coast where strangers were at once known as such, and the local commandant was greedy . . . and aware of the treasure's existence.

Then the year was 1846, and General Zachary Taylor had invaded northern Mexico and was winning victories, but was desperately in need of supplies. Steamboats were active on the Rio Grande, ferrying supplies across from the anchorage at Brazos Santiago to the waiting steamboats at Boca del Rio. The steamboats that could navigate off the coast drew too much water for the river, so all goods must be transferred.

In command of one of those waiting boats was Captain Falcon Sackett.

The war with Mexico offered opportunity for any number of adventurers, outlaws, and ne'er-do-wells, who came at once to the mouth of the river—to Matamoras, Brownsville, Bagdad, and the coastal villages. Two of these were men with one idea: under cover of the disturbance and confusion of war, to slip down to the coast and get away with the gold.

One was the last actual survivor of the original six; the second was the son of the other survivor. The first, Duval, was an old man now. He found his way to Boca del Rio, where he sought out and secured a job as cook on Falcon Sackett's steamboat. Duval was a tough old man, and luckily for the men on the steamboat, an excellent cook.

Eric Stouten was twenty-four, a veteran of several years at sea, and a fisherman for some years before that. But when he found his way to Mexico it was as an enlistee in the cavalry assigned to the command of Captain Elam Kurbishaw.

Striking south on a foraging expedition, Captain Kurbishaw led his men into the village where once, long ago, the survivors from the treasure ship had come. That night, just before sundown, Trooper Stouten requested permission to speak to the commanding officer.

Captain Elam Kurbishaw was a tall, cool, desperate man. A competent field commander, he was also a man ready to listen to just such a proposal as Stouten had to offer.

Within the hour the commandant of the village was arrested, his quarters ransacked, and the old report of the interrogation of the prisoners found. With it was a single gold piece . . . kept as evidence that what was recorded there had, indeed, transpired.

The old commandant was dead. The report and the gold piece had been found when the present man took over. A long search had been carried on, covering miles of the coast. Nothing had been found.

The commandant was released; and as he walked away, Elam Kurbishaw, who left nothing to chance, turned and shot him.

A coldly meticulous man, Elam Kurbishaw was fiercely proud of his family, and its background, but well aware that the family fortune, after some years of mismanagement, was dwindling away. He and his two brothers were determined to renew those fortunes, and they had no scruples about how it was to be done.

Alone in his tent, he got out his map case and found a map of the shore line. Military activities concerned inland areas, and his map of the coast was not very detailed. But, studying the map, Kurbishaw was sure he could find the spot from the trooper's description. Laguna de Barril, he was sure, would be the place. But, as was the case of LaFitte's men, he placed the shipwreck too far north.

One other thing Kurbishaw did not know: his bullet had struck through the commandant, felling him, but not killing him. A tough man himself, he survived.

In the quiet of Jonas Locklear's study I heard the story unfold. How little, after all, had I known of my father! How much had even my mother known? That he had gone from the mountains I knew; how long I had never known. Now I learned he had sailed from Charleston in a square-rigger, had been an officer for a time on a river boat at Mobile, and then on the Rio Grande, when Taylor needed river men so desperately.

"Elam never had a chance to look," Jonas explained. "His command was shipped south to General Miles. The way I get it, the trooper remembered the offhand way Kurbishaw had shot the commandant, and again and again he saw Kurbishaw's ruthless way, and he began to regret telling him what he had, and that gave him the idea of deserting. But first he meant to kill Captain Kurbishaw, to let what Elam knew die with him."

After all, why did he need Kurbishaw? Eric Stouten was a good hand with a boat, a fine swimmer and diver, and the vessel lay in relatively shallow water.

The night before Chapultepec he took his knife and slipped into Kurbishaw's tent. He was lifting the knife when a voice stopped him. He turned his head, to see two Kurbishaws staring at him . . . another lay on the bed.

He cried out, lost his grip on his knife, and started to turn for the door, and the two men shot him.

"How do you know they didn't find the gold themselves?" I asked Locklear.

"They didn't know where to look. The Laguna de Barril is only one of many coves and inlets along that coast.

"The difficulty was, that young trooper had talked far too much. He had, among other things, told of the other man who was still around, the other pirate who had escaped . . . and who, he was sure, was now on one of the river boats on the Rio Grande.

"If they could not immediately find the gold, they would fix it so nobody else would, and they tried to murder old Duval. That brought your father into the fight, and his first run-in with the Kurbishaws. I don't know the circumstances, but when they tried to kill Duval, Falcon Sackett put a bullet into one of them, and then Duval told Falcon his story."

Bit by bit the story emerged, and bit by bit our own plans came into being. After that hot night in Jonas' cabin none of them ever gave up going back, and after my father disappeared, the Tinker hunted for him, and Jonas, too. Neither had any luck until Will Caffrey began to spend pa's gold, and Tinker followed the trail of that Spanish gold from Charleston to the mountains.

The Kurbishaws also traced the gold, and decided to kill me for fear I might go after it.

"Cortina has controlled that area off and on for years," Jonas said, "and many of his subordinates have been thieves or worse; however, nobody wants to see that much gold slipping through their fingers.

"After that talk in the cabin of my steamboat," he continued, "we waited until the time was right, and then slipped down there to look.

"The water in many places was shallow, there were many sand bars, and their location changed with each heavy blow. Twice we went aground, several times we were fired upon. Then the war ended and we had no further excuse to be in the vicinity; and the local authorities, knowing something was hidden there, suspected everybody.

"Your father actually found the wreck and got away with some of the gold—got away, I might add, because he was uncommonly agile and gifted with nerve. And he tried to find us."

The Tinker glanced at me. "Had it been me I doubt I should have tried to find anybody, but it was Falcon Sackett, and he is a different man in every way."

Out of our talking a plan emerged. Jonas Locklear must, in any event, go to the ranch he owned on the Gulf coast. We would go with him, and then we would go to Mexico to buy cattle for a drive to Kansas, and to restock the ranch. This might call for several trips.

In this cattle-buying I should have to take first place, for either Jonas or the Tinker might be recognized, and to stay over a few hours south of the border would invite disaster.

Arrangements could be made by letter for me to pick up the herd, and then I would start north, holding them near the coast. Jonas and the Tinker would join me as cowhands, riding with other cowhands. When we had the herd close by where the treasure was believed to be, we would camp . . . and find our gold.

It was simple as that. Nobody, we believed, would suspect a cattleman of hunting for gold. It was a good cover, and we could find no flaws in it. There was water for cattle in brackish pools, there was good grass, so the route was logical.

"Are you sure," the Tinker asked me, "that your father left nothing to guide you to the ship? No map? No directions?"

"He gave me nothing when he left, and if there was a map he may have wanted it himself."

Jonas rose. "My brother-in-law may question you. You have hired to work on my ranch, that is all."

"It is settled then?" the Tinker asked. "To Mexico?"

"How about it, Sackett?"

"Well," I said, "I never saw much gold, and always allowed as how I'd like to. This seems to be a likely chance." I shook hands with them.

"I only hope," I added, "that I'm half the man my father must have been."

# Chapter 4

We fetched up to the ranch house shy of sundown. We'd been riding quite a spell of days, and while never much on riding, I had been doing a fair country job of it by the time we hauled rein in front of that soddy.

For that was what it was, a sod house and no more. Jonas Locklear had cut himself a cave out of a hillside and shored it up with squared timbers. Then he had built a sod house right up against it, built in some bunks, and there it was.

Only Locklear had been gone for some time, and when we fetched up in front of that soddy the door opened and a man came out.

He was no taller than me, but black-jawed and sour-looking. He wore a tied-down gun, and some folks would have decided from that he was a gunman. Me, I'd seen a few gunfighters, and they wore their guns every which way.

"I'm Locklear. I own this place. Who are you?"

The man just looked at him, and then as a second man emerged, the first one said, "Says he owns this place. Shall we tell it to him quick?"

"Might's well."

"All right." His eyes went from Locklear to the Tinker, and he said, "You don't own this place no more, Mr. Locklear. We do. We found it abandoned, we moved in. It's ours, we're givin' you until full dark to get off the place. The ranch stretches for ten miles thataway, so you'd best make a fast start."

Before Jonas could make reply, I broke in. Something about this man got in my craw and stuck there, and so I said, "You heard Jonas Locklear speak. This here ranch is deeded and proper, and not open to squatters. You gave us until full dark. Well, we ain't givin' you that much time. You got just two minutes to make a start."

His gun showed up. I declare, he got that thing out before I could so much as have it in mind.

"You draw fast," I said, "but you still got to shoot it, and before you kill me dead, I'll have lead in you. I'll shoot some holes in you, believe me. Now you take Cullen. When he was teaching me, he said—"

"Who? Who did you say?"

"Cullen"—I kept my face bland—"Cullen Baker. Now, when he was teaching me to draw, he said to—"

"Cullen Baker taught you to *draw?*" He looked around warily. "He ridin' with you?"

"He camps with us," I said. "What he does meanwhile I've no idea. Him an' Longley an' Lee, they traipse around the country a good deal. Davis' police, they've been hustling Cullen some, so he said to me, 'South, that's the place. We'll go south.'"

This black-jawed man looked from me to the Tinker, and then he sort of backed up and said, "I'd no idea you was with Cullen Baker. I want no trouble with him, or any outfit he trails with."

"You've got a choice," I said, "Brownsville or Corpus Christi. When the rest of them get here, I figure to have coffee on. Cullen sets store by fresh black coffee."

They lit out, and after they had gone, the Tinker looked over at Jonas. "Did you ever see the like? Looks right down a gun barrel and talks them out of it."

"Cullen did camp with us," I said, "and there's no question that he liked our coffee."

Took us until midnight to clean that place out, but we did it. And then we turned in to sleep.

Sunup found us scouting around the range. Seemed like there was grass everywhere but no cattle, and then we did come on some cows and bulls in a draw, maybe twenty-five or thirty of them lazing in the morning sun. These were wild cattle. Owned cattle, mind you, but they'd run wild all their lives and were of no mind to be trifled with.

A longhorn is like nothing else you ever saw. If a man thinks he knows cattle, he should look over a longhorn first of all. The longhorn developed from cattle turned loose on the plains of Texas, growing up wild and caring for themselves; and for the country they were in, no finer or fiercer creature ever lived. There were some tough old mossy-horns in that outfit that would weigh sixteen hundred pounds or better, and when they held their heads up they were taller than our horses. They were mean as all get out, and ready to take after you if they caught you afoot. Believe me, a man needed a six-shooter and needed to get it into action fast if one of those big steers came for him.

Times had changed in Texas. When the Tinker and Locklear had been here before, cattle were worth about two dollars a head, and no takers, but now they were driving herds up the Shawnee Trail to the Kansas railheads and paying five and six dollars a head, selling them in Kansas at anywhere from eighteen to thirty dollars each. A trail drive was a money-making operation, if a man got through.

"Tinker," I said, "if we want to get rich in these western lands we should round up a few head and start for Kansas."

He grunted at me, that was all. Treasure was on his mind—bright, yellow gold with jewels and ivory and suchlike. I'll not claim it didn't set me to dreaming myself, but I am a practical man and there's nothing more practical than beef on the hoof when folks are begging for it on the fire.

We rode down into a little draw and there was a *jacal*, a Mexican hut. Around it was fenced garden space and a corral. As we rode up, I sighted a rifle barrel looking at us over a window sill, and the man who appeared in the doorway wore a belt gun. He was a tall, wiry Mexican, handsome but for a scar on his jaw. The instant his eyes touched Locklear he broke into a smile.

"Señor! Juana, the señor is back!"

The gun muzzle disappeared and a very pretty girl came to the door, shading her eyes at us.

"Tinker, Sackett . . . this is Miguel," Locklear said. "We are old friends."

They shook hands, and when Miguel offered his to me I took it and looked into the eyes of a man. I knew it would be good to have Miguel with us. There was pride and courage there, and something that told me that when trouble came, this man would stand.

This I respected, for of myself I was not sure. Every man wishes to believe that when trouble appears he will stand up to it, yet no man knows it indeed before it happens.

When trouble came at the river's crossing, I had faced up to it with the Tinker beside me, but it had happened too quickly for me to be frightened. And what if I had been alone?

Jonas and the Tinker were impressed by the bluff I worked on the man at the sod house, but I was not. To talk is easy, but what would I have done if he had fired? Would I indeed have been able to draw and return the fire?

My uncertainty was growing as I looked upon the fierce men about me, tough, experienced men who must many times have faced trouble. They knew themselves and what they would do, and I did not.

Would I stand when trouble came? Would I fight, or would I freeze and do nothing? I had heard tales of men who did just that, men spoken of with contempt, and these very tales helped to temper me against the time of danger.

Another thing was in my mind when I was lying ready for sleep, or was otherwise alone.

After the meeting with the man at the sod house I had known, deep down within me, that I would never be fast with a gun—at least, not fast enough. Despite all my practice, I had come to a point beyond which I could not seem to go.

This was something I could not and dared not speak of. But at night, or after we started the ride south for Matamoras, I tried to think it out.

Practice must continue, but now I must think always of just getting my gun level and getting off that first shot. That first shot must score, and I must shape my mind to accept the fact that I must fire looking into a blazing gun. I must return that fire even though I was hit.

South we rode, morning, noon, and night. South down the Shawnee Trail in moonlight and in sun, and all along the trail were herds of cattle —a few hundred, a few thousand, moving north for Kansas with their dust clouds to mark the way. We heard the prairie wind and the cowboy yells, and at night the prairie wolves that sang the moon out of the sky.

We smelled the smoke of the fires, endured the heat of the crowded bodies of the herd, and often of a night we stopped and yarned with the cowboys, sharing their fires and their food and exchanging fragments of news, or of stories heard.

There were freight teams, too. These were jerkline outfits with their oxen or horses stretched out ahead of them hauling freight from Mexico or taking it back.

And there were free riders, plenty of them. Tough, hard-bitten men, armed and ready for trouble. Cow outfits returning home from Kansas, bands of unreconstructed renegades left over from the war, occasional cow thieves and robbers.

Believe me, riding in Texas had taught me there was more to the West than just wagon trains and cattle drives. Folks were up to all sorts of things, legal and otherwise, and some of them forking the principle. That is, they sat astraddle of it, one foot on the legal side, the other on the illegal, and taking in money with both hands from both sides. Such business led to shooting sooner or later.

South we rode, toward the borderlands.

Our second day we overtook a fine coach and six elegant horses, with six outriders, tough men in sombreros, with Winchesters ready to use.

"Only one man would have such a carriage," Jonas said. "It will be Captain Richard King, owner of the ranch on Santa Gertrudis."

An outrider recognized Jonas and called out to him, and when King saw Jonas he had the carriage draw up. It was a hot, still morning and the trailing dust cloud slowly closed in and sifted fine red dust over us all.

"Jonas," King said, "my wife, Henrietta. Henrietta, this is Jonas Locklear."

Richard King was a square-shouldered, strongly built man with a determined face. It was a good face, the face of a man who had no doubts. I envied him.

"King was a steamboat captain on the Rio Grande," the Tinker explained to me in a low voice, "and after the Mexican War he bought land from Mexicans who now lived south of the border and could no longer ranch north of the line."

Later the Tinker told me more: how King had bought land from others who saw no value in grassland where Indians and outlaws roamed. One piece he bought was fifteen thousand acres, at two cents an acre.

Instead of squatting on land like most of them were doing, King had cleared title to every piece he bought. There was a lot of land to be had for cash, but you had to be ready to fight for anything you claimed, and not many wanted to chance it.

Brownsville was the place where we were to separate. At that time it was a town of maybe three thousand people, but busy as all get out. From here Miguel and I would go on alone.

Looking across toward Mexico, I asked myself what sort of fool thing I was getting into. Everybody who had anything to do with that gold had come to grief.

Nevertheless, I was going. Pa had a better claim to that gold than any man, and I aimed to have a try at it. And while I was going primed for trouble, I wasn't hunting it.

First off, I'd bought a new black suit and hat, as well as rougher clothes for riding. I picked out a pair of fringed shotgun chaps and a dark blue shirt. Then I bought shells for a new Henry rifle. The rifle itself cost me $43, and I bought a thousand rounds of .44s for $21. That same place I picked up a box of .36-caliber bullets for my pistol at $1.20 per hundred.

That Henry was a proud rifle. I mean it could really shoot. Men I'd swear by said it was accurate at one thousand yards, and I believed them. It carried eighteen bullets fully loaded.

My mare I'd left back at Miguel's place. Her time was close and she would need care. Miguel's woman was knowing thataway, so the mare was in good hands.

About noontime Miguel and me shook hands with the Tinker and Jonas, and then we crossed over the river and went into Matamoras.

My horse was a line-back dun, tough and trail wise. Miguel was riding a sorrel, and we led one pack horse, a bald-faced bay. We put up at a livery stable and I started up the street after arranging to meet Miguel at a *cantina* near the stable.

One thing I hadn't found to suit me was a good belt knife, and the Tinker wasn't about to part with one of his. I went into a store and started looking over some Bowie knives, and finally found one to please me—not that it was up to what the Tinker could do.

I paid for the knife and then ran my belt through the loop on the scabbard and hitched it into place. A moment there, I paused in the doorway. And that pause kept me from walking right into trouble.

Standing not ten feet away, on the edge of the boardwalk, was Duncan Caffrey!

He was facing away from me and I could see only the side of his face and his back, but I'd not soon forget that nose. I had fixed it the way it was.

No sooner had I looked at him than my eyes went to the man he spoke with, and I felt a little chill go down my spine. I was looking right into a pair of the blackest, meanest, cruelest eyes I ever did see.

The man wore a stovepipe hat and a black coat. His face was long, narrow, and deep-lined. He wore a dirty white shirt and a black tie that looked greasy, even at the distance.

Stepping outside, I walked slowly away in the opposite direction, my skin crawling because I felt they were looking at me. Yet when I reached the corner and looked back, they were still talking, paying me no mind.

Never before had I seen that man in the stovepipe hat, but I knew who he was.

The Bishop.

It had to be him. He had been described to me more than once, and he'd been mentioned by Caffrey that night when the Tinker and me listened from the brush.

Now, nobody needed to tell me that there's such a thing as accident, or coincidence, as some call it. I've had those things happen to me, time to time, but right at that moment I wouldn't buy that as a reason for Dun and the Bishop being in Matamoras. Whatever they were here for was connected with me. That much I was sure of and nothing would shake it.

Right there I had an idea of going back to Brownsville and telling the Tinker and Jonas. Trouble was, they'd think I was imagining things, or scaring out, or something like that.

What I did do was head for the *cantina* where I dropped into a chair across the table from Miguel and said, "Enjoy that drink, because we're pulling out—tonight."

"*Tonight?*"

"Soon as ever we can make it without drawing eyes to us."

Sitting there at the table, I drank a glass of beer and told him why. Even down here they had heard of the Bishop, so Miguel was ready enough.

"One thing," he said, "we must ride with great care, for there was word that a prisoner escaped from prison and is at large to the south of here. They believe he will come to the border, and the soldiers search for him."

It was past midnight when we walked through the circle of lemon light under the livery-stable lantern. The hostler sat asleep against the wall, his *serape* about his shoulders. Music tinkled from the *cantina* . . . there was a smell of hay, and of fresh manure, of leather harness, and of horses.

As we walked our horses from the stable I leaned over and dropped a peso in the lap of the hostler.

Riding past the *cantina*, I glanced back. I thought I saw, in a dark doorway next to the *cantina*, the boot-toes and the tip of a hat belonging to a very tall man. I could have been mistaken.

We rode swiftly from the town. The night was quiet except for the insects that sang in the brush. A long ride lay before us. The cattle about which we had inquired were at a ranch southwest of Santa Teresa . . . the gold lay somewhere off the coast we would parallel.

So far as we knew, pa was the only man who knew exactly where that sunken ship lay. The Kurbishaws had killed the man who told them of it, thinking they could find it from the description. Captain Elam Kurbishaw's only map that showed the coast was vague, and had indicated only one inlet on that stretch of coast, where actually there were several. More to the point, there was a long stretch of coast that lay behind an outlying sand bar. If the ship had succeeded in getting through one of the openings in the shore line, it would be lost in a maze of inlets, channels, and bays. Looking for it would be like looking for one cow that bawled in a herd of five thousand.

"Soldiers may stop us," Miguel warned. "It is well to give them no displeasure, for the soldiers can be worse than *banditos*."

As we rode along, my mind kept thinking back to Gin Locklear and that snippy little Marsha.

Marsha was fourteen . . . she'd be up to marrying in maybe two years, and I pitied the man who got her. As for Gin, she was older than me, but she was a woman to take a man's eye, and to talk a man's tongue, too. It was no wonder Jonas set such store by her.

It lacked only a little of daybreak when we turned off the trail into the brush. We went maybe half a mile off the traveled way before we found a hollow where there was grass and a trickle of water. We staked out the horses and bedded down for sleep. Miguel took no time about it, but sleep was long in coming to me.

Thoughts kept going round in my mind, and pa was in the middle of them. I thought how pa was always teaching me things. Had he maybe taught me where that gold was, and me not knowing?

And then my mind was sorting out memories and feeling the sadness they brought.

Ma was gone. . . . Pa? Who could ever know about pa? Those were bad days for travelers and folks who went a-yondering. Chances were the Bald Knobbers had got him . . . or somebody from ambush.

I'd never believe it was them Kurbishaws.

# Chapter 5

We saw no more of the Bishop or the Kurbishaws on the trail in the next few days.

We found Santa Teresa a sleepy, pleasant Mexican village, with hens scratching in the street, and the best *tortillas* I'd eaten up to then, or for a long time after.

The *hacienda* where I bargained for and bought three hundred head of cattle was another pleasant place, and when we started the cattle back toward the border they loaned me three *vaqueros* to help until my own hands joined us—they were to meet us in camp just north of Santa Teresa.

The range from which we bought our cattle had been overstocked and the cattle were thin, but they showed an immediate liking for the grass of the coast land and its plentiful salt. We were four days driving from the *hacienda* to the camp north of Santa Teresa, but when we reached the camp there was no one there.

Here the *vaqueros* were to leave us, and here we must hold our stock until help came from the north. Five men could handle three hundred head without too much trouble when they were intent upon stuffing their lean bellies with good grass, but from there on it would be more difficult.

Scarcely were we camped, with a fire going, when we heard a rush of horses and suddenly our camp was surrounded by soldiers, their rifles leveled on us.

Their officer was a lean and savage man. He rode around the herd, inspecting the brands, then he wheeled up to the fire.

"Who is in charge here?" he asked in Spanish.

Miguel gestured to me. "The Americano. We have bought the cattle from Señor Ulloa. We drive them to Texas."

"You are lying!"

"No, señor," one of the *vaqueros* spoke up quickly. "I am of the *hacienda* of Ulloa. Three of us have ridden with the cattle to this point. Here their own riders join them. It is of a truth, señor."

The officer looked at me, his eyes cold and unfriendly. "Your name?"

"Orlando, señor." It seemed possible he might have heard the name Sackett, although it would have been long ago.

He studied me without pleasure. "Do you know Señor King?"

"We spoke with him two days ago. He was driving to Brownsville with the señora."

King was well thought of on both sides of the border, and to know him seemed the wise thing.

He considered the situation a bit, then said: "One thing, señor. A prisoner has escaped. We want him. If you should come upon him, seize him at once and send a rider for me. Anyone rendering assistance to him will be shot." Without further words, he wheeled his horse.

When they had ridden away, the *vaquero* turned to me, his expression grave. "Señor, that was Antonio Herrara—a very bad man. Avoid him if you can."

They were packing to leave, and seemed more than anxious to get away, and I couldn't find it in my heart to go a-blaming them. Surely, this was no trouble of theirs.

After they had gone there was nothing we could do but ride herd on our cattle, and wait.

Sometimes a man is a fool, and I had a feeling that when I left my mare to go traipsing after gold money I'd been more of a fool than most. I'd sure enough be lying if I said I wasn't scared, for that Herrara shaped up like a mean man, and we were in his country where he was the law.

Miguel took the first ride around, bunching the cattle for night. They seemed willing enough to rest, being chock full of good grass like they were. Me, I kept looking up trail toward the border and a-hoping for those riders.

What if Jonas and the Tinker couldn't make it? What if Herrara spotted them as escaped prisoners themselves?

"Miguel," I said, when he stopped by on his circling, "come daybreak we're pushing on, riders or no riders. We're going to head for the border."

He nodded seriously. "It is wise, *amigo*. That Herrara, he is a bad man."

The place where we were was a meadow four, five miles out of Santa Teresa and on an arm of the sea. There was brush around, and some marshy land.

"That prisoner," Miguel said, "he will not be taken easily. He killed a guard in escaping, and he has been much tortured. It is said, señor"— Miguel paused expressively—"that he was believed to know something of a treasure."

"A treasure?" I asked mildly.

"Si, señor. It is a treasure much talked of, a treasure of the pirate, La-Fitte. For thirty years and more men have sought it along the shore to the north. Most of all, Antonio Herrara and his father, the commandant of this area."

What could a man say to that? Only it made me itch all the more to get that herd moving.

"Miguel, an hour before daylight we will start the herd. Twenty miles tomorrow."

"It is a long drive, señor," he said doubtfully.

"Twenty miles—no less."

When the moon lifted, the cattle rose to stretch their legs and move around. Far off, there was a sound of coyotes, and closer by we could hear the rustle of the surf. The waters of the Laguna Madre were close by, the sea itself lay out beyond the bar, at least twenty-five miles away.

Miguel came in and, after coffee, turned in. Mounting the dun, I circled the cattle, singing softly to let them know that they were not alone, and that the shadow they saw moving was me. Nevertheless, there was a restlessness in them I could not explain, but I put it down to my ignorance of cattle.

With the first gray of dawn I stopped by to wake up Miguel.

He sat up and put on his hat, then pulled on his boots. He reached for the big, fire-blackened coffee pot, and shook it in surprise. "You drink much coffee, señor."

"One cup," I said. "I was afraid to stop for more. Something was bothering the cattle."

He emptied out the pot into his cup. "There were at least five cups in this, *amigo*. No less, certainly. I made the coffee myself, and know what we drank. It is a pot for ten men."

"Pack up," I said, "let's move 'em."

They seemed willing enough to go, and an old blue-roan steer moved out and took the lead, as he had done all the way from the *hacienda*.

As they moved, they fed; and we let them for the first two or three hours. Then we stepped up the speed a bit, because both of us wanted distance between us and last night's camp.

Most of the time I rode with a hand ready to grab a gun. From time to time I reached for that Walch Navy, and the butt had a mighty friendly feeling. Nothing feels better when trouble shapes than the butt of a good pistol.

We kept scanning the trail ahead, hoping for a sign of our riders. Lucky for us the cattle seemed to want to get away from that place as much as we did.

There were no trees. Meadows of grass appeared here and there, and sometimes there'd be grass for miles, but between the trail and the sea there was a regular forest of brush. Here and there were signs that the sea had on occasion even come this far. The last time must have been the great hurricane of 1844. If there had been another of such power since, we hadn't heard of it, but the one of '44 was well known.

The cattle drifted steadily. The heat rising from their bunched bodies was as stifling as the dust. Only once in a while did one of the steers cut loose and try to stray from the column. But for two riders it was too many cattle, and our horses would soon be worn to nothing.

Off to the right was the sea . . . that was east. As far as we were from it, I turned again and again to look that way, for though we had been close a time or two, I had never yet seen the ocean. It gave a man an odd feeling to know all the miles upon miles of water that lay off there.

Somewhere out there, lying on the bottom close in to shore, was a ship loaded with gold and silver, with gems maybe, and suchlike. Pa had found it and brought gold from it, and pa must have come back again after he left me. It would be like him to let on he was going for fur, then to trail south where the gold was. Why trap for skins, when the price of thousands of them lay off that coast in shallow water?

It set a man to sweating, just to think of that much gold. It had never really got to me until now. And after all, that was what we'd come for. We hadn't really come for a few hundred scrawny Mexican steers. . . . I wondered how long it would take that Herrara to figure that out.

Not that a few folks weren't buying Mexican stock. With the prices offered in the railhead towns, it was a caution what folks would do to lay hands on a few steers.

But this gold, now. LaFitte, he wasn't only a pirate and slave trader, he was a blacksmith in New Orleans with a shop where slaves did the work, and he and his brother . . . now how did I know that?

Had the Tinker mentioned it? Or Jonas? Jonas, probably, when we were talking. Yet the notion stayed with me that I'd heard it before.

Now I was imagining things. I couldn't call to mind any mention of Jean LaFitte—not before we came up to that plantation house after leaving San Augustine. Not before we met Jonas.

The dun was streaked with sweat and I could tell by the way he moved that he was all in. We hadn't come twenty miles, either. Not by a long shot.

Miguel dropped back beside me, and that horse of his looked worse than mine.

"Señor," he said, "we must stop."

"All right," I said, "but not for the night. We'll take ourselves a rest and then push on."

He looked at me, then shrugged. I knew what he was thinking. If we kept on like this we'd be driving those cattle afoot. We should have a remuda, and Jonas was supposed to be bringing one south. We weren't supposed to drive these cattle not even a foot after the *vaqueros* left us.

We turned the herd into a circle and stopped them where the grass was long and a trickle of water made a slow way, winding across the flatland toward the dunes that marked the lagoon's edge.

We found a few sticks and nursed a fire into boiling water for coffee. Miguel hadn't anything to say. Like me, he was dead beat. But I noticed something: like me, he had wiped his guns free of dust and checked the working mechanism.

"I ain't going to no prison," I said suddenly. "I just ain't a-honing for no cell. That there Herrara wants me, he's got to get me the hard way."

"We have no chance," Miguel said.

"You call it then," I said. "Do we fight?"

"We try to run. We try to dodge. When we can no longer do either, we shoot." He grinned at me, and suddenly the coffee tasted better.

I don't know why I was so much on the shoot all to once, but lately I'd heard so many stories of what happened in those prisons that I just figured dying all to once would be better. Besides, I didn't like that Herrara, and I might get him in my sights. Why, a man who could bark a squirrel could let wind through his skull. That's what I told myself.

Besides, I hadn't shot that Henry .44 at anything. Nor the Walch Navy, as far as that went.

We lay by the trail for three, four hours. We rubbed our horses down good, we led them to water, we let them eat that good grass. And afterwards we saddled again, and mounted up.

The steers were against it. They'd had enough for the day, and were showing no sign of wanting to go further. We cut this one and that one a slap with our *riatas*, and finally they lined out for Texas.

You don't take a herd nowhere in a hurry. Not unless they take a notion to stampede. Maybe eight to ten miles is a good day, with a few running longer than that. We'd been dusting along since four o'clock in the morning and it was past four in the evening now. When they first started, they fed along the way, so we'd made slow time. All I wanted was a little more distance. If we could get where I wanted to hold up, we'd be about twenty-five miles or so from the border.

If a difficulty developed, I figured I could run that far afoot with enough folks a-shooting after me. Anyway, I'd be ready to give it a try. I kept in mind that I'd no particular want to see the inside of one of Mr. Herrara's jail cells.

I was a lover, not a fighter. That's what I said to myself, though I'd no call to claim either. I was only judging where my interests lay.

My thoughts went to Gin Locklear—what a woman! I'd blame no man setting his cap for her, although the way I figured, it would take some standup sort of man to lay a rope on her.

That Marsha now . . . she was only a youngster, and a snippy one, but if she went on the way she'd started she might take after Gin . . . and I could think of nothing in woman's clothes it would be better for a girl to take after.

Shy of midnight we held up near salt water, with high brush growing around, and not more than four miles or so off was the tiny village of Guadalupe. Right close was a long arm of the Gulf.

"We will camp here," I said. "There is fresh water from a spring near the knoll over there."

Miguel looked at me strangely. "How does it happen that you know this?" he asked. "Señor Locklear said you had never been to Mexico."

"I—" I started to answer him, to say I know not what, perhaps to deny that I had been here or knew anything about it. Yet I did know.

Or did I? Supposing there was no spring there? How much had Locklear said?

The spring was there, and Locklear had said nothing about it. I knew that when I looked at the spring, for there, in a huge old timber that was down, there were initials carved. And carved in a way I'd seen only once before, that being in the mountains of Tennessee.

FSct

Just like that . . . carved there plain as day, like pa had carved them on that old pine near the house.

He had been here, all right. Miguel did not notice the initials, or if he did he paid them no mind. I doubt if he would have connected them with Falcon Sackett, and I was not sure how much had been told him. Something, of course . . . but not all.

Believe me, those steers were ready to bed down. We bunched them close for easy holding, and they scarcely took time to crop a bait of grass before they tucked their legs under them and went to chewing cud and sleeping.

Miguel wasn't much behind them. "Turn in," I said, "and catch yourself some shut-eye. I'll stand watch."

It wasn't in him to argue, he was that worn-out. Me, I was perked up, and I knew why. Pa had told me of this place, and I'd forgotten. Yet it had been lying back there in memory, and probably I'd been driving right for this place without giving it thought.

Now the necessary thing was to recollect just what it was pa had told me. He surely wouldn't tell me the part of it without he told me all.

When had he told me? Well, that went back a mite. Had to be before I was ten, the way I figured. He rode off when I was eleven and ma had been sick for some time before that, and he was doing mighty little talking to me aside from what was right up necessary.

It wasn't as if he'd told me one or two stories. He was forever yarning to me, and probably when he told me this one he'd stressed detail, he'd told it over and over again to make me remember. Somehow I was sure of that now.

Maybe I'd been plain tired out by the story. Maybe it hadn't seemed to have much point, but the fact was that he must have told me where the treasure was, and all I had to do was let my memory take me there.

Thing was, suppose it didn't come to me right off? I'd have to stay, and I'd need explanation for that. The fast drive we'd made would help. I could let on I didn't know much about cattle; and if anybody who talked cows to me did so more than a few minutes, they'd know I didn't know anything about them.

So I'd let on like I'd driven the legs off the cattle, to say nothing of our horses, and we were laying up alongside this water to recuperate.

That much decided, the next thing was to get my memory to operating. But the difficulty with a memory is that it doesn't always operate the way a body wants. Seems contrary as all get out, and when you want to remember a particular thing, that idea is shunted off to one side.

Rousting around, I got some sticks, some dead brush, and a few pieces of driftwood left from storms, and I made a fire. Then I put water on for coffee.

All of a sudden I felt my skin prickle, and I looked over at the dun. Tired as he was, he had his head up and his ears pricked. His nostrils were spreading and narrowing as he tried the air to see what it was out there.

That old Walch Navy was right there in my belt, and I eased it out a mite so's it was ready to hand.

Something was out there.

Me, I never was one to believe in ha'nts. Not very much, that is. Fact is, I never believed in them at all, only passing a graveyard like—well, I always walked pretty fast and felt like something was closing in on me.

No, I don't believe in ha'nts, but this here was a coast where dead man lay. Why, the crew of the gold ship must have been forty, fifty men, and all of them dead and gone.

Something was sure enough out there. That lineback dun knew it and I knew it. Trouble was, he had the best idea of what it was, and he wasn't talking. He was just scenting the air and trying to figure out for sure. Whatever it was, he didn't like it—I could tell that much. And I didn't either.

I felt like reaching over and shaking Miguel awake, only he'd think I was spooked. And you know something? I was.

This here was country where folks didn't come of a night, if at any time. It was a wild, lonely place, and there was nothing to call them.

I had taken out that Walch Navy and, gripping it solid, I held it right there in my lap with the firelight shining on it. And you can just bet I felt better.

Out there beyond the fire I suddenly heard the sand *scrooch*. You know how sand goes under foot sometimes. Kind of a crunch, yet not quite that. Heard it plain as day, and I lifted that .36 and waited.

Quite a spell passed by, and all of a sudden the dun, who'd gone back to feeding, upped with his head again. Only this time he was looking off toward the trail from the north, and he was all perked up like something interesting was coming. Not like before.

He had his ears up and all of a sudden he whinnied—and sure enough, from out of the darkness there came another whinny. And then I heard the sound of a horse coming, and Miguel, he sat up.

We both stayed there listening and, like fools, neither of us had sense enough to get back out of the firelight—like the Tinker had done that night when Baker, Lee, and Longley paid us the visit . . . and a few dozen other times along the trail.

We both just sat there and let whoever it was ride right up to the fire.

And when that slim-legged, long-bodied horse came into the firelight and I saw who it was, I couldn't believe it. Nor could Miguel. If we'd seen the ghost I'd been expecting, we wouldn't have been more surprised.

It was Gin Locklear.

# Chapter 6

She rode side-saddle, of course, her skirt draped in graceful folds along the side of the horse, her gloved hand holding the bridle reins just as if she hadn't ridden miles through bandit-infested country to get here. She was just as lovely as when I last saw her.

She taken my breath. Coming up on us out of the night so unexpected-like, and after all the goings-on outside of camp . . . I hadn't a thought in my head, I was that rattled.

It came on me that I'd best help her from the saddle and I crossed over and took her hand, but it was not until she was actually on the ground that I saw the dark shadows under her eyes and the weariness in her face.

"Miguel," I said, "you handle the horse. I'll shake up some fresh coffee."

I dumped the pot and rinsed it, and put in fresh water from the spring. Then I stirred up the fire.

"I had to shoot a man," Gin said suddenly.

Those big eyes of hers handed me a jolt when I looked into them. "Did you kill him?"

"I don't think so."

Miguel turned toward us. "It would have been better had he been killed. Now he will speak of a beautiful señorita riding alone to the south, and others will come."

"There were two men with him," she said, "but this one held my bridle when they ordered me from the saddle. They were shouting and drinking and telling me what they were going to do.

"Of course, they did not see my gun and did not expect me to shoot, but I did shoot the man holding the horse, and then I got away. One of them had hold of my saddle and he tried to grab me. He fell, I think."

"Where was this?"

"Outside of Matamoras. Only a few miles out."

Then she said, "I came to help. Jonas and the Tinker have been arrested—Jonas, at least. He was recognized."

"Recognized? By whom?"

"They came looking for him, just as if they knew he would be there."

My first thought was of Franklyn Deckrow. He was the one with the most to gain if Jonas was not permitted to return. Of course, he might have been seen by someone who remembered him from prison.

It was little enough I knew of the Deckrow deal, but from all I'd gathered Deckrow had run the plantation into debt and Jonas believed it had been done deliberately so Deckrow could later buy up the mortgages and gain possession. If so, he could have sent a rider on a fast horse to Matamoras.

"You shouldn't have come," I said. "This is no place for a woman."

"The place for a woman," she said, smiling at me, "is where she is needed. I ride as well as most men, and I have a fine horse. Also, I've lived on a ranch most of my life."

"Did you see anybody as you came along the trail?"

She looked at me curiously. "Not for miles. I've never seen a more deserted road, and if I hadn't seen a reflection of your campfire I might have gone right on by."

"You didn't circle the camp?"

"No."

Miguel was looking at me now, and I noticed he had his rifle in hand. "There was somebody around the camp. Somebody or some *thing*."

Miguel stared uneasily at the blackness beyond the fire. Neither of us liked to think there was somebody or something out there whom we could not see.

"Maybe we should go, señor?"

"No, we'll sit right here and let the stock rest up." That was my plan, but the arrival of Gin had put a crimp in it. If outlaws were going to come hunting her, we'd be in trouble a-plenty.

"Come daybreak," I said, "we'll move the herd."

"Where, señor?"

"Yonder, I think we can find a place to hold the cattle. Maybe some of the other men will get through. That Tinker—he's a sly one. If he had any warning, no law is going to latch onto him."

Gin made herself comfortable on my bed. I stirred up the fire and finished off what coffee the three of us hadn't drank, and ate a couple of cold *tortillas*.

At daybreak the wind was off the sea, and you could feel the freshness of it, with a taste like no other wind.

Wide awake, I thought of those initials of pa's. Pa had left that sign, and he'd left it for himself, or mayhap for me. He was a planning man, pa was, and one likely to foresee. . . . I think he taken time deliberately to teach me where that gold was. The trouble was, I'd gone ahead and forgotten.

Some things I did remember. He'd taught me to mark a trail, Indian fashion. Now, suppose he had marked this one? If he had, he would have added his own particular ways to it, but meanwhile, I planned to look around. If I found no sign I was going to drive that herd where I felt it should go, with no scouting for grass, or anything. Maybe out of my hidden thoughts would come the memory of what pa had taught me, to guide our way.

I taken a circle around camp, and I found no sign—nothing left by pa that I could make out.

That isn't to say I didn't find sign of another kind, and when I seen that track I felt a chill go right up my spine that stood every hair on end.

What I found were wolf tracks, but wolf tracks bigger than any wolf that ever walked—any *normal* sort of wolf, that is. These wolf tracks were big as dinner plates.

Well, I stopped right there, looking down at those tracks, and the other two came over to look. Miguel's face turned white when he saw the tracks, and even Gin kind of caught at my arm.

We had both heard tell of werewolves, and certainly Miguel knew the stories about them.

Me, I was thinking of something else. I was thinking of where those tracks were. Soon I scouted around, and a far piece away, like whatever it was had been taking giant strides, I found another track, this one set deep in the sod.

The tracks circled about the water hole at the spring. Whatever it was, it was trying to get to water, but the water had been lighted by our fire, with one of us setting awake.

All of a sudden I saw something that made me forget all about werewolves and ha'nts and such. Far as that goes, I'd never heard tell of a thirsty ghost.

What I saw was something back in the brush, and at first it didn't look like much of a find, except that there was no reason for it being where it was. It was a broken reed, and it lay right on the edge of a bunch of mesquite.

Taking up the reed, I drew it out, and you know, there were several pieces of reed stuck one into another until they were all of eight or nine feet long. Stretched out, they reached from the spring's pool to the brush nearby.

"What is it?" Gin asked.

"Somebody wanted a drink, and wanted it bad, so he made a tube of these reeds, breaking them off to be rid of the joints and putting them together so he could suck water through them. He must have siphoned water right out of the pool into his mouth while I was just a-setting there."

Nobody said anything, and I nosed around a mite, studying the brush, and finally finding where the man or whatever it was had knelt.

There, too, I found the wolf tracks.

"Two-legged wolf," I said, "wearing some kind of coarse-woven jeans or pants. See here?" I showed them the place in the brush. "That's where he knelt whilst siphoning the water."

Following the tracks back from the brush, I said, "He's big—look at the length of that stride. I can't match it without running."

I studied the reed tube again. "Canny," I said. "Like something the Tinker might do."

"We should go," Gin suggested.

"No," I said, "not without what we came after. We have come too far and risked too much."

"But how can you hope to find it?" Gin said. "You've no idea where to look."

"Maybe I have. Maybe I am just beginning to recollect some things pa told me."

The wind was blowing harder and the sky was gray and overcast. The cattle wandered to the water in small groups, then returned to the bedding ground to graze or rest. They showed no restlessness, and seemed content to hold to the low spots out of the wind.

I cut some sod with a machete, and made a wall to protect our fire from the wind, adding just enough fuel to keep some coals. Miguel was worried, which I could see plain enough, and so was Gin.

Meanwhile I was doing some figuring. Jonas was in prison, and the Tinker might well be, so that left whatever was to be done up to me. Gin was with us, which she hadn't ought to be, the country being torn up with trouble the way it was, and somewhere close by was that ship filled with gold.

Jonas needed his share to get his mortgage paid off, and the Tinker wanted his. As far as that goes, I wasn't going to buck or kick if somebody handed me some of that there gold.

Around the fire at breakfast, Miguel told me a mite about Herrara. He was a lieutenant of General Juan Nepomuceno Cortina, usually called Cheno, and part of the time he was a soldier with a legitimate rank, and part of the time an outlaw, depending on who was in power in Mexico and on his own disposition at the moment.

Of good family, Cortina had become a renegade, but one with a lot of followers. He was a shrewd fighter, risking battle only when it suited him, and running when it didn't. He was a man of uncertain temperament, but dangerous enough and strong enough to handle the pack of wolves that followed him.

Frequently, they raided across the border into Texas and had run off thousands of head of Texas cattle. Yet he had good men following him, too, and on occasion he could be both gallant and generous. But generally speaking, he was a man to fight shy of.

As for Herrara, he was one of the wolves, fierce as an Apache, and by all accounts treacherous.

Leaving Miguel by the fire, with his horse saddled, to keep an eye on the cows, Gin and I rode off through the brush, hunting the water's edge.

We hadn't far to go. A long gray finger of water came twisting through the grass, leading some distance away to a larger body of water like a bay. There we could see the white, bare bones of an ancient boat, much too small for what we were looking for . . . which, anyway, was by all accounts down under water.

My Henry was in the saddle boot, and Gin carried one also. But what I kept ready to hand was that Walch Navy. I liked the feel of that gun.

As we rode we saw nothing—only a low shore of gray-green grass, the gray water looking like a sheet of steel, the reeds bending under the wind, gulls wheeling and crying overhead. Whitecaps were showing on the water.

It might have been a world never seen by man. No tracks, no ashes of old fires, nothing man had built but the stark white ribs of that old boat.

"It's cold," Gin said.

Her face looked pinched, and the place was depressing her, as it did me.

Yet, wild and lonely as it was, the country had an eerie sort of charm like nowhere I'd ever seen. Toward the Gulf I could see the dunes of sand heaped by wind and wave, and somewhere out there was a long bar that stretched miles away to the south.

A barren desolate land. In spite of this, the place seemed to be working a charm on me.

"Let's go back," Gin said.

We turned and made our start, riding along the shore. The wind was blowing stronger, the brush and reeds bending before it. A few cold, spitting drops of rain began to fall.

The place to which we had driven the herd as in a cul-de-sac, with the sea on three sides—long arms of the sea where the water had flowed in over low ground or the working of the waves had hollowed it out.

To the east was a long, snake-like arm of the sea that nowhere was over a quarter of a mile wide. South and southwest the coves were wider.

The grass was good, and the cattle were protected by thick brush from the worst of the wind. Most of these cattle had at one time or another grazed along the shore, and like Shanghai Pierce and his "sea lions," as he called the longhorns that swam back and forth from the coast to Padre Island, they were used to the sea and were good swimmers.

"I like it," I said suddenly, gesturing toward the country around us. "It's almighty wild and lonely, but I take to it."

We drew up and looked back. The sweep of the shore had an oddly familiar look to it that started excitement in me. I frowned and tried to remember, but nothing came.

"Pa must have told me about this place," I said. "I can feel it. This here's where the gold is, somewhere about here."

"Your father must have been an interesting man."

So, a-setting there in the chill wind, I talked about him as I recalled him, powerful and dark, straight and tall. An easy-moving man who never seemed in a hurry, and yet could move swift as any striking snake when need be.

"He'd never let be," I said, "not with him knowing where that gold is. He'd come back for it. Ma never wanted him to go back.

"You see, before pa and ma met, he had trouble with her brothers, the Kurbishaws, and over this gold. There were three of them, led by Captain Elam. The other two were Gideon and Eli.

"I never got the straight of it, although from time to time I'd hear talk around the house, but they were after the gold the same time pa was, and they tried to run him off. Pa never was much on running, as I gather.

"Later on, with some of this gold in his jeans, he went to Charleston and cut quite a swath about town. And there he met ma. They taken to each other, and it wasn't until she invited him home that he met her brothers face to face and knew who they were."

"It sounds very dramatic."

"Must have been, pa being what he was and those Kurbishaws hating him like they did. I knew little about it, but I gathered more from talking with the Tinker and Jonas . . . that helped me to piece together things I'd heard as a child."

We walked our horses on, the dun's mane blown by the wind. It gave me an odd feeling to know that pa had more than likely watched and walked this same shore, maybe many times, a-hunting that gold.

Odd thing, I'd never thought of my pa as a person. I expect a child rarely does think of his parents that way. They are a father and a mother, but a body rarely thinks of them as having hopes, dreams, ambitions and desires and loves. Yet day by day pa was now becoming more real to me than he had ever been, and I got to wondering if he ever doubted himself like I did, if he ever felt short of what he wished to be, if he ever longed for things beyond him that he couldn't quite put into words.

"You'd like pa," I said suddenly. "The more I think of him the more I like him, myself. I mean other than just as a father. I figure he's the kind of man I'd like to ride the trail with, and I guess that's about as much as a man can say."

Ahead of us I saw a mite of grass bunched up, and I drew rein sudden and felt my breath tight in my throat. Gin started on, but when she saw my face she stopped.

"Orlando, *what is it?*"

It was a small tuft of grass kind of bunched up, and some other grass stems had been used to tie a knot around the top of the bunch.

There it sat, kind of out of the way and accidental-like, but it was no accident. Maybe many men used that trail marker—no doubt Indians did. But I knew one man who'd used it, and who knew I'd spot such a thing.

My pa.

"Gin"—I couldn't speak above a whisper—"pa's been here."

She looked at me, her eyebrows raised a little. "Of course, when he found the gold."

"No . . . recent. Maybe the past two or three days."

Swinging down, I slid an arm through the loop of the bridle reins and squatted down to look closer. That marker had been made within the past couple of days, for the broken grass used to tie around the bunch was still green.

Straightening up, I looked all around, taking my time. Whoever had made that marker intended for it to be seen, but not by just anybody. Nobody would see it unless he was trained to look for sign.

It stood all by itself, though. I mean, there was grass all around and some brush, but no other markers. That meant that what it was intended to mark was close by, within the range of my eyes. It was up to me to see it. Yet, looking all around, I saw nothing. The clouded sky, the gray, whitecapped water, the green grass growing just short of knee-high, the scattered brush, the reeds along the shore . . .

*The reeds!*

Reaching up, I taken my Henry from the boot. "You stand watch, Gin. Watch everything, not just me."

For two, three minutes I didn't move. I stood there beside my horse and I studied those reeds, and I studied them section by section, taking a piece maybe ten foot square and studying it careful, then moving on to another square.

Trailing the bridle reins, I stepped away from the horse and worked my way carefully through the reeds. What I had spotted was an open space among the reeds, which might mean an inlet of water, for there were several such around. However, when I got to that open place—minding myself to break no reeds and to move with care—I found a low hive, a mound-like hut of reeds made by drawing the tops together and tying them, then weaving other reeds through the rooted ones. It was maybe eight feet long by four or five wide.

Room enough for a man to sleep.

"I'm friendly," I said, speaking low but so I could be heard. "I'm hunting no trouble."

There was no answer.

Easing forward a bit, I spotted the opening that led inside, and kneeling, I eased forward. I spoke once more, and there was no response. Then I stuck my head inside.

The hut was empty.

The ground inside must have been damp, so close to the water, and it had been covered by several hastily woven mats of reeds, with grass thrown atop of them.

I backed out and stood up.

My father had taught me to build an emergency shelter just thataway from reeds, cane, or slim young trees. He taught me when I was six years old, and I'd not forgotten.

*Pa was here.*

I was sure of it now. That marker, just the way he used to use them, something to call attention, not necessarily to indicate a trail . . . and now this.

When I got back to the horse I put a foot in the stirrup and swung my leg over the saddle. Gin was waiting for me to tell her, and I did.

"Pa's close by," I said. "I've got an idea that prisoner Herrara is hunting is my father."

"You're sure he's near?"

So I told her what I had seen, and explained a bit about it.

If he was close by, he would find me—unless he was lying hurt.

Even so, he would find me or let me know some way, so I turned and we started back to the herd. We rode more swiftly now, eager to get back.

There was so much inside me I wasn't looking out as sharp as I should have. We came riding around the brush, and there were fifteen or twenty riders, and down in the middle of them was Miguel.

Miguel was on the ground, and his face was all blood. A thick-set Mexican was standing over him with a quirt in his hand. Herrara sat his horse nearby.

Only thing saved me was they'd been so busy they weren't listening, and a horse on soft sod doesn't make a whole lot of disturbance.

Lucky for me I was carrying that Henry out in the open. She swung up slick as a catfish on a mudbank and I eared back the hammer.

They all heard *that*.

Their heads came around like they were all on string, but the one I had covered was Herrara himself.

"Call that man off," I said, "or I'll kill you."

He looked at me, those black eyes flat and steady as a rattler's. I'll give him this. There was no yellow showing. He looked right into that rifle barrel and he said, "You shoot me, señor, and you are dead in the next instant."

Me, I wasn't being bluffed. Not that day. I looked right along that barrel and I said, "Then I'll be the second man to die. When I fall, you'll lie there to make me a cushion."

We looked at each other, and he read me right. Whatever happened, I'd kill.

"And the lady? What happens to her if we die?"

"We'd never know about that, would we?" I said. "I think she'd take care of herself, however, and if anything happened to her, I don't think Cheno would like it."

"What do you know of Cheno?"

"Me? Next to nothing, but the señorita's family were good friends to Cheno's family when he lived north of the border. How else would a mere woman have the courage to ride alone into Mexico?"

He was listening, and I think he believed me. Sure I was lying. Maybe her family had known the Cortina family, and maybe they never had. But I was talking to save the lady trouble, and maybe some talk for my own skin as well.

He did not like it, because it tied his hands, and he wasn't letting up yet.

"Why do you stop *here*?"

"Hell," I said offhand, "you're a better cowman than I am. I ran the legs off those steers getting them up here. I got a girl north of the border, and I wanted to get back. Those other hands never showed, so we pushed 'em hard and nearly killed our horses. We had to rest."

It was true, of course, and I made plenty of sense, and that was one thing I had planned just that way. I wanted that story to tell if he came up on us again.

"Has anyone come to your camp other than the señorita?" he asked then.

"If they did, I didn't see them. We've been hoping somebody would come by who had some *frijoles* to sell. We're short on grub."

He asked a few more questions, and then they rode off, but I'd a hunch they would leave somebody to watch, or maybe none of them would go very far.

Miguel's face was cut and swollen. He had been lashed several times across the face and struck once with the butt because he could tell them nothing.

Now he washed the blood from his face and then looked around at me. "Careful, *amigo*. That one will kill you now, or you shall kill him. You faced him over a gun and made him back up."

"Twenty-five miles to the border," I said. "Can we make it in one run? Maybe losing a few head?"

Miguel shrugged. "With luck, señor, one can do anything."

Me, I was doing some studying, and it came to me that whatever was going to happen would happen fast now. Tomorrow night—or perhaps the next—we would be driving for the border. And we'd have the gold with us.

But I wasn't thinking of that gold, I was thinking of pa. My father, whom I had not seen for eight years, was somewhere out there in the darkness.

The question was: did he know I was here?

# Chapter 7

Miguel shook me awake an hour after midnight, and I sat up, feeling the dampness caused by the nearness of the Gulf. The fire was a glowing bed of coals and the coffee pot was steaming. Gin was asleep, her head cushioned on her saddle.

"It's quiet," Miguel said, "too damn' quiet."

He looked very bad this morning, his face still swollen, and blood from an opened whip-cut tracing a way across his cheek.

"We're going to make a run for the border," I said. "You get your sleep."

He was dog-tired, and he hit the blankets and was asleep before I could drink my coffee. He'd taken time to saddle my dun before waking me, which was like him. I thought of his wife back in Texas and knew that whatever else happened, he must get back to her. And he would not go unless with me. He was that loyal.

The cattle were resting and quiet. They'd had grass and water a-plenty and were fixing to get fat. Or maybe they were stoking up for what was to come.

Among any bunch of cattle, as among humans, you will find a few staid, steady characters, and there were a couple of such steers in this herd that I'd been cultivating. These had been wild cattle; but cattle, horses, or men, no two are quite alike, and these I'd chosen showed a disposition to be friendly. It was in my mind that I might need a couple of steady steers, and these two I'd fed a few choice bunches of grass or leaves.

Truth of the matter was, I was scared. Both Gin and Miguel were looking to me, and I wasn't sure I was up to it. I had never been in a real shoot-out difficulty, and it worried me that I was trusted to handle whatever came.

Wind moaned in the brush. Finishing my coffee, I put aside my cup and, shoving the Henry into the boot, mounted up and rode out to the head, singing low. Water rustled along the shore of the inlet, sucking and whispering among the reeds and the old drift timbers. Once it spat a few drops of cold rain.

This time of night, I was thinking, would be the time to run. Herrara would have us watched, but on a cold, unpleasant night there might be a chance.

Twice I rode wide of the herd to get a better over-all look, and I rode with care, pistol to hand. There was nothing to see, less to hear.

But bit by bit something was shaping up in my mind. There was this long arm of the sea to the east of us, and that other wider arm to the west and south. We were on a point, with water on two sides. Dimly, I recalled some tracings pa had made in the earth at the back door of the cabin one day as he talked. It was like this point . . . down there on the very point he'd made a cross of some kind.

Tomorrow . . . I would go there tomorrow.

It was coming up to day when I turned back toward camp. The cattle were on their feet, most of them cropping grass. If what I thought proved true, we might be lighting a shuck out of this country come nighttime. And believe me, I wanted to be shut of it.

When I rode up to the fire I saw Gin was up and drinking coffee. How she'd managed to get her hair to looking like that, I don't know. She reached across the fire's edge to fill Miguel's cup . . . but it wasn't Miguel.

It was pa.

He was setting hunched up to the fire with a blanket over his shoulders and a cup of coffee held in both his hands. He looked thinner than I had ever seen him, his face honed down hard.

He looked up when I walked that dun into the fire's circle of light, and for a minute or two we just stared at each other like a couple of fools.

"Pa?" I said. It was all I could get out.

He got up, the blanket falling to the ground. He was a big man, even now with almost no flesh on him. He'd been that prisoner who escaped, and Lord knows how long he'd been mistreated in that prison.

"Son?" He had a hard time with the word. "Orlando?"

"It's been a long time, pa."

No words came to me, and it seemed he was no better off. He had left me a child, and found me a man. Swinging down, I trailed my reins and stepped out to face him.

He was taller than me, but raw-boned as he was now, he was no heavier than my one-eighty. He thrust out his hand I took it. "You're strong," he said. "You were always strong."

"You've had some grub?"

"Coffee . . . just coffee, and some talk with Gin."

Gin, was it? He wasted no time getting down to cases. "You'd better eat," I said. "Come daybreak, we're going down to the Point."

"Ah?" he was pleased. "So you did remember?"

"Took me a while, but it was coming to me."

"Gin said you'd recognized the shelter—and the marker, too."

"You'd better sit down and wrap up," Gin advised. "You aren't well."

She put the blanket around him when he sat down and with a tiny prick of jealousy I couldn't help but think that if pa were shaved and fixed up they'd make a handsome pair.

I got out the frying pan and mixed up some sourdough, listening to them talk the while. He had the pleasant voice I'd remembered, and the easy way of moving. Glancing over at them, it came over me that pa was *here* . . . he was *alive*.

I'd been too stunned to take it in rightly before, and it was going to take some getting used to.

His eyes were on me as I shook up that bread, and I suppose he was wondering what sort of a man I'd become. But there was something else in his mind, too.

"You speak as if you'd had no schooling," he said. "Not that it's better or worse than most men speak out here."

"We'll have to talk to Caffrey," I said. "He used your money for his own self. I've been caring for myself at your old cabin since I was twelve." Looking up at him, I grinned. "With some help now and again from the Cherokees."

"I worried about Caffrey," pa said, "but I was in a hurry to get off. And that reminds me. We'd best get out of here. If they find me with you, you'll all be shot."

"Not without that gold," I said. "We came this far for it."

"There's some all ready to go," pa said. "I've taken it out myself. The rest—most of it—will take time."

Gin looked over at me. "Orlando, I think he's right. He's a sick man. The way his breathing sounds, he may be getting pneumonia."

The word had a dread sound, and it shook me. Miguel was sleeping, but it came on me then that we'd best move the cattle a little way, like to new bedding grounds, but hold them ready for a fast move when darkness came.

"Is that gold where it can be laid hands on?" I asked.

"It is."

"We'll move the cattle on to the end of the inlet and bed down there, like for night. Short of midnight we'll make our run.'

My mind was thinking ahead. Gin probably was making the right guess, for pa looked bad. He had been lying out in the brush without so much as a coat, just shirt and pants. Even his boots were worn through and soaked.

Leisurely, we rounded up the cattle, with pa keeping from sight in the brush, and we walked them on not more than a mile. Then, late afternoon, we built ourselves a new fire and settled down as if for the night.

Rounding up those placid steers I'd been keeping my eyes on, we brought them up to camp. Then, with pa resting, we waited the coming of night.

Miguel was restless. He never was far from his horse, and he worried himself until he was taut as a drumhead, watching the brush, listening, afraid something would go wrong before we could get away.

"I'm going into Guadalupe," I said to him. "We need a couple of horses."

There was no way he could deny that, although he wished to. We had no mount for pa, and if we made a run for it, we'd be riding from here clean to the border.

Miguel shrugged. "I think it is safe enough," he admitted reluctantly, "and we have reason to get horses."

Gin had money. She had more than I did, which wasn't much, so she turned over a hundred dollars to me and I saddled up the dun. Just before I left, I walked over to where pa was lying, with Gin setting beside him. No question but he looked bad.

"You take it easy," I said. "I'll get two, three horses and come back."

"What about pack horses? For the gold?"

"Packs would make the Mexicans mighty curious, so I figured on steers. Nobody will pay any attention to the herd."

"They'll be seen."

"Maybe . . . but with horns moving, and the dust, the shifting around of the animals . . . I think we've got a chance."

It was a mite over four miles to Guadalupe, and not even a dozen buildings when I got there, most of them adobe. There was a *cantina,* a closed-up store, and the office of the *alcalde,* with a jail behind it. The rest were scattered houses and one warehouse.

In a corral were several rough-looking horses, but nobody was around. The air was chill, offering rain. At the hitch-rail of the *cantina* stood more horses, three of them led stock. I tied up the dun and went inside.

It was a low, dark room with a bar and several tables. Three men were at the bar, two of them standing together, their backs to me. A broad-shouldered Mexican with a sombrero hanging down his back by the chin-strap, and crossed cartridge belts on his chest, stood at the end of the bar, a bottle before him. He looked like a Herrara man to me. The other two were lounging with a bottle between them. The Herrara man was obviously interested in them.

Walking up to the bar, I put my elbows on it and ordered a beer.

The operator of the *cantina* accepted my money and flashed a brief smile at me, but in his eyes I thought there was a warning, an almost imperceptible gesture toward the Herrara man, if such he was.

"Holding cattle outside of town," I said suddenly. "We've played out our horses. Know where I can buy a couple, cheap?"

For maybe a minute nobody made any sign they'd heard me, and then the man next to me said, "I have three horses, and I will sell—but not cheap."

It was the Tinker.

Without turning my head, I picked up my bottle of beer and emptied the rest of it into my glass. "Another," I said, gesturing.

"I saw them," I added, "at the rail. They are fit for buzzards."

"They are good horses," the Tinker protested. "I had not considered selling them until you spoke. The buckskin . . . there is a horse!"

"I'll give you eight dollars for him," I said, and tasted my beer.

For half an hour we argued and debated back and forth. Finally I said, "All right, twelve dollars for the buckskin, fifteen for the bay—the paint I do not want."

The Tinker and his silent companion, at whom I had not dared to look for fear of drawing attention to him, seemed to be growing drunk. The Tinker clapped me on the shoulder. "You are a good man," he said drunkenly, "a very good man! You need the horses—all right, I shall sell you the horses. You may have all three for forty dollars and a good meal . . . it is my last price."

I shrugged. "All right—but if you want the meal, come to camp. Forty dollars is all the money I have."

There on the bar I paid it to him in *pesos,* and we walked outside, the Tinker talking drunkenly. The Herrara man's eyes were drilling into my back.

"He's watching us," the Tinker said as I stopped to look over the horses.

Straightening up, I looked into the eyes of the other man—Jonas Locklear. "Cortina had me turned loose," he said, "on condition I get out of the country. He didn't want Herrara to know for the present."

Mounting up, we rode swiftly from the town. By the time we reached camp it was near to sunset. Pa was up, had a gun strapped on that Miguel had taken from our gear, and he was watching the sun.

"The only place they can watch us from," he said, "is that dune. It looks over the whole country around here. It's over seventy feet high, and in this country that's a mountain—along the coast, that is. If we wait about ten or fifteen minutes, the sun will be shining right in the eyes of anybody watching from that dune. That's when we'll go for the gold."

We now mustered six rifles, a good force by anybody's count, for Gin could shoot—or said she could, and I believed her.

We made beds ready, built up the fire, and put coffee on, and grub. Miguel was cooking.

When the sun got low enough, Pa, the Tinker and me took a few canvas bags we'd brought along a-purpose, and with two steers we headed off into the brush. One of the steers showed old marks that looked like he'd been used as a draft animal sometime in the past. Both were easily handled.

As we walked, pa said, "I dove for this gold, got it out of the sand on the bottom. Most of the hull is still intact, and most of the gold will be inside, but I brought up enough to make it pay. We'll take this and run; then we'll wait for things to simmer down, and come back."

Then pa told us some about how things were in Mexico. Right about this time Cortina had gathered a lot of power to him, but he was dependent on some of the lieutenants he had, of whom Herrara was one. The situation was changing rapidly, and it had changed several times over in the period of the last thirty years. Even in the last six or seven years there had been power shifts and changes, and changing relationships with the United States.

Not many years before, a Mexican cavalry detachment had crossed the border to protect Brownsville from a Mexican bandit, a fact known to few Americans except those in the immediate vicinity.

In the northern provinces of Mexico there was much division of feeling as to the United States, and the northern country had many friends south of the border. North of the border many citizens of Mexican extraction had fought against Mexico for Texas. It was difficult to draw a line, and there was a constant struggle in process for power below the border.

Pa told me some of this, and some I'd had from Jonas while riding south when there had been time to talk.

Pa led us in such a way as to keep bushes between us and the dune he thought was the lookout post, until we arrived right down on the shore of the inlet. There on the point, right where I'd planned to look, there was where pa stopped.

"The ship," he said to me, "lies off there, in no more than five fathoms of water."

He glanced over his shoulder at the sun, then stopped and took hold of a tuft of grass and pulled on it; he caught hold of another bunch with the other hand. A big chunk of sod lifted out like a trap door, and in a hollowed-out place underneath was a tin pail and several cans, loaded with gold.

There was no time to lose. Working as swiftly as we could, we sacked it up, for the sun was going down and in a few minutes we'd stand out like sore thumbs out there on that point. Tying the sacks two and two, we hung them over the backs of the steers, and then replaced the sod. We started back as if driving two straying steers.

As darkness came we clustered around the fire, eating. Miguel and Jonas finished first and, mounting up, went out to circle the cattle. The rest of us went through the motions of going to bed. One by one the others moved off into the darkness, but Gin and me, we still sat by the fire and I stoked the flames a mite higher.

"He's quite a man," she said suddenly.

"Pa?"

"Yes. I've never known anyone quite like him."

Me, I hadn't anything to say. I didn't know enough about my own father, and there'd been little time for talking. Also, as the time drew near we were getting worrisome about what we had to do.

You bed down a bunch of steers and they'll finally settle down to dozing and chewing their cuds; but after a while, close to midnight or about there, they'll all stand up and stretch, crop grass a bit, and then lie down again. That was the time we'd picked to move them—catch them on their feet so there'd be less disturbance.

Finally we left the fire, adding some more fuel. I rigged some branches nearby so they'd sort of fall into the fire as others burned, giving anybody watching an idea the fire was being fed, time to time.

Away from the firelight, I moved up to my dun in the darkness and tightened the cinch. "You got it in you to run," I said, "you better have at it tonight."

We waited . . . and we waited. And those fool steers, they just lay there chewing and sleeping. Then, of a sudden, an old range cow stood up. In a minute or two there were a dozen on their feet, and then more.

Moving mighty easy, we started to push them. Miguel was off to one side to get them started north, and Jonas had gone up the other side.

We pushed them, and a few of them began, reluctantly, to move out. It took us a while to get them started and lined out, and we did it without any shouting or hollering.

We walked them easy for about a mile, then we began to move them a little faster. Not until we had about three miles behind us did we give it to them.

It was a wild ride. I'll say this for Gin, she was right in there with us, riding side-saddle as always, but riding like any puncher and doing her job. Only I noticed she was keeping an eye on pa, too.

It made me sore, only I didn't want to admit it. I told myself somebody had to keep an eye on him, the shape he was in. Nevertheless, I was a mite jealous, too. I reckon it's the male in a man . . . he sees a pretty woman like that and wants to latch onto her. She was a good bit older than me, of course, though a whole sight younger than pa.

We had those cattle lined out and we kept them going. After a ways we'd slow down to give them a breather, but not so slow that they could get to thinking what was happening to them. Then we'd speed them up a little. After six miles or so, the Tinker, he swung in beside me. "We'd best hang back, you and me," he said, "sort of a rear guard."

The night wore on.

Once when we came up to water we let them line out along the creek bank and drink. We had ten miles behind us then, but by daybreak we hoped to have a few more, because it wouldn't take free-riding horsemen long to catch up, and when they did there'd be hell to pay.

We had managed to keep in sight those steers carrying the gold. We'd lashed that gold in place, throwing a good packing hitch over it, and there was small danger of it falling off—nevertheless, somebody always had an eye on that gold.

The dark skies began to gray. We were more than halfway there, but we still had miles to go. The cattle had slowed to a walk. They'd have been plenty angry if they hadn't been so tired.

Pa looked awful. His face was drawn and pale, but he was riding as well as any of us. His eyes were sunk into his skull, and they looked bigger than anybody's eyes should.

We pushed on, walking them now, trying to create no more dust than we had to.

There was a place east of Matamoras where it looked like the border swung further south, and so would be nearer to us. We turned the herd that way, skirting a sort of lake or tidewater pool.

It was just shy of noon and we were within five or six miles of the border when they came at us.

It was about that time, just before they hit us, that I had my brainstorm. It came to me of a sudden and, saying nothing to anyone but the Tinker, I rode up to Gin.

"Look, you and pa take those two steers and you move out ahead. If we have to make a fight of it, we'll do it better without having to think of you."

"I can fight," pa said.

His looks shocked me, and he was coughing a lot and his forehead was wet with sweat. His cheeks were a sickly white, but I was sure he was carrying a lot of fever in him.

"Do like I say," I insisted. "You two light out and head for the border. If we have to, we'll make a fight of it and cover for you. With that money, you can help us out if we should get caught."

"If you aren't killed," pa said.

"I'm too durned ornery to die," I said. "Anyway, we got to go back to Tennessee and talk to Caffrey, you and me together."

Gin convinced him, and they taken those two steers and drove them off ahead of the herd.

They hadn't been gone more than a few minutes when we saw that dust cloud come a-helling up the road after us. The Tinker and me, we just looked at each other, and then the lead began to come our way. I was sort of glad, for I'd not wish to start shooting at folks when I ain't sure of their plans.

That old Henry came up to my shoulder sweet and pretty, and my first shot taken a man right out of the saddle. At least, I think it was my shot.

We both fired, and then we turned tail and got away from there, racing past the herd like Jonas and Miguel were doing.

We started to swing the herd and in no time at all had them turned between us and those men after us. We tried to stampede them back into those fellows, but only a few of them started—the rest were too almighty confused.

All of us were shooting, riding and shooting, and then they cut around both sides of the herd at us and our horses were too blown to run. We made our fight right there.

Dropping off my horse, I swung him around and shot across the saddle. There were guns going off all around me, and I'd no time to be scared.

"'Lando!" the Tinker shouted, and grabbed at me. "Ride and run!"

Both of us jumped for the saddle, and as we did so I saw a man wearing a black suit come out of that bunch. He had a shotgun in his hands, and as Jonas turned toward his horse he let him have both barrels.

Miguel was down, and now Jonas, and it needed no sawbones to tell me Jonas was dead. Before I could more than try a shot at that rider in the black suit, he was gone.

But not until I'd seen him.

It was Franklyn Deckrow. The Tinker had seen him, too.

We lit out. We were running all out when I felt my horse bunch up under me, and then he went head over heels into the sand, pitching me wide over his head.

Last I saw was the Tinker giving one wild glance my way, and then he was racing away.

From that look on his face, I was sure he figured me for a dead man.

Reaching out, I grabbed for my Henry, which had fallen from my hand. A boot came down hard on my knuckles, and when I looked up Antonio Herrara was looking down at me. And from the expression of those flat black eyes, I knew I'd bought myself some trouble.

It was going to be a long time before I saw Texas again . . . if ever.

# Chapter 8

The bitter days edged slowly by, and weeks passed into years, and then the years were gone, and still I remained a prisoner.

By day I worked like the slave I'd become, and was fed like an animal, and by night I slept on a bed of filthy straw and dreamed of a day when I would be free.

Always I was alone, alone within the hollow shell of my mind, for outside the small world in which I lived with labor, sweat, and frightful heat, no one knew that I lived, nor was there anyone about me to whom I could talk.

The others with whom I worked were Indians—Yaquis brought to this place from Sonora, men self-contained and bitter as I, yet knowing nothing of me, nor trusting anyone beyond their own small group.

A thousand times I planned escape, a thousand times the plans crumbled. Doors that seemed about to open for me remained closed, guards who showed weakness were replaced. My hands became curved to grip the handles of pick, shovel, or mattock. My shoulders bulged with muscle put there by swinging a heavy sledge. Naturally of great strength, each day of work made it greater, building roads, working in the mines, clearing mesquite-covered ground.

Sometimes alone in my rock-walled cell I thought back to that first day when, in a square adobe room, I was questioned by Herrara. My wrists bound cruelly tight, I stood before him.

He stood with his feet apart, his sombrero tipped back, and those flat black eyes looked into mine. He smiled then, showing even white teeth; he was a handsome man in a savage way. "You put a gun upon me," he said, and struck me across the face with his quirt.

It was the beginning of pain.

"There is gold. Tell me where it is, and you may yet go free."

He lied . . . he had no thought to let me go, only to see me suffer and die.

"The gold is gone. They took it with them."

"I think you lie," he said and, almost negligently, he lashed me again across the face with the quirt, and the lash cut deep. I tasted my blood upon my cut lips, and I knew the beginning of hatred.

That was the beginning of questioning, but only the beginning. There was gold. He knew it and was hungry for it, as the others had been before him. The original commandant, whose name I never knew, had been his uncle. In the telling, the amount of gold supposedly hidden on the shore had grown to a vast amount.

To tell him was to die, and I lived to kill him, so I told him nothing. After each questioning I was taken to a cell and left there, and each time I feared I would die; but deep within me the days tempered a kind of steel I had not known was there.

Herrara I would remember, and another man, too. I would remember Franklyn Deckrow, who had betrayed us to them, and who had killed Jonas, his brother-in-law. It was something to live for.

And I would live. No matter what, I would survive so that these men might die.

No help could come to me, for they believed me dead. Jonas had fallen, and Miguel too, although he might have somehow gotten away. They had forced me to bury Jonas, but Miguel's body was nowhere around. I hoped for him. But the Tinker had looked back and seen me lying there, and I knew he believed me dead.

Suddenly, one night, I was moved. Out of a sound sleep I was shaken awake, jerked to my feet and led away. Herrara rode beside me.

"Your friends do not give up," he said, "and they have powerful friends in Mexico, so we must take you where you will never be found."

The place to which they took me was a ranch owned by an outlaw named Flores, an outlaw who raided Texas ranches for their stock and so was ignored by the law of the province.

Duty called Herrara away to the south, so the beatings ended, but I was put to work among the Yaqui slaves. Most of the Yaqui prisoners had been sent away to work in the humid south where they soon died. Only a few were kept in the north.

The work was preferable to the cell, and I gloried in my growing strength. We were fed corn and *frijoles* and good beef, all of which was cheap enough, and they wanted my strength for the work I could do.

A dozen times I tried to smuggle messages across the border. Twice they were found and I was beaten brutally.

"Tell me," Herrara said to me on one of his sudden visits, "tell me where is the gold and you shall have a horse and your freedom." But I did not tell.

Herrara had become powerful. The outlaws supported him and he protected them and derived income from their raids into Texas. Night after night men rode away from the Flores ranch and raided over the border, returning with cattle, horses, and women.

No other Mexican came to the ranch to visit, and I gathered the outlaws were hated by those who lived nearby, but they were people cut off from authority who could do nothing.

When I looked down at my hands, I saw them calloused and scarred, but powerful. My shoulders and arms were heavy with muscle, and my mind, sharpened by endless observation and planning, was cunning as an animal's is cunning.

No day passed without its plan for escape, no possible opportunity went unnoticed by me. Always my senses were alert for the moment.

Then came another Herrara visit. The heavy oaken door grated against the stone, and he stepped inside. He held a pistol and a heavy whip, the cat-o'-nine-tails which is used aboard ship. Behind him in the doorway were two men with guns.

"It is the end," he said. "I shall wait no longer. Tonight you will tell me, for if you do not, these"—he held up the whip—"will take out your eyes."

The cat hung from his hand by its stubby wooden handle, and from its end dangled nine strips of rawhide, each with a tip wrapped in wire. It was a whip that could cut a man to ribbons, or bite at his eyes, cutting them from his head in a bloody mess.

And in that moment I knew that I could no longer wait. I must kill him and be killed.

He moved toward me, and I remained where I was, crouched in the corner with one heel braced against the wall, ready to lunge at him. My thick forearms rested upon my knees, and I waited, watching him like the cornered animal I had become.

We were at a smaller ranch, half a mile from Las Cuevas, the headquarters of Flores. It was November 19, 1875. The date is one I shall never forget.

A mistake was made that night, and upon such mistakes do men's lives depend; by such mistakes are men's lives lost—or saved. Outside my cell, beyond the walls about the ranch, beyond the border even, events had marched forward, and tonight men rode in darkness, moving along the cactus-lined trails.

As Herrara came toward me, he had his pistol ready, for he was a clever man and knew what must be in my mind. The whip was poised for a blow, but I was hard to get at, for the corner was a partial protection.

My tongue went to my lips. Within me burned a kind of cold fury, welling up from the deep hatreds that had grown within me, until nothing mattered but my hands upon his throat.

He would strike me. His bullet would tear into my flesh, and perhaps the bullets of those others in the doorway, but my hands must reach his throat. These hands that only a day or so before had bent and twisted an iron horseshoe—these hands must reach that throat and lock there. Surely, I would be killed, but surely I should kill him first.

He flipped the whip at me, but I did not move. He lifted the whip to strike downward, and he brought it down hard over my head and shoulders, but still I did not move. Suddenly his own anger burst within him, the hatred of me because I kept him from the wealth he wanted and the position it would buy, the hatred of me for holding out so long against him.

His lips curled from his teeth and the whip drew back for a mighty blow at my face. Those wire-twisted whipends would tear at my eyes. His own hatred had mastered him—I saw it in his face.

Suddenly, from outside there was a crash of gunfire, the race of pounding hoofs, shrill Texas yells.

The men at the door wheeled and ran toward the court. Even Herrara was caught, gripped by shock in the middle of his blow. And in that instant I leaped.

My left hand gripped the gun-wrist, my right seized his throat, not a grip around the neck, but the far more deadly grip of the Adam's apple and the throat itself.

His gun exploded, but the muzzle had been turned aside, and the roar was lost in the concussions of the shots outside. I smashed him back bodily against the stone wall with stunning force. My right hand gripping his throat held him on tip-toes against the stone, and my other hand gripping his gun-wrist ground his knuckles against the roughness of the stone wall.

Brutally, I ground the flesh against the stone, rasping it back and forth until he struggled to scream and his fingers could no longer grip the gun.

I released my hold upon his throat and stepped back. He struck weakly at me with the cat, but then, my feet wide, I hit with my left fist, then with my right, rolling my shoulders for the power it gave. One fist struck his ribs, crushing them; the other his face.

His head bounced against the wall, and glassy-eyed he started to fall toward me. I struck him again, and when he fell forward that time I knew that he was dead.

Quickly, I stripped off his gun belt and picked his pistol from the floor.

The passage outside the door was empty, and I ran along it, turned down another, and was in the living quarters of the ranch house. A door stood open, as it had been left when the shooting called the men out, and I smashed through it.

The room was empty and still. My footsteps padded on the bare floor as

I crossed to the gun case. Picking up a chair with one hand, I swung it and smashed the glass. I reached in for a shotgun and filled my pockets with shells.

A Henry rifle was there, and I took that also, and two belts of cartridges that hung from a chair. And then as I turned away I saw a familiar sight. In the corner of the gun cabinet was my old Walch Navy .36 with the initials C.B. scratched on it. Quickly, I took it up and thrust it into my waistband with another pistol that lay there.

No one appeared in the passage as I ran, and I went through the door to the long veranda outside. There I stopped in the shadows.

Mounted men were racing back and forth, and the red lances of gunfire stabbed the darkness. A Texas yell broke out, and a shot caught a Mexican upon a balcony. He fell head-long from it and landed nearby. The rider wheeled his horse, and in that instant he saw me.

The pistol swung at me to fire and I shouted, *"No! I'm an American!"*

He held his pistol on me. "Who are you?" His voice rang with authority.

"A prisoner. They've held me six years."

*"Six years?"*

A horse was tied to the hitch-rail and he jerked loose the tie-rope. Heavier firing sounded outside the court. *"Come! And be quick!"*

He raced from the court to where other Texas riders were milling. "Wrong place!" A man shouted at the rider beside me. "Flores' place is half a mile up the road!"

"There are two hundred men there!" I yelled at them.

The man beside me said, "Let's go!" And he led the racing retreat at a dead run down the valley.

After a mile or two they slowed to a canter, then to a walk. I glanced at the stars, and there was the North Star, beckoning us on.

"They'll be after us," the man beside me said, and there was no time for questions.

Closely we rode on, and fast, for the Rio Grande lay miles to the north. The night was cool, and the air fresh on my face. Sometimes when we passed close to a rock face we could feel the heat still held from the day's hot sun.

We slowed to a walk again, and the man I rode beside turned in his saddle and looked at me.

"Six years, you say?"

As briefly as possible, I explained. Not about the gold, exactly, but enough to let him know they had wanted to learn a secret I alone knew. When I mentioned Herrara, he nodded grimly. "He's one I'd like to find myself."

"Do not waste your time," I said. "From now on you need pay him no mind."

He glanced at me and I said, "He was using a whip on me when you came shooting into the patio, and his men rushed away."

"He is dead, you think?"

"He is dead. Without a doubt, he is dead."

"My name is McNelly," the rider said then. "These are Texas Rangers."

Thirty of them had crossed the river to strike a blow at the outlaws who were raiding ranches and stealing cattle north of the border—and sometimes south of it, as well.

Las Cuevas had long been the outlaws' headquarters, and it was Las Cuevas for which the Rangers had aimed. But mistakenly they were led to a ranch that belonged to the Las Cuevas owner, only a short distance away from the main ranch buildings. It was that mistake that had saved my life.

At the Rio Grande the riders turned on command. The outlaws were not far behind. "You, Sackett," the captain said, "go on across the border. You've had trouble enough."

"If you'll grant me the pleasure, Cap'n," I said, "I'll stay. There's men in that crowd who have struck me and beaten me, and I owe them a little. Besides," I added, "I carried off their shotgun. It is only fair that I return the loads from the shells."

Here at the river the air was still cooler because of the dampness rising from the water—and it was free air. For the first time in years I was out in the night, with free air all about me.

The outlaws came with a rush, sure they would catch the Rangers at the border before they got across the river, but they were met with a blast of gunfire that lanced the night with darting flame. One rider toppled from his saddle, and his fall as much as our fire turned their retreat into a rout. They vanished into the mesquite.

Several Rangers rode out to look at the body, and I followed McNelly. "Well," I said, "seems to me if you had to kill only one, you got the right one. That there is Flores himself."

We swam the river back to the Texas side and I followed on to their camp, which was on the bank of a creek a few miles back from the river.

Reckon I looked a sight. My shirt was in rags and the only pants I had were come castoffs they'd given me when my own played out. There I stood, bare-footed and loaded down with guns.

"You'd better let us stand you an outfit," McNelly commented dryly. "You're in no shape to go anywhere in that outfit."

They were good boys, those Rangers were, and they rigged me out. Then, to raise some cash, I sold one of them my pistol for six dollars—it was the spare I'd picked up (I'd come away with three); and I sold the shotgun for twelve to McNelly himself. The Captain had taken Flores' gold- and silver-plated pistol off the body—it was a rarely beautiful weapon.

The horse I'd ridden across the border was a handsome, upstanding roan.

"Anybody asks you for the bill of sale for that horse," McNelly commented, "you refer them to me."

The first thing I did was to head for the creek and take a long bath, getting shut of my old clothes at the same time. When I lit out for Rio Grande City, come daybreak, I felt like a different man.

Yet being free wasn't what it might have been. First off, I didn't know where to go. McNelly had heard nothing of my pa, and only remembered some talk of Jonas Locklear being dead several years back. What had become of his land, he didn't know.

So there I was, a free man with no place to go, with a rightful share in gold that might have already been spent. But something I did own, if I could find them. I owned a mare and a mule colt.

I showed up in Brownsville wearing shirt and jeans that didn't fit, a pair of boots that hurt my feet, and a worn-out Mexican sombrero. Dark as I was and wearing cartridge belts crossed over my chest, I even looked like a Mexican.

I walked into a *cantina* and leaned on the bar, and when the bartender ignored me I reached out my Henry and laid it across to touch the back bar.

"I want a whiskey," I said, "and I want it now. You going to give it to me, or do I take it after I put a knot on your head?"

He looked at me and then he looked at that rifle and he set the bottle out on the bar. "We don't cater to Mexicans in here," he said.

"You do wrong," I told him. "I'm no Mex, but I've known some mighty fine ones. They run about true to form with us north of the border—some good and some bad."

"Sorry," he said. "I thought you were a Mexican."

"Pour me a drink," I said, "and then go back and shut up."

He poured me the drink and walked away down the bar. Two tough-looking cowhands were sizing me up, considering how much opposition I'd offer if trouble started, but I wasn't interested in a row. So I just plain ignored them. Anyway, I was listening to talk at a table behind me.

"He's wise," one man was saying. "He hasn't squatted on range the way most have done. Captain King clears title on every piece he buys. That's why he's held off on that Locklear outfit—there's a dispute over the title. Deckrow claims it, but his sister-in-law disputes the claim."

"Bad blood between Deckrow and her husband, too. It'll come to a shooting."

"Not unless Deckrow shoots him in the back," I said, "that's the way he killed Jonas Locklear."

Well, now. I'd turned and spoken aloud without really meaning to, and every face in the room turned toward me.

One of the men at the table looked at me coldly. "That's poor talk. Deckrow's a respected man in Texas."

"He wouldn't be the first who didn't deserve it," I said. "You see him, you tell him I said he was a back-shooter. Tell him I said he shot Jonas Locklear in the back, and Deckrow was riding with Mexican outlaws at the time."

There wasn't a friendly face in the *cantina*, except maybe for the other man at that table.

"And who might you be?" he asked quietly. "We'd like to tell him who spoke against him."

"The name is Orlando Sackett," I said, "and I'll speak against him any time I get the chance. . . . Jonas," I added, "was a friend of mine."

"Orlando Sackett," the man said thoughtfully. "The only other Sackett I know besides Falcon was killed down in Mexico, five or six years ago."

"You heard wrong. I ain't dead, nor about to be."

Finishing my drink, I turned and walked out of the place and went across the street to a restaurant.

A few minutes after, a slender blue-eyed man came in and sat down not far from me. He didn't look at me at all, and that was an odd thing, because almost everybody else at least glanced my way.

In Rio Grande City I'd gotten myself a haircut and had my beard shaved off. I still held to a mustache, like most men those days, but it was trimmed careful. In the six years below the border I'd taken on weight, and while I was no taller than five-ten, I now weighed two hundred and ten pounds, most of it in my chest and shoulders. Folks looked at me, all right.

As I ate, I kept an eye on that blue-eyed man, who was young and lean-faced and wore a tied-down gun. Presently another man came in and sat down beside him, his back to me. When he turned around a few minutes later and he looked at me, I saw he was Duncan Caffrey.

He'd changed some. His face looked like it always did, but he was big and strong-looking. His eyes were a lot harder than I recalled, and when he put his hand on the back of the other man's chair I noticed the knuckles were scarred and broken. He'd been doing a lot of fighting. Reminded me of what the Tinker had said about the knuckles of Jem Mace, that champion fighter who'd trained him.

Caffrey looked hard at me, and he sort of frowned and looked away, and suddenly it came on me that he wasn't sure. True, I was a whole lot heavier than when he'd last seen me, and a lot darker except where the beard was shaved off, and even that had caught some sun riding down from Rio Grande City.

When I stood up and paid for my supper I saw in the mirror what was wrong. The mustache changed me a good bit, and the scars even more. I had forgotten the scars. There were three of them, two along my cheek and one on my chin, all made from the cuts of that quirt, which had cut like a knife into my flesh, and no stitches taken in the cuts.

Outside on the street a sudden thought came to me. If that blue-eyed man was a killer, and if Caffrey was pointing me out to him, then I'd better dust out. With my hands I was all right, but I hadn't shot a six-shooter, except for the other day, not in six years.

Riding out of town, I headed east, then circled and took the north road. A few days after, I pulled up at the *jacal* where I'd left the mare.

A young woman came to the door, shading her eyes at me. She looked shabby and tired. The little boy who stood beside her stared at me boldly, but I thought they were both frightened.

"Do you not remember me, señora? I rode from here many years ago—with Miguel and Señor Locklear."

There seemed to be a flicker of recognition in her eyes then, but all she said was, "Go away. Miguel is dead."

"Dead, señora?"

"*Sí.*" Her eyes flickered around as if she were afraid of being observed. "He returned from Mexico, and then one day he did not come back to me. He was shot out on the plains—by *bandidos.*"

"Ah?" I wondered about those *bandidos* and about Franklyn Deckrow Then I changed the subject. "When I was here I left a mare that was to have a colt. You promised to see to the birth and care for it."

Her eyes warmed. "I remember, señor."

"The colt . . . is it here?"

The boy started to interrupt, but she spoke quickly to him in Spanish. I now spoke the tongue well, but they were not close to me and I missed the words.

"It is here, señor. Manuel will get it."

"Wait." I looked at the boy. "You have ridden the colt?"

"The mule, señor? *Sí*, I have ridden him." There was no friendliness in his eyes. He was all of eleven or twelve, but slight of build.

"Does he run, then? Like the wind?"

Excitement came into his eyes and he spoke with enthusiasm. "*Sí*, señor. He runs."

Juana came a step from the *jacal*. "He loves the mule," she said. "I am afraid he loves it too much. I always told him you would come for it."

"You told him I would come back?"

"*Si*, señor. Miguel did not believe you were dead. He never believed it. But he was the only one. Although the señora—Señora Sackett—she sometimes thought you were alive."

"Señora Sackett?"

"Your father's wife, señor. The sister of Señor Locklear."

So Gin had married my father. She was my stepmother now. Well, thinking back, I could not be surprised. From the first, there had been something between them.

Juana came out to my horse as the boy walked reluctantly away to get the mule. "There has been much trouble," she said. "Señor Deckrow lets us to live here, but he warned us never to talk to strangers, and he said if you ever came back, to send Manuel at once to tell him."

Just then my horse's head came up and I looked around, and there stood the mule colt.

No question but what it was a mule. It was tall, longer in the body than most mules, it seemed, and with long, slim legs. But it was a mule, almost a buckskin in color, and like enough to any mule I'd ever seen.

You could tell by the way he followed that boy that there was a good feeling between them. But when I walked over, he stretched his nose to me.

"And the mare?"

"Wolves, señor, when this one was small. If I had not come upon them, he would be dead also."

Rubbing the mule's neck, I considered the situation. "Manuel," I said, "I think you and Juana should come away from here. I think you should go to San Antonio, or somewhere. You'll need to have schooling."

"How? We have no money. We have no way to go. We have only our goats and a few chickens."

"You have horses?"

"No, señor. The horses belong to Señor Deckrow."

"Ride them, anyway, and you two come away to San Antonio." I paused. "If Deckrow hears you have talked to me, there may be trouble. Besides, I want a boy who can ride the mule . . . I mean who can race him. Could you do that, Manuel?"

His eyes sparkled, but he said seriously, "*Si*, I could do it. He runs very fast, señor."

"He's bred for it," I said. "Can you go tonight?"

"What of the goats?"

"Goats," I said, "can get along. Leave them."

We didn't waste time. They'd little enough to take, and Manuel taken my horse and went out and caught up a couple of ponies in no time. He was a hand with a rope, which I wasn't. Lately I'd begun to think I wasn't a hand with anything, although all the way from Brownsville to the ranch I practiced with that Walch Navy, which I fancied beyond other guns.

The trail we chose was made by Kansas-bound cattle. Seemed to me I owed Miguel something, and I did not trust that Deckrow. So I'd be killing two birds with one stone by escorting Manuel and his mother to San Antone and getting Manuel to ride my mule for me.

"You think that mule can beat this horse?" I asked Manuel.

"Of a certainty," he replied coolly. "He can run, this mule."

So we laid it out between us to race to a big old cottonwood we could see away up ahead, maybe three-quarters of a mile off. On signal, we taken off.

Now that Mexican horse was a good cutting horse and trained to start fast. Moreover, it was an outlaw's horse, and an outlaw can't afford not to have the best horse under him that he can lay hands on. That roan took off with a bound and within fifty yards he was leading by two lengths, and widening the distance fast. We were halfway to that cottonwood before that mule got the idea into his hand that he was in a race.

By the time we'd covered two-thirds of the distance we were running neck-and-neck, and then that mule just took off and left us.

Oakville was the town where I decided to make my play, and by the size of my bankroll it was going to be a small one.

When you came to sizing it up, Oakville wasn't a lot of town, there being less than a hundred people in it, but it had the name of being a contentious sort of place. Forty men were killed there in the ten years following the War Between the States. It lay right on the trail up from the border and a lot of Kansas cattle went through there, time to time.

When we came riding into town I told Manuel and his ma to find a place to put up, and I gave them a dollar.

It was a quiet day in town. A couple of buckboards stood on the street, and four or five horses stood three-legged at the hitch-rails. When I pushed through the bat-wing doors and went up to the bar, there was only one man in the place aside from the bartender. He was a long, thin man with a reddish mustache and a droll, quizzical expression to his eyes.

"Buy you a drink?" I suggested.

He looked at me thoughtfully. "Don't mind if I do." And then he said, "Passin' through?"

"Mostly," I said, "but what I'd like to rustle up is a horse race. I've got a Mex woman and her boy to care for."

He glanced at me, and I said, "Her husband stood by me in a fight below the border."

"Killed?"

"Uh-huh. They've kinfolk in San Antone."

He tasted his whiskey and said nothing. When he finished his drink he bought me one. "Lend you twenty dollars," he suggested. "I'll meet up with you again sometime."

"What I want is a horse race." I lowered my voice. "I've got me a fast mule. If I can get a bet, I could double the ten dollars I've got. Might even get odds, betting on a mule."

He walked to the door and looked over the batwings at the mule, which was tethered alongside my roan. Then he came back and leaned on the bar and tossed off his whiskey.

"Man east of town has him a fast horse. Come sundown he'll ride in. You mind if I bet a little?"

"Welcome it. You from here?"

"Beeville. Only I come over this way, time to time, on business. I'm buying cattle."

That man had him a horse, all right, and that horse had plenty of speed, but my mule just naturally left him behind, although Manuel was holding him up a mite, like I suggested.

That ten dollars made up to twenty, and the cattle buyer handed me twenty more. "Don't worry," he said, "I made a-plenty."

He looked at me thoughtfully. "You ever been over to Beeville? There's a lot of money floating around over there and they're fixing to have some horse races come Saturday. If you're of a mind to, we might just traipse over that way. It's somewhat out of your way, but not to speak of."

"I'm a man needs money," I said. "I don't mind if I do."

"They're fixing to have a prize fight, too. Mostly Irish folks over there— Beeville was settled by Irish immigrants back about 1830 or so." Then he went on, "Powerful pair of shoulders you got there. You ever do any fighting?"

"Don't figure on it," I said, "not unless I come up to a couple of men I'm looking for."

"Gambler over there," he said, "brought in a fighter. He nearly killed the local pride, so they're drumming up another fight to get some of their own back."

"I'm no fighter," I said, "not unless I'm pushed."

"Too bad. A horse race is all right, but if you could whip this Dun Caffrey, you could—"

"I'm pushed," I said. "I'm really feeling pushed. Did you say Dun Caffrey?"

"That was the name. He's good, make no mistake, and the Bishop is his backer."

Right then I recalled those scarred and broken knuckles I'd seen on Caffrey that time down on the border. But who would ever think Dun Caffrey would turn into a prize fighter? Still, he was strong, and he handled himself well. And maybe I'd been just lucky that day down in the field when I broke him up.

Those days a saloon was not only a place for drinking. It was a meeting place, a club, a place where business deals were made, a betting parlor, and an exchange for information. If you wanted to know about a trail, or whether the Indians were out, or who had cattle for sale, you went to a saloon.

"You make your bets on the fight," I said, "but you don't need to mention any name—just tell him I'm from Oakville, or just up from Mexico."

This cattle buyer's name was Doc Halloran, and he sized up to me like a canny one. "Dun Caffrey was won six fights in Texas, and more than that in Louisiana and Mississippi. He's a bruiser, but no fool. He's a gambler, and a companion of gamblers."

"That's as may be, but if you'll back me, I'll have at him."

"Are you in shape?"

"Six years at hard labor in a Mexican prison," I said. "Yes, I'm in shape."

We went into Beeville by the back streets and Doc Halloran took me to his own house. When I got there I stretched out for a rest. Juana and Manuel, they were there, too. Doc went out to rustle some bets on a horse race and to enter my mule. And we went to talk up this fight, too.

About sundown Manuel came back from rousting around. He was a mighty serious Mexican boy. "There is great trouble, señor," he said. "I think we have been followed to this place, for Señor Deckrow is here. He rides in his carriage with the señorita, but there are many men with him."

So I sat up on the edge of the bed and looked down at my thick, work-hardened hands, thinking. It was scarcely possible they had found us so quickly, nor would Deckrow be likely to bring the señorita, as Manuel had said. That would be Marsha, the little one.

Only she would be close to twenty now, and almost an old maid, for a time when girls married at sixteen or seventeen.

"I do not think they had followed us, *amigo*. It may be they go to San Antonio. He would want riders for protection. It is said there are many thieves."

Sitting on the edge of the bed after he left, I turned my mind again to the situation. Maybe this was the showdown that had to come sooner or later. Dun Caffrey would be here, Deckrow . . . how many others?

Doc Halloran came back before midnight. His long, friendly face was serious, and he stood looking down at me. "Well, the fight is set," he said. "And we've got the mule entered in the race, but I think we've bit off more than we can chew."

"What happened?"

He touched his tongue to his lips. "I bet five thousand on the mule, but they roped me in and egged me on, and I went over my head. I've bet twenty-five thousand on you to whip Dun Caffrey."

You know, I thought he'd gone crazy. I looked up at him and listened to him say it again.

*Twenty-five thousand!* Why, that was—it was impossible, that's what it was.

"They were ready for me," he said. "After all, this is a business with them. I mentioned having a fighter, and they doubted it—said nobody would stand a chance with Caffrey. Then they kept egging me on until they told me to put my money where my mouth was. And I did."

"Doc, for that much money they'd murder fifty like us. I won't fight. Tell 'em the bet's off."

"I can't . . . they made me put up the money. They've got me over a barrel."

The Bishop . . . he would have a gang ready to tear down the ropes and mob us if it looked as if I was going to win. He would be ready for us.

"They put up their money too, didn't they?"

"Of course." Halloran paced the floor. "Sackett, if I lose this bet I'll be back punching cows. It's everything I've been able to earn or save in forty-five years. I don't think I could do it again, and I can't imagine how I was such a fool."

I got up. "Don't let it worry you. I'll fight him. I'll beat him, too. But we've got to get somebody to guard that saloon safe, if that's where the money is. If there's no other way, they'll rob the safe."

"That's just it. The Bishop has men in town. He has several who have agreed to stay in the saloon and keep watch. Sackett, we're through. We're whipped!"

There was a tap on the door, and I slid that Walch Navy out of my waistband.

"Open it," I said to Juana. "Just pull it open and stay out of the way."

She pulled the door open and a man stepped into the doorway. He was tall and very lean, with yellow eyes and gold rings in his ears. " 'Lando," he said, "I figured it was you."

It was the Tinker.

# Chapter 9

He stepped into the room and closed the door carefully behind him. The room was dimly lit, with the flickering fire on the hearth and a candle burning. The dark shadows lay in the hollows of his cheeks, and I could see little more of him than the gleam of his eyes and the shine of the gold of his earrings.

"When I heard of a man with a racing mule," he said, "it had to be you."

He stepped up to me and thrust out his hand, and a feeling came into my throat so I couldn't speak. I was not a man with many friends, but I wanted the Tinker to be one of them.

"You're heavier," he said, "and by heaven, you're a man!"

When I'd introduced him around, we all sat down. Experience had not made me a trusting man, and we'd been apart for a spell of years. But he was my friend, I was sure of that, and right now I needed him.

"The mule can run," I said, "he can really scat."

"He'll need to." He shot me a shrewd look. "Do you know whose money is against you? The Bishop's, that's whose. The Bishop's money and Caffrey's. Your Caffrey isn't only a fighter, he's a gambler—and he's a big one. The Bishop and him, they're partners."

"You know about the fight?"

"It's talked about. This is an Irish town, and you know the Irish—they love a good fight with the knuckles."

"I'll have a little of my own back. I want the hide off him, but I want to break his pocket, too. With a Caffrey, that will hurt the worst."

The Tinker was silent for several minutes, and there was no sound in the room but an occasional crackle from the fireplace and the faint hiss of the coffee pot.

We sat still around the room—the Tinker with his long, narrow face and gold earrings, Doc Halloran standing and looking long, lean and serious, with the black eyes of Juana and Manuel in the background.

"Deckrow's in town," the Tinker said finally, glancing around at Juana. "He's looking for you."

"His daughter is with him?"

"They're going to San Antonio. There's a lawsuit over the estate." He looked at me. "Your father should be here tomorrow, your father and his wife."

"He married Gin?"

"Love match—from the start. He's in great shape again and looks fine; and Gin, she's beautiful as ever. But Franklyn Deckrow claims the estate through his wife, and he claims he bought up mortgages. I don't understand lawing, but that's the way of it. The trouble will be settled in either San Antonio or Austin, but they're going to San Antonio now, then on to Austin, I think."

"I'll have to be there," I said. "I've evidence to offer."

Juana looked at me, and fear showed in her eyes. "Does he know? Señor Deckrow, does he know?"

"He knows . . . my eyes were on him and he saw it."

"Then tomorrow, when you fight?"

Doc and the Tinker, they just looked at me, and I said, "Deckrow was with Herrara's and Cortina's men that night. It was he and nobody else who killed Jonas. Shot him dead. It was Deckrow who tipped them off that we had come into Mexico after gold—they were expecting us."

"He'll kill you. He'll have to."

Looking down at my big hands, I shrugged. "He'll try."

That night I lay long awake, watching the red glow of the coals and thinking back over my life, and it didn't add up to much. I'd set out to become rich in the western lands, but going after that LaFitte gold had been my ruin. Maybe even starting west with the Tinker had been the finish of me.

When this was over I would go on . . . there were other Sacketts out in New Mexico, near the town of Mora. I would go there.

There was nobody for me here. Pa had married Gin, and he would be thinking of another family, and rightly so. It was true that I had felt strongly about Gin, but the physical needs of a man speak loud with a woman like her about, and there doesn't have to be anything else between you—although she was a man's woman in so many ways, and not only of the bed.

When I found a woman of my own, I hoped she would be like Gin. She and pa—I had seen it right off. They were for each other.

Me? Who was there for me? I was a man with nothing. A man with great shoulders and tremendous power in his hands, but nothing else. I owned a horse taken from horse thieves, and a mule bred by stealth, and nothing at all of which I could be proud. It was little enough I had in the way of learning, and in my mid-twenties I'd laid no foundation for anything.

Tomorrow there would be a horse race and then a fight, and with luck I should win one or both. Yet then there would remain the matter of surviving to enjoy my winnings. Horse-racing and fighting, these are not things upon which a man can build a useful life.

Tomorrow I would meet Dun Caffrey in the ring, with my fists. He was a skilled fighter, and I was only one with great strength and good but long-unpracticed training. If I whipped Caffrey, I'd have some of my own back; and if I could settle the matter of Deckrow and live, then I'd go west and start again as I had wished to do.

One thing I had learned in these years: I could now speak Spanish. Somewhere, at sometime in the future, it might help.

Westward I had come to grow rich in the land, but six years had passed and I had no more than at the beginning.

At last I slept, and when I awakened day had come and the coals were smoldering, with only a faint glow of red here and there. The room was empty.

Clasping my hands behind my head, I tried to organize a day that would not organize, for there were too many factors outside my grasp. Before the day was over I would have repaid Dun Caffrey what I owed him, or would have taken a fearful beating. But the greatest danger lay not in losing, but in winning. In losing I would take a beating; in winning, there was every chance I might be shot.

The Tinker and Halloran came in together. "The race will be run at ten o'clock," Halloran said. "The course is all laid out—one half-mile from a standing start."

"All right."

"The fight will be at one o'clock. Eighteen-foot ring. It's all set up in the stock corral. Those who cannot get up to the ring will find a seat on the fence."

"How many horses in the race?"

"Five, including your mule. Nobody thinks a mule can run, except a few who came in from Oakville. Right now the betting is seven to one against your mule."

From my shirt pocket I took forty dollars, every cent I had in the world. "At those odds, or anything close," I said, "you bet it on the race. If we win, bet whatever's in hand on the fight.

"Meanwhile," I said, "I'm going to take a walk around."

This here town of Beeville, along about the time we were there—you could walk three blocks in any direction and be out in the country. And some of those blocks you'd walk would be mighty sparse as to buildings.

It was a cattle-trail town and ran long to saloons and gambling houses. The folks who lived in the country around were mostly raising cattle. The rest of them were stealing cattle. Both industries were in what you might call a flourishing condition when we came into town. There was considerable money floating about town, and not an awful lot to do with it but drink or gamble. When it came to ranching, there were several successful men around Beeville; but in the cattle-rustling business the most successful man was Ed Singleton.

The town was about evenly divided between the ranchers and the thieves, and each knew the others by name and occupation. You could hang a cattle thief back in those days, but the trouble was you had to catch him at it. Singleton and those others, they were almighty sly.

There was a lot of betting on both the fight and the race, some of the folks even betting on me, sight unseen. There's folks will bet on anything, given a chance.

Quite a crowd was in town. Some, like I said, had come over from Oakville, but there was a whole crowd from Helena, too. Helena was an old stop on the Chihuahua trail and, like Beeville and Oakville, it was a rough, wild town, and those men from Helena were as tough as they come.

I walked down the street, keeping away from the knots of men arguing here and there, and finally I stopped by the corral to look at that ring. It looked big enough, and small enough, too.

A man stopped beside me, looking through the corral bars at the ring. He glanced at me out of a pair of hard, measuring eyes, and thrust out his hand. "Walton. I'm sheriff. You fought much?"

"When I had to. Never in a contrivance like that."

"He's an experienced man, and a brute. I've seen him fight." He paused. "You must think you can beat him."

"A man never knows," I said, "but when we were kids I broke his nose and his jaw. I outsmarted him that time," I said, "maybe I can again."

"This a grudge fight?"

"If it isn't, then you never saw one. His pa used to beat me, and he robbed me. This one tried to bully me around. I figure he knows a lot more about fighting than I do, but I figure there's a streak of coyote in him. It may be mighty hard to find, but I'm going in there hunting it."

Walton straightened up. "There's fifty to a hundred thugs in town that nobody can account for without considering the Bishop. I'll do what I can, but I can't promise you anything."

"In this country," I said, "a man saddles his own broncos and settles his own difficulties."

Walton walked away, and after a bit I went back to the house and saddled the roan. Time was shaping up for the race.

Manuel had led the mule out. "They want to know his name," he said. "What did you call him?"

Manuel shrugged.

"All right, call him Bonaparte, and let's hope that track out there isn't Waterloo."

The Tinker came out and mounted up, and Doc Halloran too. One of the others who showed up was a husky Irishman with a double-barreled shotgun.

"I'm a mule-skinner," he said, "and I bet on him. In my time I've seen some fast mules, and I saw this one run over to Oakville."

The Bishop was out there, and Dun Caffrey. I noticed they had at least two horses in the race.

"Manuel," I said, "how mean can you be?"

He looked at me from those big dark eyes. "I do not know, señor. I have never been mean."

"Then you've got only one chance. Get that mule out in front and let him run. Those two"—I indicated the horses—"are both ridden by tough men. One or both of them will try to block you out if you look like you'd a chance, so watch out."

"I will ride Bonaparte," he said—"it is all I can do, but it is a proud name."

They lined up, and the way Bonaparte walked up to the line you wouldn't have thought he'd anything in mind but sleep. One of those Bishop horses moved in on each side of him.

So I walked across to the Bishop. I walked up to him right in front of everybody. "Tinhorn," I said, "you better hope those boys of yours don't hurt that kid. If they do, I'll kill you."

He thought it was big talk, but he made a little move with his head and two husky shoulder-strikers moved up to me. "Caffrey will kill you," the Bishop said, his voice deeper than any I'd ever heard, "but these can rough you up a little first."

One of them struck at me, and the Tinker's training was instinctive. Grabbing his wrist, I busted him over my back into the dust, and he came down hard. Coming up in a crouch, the other man missed a blow and I saw the glint of brass knuckles on his hand. My left hand grabbed his shirt collar in front and took a sharp twist that set him to gagging and choking. With the other I grabbed his hand, forcing his arm up so that everybody within sight could see those brass knuckles.

Now, like I've said, I was an uncommon strong man before those years in prison. My fingers wrapped around his hand just above the wrist and began to squeeze, squeezing his fingers right up to a point, then I brought his hand down and let those knuckle dusters fall into the dust. At the same time I slipped my hand up a little further and shut down hard with all my grip.

He screamed, a hoarse, choking scream. And then I put my thumb against the base of his fingers and my fingers at his wrist and bent it back sharply. Folks standing nearby heard it break. Then I walked out to Manuel.

"You ride it clean, kid," I said. I spoke loud enough so all could hear. "If either of these make a dirty ride, they'll get what he got."

Somebody cheered, and then the pistol was fired.

Those horses taken out of there at a dead run, most of them cutting horses and expert at starting from a stand.

My mule, he was left at the post.

They just taken off and went away from there, but Manuel was figuring right. He held the mule back, and sure enough, those two riders to right and left crashed together. They had risked what I'd do rather than what the Bishop might do. If Manuel had been in there, he'd have been hurt, and bad.

Then Manuel let out a shrill whoop and that Bonaparte left out of there like he had some place to go and it was on fire.

He was two lengths behind before he made his first jump, but I'd never realized the length of his legs before. He had a tremendous stride, and he ran—he ran like no horse I'd ever seen.

There was no way for me to see the finish. It was a straightaway course, and several of them seemed to be bunched up at the end.

Suddenly one of the judges, a man on a white horse, came galloping back. "That damned mule!" he yelled. "The mule won by half a length!"

Back at the Mexicans' cabin nobody had much to say. The Mexican folks who owned it stayed out of sight most of the time and Juana stayed with them. I had made a bit of money and Halloran cut me in on what he'd made on the race, as well as giving a bit to Manuel. That I did too.

Those two races had made that boy more money than he and Juana had seen since Miguel died.

Me, I stretched out on the bed and lay there, resting up for the fight. My stomach felt empty and kind of sick-like, and I began to wonder if I was scared. True enough, I'd whipped Caffrey, but he was no fighter then, just a big, awkward boy, and I might have been lucky. Now he had been out among men, he had proved himself against known fighters, defeating them all, and there's no escaping the worth of experience.

Between bouts he'd had a plenty of sparring with experienced fighters, and was up to all manner of tricks that only a professional can come by. But I thought of Jem Mace, who'd taught the Tinker. He had been a master boxer, one of the great ones. Never weighing more than one hundred and sixty pounds, he had been the world's champion, defeating men as much as sixty pounds heavier.

Thinking about it, I dozed off and did not wake up until the Tinker shook me.

"Move around," he advised. "Get the sleep out of you. Get your blood to circulating."

O'Flaherty, the Irishman who'd bet on our mule, came to the house. "I've not seen you with the knuckles," he commented, "but a man with sense enough to bet on a mule is a canny one, so I bet my winnings on you."

The Tinker was carrying a pistol, a rare thing for him, and the Irishman had brought his shotgun. Doc Halloran had bulges under his coat that meant he was wearing two guns, and I slipped mine into my waistband, too.

We mounted up and started for the ring, but I'd gone no way at all when someone called out to me, and when I turned I saw it was a girl in a handsome carriage. It was Marsha Deckrow, and she was more beautiful than I would have believed anybody could be.

Pulling up, I removed my hat. "Still the servant's entrance?" I said.

She showed her dimples. "I was a child then, Orlando. I must have sounded very snippy."

"You did."

"You're stern!" She laughed at me. "I'm sorry you were in prison. My father told me about it."

"I must be going on," I said, though to be honest it was the last thing I wished to do.

"You're going to fight that awful man. My father won't let me go, even though I promised to sit in the carriage and we needn't be close. There's a knoll a little way from the corral, and we could keep the carriage there. But I'll watch. I think I've found a window."

"It is likely to be brutal," I said, "and he may whip me."

"Will I see you afterward, Orlando? After all, we're cousins, aren't we? Or something like that? Your father married my aunt."

"Do you see them often?"

"With your father feeling the way he does about pa? I should say not! In fact, we're on our way to Austin now."

I gathered the reins. The Tinker and Doc were waiting impatiently, and the time was soon. "You tell your pa for me," I said, "that he'd better drop that case. He'd best forget the whole thing. He was working for

Jonas in the beginning, and when this is over he won't even be doing that."

Her face hardened. "You're my enemy then?"

"I'm not anybody's enemy," I said, "but I know murder when I see it done. And betrayal, too."

The look in her eyes there for a minute—well, it wasn't what you'd rightly call pleasant; but then it was gone and she was all smiles. "After the fight, Orlando? Win or lose? Will you come? Pa wouldn't approve, not one bit, but if you'd come to see me . . . I'm staying with the Appletons, down at the end of the street. They hadn't room for pa, too, so he won't be there. Do come."

"Well"—she was a mighty pretty girl—"I'll see."

My stomach felt queasy when I dismounted at the corral, for there were a sight of folks sitting atop the corral fence, which had a board nailed on it all the way around so's men could look at stock when buying from the corral.

Inside, the yard had been sprinkled and then rolled or tamped until it was hard-packed. They'd set four posts in the ground and had ropes around them, running through holes in the posts.

No sooner had I got down than a great yell went up from the crowd, and there was Dun Caffrey getting out of a carriage. He wore a striped sweater, and when he peeled it off, he showed a set of the finest shoulders a man ever did see.

He was some taller than me, maybe about three inches, and had longer arms. He would weigh better than me, for I was down to two hundred and six, whilst he weighed two hundred and thirty, and carrying no fat.

Folks crowded around—men in buckboards and spring wagons, men a-horseback and afoot.

Caffrey was wearing a pair of dark blue tights and some fancy, special-made shoes for boxing or handball. I wore moccasins and black tights—these last the Tinker rustled up for me.

"They've got a set of gloves," Doc Halloran said, "and they offer to fight either way, with or without."

"Take 'em," the Tinker advised. "They protect your hands, and you'll hit even harder because of them. A lot of folks don't realize it, but a man hits harder with a bandaged hand and a glove than with a bare fist—more compact, better striking surface, and less danger of hurting your hands."

When we agreed, they brought a pair of gloves over and I shoved my hand down inside. These were three-ounce gloves, and when my hand was doubled into a fist it was hard as rock.

"We fight London Prize Ring rules," Doc explained. "You fight until one man goes down, a knockdown, slip, or throw down, then you rest for one minute, and you toe the mark when you come up for each round, and the fight is to a finish."

"He knows," the Tinker said, dryly. He looked at me. "I hope you haven't forgotten what I taught you during those months of travel. You can use a rolling hip-lock to throw him, and if you get hold of him, pound him until you're stopped."

Everybody had been taking notice of Caffrey, and when I slipped off my sweater, nobody was looking my way. I was brown as any Indian, and there were the scars of the old whip-cuts on my back and shoulders.

In spite of the difference in weight between us, I was better muscled and a little broader in the shoulders and quite a bit thicker through the chest.

Walton was to referee, and he made an announcement that he'd shoot the first man to come through the ropes or the first to try to tear down a post.

Around that ring those gamblers were gathered. Right off I could see that they'd outsmarted us, and the whole crowd against the ropes except right in my corner were his friends, and the men behind them were, too. My friends, and few enough of them there were, they were cut off, back some distance.

Suppose a whole rank started to move in on the ring? What would Walton do then?

Time was called and we walked out to toe the mark, and as soon as my toe touched it, Caffrey hit me. He hit me a straight left to the face, and it landed hard. I sprang at him, punching with both hands, and he moved around me like a cooper around a barrel. He hit me three times in the face without my landing a blow.

The crowd began to yell, and he came at me again, but this time I ducked my head against his chest and managed to hit him twice, short blows in the belly, before he put a headlock on me and threw me to my knees, ending the round.

When I walked back to my corner and sat on Halloran's knee, my lip was puffed from a blow, and there was a knot on my cheekbone. I'll give it to him. He could punch.

"Stay close to him," the Tinker whispered. "Keep your hands higher and your elbows in. Work on his body when you get the chance."

When time was called, Caffrey rushed from his corner and began punching with both hands. He hit me several times, almighty hard, but I got my head down against his chest again and hooked both hands hard to the belly. He tried to push me off then, but I stepped in fast and back-heeled him and he went down hard, ending the round.

As we went on it was nip and tuck, both of us punching hard. He was fast, and he was in good shape, and he moved well. The first six rounds were gone in fourteen minutes, but the seventh round lasted five minutes all by itself.

He'd pounded me about the head, but I wasn't really hurt. He'd drawn first blood—there was a trickle of it from my lip that had been cut against my teeth. He was unmarked, and the betting had gone up to three to one on Caffrey.

Opposite us a window had gone up in the second story of a house, and I could see a couple of women there, watching the fight. Another window in that same house was open, too, but nobody watched from it.

Round eight came up and I went out fast, slipped a left lead for my head and smashed him in the ribs. It taken his wind, and it shook him up. It was my first hard punch of the fight, and I think it surprised him. He backed off, studying me, and I stalked him. I made awkwardly as if to throw my right and he stepped in, hitting hard with his right.

My left arm was bent at the elbow, first at shoulder level, elbow near the hip, and I'd moved my left shoulder and hip over almost to the center line, while leaving my fist cocked where it was. As Caffrey threw that right, I let go with my left, letting it whip around, thrown by the tension built up by turning my shoulder forward and the weight behind it.

The blow struck high on his cheekbone and knocked him across the ring into the ropes. Eager hands shoved him back, but I was moving in on him and I struck him again with my left fist, but I was too eager with my right, and missed. He clinched and back-heeled me into the dirt, falling atop me and jerking his knee into my groin.

Throwing him off, I came up fast and mad, and hurt by that knee. He cocked his fist, and then Walton stepped in and stopped the round.

Twice after that he drove me into the ropes and once I was hit from outside the ropes, hit hard just above the kidney. I turned to complain and he knocked me down . . . a clean knock-down.

The crowd was mad now. Arguments were starting all about us, and there were several fights going close to the ring, and one back beyond it. Once, wrestling in a clinch, I thought I saw movement at that empty window, and made up my mind to speak to Doc about it.

It was bloody fighting now. Moving in, I smashed him in the mouth with a right that split his lip and started the blood flowing. In a clinch he said hoarsely, "I'm going to kill you, Sackett! Right here in this ring, I'm going to kill you!"

"I broke your bones once," I replied, "and I'll do it again!"

Catching his left arm under mine, I threw him off balance and hit him twice in the belly before I let go. We moved together, punching with both hands, and outside the ropes the crowd was shouting and brawling. Nothing could be heard above the din. Deliberately, I still pounded away at his body, but his stomach and ribs were like rock. He cut a slit above my eye and knocked me into the ropes, and there someone struck me a stunning blow over the back of the head with something like a blackjack or sandbag.

Even as I fell, Caffrey rushed at me and struck me twice in the face. I fell forward, and was scarcely conscious as the Tinker and Doc dragged me to my corner. Yet when the bell rang I was on my feet.

Now he started after me, and, still feeling the effects of the blow over the head, I could not get myself together. My punches were poorly timed and lacked force, and Caffrey rushed at me, pounding away with both hands. Getting in close, I seized him bodily, lifted him clear of the ground, and slammed him down with such force that the wind was knocked from him.

"The one in the checked suit," Doc whispered, "he's the one who sapped you."

Glancing across the ring, I saw him there, a broad-faced man with coarse features, who was wearing a black hat.

Caffrey was wary of me now, and we circled a bit, and I backed him slowly toward the man in the checked suit. That man, I noticed, had his right hand out of sight under his coat. Near the ropes I moved in, feinted, ducked a left, and landed a right under the heart, pushing him back into the ropes. Smashing another blow to the belly, I deliberately pushed him against the ropes so the men crowded there must give way, then I struck hard at his head, but off aim just enough for the blow to miss, which it did.

It missed him, but it caught the man in the checked suit on his red, bulbous nose and smashed it, sending a shower of blood over him as he fell.

We slugged in mid-ring then, slugged brutally, taking no time, just punching away. The things that the Tinker had taught me were coming back now. I stabbed a straight left to the mouth, then crossed my right to his chin. He hit me with a solid right and I staggered, but as he closed in I clinched, caught his right elbow in my left hand, and my right arm went around his body. Then I turned my hip against him and hurled him heavily to the dirt.

He was slow getting up, and suddenly I felt better. There was a cut over my eye, a welt on my cheekbone I could scarcely see over, and my lip had been split, but I felt better. I had my second wind, and suddenly all the old feeling against the Caffreys was welling up inside me. They had robbed me and enslaved me, they had treated me cruelly when there was no chance to fight back. Now we would see.

When time was called I went out fast. I feinted and hit him with a solid right on the jaw. His knees buckled, so I moved in fast to catch him before he could fall and bull him into the ropes. If he went down he would have rest and might recover. Men tried to push him off the ropes so he could fall, but I held him there and hit him with both hands in the face with all the power I had.

When he started to fall away from the ropes I caught him with another punch, and then he did fall. Turning back to my corner, my eyes momentarily caught a flash of light. Involuntarily I ducked, but there was nothing. Glancing at the empty window, I found it still empty.

The gamblers were pushing hard on the ropes, and Sheriff Walton shouted at them to hold back, but they were pushing as a mass and there was no one he could single out for a shot, and he was not the man to fire blindly into a crowd.

When we came together again in the center of the ring, I said, "Dun Caffrey, you and your folks robbed me, now I shall have a little of my own back."

He cursed me, and beat me to the punch with a left that jolted me. There was power in the man. He was a fighter—I'll give him that.

The crowd was shouting wildly, their faces red with fury at me. They had not expected me to last so long, yet here I was, in danger of beating their man.

Sweat trickled into my eye and the salt stung, and, momentarily blinded, I failed to see the right with which he knocked me into the ropes. Now it was he who held me there, and as he battered at me with both fists, several men pounded the back of my head and my kidneys from beyond the ropes. Had they left it to one man he might have done me serious injury, but so eager were they, and most of them drinking, that they interfered with one another.

I got my head down against his chest and again the great strength of me helped, for I bulled him away from the ropes and into the center of the ring.

As we broke apart, each ready for a blow, sunlight flashed again in my eyes—sunlight reflected from a rifle barrel. In the window which until now had seemed empty, a man was aiming a rifle at me.

Wildly, I threw a punch at Caffrey, deliberately throwing myself forward and off balance so that I fell to the ground, but even as I fell I heard the *whap* of a rifle bullet as it whipped past me, and then I was on my hands and knees in the dirt and all about me there was silence.

Looking up, I saw the crowd drawing back. Slumped against a ring post was a man with a round blue hole over one eye and the back of his head blown away.

In that instant, the Bishop, never one to miss a chance, sprang into the ring holding up a watch and claiming I had been off my feet for the count of ten—that I had lost, I had been knocked out.

"No!" Walton shouted, and drawing his own gun, he said, "the fight will continue. May the best man win."

The thugs and gamblers crowded back again toward the ring, shouting angrily that the fight was ended, but before they could reach the ropes, a horse vaulted over them and a man with a shotgun sat in the saddle.

"Stand back from the ropes!" His voice seemed not to be lifted above a conversational tone, but it had the ring of authority. "We'll have no interference here."

The thugs stared at the shotgun and the man who held it, and hesitated, as well they might. Captain McNelly was not a man who spoke careless words.

"I would advise you," he said, "to look about you before any violence is attempted. I am NcNelly, and the men you see are my company of Rangers. We will see fair play here, and no violence outside the ring."

Their heads turned slowly, unwilling to believe what they saw, but thirty mounted and armed men are a convincing sight, and I confess, it was pleased I was to see them.

McNelly spoke to his horse, which easily lifted itself over the ropes again. "Sheriff Walton," he said quietly, "whenever you are ready."

"Time!" Walton said, and stepped back.

It was a bloody bit of business that remained, for I found no streak of cowardice in Dun Caffrey. Many things he might have been, but there was courage in the man. He had had a few minutes of respite, and now he came up to the mark, fresh as only a well-conditioned veteran can be. For the veteran knows better how to rate himself, how to make the other man do the work and exert himself; and Caffrey was prepared to give me a whipping.

But the fighting had served a purpose with me also. No veteran of many fights, nonetheless I had sparred much with the Tinker and he had shown me many things, and practiced me in their doing, and the fight thus far had served to bring them to mind.

So if it was a strong and skilled man I still faced, it was a different one he faced now.

My muscles were loose now, my body warmed up, and I was sweating nicely under the hot sun. The rhythm of punching had become more natural to me, and my mind was working in the old grooves.

As I came in more slowly, my mind was thinking back to what the Tinker had taught me. Caffrey shot a left for my face and, going under it, I hit him with a right to the heart, rolling inside of his right. I smashed my left to the ribs, then hooked a right to the head over his left.

The right landed solidly, and Caffrey blinked. Moving in, I shook him with another right and a left. For a long minute we slugged. I could feel the buzz in my head from his punches, the taste of blood from my split lip. I saw his fist start and brushed it aside, driving my right to his chin inside his left. He backed up, trying to figure it out, but whatever else he was, Caffrey was no thinking fighter. Weaving, I hit him with both hands.

Outside, the air was filled with sound, men were shouting, cheering, crying out with anger. Not with blood lust, but with the excitement of any dramatic thing—and what could be more dramatic than a fight like this one?

He hit me with a left, but the steam had gone from his punches. I tried a light left, watching for the move I wanted. And it came again, the same too-wide left he had tried only a moment before. Only that time my right caught him coming in. My fist struck solidly on the point of his chin, like the butt of an axe striking a log, and he fell face forward into the dirt.

For a moment there I stood looking down at him. This was the man whose father and mother had cheated me and robbed me, and who had gone on to riches on the money that should have been spent for my education, the education I'd always wanted. Yet, suddenly, I no longer felt any hatred, all of it washed clean in the trial of battle.

Stooping down, I picked him up and helped him to his corner, and as I stopped him there, where of a sudden there was nobody to receive him, his eyes opened and he looked around.

Me, I let go of him and held out my mitt. "It was a good fight, Dun. You're a tough man."

He blinked at me, then held out his own hand and we stood there looking surprised, like two fools.

And then I turned and walked away and leaned against the roan, which had been led up for me. The Tinker was handing me my sweater. "Get into this," he said; "you'll take cold."

Taking it from his hand, I said, "I got to see a man."

"The one who tried to kill you? He got away."

"No, he didn't."

We walked, the Tinker and me, along the dusty street. Doc Halloran walked behind us with Captain McNelly and Sheriff Walton.

Their rig was coming down the street toward us, and there for a moment I thought he was going to try to ride right over us, but he drew up and stopped when we stopped, barring his way.

Marsha was there in the seat beside her father, and nobody else with them. They were alone, those two, but somehow I had a feeling they'd always been alone.

Deckrow's face showed nothing, but it never had. His eyes looked at me, cold and measuring, with no give to them.

"You shot and killed your brother-in-law, Jonas Locklear," I said, "and it was you tipped Herrara off that we were in Mexico, and what for."

"I do not have any idea what you are speaking about," he replied, looking at me sternly. "I am sure I would be the last man to shoot my own brother-in-law."

"I saw you shoot him," I persisted, "and Miguel did also. That's why he died. That's why you tried to kill me today."

"You ought to be ashamed," Marsha said, "telling lies about my father."

You know something? I was sorry for him. He was a little man and nothing much had ever happened to him, and with all his planning and figuring he could never make any money; while Jonas, who did all the wrong things, was always making it. And now he had to pay for it all.

Trouble with me was, I was a mighty poor hater. There was satisfaction in winning, but winning would have been better if nobody had to lose. That's the way I've always felt, I guess.

Seems to me I'm the sort of man who, if a difficulty arose, might knock a man down and kick all his teeth out, but then would help him pick them up if he was so inclined, and might even pay the bill for fixing them —although that's going a bit far.

"That property," I said, "the ranch and the house and all, belongs to Gin and your wife, unless a will said otherwise . . . not to you.

"You've no claim"—I spoke louder to prevent his attempted interruption —"and you tried to get one through murder. I will take oath, here and now and in court, that you betrayed and then shot down your brother-in-law. Furthermore," I said, and lied when I said it, "I can get Mexicans to testify they saw it.

"You sign over all claims to Gin and your wife—"

"My wife left me," he said.

"You sign over all claims or I'll have you on trial for murder."

He sat there holding the lines and hating me, but he hadn't much to say. The trouble was, he was a man with a canker for a soul, and he would be eaten away with his bitterness at failure, nor did I care much.

It is wrong to believe that such men suffer in the conscience for what they do . . . it is only regret at being caught that troubles them. And they never admit it was any fault of their own . . . it was always chance, bad luck. . . . The criminal does not regret his crime, he only regrets failure.

The Bishop was standing by listening, but I paid him no mind. There had been a time when he seemed awesome and dangerous, but that was a while back.

"You remember what I said, Deckrow," I told him, "because wherever it is this is settled, San Antonio or Austin or wherever, I'll be there."

When I came up to the house pa was there, and Gin beside him. He looked fine . . . they were a handsome couple if I ever saw one—but I was sure I'd never get around to calling her ma.

I stepped down from the saddle and slid my Winchester from the boot, and pa looked at me. "Somebody gave you a beating," he said.

"He didn't give it to me," I replied, "I fought for it."

"You'll be coming with us now? I've held your share of the gold . . . it's been waiting your return."

"Buy something with it in my name. I'll come for it one day . . . or send a son of mine for it."

"You're going back for the rest?"

"When I left Tennessee for the western lands it was in my mind to become rich with the goods of this world, but by planning and trade, not by diving for dead men's gold. I shall go on to the West."

"You still want me along?" the Tinker asked.

"We left Tennessee together. I left with you and a mule. It's fitting we hold to our course. However, we never did make a dicker for one of your knives. Now, I'd give—"

"Stand aside, Gin," pa interrupted, "there's trouble."

When I turned around it put me alongside of pa, although there was a space between us. And the Tinker stood off to one side of me.

And there facing us were the three Kurbishaws, three tall men in dusty black, Elam, Gideon, and Eli.

Pa was first to speak. "You've come a long way from Charleston, Elam . . . a long way."

"We came for you."

"You will find most of the gold still there . . . if you can get it," pa said coolly. "We've had ours."

"It isn't for gold any more," Gideon said. "There's more to it."

"I suppose there is," pa replied, his voice still cold. "You hounded your sister to death; you hunted my son."

"And now we got him," Elam replied, "—and you."

Pa didn't want it, I could see that. He was talking to get out of it, to get it stopped, but they would not listen. Strange men they were, but I'd see their like again, in lynch mobs and elsewhere. They were men who knew what I did not—they knew how to hate.

"You wouldn't try me alone," pa said. "Now there's two of us."

"Three," said the Tinker.

"We've come a far piece since then," Elam said, "and we've lived as we might, by the gun."

"Why, then," pa said, "if you'll have it no other way—"

Gideon was looking at me, so when pa drew I swung up the muzzle of my Winchester and levered a shot into him. I saw the bullet dust him at the belt line, and worked the lever again and fired. He threw his gun hand high in a queer, dance-like gesture, and then he tried to bring it down on me. I stepped forward and shot again and my bullet went high, striking at the collarbone and tearing away part of his throat as it glanced off.

The sound of shooting was loud in the street, and then there was stillness, the acrid smell of gunpowder mixed with dust, and we three stood there, facing them as they lay. The last one alive was Eli, tugging at one of Tinker's knives sunk deep into his chest.

"If that's the only way," I commented, "to get one of those knives, I'll wait."

Looking down at them, I thought it was a strange trail they had followed, those three, and how in the end it had only come to this, to death in a dusty street, nobody caring; and by and by nobody even remembering, except by gossip over a bar in a saloon.

Seemed it was just as well a man did not know where he was headed when he was to come only to this—a packet of empty flesh and clothes to end it all. In the end their hatred had bought them only this . . . only this, and the bitter years between.

It always seemed that for me something waited in those western lands, something of riches in the way of land and living, and maybe a woman. And when I found her, I wanted her to be like Gin.

Younger, of course, as would be fitting, but like her.

Somebody likely to have no more sense than to fall in love with a Tennessee boy with nothing but his two hands and a racing mule.

# MOJAVE
# CROSSING

*To Parker*

# Author's Note

As in all my previous books, the place names are those of actual places that existed as described at the time the story took place. Although a writer of fiction is under no compulsion to be as exact as I have chosen to be as to locale, I regard each of my novels as, in a sense, historical. Each water hole or spring, each valley, canyon, creek or mountain, each store, gambling house, or hotel exists now or did exist at the time.

The tanks visited by Sackett after leaving Dorinda are the White Tanks, and the well he next visited was Lost Horse Well, both of which are now within the limits of Joshua National Monument. The Hidden Valley where Sackett was loaned a horse is now visited by thousands of tourists, and they enter by crawling, as he did. The Button brothers actually used the valley to hide stolen horses (nobody yet knows how the horses were taken in or out), and they were killed, sometime later, in a gun battle in San Bernardino.

The house of Greek George was located near the intersection of Fountain Avenue and King's Road, only a block off the famous Sunset Strip in what is now Hollywood.

The local round-ups, called rodeos in California, were held in an area roughly between La Cienaga and Robertson streets, give or take a few blocks.

Although California is not usually considered a western state in the "wild west" conception of the term, few states were more so. Only Texas could have had more cattle, and without doubt the greatest of all ropers, as well as some of the finest horsemen, were the early Spanish-Californian vaqueros . . . roping grizzlies was a favorite sport.

By 1893 El Tejon Ranch, still one of the largest in the United States, was running more than 125,000 head of sheep and 25,000 head of cattle. Without doubt one of the greatest stock drives in western history was the movement, over uncharted trails, of 17,000 head of sheep from El Tejon Ranch to Montana in 1879, by Jose Jesus Lopez. This ranch is in the Tehachapis, only a few miles from the outskirts of Los Angeles.

No cattle baron ruled his empire with a harsher hand than did the "Big Basque" Leonis, of Calabasas; and the gun battles between Carlisle and

LOUIS L'AMOUR

the Kings, or that between Jim McKinney and a sheriff's posse were the equal of the OK Corral fight or any of the famous gun battles of the West. McKinney, a notorious outlaw with a number of killings behind him, shot it out in Bakersfield with Will and Burt Tibbett and Jeff Packard . . . McKinney was killed, as were Jeff Packard and Will Tibbett (the father of singer Lawrence Tibbett), Burt Tibbet killing McKinney. There was considerable testimony to the effect that Al Hulse, and perhaps another man, were also shooting at the deputies from the room where McKinney was killed.

It is an ironic fact that it was in the City of the Angels that the street called the Calle de los Negros held a record for violence and killing unequaled in the West.

# Chapter 1

When I saw that black-eyed woman a-looking at me I wished I had a Bible.

There I was, a big raw-boned mountain boy, rougher than a cob and standing six feet three inches in my socks, with hands and shoulders fit to wrassle mustang broncs or ornery steers, but no hand with womenfolks.

Nobody ever claimed that I was anything but a homely man, but it was me she was looking at in that special way she had.

Where we Sacketts come from in the high-up mountains of Tennessee, it is a known thing that if you sleep with a Bible under your pillow it will keep you safe from witches. Before they can do aught to harm you they must count every word in the Bible, and they just naturally can't finish that before daybreak, when they lose their power to hurt.

Yet when I taken a second look at that black-eyed, black-haired woman I thought maybe it was me should do the counting. She was medium tall, with a way about her that set a man to thinking thoughts best kept to himself. She had the clearest, creamiest skin you ever did see, and a mouth that fairly prickled the hair on the back of your neck.

Most of my years I'd spent shying around in the mountains or out on the prairie lands, with no chance to deal myself any high cards in society, but believe me, there's more snares in a woman's long lashes than in all the creek bottoms of Tennessee. Every time I taken my eyes from that black-haired witch woman it was in me to look back.

My right boot-toe was nudging the saddlebags at my feet, warning me I'd no call to take up with any woman, for there were thirty pounds of gold in those bags, not all of it mine.

The worst of it was, I figured things were already shaping for trouble. Three days hand-running I'd seen dust hanging over my back trail like maybe there was somebody back there who wanted to keep close to me without actually catching up. And that could only mean that trouble lay ahead.

Now, I'm no man who's a stranger to difficulty. No boy who walked out of Tennessee to fight for the Union was likely to be, to say nothing of all

that had happened since. Seemed like trouble dogged my tracks wherever
I put a foot down, and here was I, heading into strange country, running
into a black-eyed woman.

She sat alone and ate alone, so obviously a lady that nobody made a
move to approach her. This was a rough place in rough times, but a body
would have thought she was setting up to table in Delmonico's or one of
those fancy eastern places, her paying no mind to anything or anybody.
Except, occasionally, me.

She wasn't all frills and fuss like a fancy woman, for she was dressed
simple, but her clothes were made from rich goods. Everything about her
warned me I'd best tuck in my tail and skedaddle out of there whilst I was
able, for trouble doesn't abide only with fancy women. Even a good
woman, with her ways and notions, can cause a man more trouble than he
can shoot his way out of, and I'd an idea this here was no good woman.

Trouble was, there just was no place to run to.

Hardyville was little else but a saloon, a supply store, and a hotel at the
crossing of the Colorado. Most of the year it was the head of navigation
on the river, but there had been a time or two when steamboats had gone
on up to the mines in Eldorado Canyon, or even to Callville.*

Come daybreak, I figured to cross the river on the first ferry and take
out for the Bradshaw Road and Los Angeles, near the western ocean. It
was talked among the Arizona towns that speculators out there would pay
eighteen, maybe twenty dollars an ounce for gold, whilst in the mining
camps a body could get but sixteen.

It was in my mind to sell my gold in Los Angeles, buy goods and mules,
pack across the Mojave Desert and the Colorado, and sell my goods in the
mining towns. With luck I'd show profit on my gold, and on my goods as
well.

Nobody ever claimed I was any kind of a businessman, least of all me,
but if a body can buy cheap and sell high he just naturally ain't liable to
starve. Of course, in all things there was a reason, and in this case it was
the difficulty of getting either gold or goods through a country full up
with outlaws and Indians. Whilst no businessman, I was pretty fair at get-
ing from here to yonder, so I just bowed my neck and plunged in, figuring wherever a body could go a Smoky Mountain Sackett could go.

Speaking rightly, there were three kinds of Sacketts in Tennessee. The
Smoky Mountain Sacketts, the Cumberland Gap Sacketts, and the Clinch
Mountain Sacketts. These here last ones, they were a mean outfit and we
had no truck with them unless at feuding time, when we were always

---

* Now under the waters of Lake Mead.

pleased to have them on our side, for they were mean men in any kind of a shindig. But most of the time we held off from those Clinch Mountain boys.

There were some lowland Sacketts, too, living in the Cumberland Valley, but they were rich Sacketts and we paid them no mind. Pa, he always said we shouldn't hold it against them if they had money; chances were they couldn't he'p it, no ways.

All the Sacketts, even those no-account Sacketts from Clinch Mountain, run to boy-children. They had a saying over yonder that if you flung a stone into the brush you'd hit a Sackett boy, and likely, although it wasn't said, a Trelawney girl. I don't know what we Sackett boys would have done without the Trelawney girls.

But the only thing I was thinking of now was getting my old saddle-bags across the Mojave and to Los Angeles, selling as well as I could, buying as cheap as possible, and getting back to the mines.

Now, when a beautiful woman or a handsome man receives attention it is taken as a matter of course; but I was a plain man, so when this black-eyed woman started paying me mind, I checked my hole card.

Not that I'd lacked for attention where women were concerned . . . not, at least, after they came to know me. Nor could it be said that I was downright distrustful of folks. There's a-plenty of just people in the world, but the flesh is weak and man is prone to sin . . . especially if a woman is involved.

But I was packing gold, and it came upon me to realize there is something about the presence of gold that is favorable to the breathing of beautiful women. And likely this woman, with her witch-black eyes, could see right through the leather of my saddlebags.

Only I'd been storing up pleasure for myself in thinking of a time when I could set up to table and eat a hot meal I hadn't fixed for myself, and sleep in a bed, if only for the strangeness of it. And if I high-tailed it out of here now I'd miss both.

For the life of me I couldn't imagine what a woman like this was doing in Hardyville. By the looks of her, she had come upriver on a steamboat, for her clothes showed no dust, as they would had she come by stage or wagon.

When the waitress brought my food the black-eyed woman stopped her, and asked, "Isn't it time for the stage for Los Angeles?"

"Have to get them a new stage," I said.

"What do you mean?"

"It ain't a-comin' in."

All of them were looking at me now, so I said, "Seen it back yonder." I was buttering a thick slab of bread. "He who was driving is dead . . . two holes alongside his spine. The stage is laying over in the canyon and the horses gone. Two other dead men . . . passengers."

"Are you sure?" This was Hardy asking.

"The buzzards were."

"You didn't go down to them?"

"Not for more'n a minute or two. No tellin' who was laying up in the rocks with a Winchester."

"Mojaves," somebody said, "or Hualapais."

"They wore moccasins, all right, but they weren't Indians. They were Comanche moccasins, and there's no Comanches out here."

Everybody started talking all to once and I set to eating, glad to be let alone. Anyway, it was likely I'd already talked too much. One of those men who'd done the shooting might be right here in this room, although I'd cast eyes about for moccasins when I first came in, habitlike. Seems to me a man has trouble enough in this world without borrowing more with careless words.

That black-eyed woman was talking to the waitress. "But if that stage has been wrecked, how long will it be before there's another?"

"Ma'am, you'll just have to abide. The next regular stage is Thursday."

This here was Monday, and I could see from that woman's face that she had to be shut of Hardyville long before that. And it wasn't just that this was a jumping-off place—she was scared.

That witch woman's lips turned pale and her black eyes grew large, like she'd seen a ghost. Maybe her own.

She turned sharp around to me and said, "Will you take me to Los Angeles with you?"

And me, like a damned fool, and without thinking, I said, "Yes."

It never does any good for a man to cuss himself, unless maybe it helps to impress on his mind what a fool he's been, but right then and there I did a fair to middling job of cussing myself out for seven kinds of a fool. Here I was, in a running hurry to get to California—to Los Angeles, that is—and I'd burdened myself with a woman. And by the look of her she'd need coddling.

Well, I'd been fool enough for one day, and maybe I could get out of this yet. "You'll need horses," I said. "Are you packing much gear?"

"My trunk can come by stage. All I'll need will be the two carpetbags."

"My pack horse can handle them if they aren't heavy," I said, "but you'll need two ridin' horses. This here's a fast trip I'm makin'."

"Thank you," she said. "If you will get them for me, I'll pay you in Los Angeles. All I have"—she smiled beautifully—"is my stage ticket and a bank draft too large to cash here."

"I—" I started to object that I didn't have the money, but those saddlebags were pushing at my toe and I'd a sneaking feeling—with no reason for it that I could make sense out of—that she knew what was in those bags.

"All right," I said, and lost my last chance to back out of it.

No getting around it, I was upset. It was my notion to make a fast trip to Los Angeles, which was my reason for two horses, switching from one to the other. Now I had that woman to care for, and no telling what she was like on a horse.

Taking another fill of coffee from the pot on the table, I happened to look across at the bar. A man standing there was looking my way and listening to two others. There seemed to be something familiar about the biggest of them. He was a man as tall as I was, and some heavier. He was a dark, strong-looking man who wore a gun like a man who could use it. His back was to me, and he had a fine set of shoulders on him . . . he was built like a man who could punch.

That woman hadn't moved, and our tables were only two feet apart. Best thing was to get it settled right off.

"If you ride with me," I said, and I'm afraid my tone was kind of rough, "you will be ready to go, come daybreak . . . and that doesn't mean sun-up. It means the first gray in the sky."

Shoving back my chair, I got up. "Can you use a gun?"

Well, sir, she surprised me. "Yes," she said, "I can handle a rifle." And then she smiled at me, and you've never seen such a smile. "And please do not disturb yourself. I shall be no trouble to you."

Fishing those saddlebags off the floor with my left hand, I stood up, dropping a quarter on the table for my meal. Then I taken up my Winchester with my right hand and walked to the door.

A voice spoke behind me, and I had a feeling the big man had turned to look, and I knew that voice was an invitation to turn around, an invitation to trouble. Stepping outside, I closed the door behind me and stood alone in the soft desert night.

It was very still. The Colorado River rustled by out there in the darkness, and beyond the river loomed the Dead Mountains. Over there a narrow point of Nevada came down to join borders with California.

Uneasily, I looked westward into those miles of desert, and the hunch rode my shoulders that I'd see blood and grief before those miles were behind me. A fool I was to entangle myself with that black-eyed woman.

Of a sudden I realized the thing I'd ought to do was to leave now. True, the ferry was not operating, but swimming the river at this point was no new thing. Beale had done it with his camels, and fine swimmers they proved to be.

There was a light in the window of Hardy's cabin. Crossing to it, I tapped on the door, not too loud.

Being a wise man, he spoke before opening the door, but when I told I wanted to make a dicker on some horses, he opened up, but he held a pistol in his hand, which surprised me none at all.

"Yes," he replied, when I had explained myself. "I've two good horses, but they'll cost you."

He slid his gun into its holster and picked up his coat. He started to put it on, then stopped and looked over at me. "Are you taking that Robiseau woman out of here?"

"I never asked her name, nor she mine. She wishes to go to Los Angeles, and I'm riding that way."

He shrugged into his coat. "You're borrowing trouble. Look, I don't know you. You just drifted in here out of nowhere, but that woman is running from something, and whatever it is or whoever it is will bundle you into her package. I mean, they'll resent interference."

"Whatever it is," I said, "she's a woman alone, and needs help."

He didn't say any more, but led the way to the stable and lighted a lantern. The horses in their stalls rolled their eyes at me. There were only a few stalls, for his own good stock. The mustang stuff was in the corrals out back.

One of the two horses he showed me was a liver-colored stallion with a white nose and three white stockings; a long-barreled animal built for speed and staying power, and one of the finest-looking horses I'd seen, and big for this country. It would weigh a good thousand pounds and maybe a mite over. The other horse was a short-coupled gelding, mouse-colored, with a fine head and powerful hindquarters. It was somewhat smaller than the other, but all horse.

We dickered there by lantern light, but he knew I had to have those horses, and he got his price. Yet high as they came, they were worth every penny of it. He had bought them from an Army officer who was changing station. The horses had been the officer's private mounts, and the smaller one had been broken for a woman to ride.

"You made a good buy," Hardy acknowledged, "although I got my price. There's no better horses around, unless it's those you've got."

We stood in the stable door, listening to the river. "She came up on the boat," Hardy volunteered, "and just missed the stage to Prescott."

"Prescott?"

"Uh-huh. Then she changed her mind and decided on Los Angeles. Seems to me like she wants the first stage out, no matter where it goes."

He paused and we stood there in silence, with me thinking about that road west, and those men who had been following me.

There'd been a time, back along the trail, when I was not sure . . . maybe they were just traveling the same way . . . but when I left Beale's

Springs I headed up to the Coyote Wells and got in there with time to spare. Those riders never showed up, although I'd seen their dust on my trail. That could mean only one thing—they were lying out in the hills, making dry camp, just so's I wouldn't see them.

Short of midnight I had left my fire burning low, saddled up, and taken off across the hills. My trail led west, toward Union Pass; but I got a notion, and after whipsawing back and forth in the trail, I cut off through the brush toward the south. South, then west, and through Secret Pass.

At Secret Spring I made camp and slept until well past daybreak. Then, after saddling up, I had climbed to the top of the cliff and looked off to the east and north. Sure enough, there was dust and movement on my back trail. Through my field glasses—taken off a dead Confederate officer on the battlefield—I could just make out four riders.

They had ridden on by the place where I'd turned off, discovering too late that I'd cut out somewhere. Now they were scouting their back trail to find the turn-off. They were a good ten, twelve miles off and in the bottom of Sacramento Wash.

Descending to my outfit, I had mounted up and followed the Secret Pass trail into Hardyville.

Nobody had ridden in, so they were lying out again, fearful of being seen by me, which might mean that I knew them and they feared recognition.

"Whoever it is," Hardy said now, "who wants that Robiseau woman, he wants her pretty bad, and wants her himself."

There was meaning in the way he said it, and I turned to look at him. "Keep out of it, friend," Hardy went on. "Three of those men in the saloon are watching her for somebody, and they shape up like grief a-plenty for anybody in their way."

"I gave her my word."

"Your funeral."

"Maybe," I said gloomily. "I'm not a trouble-hunting man. Not a one of us Sacketts ever was."

Hardy gave a quick, funny sort of sound. "Did you say *Sackett?* Is your name *Sackett?*"

"Sure . . . do you know the name?"

He turned away from me. "Get out . . . get out while you can."

He started off, walking very fast, but when he had taken but a couple of steps he turned around. "Does she know your name? Have you told her that?"

"No . . . no, I never did, come to think on it."

"Of course not . . . of course." He looked at me, but I could not see the expression in his eyes. There was only light enough to see his face under the brim of his hat. "Take my advice and don't tell her . . . not, at least, until you reach Los Angeles—if you do."

He walked away, leaving me almighty puzzled, but convinced the time to leave was now.

# Chapter 2

When I looked into the window of the saloon the men at the bar were still drinking their liquor and talking it up. The black-eyed woman was gone.

The hotel had only four special rooms and I had latched onto one of those. The only other occupied one was the one given to the Robiseau girl, so I slipped in the back door and went to her room and tapped ever so gently.

There was a quick rustle of clothing inside, and something that sounded like a click of a drawed-back gun-hammer, and then her voice, low. "I have a pistol. Go away."

"Ma'am," I whispered right back to her, "you want to go to Los Angeles, you come to this door, an' quick."

She came, easing it open a crack. The pistol looking through the opening was no feisty little-girl pistol. It was a sure enough he-coon of a pistol, a .44 Navy Colt.

"Ma'am, if you want to get to Los Angeles, you get dressed. We've leaving out of here in twenty mintes."

I'll give her this—she didn't say aye, yes, or no, she just lowered that gun muzzle and said, "I'll be ready. At the stable?"

"The ferry," I said, "only we're going to swim it. The ferry stopped crossing at sundown."

I'd never left hold of my gold, nor my rifle, but I stepped across the hall and picked up the rest of my gear, took one longing look at that bed, and then tiptoed down the hall and out to the stable.

When I made my dicker for the horses I'd gotten an old saddle thrown in, and now I saddled up two horses.

We'd be riding those two, and leading two spare saddle horses and my pack horse. By swapping horses, we could make faster time than most anybody coming after us, and I was figuring on that.

But that wasn't the only bee I had in my bonnet. True it was that I'd never ridden those westward trails that lay before us, but I'd listened to a sight of talk about them from those who had, and it came over me that a body might strike off on a new route and make it through, if he was lucky.

That would be something to keep in mind.

She was at the river, carpetbags and all, when I got there with the horses. She had dressed in an all-fired hurry, but she didn't show it. Helping her into the saddle, I got the feel of her arm, and she was all woman, that one. She swung up, hooking one knee around the horn like she was riding a sidesaddle, and we taken off.

The water was dark, and there was more current than a body would expect. Walking our horses into the water, I pointed across. "Make for that peak, and when you get over there, don't call out. If we get separated, just stay put. I'll find you."

Holding my rifle and gunbelt high, I rode on into the water, and she followed.

I felt the stallion's feet go out from under him as he hit deep water.

He was a strong swimmer, and when I glanced back I saw that woman right behind me, her horse swimming strong too. We made it up the bank, and as I turned to glance back I heard a door slam and somebody shouted and swore.

"What the hell?" I said. "They ain't found out a-ready?"

She pulled up beside me. "Maybe the ferryman told them," she said.

"Ferryman? How would he know?"

She turned and looked at me like I was a fool. "Why, I asked him to take us across. He refused."

Me. I'd never hit a woman, but I wanted to right then. I wanted to hit her the worst way. Instead, I just turned my horse and started off into the Dead Mountains, mad enough to tackle a grizzly with my bare hands.

"Ma'am," I said roughly, "you played hell. The reason we started now was to get some distance between us before daylight. Now you've tipped them off and they will be comin' right behind us."

"But they couldn't!" she protested. "He's not—I mean, why would anybody want to catch us?"

"You know that better than me, but even Hardy knew some of those men back at the saloon were there to watch you. He told me so."

She shut up then, having nothing more to say and no chance to say it, for I led off, walking that stallion fast. Having the fresh horse was going to spell my two horses, and they could use the rest.

The trail lay white under the hoofs of the horses; the desert night was still. That liver-colored stallion went out of there like he had a fire under his tail, and I'll hand it to that black-eyed girl. No matter how she had to sit her saddle, she stayed with me.

No telling what those men wanted with her, but in these times there

were white men with bloodier hands than any Indian, and I was asking
for no trouble I could avoid with honor. Just short of daylight I drew up
and we swapped saddles to fresh horses, but it was an hour later before I
made my move.

The Dead Mountains lay behind us and I turned up a dry wash. If my
memory was working along the lines of what I'd been told, this was Piute
Wash and it ran due north for quite a spell, then a dim trail would cut
over toward Piute Spring.

There was no time for talk, and I had no mind for it, wanting only to
put distance between myself and those men back there. They might run
us down, or they might wait until the steamboat came in with whoever
was on it.

At Piute Spring, on the eastern foot of the range, we pulled up long
enough to water the horses and drink a mite ourselves. The valley ahead
of us was mostly flat-seeming land covered with Joshua trees. We went
out of the shadow of the Piute Range and into the Joshuas, and at first
they were scattered, then they thickened up. Once into the Joshuas, we
slowed down to raise as little dust as possible.

There were thousands of those trees there in the valley, and they
offered a mite of cover. From a height, somebody might have picked us
out, but nobody on our own level was likely to, so we pushed on, holding
parallel to the old Government Road from Fort Mojave.

The sun had gone before we sighted the draw I was looking for and,
riding up a hundred yards, came to Rock Spring. There was little water,
which suited me, for when we left I didn't mean for there to be any.

The Robiseau woman looked pale and drawn when I reached up to
take her by the waist to swing her down. Tired as she was, she wasn't
ready to haul down her flag. As her feet touched the ground she let her
hands rest on my forearms and said, "You're very strong."

"I'd better be."

She gave me an odd look, but I turned away and began gathering sticks
for a fire. The spot was sheltered, and there was time for coffee and a
quick meal.

This was something I'd done so often that it was no trick at all, and by
the time I'd stripped the saddles the water was boiling and the food about
ready.

"You haven't told me your name."

"Folks call me Tell."

"Only that?"

"It's enough."

"I am Dorinda Robiseau."

It sounded like a made-up name, but I'd known folks with real names that sounded made up. "Pleased to meet you."

"You haven't asked me why I couldn't wait for the stage."

"Your business."

She acted like she wanted to explain, but I had no plan to get more involved than I was. I'd been fool enough to take her along, but the sooner I got shut of her the better.

Sitting under the stars, we ate a quick meal, then finished the coffee I'd made. "There's something about a campfire . . ." she said. "I like to look into the coals."

"Take your last look," I said. "I'm putting it out." When I'd kicked sand over the coals I added, "Fool thing, looking into a fire. When you look away you're blind . . . and men have been killed thataway."

I saddled up and loaded our packs. She looked like she couldn't believe what I was doing, but I said, "If you're coming with me, get up in the saddle."

"You're going on? *Tonight?*"

"You want your friends to catch us? You can bet if I knew where this spring was, they'll know. In the desert a man's travelin' is pretty well cut and dried by where he can find water."

Whoever those men were, they must be wanting her pretty bad to follow us as they were. Of course, there was a chance they were following *me*. They might be the same outfit that had trailed me to Hardyville. There'd been a bunch of renegades drifting through the country raiding ranches or mine prospects for supplies. Somebody said they were a Frisco outfit that had come down through Nevada.

As for this Robiseau girl, she might be somebody's wife, or she might have been involved in some shady doings out California way. Anyway, they needed her bad enough to chase her.

Meanwhile, I'd been doing some pondering of the situation, and there was nothing about it to make a man content. According to what I'd been told when preparing to start westward, it was twenty miles to the next water at Marl Spring, almost due west of where we were now. Most of that twenty miles lay out on bare desert, and if we started from here now we could make it by daylight—if we didn't stray from the trail.

If we strayed . . . Well, there were bones a-plenty out there on the desert to answer that question. Moreover, I had me a tired woman, in no shape for such a ride.

In those days every saloon was a clearing house for information. Sitting around in a saloon or standing at a bar, loafing in a cow camp or riding the trail, men just naturally talked about places they'd been. It was likely to be all a body would ever get to know about trails or towns until he traveled them, so men listened and remembered.

Nobody reckoned in miles. Not often, at least. Distance was reckoned in time, and a place was a day's ride, or two days' ride, or whatever.

And many a cowhand who had never left Texas could describe in detail the looks of Hickok, Earp, Tilghman, Masterson, or Mathers. If a body wasn't able to recognize the town marshal, he'd best not try to cut any fancy didoes in western towns.

So I knew a good bit about the Mojave, although I'd not crossed it before. I knew what landmarks to look for, and the trouble to expect. Only nobody had told me I'd be crossing the wide sand with a fine-dressed woman behind me.

Well, it was twenty miles to water if I held to the trail, but there was water south along the Providence Mountains, and if we could locate one of those springs we could hole up for the night, then work our way south. We'd be taking big risks, venturing off into the desert thataway, but there was a good chance we'd leave all pursuit behind.

And so it was that when we left out of Rock Spring, we headed south.

The night, as desert nights are inclined to be, was cool . . . almost cold. There were many stars, and around us lifted the jagged shoulders of black, somber-looking mountains. We went at an easy pace, the ground being rough and the country unfamiliar, and we had to pick our way. So it was over an hour of riding before we covered the six miles to Black Canyon.

There was a spring in the canyon, but we took no time to look for it, pushing on toward the south. Getting through the canyon, which was close to impassable, was a struggle. By daylight it might have been no trouble, but at night it used up time, and by the time we covered the four additional miles to Granite Well, we were tuckered.

We made dry camp a short way from the well, bedding down on a patch of drift sand among the rocks. Rolling out my bed, I pointed at it. "You roll up there. I'll sleep on the sand."

"I've no right to take your bed."

"Don't argue," I said shortly. "I can't have you falling out of the saddle tomorrow, and what we did today will look like one of your pink tea parties to what we got ahead of us."

It was rugged, broken country, mostly rock and drift sand, with some low-growing desert brush, and I lay awake for some time, speculating on our chances of getting through. Mostly, folks went by the northern route, following the old Government Road or Spanish Trail across the desert and over Cajon Pass. But with men following us with no good intent, it seemed best to risk the run to the south.

There was another pass down thataway, or so Joe Walker had told me. The Indians had used it a time or two, and some Spanish man had gone through the pass fifty or sixty years before. It was a risky trip, but we Sacketts always had an urge to try new country, and the time was right. As for that black-eyed woman . . . she should see some new country, too. Although I wasn't sure she was going to take to it.

A time or two I glanced over at Dorinda Robiseau. She lay quiet, resting easy, as she should have, for that bed of mine was a good one, and the sand I'd spread it on was deep and free of rocks, more comfortable than many a mattress. I could only see the white of her face, the darkness of her loosened hair.

She would be a trial in the days to come, but somehow I felt better just having her there.

It worried me, though . . . why were those men chasing her? And were they the law?

Remembering the men at the bar, I doubted it. They had a bad look about them. One thing was sure: if we faced up to each other out here in this lonely desert I was going to be glad that I was packing a gun.

That big-shouldered man who had stood with his back to me . . . he worried me. Why was there something familiar about him?

I awakened with a start, coming from a sound sleep to sharp attention. Dorinda was sitting up, wide-eyed. "I heard something," she whispered.
"What?"
"I don't know. Something woke me."

My six-shooter was in my hand, and I looked first at the horses. They were standing heads up, looking off across the desert toward the east.

Rolling up, I put my six-shooter down carefully and shook out my boots —scorpions take notions to hide in boots and such like—and tugged them on.

A glance at the stars told me it was shaping up for daybreak. "Get up, and be very quiet," I said. "We're moving out."

She offered me no argument, and I'll give her this: she made herself ready in quicker time than I'd expected from any tenderfoot woman. By the time I'd saddled fresh horses, she had my bed rolled, and rolled good and tight.

Standing close in the dark, I said, "There's another spring not more than a mile over to the east. Sound carries far through a desert night."

Me, I wasn't altogether sure that whoever had made that sound was that far away, but it could be somebody searching for a water hole.

We stepped into our saddles and I led off, heading due south, and keeping our horses in soft sand wherever I could. The Providence Mountains loomed high on our right, bleak, hard-shouldered mountains.

It was rugged going, but the night was cool and there was enough gray in the sky to enable a man to pick his trail. After riding about eight miles we left the rocks behind and had the Providence Mountains still on our right, with bald and open desert on our left, stretching away for miles toward distant hills.

"We're riding south," she said.

It was a question more than a statement, so I gave her the answer. "You want to get to Los Angeles, don't you? Well, I'm leaving the trail to them. We're going south, and then west through another pass."

What I didn't tell her was that I had only heard of that pass, and had only a rough idea of where it was. I knew that a stage line and a freight road went through that pass to the placer diggings around La Paz, on the Colorado.

The sky turned to lemon over the distant mountains, a warning that the sun would soon be burning over us. Somewhere to the south there were other springs, but I doubted if they would be easily found. The desert has a way of hiding its water in unexpected places, sometimes marked by willows, cottonwood, or palm trees, but often enough right out in a bottom with nothing but low brush around, and not a likely thing to indicate water. And we wouldn't have time to spend looking.

She rode up alongside me. "You're not a very talkative man."

"No, ma'am."

"Are you married?"

"If you're wonderin' about that scar on my cheekbone, I got that in a knife fight in New Orleans."

"You have no family?"

"Me? I got more family than you could shake a stick at. I got family all over the country . . . only I am a lonesome kind of man, given to travel and such. I never was one to abide."

She looked at me curiously and, it seemed to me, kind of sharp. Then she said, "Where are you from, Mr. Tell? You hadn't said."

"No, ma'am. I hadn't."

We rode on for a couple of miles after that. A road runner showed up and raced out ahead of us, seeming glad of the company. Overhead there was nothing but sky, a sky changing from gray to brass with the sun coming up. Those mountains on our right, they were cool now, but within two hours they'd be blasting heat back at us.

"A few miles now, you keep your eyes open. We'll come up to a water hole, and I'd prefer not to miss it."

She offered no comment, and it was just as well. But she was a mighty pretty woman, and I'd have preferred riding easy with her, not worrying about folks coming up on me unexpected.

"You in some kind of trouble, ma'am?"

"I hadn't mentioned it," she said, coolly enough.

Well, that was fair. Only I was taking a risk, helping her this way.

It grew hot . . . and hotter. Not a breath of air stirred. The white sands around us turned to fire.

Heat waves shimmered a veil across the distance. We saw strange pools of water out there on the desert. Sweat trickled into our eyes. Our horses plodded along slowly; sweat streaked the gray film of dust that lay over them, and over us. Neither of us was of any mind to talk now.

From time to time I turned to look back, for we were out in the open, masked only by the shimmering heat waves and the wall of the mountain along which we rode. There was nothing behind us but heat waves and the far-off shoulder of mountain.

Cook's Well was some place along here, but we missed it, and I was of no mind to waste time in search. Blind Spring lay somewhere ahead, and if we missed that, there would be no water until Cottonwood, down at the end of the mountain chain.

Had they cut in after us? Or were they, as I hoped, riding west along the Government Road toward Marl Spring?

"It might make a lot of difference," I spoke out suddenly, "if I knew how anxious they were to find you."

She let her horse go on a few steps before she made answer, and then she said, "The man who is after me would kill you or a half dozen others to put his hands on me . . . and then he would kill me."

Well, that answered that.

At high noon we drew up and I helped her down. I switched saddles and sponged out the mouths of our horses with water from a canteen. We each had a drink, and then we mounted up again and started on.

All the long day through we pushed on, and it was coming on to dark when I finally gave up on Blind Spring. We'd been too far out from the mountain or too close in, one or the other. The water in our canteens was low, and I hated to think what would happen if we didn't find water soon. We might make it, but the horses could not; and without the horses we would be helpless.

At dusk we halted and stripped the saddles from our horses and I worked over them, rubbing them down, sponging out their mouths. Whatever Dorinda thought she wasn't inclined to say, nor was I inclined to listen.

The night came on, soft and dark, with the stars hanging easy in the sky. A cool wind blew up from somewhere, just a smidgin of it, but it felt good.

When I was finished with the horses I dug into my saddlebags for the last of the bread. It was hard and dry, but when I broke off a chunk and passed it to her, she tied into it like it was cake. We sat there on a sandbank, chewing away, and finally she said, "We're in trouble, aren't we?"

"It's like this," I said. "According to what I was told, from the point of the mountain we've got a three-cornered chance. Within three or four miles of this place there are three springs, they say, so we've a fair chance of locating one of them."

There was little time for rest, but trusting to the horses to warn us of any trouble coming, she rolled up in my bed and I hunkered down in the sand, working out a hollow for my body that came up on both sides of me, and there we rested.

In the morning, when I was pulling on my boots in the light of the last lone star, I saw Dorinda was awake, lying quiet, looking up at the star. "This country," I commented, "is hell on women and horses."

She did not turn her head or reply for several minutes, and then when I stood up to sling my gunbelt around my hips she said, "You get me to Los Angeles . . . that's all I ask."

I didn't answer her. With my bandana I carefully wiped the dust from the action of my pistol, checking the roll of the cylinder. She was asking a whole lot more than she knew, and right there I figured not to make any promises I couldn't keep.

When we had saddled up I said to her, "Just let the bridle alone. From here on, our horses might find water quicker by themselves."

Though I'd been told that Cottonwood was over the toe of the mountain from where we were, I decided to chance the other two springs, figuring there was no use wasting time in perhaps the wrong direction. So I headed south and let that stallion have his head.

For a while he plodded on, seeming uninterested in much of anything, but then a change in the wind brought his head up and he quickened his step, bearing off to the right toward what I guessed would be the Old Dad Mountains. But as we drew closer I could see there were two small ranges with a break between them.

In a little cove in the rocks we found a spring. There was a small trickle of water, and we let the horses drink their fill. After filling our canteens, we started on.

A dozen miles further along we found Willow Spring, with a good flow of water and some willows and a few cottonwoods around, most of them no bigger than whipstocks. Leaving Dorinda to freshen up, I took up my

Winchester and hiked it to the crest of the ridge, where I could look over our back trail.

There was a flat rock that lay half in shadow, and down in front of it, about six to eight feet lower, a patch of white drift sand. Sitting on the edge of the rock where the shadow had cooled it off a mite, I studied our back trail toward the end of the Providence Range.

It was hot and still. Far off over the desert a dust devil danced among the Galleta grass and the creosote brush, but I saw no dust of human make. It could be we had shaken them. Maybe we would have no trouble after all.

What made me turn my head I'll never know, but glancing over my left shoulder I caught just a glimpse of a rifle muzzle as somebody drew sight on me.

Mister, I left off of that rock like I was taking a free dive into a swimmin' hole, and I hit that heaped-up sand on my shoulder and rolled over. When I came up it was on one knee, the other leg stretched out ahead of me, and my Winchester coming up to firing position.

The echo of at least two shots hung in the hot desert afternoon. I saw a man come around a rock and I tightened my finger on that trigger and made the dust jump on his jacket.

It was no great shooting, for he was no more than thirty yards off. I'd no idea where he'd come from, but one thing I did know. He wasn't going any place else. That .44 ca'tridge bought him a free ticket to wherever the good Lord intended, and I up and scooted down among those rocks, a-duckin' and a-dodgin' and a-squirmin' among rocks and brush, my shoulders braced for a bullet that never came.

When I hit the brush I was runnin' all out, and the next thing I know there's a squeal of startled irritation and there's that black-eyed woman holding her dress in front of her and starin' at me so fierce I had a notion to go back and face those guns. But I had another notion that beat that one altogether.

"Lady," I said, "unless you want to ride out of here naked, you'd better dress faster'n you ever did. They've come upon us."

A bullet spat sand over my boots and I rolled over in the brush and laid all flat out, peeking through the willow leaves for something to throw lead at. I saw nothing.

The echoes died away, and the afternoon was hot and still as ever. I'd no idea who was out there, or how many, but when they'd started shootin' at me they opened the ball, and I was going to call a few tunes my own self.

After a moment I eased back into the willows and went for the horses. They were out of sight among the rocks, and when I got to them I stood by, waiting for that woman to come up. While I waited I kept a sharp eye out for trouble and kept thinking about that range of hills to the south . . . all of four miles away, and all of it bald desert.

Nobody needed to tell me that whatever we did, we'd have to clear out of here. There was too much cover around from which these springs could be taken under fire. When that witch woman came out of the brush, her black eyes sparking fire, I didn't wait for any fancy talk. I just taken her up by the waist and threw her into the saddle and said, "Ride, lady!" And I went up into my saddle and we taken out of there like hell a-chasin' tanbark.

Somebody started shootin', and I caught time for one quick glance over my shoulder and saw there were four or five anyway, and then two more came up out of the ground right ahead of me. I shot into the chest of the first one, firing my Winchester one-handed, like you'd hold a pistol. The other one let fly at me and damned near busted my eardrums, and then my horse went into him. I heard him scream when a hoof smashed into his chest, but I only had time to hope that hoof wouldn't get hung up on the ribs.

Swinging wide to get that woman and the other horses ahead of me, I levered three fast shots back at those men, but I didn't hit anything but desert and rock. Ricochets have a nasty whine, though, and I caught a picture of the men duckin' for cover . . . and then all they could see of us was our dust.

We had good horses, and those men in tryin' to sneak up on us had left theirs somewhere behind them. We were runnin' all out and reachin' for the shadow of the Bristol Mountains before I looked back and saw them come out of the hills, far back.

Closing in beside the Robiseau woman, I said, "Next time you take a bath it better be in Los Angeles."

# Chapter 3

It worried me that those men had come up on me from out of nowhere. Somebody in the lot of them was a tracker, or a shrewd one at judging what a man had in mind, and it left me uncertain of what to do. Having a woman with me complicated matters . . . or would if I let it.

Whatever they'd had in mind to start off with, it was a shooting matter now. There were three men down, and it was likely all three were dead, or hurting something fierce, and it wasn't likely the others would pull off and forget it.

Until now I'd been lucky—unlucky that they found us at all, but lucky in that I got off scot-free and didn't catch lead myself. Nor the woman or horses.

There was only one thing I could see to do, and that was to make them so miserable trying to catch us that they'd quit . . . if they had quit in them, which I doubted. So far it had cost them, but it was up to me to make it cost them more.

We crossed over the Bristol Mountains and headed due south for a pass in the Sheep Holes, thirty-five or forty miles off, with not a drop of water anywhere between.

On the horizon, not far ahead of us, loomed the black cone c´ vol-canic crater, and the black of a lava field. Beyond lay a wide dry lake, and I pointed our horses right at the spot where lava and dry lake joined, and we rode on.

After a while, when we looked back, the notch in the mountains through which we had come was gone, vanished behind a shoulder of the mountain. There was no sound, there was no movement but our own, and the tiny puffs of white dust that lifted from the face of the *playa* as our horses walked.

Behind us were shimmering heat waves, before us and around us the air wavered, and changed the looks of things. Small rocks seemed to tower above the desert, and the sparse brush seemed to be trees. Sweat streaked the flanks of our horses, dust rose around us. We were in a lost world, shut out from all about us by distance and by the shimmering heat.

Far off, something more than twenty miles away, loomed a blue range of hills . . . the Sheep Hole Mountains. Beyond them would be more desert and more mountains.

Would they follow us? Or, wiser than we were, mightn't they turn and ride right to Los Angeles, knowing we would come there?

Only, of course, they did not know. We might go to San Diego, or we might ride back north and go to San Francisco along the coast road.

They had to follow, and before they caught up with us I figured to lead them a chase. If they wanted tracks to follow, I aimed to show them a-plenty, and across some wild country. Only thing was, this black-eyed woman wasn't going to like it. In fact, I figured she regretted her bargain already. What waited her when those men caught up with us, I couldn't say, but it would have to be almighty bad to equal what lay ahead of us now.

Joe Walker and Old Bill Williams, mountain men both of them, had told me a good deal about the Mojave, but I'd learned of it from others as well, including a couple of Hualapai Indians I'd met in Prescott, both of whom had raided the ranchos for horses. It had been these Indians who told me most of what I knew of San Gorgonio Pass.

Desert travel was not new to me, for I'd crossed the cap rock of west Texas by the Goodnight-Loving Trail, and I'd been across the White Sands of New Mexico, as well as made a trip up the *Jornada del Muerto,* the "journey of death," so I was no tenderfoot when it came to deserts.

The desert can be a friendly place to a man on the dodge, but it is always better to hole up some place and wait for sundown. We were doing the worst thing a body could do in traveling by day, under a hot sun. The trouble was, those men back there behind us weren't about to give us any time.

Nobody knew better than me how lucky I'd been in that shindig back there, and it wasn't likely to happen that way again.

We pushed on, sagging in the saddle, the horses plodding steadily. Only me, I taken a look, time to time, to see if anything was gaining on us. Twice we stopped and I sponged out the horses' mouths and gave that Dorinda girl a mouthful of water to drink.

At sundown we could see mountains close ahead of us, and I began searching for the pass. One long arm of mountain had showed up to the east of us, and soon there was another on our right. A notch showed itself and I headed for that, glancing back one last time. There was a thin trail of something that might be dust, hanging against the sky.

In the cool dark, with a kit fox yapping somewhere up in the rocks, we rode through the Sheep Hole Mountains and made dry camp in a tiny cove.

Me, I was dead beat, and when I took that black-eyed Dorinda from her horse she could scarce stand, so I helped her to a place on the sand and kindled ourselves a hatful of fire and made coffee. Nobody needed to tell me how much she needed a hot drink, and I wasn't against the idea myself. Meanwhile, I checked out my Winchester, then my pistol. Rummaging around in my bedroll, I dug out a spare Colt, and made sure it was loaded, too.

"You killed a man back there," she said suddenly.

"Yes, ma'am. Maybe two or three."

"You don't seem bothered by it."

"They were comin' at me."

I poured out a cup of coffee for her and sat back on my heels, far enough from the fire not to be easily seen, and far enough from the crackle of the flames to hear if anything came upon us.

"I never had it in mind to shoot at any man, ma'am, but when somebody takes up a gun and comes for you in anger, he borrows grief. He was fetching trouble, so I gave him what he asked for."

She was half asleep already, and I passed her over a piece of jerked beef to chew on. "Go ahead," I told her, "it doesn't look like much, but there's a lot of stayin' quality in it."

After chewing a while myself, I said, "Carryin' a gun is a chancy thing. Sooner or later a man is put in position to use it. And a body has to figure that if somebody packs iron he plans to use it when the time comes; and if he draws it out, he plans to shoot."

I saw that she was fast asleep, so I covered her with a blanket and killed the fire. Then I went out and rubbed my horses down and gave them water, just a mite squeezed into their mouths. It wasn't much, and they wished for more; but it was all I had to offer, and it's likely they understood.

Taking my Winchester, I prowled around, and stood off under the stars, listening. This was spooky country, with big Joshua trees hither and yon, any one of which might be a man standing there. But the desert night was cool, and mean-tired though I was, it felt likely to my spirit.

Work and war never gave me much time for poetry, but there was a man in my outfit during the fighting near Shiloh who fancied it, and a time or two he'd quoted things at me from a book he carried in his shirt. I thought of it now, wishing I had some of those words he used to speak of the desert night.

Sitting down on a rock, I sort of listened and waited, studying the night with my ears, and each sound held meaning for me. Sometimes I had to sort the sounds a mite, but I knew what each one was . . . and I heard no sound of man nor horse, no creak of saddle, clink of metal, or brush of garment upon stone.

That woman back there was done in. Like it or not, we had to hole up somewhere and give her time to rest, but the worst of it was, one of those men in that outfit trailing us was a tracker and a hunter, and a sight better than most. It was that man who worried me, for if he continued to be as good as he'd been so far, we would be facing a showdown a lot sooner than I hoped.

More and more I wondered what I'd got myself into, and what Dorinda Robiseau had done to make them want her so much.

Not that she wasn't a beautiful woman, and the kind of woman any man would want. Even now, tired out as she was, she was lovely. But there was more to it than that. And the chances were good that I'd gotten myself on the wrong side of the law. Still, none of those men back at Hardyville had been wearing a badge . . . nor did they look likely to. Though all the men who wore badges through the western lands could not be said to measure up to a proper standard.

After a while I went back to our corner, checked the horses again, and burrowed into the sand to sleep.

But sleep did not come, dead tired though I was, for it came upon me that I knew mighty little about Dorinda Robiseau—not where she came from, who she was, nor where she planned to go. There was no telling about her, and all I had was my first suspicions that she was a witch woman.

Not that I place much stock in witches. All my life I'd heard tell of them, but I had never seen one, nor anything of their doings that I could swear to. . . .

Somewhere along in there, I sort of dropped off, and the next thing I knew it was daylight.

Broad, bright daylight . . .

The sun on my face awakened me, and I sat up fast and looked about.

A moment there, I couldn't place where I was, and then I saw the girl and she was a-settin' up, too.

"We slept over," I said, "and I was a fool to chance it."

About us the mountain walls lifted up steeply, in jagged, broken slopes. Up these a man on foot could climb, with some struggle and skill. Before us, and to the south, the desert lay open, masked only by a drift of sand, a pair of crowded Joshuas, and some small brush. On the horizon to the south, maybe twelve to fourteen miles off, were the Pinto Mountains.

The cove in which we were hidden comprised maybe an acre of flat ground and banked sand. There were some good graze plants in the bottom, and I had the five horses pegged out among them. Sand had heaped across the opening of the cove so that with the brush and all it was mighty near invisible from the outside, without a man riding up to the top of the sand hill.

It was that which saved us, that and the wind being so that none of the horses caught scent of one another. For when I went up to the top of the sand I could see those riders out there, not fifty yards away, and all bunched together, talking.

During the night there had been a wind stirring, not much, but enough to drift sand in this locality where it was loose, and our trail had drifted over. Evidently they had lost track of us and were talking it over to decide which was the most likely route for us.

The side of the mountain was drifted deep with that loose white sand. In some places it looked fit to bury whole sections of the range. So anybody taking a quick look our way would think there was nothing anywhere around but sand and rock.

Me, I motioned back to Dorinda to be still, and I lay there flat out on the sand with only the top of my head showing, and it screened by low brush and the base of a Joshua tree. My Winchester was with me, looking one-eyed at those men down there, ready to speak its piece if they started our way.

There was argument going on among them, but I could only guess at the words. Finally they turned and rode off toward the east and the spring at Twenty-Nine Palms.

That was the next worst thing to their finding us, because there was no nearer water that I knew of, and our canteens were shaking light with only mouthfuls of water remaining.

Lying there in the sand, I watched them ride off. By the time they reached Twenty-Nine Palms they would figure it out that they were ahead of us, and the chances were they would sit right there by the water and wait for us, knowing that sooner or later we had to show up.

Oh, they would have it figured, all right! They would know about how much water we carried, and about how fast we used it, and right this minute they could guess within a quart the amount of water we had now . . . maybe closer.

So I watched them ride away, and I knew that, riding away in the direction we must go, they carried our lives along with them. It was no easy thing, seeing them ride off, knowing the girl behind me was depending on me for a way out; and when I thought of what tomorrow would bring—the sun, the dust, the miles upon miles of desert around—I felt fear.

But there was no sense in starting off into the blazing heat of a desert day. With them ahead of us, I could, for the first time, choose our time of travel. Taking up my rifle, I slid down the sand, and then walked back to where Dorinda was resting. From my expression she must have realized that trouble was upon us. She sat up, and, dropping to one knee on the sand, I told her.

There are men who prefer to keep trouble from a woman, but it seems to me that is neither reasonable nor wise. I've always respected the thinking of women, and also their ability to face up to trouble when it comes, and it shouldn't be allowed to come on them unexpected. Many a man has sheltered his wife from his troubles, until suddenly he dies and she awakens to poverty as well as grief. So I gave it to Dorinda hard and cold.

I drew her a diagram on the sand. "This here is Twenty-Nine Palms, and beyond is the San Gorgonio Pass to the coast of the western sea. Right about there is Los Angeles."

"Aren't there other water holes? In some other direction?"

"More'n likely . . . but finding them wouldn't be easy."

She looked up at me. "We'll have to try, won't we?"

Simple as that. Sure, we'd have to try, because as well as I knew anything, I knew those men who had been trailing us would soon know they'd passed us somewhere and, as I'd thought when I watched them ride away, they would just wait for us there by the water.

Making some fire, I burned off the spines from some cholla and beavertail cactus and the horses ate them eagerly, for the pulp was moist. In Texas I've known ranchers to feed their stock that way. In this case, I was thinking more of the water they would get from it.

There was shade in the cove, and we sat tight, letting the day move slowly past. I'd made up my mind to travel no more by day, for, without anybody chasing us, there was no reason. Traveling in full desert sunlight can kill a man or a horse mighty quick without enough water . . . and we hadn't enough.

We did no talking, but I did a lot of thinking.

One time in Prescott I'd heard Paul Weaver yarning about some Mojaves who raided the California ranchos for horses and on their way back were driven from the trail by a sandstorm. With them was a Chemehuevi Indian who guided them to a hidden valley and a water hole in the canyon behind it.

This was in a country covered with Joshua trees and a weird lot of rocks piled up in all sorts of strange shapes. Near the valley there had been one formation I remembered Weaver telling about—he said it looked like a huge potato balanced on three points of rock.

There had been two other water holes he mentioned, but of their location I knew nothing—only that the Chemehuevi had known of them. It was almighty little to begin with, and I was scared.

Twice I went back up to that ridge of sand and looked off to the south, and neither time did my looking give me any room for hope. All I could see was miles upon miles of empty sand or burning rock, mostly dotted with creosote bushes, or here and there cactus or Joshua trees.

When the sun was almost down I put the saddles on our horses, and loaded up our pack horse. Believe me, those horses were ready to go. They had sense enough to know that if we were to get out alive we had to travel. And so, with the dying sun like a red ball of fire over the western mountains, we rode over the sand ridge and headed south into the empty, unknown desert.

After a while a bright star showed up, hanging above the distant mountains, and I chose it for our own, putting my horse's nose on it, and pointing it out to Dorinda.

"What mountains are those?"

"I don't rightly know. Could be the Pinto Range. There's a dozen small chains of mountains through here . . . they all look alike the first time you see them."

"You are risking your life because of me."

"Didn't figure on it."

Beauty does something for a woman—some of them, anyway. Taking a side glance at Dorinda, I could see that even out here she'd made an effort to brush up and comb out. For a girl who'd been riding and sleeping out, with no water and all, she looked almighty pert. And I could imagine how I looked, a tall man with a big-boned, wedge-shaped face, a scar on my cheekbone, and by now a heavy growth of beard. Nobody ever claimed I was pretty, but by now I sure must look like an old grizzly coming out of hibernation. The only brushing up I'd done was to beat the dust off my hat and wipe my guns off careful.

Only two things a man really needs in this country to survive, a gun and a horse. . . . Come to think of it, though, there is something else. Water.

Dorinda was thinking of it, too. She rode up beside me again and said, "However can we find water out there?"

"We've got to be lucky. In desert country you can find it up a canyon, or somewhere where the rock is faulted, or at the lowest point of a basin. But unless a body sees trees out in the bottom, I'd not chance that.

"Sometimes where a ridge pushes into the desert you'll find water, but mostly you look for trees or brush of a kind that needs water. Palm trees grow with their feet in the water and their head in the sun—that's what they say. It usually is only a little way to water if you see palms growing. Willows, cottonwood . . . they are good indicators, too.

"But you can't rely on that. Mostly a body should look for animal tracks, or birds flying, but mostly for bees. I've found that bees can lead a man to water faster than anything, but it's chancy . . . it's chancy."

I felt pretty sure there probably weren't five water holes within a hundred square miles . . . not that you could rely on. Tilting my hat brim down, I studied those hills. It was a cinch we weren't going to find anything this side of the mountains.

The night was cool. The stars hung bright above us, and the horses moved ahead, walking with a steady, distance-eating gait. Several times I opened my mouth and drank in great gulps of that cool air.

An hour passed, and then another. But the mountains seemed no nearer. We were out on the bare desert, and I worried over every bit of talk I'd heard of the Mojave, trying to recall anything that might be of help.

When, judging by the stars, two hours more had gone by, I drew up and got down, and helped Dorinda from the saddle. She was dead beat, I could feel it in her, and she sank onto the sand and just stayed there whilst I swapped saddles and talked encouragement to the horses. They were going to need it.

"How far have we come?" she asked.

"Maybe twelve miles, if you figure a beeline. More, by the way we've had to travel."

"How much further to the mountains? We'll rest then, won't we?"

"We won't rest until we find water . . . if we do."

She got up into the saddle again with some help from me, and we started on, only this time I walked. At least, I walked for the first couple of miles. When I began to stumble, as near asleep as awake, I climbed into the saddle myself.

Sometime after that, I dozed in the saddle, and when my eyes opened again the horses had stopped and it was gray in the east.

We had come up to a deep, sandy wash. Looking around, I saw that witch woman, looking like nothing but a tired girl, just sagging in the saddle and hanging on by sheer grit. My pack horse was gone.

Staring back over the desert, I figured I could see something back there, a black spot of something on the sand.

"You got anything in that outfit of yours that you can't afford to lose?" I asked.

She looked up at me, staring stupidly for a moment before the sense of the words reached her. Then she turned to look, and after a moment she shook her head.

"He may come on after us." I said. "It'll be in him to come after the other horses if he's able. They've been carrying more weight, but they're better stuff than him."

Looking up at her, I added, "Ma'am, you've got some solid stuff in you, too. You surely have."

But her lips were cracked and swollen, and there was no more spark to her than nothing. Nor in me, neither.

Right and left I looked, seeking a way through that wash. The banks were steep, and I feared to slide my horses down for fear they'd never get up after reaching bottom. At last I saw a place that looked like a broken-down bank, so I turned and headed for it. The sky was already lighter, and without water we would last no time in our condition if the sun caught us here.

We got through the wash, although I had to dismount and bully and harry the horses to get them up the opposite bank. A break in the mountains showed ahead of us, and I headed for it. From somewhere there came a burst of energy . . . most likely the last I had.

The sun was an hour old before we found shelter in the lee of a shoulder of rock. That horse of hers just quit cold, and I didn't blame him.

Dumping our saddle gear in the shade of the rocks, I stared around. There wasn't even a barrel cactus within sight, although this was the country in which they grew. Nor was there anything I could use to feed the horses or to give them a bit of moisture. There was nothing but creosote, and mighty little of that.

Sizing up those horses, I could see they weren't going to travel much further, for they were used up. Two of them, the big stallion and my own original horse, might go on for a while. Even the second horse I'd bought from Hardy . . . but that was a question. We had to have water.

Dorinda had slumped over on the sand, but me, I walked out a ways from where she lay and studied the sand. For about an hour I criss-crossed back and forth over the desert around and about, studying for tracks. Mighty few were to be seen, and none of them were bunched up and traveling the same route, which might indicate water.

Most desert creatures get along either without any water at all, or on mighty little, getting what moisture they need from what they feed on, be it plants or animals. But most will take water when they can get it, and some of them have to have it.

Finally I gave up and came back and sat down. I must have dozed off; when I woke up my throat was so parched I could scarce swallow, and when I tried to open my mouth I could feel my lips cracking with dryness. My tongue was like a stick in my mouth, and I knew our time was short.

The girl was asleep, or maybe passed out. I didn't look to see. One of the horses was stretched out on the ground, the others slumped three-legged, their heads hanging. My face felt stiff, and when I moved my eyeballs they seemed to grate in their sockets.

Catching hold of a rock, I pulled myself up and decided to try it one more time. And like before, I taken up a canteen and slung it around my neck where it couldn't slip off.

We'd slumped down at the foot of a great chunk of white granite, off by itself from the foot of the mountain. Others like it were around, and, starved for water though I was, I had sense enough to fix the shape of it in my mind . . . else I might never find my way back. Not that it was going to matter, if I didn't find water.

"I'll find water," I said out loud.

If she heard me at all, she gave no sign of it, but just lay there on the sand. So I turned and walked off.

The desert sand was white and hot, and the sunlight blazed back from the sand into my face and there was no shielding myself from it. After I had taken only a few steps I began to stagger. Once I fell against a rock and stood there for several minutes, I guess, before I got started again.

My eyes were on the sand, for I was hunting tracks. But something buzzed in my brain—something like an alarm bell of some kind—and then it was gone. Pausing, I felt my eyes blinking and I made my head turn, and there was a man standing on a rock some distance off.

As my eyes focused on him he lifted a rifle, sunlight glinted on the barrel, and he fired. Instinct made me grab for my gun, but the movement over-balanced me and I fell. That much I remember . . . and then nothing else for a long time.

Cold . . . I was cold.

Feebly, I tried to burrow into the samd for warmth, but warmth would not come. My eyes opened, and I tried to swallow. My throat was raw, and the membranes of it chafed and tightened with the attempt.

Somehow I got my hands under me and lifted myself up. It was night, it was cold, and it was very dark. Stars were out, a chill wind was blowing . . . but I was alive.

Alive . . .

I started to crawl.

Suddenly a coyote yapped weirdly, not very far off, somewhere among the rocks, and I stopped.

When I started to crawl again something moved near me and something clicked on stone.

I knew that sound. A hoof . . . but not a horse.

Forcing my stiff neck to bend, I looked up and saw it there, black against the sky for an instant. A bighorn sheep. . . .

In the half-delirium that clouded my brain I felt irritation at the thought of the name. The bighorn was no more a sheep than I was. It was a deer. It had a body like a deer, hair like a deer . . . even the same color. Only the horns were different.

I crawled on, and the blood started moving within me. Pain awakened, I felt raw and torn inside, my body ached.

The bighorn would have to have water, so there must be water near. Forcing my muddled thoughts into line, I struggled to think more clearly. The bighorn had gone into the canyon, so the water must be there . . . at this hour he would be joining others of his kind at water, or would be leaving it.

Somehow I moved on, and then all movement ceased. Something stirred in me and I tried to move on, but I could not.

And then I felt the sun upon my back, and it was hot, terribly hot. My eyes opened and I struggled. In my mind was terror—terror of death, terror of dying here, like this. . . . And there was memory of the sheep. Pulling myself to hands and knees, I stared blearily around for tracks, and found none, for I had crawled upon the rock, bare rock where I saw not even the scars from hoofs.

Suddenly something buzzed by me and sang off into the distance.

A bullet? The sound lasted too long.

Struggling on, I paused again, hearing a queer, cricket-like sound. I knew that sound. It was the croaking made by the red-spotted frog.

And I knew something else. The life of that frog was lived in canyons or in places near permanent springs or seeps.

Water was near.

With a lunge, I came to my feet as though pricked with a knife point. Wildly, I stared around, and saw nothing.

And then that sound again . . . something buzzed by me that I knew for a bee. Quickly I started after it, taking three faltering steps before realizing that the sound had died away.

Scrambling and falling among the rocks, I came upon it suddenly—a basin in the white granite, filled to the brim with water . . . and it was no mirage.

I crawled down to it and splashed water into my face, then scooped a handful into my mouth and held it there, feeling the delicious coolness, and then the actual pain as some trickled slowly down my throat.

It seemed a long time that I lay there, letting that one gulp of water ease down my raw throat. And then after a bit I tried again.

The sun was blistering hot on the granite where I lay, so I crawled into the shade alongside the water. There was room to stretch out there. Several times I drank . . . once my stomach tried to retch.

When perhaps an hour had passed, I began to think.

The girl was back there . . . Dorinda. She and the horses . . .

But there had been a man who shot at me. Or had that been delirium?

Weakly, I struggled to sit up, and then I filled the canteen. I was going back.

I had to go back. I had to know.

# Chapter 4

My old tracks were on the sand to guide me, and I found the place where I had fallen in attempting to draw and return the fire of the man with the rifle. There was a rock where such a man might have stood, some distance off, but in plain sight. Around where I had fallen there were no tracks but my own.

More carefully now—for it might not be delirium that the man had shot at me—I moved among the rocks of white granite toward the place. . . .

Gone . . .

Dorinda was gone, my horses were gone, my packs and my gold were gone. Nothing was left.

There had been four or five riders, and they had approached from the west. They had taken Dorinda, my Winchester, my horses—and they had vanished.

They must have believed me dead. Here I was, alone, on foot, and miles from any possible help.

Standing there in the partial shade of that rock, I knew that I was in more trouble than I had ever been in my life. I had a canteen of water and a pistol with a belt of ammunition. But I had no horse, no food, and no blanket. The nearest settlement of which I knew was maybe a hundred miles away to the west—a Mormon town called San Bernardino.

For the moment my canteen was filled with water, and I had recently drunk. The tank that I had found in the rocks was a half-mile back up the draw; if I retraced my steps and camped there for the night I should have walked a mile to no purpose.

Pa, he always taught us boys to make up our minds, and once made up, to act on what we decided, and not waste time quibbling about. So I taken up my left foot and stepped out toward the west and followed it with my right, and I was on my way.

But I wasn't going far at midday, which it was by now. So I walked on from one of those islands of rock to another, sometimes resting in the shade a mite, then going on to another one, but always holding to the west. And away down inside me I began to get mad.

Until then I hadn't been mad, for we Sacketts, man and boy, are slow to anger, but when we come to it we are a fierce and awful people.

Another thing Pa had taught us boys was that anger is a killing thing: it kills the man who angers, for each rage leaves him less than he had been before—it takes something from him.

When that black-eyed girl back there at Hardyville asked me to help her get on to Los Angeles, I suspicioned trouble, but woman-made trouble, nothing like this. Now those men who chased after her had got her, and they had shot at me, left me for dead. They had taken my outfit and my gold.

Well, now, that was enough to make a body upset. Seemed to me this was a time for anger, and it came upon me. It was no wild, fly-off-the-handle rage, but a cold, deep-burning anger that pointed me at them like a pistol.

They would have gone to Los Angeles, but no matter. Wherever they had gone, I would find them.

A journey, somebody said, begins with one step, so I taken that step. I was started, and before I set my foot down for the last time on that journey there would be blood on the moon.

At sundown I struck out, headed westward. My life depended on getting to water before my canteen emptied. By now they had probably left the Palms, but that was away off to the north and beyond my direction now. I was going to hold westward, and hope.

A man afoot can walk a horse down. It has been done many a time, and while I had no idea of walking them down, if I could come up to water and find food I'd not be far behind them when they reached Los Angeles.

Food . . .

My stomach was already chafing my backbone from hunger, and my belly sure was thinking my throat must be cut, it had been so long since I'd eaten. Nonetheless, I just kept picking my feet up and putting them down.

We mountain boys were all walkers. Mostly it was the fastest way to get any place back in the hills, for often a boy could cross a mountain afoot where no horse could go . . . if he owned a horse, or even a mule.

Westward the mountains lifted up maybe a thousand feet above the desert, but I'd crossed higher mountains, and if I couldn't go through, I'd go over.

Due west I walked, keeping a steady pace for upwards of an hour, then resting a few minutes and going on again. Two, three times I found rough going that held me up, but by moonrise I was close to the mountains and I picked out a narrow Indian trail or sheep trail. It showed white against the desert and between the rocks; I'd followed many such, and recognized it for what it was.

Most such trails are narrow, maybe four to eight inches wide, and usually easier to see from a distance than close up. I mean, from a cliff or ridge you can pick them out at quite a distance; but on the ground and close up they are hard to find, unless in regular use. But a body gets a knack for seeing them after a bit.

This one went south along the mountains, and I followed it for about a half-mile until it joined up with a westbound trail that cut into the mountains. Following it over and through the hills I found another spring at the foot of a granite spur that stretched out into a high mountain valley. The spring was marked by two patches of white granite, easy to see against the dark rock of the mountain.

In drift sand close by, I bedded down and made some sleep, after a long pull at the water in my canteen. Come daybreak, I drank from the spring, refilled my canteen, and took off to the westward while the sun was still below the horizon.

It came on me then if I was to eat I'd have to look sharp, or maybe lay out near a water hole of a night and try to kill something that came for water. A sheep would be best, but one more day without grub and I'd tackle a desert wolf or most anything that walked or flew—or crawled, for that matter.

It was about then that I came up to the horse tracks.

There must have been fifty in the lot, maybe more, and they were pretty well strung out. These were not wild stuff, but shod horses, most of them, and they were driven. As near as I could tell, they were driven by two men.

Right away I took to the rocks to study it out. The way it seemed to me, this was no country for an honest man to be driving horses. There were no ranches anywhere within miles, and no occasion for anybody to be moving a herd through here that I could grasp hold of. Anybody moving horses would be likely to keep to well-traveled trails and known water holes.

Then I recalled Old Bill Williams, and what Joe Walker had told me about the characters from Arizona who used to steal horses in California and drive them across the desert to sell in Arizona . . . or the other way around. Maybe somebody was still doing it.

Horses meant water; and wherever these horses were going, it was a place known to the drovers, who were heading them right across country *toward* something.

That something must mean a hide-out, a camp. And that meant grub. It also could mean a horse for me.

Hunkered down among those big old rocks, I gave study to the problem. If the men driving the horses were thieves, they wouldn't take it kindly of me to come upon them, and they might start blasting at me with firearms. Nevertheless, they would have grub, which I needed, and they would have horses.

For maybe a half-hour I held my place, and gave the time to studying the country around. You never saw such a jumble of boulders, heaped-up rock, and cactus in your life.

And then of a sudden I recalled what I'd been told about a balanced rock near a Hidden Valley, a rock like a huge potato. For there, not more than a few hundred yards off, was just such a rock.

The trouble was, in a jumble of rocks such as that a man might look for years and not find the entrance to the valley unless he was mighty lucky, or found some tracks. And there was likely a lookout somewhere up among the rocks. No matter—I had to take my look.

Right at that moment I didn't much care. I was hungry, and I was dead tired, and I had been put upon by the men hunting that woman. They had taken my outfit and they had left me for dead, and before this thing was over they would pay through their hides.

So I started to follow those tracks.

"You huntin' something?"

The voice came out of nowhere. I was smart enough to freeze right in my tracks, and when I looked up I saw a man standing there with a Winchester aimed at my belt buckle. He was a rough-looking character wearing a flat-brimmed hat and beat-up chaps.

"You're damned right I am," I said irritably. "I'm hunting three square meals and a horse."

He chuckled at me. "Now you don't tell me you come all this way afoot?"

"No," I said, "I been set afoot. And when I get up in the middle of a horse I'm headed for Los Angeles to find those who left me."

"You a Los Angeles hombre?"

"Arizona," I said. "I started over here to buy horses and goods to take back, and in Hardyville I ran into this woman."

He lowered his rifle. "You don't look like the law," he said, "so come along. We can feed you, anyway."

He walked over to some rocks and he said, "You've got to crawl." He indicated a hole where two rocks sort of leaned together, and I got down and crawled through the hole. When I stood up, I was inside of Hidden Valley.

From where I could see, it looked to be at least a half-mile long, although some of it may have been out of sight. The two walls of rock, mostly heaped-up boulders, were only a few hundred feet apart. Scattered over the bottom of the valley, there must have been sixty or seventy head of good horses.

This gent who showed me in pointed with his Winchester and we walked along the wall of rock where there were some caves and a spring . . . and lots of bees buzzing about.

There was a smidgin of fire going, and three or four gents sprawled around. They sat up when we came into sight.

"What you got there, Willie?" It was a tall man with some teeth missing. "You caught you a pigeon?"

"You think I'm a pigeon," I said, "you just stack your duds and grease your skids and I'll whup you down to a frazzle. . . . After I've been fed."

So they asked me about it, and I laid it on the line for them, having no cause to lie, and they listened. Only thing I didn't tell them was that last shot fired at me. Seemed to me they'd be more sympathetic if they figured I'd been left afoot a-purpose.

Willie put down his rifle and shook out a cup and filled it with coffee. "Start on that. Even if we decide to shoot you, you'll take it better on a full stomach."

"They'd no cause to set you afoot," the tall man said irritably.

Like the Good Book said, I had fallen among thieves, but they were a rough and ready lot, having no bones to pick with me, and no man likes it to be set afoot.

When I'd eaten a mess of beans, some sourdough bread with honey, and about two pounds of good bacon, I pushed back and relaxed with another cup of coffee.

"We'd better give him a horse, Charlie," Willie said. "If he eats like that we can't pack grub enough to feed him."

Charlie rolled a smoke, and when he had lit up he said, "Did you get a good look at any of those men?"

When I had given a description of them—and I'd not found it necessary to tell about the men killed in the gun battle further north—Charlie looked over at Willie and said, "This here friend of yours has bought himself a packet. I figure we should let him have a horse."

Willie and Charlie Button they were, and known men. Somehow they had come upon this Hidden Valley and were using it to hide stolen stock . . . I had my own hunch about that, believing they had learned of it from Peg-Leg Smith, who devoted more time to horse stealing than to losing mines.

"What I can't figure," I said, "is how you get those horses in here in the first place. That's a mighty small hole for a horse."

I didn't get an answer to this.

"You tell me you like to travel by dark," Willie said. "All right, you rest up today. When dark comes we'll give you a horse and point you right. The rest is up to you."

"I'll be obliged."

They never said ary a word about me saying nothing about their hide-out, nor did they need to.

Sure enough, Willie showed me out through the same hole by which I crawled in, and when we got outside there was Charlie and a couple of others with a fine-looking sorrel horse.

"The horse is yours," Charlie said. "You ride him on out of here."

Well, I couldn't avoid it somehow. I just looked at Charlie and said, "How good is my title to this horse?"

Charlie grinned at me. "If you're ridin' west your title is good; if you're ridin' toward Arizona, it ain't good."

Title or not, those boys loaned me a good horse. He just reached out those long legs of his and went away from there, and with the bait of grub they packed for me, I made an easy ride of it.

The hotel of Mr. Gabriel Allen was the place to put up, and when I'd paid my bit from the few dollars of gold in my pockets, I arranged for a bath and bought a razor and soap.

Nobody had got at the money in my pockets, carried for day-to-day expense, so now I went the whole hog and spent twelve dollars for a new suit of clothes. Things seemed almighty high here in the city, for I could have bought the same suit in Prescott for ten dollars. Of course, this wasn't actually the city—Los Angeles was still thirteen or fourteen miles off—but prices were the same. I spent another dollar and a half for a white shirt, and when the man offered to throw in a necktie if I bought two more, I did so.

A boy on the corner blacked my boots for a nickel, so when I finally mounted up to ride into Los Angeles I was dressed for the city, and looked elegant enough for any of those fine homes along San Pedro or Main streets.

So I rode into town and put up at the Pico House, which was the biggest, finest-looking building I ever did see. It had been opened in 1870, and was all of three stories high and built of blue granite. It stood right on the corner of Main Street and the Plaza.

The room they gave me was almost as large as our whole cabin back in the mountains, and when I had brushed up and combed my hair again, I checked my gun. Somebody owed me some horses, thirty pounds of gold, and a couple of good saddles, and I was going to have them back.

Little was my worry over that black-eyed witch girl, for once free of the desert I'd an idea she could care for herself. And so far as she knew, I was dead back there on the sand of the Mojave.

Nonetheless, it was up to me to find out if she was getting a fair shake, and in the way of doing that I would have my gold back, and my horses.

This was the biggest town I ever did see, and I'd suspect there were all of ten thousand people in it. I've heard tell of bigger towns . . . come to think of it, New Orleans was bigger; but that had been long ago, and far away.

It seemed to me no town was large enough to hide that black-eyed woman, and I was right.

First person I saw when I came down stairs into the main lobby of the Pico House was Dorinda Robiseau.

She was across the room from me and she was talking to two men, dressed-up city folks. One of them was a big young man, handsome as all get out, but somehow he looked to me like a shorthorn. Although that slight bulge on the right side of his waist in front gave me to wonder. The other man, maybe fifty-odd years old, was shorter and square-shouldered.

Walking up to them, I said, "Ma'am, I'm glad to see you made it all right."

Her back had been toward me and there was an instant when it stayed toward me. Then she turned and looked me right in the eye and said, "I beg your pardon? Were you speaking to me?"

The two men who stood with her both looked at me as if I had crawled out from under a log. The big young man started to speak, but I said, "When I got back and found you gone, I was some worried."

"I am afraid," she spoke coolly, "you have made a mistake. I have no idea who or what you are talking about."

Well, I started to explain. "Why, out there in the Mojave, ma'am, I—"

The young man broke in on me. "You heard the lady. She doesn't know you."

He turned his back to me and took her by the arm, and they walked off and left me standing there.

Felt like a country fool, I did, them turning from me like that, and when I glanced around several people were looking at me and smiling with amusement. Made me mad, deep down. And me, traipsing over the desert, fighting and all to get her to safety, and then turned down like some stranger!

The more I thought of it the more it irritated me, and then it came over me that whilst I'd found her, I still hadn't my outfit back. I started to follow after them, but they were gone, clean out of sight.

There was a black carriage going away from the hotel, and mayhap they'd stepped into that.

Anyway, I was going to get my gold.

There were a hundred and ten saloons in Los Angeles about that time, but the one I'd been told to head for was Buffum's. It was the place to hear things, and was the most elegant in town. Buffum's . . . that was the place.

Putting on my hat I stepped outside, and as I did so a man moved up beside me. He was a slender, dark young man. A Mexican . . . or a Californian.

He spoke to me quietly. "It is of a possibility, señor, that we have interests in common."

"You're doing the talking."

"It is the dark-eyed señorita has been ill, and confined to her room. I think this is untrue. I believe she left Los Angeles and was brought back."

"Mister," I said, and I stopped and looked at him with no pleasant thoughts in my mind, "I expect what the lady does is her business."

"Ah? Perhaps. The señor is gallant, but is he also wise? The lady is not to be trusted, señor, nor those about her. And they are dangerous. Dangerous to me, but just as dangerous to you also. They will try to kill you."

It went against my nature to hear evil spoken of a woman, yet had I not myself figured her for a witch woman?

"We can talk at Buffum's," I said, "if you've got anything to say. I figure there might be somebody there that I'm hunting."

"There are a hundred and ten saloons in Los Angeles, of which Buffum's is only the finest, not necessarily the best place to look."

Maybe . . . anyway, it was a place I'd heard tell of, and a place to start. Meanwhile, I had pondering to do. And it just might be this gent with me could point out some trail sign I'd missed. Leastways, he knew the town, and I did not.

It came over me that he was probably shaping truth when he declared that black-eyed girl was not to be trusted. But she had been running scared . . . of *what*?

Thinking back, I recalled something Hardy had said that night when I bought the horses from him before crossing the river. When he learned my name was Sackett he advised me not to tell Dorinda. Why was that? What had my name to do with it?

At a table in Buffum's we ordered beer and sat back to watch. The place was crowded with a mixed lot of Spanish men and frontiersmen, businessmen and farmers.

"I was born here," my friend commented suddenly. "My name is Roderigo Enriquez. I love this place, but it is changing, changing too much for my people."

As he spoke I saw across the room a man who looked like one of those I had seen that last night in Hardyville. He stood at the bar in conversation with another man whom I could not see because of those between us.

"My people are not thrifty," my companion went on, "and life in California has been too easy. They have not had to think about money, and there has always been enough to eat; so they are not able to compete in business with the Yankees. The lucky families are those into whom Yankees have married, yet even that is not always enough. As in our own case."

About that time I wasn't paying attention the way politeness demands, for I had my eyes on that man across the room. I was feeling the pistol on my hip, and was ready to move to follow him if he started to leave.

"The Yankee who married into my family was a pirate."

"I've heard of him. Joseph Chapman."

"No, this is another man. Señor Chapman is a good man, and he is a good citizen. My grandfather, Ben Mandrin, is like him in some respects. Only my grandfather was very much a pirate, and a very hard man . . . except to his family."

The man across the room finished his drink and he was not ordering another.

Shifting in my chair, I made ready to rise, but Roderigo seemed not to notice. "My people lived too easy for too many years, and now that they must compete they lack the capacity. We will lose much."

"Sit tight. Just hang on."

"No, it is not enough. The drouth we have had for two years now . . . it has placed us in debt. And my grandfather signed a note for a friend, the bank failed, and the note will soon be due. We cannot expect an extension."

Me, I was scarcely listening. My attention was all centered on the man I figured to follow, once he started to leave.

"It was Dorinda Robiseau who got him to sign the note."

That stopped me. All Roderigo had been saying had seemed small talk, had seemed like something far away from me, for I had no California land, nor did I know anybody who had any. Now it suddenly seemed to tie in somehow.

"You mean she done it a-purpose?"

"One cannot always prove what one knows, but I believe there was agreement between the directors of the bank and the man with whom Dorinda Robiseau is working. I believe that she got my grandfather to sign the note for his friend when plans had been made to allow the bank to fail."

It made a kind of sense, what he said. The bank was already in a bad way, due to drouth and the resulting loss of cattle and crops. With the bank in serious trouble, if a man showed up offering a chunk of gold money and a chance to get out from under the crash—why, those bankers would be apt to accept . . . if they had larceny in them.

Yes, this made a crooked sort of sense. All the banker had to do was go to his friend Ben Mandrin and get him to sign a note . . . with Dorinda to help.

Those old-time California folks were mighty free-handed with money . . . one man used to keep a big kettle full of it in his patio, and anybody who needed any just dipped in and helped themselves. They were pleasant, easy-going folks and living was no problem. Those around them were much as they were, so it worked out all right . . . until the gold rush and the boom that followed brought another type of man into the country.

The miners and the settlers came first, and most of them were as free-handed, when they had it, as the Californios. After them came the gamblers, the confidence men, the business swindlers.

"How much land is at stake?" I asked Roderigo.

"Over one hundred thousand acres."

It taken my breath away. In the mountains we farmed a hundred and sixty acres, and had as much around that was brush and timber, too steep to farm. Out of that quarter section we farmed we made a bare living, for there was thin soil and poor crops. But this was rich land, if irrigated.

It was no wonder they were prepared to do murder to win their game, and they could not afford to have me about stirring up trouble.

"That girl, now. What was her part in all this?"

"Old Ben is no different from the rest of us. He likes young, pretty women, and when Turner—he was the banker—came to see him he brought his 'niece' along with him."

The man at the bar turned suddenly and walked from the room, so I got up. "You save the rest of that," I said. "I've got business to attend to."

He had gone off down the street, and when I stepped out and got to the corner I saw him standing in front of what used to be the Bella Union Hotel. They'd changed the name of it to the St. Charles, but it was a place I knew. Ten, fifteen years before there'd been a big gun battle there where Bob Carlisle shot it out with the King brothers.

Anyway, that man was standing there and I started for him, figuring to get just as close as I'd need to be before he saw me. He was a little distance off, but I have long legs and I stepped fast but easy, not to scare him off.

Then he saw me and, turning, he ducked into an alley, and I went in after him . . . too fast.

As I wheeled around the corner, he was standing maybe forty feet off, and he ups with his six-shooter and let drive at me. It was point-blank range, and he should have nailed me, but he'd been running, then just skidded to a stand and fired, so he must have been a mite unsteady.

Something hit me a wallop on the head and I went down to my knees, then fell over, face down on the ground.

From somewhere I heard running feet coming up behind me, and then in the other direction, plain as a body could wish, I heard a door slam.

# Chapter 5

When I hit ground it seemed to me I was only there about a second when folks were all around me filling the breathing air with foolish questions. Lurching to my feet, I fell against the side of the building and leaned there with blood running into my eyes, trying to bring my brain into focus. All I could remember was the sound of a door slamming somewhere down the alley ahead of me.

Folks kept nagging at my attention with questions as to what happened and who shot me, but their words reached me without registering any effect. What little awareness I had was concentrated on just one idea: finding the man who shot me.

Roderigo was there trying to help, but I brushed him away. I got my two feet under me and pointed myself down that alley.

There was only one door in sight. When I got to it I leaned against the wall for an instant, sort of gathering myself for whatever was to come, and then I grasped the latch and opened the door.

The hallway down which I looked was maybe forty feet long, with two doors on the right and one on the left. The first door on the right opened into an empty store building with lumber piled on the floor, as if for building work. There was nobody in the room.

Closing the door as softly as I could, I went on to the next door on my right, which led into a clothing store. The place was empty but for the clerk and one customer.

"Did anybody come through here?" I asked.

They both looked at me, then shook their heads. "Nobody . . . ain't been a soul around," said the clerk.

The door on the left remained, and I turned to it. Opening it suddenly, I stepped inside.

Behind a desk sat the man I had seen with Dorinda Robiseau, the big young man who had guided her away from me.

"You wished to see me?"

"I wish to see the man who came in here from the alley," I said.

"I am very sorry. Nobody has come here. Is that all?"

With my left hand I wiped blood from my face. My skull was throbbing with an enormous and awful ache, hurting so that I squinted when I looked around.

There was just this big rolltop desk, two chairs, and a table. But there was another door.

"Who's in there?" I asked.

"Nobody."

He didn't like me, not even a mite. He started to say more, but I pointed at the door.

"You open it up," I said.

He leaned back in his chair. "Don't be a damned fool. I shall do nothing of the kind. Now you get out of here or I'll have you jailed . . . and I can do it."

Stepping over to his desk, I leaned across it, and I am a tall man. "Mister," I spoke mighty gentle, "you do what you're told."

He got mad then, and he started to get up. Oh, he was a man used to having his own way; it was written all over him. He was a big man and strong, and he was mad. So he started to get up, and when he was off the chair with both his hands on the arms, I caught him by the front of his shirt and vest and jerked him toward me to get him off balance, and then I shoved him back, hard.

He hit that chair and both of them went over on the floor, and I stepped quick to that door and jerked it open. Two bullets came through, their reports one right behind the other, but I was well over to one side and both missed.

That man inside the room, he had just shot into the opening door, taking no aim at all, nor seeing anything to shoot at.

"Next time," I said, "I'm going to shoot back. You going to drop that gun, or are you going to die?"

He didn't seem to like the choice much. I heard him shift his feet, and I said, "You got you two bullets. You might nail me, but I've got five and I'm not about to miss."

"I've nothing of yours," he said, and with my gun up I took a long chance and stepped into the door with my gun in my hand.

He had a notion to shoot, but when he saw that big six in my hand he had another notion that beat that first one all hollow. He taken a long look at that gun and he stepped back and dropped his pistol.

"I ain't about to pick it up," I said, "and you go ahead, if you're of a mind to."

Behind me I heard a stirring on the floor, and I moved so I could keep half an eye on that big man on the floor, too.

"Mister," I said, "my outfit has been taken. My horses and gold are gone. Now, I aim to have them all back. You boys can start talking or start shooting, and I ain't of a mind to care which."

The big man got up off the floor, but carefully, holding himself with knowledge that I might have a touchy finger on a hair-trigger. With my gun muzzle for a pointer I moved the second man over alongside the first.

"We know nothing about it," the big man said. "I have no idea what you are talking about."

"I think you're a liar," I said, "and if it proves out I'm wrong, I'll apologize and welcome. But this gent who taken some shots at me, he was there. He was in the desert."

"You've got me all wrong!"

"I sure have. And being in the desert, you know I ain't a-fooling when I hold this gun. I want my outfit, and I'm going to have it."

"You're a fool," the big man said contemptuously. "You have that gun on us, but when you leave the law will be on you, and if you shoot us, you'll hang."

"Before I hang," I said, "I'll do some talking."

They didn't like that. They didn't like it even a little. Suddenly I had a feeling that if they hadn't already marked me down for killing, I had just moved myself to the head of the list.

"Watch him, Dayton," the smaller man said, "he's good with that gun."

Dayton smiled, and it was not a nice smile. "My advice to you, my friend, is to get out of town, and get fast."

"Why, I might do that . . . given my outfit."

Dayton glanced at the other man. "What about it, Oliphant? Do you know anything about it?"

Oliphant touched his lips with his tongue. "We figured him for dead. Of course we brought his horses in."

"And thirty pounds of gold," I said.

Oliphant shifted his feet. "I don't know—"

"That's quite a lot, Oliphant," Dayton suggested coolly. "I'd rather like to know about that myself."

"I don't know anything about the gold," Oliphant said. "I—"

Well, I just eared back the hammer on that gun of mine. "You just jog your memory, friend," I said. "You just jog it a mite. If you don't, I'll be asking questions of somebody else."

Oh, he was sweating, all right! He was right-down scared, and not only of me. Apparently he, and maybe some of those others, had just kept still about that gold. But there was still fight in him.

"You'll not talk so loud," he said, "if you brace Sackett."

"*Who?*"

"Nolan Sackett. And if you don't know that name, you don't know anything. Nolan Sackett, the gunfighter."

He mistook my manner for fear, because I was some startled to hear the name of Sackett. And then suddenly the familiarity of that big-built man returned to me. Not that I knew any Nolan Sackett, nor had I ever heard the name, but the build was so like my own . . . or my brother Orrin's, for that matter, although he was heavier.

There was no Nolan Sackett I'd ever heard tell of, certainly not among the Smoky Mountain or Cumberland Sacketts.

"Clinch Mountain!"

"What's that?" They both stared at me, not guessing what I meant. And knowing no Sackett history, they could not know. But the only kind of Sackett likely to wind up in such a deal was a Clinch Mountain Sackett. They were the outlaw branch, but fighters . . . I'll give them that.

"Mister," I said, "you start talking. Where are my horses and my gold?"

"You'll have to brace Sackett if you want them." He was still thinking the name had scared me. "You ain't about to do that."

"I'll send you to do it," I said, "but if need be, Sackett can face Sackett."

They didn't get it. They just looked at me, so I told them. "Why, Sackett is my name, too. William Tell Sackett, although most call me Tell, and I'm from the mountains of Tennessee, although a different set of mountains from him. And we Sacketts don't take kindly to anyone of our name mixing in with disgraceful conduct. I'll just have to meet this here Nolan Sackett and read him from the Book."

"Your horses are at Greek George's place," Oliphant said, "out beyond Cahuenga Pass. The gold is there, too, if you can get it."

"I'll get it."

Backing to the door, I looked over at Dayton. "You stay out of my way," I said. "I don't like anything about you."

He smiled, but I knew now it was not a nice smile. There was murder in it. "You'll not live to cross the mountains," he said. "I shall see to that."

"You're too busy," I said, "trying to steal an old man's ranch."

That hit him. It was like he'd been slapped across the mouth, and he came up out of his chair, white around the lips, but I just stepped outside and pulled the door to behind me.

Roderigo was waiting for me at the end of the street, and he was worried.

"I was afraid for you," he said. "I did not know what to do."

"First things first. Do you know Greek George's place?"

"Who does not? It is there they captured the outlaw, Tiburcio Vasquez."

"Is it far?"

"Ten miles . . . only that. At the foot of the mountains."

"My horses are there. My gold also."

He glanced at me. "And you will go for them? Do you know what you do, señor? It is the place of the outlaws. And there are outlaws in the canyons all along the Santa Monica Range. You must have the sheriff, señor, and a posse."

"I carry my own posse." I slapped my holster. "And as for a sheriff—why, we Sacketts always figured to skin our own skunks, and ask no help of any man."

"I would ride with you, señor."

Well, I looked at him and figured to myself that this one was pretty much of a man. "You do that if you feel the urge for it," I said; "only come prepared for shooting, if need be."

We went for our horses, and I had an idea we'd be late if we did not hurry, for Oliphant would be sending someone, or riding himself, to warn them.

"There's a man out there name of Nolan Sackett," I said. "If anybody shoots him, it will be me."

His face paled a mite. "I did not know he was there, *amigo*," he said. "It is said that he has killed twenty-two men."

"To have killed men is not a thing of which one can be proud," I said. "A man uses a gun when necessary, and not too often, or carelessly."

We mounted up and rode up Fort Street and out of town, heading west and north along the foot of the mountains, with the land sloping off west and south away from us. We rode past irrigation ditches and orchards, and it gave me excitement to see oranges growing, for I'd never seen more than a half-dozen of them in my lifetime.

The railroad had come to Los Angeles with its steam cars, and looking back I could see a train standing at the depot. Main Street led from the depot through part of Sonora town where some of the poorer Mexican and Californios lived, mostly in white-washed adobe houses. The Plaza was set with cypresses; this side of it was the Pico House and the Baker Block, two of the show places of the town. Most of the streets where folks lived were lined with pepper trees, but when we got away from the irrigation ditches it was almighty dry. Because of the bad drouth the last two years, things were in poor shape. The grass was sparse, and there was little else but prickly pear.

With Roderigo leading, we cut over to the *brea* pits road through La

Nopalera—the Cactus Patch*—to a small tavern kept by a Mexican. Roderigo swung down and went inside, whilst I sat my horse outside and looked the country over.

Only the faintest breeze was stirring, and the air was warm and pleasant . . . it was a lazy, easy-going sort of day when a man felt called upon to laze around and do not much of anything. Only we had something to do.

West of us lay the Rancho Rodeo de las Aguas,† but looking along the edge of the mountains I saw a faint smudge of blue smoke, indicating where our destination lay. This was the adobe house of Greek George . . . the very same place where Tiburcio Vasquez had been shot and wounded as he scrambled out a window, attempting to escape.

Roderigo came out of the tavern, looking serious as all get out. "Señor, there are five men at the house of the *Griego,* but the man of your name is not among them."

Well, I was some relieved. No Sackett had ever shot another, and I wasn't itching to be the first. We'd never had much truck with those Clinch Mountain Sacketts, for they were a rough lot, having to do with moonshining and perambulating up and down the Wilderness Trail or the Natchez Trace for no good purpose. But they were fighters . . . they were good fighters.

"We'll ride over there," I said. "I figure to lay hands on my outfit."

He looked at me, and I'll give him this. He was game. He mounted up and swung his horse alongside of mine, and the only thing he did was to reach back and take the thong off his six-shooter.

"I would like you to meet my grandfather," he said suddenly. "Old Ben would like you."

"From all I've heard," I replied honestly, "I'd like to meet him."

And I'd heard a-plenty. This here was a wise old man, although not too wise to be taken in by a pretty face. But he was not alone in that.

We trotted our horses along the road that came down behind the adobe, and we swung down.

The door opened and a man lounged there, a tough, kind of taunting smile on his face. "Well, look who's here! We figured you were lyin' dead out on the Mojave."

"I take a lot of killing."

"So you do." The man chuckled. "But we never make the same mistake twice."

---

* The area now known as Hollywood.
† Now the Beverly Hills area.

While he was making talk, I was walking toward him. Roderigo, so far as I knew, had not moved from his place by the horses.

The man in the door straightened up and, grinning at me, suddenly went for his gun. He no doubt fancied himself a fast man, but I didn't even move to draw. I just fetched him a clout with one of my fists, which are big and toughened by a good many years of work with shovel, sledge hammer, and rope . . . and he never got his gun clear.

My fist caught him on the angle of his jaw and drove the side of his head against the door jamb. He slumped over and fell where he was, and at the same time I heard two quick shots from outside. Flattening against the door with my fist full of gun, I glanced over to see Roderigo holding a smoking pistol. There was a man with a Winchester slumped over a sill of the window in the ell of the house. He looked kind of dead to me.

Inside three men were suddenly reaching for the smoky beams, and a pretty Mexican girl was standing staring at me. She was young, but she was pert . . . and I'd say that her path had probably been a twisty one.

"You look like him!" She was surprised, a body could see that. "You look just like him!"

"We Sacketts favor," I said, "if it is Nolan you speak of, but I've never seen the man."

"You'll see him but once," she said contemptuously.

"Why, now. As to that, I'll speak my piece and he'll go about his business . . . elsewhere."

It was not so much a boast as a wish. I called for no shooting with kinfolk, and was surprised that he had it in mind. Only maybe he didn't.

To those others I said, "I came for my outfit . . . and the gold."

"You'll find your horses and gear yonder." A red-headed man indicated the corral and stable. "I don't know anything about any gold."

"Ma'am," I said to that Spanish girl, "stir up your fire. I reckon we're going to need it. And bring that spit over here." I grinned at those men. "I traipsed about down New Mexico way for quite a time. Those there Apaches, they know a thing or two."

The red-headed one, he wasn't worried much, but those others, they started shifting their feet and both of them broke out in a sweat.

The one I'd slugged in the doorway was fetching around, so I backed up and grabbed hold of the back of his neck with one hand and dragged him bodily into the room and skidded him across the floor.

The Mexican girl hadn't moved. I took up a poker and worried the fire a mite, then she turned and took up her shawl. "Don't you worry," she said to the others. "I'll go for Nolan and Señor Dayton."

She looked boldly at me. "This one will do nothing! He is afraid."

I chuckled at that, and it made her mad. Her black eyes flashed and she started to say something back, but I just said, "Ma'am, you sure are a pretty little baggage, but you just go get Nolan Sackett, and when you come upon him you tell him it is William Tell Sackett who is here, and to come along if he's a mind to. As for Dayton, he knew I was coming here. I saw him earlier today . . . with a man named Oliphant."

That surprised them, but she went scooting out like she was afraid I'd stop her, which I'd no mind to do. It was in me to settle things, and if they all came around so much the better.

"I have friends, señor," Roderigo said to me; "perhaps I should go for them." He paused. "There are the vaqueros from our ranch, and I believe it is a thing they would like, to find these . . . who are known to be thieves."

Now even Red was looking out of sorts, so I told Roderigo, "You go ahead. Tell 'em to bring extra rope. We may need some neckties for these boys."

Back in those days the pueblo, as everybody called Los Angeles, was a place noted for being mighty free with their hangings, legal or otherwise. Over a span of a few years there had been forty legal hangings and thirty-seven spur-of-the-moment affairs. Shootings were a daily occurrence, but, casual as the authorities were, the townspeople were notoriously short-tempered on occasion, and it required little effort to organize a lynching party.

They might not figure me for much, but they had the consciousness of their own guilt to worry them.

There was a close-up storeroom at the back of the house and, herding them all back there, I put them in and barred the door.

Outside, I located my horses, all five of them, and my saddle gear. Saddling up the horses, I found my pack, which had been gone through, but most of it nobody wanted and so it was intact. My Winchester I found in the house along with somebody else's outfit. The Winchester I took, checked the loads, and made ready for whatever might happen.

But what I wanted most was the gold, not all of it being mine. And believe me, I wanted what belonged to me. For the better part of an hour I went over that house, going through everything, hunting the gold, but I didn't find it at all.

And then I heard horses a-coming and knew I was in for shooting trouble.

From the window I watched them approach, then slipped outside and waited among the willows beside the spring. The Mexican girl was with them, and I counted six men, all heavily armed.

They came up at a fast trot, accompanied by a little dust cloud, and as they slowed their pace and spread out to surround the house the dust sort of thinned and settled down. When they actually moved up around the house the horses were walking.

Crouched among the willows, I just waited and let them come. I wasn't seeking any shooting war unless forced to it. Most particularly, I was hunting Nolan Sackett, but he wasn't among them.

All this time I was studying about where my gold might be. Oliphant had said it was here, on this place, but I had my doubts.

When those riders dismounted and went into the house I went over to my horses, mounted up on the stallion, and walked them away from there. From inside I heard argument and talk, but I walked steadily away from there, putting the bulk of the barn behind me as soon as I could, and heading for the mouth of a canyon that opened not far off.

Roderigo would be back, and until then I wasn't going to do any shooting I could avoid. I might kill the wrong man. I might kill the man who knew where my gold was.

After a minute or two they came bursting out of the door and began to hunt all around.

Sitting my saddle in a clump of tall cactus, I watched them, holding my Winchester across the saddle in front of me. Off down the valley from the direction of the Rancho Rodeo de las Aguas I could see a dust cloud that meant riders moving fast.

The men at the house started scouting around for my tracks, but there were too many horses around the place, and too many people had come and gone. They weren't going to get anywhere with that, and I wasn't much worried.

I was only worried about getting my gold back, for there were folks back in Arizona depending on me. My hunch was that wherever that gold went, Dorinda would know. Unless I was judging her all wrong, she was a girl who could keep her eye on a thing like that.

That distant cloud was coming nearer, and I guess they sighted it, too, for all of a sudden they scrambled for their saddles and rode off, scattering out.

Two of them rode past me, heading up the canyon* where there were other hangouts for outlaws.

When they had gone I walked my horses from the clump of cactus and rode back down to the ranch. Only the girl remained to greet me, and her eyes flared when she saw me.

"You know where that gold is?" I asked mildly. "You could save me trouble if you told me."

---

* Laurel Canyon.

"I care nothing for your trouble!" She tossed her head. "When Señor Sackett comes he will make a fool of you."

"He'd better hurry. My friends are coming."

She said nothing to that, for now we could hear the drum of the horses' hoofs.

"If you change your mind," I said, "you come to me. Seems a shame, a pretty girl like you, mixed up with this crowd."

She started to reply, then tightened her lips.

There were twenty wiry, tough-looking vaqueros with Roderigo, and they looked disappointed when it proved there would be no fight.

"You had better come away with us," Roderigo said, "Old Ben wishes to see you."

"Ben Mandrin?"

"*Si*." He smiled. "And the Señorita Robiseau."

# Chapter 6

The house was a long adobe with several doors opening on a veranda. The place was old and mellow. There were some huge old oaks about, and a few sycamores. The shade was a welcome thing after the long ride's heat, and I pulled up there and sat my saddle a minute or two, just looking around.

If they didn't take it away from Old Ben, this place might become Roderigo's, and I didn't blame him for wanting it. There was a feeling of lazy good will about it, from the smell of the barnyard and the jasmine around the house to the shade of the huge old trees.

The house was L-shaped and rambling, and opened on a view that showed the sea away off to the west—just a hint of it beyond the round shoulder of a hill. In between was grassland, brown now and parched from the drouth, with here and there a cultivated patch of corn or beans, or some other row crop.

A door opened and, looking past my horse's head, I saw Dorinda standing there, wearing a lovely dress and looking more beautiful than she'd a right to.

"Won't you get down and come in? Mr. Mandrin would like to see you." She turned. "Juan, will you take care of the gentleman's horse?"

Stepping down from the saddle, I whipped dust from my clothes with my hat and walked across the yard. The feeling up my spine warned me that somebody was watching—not Dorinda, and not Juan.

She held out her hand to me, smiling with her lips. It was a wide, pretty smile showing beautiful teeth, but her eyes did not smile. They were cautious, somewhat worried eyes.

"Thank you, Mr. Sackett. Thank you very much for all you did. When they came to get me we thought you were dead."

"Handy," I said.

"What do you mean?"

"Otherwise they might have made sure."

She let her eyes rest on my face a moment longer, as if trying to judge how smart I was, or how dangerous. . . .

"It was all a mistake."

"There's men dead out there on the Mojave would be surprised to hear it," I said bluntly.

When she started to answer me I cut her short. "Ma'am, I didn't come to call on you. I came to see Ben Mandrin."

His voice came deep and booming. "And so you shall! Come in, Mr. Sackett! Please come in!"

He was sitting in a great old rocker, and whatever I had expected a pirate to look like, it was not this. He had never been tall—not like me, anyway—but he was broad-shouldered, and my guess was that he had once been a mighty powerful man. It showed in the size of his bones. His wrists were as large as mine, which are ten inches around, and he had strong, well-made hands, flat across the knuckles . . . a fighter's hands.

He had a broad, heavily boned face and deep-set eyes; his heavy shock of black hair was mixed with gray. He had to be upwards of seventy years old, but he didn't look it. Only you could see at a glance that something was wrong with his legs. He had them covered by a blanket, but I could tell they were thin, almost like there was nothing there at all.

There was an old scar over one eye and another on his cheekbone, but he did not look sinister, as they say of such men. He looked like a strong old man who had lived a life.

He was old, all right, a body could see that, but I could see a whole sight more. Old as he was, and with those crippled legs, there was a lot of iron in him yet.

"So you're Sackett?" he said. "Dorry told me of you. You sound like a fighting man."

The scar over his eye held my attention, and he noticed it. "Saber," he said. "That was a long time ago, a lifetime away."

"Off Hatteras," I said, "and they thought it killed you."

Well, both of them were surprised. Dorinda turned sharply to look at me, and the old man caught the arms of his chair and pulled himself out of his slump. "Now how could you know *that?*" he said. "There were few enough who knew."

"You raided the Carolina coast too often," I said. "The man who gave you that cut over the eye was my grandfather."

He glared at me for a minute, then he chuckled. "He was a fighter," he said. "Best hand with a blade I ever saw—bar one."

He took a good look at me. "There's another Sackett here. Is he kin of yours?"

"I reckon. He's a Clinch Mountain Sackett, and we don't hold with them . . . but we aren't pirates."

There was a mighty hard look in those eyes of his . . . gave a man something to think about. Had he been a younger or even a healthier man, you'd think twice before giving sass to him. But I thought he liked this talk, and it came over me that it had probably been a time since anybody gave him back man-talk. Because of his wealth and his being crippled and all, they'd more than likely soft-talk him.

"That was a long time ago," Ben Mandrin said. "I've become a rancher and a stable citizen." His eyes glinted with a kind of tough humor. "Or hadn't you heard?"

"I heard, and I believe it . . . up to a point."

He chuckled again and, glancing over at Dorinda, he said, "I like this man."

Then he turned his eyes back to me. "How'd you like to work for me?"

"I'm not hunting work. I'm hunting thirty pounds of gold that was taken from me, and when I find it I'm riding back to Arizona. And furthermore"—I looked right at Dorinda—"I've got an idea who to ask about it."

Oh, he got it all right! Old Ben missed mighty little. He glanced at her, then back at me. "You're wrong, my friend—she has been with me."

He gestured toward a chair. "Sit down, and we'll talk a bit of ships and sabers and the Carolina coast fifty years ago . . . or how much did your grandfather tell you?"

He turned to her. "Dorinda, bring us a bottle of wine—a very good bottle, that will bring memories around us."

We sat silent then, listening to her retreating footsteps. From the sound of them, the wine must have been somewhere at the far end of the house, and it was a great way off, it seemed.

"You helped her in the desert, Sackett, and for that I thank you."

Surprised, I was, for I'd been thinking he knew nothing of her leaving the pueblo. "I went for water, and when I started back, they had her. I stumbled as one of them shot at me, and he thought me dead."

"And you lay still? She does not know that I know." He lighted a long black cheroot, then gave me a sharp glance. "Did she get your gold?"

"As to that, I couldn't say, but I would believe her a woman to know where gold was. I think"—I tried to put it so he would take no offense—"she has a nose for gold, if you'll not mind my saying so."

She came back then, walking along the veranda toward us, and we sat silent, waiting. The bottle she brought was Madeira, of a kind they call Rainwater, although no storm that I have seen brought such water from the sky.

"I would have preferred Jamaica," he said, "but it is hard to come by in California."

We tasted the wine, and it was good. I thought him a fine old man, but

I trusted the wine more than I did Old Ben Mandrin; and I trusted him a bit more than I did that black-eyed witch woman. Surely, I thought, this was a strange way for a tall and homely cowhand and miner to be treated, and it gave me an uncomfortable feeling to think that it was likely he would lose all this.

Roderigo had told me a little more during our ride from the pueblo to Greek George's ranch. Turner, the man from the bank, had relied on Dorinda to persuade Old Ben to sign the notes; and Turner would get cash from Dayton and his friends, while they would take over the note and get the ranch. Even without the note, they would have Old Ben lashed to the mast, for he was broke and down to his last bit of money.

The drouth had ruined the crops and his range, and there was nothing left for him but to yield up the rancho . . . but what would he do then, a crippled old man?

There was none of that in his talk now, for once the wine warmed his blood he talked of the old days off the Carolina coast, and of the fight with my grandfather. They had fought on a bloody deck—my grandfather being one of a make-up crew that had gone off to intercept him when there was no warship about equipped to handle the job. They had fought a desperate fight, with both men wounded and bleeding before the cut that felled Old Ben.

As we talked he kept his eyes on me, or looked off and seemed to be listening to the sound of my voice, although it was rare indeed that I had chance to speak. But it seemed to me there was something on his mind, something dark and secret that he held within himself.

Dorinda listened, and occasionally she went from the room and returned. I noticed she drank no wine . . . was there purpose in that? Or did she simply not drink at all? Sometimes she seemed impatient, wishing me to be off, no doubt, for all of our talk was taking us no place.

It was in my own mind to leave, until suddenly Old Ben said, "You must stay the night, Sackett. You can snug down here—there's room enough and more. It will be time enough to go off hunting your gold in the morning."

He looked at me sharply as he replaced his glass on the table. "Roderigo said you had planned to buy mules or horses and pack goods back to the mines to sell. Is that still in your mind?"

"When I have my gold."

He waved his hand at the broad acres around me. "They plan to take all this from me, but there's mules enough, and I could let you have some . . . for a small price. I'll have some run up for you to look upon."

He caught hold of his cane suddenly as if to get up, then stopped and said to Dorinda, "Tell them to come for me, and show Mr. Sackett to a room." He paused again as if thinking. "To Pio's room," he added.

She looked surprised, but left the room, and when she came back two vaqueros came with her. They picked Old Ben up, chair and all, and carried him from the room. When they had gone I finished my wine and put down the glass.

"I have never seen him like this," Dorinda said, puzzled and disturbed. "He has never talked so much to any stranger."

"It was because of the old times," I said. "My mention of the fight off Hatteras brought it all back to him."

Some of her puzzlement seemed to go away. "Yes, yes, that must be it," she said.

She was a beautiful woman, but now I could see a coldness there that I had not noticed so much before, although I was ever wary of her.

"But in Pio's room!" she went on. "He has never allowed anyone in that room but the old governor."

"Pio Pico?"

"They were friends . . . are still friends, I think, although he comes out but rarely now." And she said no more.

There were four of us at supper, Old Ben, Roderigo, Dorinda, and myself, but now Old Ben talked little. He broke in once to say, "There was some shooting around Mora, in New Mexico, in which some Sacketts were involved. One of them married a Mexican girl."

"They are my brothers," I said.

He ate with good appetite, I noticed, but drank no more wine—only several cups of the blackest coffee this side of Hell itself. I drank my own share, but I was used to cow-camp coffee which will float a horseshoe.

Tired, I was, and ready for the bed, and we sat about very little after supper was over.

In my room was a huge old four-poster bed, the finest bed I had ever seen, and on a marble-topped table were a bowl and a pitcher of water. There was a chair and a thick carpet on the stone-flagged floor. The room had one window, and an inner door that evidently connected with Old Ben's room.

Sitting down on the edge of the bed, I considered the situation, and none of it made sense. All I wanted was to get my gold back and get out on the trail back to the mines, yet here I was, a guest in an old Spanish hacienda, the guest of a former pirate.

True, I had my outfit back, but the country was filled with my enemies —and all through no fault of mine. Only trying to help a girl who, it now seemed, was tied in with my enemies . . . enemies I'd made because of her.

Tired of trying to figure it out, and deciding I was pretty much of a fool, I pulled off my boots, washed my face and hands, and started to undress.

And then the door from Old Ben Mandrin's room opened and he stood there, hanging on a pair of crutches, and looking at me with devil's laughter in his eyes.

He swung himself around and lowered himself into the chair. "I need help, boy. I need your help."

Me, I just stood looking at him. He was dressed for riding, in an outfit that had once fitted him, but did so no longer.

"We've got to ride nearly twenty miles before daybreak," he said. "Pull your boots on."

It looked like I was never going to sleep in a bed.

"You in shape for a twenty-mile ride?" I said.

"No . . . but I'll ride it. Leave that to me."

I could only stare at him. "Why me?" I said. "You've got men around. You've got Roderigo." And then I grinned at him. "And you've got Dorinda."

He brushed the suggestion away. "An old man's fancy. Look, son, you're young. You're strong. There will be many women for you, but for me she may be the last. I'll not be saying she's mine, for she isn't, and I am sure she has nothing of the kind in mind.

"She looks like a passionate woman, but she isn't, son. Take it from me, the great courtesans of the past—and Dorinda is like them—were never passionate, loving women. They were cold, calculating. They used the emotions of men for their own purposes, they were all show, all promises. A passionate woman gets too involved for straight thinking, she becomes too emotional . . . not Dorinda. She's thinking all the time."

"Then why not be rid of her?"

"Like I say, she may be the last beautiful woman to pay me attention. Most of us pay for love in one way or another, and I paid for her attentions by signing that note." A wolfish gleam came into those hard old eyes. "Now with your help, I'm going to serve them what they have coming."

"It don't sound right to me."

"That's why I chose you. You're honest."

I just kept looking at him. I'd grown up on stories of him, and I could see they were true. He was an old devil, but I found myself liking him. And sympathizing with him, too.

"What you got in mind?" I asked cautiously.

"A ride to the west . . . to a place out in the mountains."

"You're in no shape. Tell me what you want done, and I'll do it."

The wolf in him showed his teeth. His eyes danced wickedly. "This I shall do myself." The smile disappeared. "All I am going to do is save my ranch, and injure no man."

A moment I thought about it, but I was getting nowhere. I was no hand to ferret out the plans of other folks. Maybe I just ain't smart, maybe there ain't enough wolf in me . . . I don't know. I can face up to guns or fists, but believe me, I can't plot and figure out ways to deceive.

No use my trying to study out what he had in mind. I knew I was going to help him, because if an old man in his kind of shape had the guts to try to ride twenty miles, I was going to help him. And I knew I wanted to see the old devil outsmart those who would rob him of what was his.

"All right," I said.

"Get horses," he said, "and hurry. We've far to go."

When I started for the door, he hooked my arm with a crutch. "The window," he said. "Our doors will be watched."

The window went up soundlessly, and I eased out into the still night. Stars were out, and somewhere an owl talked in a treetop. Moving on cat feet, I made the corral where my horses were. It taken only minutes to get them out and saddled, the two best of them. Then I led them back in the darkness close to the house.

I managed to get Old Ben through the window, but he helped me some. When I lifted him to the saddle, I was sure surprised. He was light, but there was power in his arms and shoulders and hands . . . I could feel that.

Mounting up, I led off into the night, and then he took over. He could ride, all right. He put his horse westward into the mountains, and I trailed behind, fearful all the time that he might fall off and hurt himself.

The wind was cool on our faces. The black of the mountains loomed above us. We rode steadily westward, and there was no talk between us, although, worried as I was about him, my eyes kept straying his way. But he rode steadily, although with his weakened, crippled legs, I could not guess how he managed it.

These were dark and silent hills. There were cattle here, and horses, but they slept their own sleep and we saw none of them. Once, we saw distant lights . . . we slowed our pace and walked our horses carefully through the dust so as not to awaken the sleepers in the village surrounding a ranch. In those years much of the population clustered in such tiny villages gathered about the ranches.

We turned suddenly into the mountains, mounting by a narrow trail only faintly seen. The ground was lighter in shade where it was worn by the passing of men or cattle. As we climbed I fancied I could smell the sea; and suddenly, when we topped out upon a ridge, I knew it for truth. There it lay, broad upon our right, the great ocean of the Pacific.

He drew up then and looked seaward. I could not see his eyes in the darkness, but it seemed to me there was a longing in him, a longing for the deep waters.

It was in me to understand this, for I knew my own bit of longing for the wild places. I am a man not given to cities, nor the crowded walks of men. I like the long winds upon my face, the stirring of miles of grass bending before the wind, the cloud shadows upon the plain, the lure and lift of far hills.

Below us and a little behind us, dark against the moonlit sea, a point thrust into the waters. He swept a hand toward it, and along the shore. "Malibu," he said, "Rancho Malibu."

He glanced at the stars, and pushed on, although the trail was rough. By the feel of it, it was one rarely traveled. We dipped into hollows and emerged from them, and now he seemed to be doing his best to lose me, to prevent me from ever retracing my steps.

Suddenly he turned at right angles and dipped into a gap or pass in the mountains, and when he had gone but a short distance, he drew up.

"Help me down," he said, as I dismounted.

Reaching up, I lifted him from the saddle, and he sagged in my arms, then drew back.

"No crutches," he said. "They'd be no use to me here." Iron came into his voice. "Wait for me here . . . I shall be a while."

He could not walk, but crawled away into the black darkness where no moonlight fell. I lighted a cigar, cupping my hands well to conceal the point of flame, and prepared to wait.

To what strange place had he brought me? And why had he crawled off in the darkness alone?

Once, a long while after he had left me, I heard a stone rattle distantly in the night, and I knew that it fell off into space, for a long time later I heard it strike.

I was thinking that Old Ben Mandrin was no fool, and I knew that whatever he did, it was something he wished desperately to do. But he was no man to be either questioned or doubted, so I just stayed there and listened into the night . . . listening both for him, and for trouble that might come.

Several times I glanced at the stars to check the time that passed, and they gave me no comfort. It was a far ride back to the ranch for a tired old man, and daylight might find us on the trail. What then? What if they carried his breakfast to his room and found him not there? Or what if his heart failed on this ride and he died with me? Would anyone believe my story?

Restlessly, I tramped up and down, impatient for his return. Was he only a few yards off, listening, perhaps with amusement, to my restless pacing? Or had he gone far away and fallen, injuring himself? But I heard no call for help, and the night was clear and cool.

Finally, I sat down, lighted a fresh cigar with caution, and waited. I thought of what odd turns there are in the life of a man. It was strange that I should be here with this old pirate of whom I had only heard as a boy, and had known now only a matter of hours.

There were no trees here, only the black chaparral. Some of the bushes were almost as tall as a man, but most no more than waist high, yet there were game tunnels beneath them, trails long used by lion or coyote or bobcat. They formed a maze that covered all this chaparral country with hidden trails, to be followed by wild creatures or by a man, if he chose to crawl. Here, atop this ridge, the chaparral was thin, for the ridge was broken by jagged rock outcroppings or by gigantic boulders, bare and time-eroded.

The stars waned. Impatiently, I ground out the stub of my cigar and got to my feet.

The horses, heads up, ears pointed, were looking off into the night, toward the direction in which Ben Mandrin had crawled. Nostrils dilated, they looked along the ridge.

Stepping out away from them, I spoke softly, "Ben?"

No answer came.

It was too dark to see tracks, and although I had risked lighting the cigars, to hold a light while trying to make out tracks seemed too chancy. This was a high ridge, and the country was alive with outlaws. If I started out to search for him, I might miss him in the darkness. I had no idea how far he had gone, nor even if he had persisted in the direction in which he started, for that might have been only to give me a false idea.

My head was aching, for the riding had set that wound on my skull to throbbing. It hadn't amounted to much . . . a bullet that cut a furrow in my scalp and skinned away some hair, but it also left a lump there big as a hen's egg.

Waiting had given me time to think, and precious little time I'd had before for pondering. But I still didn't know who had been chasing Dorinda when I first met up with her, or why, although it began to look like she might have wanted to get out of this deal with Old Ben. But why?

What was her stake in all this? And who had got her into it? There must have been something promised to her. . . . And where was Nolan Sackett?

Most of all, where was my gold?

Again I looked at the stars. The hour was late, and there was but little time left to us. I got to my feet and walked off into the darkness, listening.

There was no sound.

He was out there alone, and something had gone wrong, I was sure of it now. It wasn't in me to abide longer with that crippled-up old man out there on the rocks and in the dark of night.

So I started out after him.

We were high up on a hog-backed ridge, with the mountains falling away toward the sea on one side and on the other a deep hollow,* what in this country they call a *potrero*, because usually those hollows are good pastureland. There wasn't much chance of getting lost up here because a man had mighty little room to move around in.

It was the dark hour that comes before daylight, and I worked my way along carefully, straining my eyes to see if he lay on the ground, passed out. A couple of times I called softly, but nobody gave back reply.

Suddenly I came to where the trail, if you could call it so, broke in two, with one way going on along the hogback, the other seeming to go out along the shoulder of an even higher ridge. That last looked a mighty bad place to go.

Here I must take a chance, for there was no time to search out both ways. The ridge would shield any light that showed from the land side, and as for the sea, I'd have to chance it. So, kneeling down, I struck a match, held it cupped in my hands, and checked the ground.

It was there, plain as a skunk on a log. The old man had dragged himself along here and taken that higher ridge trail.

Only it wasn't a trail. It was a thread of rock hung in space over several hundred feet of steep fall. Dark as it was, I couldn't see how far it was, but it was a-plenty. So I started out along that shoulder. After a while the trail widened out, then narrowed down.

I'd walked a couple of hundred yards from my horse before I stopped to call out again. And this time I heard a faint stirring up ahead of me. Whether it was game animal or man, I couldn't tell, but I moved on, and suddenly there he lay on the trail ahead of me, face down on the rock and sparse grass where he'd been crawling.

His hands were skinned and chewed up from the rocks. Beside him in the trail was a big sack full of something. I wished for the moon, which had gone from the sky a long while back. Well, there was mighty little time, so I scooped him up in my arms, and then reached down and got a hold of that sack, which was fearful heavy. Somehow, sweating and panting, I got them both back to our horses, and loaded up.

---

* Where Lake Sherwood now lies, and the valley beyond.

He came out of his faint when I was hoisting him up. "Can you hang on, or should I lash you up?"

"You start, boy, and you ride like hell. I'll stay with you."

He grabbed my wrist, and believe me, that old devil still had the power to hurt in that grip of his. "Boy," he said, "I've got to be stretched out in bed before there's anybody afoot at the ranch. Don't you worry about me. You just get me there."

I taken him at his word. Those horses were fixed up and a-raring to go, and we lit out of there fast, high-tailing it down off that mountain.

We hit that little village at a dead run, and a moment after we raced through, somebody ran into the trail and yelled after us, but we headed across the plains toward the ranch. And he stayed with me. Old and weak he might seem, but there was grit in him, and we almost ran the legs off those horses until we were within a hundred yards or so of the ranch.

There was gray in the sky and a light was going in one of the vaquero shacks, but we slipped in, and I got him back through my window. Then I got him into his own bedroom, and he locked the heavy bag in a closet at the head of his bed.

Outside, I hurriedly stripped the gear from the horses and turned them into the corral. Nobody was around, so I rubbed them down, and was working over them when a vaquero came out.

Well, he pulled up short when he saw me there working, but I just raised up and said, "*Buenos dias, amigo*." Then I added in English, "When do we eat around here?"

"*Poco tiempo*," he grunted, and went inside. So I kept on working over my horses, rubbing them down carefully, then forking hay into the corral, and going to the bin for a healthy bait of corn for each. They'd earned it.

When I walked to the house and stepped up on the veranda, Dorinda was standing there. She gave me a sharp glance and said, "You're up early."

"Now, ma'am," I said gently, "no such thing. You take any mountain boy . . . he'd be apt to be up this early. Why, back to home we'd had the cows milked by this time, or if 'twas winter, we'd be out runnin' a trap line."

"I had no idea you were from the mountains," she said, and I don't know why, but suddenly I knew she lied.

"Have you seen Mr. Mandrin?" she asked.

"Me? Is he up and about?"

She came up close to me. "Tell," she put a hand on my sleeve, "please don't think me ungrateful. I've wanted to thank you for all you did and tried to do, but it wasn't possible. You see, those men would not have understood. Someday I'll explain—"

"Don't bother," I said. "Anybody who'd try to take an old man's ranch away from him doesn't owe me anything, least of all, explanations."

She stiffened up, her face went white, and those black eyes turned to poison, quick as that. "You are a stupid fool!" she said contemptuously. "I shall explain nothing!"

She turned away from me, and I was just as pleased. I wanted no truck with that black-eyed woman, but the way I saw it, my troubles had only just begun.

About a half-hour later, when I was hungry enough to chew my own boots, they called us to breakfast, and about that time there were horses riding up outside.

One glance through the window sent me stepping back to my room to pick up a gun. It wasn't in me to wear a gun to any man's table, but this here was different. So I taken up a pistol and shoved it down behind my waistband within easy grasp.

Outside there I'd seen Dayton and Oliphant, that city man I'd first seen with Dayton and Dorinda. With them was Nolan Sackett. It was the first time I ever laid eyes on kinfolk of mine when I wasn't pleased.

There were some others, too, and one of them was a wiry, sallow-faced man with the snakiest black eyes you ever did see. He had a tied-down gun which some gunfighters favor, and a way about him that told me he figured himself a handy man with a gun.

When I walked into the dining room Old Ben Mandrin was already settin' up to table, and he looked at me just as perky as could be. "You're walking into trouble, boy," he said. "Are you with me?"

"I reckon we share enemies," I said.

Roderigo came in suddenly, and he glanced quickly at me—doubtfully, I thought, like maybe of a sudden I wasn't to be trusted.

The others showed up at the door.

"Come in! Come in!" Old Ben was smiling and easy, and it throwed them. I mean they didn't know what to make of him, for without doubt they had come to lay it on the line and tell him the ranch was theirs and he'd have to get off. You could see it in their eyes.

We all sat down to table, and me, I couldn't figure where I stood in all this. Seemed to me I wasn't getting any nearer the gold I'd lost, nor had I any clue as to where it was. And Dorinda wasn't about to tell me, if she knew.

All my life I've been getting myself tangled up where it was none of my affair, and never could figure out why. Maybe it was just that I followed the easiest line, maybe I wanted too much to do things for folks, maybe I was just easily persuaded. Anyway, I was tangled up now.

Right from the start when I saw the black-eyed woman a-settin' there looking at me, a homely man, I knew I was shaping up for trouble. Yet no sooner am I shut of her than I get tangled up with this old man, and from what I'd seen of him he was fit to care for himself. . . . Well, maybe not that night up on the mountain. If I hadn't carried him out of there he'd be waitin' for buzzards by now. But with a tough old man like that, you can't be sure.

This Dayton was a rugged man in his own way, but all polish and surface. I didn't take to him. But now he'd brought me face to face with my kin.

Nolan Sackett came in a step or two behind him, and we looked at each other across the room.

"You could be in better company," I said, right off.

He grinned at me. "Show's on you," he said. "You're one of those preachin' Sacketts."

He was as broad in the shoulders as I, and a right powerful man, maybe twenty pounds heavier, with a big chest and thick arms that swelled out his shirt sleeves until they were like to bust. His face was wider than mine, with a blunt jaw and a nose that had been broken sometime back, but he had the Sackett look to him, all right, and all we Sacketts favor, more or less.

"I never drew a gun on no Sackett," I said, "and I hope you don't fix it so's I have to."

"You could leave out of here," he said. He had a tough, insolent way about him, but he was curious, too, for here we kinfolk had met up away out in California, a far piece from the Tennessee mountains.

"You finally clean out them Higginses?" he asked.

"Tyrel fetched the last one."

"They were fighters. I mind the time two of them had me cornered up on McLean Rock, and me with a bullet in me."

"Was that you? My brother Orrin told me of it. He toted you down off the mountain, piggy-back. Ten, twelve miles."

Dayton was irritated. "We came on business, Nolan. In case you've forgotten."

Nolan ignored him. "Rose Marie Higgins came around on mule back . . . one of the Trelawney girls with her. She came to find where those Higginses were so's they could have Christian burial."

"Orrin, he went back up and dug for them both," I said, "and he spoke words over them, and read from the Book. Then he wrote them—their people, that is. He wrote them to tell where the graves were.

"Given time," I said, "we Smoky Mountain and Cumberland Sacketts always bury our dead, we bury them Christian."

"Like out on the Mojave?" Nolan said, wickedlike.

"Wasn't much time," I explained, "and I had a woman with me. Had there been time, I'd have read over them."

"Nolan . . ." Dayton was getting almighty upset over our talk.

"You came on business," Nolan said, "so get on with it."

"It concerns you!" Dayton declared angrily. "If anything goes wrong . . ."

"I know," Nolan said patiently, "if anything goes wrong I've got to do the fightin'. That's what I'm paid for. All right, you settle your affairs, and when fightin' time comes around, I'll be there."

"I hope you ain't," I said. "I never read over no Sackett, and I ain't honin' to."

"You tell me where at you keep the Book," Nolan said. "I'll be doin' the readin'."

"Come, come, gentlemen!" Old Ben, he looked as cheerful as a 'possum eatin' persimmons. "No business until after we've eaten."

"I hate to spoil your appetite, old man," Dayton said, in that nasty way he had, "but I came to foreclose. I own this ranch."

Glancing across the table, I happened to notice Dorinda. She was looking at those raw, chewed-out hands of Old Ben's like she couldn't believe what she saw.

"Your hands, Mr. Mandrin! You've hurt your hands!"

# Chapter 7

For a minute there, the room was as empty of sound as if everybody had suddenly lost their voices, even their power to breathe. Old Ben Mandrin, supposedly moving only from his bed to a chair and back again, had the palms of his hands raked and lacerated like nothing you ever saw. They weren't bandaged . . . there was no real need of that, but they were raw and plenty sore.

The question in everybody's mind but mine was, how did they get that way? And the old coot was enjoying it. Why, I don't think he'd had so much fun since the last time he made somebody walk the plank . . . if he ever did.

Dayton was studying him, his eyes hot with suspicion, and Oliphant was almighty worried. Nolan Sackett, he just threw a hard look at Old Ben's hands, then at his face, and then Nolan went to eating.

Old Ben gestured carelessly. "It's nothing, Dorinda, don't worry your mind about it."

He looked too self-satisfied to please Dayton. By all Dayton's figuring, the old man should be worried sick and begging for a way out, but there he sat, all smug and smart, those old devil eyes of his brighter than a raccoon's.

Old Ben tied into his food like he'd earned it, and there for a while nobody had anything to say. Me, I was fair-to-middlin' hungry, but most of all what I needed was sleep. There'd been none the night before, and very little for some time past, and it was going to do my eye and my shooting no good, if it came to that.

When Old Ben sat back to enjoy his coffee he said, "Old man my age doesn't have many pleasures, and what he has he figures to pay for.

"When Dorinda here started being nice to me, and seemed to set her cap for me, I knew something was in the wind. Turner had introduced her to me as his niece, but Turner had never mentioned a niece before, and when she started offering to care for me and the like, I was suspicious.

"Then when Turner asked me for a loan to keep his bank afloat, I gave

some thought to it. He'd loaned me cash a time or two a long while back
. . . or rather, his father had, and I owed the bank some help.

"Meanwhile, Dorinda was still around the place, fetching and carrying
for me of her own free will, making me more comfortable, fixing the blanket over my knees, putting a pillow back of my head, and moving about
the place, swishing her skirts.

"Think that doesn't do a lot for an old man? It did for me. Now, I had
no fancy in my mind that she was starting to care for me. Maybe when I
was fifty, or even a mite later, but not now; but I could still enjoy her
being there and watching her move around.

"You've got to admit she's pretty much of a woman, and she was always
the lady. But you've got to admit she keeps what she's got so you know it's
there."

He chuckled. "I reckon I'll miss her."

"Get to the point," Dayton said. "I want you out of here . . . today."

That Dayton now . . . he was a man I could come to dislike.

Old Ben's eyes turned on Dayton like a pair of six-shooters, and he said,
"You are to be disappointed, Mr. Dayton. I am not leaving. You are not
taking my property, which is worth fifty times that note I signed for
Turner, and which you now hold. You are not taking my property now
. . . or ever."

He had changed so sudden it startled a body. Here he was—or seemed to
be—a doddering old man talking about a young woman . . . and then his
tone changed and those old eyes of his changed, and Dayton knew right
away that he was facing into trouble.

"What do you mean?" Dayton leaned forward. "Why, you damned old
fool! That note's due and you know it, and I'm granting you no time.
Every friend you have who might lend you money is in as bad shape as
you are because of this drouth! Now you get off this ranch, and get off
now!"

That Ben Mandrin was a hard old man. He chuckled, one of the
meanest chuckles you ever heard, and he said, "Why, Mr. Dayton, I'm
going to surprise you. I'm going to pay you your petty little note . . . with
interest!"

He reached down under the table, and from between his knees, which
had been covered by his blanket, he took a sack that he set out on the
table in front of all of us.

"There it is, Mr. Dayton, figured down to the last penny . . . and in
gold."

When he set that sack down there in the middle of the table we all
heard the chink of coins, but Dayton couldn't believe it. He grabbed that
sack and jerked it open, spilling those gold coins out on the cloth.

They were gold, all right, and enough to pay off that note, that paltry little sum for which Dayton and Oliphant planned to steal more than a hundred thousand acres of land in one of the loveliest places a body could find.

No, Dayton couldn't believe it. He wouldn't believe it. He knew Old Ben was out of cash. He knew nobody around could afford to loan him money. In his own mind he had already owned the ranch and was thinking of how he could advertise back east and start selling it off, as others were doing.

That black-eyed witch woman looked at the gold, and then she looked across the table at Dayton, and those black eyes were pure poison. "So now, Mr. Dayton," she said coldly, "where do we go from here?"

Roderigo looked as surprised as any of them; only Nolan Sackett seemed to take it without any excitement. He just looked over at Old Ben and said, "All right if I finish eatin' before I go?"

"By all means," the old devil said. "Please enjoy yourselves. After all"— and he sounded mighty sarcastic—"you are my guests."

The gold lay right there on the table where it had spilled, and Roderigo couldn't seem to take his eyes from it. Nolan Sackett ate with good appetite, but the others, including that sallow devil with the black eyes, hadn't much taste for eating. Dayton started several times to speak, but each time he gave it up, for there was just nothing he could say.

Finally, Old Ben spoke up. "You have tasted my hospitality"—his voice was dry, but there was a cutting edge to it—"now *get out!* And you, Dayton—if you ever show up on my property again, for any reason whatsoever, I shall have you horsewhipped!"

Dayton almost staggered when he got to his feet, for he was a whipped man already, and it showed. Oliphant got up and, more leisurely, so did the black-eyed gunman and Nolan himself.

Dayton looked over at Dorinda. "You coming?"

"Do you take me for a fool?" Oh, she was beautiful, all right, but she had a wicked tongue. "I left you before because I knew you were a tinhorn, and you brought me back by force. If you ever try it again, I'll kill you myself!"

Old Ben chuckled, and Dayton went white as a man can get and still live, then he ducked out of the door.

Nolan Sackett leaned over the table and scooped up the gold and swept it into the sack. "Dayton," he called, "you forgot somethin'!"

Nolan paused, filling the door with his bulk. He hefted the sack in his hand, and then he turned back and looked at Old Ben. "Now I wonder," he said, kind of musing out loud, "where would a man get this kind of gold? Minted gold, and quite a lot of it, some of it old, mighty old."

He put on his hat. "This I got to contemplate . . . I got to contemplate." And he stepped outside and closed the door behind him.

Old Ben was clutching the edge of the table with both hands. Some of the abrasions and cuts had opened and there was blood on the edge of the white cloth.

"Kill him!" he said. "Sackett . . . *kill him!*"

I stared at him, and then I said, "I've got no call to kill him."

"You damned fool!" Old Ben shouted. "Kill him, I say!"

Nobody moved, and Old Ben's face turned dark with angry blood, his eyes glared, and for a minute there I thought he'd have a stroke.

"That man," he said, "will be the death of some of us. Remember what I say."

"Not me," I replied. "I've nothing at stake here."

He looked at me as if he had seen me for the first time. "Yes . . . of course. I had forgotten that."

Nobody made any comment, but I guess we were all figuring on the amount of unfinished business there was at that table. Dorinda Robiseau was suddenly on her own, but with no expectations of money like she'd had, having been promised part of this deal.

Old Ben Mandrin, whom I'd admired for his guts, suddenly began to look like a mighty mean, cantankerous, evil old man. He had saved his ranch, but he had Nolan Sackett to worry about; for however you looked at it, there had been a pretty definite threat in what Nolan said.

Nolan Sackett knew, as anybody would, that such gold had to come from somewhere. Old Ben had apparently been broke. Turner had assured Dayton that this was so. Roderigo, his own grandson, had believed him broke. Then Old Ben shows up with a sack full of minted gold and pays off his debt.

Where had the gold come from?

About that time I suddenly began to look at my hole card. And it was well that I did.

The old man had gotten that gold—of which the amount he'd paid to Dayton was only a small part—on his middle-of-the-night ride with me. When he left me on that pass and turned off along the ridge, he had gone to that gold.

Was this all of it? Or was there more?

Pushing back from the table, I got up and went to my room where I got out my gear. Something told me to get out of this house, and I wanted to . . . badly.

Roderigo followed me as I carried my gear out and dumped it on the edge of the veranda. "You're leaving?" he asked.

"Yes."

"My grandfather wishes to see you. He said he had promised you mules."

So he had . . . and I was going to need those mules. "All right," I said, and we walked back inside.

He still sat at the table, although in just the few minutes I had been gone it had been cleared. He looked tired now, and I couldn't wonder at it after all he had gone through. He had let down now, and the weariness of that long ride and the crawling among the rocks was getting to him. For the first time since I had met him, he looked his years.

"You helped me," he said when Roderigo had gone from the room, "when there was nobody else I dared call on. I'm having them drive in some mules, and I shall make you a present of twenty."

"That's a lot of mules."

He shrugged. "There are several hundred on the place. There are over six thousand head of cattle here or elsewhere that I own, and nearly a thousand horses. It is a small payment for what I owe you. Besides"—and a little of the Old Ben flashed into his eyes—"it will lighten the load on my range. Unless it rains, and rains well before summer sets in, I'll lose a good many head of stock."

He scratched out a bill of sale for the mules and passed it across the table. "Roderigo knows of this. It will be all right."

Then he hitched around his chair and looked up at me. "Did the sight of that gold make you less of an honest man?"

"I can't see that having gold has bought you very much."

He grunted. "All this? What do you call this?"

"How many people can you trust? When you were in trouble you had to reach out for a stranger to help you."

"Maybe I was a fool to do that."

"That's your problem." I folded the bill of sale and put it in my shirt pocket. "What are you going to do about *her*?"

"Can't cage an eagle, boy. She'll have to go. I could keep her here and give her anything she wanted, and soon she'd start to hate me because she'd be tied to me. You make bars of gold and an eagle will bite at them, trying to get out."

"You can see she doesn't leave here broke. Hell of a thing, for a woman to be broke."

He swung around in his chair. "You're too damned sentimental, Sackett. It'll get you nowhere. Still, if you're hunting a job you can have one here. I'll give you a working share."

"No."

"You turn down a million dollars awful easy, boy. This ranch will be worth it. You'll live to see it. Is it so easy to turn down a lot of money?"

I just looked at him, and buttoned up that pocket that held twenty mules. "Mister," I said roughly, "I could have had it last night, up there on the mountain. I could have rolled you off that cliff and come back and turned in . . . nobody would have known the difference."

"Thought of it, did you?"

"No . . . but look at it yourself."

"But you brought me back." He looked up at me, those hard old eyes appraising me. "That's why I need you here. I need an honest man."

"What about Roderigo?"

He snorted. "He's honest enough, I think, and he'd try. But he's weak . . . he's a gentleman. He would try to fight clean, and he'd lose. You'd fight them the way they'd fight you, and you'd win."

"Good-bye, Ben Mandrin," I answered him.

I walked to the door and stood there a moment, looking back at him. He had that blanket over his knees and he kept one hand under the blanket, and I wasn't going to turn my back on a man like that.

"I hope you got all you wanted last night," I said. "Nolan Sackett or somebody in that crowd could track a squirrel across a flat rock."

"So can you," he said. "So can you."

I stepped out of that door backwards . . . after one quick look to be sure the yard was empty.

# Chapter 8

She was standing near the corral when I walked out there, a rarely beautiful woman, with her black eyes and red lips, and that way she had of moving and looking at a man.

She was wearing a dark red dress that really stood out against that old pole corral, and it looked to me like she had fixed herself up kind of special. So right away I began to wonder what it was she was after.

"No one else could have done it," she said. "It had to be you." She put her hand on my sleeve. "Thank you for helping him."

That was sort of a leading statement, so I just said, "Ma'am, I've got to saddle my horse. They're rounding up some mules for me."

"You're a rare man, Tell Sackett. I wish I had known you long ago."

"You think it would have made a difference? We'd have both gone the same ways we have gone."

"What are you going to do?"

"Arizona . . . I'm headed back for the mines."

"Across that awful desert?" She shuddered. "I hope I shall never see another desert."

"It's the way I've got to go. If there's anything I want, it's back there."

"Is there a girl?"

Well, now, how could I answer that when I didn't know myself? There had been a girl. And then she had gone back east to visit some folks of hers, and when she was due to come back she just didn't come. Nor was there any letter that I ever got. . . .

Ange . . . Ange Kerry.

"No, ma'am," I said, "I don't think there's a girl. Looks to me like I'm a lonesome man riding a lonesome country, and I don't see no end to it."

"There could be, Tell."

Well, sir, I looked down into those big black eyes and saw those moist lips, and thinks I, if this here's a trap, they surely picked the right kind of bait.

"Ma'am," I said, "you're a lot of woman on the outside."

She stiffened up like I'd slapped her. "What do you mean by that?"

"Well, I sure don't cut no figure as a man knowing women, but it seems to me what you wear is a lot of feeling where it shows. I don't think there's very much down inside. I'd be like that old man in there . . . I'd as soon make love to you, ma'am, but I'd want to keep both your hands in sight. I'd never know which one held the knife."

Oh, she was mad! She started as if to slap me, her lips tightening up and her face kind of flattening out with anger. But she held herself in. She was keeping a tight rein on her feelings, and she waited for a moment or two before she replied.

"You're wrong, you know. It's just that I've not found the right man . . . I've had to hold myself in, I've had to be careful. For you I could change. I could be different."

"All right," I said suddenly, "suppose we give it a try. I'll saddle a horse for you, and you can ride back to Arizona with me. If you still feel the same way by the time we get to Prescott—"

She caught my arm again, stepping up so close I could really fill my nostrils with that sweet-smelling stuff she wore. "Oh, Tell, just take me with you! I mean it! I'll do *anything!* I'll love you like you've never been loved! I'll even go into the desert with you. I'll ride all the way to Dallas if you suggest it."

Then Roderigo rode back in with two vaqueros and they had my mules. I'll give him this—he had gone along to be sure they were the best, and they were. Every mule of them was good . . . I'd go a long way to find their equal. These were not the little Spanish mules, but big ones from Missouri, valuable animals on the frontier.

"If you like, we will hold them, señor, then they will be no expense until you are prepared to load them and go."

"I'd be obliged."

He stood there, fidgeting around while I saddled up the stallion and made ready to start for town.

"Be careful," he said, "in riding across La Nopalera. Men have been killed from ambush there."

"*Gracias.*"

One last thing he had to tell me before I rode out. He came up to me as I gathered the reins and reached for the saddle horn.

"The man who was here—the slight one with the black eyes?"

"Yes."

"He has a partner . . . a friend. That one was on the desert also, and he is the one who knows of your gold, *amigo.* I have it from them." He jerked his head to indicate the vaqueros. "There are few secrets, señor, if one listens well."

"Do you know his name?"

"Dyer . . . Sandeman Dyer."

I knew that name . . . from long ago. It stirred memories that brought with them a smell of gunsmoke and wet leather. . . .

Why is it that smells are so strongly associated with memories? But it is usually the smell that inspires the recall of the memory, and not the other way, as happened to me now.

"Do you know him?" Roderigo asked.

"Maybe . . . I'm not sure."

"Be careful, señor. It is said that he is a very dangerous man . . . and he has many friends. He rode in from the north some weeks ago, and twenty men rode with him. There have been raids and robberies since—nobody knows for sure, but it is believed that he is the one who leads them.

"He is a gunman, señor, very dangerous. He has killed a man in Virginia City, and another in Pioche of whom we know."

So I swung into the saddle and looked down at my big hands resting on the pommel, work-hardened hands, used to pick handle, shovel, axe, and rope. And to guns also.

"It does not matter, amigo. If he has the gold that is mine, and that also which belongs to my friends, I shall ask him for it."

"You wish to die?"

"Nobody wishes to die."

So I turned the stallion and rode away from the ranch, and toward the pueblo.

All that remained now was to get my gold, and the man to see was Sandeman Dyer. Or . . . was I too suspicious? Was this a trap? Had the information been planted, in hopes that it would reach me?

It was dark when I came again to the pueblo of Los Angeles, and there were lights in many homes and other buildings. I came into town by the old brea pits road, and left my horse at the town's best livery stable. And so I returned to the Pico House, and my room there.

A man with a flat-brimmed white hat sat in the lobby reading the Star. He looked at me over the edge of the paper, only his eyes showing between paper and hat brim.

My few things were in my room, to which I added my rifle and the gear recovered with my horses. Only the gold was gone now.

I was tired . . . bone-weary. I felt as if I had been drugged. Tonight I should search out Sandeman Dyer, but I was too tired. Tonight I would rest, at last, in a bed.

I peeled off my shirt, and filled the basin with water and washed, then combed my hair. Standing before the mirror I looked at myself, seeing the old scars, marks of old wounds from gun battles and from the war, and here or there the finer, thinner scars of knife wounds. Those scars showed me how lucky I had been.

It was not in me to believe myself fated to die at any given time. Deep within me I knew, having seen many men die, that no man is immune to death at any time at all. During every moment, walking or sleeping, we are vulnerable . . . I could die tonight . . . tomorrow.

Young men do not like to believe that. Each has within him that little something that says: Others may die, but not me, not me. I shall live.

Despite all those who die around him, this is what he believes. But I did not believe it, and I had never believed it from the first moment I saw a good man die, when the evil lived. I could believe in no special providence for any man. Tomorrow, when I went hunting my gold, a bullet or a knife might kill me.

But it was not in me to refrain from going. Nor could I call this bravery. My determination held none of that. It was simply because it was in me to go. I had never learned how to hang back from what it was up to me to do.

Sitting down on the bed, I reached for a dusty boot. One hand upon the toe, the other on the heel, I waited, just a moment longer. Weariness made me sag inwardly, made me cringe at the sound of footsteps in the hall outside my door.

After a moment there was a light tap on the door and, stepping across to the door's side, my hand on my gun, I asked, "Who is it?"

"A letter for you, sir. It arrived yesterday, but I expected to see you at the desk."

"Slip it under the door."

There was a moment's hesitation, and then the letter appeared. It was addressed in a flowing masculine hand, one I had never seen before.

Ripping open the brown envelope, I found a sealed letter within, and with it a short note. I read the note first.

> Mr. Sackett,
> Dear Sir:
>     When the mail from the stage you saw wrecked in the canyon was brought to us it was found to contain this letter to you, addressed in care of me. As it may be of importance, I am sending it forward.
>
>                                         Hardy

Then I opened the letter, and when I unfolded the closely written pages, I saw that it was from Ange.

Dropping upon the bed, I read it through, which I could do with a bit of work, for I'd little enough time at school in my boyhood, and read but slowly.

She had been ill. . . . She was well. . . . Did I wish her to come back? And then almost in the next sentence . . . she was coming back. She would take the first stage. She would meet me in Prescott.

I folded up the letter and thrust it into my pants pocket. Then I pulled the pants off and got into bed. Drawing the blankets up, I stretched out carefully, for the bed was made for a shorter sleeper than I, and slowly I let my long body relax against the comfort of the mattress.

Ange . . . my own Ange . . . Ange was coming west. She would meet me in Prescott.

Then I sat bolt upright.

Ange would meet me in Prescott, where I would be arriving with another woman!

Presently I lay back on the bed and tried to relax once more, but no matter how I tried . . .

Suddenly, I was wide awake. Somehow I had fallen asleep, but something, some faint noise, had awakened me in spite of my exhaustion. Starting to move, I caught myself in time. Somebody was in the room.

The door was closed. The window was open the merest crack, yet somebody was inside the room.

A faint creak told me that whoever it was stood right beside the bed. Through the slit of a scarcely opened eye I saw the loom of a dark figure, the faint gleam of light on a knife blade, and I threw myself against him, knocking him back to the floor.

Choking with fear and fury, I rolled on top of him and grabbed at his knife wrist, bending it sharply back toward the floor. I grabbed him by the belt with the other hand and heaved myself up, lifting him with me, and swung him bodily at the window.

With a tremendous crash of glass he went through it and I heard a wild, despairing yell, then the thud as he struck in the street below.

The door, I then noticed, was ever so slightly ajar. Pushing it shut, I shot the bolt and went back to bed. Cold night air blew through the broken window. Vaguely I heard excited talk in the street below . . . but I decided I wasn't interested.

Presently heavy boots rushed up the hall and there was a frenzied knocking at my door.

Lifting my head, I said, "Damn it, go away! Can't a man sleep around here?"

Somebody started to reply, and I added, "If I have to get out of bed again, somebody else goes into the street. Now you goin' to leave me be?"

There was a subdued murmur, then quiet footsteps going off down the hall. I pulled the blankets around me, and in a few minutes I was asleep.

It was broad daylight when I woke up. Sunlight was streaming in through the broken window, and I got out of bed. Still a mite foggy from the heavy sleep, I went to the basin, washed, and dressed. When I had pulled on my shirt I looked out of the window, but there was nothing in the street to show where anybody had fallen.

Now one thought and one only was in my mind. Today I was going to see Sandeman Dyer.

When I came down the steps it looked like everybody was waiting for me. The manager of the hotel—leastways I figured it to be him—came up and told me I'd have to pay for breaking the window.

"Breaking the window? Mister, I broke no window. I didn't even touch it. If you want to get paid, you find the man who went through it. You collect from him."

He started to argue, and I said, "Look, mister, I don't like to get mad. Last night was once, and far's I can see, that's enough. Maybe I should point out that you got bigger windows down here."

Well, he kind of drew back, but I stepped right after him. "Also, you might spend some of the time you seem to have to waste after me and find out how that thief had a key . . . and he had one. You in the habit of givin' keys to thieves?"

I'd spoken loud, and several of the folks standing about moved closer to listen. That man began to worry.

"Ssh!" he said. He was all of a flutter to get shut of me now. "Forget it. I am afraid I was mistaken." And he hurried off.

I turned then to look at those people around me and I said, "Anybody here know where I can find a man named Dyer? Sandeman Dyer?"

Nobody seemed to know a thing. You never saw such vague folks in your born days. Everybody had been interested up to that point, and then nobody was. In less than two minutes after I spoke that name the lobby was empty.

I went outside, where sunlight lay on the dusty street and upon the walks. Pausing on the corner, I looked across the Plaza in the direction of Sonora town . . . an unlikely place to look for Dyer.

Closer to me was the Calle de los Negros, better known as Nigger Alley, and Tao's gambling house.

Taking my time, I strolled here and there about the town, looking into store windows and watching the horse cars. Most of them seemed to be going out Spring Street to a place called Washington Gardens.

On the streets the folks themselves were a sight to behold, and when it came to the Californios themselves, you never saw such a dressed-up lot of folks. Many wore short jackets of silk, figured calico, or beaded buckskin, white linen shirts open at the neck, black silk handkerchiefs knotted loosely around the neck, and pants of velveteen or broadcloth, or some-times of beautifully tanned white buckskin, and nearly every one wore a silk sash, usually bright red. The serapes ranged from Indian blankets to fine broadcloth.

The handsome outfits these men had, made me look a poor mountain boy, even in my new twelve-dollar suit. Why, I fancy it must have taken a thousand dollars or more to get some of them dressed. And their saddles and bridles! You never saw so much silver. And two-thirds of them, I was sure, with dirt floors in their houses.

Here and there you still saw men with long hair, and some of them with it not just to their shoulders. In some cases it was braided. The younger ones had taken to trimming their hair, Anglo fashion, but not all of them.

Everywhere a body looked there were black-eyed señoritas, flirting with you with quick, teasing glances that made the red climb right up a man's neck. Me, I already had two women on my hands, when I wasn't fairly used to one, and more trouble shaping up than you could shake a stick at.

As I went about the town, everybody I asked about Sandeman Dyer was warning me about him. But I was more fearful of what would happen when I rode into Prescott with that black-eyed witch girl and found Ange a-waiting for me than I was of what was ahead of me right now. Ange was a red-haired girl, and she was one with a mind of her own, and she'd had will enough to survive in the high-up mountains of Colorado before I found her there.*

Suddenly a rider turned into Main Street from Spring, and I saw it was that black-eyed gunman who had been at Old Ben's ranch. He rode past, not noticing me, heading for the Calle de los Negros. He would be going to Dyer, I could lay a bet on it.

But just as I turned to follow, a voice spoke behind me. "You take my advice and you'll leave Dyer alone."

It was Nolan Sackett.

We stood there facing each other in the street, two mighty big men, both of us armed, and both carrying the scars we'd picked up since we left Tennessee, and a few from before that.

"If he's a friend of yours, you just tell him to hand over my gold. I got no quarrel with him."

* *Sackett*, Bantam Books, 1961.

Nolan didn't even smile. "Don't be a fool, man! You came out of that alive, and you're damned lucky. Now let well enough alone."

"I'm going after my gold."

He looked disgusted and mad all to once. "Look," he said irritably, "you're kin of mine, or I'd let you go your way and get killed. Dyer has forty men around him, and he himself is one of the most dangerous men alive."

"So he sends a man to knife me in the dark?"

Nolan had an odd look in his eyes. "Believe me, Tell, that man never came from Dyer. Dyer just couldn't care less about you."

He shoved his hat back on his head, and there was a worried look in his eyes. "For a man who says he minds his own affairs, you can pick up trouble faster than anybody I ever did see. You'd be right smart if you just climbed up on that stallion of yours and lit out for the high-up desert. There's three or four passels of folks here just a-honin' to see you dead and buried."

"You tell Dyer to have my gold ready. You go right along and tell him."

"Damn it, if you come against him you'll be facing me. I'm with him."

"Like I say, I never drew iron on ary a Sackett, but if you stand between me and what's rightfully mine they can bury you along with Sandeman Dyer."

"There'll be forty men, damn you!"

"Seems to me Dyer can't be too sure of himself if he needs all that company. You go stand beside him, Nolan, and when they bury me they can dig the grave wide enough for the lot of us."

When he had gone I stood there on the street, staring off toward the hills. Maybe I was crazy. After all, why not get into the saddle and ride away? Most of that gold was my own . . . and true, it represented my stake for the future. It represented the cattle I wanted to buy to stock a ranch in Arizona. It represented a future for Ange and me, if future there was to be.

And those other folks who lost gold entrusted to me . . . they could less afford to lose their gold than I could, although they would not lose near so much.

Nobody needed to tell me what I'd be going into, and I had no plan, no idea of what to do. Like I said, I never was much account at plotting or planning or working things out. All I know is to go bulling in and do whatever comes natural. Only thing I regretted was Nolan Sackett being there.

It went against me to fire on a Sackett of the blood. It would go hard to take lead from him, or to shoot him down where he stood. Even a Clinch

Mountain Sackett was kin, and I wanted no shooting between us. Still, he had chosen his side, and now it was up to me.

Odd thing, the way a man is. Trouble waited me there, I knew, maybe injury and death, but I turned around and started down the street, and headed right into it. Maybe I just didn't know any better.

Pausing on the corner, I taken out my six-shooter and spun the cylinder. She worked smooth and easy. A passerby gave me a sharp glance and hurried on past.

That man who took one look and hurried on was the smart one. He saw trouble and avoided it. Only he didn't have all that gold awaiting him.

Tao's place was sure jumping. I mean, there were a lot of folks there, all of them gambling or drinking. By the time I reached the bar they had me spotted. Until that moment I'd have sworn I didn't know any but one or two of the men who had followed me out on the Mojave, but right away I recognized two of them here.

The black-eyed gunman was standing at the bar when I walked up to it, and he had a taunting, challenging sort of look to him that riled me. "You tell Dyer," I said, "that Tell Sackett is here, and wants to see him."

"He knows you're here."

Two men had walked over to a table near the door, where they sat down. Two other men strolled up to a card game and stood by, watching the play. A man playing at that table glanced around thoughtfully, then laid down his hand and cashed in his chips. He got up, kind of careless like, and went out the door. He was a wise one . . . he knew enough to get out before things busted wide open.

Nobody needed to tell me, after all, where to find Sandeman Dyer. The minute I saw him, I knew him.

He was sitting at a table in a little alcove, a man of less than medium height, with square shoulders, and a kind of angular face with high cheekbones. When a body first laid eyes on him it seemed that his face was out of kilter somehow, that maybe it was misshaped, but you couldn't find any one thing about it that was wrong by itself. It was just an impression you got.

He was smiling now, smiling easy and friendly. And then I thought back to Shiloh, and I felt reason to worry, for when this man smiled he was dangerous indeed.

"Well, now, Sackett, it has been a long time. A very long time." And he held out his hand to me.

When I took it I knew how it would feel . . . cold, and clammy. For I had shaken this man's hand before, and it meant no more now than it did then. He was a great one for shaking hands. I didn't make the mistake of forgetting his little tricks; only knowing Dyer, I knew it would not be now.

Sandeman Dyer—we called him Sandy then—was a talker. He was a man with a love for the sound of his own voice. He was not only a talker, but a man who liked to parade what he knew, and he was almighty sure that he knew a whole lot more than anybody else. That easy smile of his, that easy laugh, they sort of covered the contempt he felt for anybody and everybody.

He was a bright man, all right, and a shrewd one. He was cunning like an animal . . . it was a savage cunning . . . but when the Good Lord put him together something went wrong. For he was a man without mercy, a man with cruelty so deeply ingrained in him that it was the most important part of his life. He was made up of cruelty and self-importance, I guess, in about equal amounts.

Yes, he loved to talk, to parade his smartness, but the trouble was he could stop talking awful sudden. . . . He could break off in the middle of a sentence and kill you, or have you killed.

I'd seen it happen, for back there at Shiloh we were in the same outfit. The first time I saw it happen—the first time he shot an unarmed prisoner —I thought he'd gone wild from the pounding of the guns. Cruelty was a rare thing in the war. Fireside folks who talk about war and read about it, they figure it's cruel more often than not, but it simply isn't so. When you kill in war it is usually impersonal, except when you've seen a friend shot down, and then you strike back and hard . . . if you can.

You kill in war because it is your job, and because you want to survive, and not because of any desire to kill. Cruelty takes time, and there is mighty little of that in war. But Sandy Dyer was a different kettle of fish.

The second time it was a major we'd captured, a handsome man of thirty-five, a gallant gentleman, who when trapped had surrendered. Come right down to it, he was *my* prisoner. That was what made me mad. But when Dyer started talking to him nice and friendly like, I thought nothing of it. There were six of us there, and the prisoner. But mighty soon that talk of Dyer's began to take on a nasty edge I didn't care much for, and I said so. He paid me no mind.

"Got a family, Major?" Dyer asked, ever so gentle.

"Yes. I have a wife and two sons."

"Those boys, now. They in the army?"

"They are too young, sir. One is six and one is twelve."

"Ah . . ." He looked up, innocent as a baby, and he looked right into that major's eyes and he said, "I wonder how many times your wife has been raped since this war started?"

It came so sudden we all sort of jumped, and three, four of us, we started to bust in. That major's face had gone white and he stepped forward and drew back his hand to strike, and Dyer stepped back out of reach and he said, "Major . . . you ain't never going to know."

Well, I'd heard of men getting a gun out fast, but I'd never seen it. In the high-up mountains it was mostly rifles we used, and the repeating pistol was scarce twenty-odd years old, and mighty few of us had even seen one.

He just drew that pistol and shot that major right in the belly.

Me, I knocked him down.

He hit the ground all in a heap and then he went sort of crazy. Rightly speaking, I expect he was crazy all the time. Later on, when the story was told around I began to hear of other things he'd done. Anyway, he came off the ground and rushed at me, and I hit him again.

There was trouble over that, and a sort of drumhead court-martial and he was discharged out of the service. I heard afterward he'd joined Quantrill or Bloody Bill Anderson or one of those.

And now here he was, facing me across the table, and I knew he hadn't forgotten those times I'd hit him. I also knew he was dangerous as a cornered rattler and would strike, like a rattler in the "blind," without warning.

He was no rational man, and those others with him, they would do what he said.

Under my shirt I could feel cold sweat on my body, and I was scared. This here was a man I'd hoped never to see again, and I had walked right into him. Only I had one advantage over the others he might have tangled with. I knew that when he started talking soft and easy, I'd have to be careful.

Another thing I knew. Before we parted one of us was going to die. There just couldn't be any other way.

"Thought you were an eastern man, Dyer," I said. Drawing back a chair, I sat down, but where none of them could get behind me without my seeing them. "I didn't expect to run into you out here."

"I don't expect you wanted to see me, did you, Sackett?"

"Why not?" I said carelessly. Then I added, "I hear one of your boys was good enough to bring my gold in off the desert. I take that kindly."

He smiled, and this time there was something like real humor in the smile. I could see he liked my way of putting it.

"I believe there was some mention of gold," he said, "but I understood it was found on the desert. I had no idea it belonged to you." He went on smiling at me. "I suppose you can identify it?"

Now I could see he was taunting me, being sure there was no way of identifying raw gold, but in that he was wrong. Truth was, I knew mighty little about such things, only what a body hears talking with miners and prospectors, but he didn't have to know that.

"Matter of fact," I said, "I *can* identify it. So can any good assayer. The amount of silver and other mineral associated with gold varies from place to place."

He didn't like that. Not so much because he thought I could identify the gold, as because he hadn't known this fact.

Sitting there, casual like and easy on the surface, I was doing some fast figuring. This was an unbalanced man, deadly fast with a six-shooter, and with a hair-trigger temper. A normal man can be understood to some extent; but this man, though shrewd and calculating up to a point, was apt to do some damned fool thing—some damned deadly thing—on a momentary whim. It was like sitting on a keg of dynamite with a wet fuse. You knew it was going to go, but you didn't know when.

The men he had with him were bandits, adventurers, drifters, men out to make easy money, or money that sounded easy, and they followed him because he had brains and daring, and because they feared to cross him. He had come south hunting money and trouble, and they were with him all the way.

The chances were that most of those men were good with guns. Some were renegades left over from the War Between the States, others were just outlaws he'd picked up.

The way to whip a man is to keep him off-balance, and it seemed to me my best chance to get out of this alive, or with a shooting chance, was to keep him from thinking about it.

"'Member that time we met that outfit of Graybacks on Owl Creek?" I said. Glancing across the table at the others, I went on, "I never saw the like. Dyer here was on my left. There were six of us moving up to the creek in the late evening. It was coming up to dark, and it was still . . . so still you could hear our clothes rustling as we walked.

"Dyer, he had himself a pair of Remington .36-calibre six-shooters that he spent a good part of his time polishing up. He had those guns belted on, and we all carried rifles.

"Well, sir, we were a-walking along, moving like a pack of Mescaleros, when suddenly we stepped into a clearing. And just as we done so, a party of Rebs came in from the other side, at least twenty in the outfit.

"They were as surprised as we were, only Dyer here, he acted quicker'n you could say scat. He dropped his rifle where he stood and outs with those Remingtons . . . you never heard such fire. You'd have thought he had him one of those Smith-Percival magazine pistols that fire forty shots.

"He just opened up and went to blasting with both guns at once, and that whole party cut and run . . . why, I don't think ary of us got off a shot, only Dyer. He downed three of them, wounded I don't know how many."

Folks somehow have a feeling when something is about to happen, and you'd be surprised how business had fallen off in just those few minutes since I came in. That first man who cashed in his chips, he began it. Maybe a dozen had drifted out since then.

But Sandeman Dyer was a man who liked to hear himself talked about. He sat back and ordered drinks, and we started talking up old times. Yet all the time I was realizing that the fewer outsiders were in that place, the less chance I'd have. Not that Dyer would care much for witnesses. When it came on him to kill, nothing in the world was going to stop him . . . it was a kind of madness.

The worst of it was, he was fast.

Was I quicker with a gun? I surely didn't know. The fact of the matter was, it wouldn't make an awful lot of difference, because when the shooting started, if he didn't get me the rest of them would. Only I made up my mind that no matter how much lead I took, I was going to keep shooting long enough to take him with me. For if ever a man needed to die, it was Sandeman Dyer.

So we talked the afternoon away, and finally I knew I had to let go of the bull.

What I mean is, I had a bull by the tail and I was safe as long as I hung on; but I had to let go sometime, and it was better to pick my own time than to wait until he got impatient.

So finally I said, "Well, it's been friendly, seeing you after all these years, but I've got to start back for Arizona. If you'll hand over my gold, I'll leave out of here."

His expression changed ever so little, his lids flickering just an instant as he adjusted to what I'd said. Our talk had kind of lulled everybody else into quiet. They were kind of scattered out, busy with their own activities, drinking, talking, sure there'd be no trouble.

They didn't know Dyer like I did.

"Why, sure!" He smiled at me with all the warmth of a hungry wolf. "I intended you to have it all the time." He turned his head to the man behind the bar. "Joe, open the safe and bring that sack of gold over here."

And right then, I knew.

It had to be when I put my hand on that gold . . . or when I reached the door with it.

More than likely it would be the last, for he would want to drag it out. He might shoot me in the back, but it was more probable he'd let me get almost to the door, drawing his gun behind my back, and then he'd speak to me, and when I turned he would let me have it.

In my mind, I counted the steps to the door, and it was far, much too far . . . and once I was out in the open room he'd have a clear shot at me.

Suddenly, I realized something else. The afternoon sunlight was falling through the window over our heads, and when I reached that place in the center of the room or a bit beyond and turned, I'd have the sun's glare in my eyes.

Oh, I'll not say he'd seen it that way from the beginning, although with him you never knew. All this talk, when I thought I was getting him to relax and ease off the tension a mite, all that might have been just waiting until the sun was right.

For Sandeman Dyer knew I could shoot.

He had not spoken loudly, and few had heard him except those standing close by. The idle talk on the other side of the room continued, and I heard Joe close the door of the safe and walk back across the room. He put the gold down in front of Dyer and went back to his bar.

There was no sense in wasting time now. Reaching across the table, I said, "Thanks, Sandy," and picked up the gold . . . with my left hand.

He was smiling, his eyes dancing with that odd light I remembered so well, and I knew he had not missed the left hand . . . or my right hand on the edge of the table.

And then I stood up.

All of them were waiting, expecting some word from him. One word, one move from him, and they'd fill me so full of lead folks would be staking my grave for a lead mine.

Suddenly, turning, I thrust out my hand to him. Instantly, I knew I'd done the wrong thing. I'd had it in mind to hang onto him and walk him to the door with me, but the moment my hand went out, I knew this was when he would want to shoot me. It would please that mocking devil of insanity in him to shoot me with my hand thrust out to shake hands.

He had come to his feet, smooth and easy, and he half reached to take my hand, then dropped it for his gun.

My hand was outstretched . . . too far from my gun, so I just lunged with it to stiff-arm him in the chest, but he stepped back quickly, backing into his chair.

For just an instant it had him off-balance, and I threw my left arm across my face and went crash-through the window into the alley.

Believe me, it was a wild gamble, but I hit the window with a shoulder and went through, falling full length in the alley. As I fell, my hand had grasped my gun butt, so when I hit ground my gun came up with the hammer eared back.

And there he was, broad against the window's light. His gun flamed, but he had expected me to be on my feet and he was geared to shoot high.

In almost the same instant that his gun flamed, I let the hammer fall, brought it back and fired again, so fast the two shots had but one thundering sound.

He buckled as if somebody had slugged him in the wind, and his gun went off again, harmlessly, in the air, as his finger tightened convulsively on the trigger.

Leaping to my feet, I spread my legs and shot twice more into his body as he fell back. This was one man I wanted dead.

There was a rush of feet from inside, and then a voice spoke out, stopping them.

"Leave him be." It was Nolan Sackett. "You boys just stand hitched."

Stooping down, I felt around for my sack of gold, and picked it up. Then I went up to the window. Dyer was sprawled dead on the floor, and they were just beginning to realize there was nothing to fight for.

"Any of you boys want a buy into this game?" I said. "The pot's open, and bullets are chips!"

Nobody seemed to be holding high cards, so they stood pat. I said to Nolan, "I'm riding out of here. Want to come along?"

"You go to hell," he said politely.

# Chapter 9

Sometimes the damned fool things a man does are the ones that save his bacon.

When I had my horses all together I tied lead ropes on them and started out of town, and I wasn't sorry to go. Only one thing bothered me, I'd come this far and hadn't seen the ocean sea.

It was over yonder, not too far out of my trail, so when I was heading west across La Nopalera, the big cactus patch that lay north of the *brea* road, I made up my mind of a sudden. I'd no wish to sleep the night at the Mandrin ranch, so what better than a ride down toward Santa Monica and the sea?

Of a sudden I decided to do it, for I might not come this way again. By such whims can a man's life be saved, as mine was saved that evening.

Turning off, I taken the trail for San Vincente Spring, from which Santa Monica, both the old town and the new, so I'd heard, took their water. It was a long ride, and despite the fact that I kept moving right along, it was nigh to midnight before I got where I could hear the sea.

There was a ranch house on the bluff, about a half mile back from the sea, but I was shy of folks and rode clear of it, although I was near enough that their dog barked at me.

The stars were out and a fresh wind from off the sea felt good against my face. Down at the end of the arroyo was a clump of trees, great big old sycamores, and some brush, but there were too many squatters, to judge by the campfires still going. So I turned north along the shore until I found another canyon. Up that canyon about a quarter of a mile I found a clump of trees with nobody around, and I rode in, unsaddled, and bedded down.

It was sure lucky that nobody followed me all the way out there, for I slept like a hibernating bear until the sun found my face through the leaves.

My stock had made a good thing of it on the grass in the clearing, so I taken my time getting around. My saddlebags were empty of grub, and after a bit I saddled up and rode along the shore to the town.

After stabling my horses, I got me a room at the Santa Monica Hotel, and made a dicker with the manager, a man name of Johnson, to take my gold off my hands for cash money.

When he paid it over to me he gave me a sharp look and said, "You seem to be a nice young man. If I were you I should be very careful, carrying that much money. There are thieves hereabouts."

"You don't say!" I said with astonishment. "Well, thank you kindly. I shall be wary of strangers."

They had a bath house there where folks came to take the baths, and it seemed to me a good soaking couldn't but do me good. Whilst I was in the bath I laid my saddlebags close by and my pistol belt atop them where I could lay hand on the gun mighty easy. Several folks came by and looked at me and then at that gun, and they fought shy of me. They were mostly older men, taking the baths for their rheumatism.

After a good meal I walked around town a little, looking at the schoolhouse, the churches, and the railroad, which had been built out there just a year or so earlier. Some folks were saying this would be the biggest seaport on the west coast . . . at least, the biggest south of San Francisco.

A couple of times I went around to check my horses, and from the livery stable door I studied the town to make sure that nobody was following me, or that any of that Dyer outfit had showed up hunting me.

That night I slept, and slept well, in a hotel bed. I mean I just stretched out and didn't mind it a whole lot when my feet pushed out below the covers. I was sure enough in a bed, and nobody knew where I was. However, I slept with those saddlebags under the covers with me, and a six-shooter too. You might say I was not a trusting man.

Most folks can be trusted up to a point, but it always seemed to me the best thing was not to put temptation in their way. Now that black-eyed witch girl . . . she made a business of temptation. When she was around, temptation was always in the way.

It was noontime when I showed up at the Mandrin ranch.

The way I figured, they'd be expecting me at most any other time, and I'd noticed that during dinnertime when they were inside eating, and right after when they took their siesta, the place was quiet as death.

After I thought that word, I tried to unthink it. Death was riding at my heels these days, and I didn't want to charm it to me by thinking of it.

When a man rides as much country as I have, he gets a feeling for it, and wherever he rides, he looks around to get to know it. So it was that I knew just how to come up to the ranch unseen, and I was in the ranch yard and putting ropes on my mules before anybody came out of the house.

The one who appeared was a dark-eyed man wearing a white hat.

"Howdy," he said. "You'd be Tell Sackett."

"Seems like."

"You stirred a lot of talk yonder in the pueblo. Everybody's been wonderin' what became of you."

"I'm a driftin' man, so I drifted."

He stood there trying to size me up, and as I roped my mules together for better handling, I managed not to turn my back on him, nor to seem like I was thinking of such a thing. With mules fidgeting around the way they do, that was simple enough. All the time I was debating whether I should go inside and say good-bye to the old man.

This man with the white hat had a hurt arm, and he limped a mite, too. There was a cut on his face that might have come from broken glass. He looked like a man who might have been thrown out of a window and rolled down a porch roof before falling off into the street.

When I was ready to go I led my stock around in front of the house and looked over at White Hat.

"You," I said, "let's go in and see Old Ben."

"I seen him," he said, mighty sullen. "He knows me."

"You walk in there," I advised him, "and you walk in ahead of me. Looks to me like you tripped over something too big for you already, so don't take chances on it happening again."

It didn't seem he liked that very much, but he walked in ahead of me. It might have been my suspicious mind that prompted it, but it seemed to me Old Ben was doing a lot of fussing with his blanket when I came through the door.

That black-eyed girl came down from her room, dressed for riding, an Indian girl following her with some bags and suchlike that a woman feels called upon to tote around.

"Well, Ben," I said, "this here's good-bye. It's *adios*. If you plan to see me again, you'll have to come to Arizona."

His hard old eyes studied me, and they glinted with a touch of humor mixed with what might have been respect. "You killed Sandeman Dyer," he said. "Everybody allowed it couldn't be done."

"Every man is born with death in him," I said. "It's only a matter of time."

Dorinda was standing there, and when I looked at her I saw her eyes were wider than usual, her cheeks kind of pale. I wondered about that, for she was a composed sort of girl, who didn't get wrought up by trifles.

"All right, boy!" Old Ben said. "You have a nice trip. And thanks . . . thanks for everything. Not many men would have done what you did, and without pay."

"Those mules look pretty good," I said, "that's pay enough for a lot of trouble."

Glancing over at Dorinda, I said, "You ready?"

"Go ahead . . . I want to say good-bye to Ben."

"All right," I said, and turned toward the door.

He was too anxious, that old man was. He had me dead to rights, but he was too anxious. Here I'd been ready for trouble for weeks, and expecting it from everywhere, but in that moment I forgot. But he was in too much of a hurry.

First thing I knew, there was a *whap* of something past my ear, the heavy *tunk* as it hit the door jamb, and the bellow of a gun. Me, I was headed for the outside and there was nothing keeping me. I went out that door like I had fire in my hip pockets, and I'm not ashamed to confess it.

He fired again, and the bullet just fanned air where I'd been, and then I heard the damnedest job of cussing I've heard in my born days.

Around the corner of the house came White Hat, running full tilt with a rifle in his hands. But when he got where he wanted to be, my six-shooter was looking right down his throat, and I said, "You going to drop that rifle, or am I going to drag what's left of you out in the brush for the buzzards to pick over?"

He was a man of decision who recognized the logic of my argument, and he let go of that rifle as if it was hot.

"Los Angeles is quite a ways off," I told him, "and if you're going to walk it, you'd best get started."

About that time Dorinda came out the door just like nothing had happened, and I helped her into the saddle, keeping those horses between the door and me. That was a mighty sour old man in there, and he was remembering that if anybody in the world knew where his cache of pirate gold was, it was a man named William Tell Sackett.

When we rode off I could hear him yelling for White Hat or somebody, only nobody was coming. They would, after a while, but they were bright folks, and kind of shy of shooting.

Once we were on the trail, it was pleasant to ride beside Dorinda, keeping the mules down the trail ahead of us, talking easy-like with that dark-eyed witch girl.

Not that I was ever much of a hand to talk to women. Back in the mountains where I came from I never was much on talk, and my feet were too big for dancing; but along about midnight when the girls started walking out with their friends, I was usually around and about.

Only Dorinda was easy to talk to. She knew how to lead a man on to talk of himself, and somehow she soon had me talking of the hills back home, of Ma, of Tyrel and Orrin, of the Higginses, and even of the Trelawney girls.

Those Trelawney girls lived over the mountain from us, and they had the name of being a wild, harum-scarum lot, but they kept the dust rising on those mountain trails. There were eight Trelawney girls, all of them pretty, and whilst everybody else was feuding they had no feuds with anybody.

Busy as I was now a-talking, I found time to check my back trail. A man who travels wild country gets to studying where he's coming from, because some day he might have to go back, and a trail looks a lot different when you ride over it in the opposite direction.

Every tree, every mountain, has its own particular look, and each one has several appearances, so you look back over your shoulder if you want to know country. It also helps you to live a whole lot longer. Like now.

Somebody was rising a dust back there. Not a big dust . . . but a dust. It seemed to me there were four or five horses, and they were walking just to keep the dust down so as not to attract attention.

Dorinda didn't look back none at all. She was thinking, though, as I might have expected.

"It will serve him right," she said. "He tried to have you killed."

"Who?"

"Ben Mandrin. He knows you are the only one who could ride to where his gold came from. There must be a lot more of it there, or he wouldn't have wanted you dead."

"Could be."

"He had men waiting out in the cactus patch near the *brea* trail yesterday. They were out there all day, only you dodged them somehow."

"You got to give him credit for tryin'."

"I'd like to see his face when he finds the gold gone. It will be just what he deserves."

Now I took a careful look at her. It seemed to me she was doing a lot of thinking, and I hoped my Bible was still in my saddlebags. When I turned in tonight I wanted it under my pillow.

"There must be a lot of it," she said. "He told me about a ship he sank off the coast of Panama. It was loaded with gold from Peru. He told me how they had brought it ashore and up a canyon to the hiding place. It took them a week to get it all out of the ship and up to where they took it . . . only working at night, of course."

"Now that there," I said, "would be a lot of gold."

"When we get it," she said, "we can go to New York, Paris, London . . . everywhere. And you can buy the biggest, finest ranch you can find, and stock it with the finest horses and cattle."

"I sure could . . . if I had that much gold."

"You know where it is . . . and you have the mules to carry it away."

"That old man is crippled up. No telling what will happen in the future, and he may need that gold. If he don't, Roderigo might."

She turned in her saddle and stared at me like she figured me for crazy, and I expect she was right.

"You mean you're not going after it?"

"No, ma'am, I'm not. Maybe a few years from now when that old man is dead and gone, I'll come back and look around, and if he hasn't taken the last of it, I shall."

"Why, he tried to kill you! And after all you did for him!"

"That's his way. There's a mighty hard old man, Dorinda, a mighty hard old man. Right from the start I sort of half expected it. I don't think folks have ever been very friendly to him . . . not unless they figured to get something for it."

Her eyes got narrowed down and mean. "Do you intend that for me?"

"Not necessarily. It's just the way it's been for him. But he owes me nothing. Look at the mules he gave me."

"*Mules!* When you could have all that gold?"

She took off her hat then, and the next thing I knew two Winchesters were looking over a rock at me, and I heard horses coming up from behind. Dorinda's hand dropped over mine as I reached for my six-shooter.

"There you are, boys. Make him talk."

She drew away from me, taking my gun with her. I took a careful look around, but they had me. They had me dead to rights, and there just wasn't anything I could do about it.

There were six of them, and my Winchester was in the boot, and it might as well have been back in Prescott for all the good it would do me.

"Take him, boys. He's all yours." Dorinda's black eyes showed all the witch in her now. I think she was ready to shoot me herself, only they still didn't know where all that gold was.

One thing I did know. There was no way out of this one.

# Chapter 10

The way I'd taken in leaving the ranch was north into the hills. It had been in my mind, for I'd still no stock of goods to sell at the Arizona mines, to cross over the mountains to San Francisco Ranch where Newhall was building a town. Folks said he already had the finest hotel south of San Francisco there, and the railroad and stage line passed through the town.

Goods were reported to be as cheap there as in Los Angeles . . . even cheaper, some said, because Fields, who ran the store, was trying to keep folks from riding all the way into Los Angeles to trade.

We'd ridden westward a ways and were just about to cut back into the hills and head north when these men moved down on me. No question but what that black-eyed girl had planned it that way. If I'd gone to where the old man had hidden his gold, these men would have followed and taken it from me. Now that I hadn't gone that way, they were going to force me to tell them where it was.

If I reached for my rifle I'd be dead before my hand fairly grasped the action, let alone got it clear of the scabbard. Yes, they had me dead to rights.

The place they'd picked to stop me was near a big rock at one end of a small valley . . . and I had a strong hunch this was the very *potrero* that lay below the ridge where all that gold was hidden.

It was a pretty little valley, with some fine old oaks around, and we'd stopped almost in the shade of one of them. It was a still, warm afternoon, and I could hear the birds talking it up back in the trees and brush just off the trail.

They moved in around me in a narrowing circle. I let my hands rest on the pommel and tried to see my way out, but my mind was a blank.

"He took the old man out that night, boys," Dorinda said, "so he's got to know where the gold is."

"He wouldn't take me to it. Do you think he's crazy?"

Nobody said anything, and then after a bit one of them spoke up. "How about that, ma'am?"

"How far can an old man crawl? It took them time to ride out and back, so if Old Ben left him up there, he can't have gone far. There's been no rain, so we should get a few indications of direction."

The black-eyed gunman tilted his Winchester. "You going to tell us, mister? You going to take us there?"

Well, why not? It wasn't my gold, and once they had it they'd have no further use for me. They might just let me go . . . although they might figure it best to shoot me so's I couldn't come back at them.

"Far's I know, he got it all. Else do you think I'd not be up there looking?"

"If that was all there was," Dorinda said, "he'd not have cared in the least about you seeing the place. No, it took them several nights of work to take that treasure up there from the beach, so he couldn't possibly bring all of it away in one night."

"We'd have to pack grub," I said. "It's far from here, and I'm carrying nothing. I was figuring to stock up at Newhall's place."

"He's lying," Dorinda said. "I tracked them part of the way."

Now I taken another look at her. This witch woman certainly knew a sight of things no city girl should know. She had tracked us, she said, and I had a hunch she wasn't lying about that. If she had tracked us, she must be pretty good.

"It's not far from here," she said. "I tracked them for several miles in this direction, and they couldn't have ridden much further than this."

They were all around me. There was no chance to make a move without getting killed, or at least badly hurt. My mules were over there feeding on the grass along with my spare horses.

"My guess is that we aren't more than a mile or two from it right now," Dorinda said, "and if I'd not been along he'd have gone right to it."

She turned toward a tall, tough-looking blond man. "Clymer, you and the Yaqui make him talk."

The Yaqui was flat-featured, a half-breed by the look of him, and a man who would know how to make a man die slowly. The Yaquis were said to be as good at that as the Apaches.

If I tried a run for it, there was no shelter close by. The trees were too scattered, and that big rock was almost sheer.

Time and again I'd been in tight spots, and somehow I'd come out of them, and it seemed as if this here one ought to be so easy. It was such a pleasant day, the sun made leaf shadows on the ground around, and a few high, lazy clouds drifted in the sky. There was no violence around . . . except in that ring of silent guns, aimed at me.

It shouldn't happen like this, I told myself. This is all wrong. There should be shouts and guns exploding, and fighting; there should be blood and the smell of gunpowder.

There were none of those things, and here I was, flat against a wall, with no way out.

"Get down off that horse," Clymer said. He was grinning at me, and I saw he was missing two teeth. "We're going to see what kind of stuff you got in you."

He gestured toward the Yaqui. "I seen him skin a man alive one time . . . well, almost. That feller got smart and done what we told him. Not soon enough, though, because when we let him be it was already too late."

There was a moment there when I thought about jabbing a spur into the stallion and taking my chances, but the trouble was, there wasn't any chance. Those guns just couldn't miss. Not all of them.

So I swung down, and they walked me toward a big old oak. Believe me, I was sweating. I was scared, but I was determined not to show it, and I was watching every second for the break I hoped would come. Only it didn't come.

They walked me up to that tree, and suddenly I made up my mind. If they were going to kill me they might as well get it done. One thing I knew. Nobody was going to tie me up to a tree. Not unless I was dead or unconscious.

So I made ready. If I turned fast I might lay a hand on one of those rifles, and if I had one of those I'd take somebody with me when I passed in my checks.

"Hey," somebody said. "Who's that?"

A rider was coming along the road, coming slow and easy. He was a tall man who rode well up in the saddle, and he came riding straight on.

"Hell," one of the men said, "it's Nolan Sackett!"

"Get on with it," Dorinda said irritably. "This is no affair of his."

He rode right on up to us, and despite what Dorinda had said, nobody did anything but watch him come, including me.

"Howdy, boys!" His eyes had plenty of time to take in the situation. "If you're after that gold I figure I should be in for a share."

"You're in for nothing!" Dorinda said angrily. "Get on with it, Clymer!"

Nolan, he looked over at me and grinned, and then he taken a pistol from under his coat and tossed it to me.

It was as simple as that.

He just flicked that pistol over and I reached up and snared it, and then we stood there with two guns on them, his and mine.

It caught them flat-footed and off guard. They just didn't expect anything like that, for Nolan was one of them. The trouble was, he was also a Sackett, and blood runs thicker than branch water.

Dorinda didn't cut up and scream like some women might, although she was mad enough to fight a cougar. She just looked at him and then at me.

"You boys mount up and ride," Nolan told them. "This here's a cousin of mine, or some sort of kin, and whilst I might have let you shoot him, I don't cotton to seeing that Yaqui skin no Sackett out of his hide. You boys just ride out of here and count it time well spent."

"What if we don't?" Clymer asked belligerently.

"Well," I said, "you outnumber us, but by the time we get through shootin' a whole lot of you are going to be dead, and us, too, so what will you be fighting for?"

"The hell with it," one man said, and turned his horse; and after that they just drifted away, leaving us there with Dorinda Robiseau.

"Nolan," I said, "I've got it in mind to buy goods over at Newhall's place and pack them across the Mojave to the Arizona mines. That's a lot of mules for one man."

"You got you a partner," he said.

He looked over at Dorinda. "You want to come with us, Abigail?"

"I'll see you in hell first," she said, and turning her horse, she rode off. That was no way for a lady to talk.

A few miles down the trail I said to Nolan, "You called her Abigail."

"Sure . . . didn't you know? She's one of those no-account Trelawney girls from back yonder in the hills."

Well, I'd be damned! So that was Abigail Trelawney. But it was kind of dark back of the schoolhouse that night, and I never could tell those Trelawney girls apart.